COURTNEY MERRITT

Embers of the Fallen
Paperback

The Infernal Ascendant Trilogy

Second edition

ISBN (paperback): 978-1-7640131-0-9
ISBN (hardcover): 978-1-7640131-2-3

This book was professionally typeset on Reedsy.
Find out more at reedsy.com

"For the ones who refuse to stay down, held together by sheer spite, caffeine, and an unreasonable amount of luck. You are the storm they never saw coming, the chaos in fate's careful plans. Go forth, raise hell, and make destiny regret underestimating you."

Acknowledgments

For my Grandpa—who saw magic in a wild-hearted girl with pockets full of stories and wonder. Thank you for every patient answer, every late-night walk, and every ounce of belief. You taught me that curiosity is a gift and that being different is a kind of beautiful the world needs.

To my husband—my anchor in the storm and the flame that keeps my dreams alight. Your unwavering belief in me turned whispers of doubt into echoes of courage. For every late night, every tangled plot, and every moment I wanted to give up, you stood beside me, reminding me why I began.

To my children —you are the brightest stars in my sky, the greatest adventure I'll ever have, and the reason my heart beats with both love and chaos. I hope you always chase your dreams as fiercely as the heroes in these pages.

Chapter 1

The sky was burning.

Smoke and fire churned together in a storm of ruin, the heavens painted in the glow of dying embers. The air was thick with the stench of charred flesh and the acrid bite of magic unravelling at its very core. The battlefield stretched, a graveyard in the making.

Then came the scream.

A dragon's dying wail split the air, a sound so raw and unearthly that it rattled through Seraphina's bones, setting her teeth on edge. The noble beast, once a titan of the skies, convulsed mid-flight. Its massive wings spasmed, curling inward as the cursed stone in the enemy's hands drained the very life from its body, and with a final shudder, it plummeted.

Seraphina couldn't look away.

The impact was cataclysmic. The dragon's corpse struck the ground with a sickening crack, the force sending shockwaves through the earth. The battlefield trembled, a pulse of destruction rolling outward as flesh and stone alike were torn apart. A deafening explosion of dust and blood erupted into the air, staining the sky red. Worse than the sight, worse than the sound—was the way magic itself recoiled, twisting in agony, shattering like fragile glass.

Mages collapsed, their spells unravelling into nothing more than empty whispers. The potent energy that had flowed through them turned useless.

Seraphina barely registered the warlock who staggered beside her, his once-roaring inferno of power now a dying ember. His eyes were already clouding with death. Magic bled from him like an open wound, his life force feeding the corruption that spread like a sickness. He reached for her, fingers trembling, blood bubbling from his lips. She moved on instinct, her hand darting out—too late. His body crumpled at her feet, his last breath stolen before his fingers could so much as brush her gauntlet.

She clenched her jaw, forcing down the sickening coil of rage in her chest. Around her, the supernatural were falling.

A Lycan warrior lay motionless in the blood-soaked dirt, his once-proud silvered fur darkened with gore. His claws, which had torn through countless enemies, were limp, useless. Even the immortal vampires did not escape. One snarled in defiance, his crimson eyes burning with fury before his body disintegrated into ash.

Seraphina stood amidst the carnage, her breath coming sharp and ragged. Night-black strands of hair clung to her sweat-slicked skin, tangled with soot and flecks of dried blood. Her pale blue eyes were showing the depth of her exhaustion. Viscera of friend and foe alike splattered her obsidian armour, carved with faint silver runes that once pulsed with enchantments. Her sword, a relic of dark steel kissed by ancient magic, trembled in her grip. The runes along its blade flickered, the corruption in the air poisoning the very energy woven into its core.

But she did not falter.

The battlefield was a nightmare given form. Blood slicked the ground, turning the once-rolling hills into a treacherous mire of flesh and bone. The stench of death, thick and suffocating, clung to everything. Smoke curled into the sky in ghostly tendrils, masking the stars. All around her, the fallen lay in grotesque stillness, their bodies twisted in unnatural shapes. Hollowed chests where hearts had been torn out. Limbs severed, discarded like broken dolls. Eyes wide in eternal screams.

The demons had feasted well tonight.

She swallowed hard, her throat raw. She could feel the unravelling of magic in the air—tangling, breaking apart, being twisted into something

2

unrecognisable. The enemy weapon wasn't just killing them. It stripped them of their essence. Ash and iron filled the air's taste. Smelling of ruin. The promise of extinction. Through the chaos, a low chuckle sounded behind her. A voice, smooth as obsidian, pierced the chaos. "Still breathing, I see."

A smile ghosted at the corner of her lips. Silver-grey eyes observed her; she knew it without looking. That voice always found her; even amid battle, it soothed her. Seraphina turned towards the sound of his voice, her eyes travelling over his body, checking for any wounds, as she raised her head to look him in the eye. They were standing almost chest to chest as his eyes scanned the battlefield before he glanced down with a smirk as he locked eyes with her.

Kade held her eye as Seraphina breathed in, calming her racing heart at what that smirk did to her. She was close enough to catch his scent over the smell of the battle that raged around them. He smelled of frost and smoke, like winter kissing the edge of a fire. He carried the cold with him, not of death, but of something older. Wilder. His silver hair was unbound, wild as the wind that howled across the battlefield, catching light like forged steel in moonlight.

He smelled of home, if she'd ever had one.

Seraphina took another breath, letting it blow out in exasperation, blowing the strands of hair out of her eyes.

"Unfortunately for them."

Her voice was light, but she caught the look of worry that gleamed across his face as she turned, sword gripped in her hand.

The words had barely left her mouth before she moved with lightning speed. Her blade cut through the throat of an approaching soldier, steel slicing through flesh as easily as parchment. The man choked, a wet gurgle, then crumpled at her feet. His blood pooled into the already-drenched earth. She didn't spare him a glance. She couldn't afford to mourn every soul that perished in this battle.

Her eyes looked beyond the battlefield. Where the horror awaited. A towering mass of darkness loomed in the distance. Its form shifting, writhing—abominate shadows unfurling like the birth of a nightmare. It had already gorged itself on the lives of countless warriors, and it would not stop. The Veilborn lived up to their name, consorting with demons to produce a hellish army of demons and corrupted soldiers. This war of dominance between every supernatural race and the Veilborn, felt more like an annihilation to Seraphina. If you didn't die to the corruption, you would lose your freedom and soul to their version of unity. She had lost too much already to this war, and she refused to lose more to the Veilborn.

Seraphina tightened her grip on her sword, ignoring the ache in her limbs, the exhaustion clawing at her edges. As she stepped over the twisted remains of a fallen mage, a soldier in cracked black armour loomed before her, the insignia of Alexis' army etched into his chest plate. There was something wrong. His movements were unnatural, jagged, his limbs twitching in ways that defied nature. His eyes... gods, his eyes. They glowed—not with rage, but with something worse. Corruption.

Seraphina's breath hitched at the sight. This wasn't a man anymore. Something had hollowed it out, emptied its soul, and stuffed it with something else. Kade appeared beside her as his blade penetrated the soldier in front of her. She watched as the soldier's face contorted into a scream before he fell to the ground; parts of it had disintegrated into ash. Kade yanked his sword from the corpse as it dripped with fresh blood. His voice was tight, edged with revulsion. "They aren't even human anymore."

Seraphina wanted to agree, but she felt a pang of guilt slice through her at the life that was lost for being other than Veilborn and resisting them. She didn't have time to focus on the soldier and the possibilities that always ran through her head if this war had never started. Seraphina shook her head once to clear the racing thoughts when she heard Kade's sharp intake of breath beside her. She looked towards him and saw him staring at the horizon; she followed his gaze. Then she saw it.

The weapon.

A jagged monolith, its onyx surface webbed with deep, glowing cracks, shone like a jewel and pulsed with an eerie crimson light. Seraphina knew what that was. It was Dragon's blood. It coursed through its veins like molten lava, a siphon draining the magic, the very essence of the fallen. The world faded with each beat of the monolith.

They had seen pieces before, especially throughout the war with the Veilborn, but none of this size and with this much power. They had been jewels that whispered and deadened spells, draining magic from a person. Dangerous, yes—but containable. But this... this was no shard. It was the heart of the corruption, the source. No one had imagined the weapon could ever take form like this. Not until this battle. Seraphina couldn't believe it herself until she had witnessed the power of this weapon draining the magic from the Supernaturals. The very essence of their collective beings was magic. Her breath came in quick pants. How were they going to fight a weapon that demons could use to drain their allies of the very fabric that made them? She turned to ask Kade when an unearthly roar shattered the battlefield's silence. It rattled the air like a storm on the verge of breaking, and she knew the answer. They were losing.

Kade let out a sharp exhale beside her. "Not to be dramatic, but we're probably going to die." His hands tightened on his own blades.

She glanced towards him, her blue eyes committing his figure to memory. They didn't need pretty words; Kade and Seraphina always seemed to know what the other was thinking. It was an easy friendship. She knew they were going to see this through to the very end. Seraphina turned her face back towards the battle that was roaring around them as allies tried to flee, and fight another day. She rolled her shoulders, fingers tightening around her blade. "Yeah? Well, at least we'll make it hurt." She didn't look back to look at the silver eyes watching her as she charged forward.

Her armour bit into her shoulders, each movement a sharp reminder of her exhaustion. The weight of her own body was unbearable, a sinking, dragging force pulling her closer to the abyss. Her legs burned, her vision blurred, but the pain ran deeper. It gnawed at the marrow of her bones, a relentless, crawling sense of impending doom. She felt the fractured, wrong, dying magic in the air as a sickness under her skin.

She gritted her teeth, forcing her body through the mire of blood and shattered bone. Every muscle ached, every breath cut through her like a blade, but she refused to yield. She wrenched her sword free from a soldier's chest, barely flinching as another lunged. Steel met steel, the impact rattling through her arms. She twisted, drove her knee into his ribs, slashed upward—the blade met flesh, just as she ripped the sword from the body to drive it into the corrupted soldier approaching behind her—a shadow overhead.

Seraphina barely had time to move before the dragon fell.

The impact sent a shockwave tearing through the battlefield. The ground split beneath her feet, bodies flung like discarded dolls. Dust and debris clawed at her vision. She hit the ground hard, her ribs screaming in protest. The world blurred, her head swimming, pain lancing through her body. As she tried to open her eyes against the pain, she felt a weight across her legs. Warmth seeped through her armour. She twisted, and her breath caught.

A body. A dragon rider's vacant stare met hers, inches away. He clutched the hilt of his shattered sword, his lips parted, as if someone had stolen his last words mid-breath.

Beside him, his dragon—gods, his dragon.

The once-majestic creature lay sprawled in the dirt, its golden scales dulled to lifeless grey. Its wings, once strong enough to command the sky, were broken and torn, one pinned beneath the rider's unmoving form. The sight of it, the sheer emptiness of what was once something so alive, sent something sharp and unbearable through her chest.

This was no battle.

This was annihilation.

The sky was on fire—dragons plummeted, their unrecognisable roars tearing through the night as the enemy's cursed weapon ripped the life from them mid-flight.

Seraphina had seen horrors.

But this—this was worse.

She scrambled to stand, clutching her ribs as they protested her movement. Her eyes darted in panic at the fallen corpses of the dragons and their riders. The strongest of their allies, scattered around her, drained of magic. Demons were already feasting on the corpses. Seraphina couldn't look at the graveyard of friends around her; instead, her eyes kept searching for a glint of silver amidst the devastation.

Her gaze snapped to the ridge ahead, where the towering, silver-haired warrior carved his way through the enemy with brutal efficiency. He was a blur of motion, blade flashing, magic still barely flickering around him like dying embers. But even he was slowing. His strikes, though still deadly, carried the weight of exhaustion. She felt her relief disappear when she saw it.

A monster, more nightmare than flesh, burst from the shadows behind him. Its hulking form twisted with unnatural sinew, its many eyes gleaming with malevolent hunger. Its claws, black as obsidian, dripped with something viscous. Something that sizzled when it hit the ground. A poison that defiled everything it touched.

Ignoring the pain, she surged forward. The battlefield blurred around her, her focus narrowing to a single point: Kade. The single, all-consuming need to reach him before the beast did swallowed the weight of her exhaustion. Her pulse thundered in her ears, drowning out the screams. She wove through the chaos, her movements driven by raw instinct, by desperation. The enemy closed in around her, making her lose sight of Kade. She cut them down without thought, her blade an extension of her fury, her will an unbreakable force. Every second stretched into eternity, every heartbeat another step too slow. She turned on-the-spot, eyes searching. She had been so busy cutting a path towards him she could no longer see him. Her breath froze in her throat when she realised she couldn't see Kade or the Monster that was moments from him.

"Seraphina!" The voice cut through the haze, sharp and urgent.

Kade. Her breath released all at once in instant relief.

She turned behind her, scanning the carnage until she found him—a silhouette against the chaos, silver hair streaked with blood, his twin blades dripping crimson. He was fighting his way toward her, but the tide of enemies between them was thick, a writhing mass of steel and flesh.

Behind them, something else moved. Seraphina didn't have enough time to scream a warning before the beast lunged. Kade's blade rose to meet it, but it wouldn't be enough. Not this time. The realisation was a blade to her gut, a horror too deep to bear.

She gritted her teeth, forcing her legs to move, to charge forward into the chaos. Her sword felt like an extension of herself as she sliced her way forward, her heartbeat a drum against the violence of the world. She saw Kade fight against the monster between moments of stabbing her sword in the enemy and looking towards where Kade was fighting with all he had left. Seraphina was close now; she was almost close enough to help when the world seemed to slow. Kade raised one blade to parry the attack. Exhaustion was clear in the way he hunched with his sword, trying to raise the blade high enough. As the monster lunged forward, Kade's sword was stuck in it, but the demon just kept coming. Kade's shadows couldn't save him as it lunged the second time. Time slowed as Seraphina watched the demon knock Kade to the ground and watched as Kade didn't get back up again. Her legs were moving as quickly as they could towards the demon. Seraphina didn't care that the odds of her beating it were impossible. She didn't care that they had lost the battle. She just had to reach him.

I will save him. I will not let him die alone.

Her one thought as she charged towards him.

Kade's body was on the ground, bloodied, barely moving, as the demon loomed over him, a grotesque, hulking figure of darkness. Its form was barely human, a twisted blend of muscle and shadow. Eyes glowing with a sickening, unnatural light. Its claws, razor-sharp and dripping with venom, hovered above Kade's throat, ready to strike. He coughed, weak and gasping, but his eyes—those silver eyes—locked onto Seraphina. For a moment, he seemed to find some semblance of peace in the madness.

But the demon's growl shattered that fleeting hope. A blur of malevolent force moved faster than anything she had ever seen, lunging with jaws snapping shut in an insatiable hunger. Kade barely had the strength to push himself away, his body too broken to move much, yet his eyes remained focused on her, his only lifeline in this nightmare.

Seraphina's heart slammed against her ribs as she pushed forward, her feet pounding the blood-soaked earth, each step heavy with the weight of time slipping away. Not in time. She could not reach him in time. The distance between them felt like an eternity, and every inch felt harder to gain as the demon's claws tore the air apart as it raised its claw and scraped it down Kade's chest. She watched as he jerked in pain before looking towards her. She could see Kade's lips moving, but the sound of the blood rushing in her ears was deafening. As the demon prepared its final blow, Kade's voice, faint yet powerful, reached her.

"Sera."

His voice — tired, desperate—reached into the depths of her soul, a name she hadn't heard in so long. A heavy word burdened Seraphina.

Sera. *He* called me that. The world spun, her heart broke, but she didn't stop. She couldn't.

"Kade!" Her scream ripped through the air, but the roar of battle devoured it. He didn't hear her. Or maybe he did, because just before the beast's claws struck home, he turned and his eyes widened as he reached a hand towards her.

Seraphina lunged forward, her fingers outstretched, but something shifted, something deep, primal. The tainted magic in the air grew denser, crackling with the intensity of imminent lightning, yet this time, it encompassed more than just her. It was in her. It burned beneath her skin, racing through her veins like liquid fire, igniting something she hadn't even known existed. For a fleeting moment, it was everything—power, heat, light—a force so absolute it made her bones hum and her heart stutter.

Then it exploded.

A blast of raw, blinding energy erupted from her, tearing through the battlefield like a supernova. The corrupted air recoiled, howling as the force of her power shattered the demon's form. The creature's screams split the night, but they didn't register through the overwhelming surge inside her. Magic—her magic—raged outward, untamed and unstoppable.

Overwhelming speed; then—

It was gone.

The magic vanished as suddenly as it had come, leaving her gasping hollow, scorched from the inside out. Her legs buckled, her skin felt too tight, her chest heaved like she'd just surfaced from drowning. The battlefield still raged around her, the stench of burnt flesh and magic thick in the air. The power that had consumed her only moments before was nothing more than a ghost slipping through her fingers like smoke.

Kade made a sick gurgling sound that broke Seraphina from the shock. She scrambled towards him on hands and knees, kneeling beside him as she pulled his head into her lap.

Seraphina's hands found his face, pulling him close. His silver hair, wild and matted with blood, framed sharp features streaked with dirt and pain. He locked his eyes on her, as if she were all that tethered him to this world. She had never seen him look at her like that before.

"Don't you dare die on me," she said, pressing her forehead to his as her breath fanned across his face. "You do, and I'll drag you back just to kill you myself."

A breath of a laugh. "So violent," he rasped.

He reached for her hand, rough fingers closing around hers. "You always were trouble, you know." His voice was quieter now, slipping like smoke. "My Nyx."

Her heart stilled.

That name.

A flicker of a memory, long ago. Back then, she was also covered in blood and shook with fury and exhaustion. He'd said it so matter-of-fact back then as if it defined her. The way he said it now, though, sounded final. It was as if he was telling her goodbye.

Tears slid down Seraphina's face as she held Kade against her. She hung on every breath, oblivious of the approaching sounds. She didn't sense the shadows looming. Didn't see the blade rise.

A sharp crack hit her skull.

Blunt, fast, final.

Her world tilted. The light behind her eyes burst in a haze of black and red as she crumpled forward, collapsing across Kade's chest. Her body went slack, her breath shallow. Her eyes, half-lidded and unfocused, stared into nothing.

Kade's heart lurched.

No.

Kade willed his body to move. He *had* to. Seraphina watched on through lidded eyes as Kade struggled against his wounds. His body, broken and heavy, surged with a last flicker of will.

One arm locked around Seraphina's waist to keep her from slipping to the blood-soaked earth. With the other, he forced his remaining sword upward in a clumsy, wild arc toward the hulking figure that had struck her.

The blade met resistance. A hissing sound—something, or somebody—staggered backward. But Kade's vision swam, and his strength faltered. His healing, once so reliable, was sluggish. Useless. Every wound screamed.

He bared his teeth and tried to rise again, tried to throw himself between her and the monster. A searing, blinding flash of magic hit him. His nerves screamed. His sword dropped from limp fingers.

Then—darkness swallowed them both.

Chapter 2

Seraphina's mind plunged into the abyss as her surroundings dissolved, and the ground vanished beneath her. Like sand slipping through her fingers, the present unravelled. Like a distant drumbeat, her pulse echoed in her ears as her vision darkened. Then, a whisper on the wind. Fragile yet persistent, a thread of memory lingered. She was no longer in the war-torn ruins. She was home. Back in the land of her kingdom.

As the sun set, gold streamed across the castle's high walls. The river below, snaking through the valley, shone like molten fire. The open-air balcony, framed by marble columns, overlooked sprawling gardens where statues of forgotten gods stood watch. Vines heavy with blossoms spilled over trellises in a riot of colour.

The air was heavy with life. With the distant clang of steel from the training grounds, servants murmured in the halls, their voices weaving into the soundscape. From tree to tree, birds flitted, their songs blending with the wind's whisper through ancient oaks. The scent of fresh parchment, lavender, and a hint of wisteria—a familiar comfort—clung to the stone corridors.

She felt arms wrap around her.

Alexis.

His presence was as familiar as the blood in her veins. Behind her, silent but certain, he stood, his presence grounding her in a way nothing else could. Sunlight kissed his tawny skin, smooth and warm, his dark blonde hair hanging into his eyes and his features sharp—high cheekbones, a powerful jaw, lips that curled into a knowing smirk. Effortlessly beautiful, he resembled a twilight gold carving.

Yet, his eyes. The deep blue colour. An ocean that promised both calm and ruin.

As she turned around in his arms, she noticed the light caught in his gaze, softening the intensity of his usually hard eyes. For a moment, she let herself forget everything but this, him. Close enough that she could see the laugh lines at the corners of his mouth, the way the wind played with the strands of his hair as she leaned towards him.

A silent promise passed between them as his fingers brushed hers. "Sera," he exhaled the words like a prayer, and her heart clenched. She leaned into him, pressing her forehead against his chest. His scent of cedar and steel—something his—wrapped around her. Familiar, safe.

"I never thought I'd have this," she admitted, her voice barely above a whisper.

He tilted her chin up with his fingers, making her meet his gaze. "You'll always have this," he vowed, his voice steady as iron. "Always."

She longed for his conviction. She had trusted him.

Like a windblown flame, the memory flickered. A thousand moments crashed over her. A passing smile from her father. The day her sister was born. The ringing laughter of her brother. The lull of her mother's song as she brushed her hair at night. Alexis—standing before the court, the weight of the marriage alliance hanging between them, his hand outstretched as she took the first step toward forever.

Then came her wedding day.

A mixture of nerves and wonder coiled through Seraphina as she stood at the altar, her heart hammering. Her wedding robes, deep crimson edged in gold, cascaded in delicate folds around her. Each stitch a symbol of the alliance being forged between her kingdom and his.

Alexis was radiant.

A prince of legends, dressed in ceremonial black and silver, his tawny skin warmed by the sacred flames. His blue eyes held hers with a quiet intensity, a promise unspoken, yet known. He made her feel untouchable with his gaze, as if she had found a place where she was truly seen.

He reached for her hands; she offered them. This was love. This was forever.

Though a priest spoke ancient, and binding vows, she hardly heard them. All she knew was Alexis' fingers tracing circles on her palm, his gaze unwavering, his lips parting as he spoke the most important words of her life.

"In war and peace, in blood and breath, I vow to stand beside you. You are mine, Sera, as I am yours."

She shivered. When she repeated the words, she meant them with every fibre of her being.

Their exchange of rings marked their souls as one. As Alexis leaned forward to claim his bride, she closed her eyes and stepped into eternity.

Never had she felt such joy. She had married the man that others swooned over, who had swept her off her feet and made her believe in herself again, when she was at her lowest.

The brighter one shines, the harder they burn. Seraphina had soon learnt that every day since her marriage day, for eternity, was a lie.

The memory flashed forward again, and suddenly Seraphina was there again.

Gone were the gentle scents of her childhood. In its place, smoke, bitter and suffocating. The screams—piercing and raw—bounced off the marble, echoing all around her. Seraphina staggered forward, her breath caught in her throat. Crimson drowned the castle's marble halls. Blood soaked into the white stone, turning it dark, as if the very foundation of her world was drinking in the slaughter. Fire and flesh choked the air, thick and unrelenting.

She turned, unable to find a safe place to look.

Bodies. So many bodies.

People she had known.

Loved.

Protected.

They were everywhere. Everyone she had ever known. Everyone, from the servants to the nobles, were butchered where they had been.

Red ran the rivers, which once sang with life. Soldiers trampled and burned the gardens where she once walked in peace. Above it all, the sky had darkened, as if mourning alongside her.

* * *

Seraphina ran to the only room she could think of, her family seeking refuge in. The throne room.

The large oak doors slammed into the wall as she burst through. The sight she laid her eyes upon made her stagger back, gasping. There in the middle of the bloodshed stood Alexis.

Not dead.

Not slain.

Leading them.

Seraphina fell to her knees, her heart hammering against her ribs.

The insignia of her people's destroyers showed on his silver fibre, now blackened steel. His hands, which had once caressed her jaw and offered stability, were now stained with the blood of her family.

Beneath him, her father, Sword protruding from his chest.

Shattered beside him was his crown. The king's lifeless body twisted at Alexis' feet. Her mother was not far, her robes soaked through, the delicate embroidery marred by a fatal wound.

The tears came hot and salty, leaving tracks down her face in the blood and grime.

No, this isn't real. Alexis stepped forward, towering over the ruin, his expression unreadable.

His voice calm amidst the carnage, "You should have listened, Sera." He stood over her, boots stopping just before her knees

"Give it to me."

Barely hearing him, her heart fractured beyond repair. This was it; she had gone through enough.

His lips curled in frustration, his voice rising. "Give it to me!"

She didn't understand. He desired what? What did she possess he didn't already have? What was worth killing her entire family? Her head bowed as she shrunk in on herself.

A glint of steel caught her eye. Her father's sword. The blade forged in their bloodline, passed through generations, rested mere inches from her grasp. A tremor ran through her fingers. This isn't real. This isn't happening she thought as Alexis knelt in front of her.

"Give it to me, Sera," his hands flexing—not with rage, but with need. "You aren't unaware of your true identity, but I will have that which is mine by right, wife."

He spat the last word at her as his hand grasped her hair, yanking her head back to look at him. "You will look at me when I am speaking to you, wife." He said.

The words were colder than steel, and they slithered down her spine. She didn't move. She couldn't breathe. Memories of the last year of torment under the man who was supposed to love and cherish her came flooding through her mind as she gazed at him.

"No more hesitating," he warned, leaning towards her.

Suddenly, it snapped. The grief, the rage, everything came roaring to the surface. She lunged for the sword. Her fingertips grasped the hilt as Alexis' hand tightened around her throat. The hilt fit in her grip as if it had been waiting for her all along. Alexis' eyes flashed. She had only a moment to act as she blindly thrust the sword upwards and steel met flesh. Alexis' eyes widen. His breath hitched. His hand fell from her throat as it grasped the sword that was jutting out of him. The other hand reached towards her as he stumbled, sagging against her, and she caught him. Just like she always had.

This time, however, the warmth she had taken comfort in was absent. Only the blood that spilled from his wound was left, warmth seeped into her dress as Alexis lay across her lap. His breath hitched; for a moment, his fingers grasped the blade that had ripped through his heart. A small shudder rippled through his body, almost imperceptible, before his grip slackened.

His blue eyes met hers, revealing no pain, but something far worse. Disbelief. Even now, her deed astonished him. As if he had still underestimated her. As if he had died convinced she never could. Curling around her wrist, weak but insistent, his fingers held her, his breath rattling in his throat. His lips parted—whether to curse her, to beg, to say her name one last time—she would never know. For a single cruel moment, he gazed at her as he once had. Like the man she had once loved. A ghost of something soft flickered behind his gaze. Something almost tender, almost real, and it broke her more than hatred ever could.

The scent of blood and steel filled her lungs, thick, cloying. His blood soaked through the fabric of her dress, through skin, through her soul.

She had done this. She had ended him.

It had saved nothing.

The burning of the battlefield persisted. In the distance, screams still echoed. Everything she had fought for remained in ruins around her. A sob clawed at her throat, raw, aching, and desperate to escape. Before she could, a firm hand grasped her shoulder.

With a jerk, she sat up, the haze of grief snapping like a fraying thread, causing her to flinch. Her vision blurred—red, grey, and gold—until she saw him.

Kade.

He breathed hard, his silver hair tangled with sweat and soot clinging to his sharp, bloodied cheekbones. Dents, cracks, old scars, and fresh carnage marred his blackened fibre. A soldier made of war itself. He was Alexis' bodyguard.

She braced herself for the coming blow at having killed her husband, his master. She would meet it with dignity.

Raw emotion filled his bright eyes as they locked onto hers. Something dangerous.

"You need to move," his voice was firm, leaving no room for refusal.

Around Alexis' ruined armour, Seraphina's fingers clenched. Her mouth opened, but no words came. He—he would not kill her? She couldn't even process it.

Kade's grip became firmer. "They're coming, and if you don't get up, you die here." His voice dropped, something sharp and almost desperate threading beneath the words.

"Here, Sera, is where your decision lies."

As her breath shuddered in her lungs, she stared at him. Then she looked down at Alexis. Amidst the rubble, she looked upon the man she'd cherished. What had it all been for? A bitter, empty tempest raged within her, and yearned for oblivion. Let it pull her under. Let the fire consume her, as it consumed everything else. Part of her wanted to die in this room, with her family.

Kade moved, but not to help her up or pull her from the ashes; instead, he offered something else.

A sword. Not just any blade. Even amidst the carnage, its dark surface gleamed, the etchings whispering of antiquity along its length. Midnight-dark leather wrapped the hilt, and a stone shimmering between violet and deepest black inlaid the pommel. It pulsed as if alive. She had seen this blade always by his side. It was a mark of the Dark Fae that he was and a symbol of his stance within his kingdom.

Her intake of breath was sudden and sharp. "Why?—"

Kade's jaw betrayed his emotions. "I meant it for you."

She shuddered, and a breath escaped her lips. Kade studied her, his expression unreadable. Then, softer, like a quiet vow between them—"Nyx."

The name's utterance sent a cold spark through her veins; it awakened something long buried inside her. A name of a legend amongst her people, meaning a great warrior. With trembling fingers brushing the hilt, she hesitated. The moment she touched it—something inside her unlocked. She felt a surge of ancient power, a hidden passage opening inside.

The hilt's pulsing matched her steady heartbeat. Calling her. Her breath caught.

With reverence, Kade's voice softened. "The warrior of night," his voice was audible beneath the roar of flames and distant screams. "The one who rises when everything else falls."

Swallowing hard, she slowly stood, allowing Alexis' body to lie on the ground. Kade should have called her Sera. That was what Alexis had called her. What she had always been. But Alexis was gone, and Kade did not look upon a fallen woman. He was looking at her as if she were a warrior.

This time without hesitation, Seraphina inhaled as she reached her hand towards him. She took the sword. Kade smirked, something knowing flickering through his gaze.

Turning, he uttered, "Good. Let's go."

She followed.

* * *

Losing her memories, like frayed thread, slipped from her grasp. One moment she was following Kade from the throne room and the next— nothing but darkness, a heavy, suffocating weight dragging her back into cold reality. It all shattered into the cold, unforgiving present.

A jarring shock pulsed through her as the cold stone pressed against her cheek, contrasting with the past. The raw bite of damp air replaced the waking nightmare, the smell of rot flooding her senses. Her stomach turned, bile rising as the stench of death clung to the air, thick and unrelenting. It was damp; the moisture seeping into her skin, sending a deep, bone-aching chill through her body. The air was thick with the scent of mildew, rust, and something sharper—dried blood. Too much blood.

Seraphina tried to sit, but in places she never knew existed, her body ached. Her ribs protested with each shallow breath. Every muscle screamed as she forced herself to move. Her wrists were raw where the iron shackles had dug into them, the metal biting deep. Her fingers trembled as she curled them, sticky with dried blood—hers? Someone else's? She exhaled, forcing herself back into reality, back into her body.

But it was still too much. Her mind fought against the tide of the past, but her surroundings bled into the memory she had just left—blood staining stone, lifeless eyes staring into nothing. The ghost of the battle was everywhere, whispering from the corners of her vision. The dreamlike haze of memory faded, replaced by damp, suffocating darkness. She pried her eyes open, blinking against the dim torchlight.

The cell, little more than a hole in the earth, had rough stone walls slick with condensation. A single torch burned in the bracket above, its flickering light casting long, distorted shadows across the damp ground. The air was thick, humid, and oppressive.

A groan came from the corner.

Kade.

Against the opposite wall, he slumped. A split lip marred his face, a dark bruise blooming across one cheekbone, and dried blood crusted along his jawline. Even battered and broken, he still smirked, and he still looked devastatingly handsome. She looked over his chest, searching for the wound the monster inflicted, but she only saw torn clothing.

"You're awake. It's about time, Nyx." His silver-grey eyes looked at her with an unreadable emotion held in them.

Seraphina, swallowing hard, forced a breath. "You look like shit." It seemed as if he would not discuss the last moments on the battlefield when he had called her that name. If he wouldn't, then neither would she.

Kade rolled his shoulders as he stretched, wincing with the movement. A hint of sharp teeth flashed when he grinned. "Well, you should see the other guys…"

She let out a weak, breathy snort, wincing in pain at the action. Even talking hurt. Silence stretched between them, thick with unspoken things. The battle. The loss. Their continued breathing amidst widespread death. She glanced at his wrists—wrapped in chains. Thick, rune-etched shackles. The metal gleamed with an unnatural dullness, the kind that absorbed magic rather than reflected it.

She frowned. "When did shackling Dark Fae become common practice?"

With a sigh, Kade rested his head against the wall. "Since they figured out that our healing abilities don't work with iron binding our magic."

She became rigid. "You mean—"

He gave a slow nod. "Indeed. Haven't healed a damn thing since they put these on me. They noticed the healing of the wound the monster gave me and immediately put me in irons."

A sickening feeling gripped her stomach. How many days had passed?

"How long has it been?" Her voice was a whisper.

Gone was Kade's smirk; in its place, a solemn look appeared. "Three days. You were out cold."

Three days have passed. Her pulse stuttered. Three days wasted. Three days while the war raged on outside this cell—or ended. During that entire time she dreamt of the past, three days had come and gone? A heaviness settled in her chest, pressing down like a vice. What losses occurred during her absence? Kade's voice interrupted her thoughts before she could spiral into the guilt.

"Nyx, how did you kill that demon in front of me? I haven't seen you do that before." His voice was full of wonder.

Seraphina tried to recall those moments, feeling the power in her skin, the desperate need to reach him faster, to vanquish the monster without harming him. She recalled the immense power, yet felt nothing. The power seemed nonexistent now.

"I don't know." She rolled her eyes, lips twitching in amusement. "I had a burst of power, but I don't feel any power now. Maybe it was someone else helping us for once?" Then the smile fell.

"You called me Nyx." She swallowed hard, the words catching in her throat. She had meant to say, 'You' called me Sera. But hesitation overcame her the moment the name formed in her mind. Sera had belonged to another life. Another girl. A girl who had believed in promises, in love, in forever. That girl had died in the ruins of her kingdom. So instead, she whispered—Nyx.

Kade remained silent. He looked at her, something unreadable in his silver gaze as it roamed over her face. "You are Nyx." He folded his arms, resting them atop his knees, his words deliberate. "You just forgot for a while."

Scoffing and rolling her eyes, she ignored the tightness in her chest; it wasn't the words she wanted to hear. "That's supposed to be inspiring?"

A ghost of a grin tugged at his lips. "I don't do inspiring. Just stating facts."

Exhaustion and unspoken grief thickened the silence between them. The damp chill of the cell pressed in from all sides, yet she didn't feel it. Instead, she recalled the battlefield, its deafening roars, the dragons' fall.

As she breathed out, the weight of memory tightened around her ribs. "I keep thinking about them. The dragons. The way they screamed when they died."

Kade, his silver eyes dim in the torchlight, glanced at her. He didn't speak, but the slight clench of his jaw told her he remembered too. She shouldn't have been thinking about them—about the dragons. It only made the ache worse. But the image that came to mind seared itself into her, burning into the marrow of her bones. Their fall was quite a sight. Their cries shattered the sky, their pain bleeding through the bond with their riders. As soon as their bond severed, a physical agony resembling a snapped string hung heavy in the air, and she felt it in her soul.

Witnessing the horrifying scene, she saw a rider fall to his knees, screaming as his dragon plummeted from the sky and crashed onto the battlefield. He had not moved after that. He had not needed to. His soul had already gone with it.

Her throat constricted. "I still hear them."

Kade shifted beside her, his silhouette cut from shadow and silence. His face revealed nothing, but she knew. He heard them too.

The dragons were more than beasts of fire and flight. They were the first guardians of magic, ancient sentinels bound to the lifeblood of the world itself. Now, one by one, they were falling.

Their deaths weren't just losses—they were unravellings. With every dragon that fell, the world dimmed. Magic itself recoiled, wounded, fading.

She swallowed hard, but the ache in her chest remained. "It's like the world is mourning."

Kade's jaw tightened. A shadow flickered behind his eyes. "It is."

Her voice, barely audible over the sound of the flickering torchlight, recounted the unbreakable bond between dragon and rider. "But it breaks. It shatters. And the ones left behind—" She swallowed. "They don't come back from it."

Kade didn't argue. Like her, he had also seen it. He had seen how riders who lost their dragons either threw themselves into battle to die alongside them or fell into an empty existence, as if their best parts had been torn away.

His voice broke their silent remembrance of those fateful moments. "You used to talk about Vaelrik."

Her gaze turned to him as she blinked.

Exhaling, Kade leaned his head back against the stone wall. "I never met him. But you mentioned him before, how he's the only one who can shift between dragon and man." He glanced at her then, something calculating in his gaze. "Do you think he feels it, too?"

Seraphina stopped. She had never considered that before. The idea of a bond severing was horrifying enough for dragons and riders, but Vaelrik was both. What did that mean for him?

With an admission of uncertainty, she stated, "I don't know. But if he does..." She exhaled. "Then I don't know how he's still standing."

Kade hummed. "If he's still standing."

At that, Seraphina frowned. She exhaled, but offered no reply. She didn't know. The world fractured; turmoil intensified. A weapon powerful enough to eliminate ancient magic remained unseen. Until now. Demons ran unchecked, magic twisted and rotted, and the number of warriors willing to fight dwindled every day. The idea of dragons, the oldest protectors of magic, dying in that battle scared her in a way that made her blood run cold.

A moment passed in silence as they listened to the distant, dripping water echo through the darkness. Then Kade shifted. "That weapon made everyone lose faith."

She fought back the lump in her throat with a swallow as she remembered everyone trampling each other in their bid to flee from it. "They think there's nothing left to fight for."

With a nod, Kade responded. "And maybe they're right."

Turning to him, her glare was sharp enough to cut. "Don't you dare."

He faced her gaze unflinchingly. "I'm just saying what we're all thinking."

"No," shaking her head as her pulse hammered. "You don't get to say that. Not you. Not after everything we've lost."

Kade exhaled, rubbing a hand over his face. "Since the beginning, Seraphina, we've been losing. With every battle, every fight, we scrape by with fewer and fewer left. And now we're sitting here in a cell, bound, broken—tell me how the hell that's hope?"

"We're still breathing, that's why."

For a long moment, Kade studied her, his expression inscrutable. Then a slow, tired smile tugged at his lips. "You are impossible."

A hollow laugh escaped her lips. "I prefer relentless."

With his head tilted back, Kade stared at the ceiling. "You think there's still a chance? That we can turn this around?"

She closed her eyes. Her senses still held the smell of burning flesh, dragon blood, and ruined kingdoms. The memory of firelight in the halls, laughter in the wind, and a world worth saving resonated too.

With her fingers clenched into fists, she opened her eyes. "I have to."

Kade nodded, as if that was answer enough. "I guess I do too, then."

The dim torchlight cast his sharp features in shadow. But his eyes kept their spark. His smirk held a sharp edge. "While I cherish our talks, Nyx, do you have a plan to get us out of here or should I write my will?"

With a twitch of her lips, she arched a brow. "Didn't take you for the type to leave a will, Kade. Who would you even leave your things to?"

He let out a quiet laugh, his shoulders moving as far as the chains permitted. "Good point. Not much to leave behind. Maybe I will carve a message into the wall for future prisoners. 'Beware of dungeons, demons, and bad decisions.'"

Seraphina hummed. "Sounds about right." But her mind was already calculating. Weighing possibilities. For three days, their captors had kept them alive—a duration sufficient to foster carelessness and a false sense of security. A mistake. She tilted her head. "You think I'd let some second-rate dungeon keep me locked up?"

With a cocked brow, Kade looked. "That so?"

With a grin, she stretched her stiff fingers, flexing them. Despite everything—despite the ache, the weight, the loss—there was still fight in her. "Shut up and be ready to run."

He grinned more widely. "Now you're speaking my language."

With that, the game began.

Chapter 3

The world was still spinning when Seraphina's eyes fluttered open. A sharp pulse throbbed at the base of her skull, and she tasted blood, the copper tang thick on her tongue. But the air, t was fresh. Cool wind swept through her hair, carrying the scent of pine and damp earth. No chains, no walls—only the soft whisper of leaves rustling overhead. The night's chill contrasted with the dungeon's stifling heat, pressing against her.

They had escaped. Kade was beside her, his breath uneven but steady, his silver hair streaked with grime yet still somehow gleaming in the moonlight. His fingers pressed against her arm, a solid weight anchoring her, grounding her. Warm. Real.

Yet something felt off; his normally intoxicating scent of frost and smoke was gone. In fact, he didn't have a scent at all.

"We have to move, Nyx," his voice hoarse but alert. "They'll track us."

She shook the unease from her head as she forced herself up, her limbs trembling but free. The trees stretched ahead, dark silhouettes against a sky just beginning to lighten with dawn. A hush settled over the world, as if even nature itself held its breath. Hope emerged—a feeling long absent.

She let out a shaky breath, glancing at Kade. "Didn't want the sunrise escape? It had to be the dramatic sunset escape?"

Kade smirked, shaking his head. "I intended a midday bloodbath; however, our early exit prevented it. Ruined my whole aesthetic."

She snorted but gripped his forearm, savouring the realness of his warmth. "I think I prefer your aesthetic to our last decor."

"Torture chambers aren't my style," he nodded. "Too... medieval."

She let out a fragile laugh. A strange sound fractured the quiet, altering her reality. Something was wrong. Whispers carried on the wind, felt out of place. The scent of pine twisted, morphing into something sharp and metallic. The ground yielded beneath her boots; it felt unearthly.

She looked down—

Blood. A sea of it, glistening black under the dim light. Her breath hitched as she staggered back, her boots slipping on the slick surface. Death's coppery stench filled her lungs. The trees were gone. The world had shifted, warped.

She turned to Kade, panic threading through her voice. "Kade—?"

But he did not react. He stood firm, unmoving, staring past her as if he saw nothing at all. His pupils dilated; his expression was void of recognition. "We have to move, Nyx," he repeated, the same words, the same cadence.

A chill slithered down her spine. This isn't real. She turned, searching for the trees, the path forward—but the forest had rotted into something monstrous. Twisted, jagged, skeletal forms, the trunks had twisted, their bark splitting open like gaping wounds. The sky above cracked, revealing a void that pulsed and swirled like something alive. The whispers grew louder, a chorus of voices overlapping in a language she could not understand—

Until one voice did.

"You promised me forever, Sera."

Her stomach plummeted. The world tilted, shadows swallowing the forest whole. The warmth of the escape was gone. She was not free. She had never been. Alexis's voice wrapped around her like a noose, suffocating, inescapable. A gaping void stretched before her. Then—

Agony.

A fist slammed into her gut. Her eyes flared open. The illusion shattered. Her back arched, pain searing through her ribs, the taste of iron flooding her mouth. The stone beneath her was damp and real. The chains cutting into her wrists were real. Oppressive and rank, the dungeon air suffocated her. Heavy boots struck the ground. The sharp clang of metal on stone made her flinch.

"Still holding out?" a voice thick with amusement, layered with something cruel.

The figure stepped into view. A half-demon abomination. His skin was an unnatural shade of ashen grey, veins dark as ink threading beneath the surface. Horns jutted from his forehead, their ridges cracked like old stone. His mouth, too wide, curled in a sick grin that revealed teeth—sharp and stained, made for tearing rather than speaking. His yellow eyes gleamed in the dim torchlight, slitted pupils narrowing as he crouched before her.

"You're strong," he said, tilting his head as he watched her struggle to lift herself upright on the slab. "Most break after the first day."

Seraphina spat blood onto the floor between them. "Guess I'm not 'most.'"

The demon's grin widened. "Oh, I do like you." His claws trailed along the edge of a rusted dagger at his belt. "But I wonder—how long before you beg?"

Her blue eyes met his gaze, her expression sharp despite the pain. "You'll break before I do."

The demon chuckled, low and indulgent. "We'll see about that."

Then the actual pain began as the demon slammed his clawed fist into her again. Seraphina forced her head up, blood trailing from the corner of her lips. Every inch of her body screamed in protest, muscles locked in a war between agony and exhaustion. She had nothing left to give them — nothing but defiance.

She spat blood onto the cold stone floor, forcing a smirk. "You'll have to do better than that."

The torturer's expression flickered. Amusement? Annoyance? It was hard to tell with those yellow eyes devoid of anything human. His grip tightened, knuckles cracking before his fist drove into her stomach again. Pain detonated through her core, stealing the breath from her lungs. She doubled forward, but no sound escaped her lips. She wouldn't give them the satisfaction.

Then—

A sharp intake of breath. A choked groan of pain.

Seraphina's head snapped toward the sound, her own suffering forgotten.

Kade.

He was bound, shackled to the same damn chains, but his head lolled forward, breath rasping between swollen lips. His silver hair, wild and untamed, clung to his forehead, darkened with sweat and blood. Blood now covered his pointed ears, which used to poke through the silver strands, and the tip of one ear was missing. The bruises along his jaw were deep, angry things, spreading like ink beneath his skin. His ribs—gods, they had worked him over. He wasn't breathing as he should.

A guard stood over him, a wicked blade pressed against his throat.

"You break, or he bleeds," the torturer taunted. His elongated fingers tapped the hilt of a jagged dagger, claws clicking against the metal in a slow, deliberate rhythm. It was a game to them.

Seraphina's pulse pounded in her skull. Her vision blurred—not from pain, not from exhaustion, but from sheer, blinding rage.

"You touch him again, and I will rip your spine through your throat." The words were low, raw, laced with every ounce of fury she had left.

The torturer only chuckled, shaking his head. "Brave words from someone with nothing." Then he turned so damn casually—and drove his fist into Kade's ribs.

Kade jerked against his restraints, a strangled sound tearing from his throat.

She saw red. "Kade—!"

His breath hitched, and he let out a laugh; it was hoarse, weak, but it was there. The same reckless defiance she had always known. His head lifted, one eye swollen shut, the other gleaming with something wry and unbroken.

"Nice threat, Nyx," he rasped. "Maybe try it when you're not tied up?"

It was a joke. A final desperate attempt to keep something. Seraphina clenched her jaw, forcing her shaking hands into fists. One chance at liberty. She'd destroy this whole place.

* * *

Minutes passed. Or hours. Maybe days. Pain eclipsed time.

When the guards tossed them back into their cell, she hit the stone floor hard. She couldn't feel it. The cold was nothing. The bruises? Nothing.

Kade.

She dragged herself toward him, her limbs screaming in protest. He slumped against the wall, breath unsteady. His head tipped back, his chest rising and falling in shallow, ragged intervals.

Seraphina reached out, fingers ghosting over his bruised cheek. "Kade—?"

His breath hitched, then his lips twitched. "You look awful."

Relief crashed into her as she choked on it. "You're an idiot," she blew out with a breath, slumping beside him. Adjusting her wrists so the manacles weren't digging into the already fragile skin as she settled in beside him.

"Still pretty?" Kade's voice was a rasped whisper, cracking an exhausted smirk.

"Hideous," she shot back without hesitation, but her voice was too soft, too fragile.

His lips fell down, dropping the smile as quickly as it had graced his face. For the first time since their arrival in this hell, he dropped his mask, and she gasped at his true face. Following her kingdom's fall, Seraphina spent two years with Kade, yet never saw him appear vulnerable. It scared her.

His body curled inward, shielding itself from the pain that had long since settled into his bones. His uneven, shuddering breaths showed the weight of his own being was too much. The dim light cast cruel shadows over his face, carving harsh lines into his features, highlighting every bruise, every cut, and every ounce of exhaustion darkening his silver eyes.

She hesitated.

She longed to comfort him, but terror held her back, the fear of causing further pain too strong to overcome. Kade never flinched. He was the one who kept them focused and grounded. Never faltering, not even when he betrayed Alexis for her.

His lips parted, but the words barely scraped past his swollen throat.

"Maybe I should... give them whatever it is they want." A breath. A tremor.

Seraphina's stomach twisted violently. They weren't even sure what these demons of the Veilborn wanted, but considering Kade and she were the two leading most battles, they thought it was their power or allies' locations and even their lives.

Kade's hands clenched into fists, fingers twitching, as if fighting some invisible force. His voice—hoarse, raw, stripped of all bravado—was barely more than a whisper, yet it hit her like a blade to the chest. "This won't end well, Nyx," his lashes fluttering as he struggled to keep his eyes open. "Maybe I should... give them what they want. If it means they stop—"

Her heart clenched. No. Not Kade. He always took on the role of the one who fought, teased, laughed with bloodied teeth, and defied death by spitting in its face. He made the world bleed before he let it take something from him. And yet, here he was. Worn down to nothing.

She had never seen him like this. Not just hurt. Not just exhausted.

Broken. His look, however, betrayed something beyond his pain. It was hers as well. His fierce defiance dimmed, threatening extinction.

Seraphina gritted her teeth, something inside her twisting into something violent. "No." Her voice was steel, but inside, she was unravelling.

Kade let out a ragged breath, his eyes slipping shut. "I won't let them keep hurting you."

She sucked in a sharp breath. His words were quiet, but there was something final about them. As if he had already decided. As if he had already made peace with it.

The prospect of losing him, or that he'd already accepted their fate, terrified her. She stared at him, searching his face, the shadows beneath his eyes, the raw vulnerability bleeding through the cracks in his usual bravado.

Kade. Her Kade. He was breaking. Its pain surpassed physical injury.

* * *

Time stretched thin in the dark, pressing in on them like a living thing. The cold stone beneath them leeched warmth from their bodies, and the silence between them felt heavier than the shackles that had bound them. Kade lay slumped against the wall, his breath slow, steady, but she could tell he wasn't asleep. His fingers twitched, as if reaching for something that wasn't there.

Seraphina sat close, not touching him, but near enough that he could if he wanted to. Near enough that he knew he wasn't alone.

"Nyx," Kade rasped, his voice barely more than a whisper.

She shifted, waiting.

He exhaled, muttering, "The Unseelie Court won't let me live, even if we escape."

She frowned. It wasn't the words she expected, but his tone surprised her. As if he had long since accepted it.

Seraphina stayed quiet. Kade never spoke of his past. Not really. She had only ever caught glimpses—the sharp glint of something ancient in his eyes when he spoke of magic, the careful way he never let his guard down. But this... this felt different.

"They see me as worse than the Veilborn now," his head tilting back against the wall. His silver hair, still matted with blood, caught in the faint light. "At least demons don't pretend to be anything but monsters."

He exhaled again, slower this time, dragging a hand over his face. Split knuckles showed against his pale skin, the dried blood dark. "Their weapon doesn't just drain magic," his voice shook with the effort to talk. "It warps it. It twists the very fabric of supernatural life. You've seen the way it spreads, how it taints everything it touches." His eyes slid to hers, unreadable in the dimness. "It's worse than death, Sera."

She swallowed hard, remembering the way the dragons had fallen, their bodies withering mid-air, their souls consumed by something unnatural.

"What makes you so sure?" her voice was quiet.

Kade hesitated. Just for a fraction of a second. Then — "Because I've seen something like it before."

A pause.

Her eyes met his, and her gaze sharpened. "In the Unseelie Court?" She remembered on the map the kingdom of Mournvale. She knew he hailed from Duskspire. A city of blackened spires and twisted thorns, where the sky is eternally twilight.

A humourless laugh. "Where else?"

She didn't push, didn't pressure him to keep going, but she didn't look away either. Maybe that was why he continued.

"The Unseelie thrives in darkness," his voice distant, as if recalling something from a lifetime ago. "Not just the absence of light. True darkness. The kind that crawls beneath your skin, that settles in your bones. It's woven into our rituals, our magic, and the very foundation of our existence. The Court..." His lips curled, but there was no humour in it. "The Court is cruelty refined into something beautiful."

Seraphina's hands curled into fists. She had never trusted the Unseelie. Her upbringing instilled that distrust, but hearing it from him—a former Unseelie court member—made her stomach twist.

"They don't see emotions the way you do," Kade tilted his head, watching her through lidded eyes. "To them, feelings are weaknesses, distractions. Love is a flaw. Mercy is a disease." His fingers tapped against his knee. "I was weak."

She inhaled.

"They cast me out," he said, as if it were nothing. "For protecting someone I loved."

Her breath caught in her throat. He didn't elaborate. Didn't give a name, offered nothing more. The way he said it, with his voice dipping and gaze flickering, conveyed more than words could. That was all he said. Kade fell silent after that, his head tilting back against the wall, eyes slipping shut. The weight of his past hung heavy between them, but Seraphina didn't press. Words couldn't stitch up some wounds. Instead, she just sat there, watching the slow rise and fall of his chest, listening to the steady rhythm of his breath. The silence wasn't empty; it was something solid, something unspoken but understood.

Then, after a long pause, she smirked. "Remember our first year together?"

Kade raised his eyebrows at her. "I spent most of it wondering if you would put a knife in my ribs."

She grinned, the action hurting her split lip. "You deserved it half the time." She stared off into the distance. "You called me a feral pixie with a sword."

He blinked, then let out a low cackle. "I stand by that."

She reached over and slid her hand into his bleeding one. He jolted at the contact but didn't remove his hand. "That was the first time you let yourself be real with me. No cold warrior act. No walls. Just you, bleeding and sarcastic." Her lips pulled into a small smile, full of warmth. "That's when I knew we were friends."

Kade didn't speak right away. He just watched her through swollen eyes, something unreadable in his gaze.

"This isn't over," leaning in, her face inches from his.

Kade let out a low breath, something almost like a laugh ghosting past his lips. It was hoarse, but real. "Reckless as ever," his voice was rough.

For a moment, neither of them spoke. But the air between them had shifted — the weight of his past still lingered, but it was no longer crushing. She rested her head against his shoulder as she into a fitful sleep.

Chapter 4

Seraphina woke in darkness. Her body was a ruin of bruises and bone-deep aches. Every breath scraped her ribs raw, and the air—thick with mold and iron—tasted like decay. The cell stank of blood and damp stone.

She didn't know how long she'd been here.

Days had blurred into weeks. Weeks into months. There was no sun, no moon, no rhythm to anchor her. Only the flicker of torches down the corridor, sometimes replaced, sometimes left to burn to embers. Once, she'd tried to count them. Now, she didn't bother.

The Veilborn demons made sure no one died too soon.

They were efficient that way, using their dark magic to keep their captives alive just enough to suffer again. Their healing was never mercy. They mended bones wrong, stitched wounds too tightly, and filled broken lungs with air that burned like fire. Every act of "restoration" was simply preparation for the next round.

Seraphina had learned that lesson early. She'd lost count of how many times someone had pieced her body back together—just enough to start over.

Only one thing kept her anchored through the endless cycle: Kade.

When they would come and drag her away, she could hear his voice echoing down the corridor, sometimes shouting her name, sometimes nothing but a ragged breath. They separated them only during the torture.

They always brought them back, broken and bleeding, to the same shared cell.

Every time the guards left, slamming the door behind them, she crawled to him. That instinct had become stronger than thought, stronger than pain. As long as she could move, she reached for him. Even when her arms trembled, when blood blurred her sight, she would find him.

The sound of footsteps snapped her back to the present—iron scraping against stone. The cell door shrieked open, and torchlight spilled inside.

The brute entered. The one with the gravel voice and cruelty carved into his grin. "Still breathing, little warrior?"

Seraphina didn't respond. She lifted her head instead, blood crusting along her jaw. Her eyes—dull but defiant—met his.

He laughed, crouching to grab her chin. "The master says you're taking too long to break." His breath was sour. "Let's see if you're more talkative today."

His fist crashed across her cheek. White sparks. Then black. The world tilted sideways. Chains bit into raw wrists as he hauled her up again, metal scraping skin. This was always how it went. Seraphina had become so used to the pain she sometimes didn't notice how long they would take beating her. She would stare at the cracked ceiling, counting each split in the stone.

"Maybe we'll fix you later," he said, tossing her toward the corridor. "Can't have you dying yet."

The guards hauled her up by the chains around her wrists and dragged her along the stone floor, her feet scraping against jagged edges. The torches lining the hall flared as she passed, the air thick with sulphur. Screams echoed distantly, some familiar, most not.

When they threw her back into her cell, she hit the ground hard, sliding across the damp stone until she collided with something warm and solid. Kade.

The sound that left her throat was half a sob, half a gasp of recognition.

Behind her, the guards laughed. "Touching the little warrior, she was worried her friend was dead." The Veilborn with the gravely voice said to his companion. They both let out a sick cackle as they slammed the door shut.

Silence pressed in again—thick, suffocating, absolute.

Seraphina lay there, chest heaving, the edges of her vision swimming. Her body screamed for rest, but her mind reached for him first. He's always the one. She turned her head. His face was pale beneath streaks of blood, his hair matted to his forehead. His chest rose and fell, shallow but steady.

He was still breathing.

"Thank the gods..." The words were barely a whisper.

She dragged herself closer, every movement agony. The stone tore at her skin, reopening half-healed wounds, but she didn't stop. Inch by inch, she clawed her way across the floor until her fingers brushed his wrist.

Warm.

Alive!

She pressed her forehead to his arm and let out a shuddering breath. It wasn't a relief. Not really. It was a reminder that he was still hers to protect. When she had lost everything, she still had him.

Sometimes, the Veilborn would heal him before her. They liked to show her what "hope" looked like—him waking first, calling her name, before they came to take him again. Other times, it was reversed. They fed on that cycle, that small, desperate spark of reunion, before tearing them apart again.

But they never counted on what that kind of pain could build. Every scar made her harder. Every scream she swallowed became steel in her veins.

Kade stirred, a weak sound catching in his throat. His eyes fluttered open, dazed. When they found her, his expression softened.

"Sera..."

"Don't speak," she said. Her voice was raw, the words scraping out like shards. "Save your strength."

He tried to lift the corners of his lips into a smile—faint, cracked, but real. "You look awful."

Her lips twitched. Even in this pit, they found the faintest thread of humour. A ghost of the life before.

She leaned against him. "They'll come again soon."

"I know." His voice was low. "You should just leave me here—"

"I'm not leaving you." Her tone was sharp enough to cut through the dark.

Kade's hand shifted, his fingers brushing hers weakly. "You can't keep this up forever."

"Yes," she said, quiet but sure. "I can. I will."

Because the thought of not reaching him—of being dragged back to that slab and waking up alone—was worse than anything they could do to her.

She tilted her head back, staring at the ceiling's faint cracks, the way the torchlight outside flickered through them. Her chest burned with exhaustion, but beneath it, a deeper fire simmered.

"They think they've won," she said. "That we're too broken to fight back."

Kade's gaze met hers. "Are we?"

"No." She swallowed hard. "Not yet."

For a long while, neither spoke. Their breathing fell into rhythm—the same slow rise and fall that had once marked nights spent beneath stars, not stone.

Somewhere beyond the door, a Veilborn's guttural voice echoed, followed by the faint hum of dark magic. She could feel its pull through the air, the energy that kept their bodies functioning when they should have collapsed long ago. The demons thought their healing spells made them gods. But Seraphina felt the cracks in their power, the way the magic left traces, residue she could sense deep in her bones.

They were healing them all at once, which meant that quite a few of the tortured souls today must have been too close to death for them not to need to heal everyone at once.

That thought took root quietly, somewhere between exhaustion and resolve. When she glanced back at Kade, his eyes had already drifted closed again. His breathing was shallow but steady. She brushed a hand against his cheek, careful not to wake him.

Sleep, rest while you can, she thought. Because the next time they come for us, I'll be ready.

The air buzzed faintly around her, the distant hum of residual magic still crackling against her skin. Seraphina closed her eyes, drawing in a breath that hurt more than it soothed. Every ache, every scar, every night spent crawling through the dark had led her here, to this moment, this resolve.

She would endure, because when the chance came, when the chains loosened and the door creaked open—she'd make them regret leaving her alive.

This time, when she crawled to Kade, it wouldn't be in desperation.

It would be for freedom.

Chapter 5

The scrape of metal announced the jailor's arrival against stone. A hulking figure stepped inside the cell, the door groaning open and a tray of food clattering to the floor. The air was thick with damp, carrying the sour tang of unwashed bodies and old blood. Kade shifted, his wrists raw where the iron manacles bit into his skin. The chains, etched with old magic, leeched his strength, despite his dark fae blood's ability to heal him. He exhaled, tilting his head just enough to glance at her.

Seraphina, half-slumped against the wall, rolled her shoulders, testing her bruised body. Every movement sent a new flare of pain lacing through her ribs, but she forced a smile onto her face. "Well, well, if it isn't my favourite captor. Here to charm us with your wit and fine dining?"

The jailer, a brutish man belonging to the Veilborn army, grunted. "Eat. Either do it or don't. Makes no difference to me."

Seraphina rolled her eyes and snorted. "Touching. You always know how to make a girl feel special."

The guard huffed and slammed the door behind him, the clang of iron echoing through the stones like a gavel sealing their sentence. She didn't flinch; she'd long learned that reacting gave them power. Instead, she tilted her head just enough to catch the jailer's retreating form. Coward, she thought bitterly, always quick to run after pretending they'd won something.

She exhaled through her nose, slowly and shallow. Her ribs still screamed with every breath. The bruises along her side were dark now, ugly blooms of purple and black. She could sense the places where her body had been twisted, bent too far, and broken, places that had healed enough to keep her conscious. Still, she sat upright, back pressed to the cold wall, arms resting over bent knees like a soldier at ease. *Fake it until the mask sticks.* She thought.

The silence returned, stretching wide between them. She watched Kade—his chest barely rising; the manacles digging into his wrists; the way he struggled to shift without showing pain. His face was a patchwork of bruises and old blood. He didn't look at her. Not at first. But he didn't have to. She could feel him thinking, watching even without sight. He always did that—cataloguing everything, holding it all tight like a blade he'd one day use.

She reached for the tray, fingers trembling slightly. The bread was stale enough to break teeth; the water was grey and sour. Still, she broke the bread in half and shoved it toward him.

"Eat," she said, voice hoarse.

Kade didn't argue. He took it with slow, deliberate fingers, as if any sudden motion might unravel him. Seraphina watched the way his throat bobbed as he forced it down, swallowing pain and dust in equal measure. She tried a bite of her own. It turned to gravel in her mouth. The silence it filled was worse than the sound of bones breaking. She hated the silence. That's when the doubt crept in.

All you are now, perhaps, is a shadow bleeding and spitting words at ghosts against a wall. Maybe you should have let them kill you. Perhaps that would have been simpler.

She stared at the ground between them, her pulse sluggish and thick. The aches were becoming duller, more permanent. Her body was adapting to the torment. That scared her more than anything else—that she was getting used to it.

She flicked her eyes toward him again, needing the distraction. "You know," her voice was rough but edged with her usual bite, "if I had a way to pick these damn locks, you wouldn't have to sit there bleeding like a kicked dog."

Kade's mouth curved at one side, a ghost of a smirk despite the blood on his lip. "Romantic."

Seraphina let out a breath that might have been a laugh, rasping—bitter as the bread between her teeth. Her eyes didn't leave him. If he could still smirk, still match her in words… then maybe hope wasn't entirely dead yet.

She huffed, but she shifted—the previous tension deepened, and something else replaced it. A gnawing frustration, the kind that pulled at your insides and made everything feel impossible. A strange heat simmered beneath her skin, rising like a forgotten ember. It wasn't rage. She had plenty of that. It wasn't exhaustion, though she could barely keep upright. It was something else, something foreign yet familiar, like a whisper she couldn't quite hear but could feel, threading through her veins. She blinked away the sensation, focusing instead on the thin strip of bread between her fingers. Her stomach tightened, her thoughts scattering for just a moment.

The cell around them felt like it was closing in, the damp air heavy with the weight of unspoken words and lingering danger. The days had been blurring together, each one indistinguishable from the last. Every guard shift, every metal door scrape signifies another day trapped in this stifling cage, with no hint of freedom in sight.

A sharp metallic scrape against the stone broke the quiet. Another guard was back to see if they had survived the foul food they deemed nourishment. His bulk seemed to fill the space more than usual. He sneered as he pushed the door open; the sound of his boots across the stone almost made Seraphina flinch. It was never good when more than one guard visited in the same day. She rolled her shoulders back and stared up at him in defiance.

"Still breathing? Shame," the jailor spoke in a rough voice. "Maybe we can remedy that." He said as he stepped closer towards her.

Her lips curled into a grin. "Disappointed? I would hate to think I am not living up to expectations."

The jailer let out a low, guttural chuckle as he crouched in front of her. His shadow stretched long over her, threatening to consume the small space they occupied. "Oh, you'll be plenty entertaining soon enough," his voice thick with menace.

Seraphina tilted her head, eyes narrowing with mock sweetness. "Big talk. Though I imagine you are compensating for something."

The insult landed sharp as a blade, and the jailor's lip curled in fury. He lunged for her, hands outstretched, aiming for her throat. Seraphina twisted aside just in time, her instincts taking over despite the pain. Her fingers shot up, seizing his ear, and she yanked—hard. The jailor roared, stumbling back, one hand clutching the side of his head. Something small and metallic clattered to the floor between them—a snapped clasp from the ring of keys that hung at his belt.

Her pulse spiked. Before he could recover, she dove for it, snatching the thin metal loop from the dirt before he could see.

"You little—" He reeled, blood streaking his neck, fury blazing in his eyes. "You'll regret that!" With a violent shove, he slammed the cell door, the iron reverberating through the walls before his footsteps receded down the corridor.

For a moment, silence. Then Seraphina exhaled, shaking, the sound somewhere between relief and defiance. Her fingers closed around the bit of twisted metal—small, bent, but solid. It wasn't much, but it was something. Her hands trembled as she set to work on Kade's shackles, prying and twisting the makeshift pick into the old lock. Every movement was agony. The metal bit into her raw fingertips, and her muscles screamed, but she refused to stop. She could feel Kade's faint pulse under her fingertips, the dead weight of his bound wrists and the faint shimmer of his suppressed magic pressing like a bruise in the air.

The lock resisted, then yielded, one reluctant click at a time.

She worked fast, twisting the bit of metal through the crude locks. With a soft snap, the manacles fell away with a heavy clank as they hit the floor. Seraphina slid it free from Kade's wrist, her breath catching at the sight of his skin—red, blistered where the enchanted metal had burned him. He was far weaker than she'd feared. The change was instant; the suffocating pressure around him lifted, faint but noticeable. Colour crept back into his face. His shoulders eased a fraction. The tremor in his limbs dulled. Not healed. Not whole. But free enough to breathe again as his healing abilities began working again.

He stirred, eyelids fluttering. A rough cough rattled in his throat. She leaned close, her heart hammering. "We need to move," her voice low.

"Seraphina," he rasped, voice shredded, eyes unfocused.

She steadied him with a hand against his chest as he tried to rise. "Stay," her tone lined with urgency. His eyes found hers again, and for a heartbeat, everything they'd endured hung there—the exhaustion, the fear.

"I need to get the ones on your ankles," her words came out in a rush. "They're just metal. Not iron and enchanted like the rest."

He gave a weak nod. He exhaled slowly, eyes clearing a fraction as if coming back to himself. She shifted to the chains at his ankles, her hands steady despite the anxious energy thrumming through her veins. A sudden *boom*, like thunder, ripped through the corridor.

The door exploded inward.

Three guards thundered in, boots slamming against stone, echoing like war drums. Seraphina quickly stood between Kade and the opening, but it was useless. The first guard pushed her hard, slamming her back against the wall with enough force to knock the breath from her lungs; stars exploded behind her eyes. Pain lanced through her chest, familiar and burning.

She gasped, but there was no air.

The second guard sneered, stepping closer. Scar down his cheek, grin like a predator. "Think you're clever, do you?" he said as he dragged a blade down her cheek, pressing the tip against it, not to pierce but to threaten her not to move.

She let blood spill from her lips as she smiled. "Clever enough to know none of you can spell 'clever.'"

The first guard's hand was suddenly at her throat, wrapping a beefy hand around it, squeezing hard as he pulled her against him. As he pushed her against his front, arm locking her in place around her throat, her world shrank to a narrow tunnel of pain and roaring silence. She could feel what he wanted to do next, stabbing her from behind. Still, she didn't look away from Scarface as he waved the blade in front of her eyes.

"You were very naughty, hurting one of our own. Perhaps we allowed you too much freedom, and you need to be taught a lesson."

The third stepped in, his breath hot against her cheek. "You're going to beg before we're done, sweetheart." He said as he leant against her.

She didn't flinch. That would give them too much satisfaction. Instead, Seraphina looked Scarface in the eye and spat directly in his face.

As he wiped it from his face, he raised his hand and backhanded her across the face, whipping her head to the side.

The sound of metal groaning drew the guards' eyes away from her towards where Kade had been against the wall. A loud cracking as the final shackle around his ankle gave way beneath the sheer force of his fury. He rose in one fluid, terrifying motion. The shadows clung to him as if they recognised him.

One heartbeat passed. Everyone watched the Dark Fae warrior, whose silver-grey eyes focused on the guard who was holding Seraphina. A slow smile spread across Seraphina's lips as she looked at Kade. His hair hung below his chin in silver strands. His face was healing with every moment that passed, bruises fading before her eyes. Her eyes roved over his whole body, seeing him pull himself up to his full height of 6 foot 3 inches under her gaze as she watched wounds knit back together. She noticed how his face twisted into a ferocious snarl, revealing pointed canines, as shadows flowed down his arm, inky black magic that was unique to him. Rarely had Seraphina seen him use his powers outside of extreme battles. She knew he was losing the battle with his rage.

Chaos erupted.

The third guard moved too late; Kade's fist collided with his face. Bone crunched, and the man dropped. The scarred brute didn't have time to lift his weapon; Kade's elbow smashed into his ribs, then his fist met his jaw with a sickening crunch. Blood arced across the air as the guard fell to his knees.

The first had drawn a dagger in his other hand as he kept a tight grip on Seraphina, but Kade was faster. He seized him by the throat, and the grip around Seraphina's neck loosened as she collapsed to her knees. Kade drove him backward until his skull met the stone. Hard.

She was on her knees coughing violently, her vision swimming, but she forced herself upright. Her muscles screamed. Her ribs flared. But she moved.

They *moved together*.

Kade's eyes found hers. Wild. Alive. He bent, wiped his bloodied hand on the nearest guard's cloak, he picked up and held out a blade to her like an offering. A silent pact. She took it without hesitation.

"Took you long enough," she rasped, voice shredded but amused.

"Had to make an entrance," he shot back, already bending down and stripping weapons and anything that could be useful off the remaining fallen guards. Then he stood and caught her wrist—not to drag, but to anchor. Together, they stepped over broken bodies and through the cell door into the dim corridor beyond.

* * *

The air was wrong. Heavy.

The silence stretched unnaturally long, like the dungeon itself was holding its breath.

Seraphina's grip on her blade tightened.

The cold stone floor was slick beneath their feet, each stride a gamble on blood or rot or worse. Their worn boots thundered down the winding corridor, torchlight slicing across the walls in jittery flashes. Shadows danced like dying things, twisted across the walls.

Seraphina's lungs burned, each breath serrated. But Kade was beside her, a constant. Even half-broken, she moved with purpose. Her blade gleamed in the firelight. They didn't speak as they ran. They didn't have to.

From the shadows, more guards surged forward—a wall of black fibre and dull, soulless eyes. The air reeked of blood and rust.

The first guard lunged. Seraphina pivoted sharply, ducking beneath his swing, and drove her elbow into his temple. He reeled; her blade followed through, biting deep into his thigh. His scream split the air. Another came for Kade. He caught the man's wrist mid-strike and twisted until bone snapped. A dagger flashed toward Seraphina's back—Kade moved without thought, intercepting, his blade catching the attacker's throat in a single, brutal motion.

They fought like a storm—wild, beautiful, precise. But the storm couldn't last forever. There were too many.

"This way!" She said, spotting a side tunnel branching from the main corridor.

Kade didn't hesitate. They sprinted down the narrow passage, boots pounding against the slick stone, the echoes of pursuit closing in. The tunnel funnelled them into a dead-end alcove, an old drainage arch sealed by a heavy iron gate, its bars eaten with rust but still solid.

Kade seized the handle and threw his shoulder into it. The hinges shrieked in protest, but the gate gave, swinging inward with a groan. They stumbled through. Kade turned and slammed it shut, driving the bolt home just as the first of the guards rounded the corner. The iron trembled under the first impact.

They both stood there, chests heaving, the air thick with sweat, iron, and the faint hum of Kade's magic still sparking around his hands. For a heartbeat, the world narrowed to just their ragged breaths and the thunder of fists pounding on metal.

Then Seraphina froze. Her gaze darted past him, back toward the tunnel.

"Kade—" her voice broke, hoarse. "There were other cells. I saw them. People—people were still alive in there."

Kade turned from the gate, his face pale under the dim torchlight. "We can't go back."

"We can't just *leave them*." Her voice rose, the desperation raw, trembling.

"We're not the only ones they've been torturing!"

The pounding on the gate grew louder. Dust sifted from the ceiling with every strike. Kade's jaw tightened. He took a step closer; the shadows catching the edges of his face.

"If we go back now, we die with them."

Her breath came fast, fury and grief warring in her chest. "Then maybe that's worth it!" Seraphina stepped closer, fury trembling in her voice. "That is my job. *Protect them.* I swore to—"

"What good is your oath if you die down here with them?" Kade turned towards her, his voice louder than he meant to be. "They're not *you*, Sera. Don't throw yourself away because of guilt, duty, or some bleeding ideal. You're the reason people *still believe* we can win this war. You are hope."

Her expression shattered, as if he'd slapped her.

"You think *that* makes me more important?" her voice was tight. "You think it gives you the right to choose who gets saved?"

"I'm choosing *you*." Stepping in close, his voice low. "Because if you die, there is *no war left to win.*"

Her fists clenched. "That's not your choice to make."

"No," he nodded. "But I'm making it."

For a moment, they just stared at each other.

The air between them crackled—grief, rage, fear—everything they'd both been holding back, tearing loose at once. The warmth that had always tethered them, that bond forged in fire and blood, suddenly felt paper thin. A thread stretched to breaking.

"You're not my commander, Kade." Each word landed like a blade. "You're supposed to be my friend."

She turned around, ready to go back the way they'd come, no matter the cost.

Kade's jaw flexed. For a heartbeat, he looked as though he might let her. Then something hardened in his eyes. He stepped past her, crossing the cracked stone floor to a second mechanism half-hidden in the wall, a rusted lever buried under soot and ash. Seraphina's stomach dropped.

"Kade, don't—"

He pulled it.

The world answered. A deep, hollow groan reverberated through the tunnel, rolling beneath their feet like thunder in the bones of the earth. The air warped with pressure. Dust rained in pale sheets from the ceiling. Then came the roar, stone grinding on stone as the old fortress caved in on itself.

The ground heaved. The gate they'd sealed shuddered, screamed, then collapsed inward in a violent cascade of rock and iron. A shockwave of air burst through the corridor, throwing Seraphina off balance. She caught herself against the wall, coughing through the haze.

"What did you do?" she shouted, voice cracking through the chaos.

Kade didn't look at her. His expression seemed carved from ice. "I buried it. The whole route. They can't follow us."

Her heart stuttered in her chest. "You buried *them.*"

He said nothing. The silence hit harder than any denial could have.

Seraphina staggered toward him, fury blazing hot through the dust. She shoved him hard in the chest. "You didn't even try! We could've fought—we could've freed them, Kade! We *had time!*"

"We didn't." His voice broke on the word. He turned on her then, jaw trembling with something that wasn't just anger. "You think I wanted this? That I didn't *hear* them? The chains? The screaming?" His voice, low and sharp. "There were dozens of guards down there. Maybe hundreds. We wouldn't have made it three steps before they tore us apart."

"I would've died for them," she hissed.

"I know," he said.

She tried to move past him, but his hand shot out, gripping her arm—not cruelly, but unyielding.

"Let me go."

"No."

"I said *Let me go!*"

"I'm not losing you," he growled, dragging her back as the rumble above them deepened. Cracks split the ceiling; dust fell like snow. "This isn't some noble sacrifice, Seraphina—it's suicide." His voice was rough, desperate now. "I won't watch you die for ghosts."

"They're not *ghosts*!" she shouted. Her voice cracked. "They were *people*. They still *are*. You talk about hope like I'm its goddamn vessel—well, *this* is what it means! Not running. Not abandoning people. Not making me into something I'm not, just because you're too afraid to lose me."

His face twisted. "You think I'm afraid? I've seen you cut down beasts that would make kings wet themselves. But this war? It's *bigger than you*. Then both of us. I *need* you alive."

"For what?" she spat. "So I can be your symbol? Your precious weapon in a war that's already lost too much? I'm not your fucking torchbearer, Kade. I'm not your sacrifice either."

He looked at her as if she'd just broken something inside him.

"I'm not trying to possess you, Sera," he breathed. "I'm trying to save what's left."

She couldn't stop the tears, though they burned like acid. Not grief. Not yet. Betrayal.

"You already threw it away."

Then, without warning, Kade surged forward and wrapped an arm around Seraphina's waist. Before she could react, he hoisted her over his shoulder as if she weighed nothing.

"Kade! *Put me down!*" she shouted, fury bursting out of her.

"Not until we're clear of this hellhole," he growled through gritted teeth.

She thrashed, pounding her fists against his back, kicking at the air and spitting curses like fire. Every ounce of fury, betrayal, and grief poured out of her. But he held her fast, one arm locked around her thighs, the other gripping his blood-slick blade as he charged up the tunnel.

Behind them, the stone groaned with a final death-rattle. Another quake ripped through the earth, and the passage caved in completely. The sound was deafening—stone and screams swallowed in a collapse that sealed the dead away for good.

Seraphina screamed into his shoulder, her voice raw and broken. Rage, helplessness, sorrow—it all bled out in one jagged cry.

The stairwell ahead of them spiralled upward in steep, uneven slabs, carved by hands long dead. Each step was agony. Dust clung to Kade's lungs, sweat dripped into his eyes, and Seraphina's weight—though he never flinched at it—added to the growing fire in his legs.

The further they climbed, the worse the air became. The cold, damp bite of the prison faded into a stifling heat. It pressed against them like a vise. The heat whispered of fire and ruin above. Of something *going wrong*.

At the summit, they met a door—thick oak, rimmed in iron, warped by time but still standing. Kade braced his shoulder against it. Muscles screamed. He growled low in his throat and shoved—once, twice—until, with a shattering crack, the door gave way.

They tumbled into daylight.

Seraphina staggered to her feet, disoriented. Her legs trembled beneath her. Kade reached to steady her, fingers lingering on her arm as if afraid she might collapse entirely.

Before them stretched the remains of what had once been life.

The village was gone. Where bustling homes and golden fields once sprawled in safety beneath the castle's shadow, now stood only blackened husks. Ash. Burnt timber twisted like bones. The fields were grey and cracked, no longer golden, no longer alive. Just dust.

She took a step forward. The ground crunched beneath her boots; bone dry. Foreign. Her eyes scanned the ruin, searching for something that wasn't there. Hope, maybe. A survivor. A sign.

There was none.

Kade exhaled beside her, the sound hollow, broken. "We lost."

She didn't speak. Her eyes stayed fixed on the horizon, where nothing moved. Her heart thudded in her chest as if it were trying to remember how to feel. Everything they'd bled for, fought for—every sacrifice—all for this.

Silence fell over them.

Chapter 6

The world was a graveyard.

Seraphina's boots crunched against the ashen soil with each step, the sound of her movement the only thing breaking the oppressive silence that hung heavy in the air. The stench of death and fire lingered, mixing with the scorched earth beneath her feet. The land stretched before them, broken, empty, and lifeless. What had once been thriving villages were now little more than charred husks, their skeletal remains clawing at the sickly red sky above. Bodies, discarded and forgotten, lay where they fell, some twisted in grotesque positions, others impaled on blackened spikes as grim warnings. There were no birds soaring overhead, no insects buzzing in the remnants of the fields—only the whisper of the wind, cutting through a kingdom that had already forgotten its name.

But Seraphina hadn't forgotten. She couldn't. Not after everything she had lost.

Valtheris, the kingdom of humans, once stood as an unbreakable force in the world. Mist-shrouded mountains formed an impenetrable barrier. Its rivers, silver-threaded and deep, had nourished its people, their clear waters running with life and vitality. Dunmara, the capital, pulsed with life; a vibrant, sprawling castle city where the supernatural and mortal worlds lived together, magic and steel defending their shared existence.

Now, the rivers ran black with blood, their waters stained by the death that had poured into them from the fallen. The mountains endured, but even they seemed quieter, hollowed out. As if they too mourned. Dunmara burned. Its proud spires crumbled into ash, smoke curling into the blood-soaked sky. Nothing remained but ruin.

She staggered slightly as she walked, her steps uneven, her boots catching on the cracked earth. Every breath stung her throat, raw from smoke and screaming. Her left side throbbed with each motion, the bruised ribs from the earlier battle grinding with protest. Cuts lined her skin, sticky with dried blood. Some was hers, some not. Her arm was bound tight with part of Kade's tunic for a gash she hadn't even felt until after they'd escaped, adrenaline masking the pain that now gnawed its way back with a vengeance.

But it was the weight in her chest that hurt the most.

She was still thinking of them. The ones they'd left behind. The quiet faces of the prisoners haunted her thoughts. Her mind returned to the moment he'd grabbed her—hoisted her over his shoulder, carrying her like dead weight through fire and stone. She'd fought him then, but deep down... even in that moment, she'd known why he did it.

Because if he hadn't, she would've stayed. Would've burned with them. Maybe part of her still wished she had.

Kade walked beside her, his steps heavier than usual. He limped now, a wound on his thigh slowing him. Even his healing abilities were fading with his exhaustion, and every movement caused him pain. Yet he hadn't complained, not once. The silence between them had grown, fed by exhaustion and guilt, by everything they hadn't said since the prison walls fell behind them.

They hadn't touched since. They exchanged only brief glances.

Kade was still the one who'd pulled her from the fire. Still the one who'd kept her alive. Yet now, he was also the one who abandoned the rest. Actually, she didn't blame him. She knew he had done what he believed was right. She even agreed with him. But that didn't stop the ache. It didn't ease the guilt that curled like smoke in her lungs.

Kade broke the stillness, his voice low but firm, cutting through the silence like a blade dulled by sorrow. "We can't just wander aimlessly."

Seraphina blinked. His voice snapped her out of the spiral. She looked at him then—truly looked. Saw the bruising under his eyes, the way his breath caught, the stiffness in his shoulder from carrying her, fighting for her, protecting her when she didn't want to be saved. Sweat and dirt matted his silver hair, and his face was gaunt and worn from the struggle, but his piercing eyes still burned with the calculating sharpness she relied on. Even amid this endless suffering, when everything seemed lost, Kade was already thinking ahead. He always had.

She ran a hand through her tangled hair, pushing a stray lock away from her face. "Where else is there to go?"

Kade's gaze shifted to the horizon, where the skeletal remains of Dunmara's towers stood like the gravestones of a fallen empire. He spoke in a measured tone, choosing his words carefully but firmly. "Anyone who survived will be found there. The enemy would keep their prisoners in the capital."

The idea made her stomach turn. She could already picture it—the way their captors treated the supernatural, the cruel collars forged from cursed steel that suppressed magic, the brands seared into their flesh like permanent reminders of their torment. Magic siphoned away until nothing remained but husks of what they once were. If there were survivors, she knew they were suffering in unimaginable ways.

A knot twisted in her gut, but she pushed the feeling aside, forcing herself to focus. "We could circle the outskirts," her voice low but steady. "Watch the patrols. If there's even a chance of freeing anyone—"

Kade snorted, his boots kicking up dust as he slowed his pace. "You think we can break into Dunmara and save them all?" Scepticism coloured his voice, yet an undercurrent of fear threaded through it. He wasn't laughing at her—not really. Fear gripped him, because he knew she would try.

Seraphina met his gaze, her eyes hard. "If it were me in chains, wouldn't you try?"

His expression darkened, a shadow passing over his features as if the very thought had pulled him into deeper, more painful memories. She didn't need an answer—she knew it. Had lived it.

"You know the answer to that," a curse slipping through clenched teeth. "If we do this," his voice quieter now, lower—meant only for her. "We make a plan. I won't stop you, Sera... but I won't watch you get yourself killed either."

A breath caught in her throat at the sound of her name—*Sera.* It felt strange on his tongue, like a memory they hadn't touched in too long. Her chest ached with the weight of it.

She looked at him. He was paler than usual. His eyes held hers, and in their silver depths, she saw his determination to keep her safe. He kept moving. For her. Because of her.

"Then we go." Her voice sharp with resolve, honed on the grindstone of loss. Cold. Unyielding. Beneath it, she allowed space, hope living there.

Kade's gaze flickered to her, and for a moment, something passed between them. A quiet, unspoken vow. He muttered something under his breath, half frustration and half surrender, but he didn't argue.

They walked on, weaving through the skeletal remains of Valtheris, the once-thriving kingdom now reduced to ash and bone. As they progressed, conditions deteriorated. The earth itself appeared to recoil from the devastation, warping the surrounding land. Blackened and crumbling, the stone walls of the villages were nothing but hollow shells. The wind carried with it a strange, unsettling hum, as though the world itself was mourning. Death extended beyond the land. The breath and spirit of Valtheris and Dunmara's former residents lingered.

Someone defaced the once-proud statues, shattering their marble faces and erasing their names from history. Valtheris's proud figures lay ruined, their identities lost, as if erased. Streets that had once bustled with life, the sound of laughter and trade echoing through the air, now held only the remnants of battle—discarded weapons, the glint of broken steel caught in the flickering light of dying fires, bloodstains dried into the cobblestone, their crimson hue a stark contrast to the ashen landscape. The chaos trampled banners that had once waved proudly into the dirt, muting and tearing their vibrant colours—remnants of a kingdom's lost identity.

Seraphina exhaled sharply, tasting the metallic sting of blood in the air, thick and nauseating. It was the scent of destruction, of everything she had once fought to protect, now reduced to ash and ruin. Is this what we fought for? Her heart clenched at the thought. She defended the kingdom, protecting its walls and citizens from destruction. But now it was gone, its soul gutted, its heartbeat silenced. She had failed. Valtheris had fallen.

* * *

They reached the capital by nightfall. The broken walls remained a defiant challenge. Draped like fresh scars over the ruined kingdom, the enemy's banners, with their ugly and unfamiliar insignia, hung from shattered towers. The enemy defaced the once-proud gates, carved with the sigils of old rulers, burning away their intricate designs under the weight of conquest. The land bore the mark of an irretrievable destruction.

Fires flickered in the streets, their orange glow casting grotesque shadows across the broken remnants of Dunmara, dancing on the twisted, burnt-out husks of what had once been a proud city. The people moved like ghosts, their bodies thin, hollow-eyed, and their spirits broken by the relentless onslaught. Their enslavers bound them in chains, reducing them to little more than animals; others waited, waiting for their turn to be dragged into the hell that had already claimed so much of their world.

The supernaturals—those who had once walked proud and untouchable— now dragged their feet through the streets, chained and branded, their power stripped from them. Their bodies rotted, with skin stretched tight over brittle bones. The enemy had hung others on the gallows, leaving their broken bodies to sway lifelessly in the wind like twisted trophies. Seraphina clenched her jaw, her fingers curling into fists so tightly her nails bit into her palms. Rage burned through the exhaustion, bitter. It was an abomination. She would never forget this tragedy, not while she still lived.

"I should have died before seeing this." Kade's voice was low, thick with the weight of his own silent fury. His eyes, normally so calm, were now clouded with a storm she had seen many times before—a storm born from years of fighting, of seeing everything they had fought for crumble into dust. "They will watch the main roads," his voice a quiet command, filled with that steady resolve that never faltered. "We need to keep moving."

Seraphina nodded, though every muscle in her body screamed for vengeance, for justice. Now wasn't the time. She forced herself forward, putting one foot in front of the other, pushing against the tide of despair that threatened to drown her. They had come this far; there was no turning back. While navigating the broken streets of Dunmara, her fingers continued to throb with the desire to spill blood and eradicate any signs of the enemy. Surviving wasn't enough. She couldn't let it end like this. Not with so much loss.

A sudden crash shattered the silence, echoing down the alleyway like a gunshot—a body slammed into a crumbling stone wall, sending dust and shards of old mortar tumbling to the cobblestones. The impact left a human-shaped dent, and the figure crumpled forward with a groan, blood smearing where its shoulder dragged on the rock.

A dishevelled man staggered into the alley, panting like a hunted beast. His chest heaved, ribs sharp beneath torn cloth, and every breath came with a wince. Dark curls clung wetly to his brow, matted with blood and grime, framing a once-arrogant face now carved with exhaustion. His olive skin showed bruises, splits, and black marks in areas that hadn't healed correctly.

Seraphina's breath hitched.

Evander.

There had been a time Evander had swaggered into every fight like the gods owed him victory. Now he could barely stay upright. He was a ghost made flesh—yet thinner, harder, and cracked at the edges. Though his eyes once blazed with mischief, they still held a flicker of that flame, but too much pain buried it. It pierced her like shrapnel.

A group of enemy soldiers slinked out of the shadows behind him, sneering and laughing, their blades glinting like teeth. One kicked Evander behind the knee, forcing him to stumble forward. He barely caught himself.

"Still got some fight, huh?" the soldier let out with a sneer, raising his sword.

Seraphina moved like fury made flesh. Her dagger kissed the soldier's throat, opening it in a wide arc of red. Blood sprayed the alley wall. The others barely registered the motion before Kade was on them, a blur of shadows and steel. His blades sang a brutal hymn, cleaving through fibre as if it were parchment.

One lunged at Seraphina; she ducked, spun, and drove her blade into his ribs, twisting cruelly. Another tried to grab her; he lost a hand. Kade swept low, knocked another soldier into the stone, then rammed his sword through the man's back with a sickening crunch.

When silence fell again, it was wet, jagged.

Evander collapsed to his knees, coughing hard, spitting blood into the dirt. Yet—he grinned. A rough, almost manic smile cracked across his bloodied lips.

"...About damn time."

She dropped beside him, her hands hovering over his wounds, unsure where to start. "You're alive."

"Barely." He wheezed, blinking hard. He gazed up at them through his unruly hair. "Thought you two were dead."

Kade, while using a corpse's shirt to clean blades, spoke in a tight tone, "We thought the same."

Evander glanced at him. "You look like shit."

"You resemble someone who failed a wager involving a Minotaur."

"Fair." Evander let out a cackle, then let out a low groan. Clutching his ribs.

"Laughing hurts. Gods, this hurts."

Kade crouched beside them, glancing at Seraphina. "You gonna patch him up or just let him bleed dramatic poetry in the dirt?"

Evander jabbed a finger weakly in Kade's direction. "You hear that, Sera? He *missed me.* That's love."

"Oh, I've missed this," Seraphina let out a sigh as she reached into

Evander's pack that was always on his hip, knowing she would find supplies in there. He was always the best prepared. Sure enough, she found them. She gently began pressing bandages to his side, though her hands trembled slightly. "The mutual insults. The over-inflated egos. It's like nothing's changed."

Evander met her eyes. "But everything has, hasn't it?"

She didn't look up at him as she worked to stop the bleeding.

His gaze turned inward. "They captured you... then you disappeared. Months, Seraphina. We thought the weapon had devoured you."

Kade's brow furrowed. "Wait—months?"

Evander nodded grimly. "So much time passed after they took you guys that you were both presumed dead."

Seraphina swallowed hard, letting that sink in. "Did this destruction result from corruption?" Sera's hand waved around them.

Evander's jaw tightened. "It's spreading. The weapon is only part of it. The demons amplify it. They twist magic at its roots, like a rot infecting everything. Some supernaturals die the moment they draw near. Others... lose themselves. Turn. Their minds snap, their magic bends. They're still breathing, but they aren't who they are. Not anymore."

"What do you mean, *not them*?" Kade looked at Evander, frowning.

"I mean, they wear the same face, same voice—but something else is inside." Evander's eyes cut to Seraphina. "But not you."

She blinked. "What?"

"I saw it," his voice low and certain. "On the field. Everything should've been lost—dragons falling, magic failing, demons everywhere—you *burned* through it. I saw the weapon's aura hit you. It should've crushed you like it did the others. But it didn't. You resisted it... no—*you destroyed it.*"

Seraphina shook her head slowly, unsure if she even believed him. "I remember nothing like that. Just... Kade. That demon monster was about to kill him. I didn't cast anything. I ran, and something burst out of me. I didn't even think. There was just heat, and light, and—"

"—and the corruption shattered," Evander finished. "I felt it break."

Kade's expression darkened slightly, his jaw tense. "That shouldn't have been possible. Anything that close to the weapon—hell, even I couldn't summon shadows near it. At the end, when I was bleeding out... I tried. Nothing came."

Evander's brow furrowed. "You? But your magic's ancient."

"Exactly." Kade's eyes were sharp as he observed Evander. "Didn't matter. It failed."

They both turned to Seraphina.

She lifted her hands slightly, palms trembling, empty. "I don't feel it now. There's nothing. No spark, no pull. Just... silence."

Evander's eyes narrowed as he studied her, like trying to solve a riddle written in a dying language. "You never had magic before, Sera."

She shook her head. "No. I shouldn't."

"Then maybe..." Evander's voice softened, but there was a strange awe beneath it. "Maybe you're something more."

A long beat of silence.

Kade didn't flinch. "She is."

Seraphina turned toward him, searching his face.

Evander's gaze moved among them, a glimmer of recognition rising.

Kade was staring at her too now, something unreadable in his gaze. He quickly averted his eyes when Seraphina looked up at him.

She turned to him. "What did you mean? When you said I was *more?*"

Kade didn't blink. "Nothing. You're stubborn. It's not magic, it's just you refusing to die."

"Liar," Evander coughed, smirking. "You've always been a terrible liar."

Kade stood up abruptly, scanning the alleyway as if he found the conversation boring. "She'll figure it out."

Seraphina stared at his back, unsettled. "Figure *out what?*"

"Doesn't matter right now." His usual smooth tone was sharp. "We have to move. Provided Evander is correct, there's no time."

Evander coughed again, grimacing. "Still charming."

"You want me to carry you?" Kade smirked at him, a familiar glint in his eyes.

"You'd drop me out of spite."

"Only halfway."

Seraphina let out a groan, rolling her eyes. She never grasped the dynamics between Kade and Evander.

Evander reached up weakly, catching her wrist. "I'm going to the rebels. They need to know what we've learned. There's still a resistance out there. I have to believe that."

"We'll get you there."

She turned the arm he was holding to grasp his wrist, almost shaking hands on the promise but also to lend the warrior a hand up.

Kade glanced over his shoulder. "Unless you die of sarcasm first."

Evander grinned, even through the blood. "If I go, I'm taking you with me."

Seraphina helped him to his feet, their limbs shaking.

The capital, distant, mimicked a rotting, hollow corpse. She looked at it and whispered, more to herself than to them.

"We fight. We endure. We rebuild."

Kade stood beside her in silence, blades slung across his back, eyes haunted.

Evander leaned on her, breath shallow, muttering, "But gods help us, we better win. I will not perish alongside you two fools debating martyrdom."

Chapter 7

They hid in an abandoned temple, a forgotten ruin just beyond the smouldering city. The air inside was thick with dust, carrying the scent of old stone and decay, the smell that made you feel like the walls were closing in with the weight of history itself. Moonlight filtered through the gaping cracks in the ceiling, spilling like liquid silver across the cold stone floors, illuminating faded murals of gods long abandoned, their once-vibrant faces now little more than shadowed outlines in the dark. The silence was oppressive, as though the very air mourned the loss of the temple's former life.

Evander leaned against one of the cracked columns, his breath shallow but steady, the rise and fall of his chest a reminder that, despite everything, he was still here. Grime covered his body; his once-strong frame, now leaner, bore bruises and cuts, but his hazel eyes still burned with defiance. The fire that had once fuelled his roguish charm now flickered faintly, but it was there.

Seraphina watched him in the dim light, her thoughts tangled. He was a ghost from her past made flesh, another life she had thought lost forever. The weight of his presence was like a distant echo in her chest, reverberating in the hollows of her heart, stirring up old memories she wasn't ready to confront. She wanted to ask him everything—how he had survived, who else had made it, what their next move should be. But the words wouldn't come. "Get some sleep."

Evander gave her a weak smirk, tilting his head back against the stone, his tangled dark curls falling over his forehead. "Miss your charming company?"

Her lips twitched, a fleeting ghost of a smile, but it faded as quickly as it came. There was something heavy in the air between them, a subtle shift in the space that no amount of humour could chase away. His gaze softened as he watched her, and for a moment, it felt as though the years between them simply vanished. No war, no betrayal, no bloodshed—just the two of them, standing in the quiet of this ruined place, as if nothing had changed.

Evander sighed deeply, letting his head rest against the cold stone. "You've changed, Sera."

The sound of her old name clawed at something buried beneath her fibre. No one called her that anymore. Only him. She didn't let it show. "So have you."

He gave a low laugh, touched with something heavier than weariness. "I suppose we all have."

His gaze drifted to the firelight, where Kade lay sprawled in the dirt. For once, the silent sentinel had let exhaustion win. His chest rose in a steady rhythm, his silver hair spilling over one arm like a streak of moonlight against the dark. Seraphina tried not to look too long.

Evander's smirk was tired now, drawn and tinged with something unsaid. "So, the brooding shadow follows you everywhere now?"

Seraphina snorted. "You sound jealous."

"Hardly." He winced, touching bruised ribs. "Just thought no one would survive your sharp edges long enough to get close." His tone shifted slightly, curiosity laced behind the casual jab. His eyes flicked back to Kade, more cautious now. Measured. "He does, though. Stays close. Watches you."

"It's not like that." The words leapt out too fast, too defensively.

Evander raised a brow slowly and deliberate. "Didn't say it was."

She opened her mouth, then shut it again. The silence stretched. The fire cracked, but the quiet between them deepened. His stare wasn't mocking—it was knowing. Like he'd seen things she hadn't dared admit.

He tilted his head. "You ever wonder if *he's* the one keeping a distance? Not you?"

Her breath caught.

"I've seen the way he looks at you," Evander's voice was gentle. "Like you're the last piece of light in whatever darkness he's clawing through."

Seraphina let her eyes fall to the fire, voice quieter now. "He protects me because he has to. Because of who I was. Not because of who I am."

Evander studied her face. "You think he's protecting a symbol?"

"Yes." She hesitated. "No. I don't know." She shook her head, frustrated at the knot in her chest. "We've fought side by side for years, Evander. Years. Still... I don't think I know him."

Her voice dropped, a near whisper. "Not really."

Evander leaned forward, elbows on knees. "You're not wrong to question. Kade's not like the rest of us."

"What do you mean?"

"I mean..." Evander paused, choosing his words. "There are whispers, old stories about his kind. He's not just some cursed immortal with a sword. He's older than you think. Darker, too."

She blinked. "Dark fae?"

Evander gave a slow nod. "The kind that doesn't let people in. The kind that carry lifetimes like scars."

A chill crept through her bones, but not from fear—something deeper. Unease. Ache.

"He's buried things." His eyes fixed on the flames. "Deep. Maybe he's keeping you at a distance because he's afraid of what you'll find if you get too close."

Seraphina swallowed. Her fingers twisted in her lap. "So he's protecting me... from *himself*?"

"Maybe." Evander's voice softened. "Or maybe he just doesn't believe he's allowed to want something good. Like you."

Her heart beat too loudly in her ears.

Evander looked at her with something like pity. "He'd burn the world down for you, Sera. But maybe he doesn't think he gets to *stand in the ashes* with you after."

Her breath hitched, and she hated that it did.

"You need someone." Evander's eyes held her blue ones. "Even if you'll never admit it. And maybe, just maybe—so does he."

He leaned back again, eyes sliding shut almost absently. "Just be careful. Because if he ever breaks… I don't know what part of you he'll take with him."

Across the fire, Kade stirred faintly, just enough to make her heart stutter. In that moment, surrounded by silence, smoke, and the ache of unspoken things, Seraphina realised how close he was and at the same time how far.

Unable to trust herself to speak correctly. Instead, she tore off a piece of hard, stale bread from their supplies and passed it to him. He took it without protest, chewing slowly as if it were the last meal he'd ever have. For a while, they sat in silence, the only sounds being the distant wind that whispered through the cracks in the temple walls. It carried with it the faintest trace of smoke, the lingering scent of destruction from the burning city beyond. The reminder of all they had lost.

Evander studied her quietly, the flickering firelight softening the lines of his weathered face. His eyes held something rare—gentleness, yes, but more than that. Understanding. Recognition.

Then, after a long silence that wrapped around them like a second skin, he spoke—softer this time, as if he didn't want to startle the moment.

"I heard what happened."

Seraphina's hands stilled, the rough bread crumbling between her fingers. The air shifted, heavier now. Charged.

She didn't ask what he meant.

She didn't have to.

Alexis.

Evander exhaled, rubbing the back of his neck as if the weight of the world had settled there. "It wasn't your fault, Sera."

Her jaw tensed, fists clenched tight in her lap. The fire snapped and cracked, but she said nothing. Couldn't.

The ache was indescribable. Just a burn that never stopped.

"You loved him." His voice was quiet—gentle, yes, but also reverent. Careful, like the words themselves could break her. "That is not a weakness."

Her throat tightened. The tears threatened—but she swallowed them down. She'd done that so many times now, it was second nature.

"I should've seen it," her voice was thick with the emotion she tried to hold in. "The signs. The way he—"

"No." Evander shook his head, his tone firm, eyes dark with something old and aching. "Love's not about seeing betrayal before it comes. It's not a war tactic. It's trust. That's the risk—you give someone the power to destroy you, and you pray they don't."

Her breath hitched, the grief clawing its way up her ribs again, raw and relentless. But still—no tears. She wouldn't let herself break. Not here. Not now.

Evander leaned forward, elbows on his knees. When he spoke again, it was softer. Almost a confession.

"For what it's worth… I'm glad you survived."

She looked away, staring into the fire as if it might have answers she didn't.

"Surviving isn't the same as living."

There was a beat of silence. Then a faint chuckle from his side of the fire—rough, but real.

"No," he nodded. "But it's the first step."

A quiet beat passed, then, with a crooked smile, "You know, I still remember that storm of a girl in a dress too big for her, trailing after me and your brother with a wooden sword and fire in her eyes."

Seraphina huffed, sitting beside him now. "I did *not* trail."

Evander snorted. "Sera, you were a menace. You were supposed to be learning embroidery. Instead, you were sneaking into the barracks, bruising your knuckles and begging us to teach you how to fight."

Seraphina's lips tipped up into a smile despite herself; the memory glowed warm and bittersweet in her chest. "I beat you once."

His head twisted toward her, mock horror dawning. *"You did not."*

"I did."

"Your brother had just knocked the wind out of me! The blow disoriented me."

"Excuses," she leant towards him, nudging him with her shoulder.

Evander groaned. "Fine. Just that one time." His smile faded into something quieter, gentler. "But you got better. Damn fast. A cage wasn't meant for you, Sera. Not silk dresses or courtly smiles. A blade and a battlefield were always your destiny. You just didn't know it yet."

Her chest ached, the warmth of those days twisting into sorrow. They'd been children, untouched by war. Her brother's patient hands guiding hers on a blade. Evander, grumbling but amused. Her entire world was still intact.

Back when Alexis had been kind. Or at least… when she believed he was.

Evander followed her gaze across the fire. Kade lay motionless in the shadows, face partially lit, silver hair catching the flame's edge like starlight. Evander watched him for a moment longer, then spoke, voice low.

"Never liked Alexis."

Seraphina shot him a warning look. "And Kade?"

He gave a one-shoulder shrug. "I didn't say that."

"You tried to stab him."

"Minor detail." He waved it off. "He was part of Alexis's faction. Tensions were high. Steel clashed." His smirk curled at the edges. "But Alexis? Too polished. Too pretty. He played the perfect prince, said all the right things, never showed a crack."

He looked back at Kade, tone shifting.

"Kade's different. There's darkness there, sure. But it's *honest.* And it doesn't scare you. It never did."

Seraphina let the words wash over her; her silence spoke volumes.

Evander stretched his legs with a grunt, wincing as something popped.

"You always did like a challenge."

Seraphina rolled her eyes. "You're projecting."

"Maybe. Or maybe I've just been watching. You and Kade? You fight like you've been doing it for years—like your bones know where the other one will be. When you first came back after the fall, you wouldn't let anyone touch you. You didn't even let me near. And him? He was a ghost, just scars and shadows."

He leaned back, voice tinged with memory. "Yet somehow, every time I saw one of you, the other wasn't far behind. It didn't matter in the battle. It didn't matter what the odds were. You always came back."

His eyes met hers, calm now.

"That kind of bond? It doesn't just happen. Not by accident."

Silence again. But it wasn't uncomfortable—it was weighted. Grounded. Full of things they weren't quite ready to say.

After a long while, Evander's gaze drifted to the flames again, voice lowering.

"You remind me of your brother."

Her heart skipped a beat.

"The way you carry the weight of others. The way you step into danger without hesitation. He would've been proud of you."

Something cracked quietly inside her.

For the first time that night, she didn't push the grief away.

She let it settle. Let it sit beside her in the silence.

Because maybe, for once, she didn't have to carry it alone.

Evander didn't push, just shook his head with a small, weary smile. "Stubborn. Pushing forward, always fighting as if it's the last thing to do. Your sister—"

Her stomach clenched. Seraphina's fingers dug into her palms. The fire crackled, the shadows shifting along the cavern walls.

"Don't." Her voice was barely above a whisper.

Evander studied her for a long moment, then sighed, leaning his head back against the stone. "Alright." But the way he said it, the way his gaze lingered on her—it wasn't the end of the conversation. Not really.

The silence stretched again before Evander huffed a quiet laugh, tilting his head toward Kade. "So, what's stopping you?"

Seraphina frowned. "Stopping me from what?"

"You and him." He nodded toward Kade's sleeping form. "I've seen the way he looks at you, Seraphina. I've seen the way you pretend you don't notice."

She exhaled. "You're reading too much into it."

Evander just hummed, unconvinced. "Right. Because I've never known you to run from something before."

Seraphina's jaw tightened. "He's not interested."

Evander only grinned. "You always were the last one to see what was right in front of you."

Across the fire, Kade stirred slightly in his sleep, brow furrowing as if he could feel the tension in the air, even unconscious.

Her heart skipped a beat. His words had landed like a blow. The mention of her brother, Lucanis—a name she had tried so hard to bury—carried a weight she hadn't expected. The memory of him—his laughter, his steady belief in her, his protection—threatened to crack her composure. But she held firm. She swallowed the lump in her throat.

"You remind me of him," her voice was soft as she leant forward. "You were at his side until the end, where you were needed."

Evander didn't speak right away, but the ghost of a smile lingered on his lips as he nodded. "He never doubted you, you know." His voice was softer now, distant. "No matter what people said, no matter the odds, he always believed you'd survive this war."

She clenched her jaw, forcing herself past the sudden tightness in her chest that his words had caused.

Evander exhaled slowly, his eyes drifting shut. "Maybe it's time you started believing it, too."

* * *

The fire had burned low, and Evander had long since drifted into sleep.

But Seraphina couldn't. Not after what he'd said.

She crossed the campsite in silence, crouching beside Kade, her gaze tracing the powerful line of his jaw, the strands of silver hair caught in the moonlight. Even in sleep, he looked like something carved from shadow and starlight.

Her hand hovered just above his brow.

"You don't let anyone in," her voice was a whisper. "Not really. Not even me."

"I let you closer than most."

His voice was low—gravel and shadow—yet gentle. Her breath stilled as his eyes blinked open, glinting faintly in the firelight.

"You weren't asleep."

"I was. But I always know when you're near."

A beat of stillness passed between them.

She sat down beside him, folding her arms over her knees, suddenly unsure what to say now that he was looking at her with that unreadable gaze.

"You don't talk about your past." She gave him a quick glance. "I don't even know how old you are."

"That's probably for the best."

"That's not an answer."

"No," he huffed. "It's not."

She turned her head to face him fully. "Evander says you'd burn the world down for me."

His gaze flickered, but he didn't deny it.

"I don't want a world burned to ash," Seraphina let her gaze travel over Kade's form, "I want to *understand* the man who walks beside me every day."

He sat up slowly, stretching his long frame, then he looked at her—truly looked at her.

"I'm not a man, Seraphina," The words came out low. "Not entirely. Not anymore. The things I've done to survive… they would change how you see me."

"I don't know who you are."

"That might be the only reason you're still beside me."

The honesty in his voice hurt more than any blade. Yet beneath it, she heard something else.

Fear.

He feared *her*, not because of her power or what she represented in this war—but because she saw him. Because if she *really* looked, she might leave.

"I'm not afraid of you." Her voice was firm.

He gave her a sad, crooked smile. "Maybe you should be." With that, he rolled over, turning away from her and ending the conversation. Sera just huffed and made her way back to her side of the fire, careful not to wake Evander's sleeping form. Pulling her discarded coat, which she had pilfered in the market square, over him with a soft smile of fondness for the man who reminded her so much of her childhood and beloved brother. Sera went to sleep for the first time in months with the feeling of hope that the next day might just be better.

Chapter 8

She never heard them coming.

The first blade hissed through the air, missing her cheek by less than a breath. It struck stone with a scream; the sound ringing out like a warning shot, a death knell that shattered the brittle peace clinging to the temple. For a moment, everything held its breath. Then the eruption came as Evander, Kade and Seraphina scrambled out of their makeshift beds.

A second blade followed, then another. The clash of steel exploded in the silence. Shadows spilled into the sanctuary like ink, fast and ruthless. Shouts burst through the air, guttural, the curses of men who'd long since forgotten mercy.

Steel met steel beside her—Kade, already in motion, already a storm. His blades arced like lightning, the impact of his first strike sending sparks against the columns. He didn't speak. He didn't need to. This was vengeance.

Seraphina ducked a blade, twisted, and drove her sword through the ribs of a man whose eyes widened too late. Blood sprayed warm against her neck. Another charged, she met him with a scream of steel. Her body moved on instinct—fuelled by rage, by panic, by something too wild to name.

Evander moved behind her, but it was wrong—his steps unsteady, his grip faltering. Evander was just beginning to recover. He should have stayed back. He should have *lived.*

Out of the chaos, a blade surged forward. Not toward him. *Toward her.*

She saw the gleam of it—a deadly arc aimed at her exposed back.

Evander saw it too.

She would remember the choice forever. His eyes flickered. The second of hesitation. The way his gaze locked onto hers across the smoke and softened. No fear. Only *peace.*

He *moved.*

With a grunt of effort and pain, he launched himself between her and the oncoming death.

Steel met flesh.

The sound was final. A sickening, wet thud that silenced everything inside her.

Seraphina's scream ripped from her throat before she even knew she was screaming.

She caught him as he fell, knees crashing against the blood-soaked stone. His body was warm, shaking, and already slick with red. Her hands pressed against his chest, too much blood. Far too much.

"Evander—*no.* No, no, no, *don't you dare—*" Her words trembled, breaking against the weight in her chest.

He groaned, his face twisting in pain, but somehow—*somehow*—he smiled. "Didn't... think you'd... see that one..."

"Why?" holding her breath, tears already blurring her vision. "Why would you *do* that?"

He coughed, blood dribbling from the corner of his mouth. "Had little left... figured I'd... spend it well."

Behind her, the clash of battle still rang, shouts, steel on steel. But it was *closer now.* She heard Kade, grunting with effort, his blades cutting through the last wave of men. Each death punctuated by silence. One by one, he was ending them.

But she couldn't look away. Couldn't leave this moment. Couldn't *leave Evander.*

"You were supposed to live." Her voice shook, her fingers pressed hard over the wound, as if sheer will could seal it. "We were going to *fix* this. Together."

Another harsh breath. His hand trembled as he reached for her, fingers curling weakly against her wrist. "You... always needed more time. I just bought you some."

"*Stop it.*" Her voice broke, rising in desperation. "Don't say goodbye. Don't do that to me."

He gave a breathy laugh, a wheeze, wet with blood. "Kade's... still got you. He'll... hate me for this." His lips curved up, bloody and broken. "Tell him... not to forget me..."

A blade clanged behind her, another death. The last one, maybe. She could hear Kade's boots drawing closer, slower now. The fight was almost over. But for Seraphina, it had already ended.

Evander's eyes fluttered, unfocused.

"Stay," the words squeezed out through her tears. "Evander, *stay with me.* Please, gods, please—*don't leave me like this.*"

She couldn't bear another person from her past leaving her.

He drew one final breath, a slow, fragile thing. "Sera..." His lips moved, but no sound followed.

His hand slipped from her wrist.

His chest stilled.

Stillness.

But not peace.

Only the suffocating finality of loss.

She choked on a sob, her fingers curling into his tunic, holding him close. Seraphina thought that by holding tight enough, she could undo it. The temple reeked of blood and burning, of death and despair. Her heart was collapsing, one breath at a time.

Then—Kade.

He dropped beside her without a word, his presence wrapping around her like fibre. She barely registered the blood smeared across his face, the fury still glowing in his eyes. His hands gripped her shoulders, grounding her, but she couldn't feel them. Couldn't feel *anything.*

Her breaths were coming too quickly; she hyperventilated.

Until his palms cradled her face. Rough, trembling, warm. His thumbs brushed her cheeks, and only then did she fuelled she was crying. Silent, endless tears that wouldn't stop.

She raised her eyes, locking them onto his and saw her feelings reflected at her.

Grief. Rage. Helplessness.

But beneath all of it, nestled in the stormy grey of his eyes, was a sorrow so deep it mirrored her own. A shared devastation neither of them had the words for.

Beneath his calloused fingers, her pulse thrummed, a fragile rhythm. Her breath caught, trembling. She could barely see, the blur due both to tears plus the heaviness of it all.

He was so close.

Too close.

She could see every line of tension in his jaw, the faint twitch of muscle as he swallowed back words he wouldn't say. The silver in his eyes flickered with emotion, rage burning at the edges, concern rooted deep. For a moment, just one fleeting heartbeat, the world fell quiet.

No war. No loss, just *them*.

He lent his forehead against her own. His scent was overwhelming her, calming her racing mind as his touch soothed her heart. Seraphina closed her eyes as his breath fanned against her face, his nose rubbed against her own as she tilted her head up, his lips barely brushing against hers from the movement, and she held her breath.

Then he pulled away.

Abrupt. Careful.

Like touching her had hurt.

Her breath hitched, sharp and sudden, but he didn't look at her. He turned, his shoulders tight, the space between them aching with unspoken things. The warmth of his hands still lingered on her skin like a fading echo, but the chill that followed cut deeper than steel.

He was still there. Only a step away.

But she'd never felt farther from him.

Chapter 9

The rain had stopped, leaving the air thick with a cool mist clinging to the ground as Seraphina continued her work. The shovel scraped against the earth with a hollow sound, as though even the ground mourned the loss of another soul. She had dug deeper than she ever intended, her hands raw, her knuckles white from the pressure. Each blow tore at her, leaving a sickening feeling that her grief was unbearable.

Evander deserved better than this. She thought about it again, as she had a thousand times before. Better than the dirt. Better than the war that had claimed him. They had been more than comrades; they had been a family in a way that transcended blood. Shared pain and loss of life in the heat of battle forged this bond. Now, only his lifeless body remained, along with the hollow ache in her chest.

Her fingers trembled, the cold earth slipping through her fingers as she dug to cover the grave she had made. She couldn't let herself stop—not yet. Tears were a luxury she couldn't permit. She couldn't afford to let the sorrow overwhelm her. She couldn't afford to let herself break.

Is this the price? The thought echoed in her mind, bitter and raw. Is this what we fight for? She buried her loved ones like dogs in the dirt, witnessing the world crumble around her as those she cherished perished one by one. It was too much. She was exhausted. A crushing weight threatened to overwhelm her.

The shovel finally hit the bottom of the mound of dirt piled high around the grave, and she paused, staring at the freshly dug earth. She remained motionless. Seraphina let out a shaky breath, stepping back from the grave. Her eyes burned, but she refused to cry. Not now. Not with everything still left undone.

Her mind, however, betrayed her as it drifted back to thoughts of Alexis. The name felt like acid on her tongue. What was it he wanted? What was worth all this destruction, this endless bloodshed that his Veilborn army continued after his death?

She couldn't make sense of it. She couldn't make sense of him. Power? Control? What had he always wanted? What had driven him to this madness? He had been clever, calculating, but now he was something else entirely. Dangerous. Terrifying. No one knew her better than he did. He knew what would break her. He knew how to twist her emotions and use them against her. Nothing else terrified her as much.

What is he after? He is dead. She saw him die, so why is his army still coming for her? She gritted her teeth; the question gnawing at her as she stared at the grave. The uncertainty felt like a disease eating away at her insides. She couldn't figure it out. It made her feel weak, vulnerable.

A soft rustle of footsteps broke through the heavy quiet, brushing against the edge of Seraphina's grief like wind across broken stone. Her muscles tensed, hand falling instinctively to the hilt at her side—but she stilled when she saw him.

Kade.

He stood a few paces away, silhouetted against the thinning dusk, eyes shadowed but unmistakably soft. Not with pity—she would've hated that—but with sorrow. A sorrow that echoed her own. He didn't speak at first, and for a heartbeat, the silence between them deepened, aching and fragile.

She turned back to the grave. The freshly disturbed earth, the stillness, the way the wind no longer stirred as it had before. Evander was gone. Buried beneath a thin layer of soil that could never hold the weight of what he had meant.

"Seraphina," Kade's voice was rough from dust and fatigue, but gentled at the edges. "We need to go. It's not safe here."

She didn't look at him. "I know."

Despite that, she didn't move.

Leaving felt like a betrayal. The grave was finished, just a mound of stone and soil, unmarked. Unworthy of him. Walking away would be another kind of death. One she wasn't ready for.

"I don't need your comfort, Kade," her voice brittle as frost. "I can't leave yet."

He didn't flinch. "I'm not here to comfort you." He just watched her with the same quiet weight in his gaze. "But if you need to say something before we go, I'll listen."

"I don't." Her voice faltered, and for a second, her façade cracked. The way he'd held her when Evander collapsed in her arms haunted her. The way his presence had anchored her, made her feel like she hadn't fallen apart completely.

But she had.

She crouched beside the grave again, fingers curling into the soil. Her breath trembled. "He was just a boy when I met him. Reckless. Brilliant. He believed in everything I didn't. I kept him close because he reminded me of who I used to be."

Kade didn't speak, but she felt him inch a little closer. Just enough for her to feel his warmth on her back, like a shield she hadn't asked for.

"I buried my hope with him," she released the dirt in her hand as it drifted back over the grave. "I don't know if I can get it back."

Still, he said nothing. But he stayed. And somehow, that was more than enough.

She curled tighter into herself, pulling the edges of her cloak close until the worn fabric pressed against her lips. The ground beneath her was cold, unyielding, but not as cold as the ache in her chest. There would be no peace for her tonight. No sleep. Just silence and the weight of memory.

Her body remained still, unmoving, but her thoughts refused to settle. Every flicker of flame from the dying fire cast dancing shadows across her closed eyes, like echoes of wraiths in the dark. She kept her breathing slow, measured—not quite feigning sleep, but not willing to engage the world around her either.

Kade stirred beside her.

She didn't open her eyes. She didn't flinch when his presence leaned in closer. For a moment, there was nothing. Just the sound of his breathing and the whisper of wind brushing over the hilltop grave.

Then his fingers brushed gently against her temple, sweeping a loose strand of hair away from her face.

His touch was tentative, barely there. A moment suspended between comfort and restraint, as though he feared even this simple act might shatter her completely. He thought she was asleep—he had to—but his touch lingered too long to be purely practical. It was reverent. Painfully gentle.

Her breath caught, but she didn't move. She couldn't. If she did, the moment would collapse under its own vulnerability.

"I chose you because you're not afraid of the darkness," Kade's voice was raw and weighted with something deeper. "You stand in it without flinching. Without running. But I know you're still afraid... of what's left inside."

The words landed like stones across her ribs. She stayed quiet, eyes closed, heart beating a little too loudly in her chest. He didn't know how close he was to the truth. Or maybe he did. Maybe that was what terrified her most.

She wasn't afraid of dying.

She was afraid of what she might become if she lived long enough.

Alexis... he had embraced that darkness.

The Veilborn army had not always existed as it does now. Centuries ago, long before the war, the wraiths had been nothing more than whispers in the shadows, remnants of lost souls banished to the Veil between life and death. The Seelie and Unseelie courts had warred over the lands beyond mortal reach, their blood feuds eternal, their alliances fragile. When the Unseelie sought dominion over both worlds, they made a pact with the wraiths, allowing the spirits to merge with their warriors, creating beings neither living nor dead. Corrupted, unkillable.

That dark kingdom had risen and fallen, its power buried with time—until Alexis unearthed it.

Somehow, impossibly, he had bound the wraiths to his will, forging an army of Veilborn soldiers who did not bleed, did not tire, and spread decay with every step. They were not just warriors; they were a plague. When they killed mortal men, their essence seeped into flesh and bone, hollowing them out, twisting them into something monstrous. A single Veilborn could infect an entire battalion, turning once-loyal soldiers into mindless husks of corruption.

From Unseelie failures, Alexis forged a kingdom—a nightmarish stronghold where he commanded wraiths, the Veil at its thinnest. Now, he wielded them like an extension of his own will.

The thought made Seraphina's stomach twist. How? How had he managed it? It's impossible to truly control wraiths. The Unseelie could only trade power for service. But Alexis... Alexis had done something more. He had bound them, enslaved them.

Now, the army hunted her. As she heard Kade's breath settle back into a rhythm, she let her mind wander.

Their laughter, quiet garden moments, and his penetrating gaze were vivid memories for her. But that was before the war, before she realised Alexis had never truly been the man she had thought he was. He had changed, and so had she. But she hadn't known. That was the most painful part. She had trusted him. She had believed in him.

The quiet crackling of the fire seemed to mock her as the memory burned deeper into her mind. She discovered that the peaceful days were only an illusion, leaving her with the shattered pieces of a nonexistent kingdom. Alexis now held a hostile role, which caused her chest to constrict, feeling as if everything would overwhelm her. How had she been so blind? How had she let him twist everything they had, everything she had believed in, into something dark and twisted? It felt as though a part of her soul had died that day. Her hand clenched involuntarily, fingers digging into the dirt at her side. No, she wouldn't allow herself to crumble. Not now. Not when so much was at stake. The bitterness tasted like ash in her mouth, and the anger simmered beneath the surface, a constant reminder of what she'd lost.

As the fire flickered in the darkness, she focused on the present. She couldn't dwell in the past. Not now. Not with Alexis' army hunting her, and not with the looming shadow of the world's destruction hanging over her head. The future seemed as bleak as the surrounding night, and every plan she thought of felt futile. What could they really do to stop the Veilborn army? Could they contend with an enemy, harming their realm's magic?

As she formed the plan, Seraphina's heart also ached with quiet sorrow, for what she had lost, and for what was to come. The path ahead was treacherous, cloaked in shadows, both old and new. Yet, one hope remained, worn and nearly forgotten: a warrior she knew.

He had been more than just a companion in battle. He was the presence that anchored her, once. Someone whose smile had meant safety, whose voice could break through the noise in her head. Memories, bright and painful, still glowed like embers within their layered history. She had not seen him for years. Not since the fire, not since the ruins.

If she found him again... it would hurt. It would be like reopening a wound she'd tried too long to forget. But it might also save them.

Finding him wouldn't be easy. She didn't even know if he still lived. But she had to try.

She couldn't do this alone. Not anymore. The burden of her choices, her survival, the endless war—it was no longer hers to bear in solitude. Though she loathed the idea of depending on someone, especially someone from her past, she knew it was unavoidable.

Her gaze drifted sideways.

Kade.

The soft rise and fall of his chest, the silver gleam of his hair in the firelight—it stirred something fragile in her. He was constantly beside her, a help she could never repay. She didn't know what they were, or what they could be. But he was here.

Somehow, that mattered.

* * *

The wind turned colder at dawn.

They stood now at the edge of the burial site, surrounded by mist and old trees that bowed like mourners. A simple rock rested beneath her fingers as she bowed her head in silent prayer.

Evander.

She traced the rock, wishing she could add more; he deserved more. A hollow ache twisted in her chest. He had died so that she could live. She did not deem herself worthy of that offering.

The grief was old, but it hadn't dulled. It permeated her being, her gait, every inhale within this broken domain.

"Seraphina."

Her name cut through the fog like a blade softened with velvet. She didn't turn at first. The sound spoken by that voice unravelled something carefully held together. She swallowed hard.

Eventually, she looked up.

Kade stood among the trees, bathed in the low gold of the rising sun. The light caught the silver in his hair and the sharp edge of his silhouette— warrior, protector; he looked as if he belonged to another world. A world that hadn't yet bled.

She wanted to look away. But she didn't.

He whispered. "We must go."

She nodded, brushing her fingers once more across the grave before straightening. The weight of her loss settled deeper into her spine, but she carried it without flinching. She always had.

She turned and walked toward him, boots crunching against frost-laced ground, her cloak whispering behind her like a memory. Kade didn't speak as she approached, but when she passed him, he fell into step beside her.

No questions. No demands. Just presence.

Chapter 10

Days had slipped by, uncounted and weightless, as they journeyed beneath a sky slowly shifting from summer's blaze to autumn's quiet hush. The sun no longer scorched as it once had; now, its warmth lingered gently on their backs, tempered by the cooling breeze that rustled through amber-tinged leaves. Even the light had changed—less harsh, more golden—as if the world itself was exhaling after a long, stifling breath.

Though Seraphina could not name how many days had passed, her body bore the memory of each one. The soreness in her shoulders, the ache in her feet, the raw spots rubbed by the seams of worn leather boots—these were the rhythms of the road. Each sunrise bled into the next, stitched together by fatigue and the relentless press of forward movement.

The surrounding forest grew denser with every step. Its canopy of tangled branches stretched overhead, forming a narrowing corridor of shadow and light. Beneath their boots, the earth had softened with fallen leaves and damp moss, the air thick with the smell of rich soil and the unmistakable scent of rot, like the forest itself was slowly turning in on itself, preparing to sleep.

Though they had both healed, the signs were slow and subtle. Kade walked steadier now, no longer wincing at every incline or staggered root. Colour had returned to his face, and the lines of strain around his mouth had softened. More telling still was the way his magic flickered back to life—a faint glow at his fingertips when he thought she wasn't watching, or the way the surrounding shadows seemed to respond when danger drew near.

But Seraphina *was* watching. She always had.

As they set camp, "You're holding back," her voice low, barely above the whisper of wind in the trees. "You've got your strength back. Why aren't you using it?"

Kade didn't look at her. He merely fed another log into the fire, the glow painting his face in molten gold and shadow. "Because I don't trust it," he said curtly. Heavy.

She didn't press him. Not then. But the distance between them—once born of pain and circumstance—now felt like a choice. That stung more than she cared to admit.

By day, they moved together in silence, their footsteps in sync, the quiet between them loud with unspoken words. Kade stayed close, never more than a few strides away, but never quite *with* her, either. His presence was a shadow at her side, constant but unreachable, and it reminded her too much of things she had lost. Of things she didn't know how to reclaim.

The road narrowed again as they crossed a ravine choked with moss-covered stones and twisted vines. The trees leaned inward, their boughs clawing toward one another like brittle bones.

Suddenly a screech—sharp and unnatural, splitting the hush like a blade. The forest held its breath. A flurry of wings rustled above, unseen but far too close. Every instinct in her screamed. Her fingers slid to the hilt of her sword, breath shallow, every muscle drawn taut.

Snap. A branch broke. Deliberate. Near.

Before she could move, Kade's hand clamped around her wrist, the heat of his palm grounding and startling all at once. She startled, but didn't pull away.

"Stay close." His voice was steel wrapped in velvet, quiet but commanding.

Then, the first creature stepped out of the dark. Twisted flesh, jagged bone, eyes burning with sickly yellow light. Corrupted soldiers—bodies mangled by whatever dark force had taken hold of them. They moved like marionettes on frayed strings, their joints jerking unnaturally. But their intent was unmistakable.

Death.

The stench of decay hit her first, thick and suffocating, like meat left to rot under the sun. Something black and alive throbbed in the veins of their once gleaming, now tarnished and cracked fibre. A soldier's jaw hung slack, broken, his teeth bared in a grotesque mockery of a grin.

Seraphina swallowed back the revulsion crawling up her throat. Her fingers curled tighter around the hilt of her blade.

The moment Kade's sword met the first of them, Seraphina was already moving. She didn't hesitate. Her blade found flesh, slicing through the rotted throat of the closest abomination. Blood splattered across the ground, hot against her skin. The battle was brutal and swift. Adrenaline pounded through her, sharpening every sense, making her feel alive in a way nothing else did. Yet through it all, she felt Kade—a shadow at her back, his movements precise, deadly and protective. His silver hair whipped around him as he fought, a stark contrast to the darkness and the blood. When their hands brushed—just for an instant—it sent a shock through her that lingered too long to be ignored.

As quickly as it had begun, it was over. The last creature collapsed in a grotesque sprawl, its body a ruin of torn sinew and curling smoke. Silence fell like a shroud—thick, suffocating. In some ways, it was worse than the chaos. Too still. Too knowing.

She wiped her blade clean on the edge of her cloak, though the blood had already dried. Her breath came fast, too shallow, chest tight with the remnants of adrenaline.

"You okay?" Kade's voice cut through the quiet, low and steady— meant to be casual. But she caught the shift in his gaze. That flicker of something... softer. Sharper.

"I'm fine." The lie slipped from her lips, practised and easy. Her heart was still pounding. From the fight. Or from the look in his eyes. She didn't want to know which.

The stench of death thickened the air—cloying, putrid. Around them, the corrupted corpses lay in twisted heaps, their flesh leaking black ichor like spilled ink soaking into parchment. They couldn't leave them like this. They never could. Not if they wanted the ground to stay clean, not if they wanted to keep the rot from waking again.

She scrubbed a filthy hand across her brow, smearing blood and sweat into the grime caked on her skin. Her whole body ached, bone-deep fatigue making her fingers tremble. Kade handed her a torch. She took it without a word.

This was the part that always felt harder. Not the fight. The aftermath. But she'd learned how to survive it.

"You ever notice," she said, "how fast the mind learns to make space for horror?"

Kade didn't answer. He didn't have to.

"I used to throw up after a fight," she continued. "Shake so hard I couldn't hold my sword. I remember my first kill... a boy; his eyes were blue."

Biting her lip, she shoved the memory of it so fast it scraped the inside of her skull. "Anyway," she looked away, "that was a lifetime ago."

She stepped forward and touched the flame to the nearest body. The fire took with a violent hiss, curling up and around the corrupted flesh like it was starving for it. The stench of burning meat filled her nose, smoke stinging her eyes. She swallowed hard.

It never got easier.

Yet... she had grown used to it. She hated she had.

They always did this. Burned the bodies. Salted the ground. Cleansed what they could before the corruption could take root. It was necessary. Practical. A ritual of survival carved from necessity.

The fire crackled, casting flickering shadows across their faces. Kade stood beside her, jaw set, torch still burning in his hand. The muscle in his cheek twitched once before he turned and tossed the flame into the growing pyre.

"Let's move," his voice like gravel—rough and low and worn from too many unspoken things.

They walked in silence; the night stretching long and cold around them. No words. Just the rhythmic scuff of boots over damp ground, the whisper of wind through skeletal trees, and the far-off sound of something moving just beyond the edge of light.

By the time they made camp beside a narrow stream, the moon hung high and pale. The fire crackled low. Neither of them said much, but Seraphina sat staring into the flames, watching the dance of light like it might teach her something.

She wondered, not for the first time, if she was still herself beneath the fibre she wore inside. Or if she'd burned with one of those bodies long ago. Seraphina sat with her knees drawn up, arms draped over them. Across from her, Kade worked silently, stripping bark from a branch, his movements methodical as he sharpened it into a makeshift spear.

She shifted, wincing as pain lanced through her ribs. The bruises from their last fight still hadn't fully healed, and her body was a tapestry of aches and half-healed wounds, reminders of every battle, every blow she had taken. Beneath it all, the deeper wounds—ones that no amount of rest could mend. The remnants of their time in captivity still lingered, ghosting through her muscles, an ever-present ache.

They had been travelling for days since they had left Evander's grave; they had almost reached the borders of Valtheris and were currently in the ancient forest that separated the human kingdom from that of the Fae kingdom of Elarion.

As she pondered where they should look for her ally, her eyes drifted to Kade. His tunic pulled taut over his broad shoulders as he moved, firelight shifting across the sharp angles of his face. His silver hair, darkened at the roots with sweat and dirt, framed his unreadable expression. She hadn't allowed herself to look before. Not really. Now, in the flickering glow, she did. The realisation struck like a slow, creeping ache.

She had always known Kade was striking—too sharp, too ethereal for a man who had seen as much bloodshed as he had. But there was something else now. A quiet strength. A steadiness that shouldn't have felt so grounding. The firelight turned his eyes molten, unreadable.

Then he looked up, meeting her gaze. Seraphina forgot how to breathe. She forced herself to look away, fingers curling into the dirt. This wasn't real. She was tired. That was all. War-weary and frayed at the edges. But then why did her chest feel so tight?

Kade exhaled, dragging his blade along the wood one last time. "We need to move before dawn." His voice was steady, but she heard the rough edge of exhaustion beneath it.

She nodded. "We'll take turns keeping watch."

He arched a brow. "You trust me not to let you get killed in your sleep?"

That should have made her roll her eyes. Should have made her snap back. Instead, the words twisted something in her chest.

"I trust you," she admitted before she could stop herself.

Kade stilled.

Something flickered across his face—something unreadable—but he only nodded. Setting the spear aside, he leaned back against the ground, gaze flickering to the stars beyond the treetops.

The silence stretched. Seraphina told herself it was just another night. Just another battle survived. Then why did it feel like something had shifted between them—something fragile, something inevitable?

She lay down, exhaustion pressing heavily upon her. The moment she closed her eyes, the darkness swallowed her whole.

Alexis was there again. His face, once so familiar, was now cold, unrecognisable. The warmth in his deep blue eyes had given way to shadows. A stranger wearing the face of the man she had loved.

"Your destiny was never to save this world, Seraphina." His voice was smooth and deep as he spoke. *"You were just a pawn. A tool."*

The words struck like a blade to the chest, sharp and twisting. She tried to move, to speak, but her body refused to obey. Panic clawed at her throat.

"You should have known," he continued, his tone mocking, distant. *"Everything you thought you knew was a lie. Fate never intended you to be the hero. Not for him. Not for this."*

The world around her fractured, reality warping into chaos. Flames devoured the kingdom she once called home. Bodies lay strewn across the battlefield—lifeless, nameless. Amid the inferno—Kade. Standing, watching, as if he too were burning. Then came the laughter—cold, cruel. Alexis' laughter.

Seraphina *gasped*, a broken, guttural sound tearing from her throat as she jolted upright. The fire's dim glow pressed in, flickering against the jagged lines of the cave wall like the ghost of flames past. Sweat clung to her skin, soaked through her shirt, her breath dragging harshly through clenched teeth. Her hands scrabbled for something—anything—before finding the threadbare blanket tangled around her legs. She yanked it closer, anchoring herself to the now.

She was awake.

But the nightmare had claws, and they didn't let go easily.

Beside her, the silence cracked.

"You're awake," came Kade's voice—quiet, low, with an edge like steel dulled from overuse. He didn't move to her, didn't rush. He was already sitting up, cross-legged in the firelight's flicker, the faint glint of the dagger he'd been working on catching in the low light as he placed it down with deliberate care.

She didn't answer.

The dream still pressed in—an echo of blood and fire and screams that had long since burned into her bones. She could still feel the cold metal of Alexis' circlet against her fingers, the warmth draining from his body in her arms. Still see the way the sky cracked open when the dragons fell.

Even now, with breath in her lungs, her mind reeled as if it were still there. Still *losing*.

She drew her knees to her chest, wrapping her arms tightly around them. The fire popped beside her; the warmth was too distant to matter. Shadows danced across the stone—twisting, flickering things that looked too much like the ruins she had clawed her way out of.

Kade's voice cut clean through the dark. "You're not alone, Seraphina."

The way he said her name made her flinch.

She turned slowly. Their eyes met.

There it was again—that pull. The thread between them, invisible and unrelenting, stitched with everything they refused to name.

Kade's usual aloof mask cracked. He was watching her too closely, as if trying to decipher some code etched into the shadows under her eyes.

She hated how exposed she felt. Hated how he could see her like that.

She exhaled long and quietly, dragging a hand down her face. "You have something to say, Kade? Or are you just going to watch me like I might shatter?"

He didn't answer. Just picked the dagger back up and resumed the slow, rhythmic drag of a whetstone against its edge.

She scoffed, biting down the tremble in her voice. "Gods, you're insufferable." She hated the way her body reacted to Kade's presence. Like a thread being pulled too tight. She turned her body away from him after the words left her mouth.

The sound of sharpening metal stopped. Then—he moved.

Too fast.

Too close.

In one breath, he was kneeling in front of her. She stiffened, eyes narrowing as he reached out, fingers brushing her jaw. The touch was light, but it seared.

His hand tilted her face toward him, his gaze raking over her features with terrifying focus.

"I hate watching you suffer," his voice rough, low, intimate in a way that made her pulse skip.

She should have pulled away. Should have spat something cruel, cut him down like she always did.

But her heart stuttered, and she stayed still.

His thumb skimmed her cheek, calloused and hesitant.

"You don't get to touch me just because I scream in my sleep," her voice cool but trembling at the edges.

His jaw twitched. Still, he didn't let go.

"Oh?" he raised an eyebrow at her. "So now there are rules?"

"There *were* always rules," she shot back, eyes flashing. "You—you don't get to break them just because you suddenly remember you have a heart."

Kade leaned in, his breath brushing her lips, maddeningly close. "You think this is about *pity*?"

"Isn't it?" Her voice cracked like ice.

His hand slid to cup the side of her neck, fingers threading into her hair. Gentle.

"You think that means you get to touch me now?" she repeated, slower this time, almost mocking, almost begging—*daring*.

A flicker of something feral lit behind his eyes. "I think you want me to."

Her lips parted. The air between them turned molten.

"Arrogant bastard."

"I've been called worse," he said, and gods, he smirked—just enough to unravel her.

She shoved his chest hard enough to make him shift back an inch. "Don't get cocky just because I didn't slap you."

Kade's smirk didn't falter. "That was mercy?"

"No. That was *curiosity*."

His brow arched, silver hair falling into his eyes. "Then let me satisfy it."

Then—his mouth crashed into hers.

It wasn't soft. It wasn't sweet.

It was war.

A desperate, aching collision that spoke in bruises and breathless groans, in the touch that tried to memorise every scar. His hand twisted in her hair as he deepened the kiss, the other bracing her back, anchoring them both. She grabbed his tunic in both fists, pulling him down with her until the world disappeared beneath the weight of him, of this.

She kissed him as if she were drowning. Like he was the only air left.

She felt it—the way his hands trembled, the way he clung to her like she'd vanish if he let go. His scent filled her head—steel, spice, and shadows. She drank him in, fingers threading through his silver hair, desperate to burn away everything else. It felt as if the tension between them suddenly melted.

But then—

He tore away.

As fast as he'd come to her, he *ripped* himself back. His breathing became ragged. His eyes were wide, and his face—haunted.

"That—" His voice was raw, wrecked. "That shouldn't have happened."

The words hit her like a slap.

Of course.

Her jaw tightened. Fingers curled into fists, nails biting skin. She sat up straighter, ice settling over whatever warmth had bloomed.

"Coward,"

His gaze snapped to hers. "Don't."

"Don't what?" She glared at him, chest heaving. "Don't call you out for running? Again?"

Kade stood abruptly, jaw clenched, eyes stormy.

"Don't make this a game, Seraphina. *Not this.*"

She laughed—a bitter, broken sound. "Why not? Everything else is."

"You know why."

"Do I?" she said, rising to her feet. She had to glare up at him. "Because from where I'm standing, all I see is a man who kisses like he means it—then runs like a boy too scared of what comes after."

Kade looked like she'd stabbed him.

"Tell me you didn't want that." She glanced down as she spoke.

She waited a breath of a moment before locking her blue eyes on his grey ones.

"Say it." She challenged.

He didn't. Couldn't.

His eyes hardened as he turned. Walked away.

"Coward." She breathed out.

Seraphina stood there, the embers behind her flickering low, her body aching from too many truths.

Chapter 11

Dawn spilled across the land in streaks of cold gold and bruised blue, the light catching against the jagged ridgelines like the edge of shattered glass. Shadows stretched long and lean, clawing at the scorched earth as if reluctant to let the night go. The fire was long dead, reduced to nothing but glowing embers and a lingering bite in the air that clung to Seraphina's skin like ghost hands.

She hadn't slept. Not really.

Echoes filled the night—half-formed voices from a past too bloodied to mourn properly, and Kade's nearness made rest impossible. Every shift of his weight, every breath he took, was a presence she couldn't ignore.

She rolled her shoulders, the ache in her muscles bone-deep, tendrils of unease twisting around her spine. Something was *wrong*. The quiet of the morning felt... too still.

Then she saw it.

Half-buried in the grey dirt, nestled among scattered stones and brittle grass—a feather. But not any birds. This one was long, dark red, almost rusted, and barbed like a horned blade. Not from this world. Not of anything natural.

She froze.

Before she could call his name, Kade was already beside her, crouching low like a predator mid-stalk. His fingers brushed over the spiked quills, and he turned it slowly, letting the morning light catch the edge. The feather gleamed *too sharply*, like it had tasted blood.

His jaw clenched, and the familiar flicker of cold calculation passed through his silver eyes.

"We need to move."

Seraphina's voice was quiet. "What is it?"

"A *tracking demon*," he said, slipping the feather into his belt like a grim token. "They're scouts. They shed feathers like this to mark a trail. If we found this one, another's not far behind."

Her blood ran cold. "So they're following us?"

He gave a tight nod, standing again and scanning the horizon.

Seraphina's fingers curled into the soil where the feather had fallen. A silent vow.

Something had changed. Not just in the air—but in her. In a way, her chest tightened whenever he was near.

She hated it.

Hated how the early light turned his silver hair into molten moonlight.

How his tunic clung to the lines of him—strong, silent, dangerous.

How his eyes flicked toward her like he *knew* about the ghosts that clung to her.

Gods help her. She hated the way she'd wondered—*just once*—what it would feel like to be held by hands that didn't belong to a memory.

She stood abruptly, voice too sharp. "Let's move."

She didn't wait for him to agree.

* * *

The silence between them stretched as they walked, boots crunching over loose gravel and brittle roots. The air thickened with the weight of what remained unspoken.

That feather had stolen whatever peace the morning offered. Kade kept them moving at a brutal pace, one eye always on the trees, on the sky, like danger would drop out of either.

Eventually, the forest thinned, and a broken road revealed itself beneath their feet—the old trade path between Valtheris and Elarion. Once smooth stone and polished markers. Now cracked and devoured by moss, split by tree roots and long-abandoned.

The air here smelled of burnt ash and rain-soaked earth—a storm had passed, leaving the road slick and treacherous. Her foot slipped in the muck, and she barely caught herself, biting back a curse as an icy wind howled through the trees.

Kade didn't stop. He hadn't stopped all morning.

Just when she was about to snap—ready to demand they rest, even just for a moment—dark figures erupted from the treeline.

They moved with broken grace, limbs twisting at wrong angles, mouths slack, black veins pulsing beneath stretched skin. They weren't human anymore. Whatever had been human in them died long ago. These were corrupted husks and puppets made of decay and pain.

Seraphina's sword was in her hand before her mind caught up. A muscle memory more reliable than breath.

The first creature lunged with a garbled shriek, and she met it mid-step—her blade cleaving through flesh that no longer bled red. Black ichor sprayed her arm—thick, oily, rancid. The scent hit her throat like poison.

Another came from behind. She pivoted, ducked, rolled. A blade hissed past her cheek.

Beside her, Kade became a force of nature.

Silver hair flying, dual blades singing through the air. Every movement he made was vicious and elegant. Efficient. Lethal.

They fought in sync. One body, two weapons.

It should have comforted her. That rhythm. That instinctive trust.

Instead, it *unnerved* her.

He had kissed her. Now he moved through death and blood as if it had never happened. Like it had meant nothing.

Her chest burned as she cut down another.

She couldn't help but wonder—

Was it nothing?

It gnawed at her—the way he had pulled away, the way he had looked at her like she was something he had to let go of. Even now, he fought beside her with the same simple confidence he'd always shown, as if nothing had changed. As if her entire world had tilted and refused to right itself.

A clawed hand raked across her shoulder, tearing through fabric and skin. She bit back a curse, the pain sharp but distant. She slammed her blade forward, felt the sickening crunch of impact as her attacker crumpled.

A shadow loomed behind Kade. She moved without thinking.

"Kade!"

He turned just as she slammed into him, knocking them both to the ground as something massive crashed into the space where he had been standing. A twisted abomination of flesh and bone, its eyes hollow pits of red fire.

For a moment, there was only the weight beneath her. His hands had caught her waist on instinct, steadying her even in the fall, fingers curling slightly into the fabric at her sides. The warmth was a stark contrast to the frigid night air. The rise and fall of his chest beneath hers sent something sharp and desperate twisting in her ribs.

A mistake. A distraction. Seraphina shoved off him, rolling to her feet, and drove her blade straight into the creature's throat. It let out a shriek before slumping into the dirt. She turned back, heart pounding too fast for reasons she refused to name.

Kade pushed himself up, wiping blood from his cheek with the back of his hand. He arched an eyebrow at her. "If you wanted to be on top, Nyx, you could've just asked."

Her blade nearly slipped from her fingers. "Go to hell."

He grinned, teeth gleaming. "Oh, darling, we're already there."

The fight ended in a blur of steel and blood, but the weight of it didn't lift when the last enemy fell. It settled deeper, pressing against her ribs. The corrupted bodies lay strewn across the ground, their forms barely human anymore. Yet, as she stood among the carnage, her stomach twisted. They had been civilians. People. She knew that much.

She had cut them down, anyway.

A sickening nausea clawed up her throat, but she swallowed it back, forcing herself to breathe. This wasn't new. She had fought in too many battles to count, seen too many horrors. But this—this was different. Their faces showed no rage or battle lust. They had been hollow. They hadn't chosen this fight.

She wiped a shaking hand across her face, smearing blood and sweat into her skin. The war was still going on. No matter how many she cut down, how many battles they won, it didn't stop. And she was so god-damned tired.

Kade stretched beside her, rolling his shoulders like he hadn't just faced death, like this was routine. Maybe it was. He glanced at her, and for the briefest second, his expression faltered. Just a flicker of something—concern? But then it was gone, masked behind that infuriating smirk.

"You look like you're about to brood." His voice was light, teasing. "Should I be worried?"

She turned away before he could see the truth in her eyes. "Shut up, Kade."

He only chuckled, retrieving his fallen daggers. Like nothing had happened. Like she wasn't standing there, drowning in the weight of it all.

She hated him for that. For making it so damn easy to pretend.

In making her wish, she could do the same.

* * *

By the time they made camp that night, Seraphina sat by the fire, gaze unfocused on the flames, listening to the quiet sounds of Kade sharpening his blades nearby. It was a simple thing. A sound she had heard countless times before. But tonight, she found herself watching him—the way his fingers moved over the whetstone, the flicker of firelight catching against the silver of his eyes, the line of his throat when he tilted his head just slightly.

It made something in her chest twist painfully. She closed her eyes. When did this happen?

The answer came too quickly. Somewhere between the blood and the banter. He looked at her in those moments as if she weren't broken. Guilt followed, swift and sharp. Because Alexis had once looked at her the same way. The thought sent a chill down her spine.

Seraphina exhaled sharply and turned her focus to her injured shoulder. The torn fabric stuck to the wound, the dried blood making every movement ache. She gritted her teeth and peeled it back, revealing deep claw marks, swollen and angry. She poured water from her flask over it, biting back a hiss as the cool liquid met torn flesh. Digging into her pack, she pulled out a small jar of salve, its scent of herbs and something faintly metallic filling her nose. With practised movements, she spread the balm over the gashes, wincing as the sting turned to numb relief. It wasn't much, but it would hold until morning. Wrapping a strip of cloth around her shoulder, she flexed her fingers, testing the tightness, then let her head drop back against the tree behind her. The exhaustion was unbearable.

Sleep claimed her before she could chase it away. The nightmare came instantly.

Alexis stood before her, bathed in silver light, just as he had been in the days before everything fell apart. His tawny skin glowed beneath the moon, his deep blue eyes drinking her in with quiet adoration.

For a breath, she wanted to believe it was real.

Then he smiled.

It was wrong. Twisted. Too sharp. Too knowing.

"You're slipping." Stepping closer, he spoke in a harsh voice. "You see him, don't you? Do you think he can save you?"

Her heart pounded against her ribs. "This isn't real."

His hand ghosted over her cheek. "Neither was he."

She tried to step back, but the ground beneath her feet twisted, shifting into something unnatural. Shadows bled from the edges of the dream, creeping in, filling the spaces where light should have been. The air thickened, suffocating, the scent of charred wood and blood rising around her. Alexis' figure flickered, distorting like a mirage. His deep blue eyes darkened—black, swallowing the colour, endless and hungry.

A voice not quite his echoed from the shadows. "You thought I was gone?"

A chill crawled down her spine. This wasn't just a dream.

Something was watching her.

She woke with a ragged gasp, her lungs burning as if she had been drowning. The world bled back into focus in fragments—the rough bite of dirt beneath her nails, the sharp scent of charred wood and damp earth, the rhythmic crackle of the fire. But beneath it all, something else lingered. A ghost of a scent, something familiar and cruel—sandalwood and steel, just like Alexis.

The dream shattered as dawn bled across the world in hues of bruised lavender and pale gold. Seraphina's eyes snapped open, breath caught in her throat, the phantom screams of the nightmare still echoing in her ears. Cold sweat clung to her skin. She sat up sharply, the earth beneath her damp with dew, the fire beside her long dead—only curling smoke and ash remained.

She scrambled upright, her pulse hammering, breath coming too fast. Cold sweat slicked her spine. Her throat was raw, as if she had been screaming.

A steady voice cut through the haze. "Breathe, Nyx."

Kade.

He crouched beside her, his silver eyes dark with something unreadable, something dangerously close to concern. But he didn't reach for her. He had learned better by now.

She sucked in a breath, forcing herself back into her body, forcing herself to let go of the ghostly hands still clinging to her mind. The fire crackled, its warmth brushing against her chilled skin, but it did little to shake the lingering terror. She felt as though the nightmare dragged her body through it, as if Alexis' touch had seared her cheek, and his whisper settled in her bones.

A low breeze whispered through the trees, and with it, something shifted.

The air was still.

She froze.

A presence lingered—unseen, but heavy, coiling around her senses like smoke.

In one swift, instinctive motion, Seraphina rolled to her feet and reached for her daggers, falling into a low, balanced stance. Her muscles burned with fatigue, but adrenaline surged through her veins like wildfire. She wasn't alone.

Beside her, Kade was already upright, sword unsheathed in one fluid movement, his silver eyes scanning the tree line. His stance was coiled tension, every inch the warrior she had fought beside countless times.

The shadows beyond the treeline thickened, pressing inward, drawn by a gravity none of them understood.

Then the darkness moved.

A figure stepped from the forest, tall and broad, its silhouette cutting through the early light like a blade. His presence filled the clearing like thunder—silent but overwhelming. A cloak of black clung to his shoulders, swirling around him like smoke, but it did little to hide the lethal grace in his steps or the sheer power in his frame.

His hair, jet-black and threaded with strands of ember red, shimmered like coal catching fire. When his eyes lifted—molten gold, bright and burning—they locked onto Seraphina.

She stilled.

Her grip on the daggers tightened as her body screamed to act—but her heart... her heart faltered.

She knew those eyes.

That familiar smirk curled at the corner of his lips.

He was beautiful in a way that was impossible. Ethereal. Dangerous. His sharp jaw, high cheekbones, that damned air of effortless arrogance made her chest twist in a way it hadn't in years. The firelight caught against his features as he stepped fully into view—part shadow, part flame, all memory.

"Little Flame," he said, voice deep and smooth, wrapping around her like a velvet noose. "Still so quick to bare your blades."

Her breath hitched.

That name. That voice.

She didn't need to look twice.

Her vision blurred with recognition, the ground seemed to shift beneath her feet. The blade trembled in her hands.

"Vaelrik," she whispered.

Kade's stance snapped tighter. "Who the hell is this?"

But Seraphina didn't answer. The world narrowed, the sound of Kade's voice barely a flicker in the background.

Vaelrik stood before her—not a memory, not a ghost, but real. Alive! Changed.

He was no longer the warrior she'd once loved. He felt older now. Larger. Like something carved from storm and flame. His presence rolled through the space between them like an ancient tide—terrifying, magnetic.

Yet—for the first time in so long—Seraphina could breathe.

Her daggers lowered slowly, slipping back into their sheaths with a soft hiss. Her legs moved before her mind could catch up—one step, then another. Then she was running.

Vaelrik's arms were already open when she collided with him.

He caught her as though he had never stopped waiting, his body solid and burning with impossible heat. The impact knocked the air from her lungs—but it didn't matter. His arms wrapped around her like fibre, and for a moment, for one fractured breath in time, the war in her heart stilled.

He lifted her off her feet, burying his face in the crook of her neck, and she held on like she might fall apart if she didn't.

Smoke. Sandalwood. Fire. It was him. Gods, it was *him*.

Her fingers curled into the coarse weave of his cloak, clutching him with desperate strength, grounding herself in the warmth of his chest and the heartbeat thundering beneath it. That same heartbeat she once pressed her ear against as he whispered promises between battles, when the world was quieter, softer.

Once, he had laughed so freely it filled every dark corner of her life with light. Once, he had stood between her and every blade, telling her with a smirk that dragons didn't bow to fate.

But something had changed.

He was warmer now. Not just in body — his magic, once a steady flame, now crackled like an inferno beneath his skin, barely restrained. She could feel it pulsing through him, like a storm waiting to be unleashed. His arms only tightened—like he didn't trust the world to let her go again.

Time had carved itself into him. She could feel it in the strength of his hold, the weariness beneath it, the way he clung to her like he feared she might vanish if he blinked.

Yet... the way he held her?

That was unchanged.

She buried her face in the crook of his neck. "I thought you were dead," she whispered, voice raw and uneven, like the words had clawed their way out of her chest.

His breath trembled against her skin. "Not dead, Little Flame," he murmured, voice hoarse, edged with something sharp and quiet. "But you almost made me wish I were."

Her heart cracked open.

She didn't know how long she stood there, wrapped in the silence and the scent of ash and memory, but the world eventually bled back into her awareness.

A sharp scoff cut through it like a blade.

She pulled back, not fully, just enough to glance over her shoulder—and found Kade watching them. He still held his sword, but his fury burned hotter than any flame. His jaw was tight, his body a live wire of restrained violence, the look in his eyes could have cut steel.

He looked as if he wanted to break something. Preferably Vaelrik's face by the intensity with which he was staring.

Vaelrik, of course, noticed—and was thoroughly unimpressed. He tilted his head, still holding Seraphina with maddening ease, golden eyes flicking lazily toward the source of the interruption.

The smirk returned as if it had never left. Gods, she had *hated* that smirk.

She also had missed it.

Kade's glare was thunderous. "So, we're just hugging strangers now? That a new habit of yours, Nyx?"

Seraphina stiffened slightly, suddenly aware of how intimately Vaelrik still held her—one arm looped firmly around her waist, the other splayed across her back as if daring the world to take her.

Vaelrik didn't look away from her. "Who is he to you?" Kade asked, his voice low, each word precise, controlled—but only just.

Vaelrik finally deigned to meet Kade's eyes. He didn't bother hiding the amusement in his expression. "So, this is the infamous Kade." His voice curled with mockery. "I must admit, I expected... more."

Kade's knuckles whitened around his sword. "You've got a lot of nerve walking in here like I won't gut you where you stand."

Vaelrik's hold on Seraphina loosened—just slightly—as he leaned closer to her ear, his voice dropping into something silk-wrapped and dangerous. "Does he always talk this much, or is he trying to impress you?"

"Vaelrik," she said sharply, placing a hand on his chest and stepping back. Her skin still tingled where they'd touched. "That's enough."

His golden gaze softened just a breath as he looked down at her—but the tension between him and Kade crackled like lightning.

"How did you find us?" she asked, grounding herself in the question, needing answers more than the past.

Something flickered across his face. Just for a heartbeat. Then it was gone, masked beneath that damn arrogant grin.

"You didn't think I'd lose track of you that easily, did you?" he said. "I have eyes everywhere. You, Little Flame..." his gaze dragged down her, filled with heat and something unreadable, "you leave chaos like breadcrumbs."

Her pulse skipped, caught between fear and something far more dangerous.

"That doesn't answer my question."

He leaned in, just enough that only she could hear. "I never stopped looking."

Kade scoffed. "We're supposed to believe you're here to help?"

Vaelrik's gaze flicked back to him, and his smirk returned, slower this time, more deliberate. "Believe what you want. But if I wanted you dead, you'd already be on the ground bleeding."

Seraphina exhaled sharply. "Enough. If we're going to survive this, we don't have time for posturing." She met Vaelrik's gaze, her voice hardening. "You say you've been watching. Then tell me—what exactly are we up against?"

Vaelrik's smirk faded, replaced by something far more serious. "Something worse than you've ever faced."

Just like that, the fire's warmth was no longer enough to chase away the cold settling deep in Seraphina's bones. It slithered in like smoke under a door—slow, insidious, familiar.

The tension coiled around her like a noose.

It was volatile.

It was electric, waiting for a single spark to ignite the storm.

Vaelrik tilted his head ever so slightly, his golden eyes gleaming with something too knowing—an unsettling awareness that scraped across her mind like claws on stone. She knew he couldn't read her like others. Her shields had always held. But he *felt* her. He always had. It was in the way he looked at her now, like he could taste every shadow of her thoughts on the air.

The firelight danced across his features, throwing long shadows and sharpening the cruel lines of his face. He looked untouched by time, and yet more dangerous than she remembered—like the years had only refined the beast beneath the skin. His smirk was infuriatingly familiar, curved with the same arrogant ease that had once unravelled her.

Still… a part of her twisted at the sight of it. At *him*.

Beside her, Kade shifted. She could feel it in the subtle tremor of his restraint, the pressure in the air that pulsed with his anger. He lowered his sword but shifted his stance, ready and tense. Always protective of her. Always watching.

"You want to explain who this is?" Kade's voice cut the silence, low and laced with steel. There was no mistaking the distrust behind his words.

Seraphina forced herself to breathe evenly, to keep her voice steady. Her heart, however, was anything but. It beat too fast, too loud—caught somewhere between the past and the present, pulled in two directions.

Her gaze returned to Vaelrik. He had once been her everything. Her home. Her undoing. Now he was a ghost in the flesh, dredging up a life she'd buried.

"An ally," she said, but the word came out brittle—an empty thing, half-hearted and unconvincing.

Vaelrik's laughter was soft and venom-laced, curling through the air like smoke from a dying flame. He stepped closer, the air between them shifted—too warm, too intimate. "An ally, is it?" his voice silken and cruel. "You used to call me something sweeter than that."

The memories slammed into her like a wave. Pet nicknames. The nights tangled in whispered promises and breathless confessions. The way his voice had once soothed her when the world fell apart.

She clenched her fists, forcing herself not to flinch, not to fall.

Kade's grip on his sword tightened. His eyes didn't leave Vaelrik's, but Seraphina could feel the way his fury simmered just below the surface—quiet, controlled, but barely. He was ready to tear the dragon shifter apart.

She didn't look at him. Couldn't. Because if she did, he'd see everything.

Instead, she faced the ghost of her past—the one who knew too much and wore every memory like fibre. Vaelrik hadn't changed. Not truly. His presence was still too large, too consuming. Despite herself, despite everything, her chest ached at the familiarity.

"You've changed," she said, her voice quieter than she intended, fragile and raw.

For a breath, Vaelrik's smirk cracked, just slightly. His eyes flickered—

just once—with something real. Regret? Pain? She couldn't tell. It vanished before she could name it.

"So have you, Little Flame," he replied.

her breath hitched. *Little Flame.*

Gods, that name. It tore through her like a blade. It was who she used to be, the version of herself that had dared to hope—before the fall, before the betrayal. Before Kade.

She hated the part of her that wanted to hear it again.

Her chest tightened, the confusion burned hotter. She'd moved on. Hadn't she? Through the collapse, he remained, unlike everyone else. He had seen her at her worst—and loved her anyway. He was her strength; her anchor.

Yet, standing in front of Vaelrik, the past didn't feel dead. It felt *unfinished.*

She drew in a breath, straightened her spine, forced steel into her voice. "We don't have time for reunions. If you're here, it means you know something."

Vaelrik's expression shifted, the arrogance returning like a mask sliding into place. His gaze sharpened with purpose. Slowly, deliberately, he reached into the folds of his cloak and drew out a silver amulet. It shimmered with ancient runes, pulsing faintly like a heartbeat.

It thrummed with magic—old and alive.

"They're hunting more than just you," Vaelrik said, his voice darker now, clipped and cold. "They want this. I pulled it off the corpse of a demon who kept chanting about needing it for their master."

Seraphina stared at the amulet, but her mind was spinning. The enemy, the threat—it was all important. But in that moment, all she could feel was the gravity pulling her in opposite directions.

Kade. Vaelrik.

Past. Present.

Home and heartbreak.

She didn't know which way was forward anymore.

Seraphina frowned, stepping closer, instinctively reaching out. The amulet thrummed softly, as if it had a heartbeat of its own, and she felt a strange unease stir in her chest, like the stirrings of an old, forgotten fear.

Kade's suspicion was clear as he stepped forward, his eyes narrowing. "What is it?"

Vaelrik's gaze flicked to him, and a faint, almost amused smile curled his lips. "A key."

"To what?" She pressed, her pulse quickening.

Vaelrik's smirk deepened, but there was something darker in his eyes now, something that made Seraphina's stomach tighten. "To a power that should have died long ago."

Kade scoffed, stepping back, the distrust etched into his every movement. "You expect us to trust you?"

Vaelrik shrugged nonchalantly. "Trust? No, but we don't have the luxury of choosing our allies, do we?"

Her teeth ground together, frustration flaring hot in her chest. Damn him—he was right. The world had never given her the luxury of peace, let alone clarity. But that didn't mean she had to welcome the past as it strutted back into her life with that smug look in his golden eyes. Gods, he *knew* he got under her skin. He always had.

But Kade wasn't finished.

"Oh, how convenient," he drawled, his voice like ice over steel. "You show up now, right when they're closing in—holding exactly what they want. Suspicious, don't you think?"

Vaelrik sighed dramatically, rubbing the bridge of his nose with deliberate annoyance. "I'd forgotten how exhausting the suspicious ones are. Trust issues, was it?"

Kade took a step forward, his body coiled tight with aggression, fingers twitching at his side. "Try saying that again. See what happens."

The air pulsed—taut, volatile. Even the fire dimmed as if the room itself was holding its breath.

"Enough," Seraphina snapped, her voice cutting clean through the rising storm. "Both of you."

They froze, but the tension between them crackled like lightning, itching for a place to strike.

Seraphina's heart thudded painfully. Old wounds clawed their way to the surface, raw and unhealed. She didn't want this—didn't want to feel the pull of familiarity Vaelrik brought with him, nor the confusing safety Kade had become. The past and present stood on either side of her, both demanding, both dangerous.

She... she didn't know who she was in between them anymore.

She stepped forward, positioning herself between them, a living barrier barely holding back the tide. "We don't have time for this dick-measuring contest. If they're after the amulet, then we can't stay here. Not another second."

Vaelrik raised a brow, the corner of his mouth twitching. "Giving orders now? You've always had a talent for taking charge."

His voice was low, teasing, just a *hint* too familiar. She didn't rise to it. She couldn't.

She walked past him, letting her steps carry her away from both the pull of nostalgia and the gravity of what stood behind her. She spoke in a clipped but steady voice. "The mission comes first. Everything else can burn."

Behind her, Kade muttered something—low, dark, and furious—but she didn't turn around. Couldn't.

"Are you coming, or would you rather stand there and compare egos?" she called over her shoulder, the command in her voice laced with steel.

Vaelrik hesitated for the briefest moment, then fell into step beside her, his movements fluid, annoyingly at ease. "Lead the way, *Little Flame*," he murmured.

The nickname dug under her skin like a blade honed in memory.

She felt Kade's eyes boring into her back—felt the weight of unspoken questions, the ache of something unsaid. But she didn't look. She couldn't. Because if she did, if she *chose* one, then the illusion of control would shatter.

Seraphina wasn't ready to shatter.

Chapter 12

Time had slipped by in fragments measured in whispered confessions and the crunch of boots on forgotten roads. Since Vaelrik had joined them, the nights had filled with the sound of his voice—velvet and razor-edged—spinning tales of war beyond their prison walls. Of shattered alliances. Of mighty factions ground to dust. The world had not paused in their absence. It had only grown crueller.

They passed through the remnants of an old outpost, its crumbling stone walls bearing the scars of battles long past. Tattered banners hung like ghosts, threads unravelling in the wind. The scent of damp earth mingled with old, clinging magic—faint, but still potent enough to stir something buried in Seraphina's chest. Roots and ruin fractured the ground beneath their boots, splitting the stone, as if the land itself had tried to forget what had happened here.

Kade led the way, silent and vigilant. The moon caught in his silver hair, casting an almost ethereal light around him. But she saw what the moon didn't. The tension was in his shoulders. The way his hand lingered near his blade a heartbeat too long. He wasn't just watching for danger. He was watching *him*.

Vaelrik's gait was unhurried, graceful in a way that made it look like he belonged among the dead—like he *remembered* them. "This place," he murmured, eyes scanning the ruins, "once stood proud. Until it was ground beneath a greedy king's heel."

Seraphina glanced sideways. "You fought here?"

"I did," he said, tone unreadable. "But not for the crown. I fought to burn it down. Mortals should never have held the leash of my kind. You know that, don't you, *Little Flame?*"

The nickname slid over her skin like smoke and ash—intimate, and entirely unwelcome. Once, it had been whispered into her hair in the dark. Now it tasted like blood.

Ahead, Kade stiffened. His hand curled tighter around his sword hilt. He didn't turn, but the surrounding air darkened, pulsing with silent fury.

Vaelrik noticed. "Ah," he said smoothly, "I didn't know you were travelling with an *Unseelie.*"

Seraphina blinked. "You can sense him?"

Vaelrik chuckled, low and cold. "Of course. His ears give him away, sure, but it's the *stain* that lingers. Your kind carries it like a curse," he added, his gaze sliding to Kade. "And yet here you are—by her side. Not a captor. As... something else. Curious."

The tension snapped taut. Kade turned then, slowly, like a predator scenting blood. "You know nothing about me."

Vaelrik tilted his head. His smirk remained, but something darker rippled beneath it. "No," he said softly, "but I've met your kind before. Centuries ago, one of your courts tried to bind my power. Said it was for the good of the realm. I tore their envoy's heart out with my teeth."

A beat passed. Then another.

Kade's knuckles whitened on the hilt of his blade.

"I heard about that," he whispered, voice low like thunder far off on the horizon. "When I came home from training, it was all anyone could talk about. An emissary was ripped to pieces mid-mission. No one knew why. The court spun it into silence, said it was her mistake—said she'd overstepped."

Vaelrik gave a lazy shrug, his golden eyes sharp with memory. "She did."

Kade's head turned slightly, his profile half-shadowed by the moonlight. "It was one reason I joined the military. After that, I stopped believing in

112

diplomacy."

Seraphina furrowed her brow. "You knew her?"

"I didn't know who it was exactly..." he murmured, his voice trailing off. "But the details... the runes, braided red hair, the silver cuffs, the peace offering turned to blood..."

Vaelrik smirked, something cruel flickering at the edge. "Oh, spare me your tragic revelations. What do you care? Emissaries die all the time."

Seraphina scoffed. "Exactly. Why would you care so much about an emissary being killed four hundred years ago?"

Kade turned to face her fully then. His expression unreadable. Still. Too still.

"Because," he said, voice calm in a way that made her chest tighten, "four hundred years ago... I was married."

The world stopped.

Kade's eyes met hers, and there was something raw and hollow behind them.

"She was my partner," he said, each word sharp and spare. "She wore silver cuffs because she hated gold. Said it looked too gaudy on her skin. She braided her hair herself every morning, but when I was home, she let me do it. She thought we could help your kind. That we could make peace."

His voice cracked—not loudly, not messily. Just enough to shatter something inside her.

"And she died with her heart ripped out," he finished, "because she believed you could be saved."

The silence was absolute. Even the wind seemed to stop.

Seraphina opened her mouth. Closed it again. Her throat burned.

Vaelrik didn't speak. His smirk had faded, eyes narrowing, not in guilt— but in something colder. Recognition.

It was Seraphina who finally whispered, "Kade... I didn't know."

"I know." His voice was steady, but not unbroken. A thread of something quieter, older, curled at the edges.

Vaelrik exhaled—long, drawn-out. It was a sound that didn't come from lungs, but from centuries buried beneath ash and memory. "She shouldn't have tried to chain me."

Kade's jaw tensed, teeth grinding against a silence he hadn't wanted to break. "She thought it was the only way. You were tearing through cities, Vaelrik. Leaving nothing but fire and shadows."

"She was right," Vaelrik said evenly. "She was wrong."

No heat. No defensiveness. Just truth, stripped bare of sentiment.

Kade looked away. His shoulders sagged with the weight of too many unspoken nights. "I hated you for it. Still do, most days."

Vaelrik didn't argue. Didn't ask for forgiveness. He only nodded, slowly and deliberate. "I know."

The quiet that followed wasn't empty. It was dense—thick with old grief and half-healed betrayal, like a wound that didn't bleed anymore but still stung when touched.

Then Vaelrik turned.

His gaze landed on Seraphina—sharp, precise, but lacking the malice it once might have carried. Something old flickered there. Not quite affection. Not quite distrust. Something in-between.

"I know Seraphina was never one to follow orders," he said, the ghost of a smirk tugging at one corner of his mouth. "Let alone tie herself to the shadows."

The smirk faded.

His tone changed, cooled.

"So tell me, Seraphina—how did you come to be with him?"

The question hung in the frosty night air like a blade half-drawn.

Seraphina stilled mid-step. Her breath curled in front of her like smoke, and for a heartbeat, she didn't answer. The ground beneath her boots felt unsteady, like the ruins themselves had shifted in response.

"It's a long story," she breathed.

Vaelrik tilted his head, golden eyes narrowing slightly as they studied her—not like a stranger, but like a puzzle half-solved. It wasn't curiosity alone that shaped his silence—it was familiarity. Recognition. She saw it in the crease of his brow, in the way his eyes searched hers like a map he once knew by heart.

He stepped back.

Not physically. Emotionally. Strategically. He didn't press, that restraint hit her harder than a thousand accusations. Vaelrik had always known *when* to push. He was never reckless in his probing. He simply planted the question like a seed—and waited.

His gaze lingered a moment longer, the unspoken promise of *we will revisit this* glinting behind his smile before he finally turned away. His eyes swept across the shattered remnants of stone towers and shattered keeps. When he spoke again, it was quieter. Almost wistful.

"You're brooding," he murmured, amusement threading through his voice like smoke.

She scoffed under her breath, shaking her head. "You think everyone's brooding?"

"Because most of you are," he said, tone lilting with dry amusement. "Though you—" he gestured lazily, "—you're not subtle. You glare at the back of Storm Cloud's head like you're trying to set it on fire."

She almost laughed, but the sound caught in her throat. Had she been? She hadn't noticed. Or maybe… maybe part of her had.

Vaelrik moved beside her, his steps smooth and soundless. He walked too close—close enough to remind her of other nights, other roads, where they had walked side by side with the trust forged in blood and flame.

But that was then.

Still, his presence felt protective. Familiar. Unwanted.

She shifted slightly to the side. Not enough to be obvious. Just enough to reclaim a sliver of space. But Kade noticed.

He always did.

His shoulders drew tighter, and his hand drifted nearer to his blade—not in fear, but in tension, in instinct. He flicked a glance over his shoulder, in that moment, she saw it: not jealousy, not exactly. Something deeper. Something older. Feeling cautious about something. His eyes met hers, unreadable, then dropped to Vaelrik with a flicker of restrained calculation before turning away again.

He didn't like this. He didn't like the way Vaelrik moved with her. Didn't like that they shared a language built on silence and fragments.

Seraphina's jaw tightened. She focused on the road ahead, the fractured moonlight painting the ruins in hues of silver and sorrow. The wind tugged at her hair, whispering of the past she wasn't ready to speak aloud.

Vaelrik hadn't changed.

Yet, he had.

He still looked like the devil carved into a dream—golden-eyed, sharp-boned, danger and desire wrapped in silk and shadows. But the softness that once lived behind his eyes was gone, burned away into something colder. Sharper. There was an edge to him now that hadn't existed when they were younger—when they had danced between choices instead of consequences.

"Whatever you're thinking," she muttered, "stop."

Vaelrik didn't respond right away. When he did, his voice was low, almost too soft. "You asked me once if monsters could mourn."

She frowned, thrown by the sudden shift.

His gaze remained fixed on the stones as he continued, "I never answered."

His golden gaze looked at her. "I was unaware then. I know now."

The quiet stretched between them like a wire pulled taut. Kade slowed his steps just enough to hear his profile sharpening in the moonlight.

Seraphina's voice was barely a whisper. "What do you mourn?"

But Vaelrik didn't answer.

Not yet

Chapter 13

It felt like hours had passed in the silence that followed when suddenly Kade motioned for them to halt, dropping into a crouch. His fingers sifted through the dirt, muscles coiled beneath his dark leathers. He is always a warrior, always ready. His gaze flicked up, sharp and focused. "We're not alone."

The words sent a ripple through the air.

A growl rumbled through the silence, low and guttural—a sound that did not belong to the living. It reverberated against the ruined stone, crawling up Seraphina's spine like ice.

The air thickened, laced with the stench of decay and sulphur. Shadows slithered unnaturally, stretching and curling where they shouldn't. The ruins breathed around them; the darkness coming alive.

Seraphina's pulse quickened. Not just because of the sound, but because she had felt this before. That shift in the air. That moment before the world turned to blood and death.

Vaelrik had already moved, his stance shifting—protective, instinctual, right at her side. The way he used to. The way Kade had for the past two years.

A muscle feathered in Kade's jaw, but there was no time for anything more.

Something moved.

A flicker in the darkness—then it was there.

A grotesque fusion of beast and shadow, its form barely held shape as it lurched forward. Its maw gaped wide, jagged teeth glistening with thick, inky saliva. Its clawed hands twitched with anticipation, tendrils of darkness peeling from its flesh like smoke.

Seraphina barely had time to draw her blades before it lunged.

Kade was the first to move, his sword slicing through the air in a deadly arc, cleaving through the creature's chest. Black ichor splattered across the ground, sizzling as it met the stone.

Seraphina twisted narrowly, dodging a second creature as it barrelled toward her. Her dagger found its mark, sinking deep into its throat. Hot blood poured over her hand as the creature thrashed violently before collapsing in a heap. Vaelrik fought beside her, a storm of flames and fury. His fire licked at the abominations, turning them to ash.

The battlefield erupted into chaos—snarling beasts, flashing steel, the stench of burning flesh, and the shrill screams of the fallen. But beneath the cacophony of war, something darker stirred—something ancient and cruel, worming through the frayed edges of Seraphina's mind like rot beneath a wound.

Then she heard it. A whisper, soft as silk and twice as venomous.

Sera... Sera...

Her breath hitched, her pulse faltering. The world twisted at the edges. Blood-soaked stone gave way to marble floors. Smoke thinned into perfumed air—sweet myrrh and rose petals. Suddenly, she stood barefoot in the palace hall, golden light spilling through the stained glass windows. It was beautiful, it was wrong.

Her skin prickled.

The warmth of fingers brushed over her wrist—gentle, familiar, possessive. A kiss ghosted across her lips. She knew the shape of that mouth.

But it felt like ash.

Did you think you could forget me?

A tremor of dread crawled up her spine. Her knees locked, her throat tight. No. No, not here. Not again.

The memory swallowed her whole.

The vision darkened—the walls seemed to bleed shadow, dripping like black tar. A figure emerged from the gloom — tall, regal, haloed by flickering candlelight.

Alexis.

His deep blue eyes once held the constellations for her. Now they were fathomless pits—flat, cold, soulless. The memory of him used to bring peace. Now it only brought bile.

He smiled. Not warmth. Not love. Something else. Possession.

Then—

A movement behind him.

Her sister.

Elira.

Bound, trembling, her eyes wide and brimming with silent screams. Her face was streaked with ash and blood. Elira had always been delicate— soft-spoken, sun-kissed and birdlike in her movements, too kind for court games. She had hidden behind Seraphina's skirts as a child and grown into a young woman of wild laughter and soft rebellion.

Now she was barely standing.

"Please," Seraphina breathed. "Let her go. She's done nothing."

"She saw too much," Alexis said, calm.

Seraphina surged forward, desperation tearing through her—but the world moved slower than her heart.

Too slow.

The silver flash came with cruel elegance.

A blade. Sharp. Merciless.

Elira's gasp.

The wet thud of steel into flesh.

That horrifying, pregnant silence before a body falls.

Her sister crumpled, blood blooming across her chest in a grotesque flower.

Seraphina screamed. The sound came from a place deeper than her lungs, deeper than her soul—an animal wail of grief so fierce it splintered her mind. She caught her sister just as she collapsed, hands slipping in blood. Elira's eyes blinked once—twice—then stilled, wide and glassy, staring through her.

"No—no—stay with me, baby bird, please," her voice cracked, raw with denial.

A hand.

On her ribs.

Pressure.

Pain.

Blinding electric agony shot through her body. Her vision turned white. Her body arched.

She looked down.

The blow buried the blade in her side. Her own blood gushed hot and wild across Alexis' hand.

His breath brushed her ear as he leaned in. *"You were always so easy to fool, Sera."*

The betrayal struck deeper than the blade.

She couldn't scream. Couldn't breathe. Just—why?

Why her sister? Why this?

Her knees hit the stone. The candlelight flickered and faded. The hall shattered.

The pain was real. Now. Present.

A voice—urgent, frantic—broke through the nightmare like a lance of lightning.

"Seraphina! Stay with me!"

Kade's voice.

Real.

Her name in his mouth was salvation—ragged and raw, cracked with desperation. It sliced through the fog of her fractured mind like lightning in a storm.

"Seraphina!"

She blinked. Once. Twice. Her chest heaved, lungs burning. The battlefield slammed back into focus.

Moonlight fractured over pools of blood. Screams rang through the air like broken bells. The stench of death clawed down her throat—smoke, rot, something darker, older.

She wasn't at the palace.

Elira wasn't here. Alexis wasn't here.

But the wound? The wound was.

She staggered to her feet, body trembling, every muscle screaming for rest. Her breath came in gasps, each one a battle against collapse. But she *couldn't* fall. Not now. Not when she had already lost too much.

Her gaze found Kade—tall, silver-haired, a slash of moonlight against the night. His normally unreadable eyes blazed with panic. Not for himself. For her. He had seen her falter, seen the ghost clawing at her mind—he had called her back.

She swallowed the bile rising in her throat and forced herself upright.

There was no time.

A blur of shadow lunged at her.

A demon—its mouth filled with blackened fangs, eyes like sunken coals. Seraphina didn't think. She moved. Instinct took the reins, honed over years of war and pain. She threw herself in front of Vaelrik—young, defiant, untested, but loyal. Her blade flashed, catching the creature mid-leap. The dagger slammed into its skull with a wet crunch. It spasmed, twitched—and fell still.

Vaelrik exhaled a shaky breath, disbelief written in the furrow of his brow. His lips twitched in the briefest flicker of admiration, but there was no time for words.

The wind bit at her back, cool against sweat and blood. She turned, already knowing the pain was coming.

A jagged edge of her cracked fibre sliced across her side. She hissed through clenched teeth. Crimson leaked from the gash, hot and sticky.

She didn't stop.

Then *it* came.

A hulking demon—twice the size of the last—emerged from the smoke. Bone jutted from its back like broken wings, its blade slick with a black

121

venom that shimmered like oil.

It didn't hesitate.

The blade sank into her side.

She choked on the scream, staggering backward. Poison scorched through her veins. Ice and fire fused into agony. The creature leaned close, its voice a hiss of broken glass.

"Foolish girl."

She didn't answer.

She couldn't.

Her focus was slipping, her limbs heavy, her heartbeat a war drum in her ears. But her gaze—her mind—locked on Vaelrik.

A memory surged forward. A promise whispered beneath starlight, their backs pressed to the earth, breath fogging in the cold.

"You'll protect me, right?"

"With everything I am."

That promise was a tether, holding her above the tide.

She would not break it.

Her ribs screamed. Her chest burned. But her vow burned hotter.

Another beast lunged. She moved before she knew it, driven by will alone. Her legs nearly buckled, but she surged forward, slicing her blade upward, catching it beneath the jaw.

It fell.

But something else moved behind Vaelrik.

Something *bigger*.

She saw it before he did—a shadow splitting from the smoke. Long limbs, too many eyes, a maw stretching wide with hunger.

Time fractured. She lunged. Her blade found the creature's throat—metal piercing rot and magic. It shrieked, flailing, before crumpling at Vaelrik's feet.

Victory for a breath.

Then *pain*. A second beast—a trick.

The poisoned claw tore through her chest. Her world exploded in red. The force threw her back. Her fibre shattered, bones cracking under the force. Fire consumed her nerves as the venom twisted through her blood, unmaking her from the inside.

She landed hard. Her body spasmed. Every breath a torture. Every second is a choice to keep living. Her chest constricted, every breath a struggle. She could feel the poison working its way through her, a heavy, suffocating presence sinking deep into her skin. Her blood felt cold, her vision flickering. The world tilted.

Her body was breaking.

Kade's hands were on her again, pulling her back, his grip iron-tight. His silver eyes were wide, fear written across his face.

"Stay with me, Sera. Don't you dare—" His voice cracked, desperation and anger tangling in every word. But it was more than that. There was something raw there. Something fragile. She could see it in the way his hands shook, pressing against her chest where the venom seeped deeper. He was terrified.

She smiled weakly at him, but the smile barely formed before the world spun again.

Vaelrik's voice broke through the haze, a flame igniting in the air. He surged forward, his golden eyes blazing as he ripped through the demon with a burst of fire. The creature disintegrated in seconds, reduced to nothing but charred remnants. But that wasn't enough. Not for her.

Her vision blurred again, the sounds of battle distant, muted, as though underwater. She could feel Kade's frantic hands at her wrist, could hear the muttered curses from Vaelrik, but the world was fading.

The venom was everywhere now, crawling beneath her skin, making it feel like her body was being pulled apart. It twisted and turned, each beat of her heart sending waves of agony through her chest. Her limbs felt heavy, her bones like brittle glass.

The last thing she remembered was Kade's voice, soft, raw, desperate in her ear.

"Not like this," he whispered, a broken plea in his voice. "Not like this, Sera."

But she had already decided. The blackness was creeping in, seeping around her vision, smothering everything.

She could feel herself slipping, but the promise held her.

"I promised..." she whispered, barely audible, her lips cracked from the effort. "I promised... I'd protect him."

Then everything went black.

Darkness clung to her like a second skin, suffocating her senses, dragging her down into an abyss of nothingness. The waves of heat came again—flickering at the edges of her awareness. She felt the faintest stirrings of hands, of something pulling her back.

Rough. Calloused. Cool.

Kade's voice reached her, tight with frustration. "She's not healing fast enough."

Vaelrik's voice was sharp, but laced with something softer, deeper. "I'm aware. Unless you've suddenly developed the ability to purge dark magic, I suggest you let me work."

A curse fell from Kade's lips, frantically pacing. "Damn it, she should be healing. This isn't normal."

Vaelrik's tone softened ever so slightly. "You think I don't know that? This poison is older than anything I've ever felt. Corruption, not magic, is the issue. It's too much. It's working too fast."

Kade's breath caught, a tight, shuddering exhale. His hands trembling, he found hers again. "Sera... please."

But Seraphina was too far gone. The blackness swallowed her whole.

The world around Seraphina blurred as the dream took hold, the memories surfacing against her will, just like the poison still writhing in her veins. She felt herself slipping, but not into unconsciousness this time. Instead, she was drowning in the past—the warmth of a promise made, the weight of it.

"I promise, Vaelrik. I'll protect you, no matter what."

She spoke the words with the conviction of someone who had nothing left to give, but still offered everything. The words burned themselves into her soul. She was young then, fresh in the heat of battle but still innocent in her trust. The image of Vaelrik, with his sharp eyes and proud stance, was still clear in her mind, though the edges of the memory now flickered with doubt.

The dream faded like a flickering flame, the sharp sting of reality rushing back to her. The stone walls, the air thick with exhaustion, the bitter taste of betrayal—it all returned, harsh and immediate.

Seraphina's throat tightened as she blinked rapidly, trying to clear the fog that was clouding her thoughts. She tried to focus, but it was as if the weight of the world was pulling her under. The dim candlelight flickered in the small room, casting long shadows over the cold stone walls. The air was thick with silence before Kade's voice broke through.

"There she is," he murmured, the words soft but laced with an edge of concern. His silver hair was tangled; he softened his usually hard face and furrowed his brows as he studied her. He was kneeling beside her, one hand resting lightly on her forehead, his thumb brushing across her skin in a way that made her heart stutter. As she tried to sit up, she found herself unable.

The world tilted as Seraphina stirred again, her body heavy with exhaustion, the pain from her wounds seeping through every inch of her. Her chest ached, the tight bandages around her ribs a constant reminder of the brutal stab wound she'd taken. The claw marks that marred her chest were raw and angry beneath the bandages, and every movement sent a shiver of pain through her body. She could still feel the poison coursing through her veins, a lingering ache that dulled her senses and made everything feel far away.

"You're still alive," Vaelrik muttered from across the room, voice dry. "And that's something we weren't sure of for a while."

Seraphina let out a shaky breath, shaking her head as she tried to ignore the exhaustion clinging to her every movement. "I'm not sure I should be." Her voice was weak, barely above a whisper.

Kade snapped his attention toward her. "Don't talk like that. You don't get to give up on us."

Seraphina couldn't help but laugh bitterly. "You're one to talk."

The air between Kade and Vaelrik crackled, as it always did when they were together. The tension was palpable, thick enough to suffocate anyone who dared to stay too close.

"What... happened?" she rasped, her voice barely a whisper.

Kade exhaled sharply, his grip tightening just slightly on her wrist. "You froze in the middle of the fight. What the hell happened?"

Her pulse quickened as she tried to recall the battle, the blur of demon claws and blood-soaked earth. But it wasn't the battle that haunted her now; it was the vision, the voice. *Alexis.*

"I... I heard a voice," she murmured, her mind struggling to make sense of it all. "It was Alexis. He spoke to me, and I..." Her words faltered as the memory gripped her tightly again—the golden light, the warmth of his presence, the unbearable sadness that had flooded her chest. She fought against the weight, pushing it back.

Kade's brow furrowed, his gaze intense as he leaned closer. "Alexis? That makes little sense. He's—"

"I know," she cut him off sharply, a tremor in her voice. "It makes little sense, but I heard him. It was like... like he was inside my head." Her fists clenched as she shut her eyes, trying to escape the ghost of his voice. "It was the only thing I could hear. It... stopped me in my tracks."

Kade's face was a storm of frustration and concern. "That's why you froze?"

Her heart ached as she nodded, the crushing weight of the memory still pressing against her chest. "Yes. I couldn't... I couldn't fight against it."

For a moment, there was nothing but the soft sound of her breathing and Kade's harsh exhale. Then, as if realising something, he softened his grip, his eyes searching her face, a flicker of vulnerability in his gaze that she rarely saw.

"I hate to admit it, but... I'm glad you're still here, Sera," Kade muttered, almost gruffly, his mask slipping just for a second. He looked away quickly, rubbing the back of his neck. "But damn it, you can't just keep doing that. You can't sacrifice yourself every time."

Before Seraphina could respond, a low voice interrupted them.

"Well, well, well," Vaelrik's voice came from across the room, the usual sardonic tone replaced by something more sincere. "The brooding idiot's actually showing a softer side."

Seraphina turned her head slowly toward him, her muscles protesting with every movement. Vaelrik was standing by the wall, arms crossed, but his eyes had softened as he met her gaze.

"You saved me," he breathed, the words almost surprising in their tenderness. "I'm... grateful for that. But don't do it again, Seraphina. Don't sacrifice yourself for the rest of us. We need you. You don't get to throw your life away."

Seraphina's chest tightened, her breath coming in shallow gasps. She wanted to argue, to tell them that time was running out, that they had to move. But her body, aching from the poison and the physical toll of the fight, betrayed her.

"I can't..." she began, but Vaelrik held up a hand.

"No. Rest." His tone was commanding, but there was a gentleness beneath it. "We didn't spend all those days healing you for you to run off and try to save the world again. You need to take a moment and breathe, Seraphina."

Her eyes narrowed, her mind struggling to fight against the truth in his words. "We don't have time for a rest."

Kade's voice, rough but filled with resolve, cut in. "You're not going anywhere, Nyx, not until you can stand without collapsing."

Vaelrik rolled his eyes dramatically. "And there it is. The woman who never listens. But I'm with Silver on this one. Time's not on our side, but neither is your health. We all need you in one piece." He grinned, his usual arrogance returning. "You're no use to anyone if you're dead on your feet."

She let out a breath, feeling the weight of her wounds again. The stab wound to her chest burned with every breath she took, the pressure on her ribs reminding her of just how close she had come to losing everything. The claw marks along her side throbbed in tandem with the pounding in her head. She felt utterly exhausted, and yet... the urgency that tugged at her still wouldn't relent.

She let her eyes close for a moment, willing herself to push through the pain. But every inch of her body screamed in protest, she knew, deep down, that she needed to rest. There would be no saving anyone if she didn't.

"I'll be fine," she muttered, her voice thick with fatigue. "I just need... time."

Kade shot her a warning look. "No, Sera. You need time to heal. We need to make sure this doesn't happen again."

Vaelrik's gaze softened, his usual bravado slipping away. "You're not the only one who's been through hell. But we'll all be dead if you push yourself too far." He stepped closer, his voice quieter now, more sincere. "I'm glad you're still here. Just... don't do that again."

Seraphina couldn't muster a response. Instead, she lay back against the pillow, the weight of her body, the pain, the ever-present sense of dread wrapping around her once again.

Her eyelids fluttered shut, just as the darkness pulled her under, she heard Kade's soft voice.

"Rest. For once, just... rest."

Without warning, the dream swept over her, dragging her deeper into the past—a past she had buried so far within herself that it had almost faded completely. The dream pulled her from the present, the battle, the heat of Kade's touch, into a distant, unreachable warmth.

Golden light spilled over her, soft as the last kiss of sunset, drifting through the trees where Vaelrik held her. His touch was a fleeting echo of safety, a promise that no darkness could breach.

But then the fire came.

It tore through her world—relentless. A searing wall of destruction that devoured everything. Vaelrik's form was ripped from her grasp, swallowed by the shadows. The feel of dark magic stung in the air.

She screamed at him. Desperate. But there was no answer—only the roar of flames, the crunch of burning wood, the suffocating weight of loss.

In the real world, her body jolted, breath ragged, as if still caught in the flames. Kade's hand tightened around hers, his gaze snapping to Vaelrik. "What the hell is she dreaming about?"

Vaelrik didn't answer at first. His brow furrowed as he reached—reluctantly—into her mind. He felt like an intruder trespassing on sacred ground, the ease with which he entered chilled him.

"Me," he said finally, his voice hollow.

Kade's jaw tensed. "You can read her thoughts?"

Vaelrik rolled his eyes, though his tone was dry, not cruel. "I'm not a god, Kade. It's not like I can just dip into anyone's mind on a whim. Most supernaturals have natural wards. Walls. Even you, for all your broken bits, have layers I can't sift through."

He gestured vaguely at her, his expression tightening. "But mortals? They're different. Seraphina—she's not shielding right now. She's feverish, fractured. Her defences are completely down."

"So you're saying it's because she's weak?"

"Don't get noble on me. It's not her fault. Normally, I wouldn't even *try*." His voice dropped, bitterness threading through it. "I respected her mind. I have always done so. But now, it's like she's crying out and no one's listening. I'm just... hearing what's already pouring out."

Kade didn't look convinced. His fingers flexed against hers. "But you *did* try."

Vaelrik didn't flinch. "Wouldn't you?"

Seraphina whimpered in her sleep, her fingers twitching as though reaching for something beyond her grasp. "Vaelrik... don't leave me."

The name hit Kade like a blade to the gut. He had no right to feel jealous. But there it was—gnawing. Raw.

"She loved me once," Vaelrik murmured, eyes still fixed on her. "But they tore me from her. Not by choice."

Kade growled under his breath. "How do we wake her?"

Vaelrik finally looked at him, something unreadable passing between them. "You think you can save her? That you're the hero in this story?"

Kade snapped, "She doesn't belong to you."

Vaelrik smirked, but it didn't reach his eyes. "No. But she'll never belong to you, either. You feel it, don't you? That wrongness inside you? You *know* she's meant for more than either of us."

Their words dissolved into silence as Seraphina twisted in her fevered dream, trapped in a memory not even death could pry free. Her body trembled with exhaustion, her breaths short and desperate.

Kade's eyes stayed locked on her face, on the signs that she was still fighting. Still *herself.* "I won't lose her."

Time folded around her.

She drifted.

A tetherless nothingness cocooned her, the weight of days—or perhaps weeks—pressing like fog behind her eyes. Dreams bled into reality. Voices murmured through the haze—some tender, some sharp, some cold as frost. She thought they were memories. Echoes. Fragments of something her mind had conjured to survive.

But they were real.

She heard Kade's low voice, urgent and aching. She heard Vaelrik— mocking, amused, sometimes distant. Other times... *too* close.

Through it all, Seraphina floated, unsure which voices belonged to the world, which belonged to her unravelling mind.

Then—clarity.

It came slowly, cruelly, like a blade pressing to the skin. Her cheek felt a sensation of warmth. The stiffness in her limbs. The dull ache of healing. Something had shifted. The fever had broken. Her mind, no longer fully submerged, began clawing back at what it had lost.

She dismissed the voices as a dream, but fragments of conversations she was never meant to hear created a complete picture. Kade's fear. Vaelrik's bitterness. Arguments laced with old wounds and deeper truths.

Vaelrik's voice, sharper than the rest.

"She loved me once... But they tore me from her. Not by choice."

"You think you can save her?"

"She'll never belong to you, Kade."

Her heart pounded. Her fingers twitched.

Those hadn't been hallucinations.

She *had* heard them.

They had *been here.*

Worse—*he* had been in her head.

A spike of dread coiled in her chest.

Vaelrik.

Her dream hadn't been just a memory. She could feel it now, the remnants of a presence not her own, rifling through her soul like old parchment. Her secrets—exposed. Her pain—watched.

Her stomach turned.

The horror crawled up her throat as realisation sank in.

He *read* her.

He'd *seen* everything.

The fire, the screams and the loss she buried so deep she couldn't find it without bleeding.

A soft murmur of voices floated to her once again, followed by the gentle echo of footsteps. Her chest tightened, and with great effort, she forced her eyes open. The world swam, dim and golden. Her vision blurred, then cleared—revealing Kade standing over her, eyes shadowed but shining.

"Seraphina?"

His voice was low. Softer than she'd ever heard it.

Something broke inside her.

She tried to speak, but her throat burned; her body was still fragile. All she managed was a dry, cracked rasp.

"...Kade..."

Her voice trembled with more than just exhaustion.

A brief touch of his fingers brushed her hair from her forehead, the warmth of his presence seeped into her, making her heart thud painfully. "You're awake. Thank the gods... you scared the hell out of me," he said, his voice tight with emotion.

"I've scared worse..." she whispered, forcing a smirk that quickly morphed into a grimace. It felt foreign on her lips, a ghost of her old self slipping away. The bitter truth settled deep inside her bones—she wasn't the same.

Kade didn't laugh. Instead, his hand pressed hers, solid, grounding. "You've been through a lot. You need to rest. We'll—"

"No." She shifted, a sharp pull of pain shooting through her chest, but she couldn't lie still. She couldn't afford to. Not again. "Tell me what happened. Where are we?"

Kade gently pushed her back down, but she resisted, the need to know overriding everything else. She forced her gaze up to him. His face was haggard, his jaw tight, his eyes shadowed with fatigue. Yet there was something else there too—something softer, almost vulnerable. She saw it now, guilt twisted in her chest. She had done this to him. To both of them.

"I need to know," she demanded, her voice gaining strength.

Kade squeezed her hand. "You're safe now, Seraphina. We're in a healer's hut on the edge of the forest. Couldn't stay in the city—it's too dangerous, especially with the demons invading Sylvaris, and I didn't want to risk it."

She nodded slowly, the information sinking in, but unease lingered. They'd survived, yes, but she knew deep in her gut that this wasn't over. She closed her eyes again, trying to steady herself, but the dizziness and the memories of everything—the battle, the fever, the pain—swirled in her mind. It all felt so close, like it had all happened in one suffocating breath. But then, the crackling fire, the steady rhythm of Kade's presence beside her, grounded her. It was something. It was enough.

"I don't feel like myself," Seraphina whispered, her voice fragile. The words hovered between them, raw and unguarded.

Kade's gaze softened, and he brushed his thumb gently over her hand. "You're more yourself than you've been in a long time," he said, his voice thick with meaning. "I've seen you fight. You're not done yet. We'll fix this. Together."

Her gaze softened, and she let his words settle deep in her chest. He wasn't just a warrior—he was her anchor. For all the damage she had endured, for all the pain, he was the only thing that felt real now.

"But how?" Her voice cracked, filled with desperation. "I don't know how to move on. I don't know how to pick up the pieces of myself."

Kade hesitated, his gaze drifting to the fire before returning to her. "We do what we've always done. We survive."

The weight of his words wrapped around her like a fragile promise. It wasn't enough to heal the wound, but it was something. Something to hold on to. She closed her eyes again, exhaustion pulling her under, but before she could drift back into unconsciousness, the sound of footsteps echoed from the doorway. A figure stepped into the dim light.

"Would you look at that?" Vaelrik's voice broke through the quiet, rough but laced with dry humour. He was back, his tall frame filling the doorway, gleaming with new armour and an ominous scowl.

"Had to get something for your stench," he muttered, eyeing Seraphina. "Can't have you going around smelling like a field of dead bodies. The healers wouldn't touch you if they caught a whiff."

Seraphina glared at him, the corners of her lips curling into a faint, tired smirk. "Glad to see you still have your sense of humour."

Vaelrik chuckled, tossing the medical supplies onto a nearby table before striding over to her. He eyed her critically. "You've slept enough. Time for a bath. You stink."

She chuckled softly, despite herself. "I can hardly wait."

Chapter 14

The days that followed blurred into one another, an agonising process of recovery stretched out beneath the weight of time. Her body mended slowly—painfully. The bruises faded from deep violet to dull yellow; the cuts knitted closed, and eventually, the fever broke, leaving her drenched in sweat and hollowed out. But her mind... her mind remained splintered, adrift in shadows.

She slept more than she was awake. At first, the sleep was a void—dreamless, barren. But then the whispers came, threading through her rest like tendrils of smoke. Voices, she thought she imagined. Names she didn't remember speaking. Sounds that didn't belong to dreams at all.

Sometimes, she opened her eyes to find Kade beside her, his form a silhouette against the flickering hearth, silent and vigilant. Other times, she stirred only enough to register the quiet rhythm of Vaelrik's footsteps echoing through the keep—unseen but ever-present. The world outside moved on without her.

Autumn bled around her. She watched it through the high, frost-blurred windows when she could hold herself upright—first the turning of the leaves, then the rustling rainstorms that came with the shift in the air. Trees shed their golden crowns. Winds howled. The sun hung low on the horizon, weak and tired.

Her limbs trembled the first time she tried to sit up alone. Days passed before she could walk the length of the room without falling. Her lungs protested each breath of the chilled air, her muscles burned, and her pride screamed louder than them all. But step by step, she moved forward. Slow. Unrelenting. Stubborn.

By the time she could eat without Kade's steadying hand, the nights had grown longer, colder. The last of the autumn warmth clung to the daylight like a dying ember, flickering before winter claimed it fully.

One of those late autumn nights had brought the lake.

She'd insisted on cleaning herself. The scent of sweat, blood, and captivity had sunk into her skin, and it had to go. But the water was bitterly cold—ink-black and still under the moonlight, its surface fractured only by her trembling attempts to cleanse herself. Her body, though healed in appearance, betrayed her strength. She had fallen to her knees, arms shivering violently as her breath caught in her throat.

Kade had been there. Silent. Unmoving.

Until he sighed.

Without a word, he had stripped off his tunic and waded in. She'd snapped at him—of course she had—but it was a feeble protest. One look at her and he had lifted her easily, bracing her weight beneath her arms like she was no heavier than a sack of grain.

"I can do it myself," she had muttered, shame and stubbornness burning beneath her skin.

"Of course you can," he had said, tone bone-dry. But he didn't let go.

His hands had been steady, his movements careful. No teasing. No heat. Just warmth—quiet and infuriating and real. He held her upright as she washed, combed the blood from her tangled hair with his fingers, rinsed the grime from her skin like she was something fragile. Something *worth* saving.

For the first time in weeks, she had felt clean.

Then Vaelrik had arrived.

"Well, well, well," he'd called from the shore, arms folded and golden eyes glinting. "Isn't this cosy? Should I come back later, or are we embracing nudity as a team-building exercise now?"

135

Seraphina had wanted the lake to swallow her whole.

Kade had tensed immediately, drawing back as if burned. His hands vanished from her body in an instant, and she had nearly collapsed without his support. He tossed her a towel, jaw clenched, retreating into that cold, unreadable silence he wore like a second skin. Vaelrik, of course, hadn't shut up for a moment.

Now, standing tall and steady in front of the old mirror, Seraphina traced her fingers across the new armour Vaelrik had brought her.

The memory faded into the edges of her mind, swallowed by the reflection staring back at her.

The armour was nothing like the one she'd worn in the past. This one moulded to her like a second skin—sleek, black leather reinforced with woven steel filaments that shimmered like shadow in the firelight. It was light, flexible, deadly. No more rusted plates. No more deadweight.

She shifted her stance, rolled her shoulders, flexed her fingers.

No restrictions. No hesitation. She was stronger now.

Outside, winter had come.

Frost lined the edges of the windows. Snow clung to the rooftops in thin, crisp layers. The wind that snuck through the stone corridors bit at her skin with icy teeth. Time had passed. The world had turned. And she had endured every second.

"I have to admit, I had my doubts," she murmured, admiring the quiet precision in the design.

Vaelrik grinned from the doorway, arms crossed. "What, you thought I'd bring you something hideous? I have *standards*, darling."

"It's… fitted," she noted, tugging at the high collar. "Too fitted."

He smirked. "Custom made. I took some liberties with the measurements. You can thank me later."

She shot him a look, but there was no real bite to it. The armour was perfect. It moved with her, felt like a second skin. It wasn't just armour—it was a promise. A return to strength. She had spent too long being weak. Too long trapped in her own body's failures.

As she fastened the last of the straps, her gaze flickered to Kade. He hadn't said a word about the armour, but she could feel his stare like a tangible weight. His jaw was tight, his expression unreadable. She thought of the lake. Of his hands steadying her. Of the way he had pulled back the moment Vaelrik had appeared. Something inside her clenched. She had no time for that. No time for emotions that muddied the waters of survival.

So she forced a smirk, adjusting the cuffs of her sleeves. "Well, gentlemen. Shall we?"

Vaelrik grinned, leaning against the doorframe with that usual mischievous glint in his eyes. "Finally. I was thinking you enjoyed lying around half-dead."

Kade remained silent, his gaze steady, though it lingered just a moment longer than usual before he turned away. Seraphina exhaled slowly, rolling her shoulders, her fibre settling with a familiar weight. She was ready for whatever lay ahead. The ache in her limbs, the shadowed remnants of the nightmares—she would push through them, as she always did.

But Kade spoke up before she could move, his voice low and firm.

"We can't just wander aimlessly. We need a plan. A clear direction."

Vaelrik's sharp golden eyes met his, the playful edge to his tone dimming slightly. "Of course. And the first thing we'll need is supplies—more than what we've got. You think this stash of dried meats and herbs is going to get us through?"

Seraphina's thoughts snapped into place. She'd been running on instinct for so long. Now, with her body finally responding to her commands, the realisation hit her hard. "None of what we need is anywhere nearby," she said, her voice steady but matter-of-fact. "The cities and villages here won't have it. We'll need to head north—toward the trade routes."

Vaelrik raised an eyebrow, clearly intrigued. "Trade routes? So we'll be risking tundra and blizzards for merchant carts filled with whatever scraps they're willing to part with?"

"Exactly," Seraphina said, her expression hardening with resolve. "The trade cities are the best bet. We'll find what we need there—or at least what's closest."

Kade crossed his arms, his jaw tightening. "We're already at the mercy of winter. Travelling north won't be easy, and the roads are treacherous."

Vaelrik let out a small laugh, clearly unfazed by the challenge. "Well, I'll be fine. As a dragon, I can keep both of us warm enough. You, though…" He glanced at Kade with a wicked grin. "You probably prefer the freezing cold for your heart, eh?"

Kade scoffed, his expression unreadable, but the sharpness in his gaze spoke volumes. "Don't flatter yourself. I'm more than capable of surviving a little cold."

"Ah, but will your *heart* survive, I wonder?" Vaelrik teased, his tone dripping with mockery. He stood straighter, looking at Seraphina. "So, we're heading north, then. No turning back?"

She nodded, her resolve firm. "We're heading north. No matter the cold. We get what we need, then we move forward. The rest will fall into place."

With that, Kade's expression softened ever so slightly, the lines of tension around his eyes easing. He didn't speak, but the unspoken understanding between them was clear. He'd follow her wherever she went.

Vaelrik slapped his hands together, grinning widely. "Alright, let's move out. If we're lucky, we might find some warm drinks on the way."

Kade and Seraphina shared a glance, the weight of what lay ahead hanging heavily in the air, but neither of them spoke. They simply gathered what they could, preparing for the journey northward.

Chapter 15

The nights had grown longer.

Weeks had passed since that night—the one none of them talked about. The incident had become just another unspoken thing buried beneath miles of frostbitten road and too many silences. They'd made it through bandit territory, crossed river after frozen river, pushed through skeletal woods that howled with wind instead of wolves.

And now, they were deep in the heart of winter. The cold clung to everything. Days bled out in silver and grey before dusk swallowed them whole. Each night hit harder, settled deeper into their bones. But this one—this night—was different.

Clear skies. Sharp stars. No wind. Just the brittle hush of snow underfoot and the faint crackle of a small, carefully built fire. The cold that made your breath feel heavy in your chest. The kind that made silence louder.

Kade sat a little apart from them, as he often did now. Distant. Controlled.

Vaelrik stretched lazily by the fire, tossing a twig into the flames. "You've been quiet lately, Kade."

Kade didn't respond.

Vaelrik smirked. "I mean, quieter. Even for you."

Kade's eyes flicked toward him, unreadable. "I have had little to say."

"That's not it," Vaelrik murmured, watching him like a cat watching a wounded animal trying to walk without a limp. "It's your magic. It's off. Not leaking exactly—but twitchy. Like it wants to move, but you keep strangling it."

Kade didn't answer, but his jaw tightened. Just slightly.

Seraphina, bundled in her cloak beside the fire, said nothing. She didn't look at him, but she felt the shift—how cold his power had gotten. How sharp.

Vaelrik went on as if just chatting about the weather. "You know, if you keep bottling it like that, eventually it's going to find a crack. And when it does…" He blew out a breath between his teeth. "Boom."

"Shut up," Kade muttered, low.

Vaelrik just grinned, unfazed. "Touchy."

Seraphina glanced up. "Both of you. Enough."

Just like that, they fell quiet again. The fire snapped softly. Snow drifted lazily from the top branches above. The peace that never lasted long.

That was when it happened.

The hairs on the back of Seraphina's neck rose first—a familiar tingle at the base of her spine. Not magic. Not yet. Just instinct.

A footstep. Soft. Too soft for any normal traveller on snow.

She rose slowly, eyes scanning the shadows beyond the firelight. "We're not alone."

Kade was on his feet in an instant, shadows curling faintly at his fingertips.

Vaelrik sighed. "Can't we have *one* quiet night?"

But Seraphina was already moving, slipping her hand to the hilt of her blade, eyes narrowing as a shape formed from the dark—tall, cloaked, and entirely too calm for someone walking into armed strangers at night.

The stranger didn't speak.

Didn't flinch.

Just stood there at the edge of the firelight, half in shadow, frost shimmering on their shoulders like dust from another world.

"I need help," he said, his voice raw, breathless. "They're coming. The bandits—they—they're close."

The tension shifted, and Kade's protective instincts flared. Seraphina straightened, her smile fading as her gaze flicked to Kade, then back to the stranger.

"Get him a seat," she instructed, "and tell us everything."

As Kade helped the man to the campfire, Seraphina glanced at Vaelrik, who was watching her closely. Seraphina might have a way with words, but the battle ahead was not one of words. It was one of blood and survival.

The stranger slumped heavily against the fire pit, breathing unevenly, his eyes darting nervously between Seraphina, Kade, and Vaelrik. The flickering flames cast deep shadows on his face, exaggerating the desperation in his eyes.

Seraphina crouched in front of him, her voice soft but commanding. "Take a deep breath. You're safe for now, but we need to know who's coming and why."

The man swallowed hard, his eyes shifting toward the edge of the camp, as if expecting the shadows themselves to rise and drag him back into the night. His voice trembled when he spoke. "It's the bandits. Not just any bandits—them. They've been raiding villages for weeks. They take what they want, burn the rest. But they've started moving faster... closer to here. I think they're hunting something." His gaze flicked to Kade, then back to Seraphina. "I think they're hunting you."

The words hung in the air, thick with an ominous weight. Kade's eyes narrowed, the tension snapping back into his posture. His instincts screamed they were being watched, the hairs on the back of his neck standing at attention. Seraphina's expression remained unreadable, but her hand clenched around the hilt of her sword, a reflex of readiness.

"Who exactly are these bandits?" Kade asked, his voice low, controlled—though there was an edge to it now.

"They're not just any thieves," the man said, his voice growing quieter, as if the very mention of them could summon them. "They have magic, dark magic. It corrupts everything it touches. The land. The air. And they can see things... things that aren't meant to be seen."

Seraphina's gaze flicked toward Kade, then Vaelrik, before locking on the man again. "What kind of magic?"

He trembled. "I've heard rumours. They're led by a warlock. He has something... something powerful. A stone, an artefact of sorts. I don't know the details, but it's like nothing I've ever seen. It burns with dark fire, and they say it can steal your soul."

The firelight flickered, casting a ghostly glow on the man's face. It was clear the toll of fear had weighed heavily on him, and his breathing was quickening again.

Kade stood abruptly, his muscles coiling like a spring. He knew, as they all did, that it was just a smaller version of the monolith that had destroyed everything in the battle. "If they're after us, we need to move. Now."

Seraphina rose to her feet, moving toward the pack at the edge of the camp, her mind already working through the options. "We can't outrun them, Kade."

"We can hold them off," Kade said, his voice edged with a confidence that Seraphina knew all too well. "At least long enough to get the upper hand. They won't be expecting us to fight back."

Her gaze was steady, unwavering as she turned back to him. "And if they do?"

He met her gaze with a silent intensity, his jaw tight as his hand flexed around the hilt of his blade. "Then we do what we do best."

Seraphina nodded. She knew what that meant. It was a fight. A battle with no mercy for the weak. They would stand their ground or die trying.

"Vaelrik," she said, her voice sharp. "What do you know about these bandits? Any weaknesses we can exploit?"

Vaelrik tilted his head, his eyes narrowing in thought. "They're not invincible. The warlock's magic has limits. It can't bend the natural world entirely—there are still things that can break through. But we'll need to draw them out, isolate the leader. The rest of them are just foot soldiers."

Seraphina turned to the man, who was now visibly sweating, his hands trembling in his lap. "You can go if you want," she said, her tone surprisingly gentle. "We won't force you to stay and fight."

The man glanced up at her, gratitude and fear warring in his eyes. "I can't go back. They'll kill me if they know I warned you."

"You'll be safer with us," Kade said quietly. "We're not leaving you behind."

There was a beat of silence before the man nodded, resignation settling in.

Seraphina turned to Kade, her expression unreadable, but something flickered in her eyes. "We need a plan. Fast."

Kade moved toward the edge of the camp, his hands already working through the strap of his pack, pulling out weapons and tools. "I'll scout ahead. We'll set up a perimeter, and I'll keep my eyes on the horizon. They'll want to get close before they strike. We can use that against them."

"Good," Seraphina said, her gaze cold, calculating. "We need to make sure they don't think they can corner us."

"I'll stay with the man," Vaelrik offered, his voice smooth, though there was something calculating in the way his eyes flicked between Seraphina and Kade. "I'll make sure he's taken care of."

Seraphina nodded, her thoughts already racing, putting together the pieces. She glanced over at Kade as he prepared to move out. Her gaze lingered a moment, but the decision was already hers. She couldn't afford distractions. Not now.

"You know what to do," she said. "Stay sharp."

Kade's mouth twitched upward at the corner, though the rest of his face remained tight. "Always, Nyx."

With a final glance back at her, Kade vanished into the darkened woods, his figure swallowed up by the night.

Seraphina turned to Vaelrik. "Get him to safety." She ordered.

He raised an eyebrow but said nothing as he moved toward the stranger, offering him what little comfort he could.

Seraphina drew her sword and stepped into the night, the weight of her thoughts heavy but focused. She had no intention of letting anyone die on her watch—not again. Not this time. The fire crackled behind her as she disappeared into the shadows, the air thick with the scent of impending violence.

The night was unnervingly silent as Seraphina moved through the dense trees, her footsteps barely a whisper against the earth. She stayed low, her senses sharp, feeling the chill of the air as it wrapped around her. The shadows, deep and oppressive, seemed to pull at her, but she pressed forward, determined. The deeper into the forest she went, the more her mind raced—how long until Kade would return? Were they being followed? How much time before the bandits would reach their camp?

She could feel the weight of her sword against her back, the familiar presence of the blade giving her a sense of purpose. Each breath she took was steady, measured, even as her heart pounded in her chest. The stillness of the woods only heightened the sense of danger that lurked just beyond her reach.

Her thoughts flashed to the stranger's warnings. The warlock... the dark magic... They weren't just simple raiders. This was something far more dangerous, something they wouldn't easily defeat. But Seraphina didn't have time to consider that now. Every minute counted. She had to get to the edge of the forest before they made their move, and if they were already there, then they had to be prepared.

In the distance, the faint rustle of leaves caught her attention. She froze, her hand instinctively going to her hilt. The sound was soft, almost imperceptible, but it was there. She crouched low, scanning the area, her eyes narrowing as she focused on the shadows. There, just on the edge of her vision, a figure moved between the trees. It wasn't Kade.

Her heart skipped a beat, and the hairs on the back of her neck stood up.

"Vaelrik," she murmured under her breath, he must have gotten the stranger to safety. Shifting her weight, ready to draw her sword. She waited for another sign, another movement. Her eyes flicked to the surrounding space, every shadow a threat. The moment stretched, an eternity of silence before—

A figure stepped out from behind the trees, and her grip on her sword relaxed.

Kade.

He moved toward her with a confident, silent stride, his silver hair barely visible in the lack of moonlight. His eyes locked on hers as he came closer, a quick but meaningful glance that told her everything. He was okay. They were still in control—for now.

"Bad news," Kade said quietly as he came to a stop beside her. His voice was calm, but there was an edge to it, a warning that pricked at Seraphina's instincts. "They've already set up a perimeter. They're closer than I thought. The warlock's men are already scouting the area."

Seraphina frowned, her lips pressing together as she absorbed the information. She glanced at the dark horizon. "How many?"

"Enough," Kade replied, his gaze flicking toward the trees in the distance. "Too many for us to take head-on, especially if the warlock is with them."

Seraphina's jaw tightened. The warlock. That name hung in the air like an unspoken curse. She knew deep in her bones that facing him would be the real challenge. The bandits were dangerous, yes, but it was the dark magic that made this mission deadly. And if they underestimated the power of the warlock, they would all pay the price.

"We need a distraction," she said, her voice low but resolute. "Something that'll draw their attention away from the camp and give us a chance to take them down before they can regroup."

Kade's lips twitched into a grim smile. "I can manage that. But you'll have to stay on your toes. It won't be pretty."

"I don't need it to be pretty," Seraphina said with a steely determination in her eyes. "Just effective."

The two of them exchanged a look, an unspoken understanding passing between them. They didn't have the luxury of time. Seraphina turned away, ready to move back to the camp, when a voice cut through the night.

"They're coming," Vaelrik's voice rang out from behind her, sharp and urgent. "It's too late to leave. We need to fight."

Seraphina didn't hesitate. She drew her sword, her focus narrowing on the task ahead. There was no turning back now. No more running. They had to fight, and they had to win.

"Get ready," she said to Kade, her voice cool and commanding. "Stay in the shadows. We don't attack until they're close enough to feel the heat of the fire."

With a sharp nod, Kade disappeared into the night again, his figure blending into the darkness. Seraphina moved to the edge of their camp, crouching low behind the cover of the trees. The firelight flickered behind her, casting long shadows over the ground. She scanned the perimeter, her senses stretched tight, waiting.

Then she heard it. The faintest sound—footsteps, soft and deliberate, but growing louder with each passing second. The bandits were closing in. Seraphina took a deep breath and silently signalled for Vaelrik to get into position. The plan had to work. There was no room for error.

The first of the bandits crept into view, his movements cautious but sure. He stepped into the clearing just as the breeze picked up, the scent of the fire mixing with the sharp tang of sweat.

Without warning, Seraphina sprang into action, her voice cutting through the tension like a blade.

"Now."

Chaos erupted the moment Seraphina's command sliced through the air. The crackling fire at the centre of the camp flared high as Vaelrik ignited the signal—an explosion of flame that sent the bandits stumbling back, their eyes temporarily blinded. The very ground seemed to shake as Seraphina moved with a predator's grace, her sword flashing in the firelight.

The first bandit barely had time to register her presence before she was upon him. With a swift, clean strike, she disarmed him, sending his blade clattering to the ground. He barely had time to cry out before her foot slammed into his chest, sending him sprawling into the dirt. More appeared, their weapons drawn, panic flashing in their eyes as they tried to regroup. But Seraphina didn't give them the chance. She was everywhere—flashes of steel, quick movements, her presence a blur of calculated violence. Each strike was purposeful, ruthless, a deadly dance in the camp's chaos.

Kade emerged from the other side of the camp, moving like a shadow, his long silver hair catching the light of the fire as he launched himself into the fray. He was faster than any of them expected, his blade cutting through the air with lethal precision. Each strike seemed to take down a bandit with ease, leaving behind a wake of broken bodies.

Seraphina's eyes never wavered as she cut down another opponent, her senses sharp, constantly assessing, constantly adapting. She could feel the bandits' fear, their hesitation. The bandits were unprepared for this kind of fight. But even as she dispatched one enemy after another, a sinking feeling gnawed at her gut. This wasn't just a random group of raiders. Their actions showed coordination. They were too skilled to be mere thieves.

A flash of dark robes at the edge of the battle confirmed her suspicions. The warlock. The source of the dread that had been hanging over them. He moved with unnerving calmness, standing just outside the chaos, his dark magic rippling through the air like an invisible force. With a flick of his wrist, the air seemed to shimmer, the earth beneath Seraphina's feet suddenly unsteady.

She had no time to react before the ground beneath her seemed to split open with a crack, as if the earth itself was being torn apart. She stumbled, her legs nearly buckling as the shockwave hit. The bandits seemed to hesitate for a moment, stunned by the warlock's power.

"Get down!" Kade shouted, his voice strained but urgent.

Seraphina rolled to the ground just as the warlock unleashed a wave of dark energy, sending tendrils of shadow crashing into the camp. The surrounding trees seemed to warp and twist, their branches reaching out like hands desperate to claw at the intruders. She felt the heat of the magic as it passed by her, a searing, unnatural warmth that made her skin prickle. Her heart raced, the danger of this battle now more apparent than ever. They had to end this—quickly.

"Kade!" she shouted, struggling to regain her footing as she pushed herself up. She could feel her sword vibrating in her grip, the weight of the magic in the air affecting her every move. But Kade was already ahead of her, his silver blade flashing as he barrelled toward the warlock with a fury that matched her own. He met the warlock's magic with a force of his own, his strikes deflecting the dark tendrils that came at him like living shadows. The air crackled with the clash of power, each strike a battle for control. Seraphina didn't hesitate. She sprinted towards the warlock, her feet pounding against the earth, her sword raised high. Every step felt like it brought her closer to the edge of destruction.

The warlock turned just in time to see her approaching. His cold eyes locked onto hers, and for a moment, she saw something—a flicker of recognition, a brief spark of fear. But before she could react, he raised both hands, and the surrounding shadows seemed to surge with life, enveloping her like a choking fog. She couldn't breathe. The air thickened, pressing against her chest, her heart hammering as if it were going to burst. The magic held her in place, binding her as if she were trapped in a vice, despite her swinging her sword with all her strength.

"Kade!" she gasped, her voice strained with the effort to speak.

Kade's figure appeared next to her, a blur of movement as he pushed through the magic. His hand grabbed hers, pulling her close, and with one mighty swing of his blade, he shattered the tendrils that held her in place. The shadows screamed as they disintegrated, but the warlock was already pulling back, his face twisted with fury.

"Run!" Kade shouted, pulling Seraphina back toward the forest, his hand firm on her arm. "We have to get out of here!"

The ground beneath them shifted again, more dark magic crashing against the forest, but they couldn't stop. Not now.

Kade glanced over his shoulder, his silver eyes wide with urgency. "Keep going! We need to lose them!"

The wind howled through the trees, carrying the scent of burning wood and the bitter tang of sweat. Seraphina's muscles screamed in protest as she pushed herself harder, but there was no time to slow down. The distant echoes of the warlock's enraged shout reverberated through the forest like a death knell. She could almost feel the weight of his magic chasing them, the oppressive force that lingered in the air. The darkness was closing in.

Kade's breath was heavy beside her, his grip tight on her arm as they sprinted through the underbrush. His silver hair whipped behind him like a banner in the wind, his body an effortless blur of speed and strength. But Seraphina could see the strain in his eyes, the faintest flicker of doubt. He knew how close they were to the edge.

"We need to make it to the cliffs," Kade grunted, his voice low but urgent. "There's a cave system there. We can lose him in the tunnels."

As they neared the base of the cliffs, the forest grew darker, the trees thicker and more tangled. The air was cooler here, but the heavy pulse of dark magic still hung in the atmosphere like a storm waiting to break. Seraphina glanced over at Kade. His eyes were scanning the path ahead, his movements sharp and calculating, but there was something else— something unspoken between them.

"Are you alright?" she asked, her voice barely a whisper, even though they were both struggling to catch their breath.

He didn't respond immediately, but then he gave her a fleeting glance, a slight smirk tugging at the corners of his lips. "I'm not the one who just got my life force drained by a warlock," he said, his tone light but strained.

The banter was a fleeting relief, but it did little to ease the weight of the situation. They were running out of time, and the warlock wasn't far behind. As they reached the base of the cliffs, Seraphina scanned the rocky landscape. The narrow path leading up to the caves was barely visible in the dark, and it would be treacherous to climb in its current state. The warlock's magic had drained her more than she'd like to admit, and her muscles felt heavy.

The climb was steep and exhausting. Slick with moisture, the rocks beneath their feet added to the growing intensity of the wind, a sound almost drowned out by their pounding hearts. The caves were just ahead, but each step felt like it was dragging them further from safety. With one final push, Kade hauled her over the lip of the cliff, his arm around her waist, steadying her. They stumbled into the relative shelter of the cave entrance, breathing heavily, both of them covered in dirt and bruises.

The cave was cold, the air thick with the smell of earth and stone. They paused, taking in the moment of respite, but neither of them dared to stop for long. The sound of footsteps, slow and deliberate, echoed from outside the entrance.

Seraphina's breath caught in her throat. They hadn't lost him.

"Kade," she breathed, her voice full of concern. "What if we don't make it?"

Kade turned to face her, his expression unreadable for a moment. Then he placed a hand on her shoulder, a surprising gentleness in his touch. "We'll make it. We have to."

His words were reassuring, but Seraphina could feel the weight of their situation pressing down on them both. The warlock wasn't just an enemy. He was a force of nature. His power was unyielding, and they were running out of options.

Seraphina gripped her sword tighter, the familiar weight grounding her. "Then we fight."

Kade's lips quirked into a grin, though his eyes betrayed the same flicker of doubt she had seen earlier. "Wouldn't have it any other way."

As if summoned by their desperation, the ground trembled again. The warlock's voice echoed through the cavern entrance, cold and mocking.

"Did you really think you could escape?"

Seraphina's grip on her sword tightened. She exchanged a look with Kade—one of grim determination. The battle was far from over, but they couldn't afford to run anymore. The warlock's power rippled through the air, and the tension in the cave was almost unbearable. They could feel the danger closing in, but this time, they would stand their ground. There was no other choice.

"Get ready," Seraphina whispered, her voice steady despite the fear gnawing at her insides.

Resolve laced Kade's smirk. "After you."

"I know you're there," the warlock's voice rang out, low and cold. It reverberated through the cave walls, mocking them. "You can't hide from me forever."

Without warning, the ground beneath them shuddered. The very earth was alive with the warlock's power. The warlock's power pulled rocks from their foundations, sending them tumbling through the air in a deadly dance, causing them to crack and groan. Seraphina ducked narrowly, avoiding the jagged shards that whizzed by, and instinctively, Kade's arm was around her, pulling her further into the shadows of the cave.

"We have to stop him before he brings the whole place down," Kade hissed, his voice strained with urgency. He glanced around, calculating their options in a split second.

Her mind raced. She knew Kade was right. The warlock's fury was destroying everything in his path, and unless they acted immediately, it would bury them. The walls glowed faintly, an eerie, unnatural light pulsing from the cracks. Shadows moved unnaturally, creeping across the walls like the limbs of some massive beast, and took a strike at Kade, knocking him over and causing deep gashes on his chest.

"Do you think you can defeat me?" the warlock asked, his voice like a jagged blade against her thoughts. "You are nothing but ants beneath my feet."

"Then let me crush you like one," Seraphina muttered, more to herself than to him. She stepped forward, pushing Kade behind her. He staggered back, too weak to protest.

But before she could strike, the warlock's next blast of magic slammed into her—violent and scorching, knocking the air from her lungs as shadows flared and cracked around her like lightning through storm clouds.

The force of it threw her back, her body slamming against the cold stone wall. Pain radiated through her, but she ignored it, pushing herself upright with a growl. Her sword was heavy in her hand, but it felt right. The weight was familiar, a constant in the chaos. It was more than just a weapon—it was a promise.

The warlock's eyes narrowed, watching her movements with cold amusement. "Come then, warrior. Show me what you've got."

Seraphina didn't hesitate. She ran forward, the sound of her boots hitting the stone floor a rhythmic drumbeat in her ears. Her sword glinted in the dim light, a streak of silver, and she raised it high as she closed the distance. His face twisted in frustration, and for the first time, there was fear in his eyes. Just as Seraphina's sword struck with all the power she could muster, a new energy filled the cave—an oppressive, almost tangible presence that cut through the air like a blade. The warlock's magic flared to overpower her, but then something else shifted, something that made the very ground beneath her tremble with anticipation.

A deep, guttural growl reverberated through the stone, and out of the shadows stepped a figure. Tall, imposing, with dark armour that seemed to absorb the light, his eyes glowed faintly with a malevolent golden-red hue. Vaelrik. The surrounding air was thick with raw power, a coldness that made the already oppressive atmosphere seem even more suffocating. He was a force of nature, an embodiment of destruction, yet there was a calmness about him—a control that was terrifying in its own right.

The warlock's smirk faltered, his attention momentarily diverted. "You," he spat, voice dripping with disdain. "What are you doing here?"

Vaelrik's voice was a low, rumbling growl, his tone laced with malice. "I'm here to end this, warlock."

In one swift motion, Vaelrik raised his hand. It extended into a claw. A wave of fire rippled outward, a pulse that sent a tremor through the cave. The warlock staggered back, barely staying upright as the power collided with his, and for the first time, Seraphina saw him flinch—something she had never thought possible.

She didn't hesitate. Seeing the warlock off-balance, she closed the gap in an instant, her sword flashing as she slashed toward him again.

"Now, Seraphina," Vaelrik growled, his voice low but commanding. "Strike him while he's weak."

Her instincts screamed at her to listen, and without a second thought, she did. With a roar, she lunged forward, her sword cutting through the air with the precision of a predator. The warlock screamed in agony as the blade met its mark, the sound ringing through the cave like the death knell of his arrogance. The blow pushed his body back, crumbling it under its force, but his burning, hateful eyes locked onto hers with an almost manic intensity. There was no more struggle, no more fire in his eyes. The warlock's body crumpled to the ground, lifeless, his reign of terror over.

For a moment, the cave was eerily silent, save for the heavy breathing of the three of them. Seraphina stood there, her heart still racing, her body trembling from the exertion. She turned to Vaelrik, who had already taken a step back, his expression unreadable. The red glow in his eyes had dimmed, but the darkness still lingered around him.

"Thank you," she said, her voice steady but laced with gratitude.

Vaelrik gave her a single, brief nod, his gaze flickering to Kade, who had stepped forward, eyes narrowed. "This is far from over."

Seraphina frowned, her brow furrowing in confusion. "What do you mean?"

Vaelrik didn't answer immediately. Instead, he turned his attention to the warlock's body, and a flicker of something—regret?—crossed his face before disappearing into the shadows.

"The warlock may be dead, but there are others," he said finally, his voice colder than before. "Other forces, darker and more powerful. You've only scratched the surface."

Kade stepped up beside Seraphina, his voice low but determined. "How do you know that?"

Vaelrik's lips curled into a ghost of a smile. "You'll need more than just swords to end this."

Seraphina met his gaze, a silent understanding passing between them. She didn't need to question how he knew or why he recognised the warlock. She understood he had a past that he was not yet ready to talk about.

Chapter 16

The nights had grown longer.

Weeks had passed since that night—the one none of them talked about. The incident had become just another unspoken thing buried beneath miles of frostbitten road and too many silences. They'd made it through bandit territory, crossed river after frozen river, pushed through skeletal woods that howled with wind instead of wolves.

Now, they were deep in the heart of winter. The cold clung to everything. Days bled out in silver and grey before they were swallowed whole by dusk. Each night hit harder, settled deeper into their bones. But this one—this night—was different.

Clear skies. Sharp stars. No wind. Just the brittle hush of snow underfoot and the faint crackle of a small, carefully built fire. The kind of cold that made your breath feel heavy in your chest. The kind that made silence louder.

Kade sat a little apart from them, as he often did now. Distant. Controlled.

Vaelrik stretched lazily by the fire, tossing a twig into the flames. "You've been quiet lately, Kade." Vaelrik smirked. "I mean, quieter. Even for you."

Kade's eyes flicked toward him, unreadable. "I haven't had much to say."

"That's not it," Vaelrik murmured, watching him like a cat watching a wounded animal trying to walk without a limp. "It's your magic. It's off.

Not leaking, exactly—but twitchy. Like it wants to move but you keep strangling it."

Kade didn't answer, but his jaw tightened. Just slightly.

Seraphina, bundled in her cloak beside the fire, said nothing. She didn't look at him, but she felt the shift—how cold his power had gotten. How sharp.

Vaelrik went on, as if just chatting about the weather. "You know, if you keep bottling it like that, eventually it's going to find a crack. When it does…" He blew out a breath between his teeth. "Boom."

"Shut up," Kade muttered, low.

Vaelrik just grinned, unfazed. "Touchy."

Seraphina glanced up. "Both of you. Enough."

Just like that, they fell quiet again. The fire snapped softly. Snow drifted lazily from the high branches above. The kind of peace that never lasted long.

The hairs on the back of Seraphina's neck rose first—a familiar tingle at the base of her spine. Not magic. Not yet. Just instinct.

A footstep. Soft. Too soft for any normal traveller on snow.

She rose slowly, eyes scanning the shadows beyond the firelight. "We're not alone."

Kade was on his feet in an instant, shadows curling faintly at his fingertips.

Vaelrik sighed. "Can't we have *one* quiet night?"

But Seraphina was already moving, slipping her hand to the hilt of her blade, eyes narrowing as a shape began to form from the dark—tall, cloaked, entirely too calm for someone walking into armed strangers at night.

The stranger didn't speak.

Didn't flinch.

Just stood there at the edge of the firelight, half in shadow, frost shimmering on their shoulders like dust from another world.

"I need help," he said, his voice raw, breathless. "They're coming. The bandits—they—they're close."

The tension shifted, Kade's protective instincts flared. Seraphina straightened, her smile fading as her gaze flicked to Kade, then back to the stranger.

"Get him a seat," she instructed, "Tell us everything."

As Kade helped the man to the campfire, Seraphina glanced at Vaelrik, who was watching her closely. Seraphina might have a way with words, but the battle ahead was not one of words. It was one of blood and survival.

The stranger slumped heavily against the fire pit, breathing unevenly, his eyes darting nervously between Seraphina, Kade and Vaelrik. The flickering flames cast deep shadows on his face, exaggerating the desperation in his eyes.

Seraphina crouched in front of him, her voice soft but commanding. "Take a deep breath. You're safe for now, but we need to know who's coming and why."

The man swallowed hard, his eyes shifting toward the edge of the camp, as if expecting the shadows themselves to rise and drag him back into the night. His voice trembled when he spoke. "It's the bandits. Not just any bandits—them. They've been raiding villages for weeks. They take what they want, burn the rest. But they've started moving faster... closer to here. I think they're hunting something." His gaze flicked to Kade, then back to Seraphina. "I think they're hunting you."

The words hung in the air, thick with an ominous weight. Kade's eyes narrowed, the tension snapping back into his posture. His instincts screamed they were being watched, the hairs on the back of his neck standing at attention. Seraphina's expression remained unreadable, but her hand clenched around the hilt of her sword, a reflex of readiness.

"Who exactly are these bandits?" Kade asked, his voice low, controlled— though there was an edge to it now.

"They're not just any thieves," the man said, his voice growing quieter, as if the very mention of them could summon them. "They have magic, dark magic. It corrupts everything it touches. The land. The air. They can see things... things that aren't meant to be seen."

Seraphina's gaze flicked toward Kade, then Vaelrik, before locking on the man again. "What kind of magic?"

He trembled. "I've heard rumours. They're led by a warlock. He has something… something powerful. A stone, an artefact of sorts. I don't know the details, but it's like nothing I've ever seen. It burns with dark fire, they say it can steal your soul."

The firelight flickered, casting a ghostly glow on the man's face. It was clear the toll of fear had weighed heavily on him, his breathing was quickening again.

Kade stood abruptly, his muscles coiling like a spring. He knew, like they all did, that it was just a smaller version of the monolith that had destroyed everything in the battle. "If they're after us, we need to move. Now."

Seraphina rose to her feet, moving toward the pack at the edge of the camp, her mind already working through the options. "We can't outrun them, Kade."

"We can hold them off," Kade said, his voice edged with a confidence that Seraphina knew all too well. "At least long enough to get the upper hand. They won't be expecting us to fight back."

Her gaze was steady, unwavering as she turned back to him. "If they do?"

He met her gaze with a silent intensity, his jaw tight as his hand flexed around the hilt of his blade. "Then we do what we do best."

Seraphina nodded. She knew what that meant. It was a fight. A battle, with no mercy for the weak. They would stand their ground or die trying.

"Vaelrik," she said, her voice sharp. "What do you know about these bandits? Any weaknesses we can exploit?"

Vaelrik tilted his head, his eyes narrowing in thought. "They're not invincible. The warlock's magic has limits. It can't bend the natural world entirely—there are still things that can break through. But we'll need to draw them out, isolate the leader. The rest of them are just foot soldiers."

Seraphina turned to the man, who was now visibly sweating, his hands trembling in his lap. "You can go if you want," she said, her tone surprisingly gentle. "We won't force you to stay and fight."

The man glanced up at her, gratitude and fear warring in his eyes. "I can't go back. They'll kill me if they know I warned you."

"You'll be safer with us," Kade said quietly. "We're not leaving you behind."

There was a beat of silence before the man nodded, resignation settling in.

Seraphina turned to Kade, her expression unreadable, but something flickered in her eyes. "We need a plan. Fast."

Kade moved toward the edge of the camp, his hands already working through the strap of his pack, pulling out weapons and tools. "I'll scout ahead. We'll set up a perimeter, I'll keep my eyes on the horizon. They'll want to get close before they strike. We can use that against them."

"Good," Seraphina said, her gaze cold, calculating. "We need to make sure they don't think they can corner us."

"I'll stay with the man," Vaelrik offered, his voice smooth, though there was something calculating in the way his eyes flicked between Seraphina and Kade. "I'll make sure he's taken care of."

Seraphina nodded, her thoughts already racing, putting together the pieces. She glanced over at Kade as he prepared to move out. Her gaze lingered a moment, but the decision was hers already. She couldn't afford distractions. Not now.

"You know what to do," she said. "Stay sharp."

Kade's mouth twitched upward at the corner, though the rest of his face remained tight. "Always, Nyx."

With a final glance back at her, Kade vanished into the darkened woods, his figure swallowed up by the night.

Seraphina turned to Vaelrik. "Get him to safety." She ordered.

He raised an eyebrow but said nothing as he moved toward the stranger, offering him what little comfort he could.

Seraphina drew her sword and stepped into the night, the weight of her thoughts heavy but focused. She had no intention of letting anyone die on her watch—not again. Not this time. The fire crackled behind her as she disappeared into the shadows, the air thick with the scent of impending violence.

The night was unnervingly silent as Seraphina moved through the dense trees, her footsteps barely a whisper against the earth. She stayed low, her senses sharp, feeling the chill of the air as it wrapped around her. The shadows, deep and oppressive, seemed to pull at her, but she pressed forward, determined. The deeper into the forest she went, the more her mind raced—how long until Kade would return? Were they being followed? How much time before the bandits would reach their camp?

She could feel the weight of her sword against her back, the familiar presence of the blade giving her a sense of purpose. Each breath she took was steady, measured, even as her heart pounded in her chest. The stillness of the woods only heightened the sense of danger that lurked just beyond her reach.

Her thoughts flashed to the stranger's warnings. The warlock... the dark magic... They weren't just simple raiders. This was something far more dangerous, something they wouldn't easily defeat. But Seraphina didn't have time to consider that now. Every minute counted. She had to get to the edge of the forest before they made their move, and if they were already there, then they had to be prepared.

In the distance, a faint rustle of leaves caught her attention. She froze, her hand instinctively going to her hilt. The sound was soft, almost imperceptible, but it was there. She crouched low, scanning the area, her eyes narrowing as she focused on the shadows. There, just on the edge of her vision, a figure moved between the trees. It wasn't Kade.

Her heart skipped a beat, the hairs on the back of her neck stood up.

"Vaelrik," she murmured under her breath, he must have gotten the stranger to safety. Shifting her weight, ready to draw her sword. She waited for another sign, another movement. Her eyes flicked to the surrounding space, every shadow a threat. The moment stretched, an eternity of silence before—

A figure stepped out from behind the trees, her grip on her sword relaxed.

Kade.

He moved toward her with a confident, silent stride, his silver hair barely visible in the lack of moonlight. His eyes locked on hers as he came closer, a quick but meaningful glance that told her everything. He was okay. They were still in control—for now.

"Bad news," Kade said quietly as he came to a stop beside her. His voice was calm, but there was an edge to it, a warning that pricked at Seraphina's instincts. "They've already set up a perimeter. They're closer than I thought. The warlock's men are already scouting the area."

Seraphina frowned, her lips pressing together as she absorbed the information. She glanced at the dark horizon. "How many?"

"Enough," Kade replied, his gaze flicking toward the trees in the distance. "Too many for us to take head-on, especially if the warlock is with them."

Seraphina's jaw tightened. The warlock. That name hung in the air like an unspoken curse. She knew, deep in her bones, that facing him would be the real challenge. The bandits were dangerous, yes, but it was the dark magic that made this mission deadly. If they underestimated the power of the warlock, they would all pay the price.

"We need a distraction," she said, her voice low but resolute. "Something that'll draw their attention away from the camp and give us a chance to take them down before they can regroup."

Kade's lips twitched into a grim smile. "I can manage that. But you'll have to stay on your toes. It won't be pretty."

"I don't need it to be pretty," Seraphina said with a steely determination in her eyes. "Just effective."

The two of them exchanged a look, the unspoken understanding passing between them. They didn't have the luxury of time. Seraphina turned away, ready to move back to the camp, when a voice cut through the night.

"They're coming," Vaelrik's voice rang out from behind her, sharp and urgent. "It's too late to leave. We need to fight."

Seraphina didn't hesitate. She drew her sword, her focus narrowing on the task ahead. There was no turning back now. No more running. They had to fight, they had to win.

"Get ready," she said to Kade, her voice cool and commanding. "Stay in the shadows. We don't attack until they're close enough to feel the heat of the fire."

With a sharp nod, Kade disappeared into the night again, his figure blending into the darkness. Seraphina moved to the edge of their camp, crouching low behind the cover of the trees. The firelight flickered behind her, casting long shadows over the ground. She scanned the perimeter, her senses stretched tight, waiting.

Then she heard it. The faintest sound—footsteps, soft and deliberate, but growing louder with each passing second. The bandits were closing in. Seraphina took a deep breath and silently signalled for Vaelrik to get into position. The plan had to work. There was no room for error.

The first of the bandits crept into view, his movements cautious but sure. He stepped into the clearing just as the breeze picked up, the scent of the fire mixing with the sharp tang of sweat.

Then, without warning, Seraphina sprang into action, her voice cutting through the tension like a blade.

"Now."

The night erupted.

Chaos erupted the moment Seraphina's command sliced through the air. The crackling fire at the centre of the camp flared high as Vaelrik ignited the signal—an explosion of flame that sent the bandits stumbling back, their eyes temporarily blinded. The very ground seemed to shake as Seraphina moved with a predator's grace, her sword flashing in the firelight.

The first bandit barely had time to register her presence before she was upon him. With a swift, clean strike, she disarmed him, sending his blade clattering to the ground. He barely had time to cry out before her foot slammed into his chest, sending him sprawling into the dirt. More appeared, their weapons drawn, panic flashing in their eyes as they tried to regroup. But Seraphina didn't give them the chance. She was everywhere—flashes of steel, quick movements, her presence a blur of calculated violence. Each strike was purposeful, ruthless, a deadly dance in the camp's chaos.

Kade emerged from the other side of the camp, moving like a shadow, his long silver hair catching the light of the fire as he launched himself into the fray. He was faster than any of them expected, his blade cutting through the air with lethal precision. Each strike seemed to take down a bandit with ease, leaving behind a wake of broken bodies.

Seraphina's eyes never wavered as she cut down another opponent, her senses sharp, constantly assessing, constantly adapting. She could feel the bandits' fear, their hesitation. The bandits were unprepared for this kind of fight. But even as she dispatched one enemy after another, a sinking feeling gnawed at her gut. This wasn't just a random group of raiders. Their actions showed coordination. They were too skilled to be mere thieves.

A flash of dark robes at the edge of the battle confirmed her suspicions. The warlock. The source of the dread that had been hanging over them. He moved with unnerving calmness, standing just outside the chaos, his dark magic rippling through the air like an invisible force. With a flick of his wrist, the air seemed to shimmer, the earth beneath Seraphina's feet suddenly unsteady.

She had no time to react before the ground beneath her seemed to split open with a crack, as if the earth itself was being torn apart. She stumbled, her legs nearly buckling as the shockwave hit. The bandits seemed to hesitate for a moment, stunned by the warlock's power.

"Get down!" Kade shouted, his voice strained but urgent.

Seraphina rolled to the ground just as the warlock unleashed a wave of dark energy, sending tendrils of shadow crashing into the camp. The surrounding trees seemed to warp and twist, their branches reaching out like hands desperate to claw at the intruders. She felt the heat of the magic as it passed by her, a searing, unnatural warmth that made her skin prickle. Her heart raced, the danger of this battle now more apparent than ever. They had to end this—quickly.

"Kade!" she shouted, struggling to regain her footing as she pushed herself up. She could feel her sword vibrating in her grip, the weight of the magic in the air affecting her every move. But Kade was already ahead of her, his silver blade flashing as he barrelled toward the warlock with a fury that matched her own. He met the warlock's magic with a force of his own, his strikes deflecting the dark tendrils that came at him like living shadows. The air crackled with the clash of power, each strike a battle for control. Seraphina didn't hesitate. She sprinted towards the warlock, her feet pounding against the earth, her sword raised high. Every step felt like it brought her closer to the edge of destruction.

The warlock turned just in time to see her approaching. His cold eyes locked onto hers, and for a moment, she saw something—a flicker of recognition, a brief spark of fear. But before she could react, he raised both hands, the surrounding shadows seemed to surge with life, enveloping her like a choking fog. She couldn't breathe. The air thickened, pressing against her chest, her heart hammering as if it were going to burst. The magic held her in place, binding her as if she were trapped in a vice, despite her swinging her sword with all her strength.

"Kade!" she gasped, her voice strained with the effort to speak.

Kade's figure appeared next to her, a blur of movement as he pushed through the magic. His hand grabbed hers, pulling her close, with one mighty swing of his blade, he shattered the tendrils that held her in place. The shadows screamed as they disintegrated, but the warlock was already pulling back, his face twisted with fury.

"Run!" Kade shouted, pulling Seraphina back toward the forest, his hand firm on her arm. "We have to get out of here!"

The ground beneath them shifted again, more dark magic crashing against the forest, but they couldn't stop. Not now.

Kade glanced over his shoulder, his silver eyes wide with urgency. "Keep going! We need to lose them!"

The wind howled through the trees, carrying the scent of burning wood and the bitter tang of sweat. Seraphina's muscles screamed in protest as she pushed herself harder, but there was no time to slow down. The distant echoes of the warlock's enraged shout reverberated through the forest like a death knell. She could almost feel the weight of his magic chasing them, the oppressive force that lingered in the air. The darkness was closing in.

Kade's breath was heavy beside her, his grip tight on her arm as they sprinted through the underbrush. His silver hair whipped behind him like a banner in the wind, his body an effortless blur of speed and strength. But Seraphina could see the strain in his eyes, the faintest flicker of doubt. He knew how close they were to the edge.

"We need to make it to the cliffs," Kade grunted, his voice low but urgent. "There's a cave system there. We can lose him in the tunnels."

As they neared the base of the cliffs, the forest grew darker, the trees thicker and more tangled. The air was cooler here, but the heavy pulse of dark magic still hung in the atmosphere like a storm waiting to break. Seraphina glanced over at Kade. His eyes were scanning the path ahead, his movements sharp and calculating, but there was something else— something unspoken between them.

"Are you alright?" she asked, her voice barely a whisper, even though they were both struggling to catch their breath.

He didn't respond immediately, but then he gave her a fleeting glance, a slight smirk tugging at the corners of his lips. "I'm not the one who just got my life force drained by a warlock," he said, his tone light but strained.

The banter was a fleeting relief, but it did little to ease the weight of the situation. They were running out of time, the warlock wasn't far behind. As they reached the base of the cliffs, Seraphina scanned the rocky landscape. The narrow path leading up to the caves was barely visible in the dark, it would be treacherous to climb in their current state. The warlock's magic had drained her more than she'd like to admit, her muscles felt heavy.

The climb was steep and exhausting. Slick with moisture, the rocks beneath their feet added to the growing intensity of the wind, a sound almost drowned out by their pounding hearts. The caves were just ahead, but each step felt like it was dragging them further from safety. With one final push, Kade hauled her over the lip of the cliff, his arm around her waist, steadying her. They stumbled into the relative shelter of the cave entrance, breathing heavily, both of them covered in dirt and bruises.

The cave was cold, the air thick with the smell of earth and stone. They paused, taking in the moment of respite, but neither of them dared to stop for long. The sound of footsteps, slow and deliberate, echoed from outside the entrance.

Seraphina's breath caught in her throat. They hadn't lost him.

"Kade," she breathed, her voice full of concern. "What if we don't make it?"

Kade turned to face her, his expression unreadable for a moment. Then he placed a hand on her shoulder, a surprising gentleness in his touch. "We'll make it. We have to."

His words were reassuring, but Seraphina could feel the weight of their situation pressing down on them both. The warlock wasn't just an enemy. He was a force of nature. His power was unyielding, they were running out of options.

Seraphina gripped her sword tighter, the familiar weight grounding her. "Then we fight."

Kade's lips quirked into a grin, though his eyes betrayed the same flicker of doubt she had seen earlier. "Wouldn't have it any other way."

As if summoned by their desperation, the ground trembled again. The warlock's voice echoed through the cavern entrance, cold and mocking.

"Did you really think you could escape?"

Seraphina's grip on her sword tightened. She exchanged a look with Kade—one of grim determination. The battle was far from over, but they couldn't afford to run anymore. The warlock's power rippled through the air, the tension in the cave was almost unbearable. They could feel the danger closing in, but this time, they would stand their ground. There was no other choice.

"Get ready," Seraphina whispered, her voice steady despite the fear gnawing at her insides.

Resolve laced Kade's smirk. "After you."

"I know you're there," the warlock's voice rang out, low and cold. It reverberated through the cave walls, mocking them. "You can't hide from me forever."

Without warning, the ground beneath them shuddered. The very earth alive with the warlock's power. The warlock's power pulled rocks from their foundations, sending them tumbling through the air in a deadly dance, causing them to crack and groan. Seraphina ducked, narrowly avoiding the jagged shards that whizzed by, and instinctively, Kade's arm was around her, pulling her further into the shadows of the cave.

"We have to stop him before he brings the whole place down," Kade hissed, his voice strained with urgency. He glanced around, calculating their options in a split second.

Her mind raced. She knew Kade was right. The warlock's fury was destroying everything in his path, unless they acted immediately, it would bury them. The walls glowed faintly, an eerie, unnatural light pulsing from the cracks. Shadows moved unnaturally, creeping across the walls like the limbs of some massive beast and took a strike at Kade, knocking him over and causing deep gashes on his chest.

"Do you think you can defeat me?" the warlock asked, his voice like a jagged blade against her thoughts. "You are nothing but ants beneath my feet."

"Then let me crush you like one," Seraphina muttered, more to herself than to him. She stepped forward, pushing Kade behind her. He staggered back, too weak to protest.

But before she could strike, the warlock's next blast of magic slammed into her—violent and scorching, knocking the air from her lungs as shadows flared and cracked around her like lightning through storm clouds.

The force of it threw her back, her body slamming against the cold stone wall. Pain radiated through her, but she ignored it, pushing herself upright with a growl. Her sword was heavy in her hand, but it felt right. The weight was familiar, a constant in the chaos. It was more than just a weapon—it was a promise.

The warlock's eyes narrowed, watching her movements with cold amusement. "Come then, warrior. Show me what you've got."

Seraphina didn't hesitate. She ran forward, the sound of her boots hitting the stone floor a rhythmic drumbeat in her ears. Her sword glinted in the dim light, a streak of silver, she raised it high as she closed the distance. His face twisted in frustration, and for the first time, there was fear in his eyes. Just as Seraphina's sword struck with all the power she could muster, a new energy filled the cave—an oppressive, almost tangible presence that cut through the air like a blade. The warlock's magic flared to overpower her, but then something else shifted, something that made the very ground beneath her tremble with anticipation.

A deep, guttural growl reverberated through the stone, out of the shadows stepped a figure. Tall, imposing, with dark armour that seemed to absorb the light, his eyes glowing faintly with a malevolent golden red hue. Vaelrik. The surrounding air was thick with raw power, a coldness that made the already oppressive atmosphere seem even more suffocating. He was a force of nature, an embodiment of destruction, yet there was a calmness about him—a control that was terrifying in its own right.

The warlock's smirk faltered, his attention momentarily diverted. "You," he spat, voice dripping with disdain. "What are you doing here?"

Vaelrik's voice was a low, rumbling growl, his tone laced with malice. "I'm here to end this, warlock."

In one swift motion, Vaelrik raised his hand. It extended into a claw. A wave of fire rippled outward, a pulse that sent a tremor through the cave. The warlock staggered back, barely staying upright as the power collided with his, for the first time, Seraphina saw him flinch—something she had never thought possible.

She didn't hesitate. Seeing the warlock off-balance, she closed the gap in an instant, her sword flashing as she slashed toward him again.

"Now, Seraphina," Vaelrik growled, his voice low but commanding. "Strike him while he's weak."

Her instincts screamed at her to listen, without a second thought, she did. With a roar, she lunged forward, her sword cutting through the air with the precision of a predator. The warlock screamed in agony as the blade met its mark, the sound ringing through the cave like the death knell of his arrogance. The blow pushed his body back, crumbling it under its force, but his burning, hateful eyes locked onto hers with an almost manic intensity. There was no more struggle, no more fire in his eyes. The warlock's body crumpled to the ground, lifeless, his reign of terror over.

For a moment, the cave was eerily silent, save for the heavy breathing of the three of them. Seraphina stood there, her heart still racing, her body trembling from the exertion. She turned to Vaelrik, who had already taken a step back, his expression unreadable. The red glow in his eyes had dimmed, but the darkness still lingered around him.

"Thank you," she said, her voice steady but laced with gratitude.

Vaelrik gave her a single, brief nod, his gaze flickering to Kade, who had stepped forward, eyes narrowed. "This is far from over."

Seraphina frowned, her brow furrowing in confusion. "What do you mean?"

Vaelrik didn't answer immediately. Instead, he turned his attention to the warlock's body, a flicker of something—regret?—crossed his face before disappearing into the shadows.

"The warlock may be dead, but there are others," he said finally, his voice colder than before. "Other forces, darker and more powerful. You've only scratched the surface."

Kade stepped up beside Seraphina, his voice low but determined. "How do you know that?"

Vaelrik's lips curled into a ghost of a smile. "You'll need more than just swords to end this."

Seraphina met his gaze, a silent understanding passing between them. She didn't need to question how he knew or why he recognised the warlock. She understood he had a past that he was not yet ready to talk about.

Chapter 17

Kade's point of view

The road stretched endlessly before them. The frozen trail kicked up flakes of snow with each step, the low hum of tension hanging in the air like a dark storm cloud. Vaelrik was rummaging through his pack for the map he got in a small village along the road. He was muttering to himself about the uselessness of this journey. Seraphina had to hide a small smile at him, muttering about following "The Brooding Princess" into the unknown. Kade walked a few paces ahead, arms crossed, his thoughts a tangled mess of frustration and bitterness. They'd barely exchanged words since the warlock's death, and honestly, that suited him just fine. Silence alone kept the sharp pain of her repeated rejections at bay.

Kade could almost feel Vaelrik's smug smile, and it made his stomach churn. He didn't want to hear it. Didn't want to hear how easily Seraphina was falling back into Vaelrik's poisonous web. He didn't want to acknowledge the unease gnawing at him, the thing that tightened his chest every time the two of them spoke. The rest of the day passed in a blur, with Vaelrik's insufferable remarks echoing through Kade's mind. Every time the man leaned too close, every soft whisper in Seraphina's ear, it sent Kade's temper spiralling higher.

As night fell, the campfire crackled around them, its flames flickering weakly as if they too sensed the heaviness in the air. Shadows stretched like dark tendrils across the clearing, the night feeling too still, too oppressive—a silence laden with things unspoken. Kade stood beyond the firelight's embrace, eyes locked on Seraphina. She sat on a large stone, her body turned slightly to face the flames. Her posture was stiff, guarded, as though the fire's heat could not reach the coldness that had taken root between them.

Even in the dim glow, she was stunning—her hair like silk against the night, the graceful lines of her body softened by the flickering light. But under that surface, Kade could feel the distance growing, creeping between them with every passing second. His chest tightened, an ache, a gnawing hunger to close the gap, to pull her back to him. But he couldn't. The thought of touching her—of letting himself fall back into her warmth—terrified him.

Unseelie. The word echoed in his mind: bitter, unforgiving. She deserved better than him. He wasn't even a normal Dark Fae anymore. He was darkness — blood-stained, broken, and hollow. Anyone who approached him would suffer. Like everything else, he would destroy her. She just didn't know it.

Frustration coiled tight in his chest. How could she want someone like him? How could she want the thing he had become?

"Seraphina…" His voice was barely a whisper, quiet against the crackle of the fire.

She looked at him over the flames and stood, moving toward him with purpose, her steps steady. She was a force, and it terrified him. He wanted her to stop, to turn away, but there was something in the way she held herself—an unyielding strength that reached out to him. She wasn't afraid.

"I need you to understand," he croaked, his throat tight. "I'm not… not good for you." His words trembled, breaking as it left his lips. "You deserve better. Someone who can love you without bringing darkness into your life."

Her gaze softened, not with pity, but with something deeper, something more dangerous. Compassion. Her hand reached for him, fingers brushing against his arm, warm, grounding. "Kade," she said, her voice steady. "Don't you see? I'm not afraid of the darkness in you. I see the light, even when you can't. And I want you. Just as you are." She moved closer, and he swore the ground beneath him trembled. He was losing himself in the pull of her presence. "I'm not going anywhere."

Her words cut through him, but they weren't the balm he thought they'd be. No, they were a thread wrapping around his chest, tightening, pulling him toward something he wasn't ready for.

"I can't…" His voice broke again, a raw tremor of vulnerability. "I can't let you love me. Not like this. Not with the monster that I am."

Her hands found his face, soft against his harsh features, lifting his gaze to meet hers. There was nothing but understanding in her eyes — nothing but certainty. "You're not a monster," she whispered, her breath warm against his lips. "You're Kade. I see all of you. And I choose you. Just as you are."

A shudder ran through him, and for a moment, just a fleeting moment, he let himself feel it—the warmth of her closeness, the weight of her acceptance. Maybe she was right. Maybe she could handle the darkness within him. But could he be the man she needed? Could he ever be enough for her?

He pulled her into his arms, his hands trembling as he held her, as though she might slip away if he didn't hold tight enough. "I can't hurt you," he whispered into her hair. "I can't let you love me. Not when I'm like this."

Her arms wound around him, her fingers pressed against his chest as though she could feel the storm churning inside him. "You can, Kade," she said, her voice steady, unwavering. "You just have to trust me."

For a moment, he did. He trusted her. But in the same breath, his fears rose again like a tidal wave, crashing over him.

"I don't deserve you," he muttered, the words slipping out before he could stop them. A sickening wave of regret crashed over him as soon as the words left his mouth.

Seraphina's touch faltered, her breath catching in her throat. Her eyes hardened, a storm of frustration and pain clouding her gaze. "Do you not understand?" she snapped, the fire in her eyes burning. "You think you're a monster? You think you're unworthy of love." She shook her head, her anger palpable. "But you're wrong, Kade. You're wrong."

Kade took a step back, his chest tightening, a mix of guilt and panic clawing at him. No, this wasn't what he wanted. He wanted to pull her closer, but the words he couldn't take back hung between them like a blade.

She stepped closer still, her presence like a tidal wave, her heart laid bare for him to see. "I've never asked for perfection," she continued, her voice low, edged with pain. "All I've ever wanted was you. But you keep pushing me away. Keep telling me I'm not worth your love."

Her words hit him harder than anything else ever could, each one a stab to his bleeding heart. But it was the truth. She had wanted him. And he had pushed her away, again and again.

He just couldn't tell her the real reason. Not yet. Not with the storm that loomed closer with every step they took. If she knew what was inside him—what was coming—it would destroy her.

This… this was as much as he could give.

Kade, don't be selfish. The thought struck like lightning. He had to push her away. For her safety. For all their sakes.

And he knew exactly the words that would do it.

"Is that the truth? You don't want me because you think I can't handle you?" she asked, stepping closer, her chest rising and falling with the force of her emotions. "Well, I can handle you, Kade. I choose you."

Without hesitation, she reached up, pulling his face toward hers, her lips meeting his in a kiss that shattered every wall he'd built. For a heartbeat, he didn't move. Just let the fire of her touch thaw the cold he'd wrapped himself in.

But then—

He pulled away sharply, his grip tight on her shoulders, as if he didn't hold on, he'd fall apart.

His voice came out like a blade. "You must give your love freely, Seraphina. Sharing it with everyone."

He saw her flinch—but forced himself to go on.

His gaze turned bitter, exactly how he needed it to sound. "I've seen the way you and Vaelrik have been all over each other. Don't stand here and pretend that you haven't."

The words struck her like a thunderbolt. She froze, shock and fury warring across her face. Without warning—her fist collided with his jaw, the sound echoing in the night.

"You bastard!" she spat, her voice thick with rage. Her chest heaved with the weight of her anger, and without another word, she stormed off, disappearing into the darkness.

Kade stood there, heart pounding, his cheek stinging where her fist had landed. Regret crashed over him, but his pride—his pride—held him in place. He couldn't follow her. Not now.

As if fate itself had a twisted sense of humour, Vaelrik appeared from the shadows. Leaning casually against a nearby tree, he smirked at Kade, amusement gleaming in his eyes.

"Well," Vaelrik drawled, "that was painful. I've seen men face death and still hold their pride. But that? That was brutal." His smile widened, with a malicious glint in his gaze. "It was like watching someone pull a sword from a wound while it's still bleeding."

Kade's hands shook, rage boiling beneath the surface. "You think this is funny?" His voice was sharp, but it felt hollow—empty.

Vaelrik's grin softened, almost sympathetic. "Funny? No. Pathetic? Yes."

Kade's jaw tightened, but his chest ached, too tight to bear. He couldn't respond. Not now. Not when everything felt like it was slipping through his fingers.

Chapter 18

Seraphina's footsteps were hard and sharp as she stormed away from Kade, fury boiling inside her chest so fiercely it was hard to breathe. She barely registered the ground beneath her feet—her mind was a whirlwind, each thought spiralling into the next, louder and heavier than the last. *How dare he?* The words echoed like venom, each repetition twisting deeper into her chest.

She felt like she was on fire, as if her skin suddenly felt too tight for her. She felt *it*.

The magic. That *magic*.

It thrummed to life beneath her skin, sudden and blistering, humming through her veins with a ferocity she hadn't felt since the battlefield.

No, it couldn't be back—not after everything. Not now.

The disbelief was a fleeting thought, barely formed before it was swept away by the tide breaking loose inside her. Panic slammed into her like a tidal wave. Her breath hitched, coming faster, more shallow, her throat tight.

It was too much. *Everything* was too much.

The war. The prison. The tortures. Evander's lifeless eyes stared back at her.

The endless killing. The nightmares that clawed through her sleep. The weight of survival.

It all surged at once, crashing through her ribs like thunder, unravelling her from the inside out. She stumbled, clutching her arms around herself as if that might hold her together. But she was breaking. Coming apart at the seams.

She wanted to scream—to tear the world down to match the chaos inside her—but even that felt empty. Like everything else.

Her hands were shaking now, her fingers twitching with the need to release the energy that was writhing inside her. The anger, the power—it all tangled together, suffocating her, drowning out everything else. She felt like she was on the edge of something she couldn't control, a storm waiting to burst. Just as her control was slipping, a voice cut through the chaos—a low, soothing murmur that held her in place.

"Seraphina…"

The sound of her name was like a tether, pulling her back from the brink. She spun, her heart hammering in her chest, only to find Vaelrik standing in the shadows. His dark hair shimmered faintly in the moonlight, his figure somehow calm amidst the chaos swirling around her. His golden eyes were steady, unflinching, as if he had seen this before.

"What are you doing here?" She breathed, her voice trembling with the strain of holding herself together.

"I was drawn to the storm," he said, shifting his gaze to her hands where the power crackled in vivid bursts. He took a careful step forward, his expression unreadable, but there was something there—something comforting in the way he stood. "I know what this feels like."

Her chest tightened, and she couldn't hold back a bitter laugh, a sound full of frustration and disbelief. "You know what this feels like?" She took a step back, the surge of power beneath her skin almost unbearable. "I can't control it. It's like I'm going to tear everything apart."

Vaelrik's eyes softened, a flicker of understanding crossing his face. He didn't step back, didn't flinch at the raw intensity of her magic. Instead, he moved closer, carefully, until there was only a hair's breadth between them. She could feel the heat, his presence grounding her in a way she hadn't expected.

"I understand more than you think," he whispered. "When I first shifted into my dragon, it was just like this. I couldn't control the fire inside me—the rage and the magic. It consumed me. I couldn't stop it, no matter how hard I tried."

His words struck a chord within her. The vulnerability in his voice caught her off guard. For the first time, she saw the depth of what he was saying—not as a mentor, not as a soldier, but as someone who had lived through the very thing she was facing.

"I didn't have anyone to help me then," Vaelrik continued, his voice still steady, still calm. "But you do. You can do this, Seraphina. You're stronger than you know."

She swallowed hard, her hands still trembling at her sides. The power was still there, crawling beneath her skin, but his presence—the warmth of him, his quiet assurance — was like a balm to the fury. She wanted to push him away, to hide from the truth of his words, but something in his gaze kept her from doing it.

"You have the control," Vaelrik said softly, stepping even closer. He reached out, his hand gentle as it brushed against her trembling fingers. "It's not about stopping it, Seraphina. It's about embracing it. Accepting it. You're not broken, and you're not a monster. This power inside you? It's part of who you are. And you can learn to control it, just like I did."

Her breath caught in her throat as his words sank in, the storm of emotion swirling inside her suddenly stilling, just for a moment. His touch was steady, like an anchor she hadn't known she needed. She had spent so long fighting against herself, against the power that surged within her. But now, with him standing there, his warmth bleeding into her own frozen heart, it felt... possible.

"I don't know if I can," she whispered, the vulnerability in her voice betraying her.

"You can," Vaelrik said firmly. "I'll help you. I won't let you burn yourself out."

Seraphina looked up at him, meeting his gaze. There was no judgement there, no pity—only understanding, only support. His presence surrounded her, offering a safe space for her to feel the magic, to accept it without fear.

"I won't let you go through this alone," he added, his voice quiet but resolute. "You don't have to carry this burden by yourself."

For a long moment, they stood there, the air between them thick with unsaid things, with a kind of understanding that transcended words. Seraphina's chest still ached, still pulsed with the leftover echoes of her magic, but now, it didn't feel so impossible to contain.

Her breath evened out as she drew in a shaky inhale, letting his words settle inside her. Slowly, she let her hand fall to her side, the power there still wild, still crackling, but no longer threatening to overwhelm her. She wasn't alone. And maybe... maybe she could control it after all.

A heavy silence stretched between them, filled with unspoken words, yet something changed in that space. She could feel it—a subtle tension that hadn't been there before, like the quiet before a storm, but this time, it wasn't angry or destructive. It was... hopeful.

Vaelrik's presence anchored her in ways she hadn't expected, his warmth a soft beacon cutting through the storm inside her. He didn't pull away when she faltered; instead; he was steady, unyielding in his belief. For the first time in a long time, Seraphina felt something inside her loosen, as though the storm was slowly receding, one breath at a time.

"You're not alone," he repeated, his voice a whisper that seemed to echo in her chest.

She nodded slowly, her hand moving to meet his, her fingers grazing his palm like a tentative surrender. The magic beneath her skin hummed gently now, the flickers of wild power gradually ebbing into something more manageable.

Vaelrik's eyes softened as he stepped closer, his gaze fixed on hers with an intensity that made her heart beat just a little faster. He cupped her hand more firmly in his, his touch grounding. "I've seen you fight. You don't need to fight this anymore. Embrace it, Seraphina. It's a part of you. I'll be here, guiding you through it."

His words were like a balm to the rawness inside her. He spoke as though he truly believed in her, in this — the magic that was new and scared her, the strength she tried so hard to control. It wasn't a weakness to embrace it. It wasn't a loss of herself.

"Take a deep breath," Vaelrik said softly, his voice low and steady, as though guiding her through something ancient and primal. "You have the power to bend this to your will, not the other way around."

She closed her eyes, focusing on the deep, steady beat of her own heart. She took in a slow, measured breath, feeling the surge of magic still fluttering beneath her skin, but now—now it didn't feel so threatening.

The storm inside her settled, and for the first time, she wasn't afraid of it. She wasn't afraid of herself. When she opened her eyes again, Vaelrik was watching her with a quiet pride, his expression softening even more.

"That's it," he murmured, his voice just above a whisper. "You're understanding. It's about control, yes, but it's also about trust. Trust in yourself. Trust that you're more than just the magic. You're the one who holds it, Seraphina. Remember that."

Her breath caught in her throat, the last pieces clicking into place as his words settled into her soul. She was the one who held it. The magic didn't define her; she could bend it to her will, and with that thought, the power within her rippled again—strong, but this time, with purpose, with intent.

She glanced at Vaelrik, her eyes searching his for any trace of doubt, but there was none. Only certainty. Only trust.

"I didn't think I could. This is all so new. I've never been able to do magic, and the one time it has happened, it was that one burst, then I never felt it again. It's never been so… alive," she admitted, her voice barely audible, her heart still racing.

Vaelrik's thumb brushed across the back of her hand in a comforting motion. "I know. But now you control it, and as you use it more, the more you can understand your new power."

There was something in his gaze that made Seraphina feel like she was standing on the edge of something new—something that could change everything. She wasn't sure what it meant, but in that moment, she realised she didn't have to fight it. She didn't have to do everything on her own.

The fire of magic was still alive within her, but now, it felt less like a curse and more like a gift—a gift she could wield, control, and protect.

"Thank you," she said, the words catching in her throat, but she meant them more than she had ever meant anything.

Vaelrik's lips quirked upward, and for the first time, it wasn't a smirk or a teasing grin—it was something softer, something warmer. "Don't thank me yet. We're not done. You still have a long way to go."

Seraphina's mouth twisted into a half-smile, the first sign of a true, unguarded moment between them.

"I'll take it one step at a time," she said, the words feeling stronger as she said them.

For a moment, the world outside seemed to disappear. The chaos of the battle, the looming threats—all of it felt miles away.

"I told you," Kade's voice rang out, dripping with something she couldn't quite place, but the sting was unmistakable. He was standing at the edge of the clearing, arms crossed tightly over his chest, eyes narrowed with a kind of scorn. "You give your love so easily. All this... this is just another example. You trust him, just like you trusted me. But it's different now, isn't it?"

Seraphina's blood boiled. *How dare he?* She thought. *First he says he is a danger to her than accuses her of what? Sleeping around? Is this a new technique to keep her distant?*

She could feel her magic pulsing, urging her to act, to unleash all the energy that had been building inside her since the fight began. The world blurred around her, her vision narrowing as her heart raced, her power flaring dangerously.

"Don't," Vaelrik warned, stepping forward and placing a hand on her arm, his voice low but firm. "He's trying to provoke you."

But Kade wasn't finished. "Oh, please, I don't need you to defend me. She's just like this with everyone who can give her what she wants. This isn't about friendship, Vaelrik. This is about something else. Isn't it, Sera?"

The last word hung in the air like a challenge, but Seraphina was already feeling the recent surge of magic rise, threatening to spill over. She wanted to yell, to throw everything at him—she wanted to silence him, make him feel what she was feeling. The urge to let loose was almost too much to fight. But before she could even take a step toward Kade, Vaelrik was already there, his body positioned between them, his voice calm yet insistent.

"I don't think you've ever seen her with friends, Kade. This is who she is. She gives herself freely, loves without limits. It's a strength, not a weakness. Maybe you should try it sometime."

Seraphina froze, the words sinking in like a cool wind against her overheated skin. But Kade wasn't having any of it.

"You don't know her like I do!" Kade shouted, his face flushed with anger. "You think you understand her, but you don't. She's out of control, and you're just enabling it—just like everyone else! You're letting her go wild."

Vaelrik turned to her. "Ignore him love, he is just acting on jealously and fear. You know that."

Seraphina felt the anger within her flare once more. This time, she couldn't stop it. The power beneath her skin was no longer a whisper—it was a roar, eager to be unleashed, threatening to consume everything in its path. Her hands clenched into fists, and she could feel the heat rising. But just as she felt the explosion of power bubbling up within her, Vaelrik's hand shot out, gripping her wrist firmly.

"Control it," he said, his voice steady but tinged with urgency. "Please. You'll regret it if you hurt him."

The words barely reached her. All she could feel was the pull to release everything, to give in to the magic and let it destroy. She opened her mouth, but no sound came out— just the overwhelming rush of power inside her. She couldn't hold it back anymore. She could feel fire licking at the edges of her skin.

Then, in an instant, everything changed.

Vaelrik shifted, his body rippling with energy, his form morphing into something monstrous. In a split second, the man she had known was gone, replaced by a towering crimson dragon, its scales shimmering like molten fire, wings unfurling with a terrifying grace.

Before Seraphina could even react, Vaelrik's enormous wings wrapped around her, cocooning her in warmth, in power. She felt her magic surge forward, a violent torrent of energy, Flames exploded out of her—but instead of destroying, it collided with Vaelrik's protective wings, absorbed by him, swallowed whole.

Seraphina wasn't worried about Vaelrik's Crimson dragon. It felt like home to her, familiar and safe.

Her breath hitched, and she froze. "Vaelrik?" She whispered, panic rising in her chest. She could feel her magic beginning to wane, but her heart was still hammering in fear. "Did I hurt you?"

Through the powerful, roaring thrum of her magic, a voice—calm, strong, reassuring — echoed in her mind.

I'm fireproof, little flame. Don't worry. You didn't hurt me.

Her eyes shot open, meeting the glowing gold of Vaelrik's dragon eyes. He was standing tall, wings extended behind him, the sheer size dwarfing the surrounding space. The force of her magic had not harmed him. Instead, he had absorbed it, taking it on himself. She forgot how magnificent his dragon form was. The way the scales caught the moonlight and shimmered crimson made her want to reach out and stroke them. Regardless of everything she knew about dragons and not touching them, she knew Vaelrik would allow it.

As she rubbed a hand across a spot on his foreleg, she felt him hum at the connection. "Your dragon still looks the same as I remember when I was young." She whispered.

You may also remember that I tried to set you on fire for daring to approach me. His voice was loud and rough in her mind, but full of warmth.

Seraphina blushed at the memory, recalling how she got the nickname of Little Flame.

Vaelrik's enormous head shifted away from her, and his golden gaze settled on Kade. For the first time, the fierce, untameable power of the dragon seemed focused solely on him.

"I didn't do this for you," Vaelrik said, his voice low and cutting through the air like a blade. "I did it for her." He stepped forward, his enormous form moving with a fluid grace, every movement carrying the weight of someone used to command. His gaze never left Kade, sharp and unyielding. "You'll do well to remember that."

Kade, taken aback, flinched at the intensity of Vaelrik's words. The words hung in the air for a moment, heavy and laden with meaning.

As her panic subsided, she looked up at the dragon before her, the mighty crimson creature that had shielded her. The power still thrummed within her, but it wasn't boiling her from the inside out now.

"Thank you," she murmured, the words more for herself than for him, her voice barely a whisper as she pressed her hands against the dragon's massive scales, seeking reassurance in the warmth of his power.

Vaelrik's golden eyes softened just a fraction before his massive form shrank back down, returning to his human shape, though his aura still radiated strength.

"You're welcome," he said simply, his tone warmer than it had been before. But his gaze flicked briefly back to Kade. There was something in the air between them now—a challenge, a spark that hadn't been there before.

Seraphina's heart was still pounding, but she knew something had changed. Vaelrik's arms were still around her. Seraphina's breath steadied, the last remnants of her magic dissipating into the cool air. Despite the calm that slowly washed over her, a new tension had settled between them—an almost tangible weight. Kade stood in silence, his expression dark, and she could feel his gaze on her, the storm of emotions there impossible to ignore.

For a moment, everything was still.

Vaelrik looked down at her, his dark hair falling across his eyes as he took a step away, golden eyes assessing her. Though the surrounding air still vibrated with the power of the dragon just unleashed. He gave her a small nod, the slightest of affirmations, and she couldn't help but feel a rush of gratitude. His protective gesture, while powerful, hadn't come without its cost, and that thought lingered in her chest like a heavy stone.

He'd taken the brunt of her uncontrolled magic, and yet there was no anger in his eyes, no judgement. Only understanding.

Her gaze shifted to Kade, whose face was hard, set in a grimace that only deepened the knot in her stomach. The moment stretched on, thick with unspoken words.

"You really think I need you to defend me, Vaelrik?" Kade's voice cut through the silence, sharp as a blade. His words were low but filled with venom. "You really think that's going to change anything?"

Seraphina's chest tightened. She could feel the flare of Kade's anger, raw and desperate, and it made her stomach twist. This wasn't about her anymore, not entirely. It was about something deeper—something she couldn't quite put her finger on, but that gnawed at her insides.

Vaelrik stood tall, unmoving. "It's not about defending you, Kade. It's about her. She deserves better than what you're throwing at her right now."

The words hit her harder than she expected. She had spent so much time trying to understand the dynamics of her relationship with Kade—his feelings, her own—and here it was, laid bare in a single sentence.

But Kade wasn't backing down. "She doesn't need protection from me. She needs to see it, Vaelrik. That's the problem with her, isn't it? Always giving everything without considering the consequences. You're so eager to shield her from everything, but you're making her weak." His words were bitter, filled with a growing rage that was hard to ignore. "She's not the same person I—"

Kade's voice faltered for just a split second. Seraphina caught the hesitation. That crack in his armour—the hint of something deeper, more painful, that he was trying to bury.

But before she could process what he meant, Vaelrik took a step closer, his eyes narrowed and his voice low with an edge of finality. "Enough, Kade."

The air between them hummed with the weight of his words. Kade took a step back, his eyes flashing with frustration, but there was nothing more to be said. Vaelrik had drawn a line.

It caught Seraphina in the middle of it all. She wanted to scream and shatter the tension with her voice, but she could only stand there, feeling small under the weight of everything they had said.

Instead, she looked to the ground, her hands trembling slightly. "I don't want this," she murmured, more to herself than anyone else. "I don't want to be caught in the middle of this."

For a long moment, no one spoke.

Vaelrik's gaze softened, the dragon's fierce edge replaced by something gentler, though no less intense. He gave her a small, almost imperceptible nod. "You don't have to, little flame. You never have to."

The words hung in the air, and Kade's eyes flicked to Seraphina, a flash of something painful crossing his features—something regretful, maybe even broken—but it was gone in an instant. His walls slammed back up, and he turned away without another word.

Seraphina stood there, her heart pounding in her chest. She didn't know what to do with herself. She didn't know what to feel. Kade's words still echoed in her mind, leaving a hollow ache in their wake. Vaelrik's gaze softened as he turned back toward her, his eyes steady and warm. But there was something there that was hard to ignore—something like understanding.

Chapter 19

The landscape stretched out before Seraphina in a haze of greys and muted greens, the jagged cliffs in the distance reminding her of how close they were to the dragon territory—Drakorath—also reminding her of the walls she'd built inside herself. Her mind buzzed with noise—Kade's broken words, Vaelrik's quiet manipulations, and the fire of something else coursing beneath her skin, too hot to ignore.

What is this? She thought bitterly, rubbing her temples as though the answer would just appear. She was ignoring them both. It was easier this way, less complicated. But that didn't stop the constant ache in her chest or the pull toward the men she'd tried to push away.

Stop thinking about him. Both of them.

The power—it was burning, a heat that prickled her skin and thrummed like a pulse, just under the surface. She clenched her fists, willing herself to focus on the world around her. She needed to clear her head. This hunger was unfamiliar, unlike anything she'd felt before. The magic—no, it wasn't just magic—seemed to take on a life of its own, always just out of reach. It was her life force pushing to the surface, ready to tear free. She couldn't control it, couldn't understand it, but the power was so raw, so consuming.

Vaelrik stepped beside her, the lightness of presence a stark contrast to the turmoil inside her. "You know, you're still avoiding me, hmm? Not a fan of company today?"

Seraphina didn't look at him, her eyes fixed straight ahead. "I'm not in the mood to talk," she muttered, her voice flat, devoid of the usual sharpness.

Vaelrik smirked, his gaze never leaving her face. "Not even a little banter?" He leaned closer, his breath warm against her ear. "Kade still sulking in the back? You're certainly giving him the cold shoulder."

Her mouth tightened at the mention of Kade, her stomach knotting. She refused to acknowledge the tension in her chest. "I'm fine. You're wasting your time."

A beat of silence passed before she finally spoke again, her voice quieter this time. "How did you even do that? Talk aloud like this—in your dragon form, I mean. I thought it was all telepathic."

Vaelrik tilted his head, a glint of pride flickering in his golden eyes. "Most of us can't. It took me centuries to master—refining the magic, reshaping my throat, syncing voice to form without the telepathic bridge. It's... not pleasant. But I like the effect."

She glanced at him, despite herself. "You did all that just so you could keep talking shit while flying?"

He grinned, teeth sharp and gleaming. "Well, that—and I find it gratifying to systematically awe and annoy everyone."

She shook her head, the corner of her mouth twitching before she buried the expression again. "You're impossible."

He chuckled, unbothered.

She rolled her eyes, ignoring him completely. But his words stuck with her. She was restless, a tremor running through her limbs that she couldn't shake. What had happened to her? Why was the air so thick with... something? Her heart thundered, and the power simmered beneath her skin, sparking with every step. No. Not now.

The sound of Kade's footsteps reached her ears, but she didn't dare glance back. She felt the heat of his stare, even from behind. The last thing she needed was his pity. Or his concern. Or... his presence. She couldn't breathe when he was near. She couldn't think. He did not know what he was doing to her.

Before she could stop herself, she shot her hand into the air behind her, flipping Kade off in one swift motion.

Vaelrik's laughter was low and dark beside her. "Well, that's one way to tell him where he stands."

Seraphina said nothing, her lips pressed tight as the words burned on the tip of her tongue. I'm not yours to save, she thought, her fists clenching again. Neither of you.

The power burned under Seraphina's skin again, fierce and untamed, crackling through her veins like wildfire. It was growing—more intense with every passing hour. It gnawed at her, hungry and restless, demanding to be understood, yet every time she reached for it, it slipped from her grasp like water through her fingers. She had never been one to rely on magic, never needed it—not in the way others did. But now...

What is this?

Her steps faltered as the question echoed in her mind. The power was inside her — pulsing, alive—and it terrified her. She had always prided herself on her physical strength, her combat skills, and her will. But this... This was different. It was foreign. It was magic.

Jessamine. The name echoed like a ghost in the corners of her thoughts.

Vaelrik noticed the change in her posture, the subtle shift in her expression as she slowed her steps, though her face remained impassive. He had seen it before: that faraway look in her eyes meant she was lost in a memory she would rather forget.

"You seem... distracted," Vaelrik commented, his voice smooth as silk but with a certain edge.

The name slipped from her lips without warning, barely a whisper on the wind: "Jessamine." Seraphina stiffened, as if surprised, though she wasn't sure why.

Vaelrik's smirk tugged at his lips, his gaze cool and calculating as always. "You seem to ask for help, though. I thought you, of all people, would know better than to trust magic wielders."

She glared at him, but the question still lingered in her mind. Should she seek the magic wielders? Maybe they could help her understand what was happening—what this power really was. But Jessamine? She hadn't seen her in years, not since that… incident. Jessamine had been part of the magic world Seraphina had never quite belonged to, and now, with this power surging through her, the lines between her past and present felt blurrier than ever.

Vaelrik smirked, leaning against the trunk of a tree as he studied her. "It's strange, isn't it? You—Seraphina, the warrior with a heart colder than steel—saving a witch. What made you risk everything for her all those years ago?"

The question hung in the air like a challenge, but Seraphina didn't flinch. Her eyes flicked briefly to Kade, who was trailing behind, his gaze ever-watchful, always aware of where she was. He was being overprotective again. He did not know how to stop treating her like a delicate flower that needed guarding. But then again, it had always been that way. Since the first time they met, Kade had never let go of the idea that she needed saving.

But she didn't need saving. Not this time.

She turned her focus back to Vaelrik. "I didn't save her. I helped, and I paid for it."

Vaelrik raised an eyebrow. "Ah, yes. The punishment was from her master. I recall the scar on your ribs… quite the souvenir."

Seraphina's hand instinctively brushed over the long scar hidden beneath her tunic, her fingers lightly grazing the rough skin that still stung. She had earned it. She had taken the punishment from Jessamine's master, the cruel warlock who'd made sure Seraphina suffered for daring to interfere. But she had never regretted it. Dark forces, far older than she could comprehend, had cornered Jessamine, and Seraphina couldn't let the girl die.

But what Vaelrik didn't understand—what no one seemed to understand—was that the cost of that decision wasn't just the scar. It was the weight of a life she had carried, and the price she still paid for it.

"She didn't deserve that," Seraphina said quietly, her voice more vulnerable than she intended. "No one does."

Vaelrik's smirk faltered for a moment, but only for a heartbeat. "And what if she doesn't want to be found now? What if looking for her is pointless?"

Seraphina didn't respond immediately, her gaze drifting through the trees. Her thoughts had gone dark again, the weight of years pressing on her shoulders. Jessamine had vanished after that, disappearing without a trace. She had tried to find her once, but it was like chasing shadows. Jessamine had told her of a way to find her when she needed it, had given her something to help, but Seraphina never understood it.

She shook her head, clearing her thoughts. "It doesn't matter." Her tone was firm, but the doubt still lingered in her chest, clawing at her insides. "We have other things to focus on."

Vaelrik was silent for a moment, clearly mulling over her words. "Of course." His voice was casual, but Seraphina caught the flicker of something in his eyes—curiosity, maybe. He was never one to leave things alone.

Kade's voice broke through the tension, sharp and protective. "If you're going after her — whoever she is—I'm coming with you."

Seraphina rolled her eyes without thinking, her lips curling into a smirk that didn't reach her eyes. "I never asked for your protection, Kade."

He didn't flinch at her words, his gaze unwavering as he caught up with her. "You might not ask, but I'll be there anyway."

The defensiveness in his tone was familiar, and it grated on her nerves.

"Why can't you just let me deal with things on my own?" her voice low, but sharp.

Kade's expression hardened, though he didn't respond right away. His steps slowed as he walked beside her, the weight of his concern pressing down on her like a storm cloud.

* * *

As the day wore on, their journey continued with quiet determination.

The air had taken on that still, heavy quality that always came before a storm—thick with moisture, humming with distant thunder. Skies, once a pale winter grey, darkened to an ominous charcoal, clouds swelling and rolling in like an unstoppable tide. The wind bit at their cloaks, tugging hair into eyes and stinging cheeks with icy promise.

Despite the worsening weather, no one suggested stopping. They pressed on, boots squelching in the mud, shoulders hunched against the chill. But with each step, the rift between Kade and Seraphina widened. The space between them had become more than physical. Unspoken words remained buried, and both used silence as fibre they dared not remove.

Then—

"By the flames. Is that a cabin?" Vaelrik's voice cut through the tension like a fiery blade. He surged ahead, eyes gleaming with something dangerously close to joy. "Tell me that's a roof I see and not another hallucination caused by weeks of damp travel and tragic company."

He ran up the slope with barely contained glee. "Please, let it not be another night of rain soaking my magnificent hair."

Seraphina blinked up at the crooked silhouette ahead—a cabin, weathered and half-sunken into the ground, like it had long since given up standing tall. Yet it stood. Somehow. Nestled in a dip between two snow-dusted hills, surrounded by a fringe of bare trees that whispered in the wind, it looked like a forgotten piece of another life.

The cabin's slanted roof had a moss patch where shingles were missing. Ivy curled possessively around its crumbling exterior, and the chimney leaned precariously, as though sighing under the weight of years. Still, it was shelter.

As they approached, even Kade's usually impassive expression softened with the smallest flicker of relief.

Seraphina reached the door first. It groaned on its hinges as she pushed it open; the wood swollen with moisture and age. Inside, stale air greeted them—dust and mildew, but no rot. A good sign.

The single room was simple and empty, save for a collapsed chair in the corner, the broken remnants of a table, and a long-forgotten hearth that begged for a fire. Faded light trickled in through the slats and cracks, casting long shadows that shifted with every breath of wind.

Vaelrik ducked through the doorway with exaggerated care, sniffing the air dramatically. "It's paradise," he declared, voice reverent. "A bed of wood planks and not a single drop of rain on my hair. I might cry."

Seraphina rolled her eyes, but already she was unbuckling her damp gear, her hands finally ceasing their cold-induced shaking.

"We can rest here for a while," Kade said, his voice quieter now, the urgency of their quest weighing heavily on him. "I'll check the perimeter."

Vaelrik dropped his map and supplies on the table that they had secured in the previous village. Clearly they needed a plan, wondering aimlessly away from who captured them and as far from the corruption was no longer a workable plan. Vaelrik had told them as much when he bought the map.

"Right, let's make some plans," she muttered, scanning the map with sharp eyes. She pushed aside the pull of the past, even though it still held her attention. There were more pressing matters at hand.

Vaelrik wandered over to the old fireplace, crouching to examine the remains of a cold fire pit. "A place to rest and no one to stop us... this is becoming far too easy," he murmured, his voice low and playful. He glanced back at Seraphina, his golden eyes flickering with amusement. "I hope you're not getting too comfortable."

"Focus, Vaelrik," Kade snapped, though his words lacked their usual bite. He was losing patience, and Seraphina could see it in the way his fingers tightened on his weapons, the subtle tension in his frame.

Seraphina took a deep breath and spread the map further, pulling a few tattered notes from her pack as she pieced together the path they would take. Her fingers brushed the edge of the map, tracing routes with the tip of her finger, calculating their next move.

The soft murmur of the forest outside was a far cry from the tension simmering within the cabin. The sun was beginning its slow descent, casting long shadows across the dusty wooden floor as the trio huddled around a rickety table.

Kade was the first to break the silence, his voice steady but edged with urgency. "We need to get to the fae kingdom of Elarion," he said, eyes narrowing as he traced a route on the map with his finger. "They're our best bet for alliances—information, resources. We need safety, and we need it quickly."

Vaelrik scoffed from across the table, his golden eyes glinting with something darker. "Safety?" he mocked, leaning back in his chair, his long dark coat pooling around him. "The fae will want a price for their help, Kade. And we both know that price is rarely in our favour. Also, from what we saw of their kingdom, the corruption is strong, and demons have overrun the outer villages. No, we go to the dragons, In the heart of Darkroaath. Their power is unmatched. We could tip the scales in this war."

Seraphina's eyes flicked between the two, her hand tightening around the edge of the map. The sharpness in their voices cut through the cabin's warmth, and she could feel her frustration building. Kade, ever the tactician, thought in terms of logic and alliances. Vaelrik, driven by his thirst for power, was ready to chase after whatever would give him an edge.

"I'm not going to the fae or the dragons." Seraphina's voice cut through the argument like a blade, firm and clear. "I'm going home."

Kade looked up sharply, his brow furrowing in disbelief. "What do you mean, 'home' — the kingdom of Eryndral is nothing but ruins?" he asked, voice laced with confusion.

Her eyes locked onto his, a determined fire burning deep within them. "My city, Caelvaris, it might be ruins," she said, her gaze unwavering. "Something is calling me there. It's where I need to go."

There was a heavy silence. Kade opened his mouth, but Vaelrik beat him to the punch, a smirk curling on his lips. "Ah, the heart of a queen," he mused. "The ruins, the ghosts of what once was. A fitting pilgrimage, but foolish."

Kade's hands clenched at his sides, frustration and concern warring within him. "Seraphina, this is madness. There's nothing left there but destruction. We need to be smart. We need allies, not ghosts."

But Seraphina didn't waver. She pushed the map aside, her fingers brushing the worn leather of her armour as if gathering her resolve. "I don't care about allies right now, Kade. I care about what's calling me home. Whatever's left, whatever's waiting there — that's where I'm going."

The tension in the room thickened as Kade stared at her, his expression a mix of frustration and understanding, but no agreement. Vaelrik's eyes glittered with a dangerous amusement as he leaned in, voice low and sly. "So, it's decided, then?" he asked, almost as if he already knew the answer. "We go to the ruins. Not for power, not for allies, but because Seraphina's heart demands it."

She nodded once, the decision final. "Yes. It's where I belong."

Kade let out a long sigh, rubbing his temple. "Fine," he said, voice tinged with reluctant acceptance. "We go to your ruined kingdom. But we leave at first light. At least it is close to where we are."

Vaelrik grinned, his golden eyes gleaming with approval. "Now that we've sorted this out..." He stretched out lazily, eyeing the lone bed in the room. "I believe that bed is mine for the night. And, little flame," he added with a teasing smirk, "perhaps you'll join me?"

Seraphina rolled her eyes, her lips curling into a playful smile. "I think I'll pass," she said, her voice light but firm as she moved to the floor, curling up on the cold wood instead. "Maybe Kade would like to join you if you get cold," she teased.

Kade's eyes widened, his face reddening as he shot her a glare. "I'm fine," he muttered, moving to the far side of the room. He crossed his arms over his chest, still too tense to relax in the cramped space. Vaelrik let out a low chuckle, watching the interaction with an amused glint in his eyes.

For a moment, the tension eased — they forged a fragile truce of sorts, sealing it with humour and the unspoken understanding that the road ahead would be just as complicated as the one they had gone through. Seraphina settled into her makeshift bed, her eyes flicking toward the window, the last light of the day creeping across the horizon.

Tomorrow, they would leave for the ruins. For home. Whatever lay beyond those broken walls, she was determined to face it. But for tonight, as the fire crackled low, and the night deepened, they found solace in the silence between them. And Seraphina let the distant call of her kingdom fill her thoughts, knowing that no matter what, she would follow it to the end.

* * *

The faintest light of dawn crept through the cracks in the cabin's wooden walls, casting soft shadows across the floor. The night had passed in a slow stillness, broken only by the occasional crackle of the fire and the hushed sounds of the forest beyond.

Seraphina stirred, her body stretching lazily as the fog of sleep clung to her mind. She fluttered open her eyes, and for a moment, she was disoriented. The cool wooden floor beneath her was hard, but there was something else—something warm and solid against her head. She blinked a few times, confused, before realising she had somehow worked her way onto Kade's lap. Her breath caught as she looked up at him, still deeply asleep, his face serene, framed by the unruly strands of his silver hair. The steady rise and fall of his chest soothed her, and for a moment, she simply watched him, mesmerised by the peaceful beauty of his sleep.

It was strange—seeing him like this, without the usual tension or the constant readiness for battle. There was a softness in his features now, a rare vulnerability that he only ever showed when he thought no one was looking.

Her gaze lingered on him, and it felt like time slowed.

"You're staring," came a voice, soft and hushed, but with a hint of amusement.

Her heart leaped in her chest as she froze. She looked up to meet Kade's eyes, half-lidded, a lazy smile tugging at the corner of his lips.

Her face flushed, and she rubbed her eyes, still groggy. "I... I don't know how I got here," she mumbled, half in embarrassment, half in confusion.

194

Kade chuckled softly, his voice thick with sleep. "It's alright, Nyx. Just go back to sleep. It's still early."

Despite his words, his hand drifted to her hair, his fingers running gently through the strands. The simple touch sent a shiver down her spine, his fingers moving with a slow, almost reverent touch as if he were savouring each moment.

She felt her heart flutter at the unexpected tenderness of his gesture, the intimacy of the moment catching her off guard. Her eyelids grew heavy again as Kade's fingers worked through her hair, the rhythm soothing and comforting, almost as if he were weaving peace into the strands.

"You know," he murmured, almost to himself, his voice low and full of affection, "I fucking love your hair."

The words sent a rush of warmth through Seraphina, but before she could fully process them, she felt herself sinking back into the comfort of his lap. The sound of his voice, the sensation of his fingers in her hair—it was too much. Her eyes closed once more, and with a soft exhale, she drifted back into sleep.

This time, it wasn't just the exhaustion that pulled her under. It was the sense of calm, the overwhelming comfort of Kade's presence, his quiet affection, and the unspoken connection that seemed to deepen with every passing moment. She let herself fall back into the warmth, letting go of the world for just a while longer.

Kade's fingers continued to work through her hair, the gentle motion a steady lullaby. Seraphina let herself sleep again, her heart lighter than it had been in weeks.

The morning light had fully crept into the cabin by the time Seraphina slowly stirred from her second slumber. The warmth of Kade's lap and the soft motion of his fingers through her hair had lulled her back to sleep, but now the world was pulling her from the depths of rest. She blinked, her mind still heavy with sleep, as she realised that the position she was in hadn't changed—her head still rested on Kade's lap, and her body was curled on the floor beside him.

But this time, it wasn't just the sound of Kade's breath filling the space.

There was another sound—a deep, amused chuckle.

"Well, well," came a familiar voice, dripping with playful sarcasm. "Look at this. I'm not sure who's more comfortable here."

Seraphina groggily lifted her head, blinking as her eyes adjusted to the morning light. Kade remained seated on the floor, his back against the wall, his body relaxed despite the awkward position. He had fallen asleep like that, still keeping his hand in her hair as she rested against him.

"Vaelrik?" she groaned, rubbing her face, still half-dazed.

Vaelrik, who had been watching from the corner of the room, leaned casually against the wall, his arms crossed over his chest. A mischievous grin stretched across his face as he took in the sight of the two of them. "I see you two are making yourselves cosy." His voice was dripping with humour, and there was a glint of mischief in his eyes.

Seraphina narrowed her gaze at him. But it was hard to be serious about the absurdity of the situation. She sat up slowly, blinking the sleep away.

Vaelrik's grin widened as he stepped closer. "You know, little flame, I'm jealous looking for someone to play with my hair next time. I'm sure you would be happy to help." His tone was playful, teasing, the banter that only Vaelrik seemed capable of pulling off.

Seraphina shot him a look, one eyebrow arched in amusement. "I'm sure I'll pass, but maybe Kade will help you," she said, her voice still thick with sleep, though the edges of a smile tugged at her lips.

Kade, now fully awake but still with the remnants of a sleepy haze in his eyes, glanced up from where he had been, idly watching the interaction. His lips curled into a grin, though there was a sharpness to it. "I'm much more likely to hit him upside the head, though, if he keeps talking," he muttered, his voice low and filled with a quiet amusement.

Vaelrik gasped in mock horror, his eyes wide with exaggerated shock. "Oh, my dear friend, you wound me!" he said dramatically, clutching his chest as though Kade's words had pierced him. "How could you think such a thing? I'm wounded, deeply wounded."

Kade shook his head, his grin never leaving his face, as he nudged Seraphina with his elbow. "It's not like he doesn't deserve it," he said with a smirk, the light teasing tone clear in his voice.

She chuckled, the tension from the night's events easing with the playful banter. It was a moment of normalcy, of simple camaraderie, but she appreciated it more than she could say.

"Alright, alright," she said with a shake of her head, brushing her hair from her face as she stood up. "Let's get going. No time for jokes." But despite her words, a small smile tugged at her lips.

Vaelrik smirked, brushing imaginary dust from his shoulder.

"Fine, fine—but next time you two start eye-fucking like it's a bard's tragic love ballad, I'm braiding your hair, Kade. Maybe even add a feather. For *flair.*"

Kade blinked once, his grin faltering into a puzzled scowl.

"Why are you so obsessed with touching my hair?"

Vaelrik raised his hands innocently, eyes wide with exaggerated wonder.

"Oh, I don't know," he said, then dropped his voice into a pitch-perfect imitation of Kade's low drawl.

"'I fucking love your hair, Seraphina.'"

Seraphina choked on her breath, her face going crimson.

Kade stared at Vaelrik, stunned into silence for half a second before a deep groan escaped him.

"You little snake," he muttered, running a hand down his face. "You were *awake?*"

"I'm *always* awake when something interesting is happening," Vaelrik said with a grin that could outshine the moon. "Honestly, it was the most romantic grunt I've heard in weeks."

Seraphina turned away quickly, trying—and failing—to hide her flustered smile.

Kade grumbled something under his breath that sounded suspiciously like a curse, pulling his cloak tighter around him.

"Remind me why I haven't thrown you into a ravine yet."

Vaelrik adjusted the strap of his pack with a lazy flourish, glancing sidelong at Kade.

"Face it, I'm the real backbone of this little trio. Comic relief, devastating charm—and clearly, *better hair.*"

Kade scoffed, his tone dry as old steel.

"Keep talking, Vaelrik. One day you might actually convince yourself."

"Oh, I don't need convincing," Vaelrik shot back with a grin. "But I wonder—if I told Seraphina I loved *her* hair, would you finally try to kill me in my sleep, or just glower harder?"

Kade's jaw flexed, a sharp flash in his eyes.

"Try it, and we'll find out."

Seraphina let out a strangled laugh, the tension crackling between them like the spark before a fire.

Seraphina shook her head, warmth flickering through the chaos. For just a moment—sharp, ridiculous, and tangled with unspoken things—they weren't fighters clinging to the edge of the world.

They were *them.*

Somehow, that made all the difference.

Chapter 20

It had been a long and relentless journey; The surrounding air grew colder as the days passed, the wind sharp against their skin, the weight of the world pressing ever more heavily on Seraphina's shoulders. But they could not stop—not yet. Not until they reached her home.

The ruined palace loomed before them now, its broken walls standing like ancient, gnarled bones. It had once been the heart of the kingdom, the beating pulse of a thriving land now lost to time and tragedy. And here, amid its shattered grandeur, Seraphina felt it all—the sorrow, the anger, the betrayal. Old stone, dust, and something more sinister—memory—filled the air in the ruined palace. Scorching marred the walls; long ago, rot consumed the grand tapestries, leaving only torn remnants clinging stubbornly to their mounts. In the broken marble and shattered chandeliers, echoes of a past life lingered, whispering to Seraphina as she walked through the remnants of her childhood home.

Every step she took brought her closer to the heart of the devastation. The throne room. She could almost hear the laughter and the murmurs of court life, could almost feel her parents beside her, their warmth and strength still in her bones. The memory was so vivid, it almost hurt. The throne room loomed ahead, its grand double doors still standing, but barely. Fire had splintered and worn them, blackening them. The weight in her chest tightened. This was where it had happened. She hesitated, fingers grazing the carved wood, the once-intricate designs now barely discernible beneath the scars of time and battle.

"This is it, isn't it?" Vaelrik's voice was almost casual, but there was something sharp underneath, something knowing.

Kade shifted behind her, silent. Watchful.

Seraphina inhaled, gathering her strength, and pushed forward. The doors groaned as they opened, revealing the ruined throne room. The sight stole the breath from her lungs.

What was once a majestic chamber, ruled by generations of kings and queens, had become a graveyard of its former glory. Jagged remnants of the stained-glass windows, once bathing the room in warm light, catch the dim glow of the setting sun. The cracked dais, where her parents once sat, mocked what had been with toppled thrones, one still barely upright. And there, upon the floor, the dark stains remained. Time had worn them, but she knew. She would always know.

Her mother had fallen there. Her father was beside her. And standing over their bodies had been Alexis, her husband—the man she had trusted.

Seraphina clenched her fists, nails biting into her palms. The ghosts of that night pressed against her—the sound of her mother's final breath, the sickening wet gurgle as steel met flesh, her own screams ringing in her ears. She swallowed it down. The past would not break her. Not now.

Vaelrik, for once, was quiet as he strode forward, gaze sweeping the room. His usual smirk was absent as he knelt near the dais, brushing away debris with lazy fingers. Then he stilled.

"Well, well," he murmured, reaching into his cloak. From its depths, he pulled free the amulet—the one he had been carrying since she had met him.

Seraphina had always thought there was something strange about it, an unspoken weight to its presence. Vaelrik had called it a key, but to what, he had never truly explained. Now it pulsed. A slow, rhythmic glow thrummed beneath its surface, the once-dull gemstone at its centre coming alive with an ethereal white light.

Vaelrik's grin returned, sharp and amused. "Looks like we found the lock."

Seraphina stepped forward, drawn to it. She saw the inscription on the stone. How had she never noticed this before?

Here, the answers will be unlocked with the key and the hope of the kingdom

"Let me hold it."

Vaelrik hesitated. "Not usually in the habit of handing over priceless, possibly dangerous artefacts, but... since you asked so nicely." His tone was teasing, but there was something else there. Curiosity. Maybe even anticipation.

He dropped it into her palm.

The moment it touched her skin, the world exploded in light.

A blinding, brilliant radiance burst from the amulet, consuming the throne room in a white glow. The air trembled, thick with something ancient and powerful. Seraphina felt a jolt deep in her core, as though something had awakened within her.

Then, as suddenly as it had appeared, the light condensed, shrinking, taking shape. When the glow finally dimmed, a creature hovered before her.

It was small—no larger than a cat—its body slender and covered in pristine silver scales that shimmered like frost-kissed silver. Delicate wings, almost translucent, beat the air, keeping it aloft. Its eyes, piercing, intelligent gold, fixed on her.

A dragon.

A tiny, impossibly perfect dragon.

The silence stretched thick with disbelief.

Then Vaelrik, ever incapable of letting a moment be sacred, grinned. "Well. That's adorable."

The dragon huffed, somehow looking indignant despite its size. "I am not adorable."

Seraphina's breath hitched. The voice—clear, strong, edged with the weight of something ancient—echoed in the chamber. His mouth never opened, but it spoke in her mind—everyone's mind.

The dragon narrowed its gaze at Vaelrik. "And you. You are an insufferable thief."

Vaelrik placed a hand on his chest, mock offended. "Thief? I prefer the term 'opportunist.'"

Seraphina found her voice, though it came out hoarse. "Who... what are you?"

The dragon turned to her, its expression shifting. Softer. Almost... warm.

"I am Aurion," it said.

The name struck a chord with her. A story whispered in her childhood, a name spoken with reverence. A name her father had mentioned when he called her the hope of the kingdom.

"My father..." she whispered.

Aurion dipped its head. "And his greatest ally."

Realisation dawned. "He created you?"

"In part." Aurion's wings flexed. "Your father and his ally, the great dragon Vhastir, created this amulet as a link—a way for you to always have someone who knew the secrets of the royal bloodline, someone to protect you." Its gaze turned sorrowful. "But it was lost to you when your kingdom fell. I have been waiting. Watching. But I could do nothing until you held me once more, here, to activate the magic."

Seraphina's heart pounded. A thousand questions warred in her mind.

"Why now?" she asked. "Why not before?"

Aurion's expression turned exasperated, and she had the distinct feeling it was rolling its eyes.

"Do you think I enjoyed sitting in Vaelrik's pocket, listening to him talk to himself?"

Vaelrik smirked. "Oh, I knew you could hear me. My ability to sense magic has some upsides, it seems."

Aurion ignored him. "I have always been with you, Seraphina. But the magic binding me to this form could not fully awaken until you touched the amulet."

Kade, who had been silent through all of this, finally spoke. His voice was low, wary. "And what exactly are you supposed to do now?"

Aurion turned, and the air in the room shifted.

The tiny dragon stared at Kade with an intensity that was almost unsettling. Then, to Seraphina's utter shock, its voice echoed in her mind alone.

Oh, I despise him.

She blinked. What?

Sarcasm laced Aurion's mental voice.

I had to watch this man reject you. Do you have any idea how frustrating that was? If I could've strangled him, I would have.

Seraphina barely stopped a laugh from escaping.

Kade scowled. "What?"

"Nothing," she said too quickly.

Aurion smirked in that infuriatingly knowing way. "Oh, I like you, Seraphina. We're going to have fun."

Vaelrik clapped his hands together. "Fantastic. We've got a sassy, pocket-sized dragon and a family mystery. Shall we?"

Seraphina gazed at the ruins of her past, at the tiny dragon who had once been meant to protect her, and at the men who now stood beside her.

For the first time in a long while, something inside her didn't feel so broken.

She curled her fingers around the amulet.

"Yes," she murmured. "Let's."

Heavy silence suffused the corridors of the ruined palace, broken only by the faint echo of their footsteps against the cold marble floor. The deeper they ventured, the more the devastation softened. The outer halls bore the brutal scars of war—blackened walls, shattered stone, and the eerie remnants of a once-great kingdom. Yet, the heart of the palace seemed spared the full wrath of destruction, and the inner chambers fared better.

Seraphina's fingers brushed the cool stone, tracing the faint carvings half-buried under layers of dust. Here, in this forgotten corner of her past, something still lingered — something that had withstood the ravages of time.

Vaelrik's voice broke the stillness, low and thoughtful. "Well, would you look at that? Still intact."

He wasn't wrong.

The room they entered was vast, its high ceilings once adorned with delicate frescoes — now faded, but still able to tell a story. Scenes of dragons coiled around kings and queens, a union of beasts and monarchs immortalised in paint and gold leaf. Heavy wooden furniture, though cloaked in dust, stood resilient, untouched by the years. At the far end, a grand fireplace—carved with intricate sigil's—loomed, the embers of an old fire still lingering in the stone, as though holding onto the last remnants of warmth.

Seraphina exhaled slowly, her voice barely above a whisper. "Someone must have sealed it off."

Kade gave a quiet nod, his eyes scanning the room with a steady calm. "Protected from the worst of the attack."

Vaelrik, never one to stay still for long, flopped into a chair with nonchalant ease, tossing his boots onto a nearby table. "A little dusting, this place could be a five-star inn."

Seraphina rolled her eyes at him, but the tension in her shoulders loosened just a fraction. She unclasped her cloak, letting it fall over the back of a chair, then drew the amulet from around her neck. Her fingers lingered over it for a moment before she lifted it to her chest.

The moment the amulet touched her skin, Aurion reappeared, his tiny form materialising in the air with an almost imperceptible shimmer.

"Finally," the dragon huffed, his voice laced with impatience. "I was wondering if you'd wear me like a pretty trinket all night."

Seraphina's lips twitched with amusement. "I'm still deciding whether you're a trinket or a pest."

A tiny clawed hand flew to Aurion's chest, his eyes widening in mock shock. "How dare you! I am a noble guardian, a trusted advisory, a beacon of wisdom."

Vaelrik smirked, lounging in the chair with his arms behind his head.

"A very loud pocket dragon, that's what you are."

The dragon puffed up, hovering in the air with an air of offended dignity. "Loud? I am magnificent."

Seraphina couldn't suppress a small laugh. The weight of everything — her past, the endless journey — lightened, if only for a moment.

She interrupted before Aurion could respond. "Why did my father create you?" She tilted her head, watching the tiny dragon curiously. "What was so dangerous about ruling that he thought I needed an immortal little lizard as my guardian?"

Aurion sniffed, clearly unimpressed with the term lizard, but he landed on the back of a chair, curling his tail around himself.

"Your father was no fool," he said. "He knew the throne was a dangerous place. And he was right." His golden eyes flickered with something ancient. "Fate intended you to rule. But there were forces that would see you fall before you even had the chance. I was a dragon who was dying. They asked me to do this to save my soul. I gave my full consent to the king of dragons, as this was preferable to dying, and I still keep all my power just to help you specifically now."

Seraphina frowned. "Like Alexis." Seraphina ignored the dragon's past because she was more interested in finding out what secret her father wasn't telling her.

Aurion's tail flicked sharply. "Among others."

Kade, silent until now, leaned forward, his voice measured. "Why didn't you warn her? If you were supposed to protect her—"

Aurion gave him an unimpressed look. "Oh yes, I will just ignore all the magical laws that govern my existence and interfere in ways I was explicitly forbidden to. That worked out so well the last time dragons meddled in royal affairs."

Kade's jaw clenched.

Vaelrik snickered. "Kade, I think you've made a new friend."

Aurion turned back to Seraphina, as if the others didn't exist. "Your father and Vhastir knew a ruler is only as strong as the knowledge they wield. This palace and your kingdom are founded on alliances, betrayals, and power. I was your guide to ensure that you never walked into a battle unprepared. Upon being placed with you, I was to protect you."

Seraphina exhaled, trying to imagine what her life would have been like had she known all of this before.

"If you were supposed to guide me," she said, "then why was Vaelrik the one carrying you around?"

At this, Aurion turned his full, scorching glare on the thief.

"Because he found me on a black market, where a backstabbing smuggler unceremoniously dumped me after stealing me from the battlefield."

Vaelrik held up a hand, grinning. "In my defence, I did not know I was carrying around a talking relic at the time."

Seraphina's head snapped toward him, eyes narrowing. "You told us you got it from a demon. That you didn't know what it was."

Vaelrik's grin faltered, replaced by a flicker of something darker. "I didn't lie," he intoned. "A dead demon led me to it. I could sense the magic, sure, but nothing else. Not like I knew it had a damn soul trapped inside."

Aurion's voice cut like frost. "You never cared to look deeper. Typical."

Kade leaned back against the fireplace, watching them all, his expression unreadable. She could see the tension in his shoulders, the way his hands flexed against his crossed arms.

Aurion flicked his tail, to Seraphina alone, whispered in her mind.

He's sulking. Good. I hope he broods over it for hours.

She could barely stop herself from laughing.

Why do you hate him so much? She asked, half-amused, half-curious.

Aurion let out a long, suffering sigh. *He had you, and he let you go. Do you have any idea how frustrating it was watching you pine over him? He could have had everything, and instead, he* —the dragon made an indignant noise. *I can't even say it. It offends me.*

Seraphina shook her head. *You're ridiculous.*

And you have terrible taste in men.

Excuse me?

Case in point, your dead husband.

She pursed her lips, resenting that he might have a point.

206

Kade, who had been watching them closely, scowled. "I don't like it when you two do that."

Vaelrik grinned. "When they do what?"

Kade gestured vaguely between Seraphina and Aurion. "That silent talking thing."

Aurion flicked his wings. "Oh, I love it annoys you."

She smiled sweetly at Kade. "Maybe if you had been nicer to me, you could have your own mind-talking dragon."

Aurion crossed his tiny legs. "Absolutely not. I would rather wither into dust."

Vaelrik looked entirely too entertained.

Seraphina sighed, leaning back in the chair, fingers brushing against the amulet.

The fire crackled, its warmth seeping into the room. For all the barbs and arguments, for all the weight of history pressing against them, she felt... something she hadn't in a long time.

A piece of home.

She let her eyes close for a moment, the weight of the past still there, but not unbearable.

* * *

The fire crackled low, casting long shadows against the frescoed ceiling. The scent of old books, scorched stone, and lingering embers settled in the air, mingling with the weight of memory. Seraphina traced the edges of the amulet absentmindedly, her mind still whirling with everything Aurion had revealed. Her father had prepared her for a battle she never got the chance to fight. And now, here she was, piecing together the remnants of her past with a tiny, sarcastic dragon perched on her shoulder.

The silence stretched until Aurion—clearly unable to tolerate it any longer—let out a dramatic sigh. "As much as I adore reminiscing about the past, you need to think about the future. You need allies. A haven. A kingdom doesn't rebuild itself on good intentions and sheer willpower alone."

Seraphina exhaled sharply. "And where do you suggest I find these allies? The allies I had either betrayed me or were slaughtered.

Aurion's golden eyes gleamed. "Not all of them." He paused as if savouring the moment. "You need to find your Uncle Dylan."

Silence.

Vaelrik smirked. "Oh, I know him. Called his kid a runt once. He tried to rip my throat out."

Kade pinched the bridge of his nose. "Of course you did."

Aurion gave Vaelrik a long, unimpressed stare. "Frankly, I'm amazed you're still alive."

Vaelrik grinned.

Kade blinked between them, confusion flickering across his face. "Wait, you've had an Uncle Dylan this whole time, and now we're just hearing about him?"

She raised an eyebrow. "Didn't you listen when Vaelrik and I spoke about this in the woods?"

Kade had the decency to look down, feeling the sting of his forgetfulness. "In my defence, I ignore Vaelrik a lot," he muttered.

Seraphina sighed. "He's not actually my uncle. He was my father's closest advisory—his most trusted friend. When I was little, I called him 'Uncle Dylan,' and it just… stuck."

Kade absorbed this, then sighed. "Right. Of course. Because why would anything be simple?"

Vaelrik, looking deeply entertained, leaned back. "Oh, this is fantastic. Not only do we have a lead, but it's someone who probably still wants to kill me. I love that for us."

Aurion flicked his tail. "Truly a tragedy."

Seraphina rolled her eyes. "Alright, enough. Aurion, why would my father send me to Dylan?"

Aurion's golden gaze sharpened. "Because he knew this day would come. Dylan has survived because he knows how to stay hidden. He may not be blood, but he would die before betraying your father's memory. If anyone can help you reclaim what is yours, it is he."

She clenched her jaw, weighing his words carefully.

Kade, ever the realist, frowned. "And the Lycan shifters? They're not exactly known for their hospitality."

Vaelrik smirked. "Oh, don't worry. If they kill us, they'll do it quickly."

Kade glared. "You are not helping."

Aurion, utterly unimpressed by the entire conversation, turned to Seraphina. "Find Dylan. He will know what to do next."

Seraphina nodded slowly. It was a risk, but one she had to take.

Then Aurion's voice slipped into her mind, low and wry. *As long as the amulet touches your skin, we can communicate like this. I'd prefer to keep that our little secret. These two are insufferable enough already—I refuse to share all of my wisdom with them. As your magic grows and so to our connection will and we won't need the amulet.*

Seraphina's lips twitched. *You don't want to share, or you don't want Vaelrik to torment you?*

Both Aurion admitted *yes, my power is connected to yours before you ask. As you grow stronger, so will I. The amulet is attuned to you. The more you reclaim what was taken from you, the more I will protect you and teach you.*

She exhaled, absorbing the weight of his words. There was so much she still didn't know—about herself, about her past.

Kade, still unimpressed with the plan, muttered, "This is reckless."

Vaelrik smirked. "Ah, my favourite kind of plan."

Aurion huffed. "For once, I actually agree with him."

Seraphina rolled her eyes and stood up. "Well, reckless or not, we have a new destination. Get some rest — we leave at dawn."

Vaelrik grinned. "Oh, I love when you sound commanding. It's queenly."

Kade sighed, clearly bracing himself for whatever fresh disaster awaited them.

Chapter 21

Exhaustion and unspoken tension shrouded their trek toward Veyldorn, the last Lycan stronghold, blurring the days into a fog. Endless land stretched before them—rolling hills marred by the scars of war, forests gutted by fire, and rivers thick with the remnants of the fallen. The air hung heavy with the stench of charred earth and old blood, but beneath it all, the stubborn scent of damp pine lingered, as if the land itself refused to yield to ruin.

The sky above was a tapestry of shifting greys, heavy clouds threatening rain, but never quite delivering. Somewhere in the distance, dragon cries echoed—a reminder that they were not alone. Not yet. Seraphina's thoughts fractured between past and present, struggling to stay anchored in the now. Kade remained distant, his gaze always fixed forward, his focus unshakeable. It should have been enough. She should have been grateful for his discipline, his unyielding presence.

But she watched him. Every time he moved, her pulse betrayed her—the rhythmic tilt of his canteen to his lips, the effortless way his throat worked as he swallowed. It was nothing. It was everything. And she hated herself for it.

If you're going to lust after him, at least try to be subtle.

She stiffened at the voice in her mind

Stay out of this, Aurion.

The small dragon, perched smugly on her shoulder, flicked his tail in amusement. *Oh, but I can't. You forget, Seraphina, I hear everything. Every thought. Every little sigh you swallow down when he so much as—*

Shut up.

A chuckle rumbled through her mind, warm and teasing. *You mortals and your pointless denials.*

She could practically feel his satisfaction, a little menace coiling through his words. She threw a glare at him, but he merely preened, his silver scales glinting in the dim light.

She forced her mind to focus elsewhere, but it didn't help.

Kade moved with lethal grace, every motion precise—whether he was stringing his bow, gutting their kills, or — damn him—splitting firewood. She had to bite the inside of her cheek as she watched as the axe swung in clean, powerful arcs, the muscles in his arms flexing with each stroke, the sound of splintering wood ringing in the still air. It was maddening. He was maddening.

Aurion hummed in her ear. *Perhaps if you simply tackled him to the ground and had your way with him, this would be easier for all of us.*

Seraphina nearly tripped over a root. *You—*

A low chuckle to her right made her scowl even deeper.

Vaelrik.

The golden-eyed dragon shifter had been watching her for far too long, and the smirk curving his lips told her he knew exactly what was going through her mind.

"You're thinking about him again," Vaelrik drawled lazily, his voice a teasing purr.

Seraphina shot him a sharp glare. "And you're annoying again."

He merely grinned. "Admit it, princess. You want him."

Aurion chirped. "Finally, someone with sense."

Her blood boiled. She was going to kill them both.

"I want a moment of peace," she muttered, adjusting her grip on the hilt of her sword.

Vaelrik chuckled, utterly unbothered. "You don't make a habit of denying what you want, do you?"

Seraphina exhaled sharply. "You certainly don't."

"Why should I?" Vaelrik stretched, his movements slow, predatory. "When I see something I want, I take it. It's really that simple."

Aurion snorted. *Oh, the arrogance of dragons! Truly, it's inspiring.*

Seraphina shook her head, trying to focus ahead. Kade was still up front, scouting as always, his figure half-obscured by the trees. He was quiet. Too quiet. The tension between them had thickened into something palpable, a weight neither of them acknowledged, but both could feel pressing against their ribs.

Aurion sighed, curling his tail around himself. *And yet, here we are. You, suffering. Him, brooding. Vaelrik, being insufferable. Truly, the gods have cursed me.*

Seraphina rolled her eyes. "No one forced you to come, you know."

Aurion sniffed. "Someone has to witness your misery firsthand."

Vaelrik snickered. "The tiny one's not wrong."

Seraphina glared at them both. "I hate you."

Aurion yawned. *No, you don't. But if you want to keep lying to yourself, be my guest. I'll just be here. Listening. To everything.*

She groaned.

This journey was going to kill her.

The night stretched long, shadows twisting beneath the stars as the fire crackled between them. Kade sat brooding on one side, his back stiff, while Vaelrik lounged beside Seraphina, too pleased with himself for the chaos he was stirring.

"You should smile more, little flame," Vaelrik murmured, his voice low, teasing, leaning closer to her. "It suits you."

She snorted, tilting her head to the side. "I do smile. Just not when you're around."

Vaelrik smirked. "Lies. You're smiling right now."

Damn him. She rolled her eyes, nudging him with her elbow. "You just like to hear yourself talk."

"I like many things," he said smoothly, his golden eyes flicking toward

Kade, whose grip on his dagger tightened. "But watching you pretend you don't enjoy my company might be my favourite."

Kade exhaled sharply. "Do you ever shut up?"

Vaelrik placed a hand mockingly over his heart. "Oh, look at that. He speaks. I was thinking you'd forgotten how, oh brooding one."

Kade's glare darkened. "Keep running your mouth, and I'll help you shut it."

Aurion, the tiny dragon, preened atop Seraphina's shoulder, letting out a dramatic sigh.

Finally. I was wondering how much longer this slow-burning disaster would last. His tail lazily swished, amusement glinting in his bright eyes. "Please do," he said drily. "I'd love to see you try."

Seraphina rubbed at her temples. "Why are men so exhausting?"

"I prefer dragons personally," Vaelrik said with a sharp grin.

Kade's fist clenched. "Do you have a point to all this, or are you just determined to be unbearable?"

Vaelrik leaned back on his elbows, stretching with the grace of a predator basking in superiority. "Oh, I have plenty of points. None you'd understand, storm cloud."

Kade was on his feet in an instant. "Say that again."

Vaelrik laughed, unbothered. "Oh, you have some fight in you. I was thinking Seraphina had drained it all from you."

Kade moved before he could think better of it, but Seraphina was faster, stepping between them to stop things from escalating. She placed a firm hand on Kade's chest, meeting his furious gaze with an even one.

"Let it go," she hissed.

His breath was uneven, his entire body taut as if holding back a storm. But at her touch, something flickered in his eyes. Something raw. Something that made her chest ache.

He exhaled sharply, then turned on his heel, storming off into the dark.

Vaelrik let out a low whistle. "Didn't know he could take orders. That was impressive."

Aurion, ever the instigator, stretched his wings and yawned theatrically.

Well. That was delightful. So much tension, so little resolution.

Vaelrik simply chuckled, standing and moving toward the edge of the camp. "I'll take first watch," he murmured, his usual playfulness replaced with something quieter, unreadable.

She shot him a glare, but before she could speak, Aurion spoke in her mind, smug and amused. *You know, if you'd just let yourself kiss him, I wouldn't have to listen to all this unbearable tension.*

She groaned internally. *You hear everything, don't you?*

Oh yes, Aurion purred. *And I plan to remind you of it at every opportunity.*

She huffed, settling on her bedroll as the fire flickered lower, Aurion curling up beside her.

For a while, she stayed silent, letting the night settle around them. But as exhaustion weighed on her, she sighed, running a hand over Aurion's tiny frame.

"I'm tired," she admitted softly. "Tired of wanting something that isn't mine to have."

Aurion lifted his head, blinking at her. "You mean Kade."

She nodded, throat tightening. "I wish I could just turn it off. Stop feeling so much."

Aurion nuzzled against her hand in a rare show of comfort. "That would be a shame," he breathed. "Your heart makes you strong. You could tell him how you feel, you know."

Seraphina swallowed. "It's also what gets me hurt." A bitter laugh escaped her. "And what would that change? He made his choice."

Aurion hummed thoughtfully. *Perhaps. Or perhaps he's just afraid of losing you. Just like you're afraid of losing him.*

Her throat tightened, but she shook her head, unwilling to let the emotions take hold. "I can't afford to think like that."

Aurion's golden eyes softened, his sharp wit momentarily absent. *You're stronger than you think, Seraphina. Even if you have terrible taste in men.*

She snorted, nudging him lightly. "You're impossible."

Aurion tilted his head, voice smug again. "Well, maybe stop falling for brooding idiots with too much baggage."

She let out a tired laugh, shaking her head. "I hate you."

"No, you don't," he said smugly. "Now get some rest. You've got more terrible choices to make tomorrow."

Unbeknown to them both, Kade stood just beyond the tree line, hidden in the darkness. He had heard every word. And for the first time in a long while, he wasn't sure what to do about it.

Chapter 22

The night had been suffocatingly still—oppressively quiet, as if the world itself were holding its breath.

Then it shattered.

Seraphina jolted awake, heart thrumming like a war drum. Chaos erupted around her. The air had curdled into something toxic—thick with the acrid tang of sulphur and the metallic sting of blood. It scalded her lungs with every breath. The stench of rotting flesh clung to her skin, invasive and cloying, forcing bile to rise in her throat.

The campfire had withered to a scatter of dying embers, casting a feeble light on the carnage. Shadows writhed just beyond the flickering glow— no longer shapeless, but solid, snarling forms that moved like nightmares given flesh.

"Demons."

Kade's voice cut through the din—a low, guttural snarl, more beast than man. His silver hair clung to his brow, damp with sweat, and his eyes glinted like twin blades catching moonlight. Every line of his body was taut, ready, as he scanned the darkness. But it was too late—the enemy was already upon them.

The first wave hit like a storm.

Twisted limbs burst from the trees, dragging behind them grotesque bodies stitched from horror. Claws like scythes gleamed in the dark.

Mouths filled with rows of needle-like teeth snapped hungrily, a cacophony of inhuman shrieks rising with each charge. The demons moved as one—a relentless, writhing tide of monstrous hunger.

"Hold the damn line!"

Vaelrik's voice boomed across the clearing, thunderous and commanding. He was already in motion, golden eyes blazing with fury. His blade sang as it tore through demonic flesh, each strike honed by centuries of war. But even he, the battle-scarred legend, was faltering beneath the weight of their numbers.

Kade moved like liquid shadow—his twin blades a blur, dancing through the melee. He struck with precision, each motion elegant, devastating. His fae-like speed made him nearly untouchable, yet the swarm pressed closer, relentless.

Seraphina's breath hitched, her pulse thrumming in her ears. There was no time to think. Her sword was already in her hand, her body responding before thought could catch up. She ducked beneath a hooked claw aimed for her throat, twisted, and drove her blade deep into the chest of a snarling demon. It shrieked as its acidic blood spilled, sizzling against the dirt in violent spits of steam.

To her left, Vaelrik carved a path through the horde, his massive frame a wall of fury. "Little Flame!" he roared, his sword cleaving through a horned beast in a single, brutal arc. "I can't hold them all!"

Seraphina pivoted, her sword flashing through the neck of a leaping fiend. The creature's head spun into the dark as its body crumpled at her feet. Her muscles screamed in protest, already aching. Her voice rang out through the madness:

"Then we don't hold—we end them!"

The night screamed back.

A deafening roar split the sky. Seraphina turned just in time to see Vaelrik change. In one heartbeat, he was a warrior drenched in blood. Next, his body twisted and stretched, red scales erupting as his bones cracked and reshaped. Wings burst forth, vast and terrible, scattering the enemy with their sheer force. He reared back, a creature of legend reborn,

217

and roared—a sound of wrath, of fire, of ancient power not meant for mortal ears.

But his freedom was brief.

Chains flew from the shadows—thick bands of black iron glowing with runes that pulsed like dying stars. They struck with unnatural speed, coiling around Vaelrik's limbs, his wings, his neck. The moment they touched him, the air burned hotter. They sizzled against his scales, searing through flesh with a sound like sizzling meat.

His cry of agony cracked the heavens.

Seraphina staggered, her chest constricting as the voice of Aurion echoed in her mind, frantic and raw.

They're hurting him! We have to—

"I see it!" she snapped aloud, driving her sword through the skull of the nearest demon. She didn't need to be told. She had already locked her eyes on Vaelrik, whose form was writhing in the grip of those cursed chains.

She surged forward, every step a defiance of the despair clawing at her throat. The ground trembled beneath Vaelrik's struggle, his colossal form dragged down inch by inch. His wings were bound, crushed against his body. The air stank of scorched scales and dark magic.

"Vaelrik, hold on!" Seraphina shouted, her voice torn and raw, throat burning with desperation.

The demons were everywhere—thick and snarling, a tide of shadow closing in. Her arms ached, her blade slower than it should've been. She fought like a flame guttering against the wind, slashing, twisting, bleeding. Every breath came ragged. Every step was a struggle. They were going to tear her apart. Seraphina staggered.

One demon struck hard—claws raking across her ribs, sending her crashing to her knees. Her sword fell from her fingers. Another lunged toward her, its fangs bared, ready to rip through her throat.

Then—she saw him.

Kade.

Across the battlefield, their eyes locked. His chest heaved, face smeared with blood and smoke, blades dripping black with ichor. But it was the *stillness* in his gaze that froze her. Not panic. Not helplessness. Something else. Something old.

Aurion whispered, almost broken in her mind. *He's about to do something no one should ever see.*

Her eyes widened.

Kade moved.

He didn't shout. Didn't scream. He *snapped*.

The shift was instantaneous.

The ground beneath him cracked with a low groan, as if the earth itself recoiled. Shadows surged outward in jagged lines, drawn to him like smoke pulled into a storm.

"You dared to touch her," he said, voice low—too low, laced with venom and fury. It wasn't a shout. It was a death sentence.

Magic bled off him in black, rippling waves—heavy and wrong. It wasn't just darkness—it was ancient, corrupted. The kind that seeped into your bones and *stayed*. It didn't glow—it *devoured*. The temperature dropped, the air thickening, pressing down like the calm before a catastrophic storm.

Vaelrik's roar split through the battlefield, a sound of fear, not rage. "*Kade, no! Don't do this! Not like this!*"

But it was already happening, and Seraphina felt confused because everyone else already seemed to know.

Seraphina, gasping for air, pushed herself upright. She could feel the shift in the world. Her fingers trembled, not from exhaustion—but from something primal. *Terror.*

The demons paused—just for a heartbeat—but even that hesitation was unnatural. It was as if *they* knew what he was. What was coming?

His eyes—those silver-grey eyes that once looked at her with warmth—had gone flat, unreadable. A void had taken root in him, and from that void came power.

The battlefield bent around him, shadows stretching, distorting, reality beginning to unravel at the edges. The cursed magic he had buried—kept locked away to protect her, to protect *everyone*—was now unchained.

Seraphina felt it hit her like a tidal wave—thick, suffocating. People shouldn't wield magic like this, or they'll lose pieces of themselves. And he was giving himself to it.

To *save her.*

Her pulse thundered in her ears. She wanted to scream his name, to stop him—but the words caught in her throat, drowned by the rising roar of his unleashed power.

A violent surge erupted from him—an explosion of raw, dark force. The raw, dark force flung demons like rag dolls. The earth cracked. Lightning split the sky, not light but black and red, searing into the heavens.

His twin blades pulsed with the same twisted energy, their edges tearing the air itself.

Seraphina could do nothing but watch.

Not as a warrior. Not as a leader.

As the woman he was about to destroy himself to protect.

Kade's eyes—the voids that had once been grey—burned with an unnatural fire. His mouth twisted into a grin, dark and wild, as if he had embraced the very thing that had haunted him for so long. He was no longer the man she knew. This was a weapon — untethered, dangerous, and terrifying.

"Kade..." she whispered, shocked. She knew he would hear her.

"I warned you all." Kade's voice was a low, guttural rumble, dripping with ancient malice. He looked at Seraphina when he heard his name, his dark eyes meeting her blue ones. "If this is the price for you, then I'll pay it every damn time."

He lifted his hand, and the earth beneath him cracked open, fissures of blackened stone running like veins through the ground. The demons were no longer the predators. Now, they were prey.

Kade stepped forward, the air around him twisting, pulling at the fabric of the world. He moved with purpose, with hunger. His blades, now glowing with dark magic, cut through the demon ranks like they were nothing more than paper. Blood and ichor sprayed, sizzling against the night.

Seraphina's mind reeled. She could see it now—each slash, each swing was a part of him breaking free, tearing away the last remnants of the man he had been.

"Stop!" Vaelrik's voice cracked through the chaos, full of desperation. "Kade, you're losing yourself!"

But Kade didn't stop. He couldn't. The power coursing through him was too much—too potent to be out of control. He was unstoppable now, a force of destruction, and nothing could hold him back.

Seraphina's hands shook. She wrestled with the need to stop him, to save him from the abyss he was falling into, and the overwhelming terror of what he was capable of now.

But it was already too late. The dark magic had taken root in him. She could see it — the way the power twisted his form, his mind, his very soul.

"Not like this," she whispered, her voice barely audible, even to herself.

Suddenly, the ground rumbled again. From beneath the earth, massive black tendrils shot up, writhing like serpents, tearing through the battlefield with a mind of their own. The demons recoiled in fear, attempting to retreat, but found themselves trapped. The tendrils coiled around them, pulling them back into the earth, crushing them into the ground like insects beneath a boot. Seraphina could hear their screams, but it was distant—muffled by the deafening pulse of Kade's magic. With a final, earth-shattering scream, the battlefield went silent.

Seraphina's heart hammered in her chest, each beat louder than the last. The surrounding air crackled, thick with magic and despair. She had seen Kade drift further into the abyss before, but this—this was something else entirely.

She couldn't stand it. She couldn't let him go.

"Kade!" She screamed his name again; her voice was hoarse and raw with fear.

He didn't respond. A swirling storm of black magic consumed him, veiling his eyes in shadow. But she saw it—that flicker. A flash of recognition. The faintest glimmer of the man she cared for, buried deep beneath the darkness, threatened to devour him.

She didn't hesitate.

She spun, slicing through Vaelrik's chains with a crack of steel and fury. The moment the last shackle hit the ground, she turned toward Kade, her body moving before her mind could stop her. Her sword slipped from her hand, forgotten in the dirt. She didn't need it. Not for this.

All she needed was *him*.

"Aurion," she whispered in her mind, pleading. *"Please—what do I do? How do I reach him?"*

The dragon's presence stirred; his voice was ancient and uncertain. *"I... I don't know, Seraphina. I've seen the magic of kings and tyrants, of cursed gods and broken souls. But I've never seen an Unseelie fae burn with power like this. This isn't just darkness—it's something else."*

Her heart clenched.

"You mean he can't control it?" she asked, her thoughts a scream barely contained.

Aurion's silence answered for him.

"No!" Vaelrik roared behind her, his voice sharp with panic. He surged to his feet, staggering. "Sera—*get away from him!* He's unstable. If he loses control—if you can't reach him—we're all dead. That power isn't just turning on the enemy; it's warping everything."

But Seraphina didn't stop.

She surged forward, slipping between tendrils of wild magic, her boots skidding on the cracked earth. Her hands found Kade's face—hot and feverish beneath her touch. Her fingers trembled, pressing into his skin as if she could anchor him there, tether him back to *her*.

"Kade," she whispered, barely more than breath, "come back to me."

His entire body was a battlefield—veins surging with corrupted energy, breath ragged and shallow, muscles trembling as if trying to hold something *in*. His pulse raced under her fingers, frantic, as though his soul itself was tearing apart.

But he didn't pull away.

Not yet.

She pressed her forehead to his, her tears sliding down to meet his burning skin, vanishing on contact like embers swallowed by wind. A sob tore from her throat—a sound full of helplessness, fury, and aching devotion—but she didn't falter. Her body had moved without thought, her soul dragging her toward him with the sheer gravity of a forgotten truth.

She hadn't chosen this.

Something inside her had *recognised* him. Not as a lover. Not as an ally. As something deeper—an echo of herself, a tether written in a language older than blood, older than memory.

The magic within her stirred violently now, no longer gentle but *demanding*. It surged like molten gold beneath her skin, blooming from her fingertips in luminous threads that shimmered and cracked the surrounding air. She didn't command it. It was instinct—raw, primal—pulling her into him like a celestial force bent on reunion.

She didn't understand it. But she knew it.

The bond she felt—*that impossible, beautiful thread*—wasn't one forged in words or history. It felt like the connection born on battlefields, through fire and ruin, hardened by pain and carved by loyalty. Her magic had found *him*, and it knew him. It clung to him like a drowning soul to the shore.

She poured herself into it. Every broken shard of her soul, every flicker of her light, her love, her rage, her hope—*all of it.*

"Kade," her voice fractured, breath hitching. "Come back to me. Please."

Her lips met his—trembling, uncertain, but filled with desperate purpose. Not a kiss of romance. A promise. A cry for the man she *knew* was still in there, clawing for breath beneath the black tides.

And for the briefest heartbeat—he responded.

His mouth softened, hesitating against hers, the trembling warmth of a dying ember in a frozen world. Against her waist, his fingers twitched, tightened, pulled, and clung. His body shuddered, and for just an instant— an aching, breathless instant—his eyes flickered.

Silver. *His* silver. Blazing through the abyss like the last star before dawn.

A whisper of him. A breath.

Then—gone.

Aurion's voice pierced the moment, sharp with dread. *"Seraphina—stop! You're burning yourself out!"*

But she couldn't. She wouldn't.

Her power roared from her in golden waves, wrapping around Kade, wrapping around *them*, threading into the fabric of his soul. It was more than love. More than memory. It was creation. Destruction. *Reckoning.*

The world fell away. There was only him.

Her veins felt like fire. Her bones cracked with light. The threads of her magic frayed at the edges, pulled too tight—burning her from the inside out.

"She's channelling something sacred," Vaelrik growled, his voice thick with fury and fear. "It's not just magic. It's *life-force*. She'll die if she keeps going!"

"Then stop her!" Aurion's scream broke like thunder through her mind, terror in every syllable.

Then—impact.

Vaelrik slammed into her, a wall of force and panic. Her bond with Kade shattered midstream, snapping with a soundless cry of agony. Seraphina's body hit the ground hard, convulsing as her magic violently recoiled. Golden threads disintegrated in the air around her like ash in a storm. She screamed, the pain of separation tearing her open like a blade through her chest.

Her hands clawed at the dirt, reaching blindly toward him. *"No!"*

But it was gone.

The connection. The warmth. The moment. The world tilted violently, as if the very threads of reality recoiled from what had just happened. Her magic, once radiant and fierce, now unravelled inside her like a tapestry ripped at the seams. It tore through her chest, raw and merciless, leaving her breathless. Her knees buckled. The golden threads that had once stitched her to Kade frayed into ash and scattered like dying fireflies.

She crashed onto the earth. The impact jarred her bones, the cold dirt biting into her skin like punishment. Her body convulsed with the shock, golden light flickering out in weak, fading pulses. The surrounding air crackled, thick with the scent of scorched magic and burnt grass, and her lungs couldn't draw enough breath. Everything felt hollow, like she'd given her soul and found only silence.

She lifted her head with a trembling effort, vision swimming. And there—through the haze of pain and magic gone awry—was Kade.

He looked up slowly, as if pulled from the depths of a nightmare. His skin was pale, sweat-slicked, and trembling. Light now flickered in his eyes, silver piercing the black. His mouth parted. He struggled to speak, as if his throat still belonged to the shadows.

One word. A whisper. A memory.

"Sera..."

The name. Her name. Not Nyx. Not a warrior's title. But *Sera*. Something fragile. Something from another life. A name she hadn't heard from his lips since the world unravelled.

Her heart clenched violently, the sound hitting her harder than any blade could. It was a lifeline thrown across a chasm—but it didn't reach her in time.

She reached for him, fingers trembling with magic that barely held form. A fading echo of something ancient and profound, she could still feel their bond. She'd trusted it. She hadn't questioned the pull she felt toward him from the beginning. Her magic *knew* him. It had reached for his instinctively, wrapping around his essence like ivy to stone, believing in a bond that could only exist through years of battle-forged loyalty and pain survived side by side.

But that was the lie—*she'd assumed*. Her magic had responded to him not with logic, but with raw, ancient recognition. Two flames drawn to the same spark. She had *felt* him. And that had been enough.

Until it wasn't.

Vaelrik's snarl shattered the moment like glass. He stepped between them, his aura a wall of fury. "Not another step," he growled, eyes wild with a protectiveness that startled even her.

Aurion's voice rang out like a sword unsheathed. "You're lucky to be alive, Kade. But if you ever put her through that again, I *swear* I'll end you."

Seraphina lay crumpled, watching, helpless—but not powerless. No, this… this had been her *choice*. She had thrown herself into that bond. She had *believed*.

Kade stumbled backward, his breath ragged, his form shuddering under the weight of his returning self. His gaze flickered toward her—just briefly—but in it was a storm. Confusion. Guilt. Pain.

His eyes… they weren't the same. The silver had returned, but it was darker now, clouded with something hollowed out. It was as though a part of him had died; perhaps it had.

He stood swaying, caught in the aftermath of something he didn't yet understand. His fists clenched at his sides, knuckles white, but he didn't come to her. He didn't speak again. The space between them stretched and widened, each breath making it worse.

Then—he turned.

His back to her was more final than a sword in the chest. A chasm. A void. One she couldn't cross. Not now.

She reached out, her fingers aching to touch, to *feel*, but her body refused her. Her magic was gone. Empty. Nothing but scattered fragments trying to reassemble into a shape that could stand.

Vaelrik's voice came again, sharp and suspicious. "What the hell are you?" His glare narrowed, cutting through Kade like a dagger. "You're not just a Dark Fae. What *are* you?"

Kade's body stilled.

For a moment, silence reigned—so thick it felt like the world itself was holding its breath.

Then, quietly, through clenched teeth, "I am one of the last remaining Dark Fae Princes." Of the Unseelie Court.

Shock rippled through the air.

He didn't look at them. His eyes found Seraphina's instead—tortured, ashamed. "I'm something you'll never understand. Nor do I want you to try. But thank you… for pulling me from her."

The words struck like a blade. *From* her. As if she were poison. As if what they'd shared wasn't salvation, but destruction.

His gaze lingered for just a second longer—then he vanished, slipping into the shadows of the trees like a ghost.

The ache in Seraphina's chest bloomed into something unbearable.

Vaelrik was suddenly beside her, kneeling down, his voice uncharacteristically soft. "You okay, little flame?"

She shook her head, blinking back tears. "He's gone again, Vaelrik."

Vaelrik exhaled, brushing a hand gently across her hair, his thumb grazing the ash-streaked edge of her cheek. "Yeah. He is. But *I* see you, Seraphina. I'm not going anywhere."

She tried to speak, but only a shallow breath escaped. Her body trembled from the strain, her vision dimming at the edges.

Aurion landed beside her, frowning. "She's near burnout. Her magic reserves are empty. She needs rest—now."

Vaelrik didn't hesitate. He scooped her up, her body limp against his. He cradled her like something precious. She barely had the strength to protest.

He smirked down at her, voice warm with forced levity. "Guess I finally get to carry the little flame. You always did like making a dramatic exit."

Aurion rolled his eyes. "Less talking. More moving."

As they moved away, Seraphina's head lolled against Vaelrik's shoulder. Her eyes fluttered shut, and the weight of rejection settled like a stone over her heart. Kade still watched from the shadows—hidden, silent. Torn.

She had kissed him.

She had given him everything.

But was it enough?

Was it ever?

Chapter 23

That night, beneath the cold watch of the stars, Seraphina lay still, her mind a battlefield. Memories clawed at her, dragging her into the darkness where Alexis stood—his face twisted, eyes once warm, now glowing with cruel malice.

"No one will ever love you, Seraphina. Not after everything you've lost."

The words coiled around her heart, choking her. She reached for him— desperate for what once was—but he vanished like smoke, leaving only the echo of his laughter.

She gasped awake, the frosty night air biting her skin. Above, the stars blinked indifferently.

"No more." Her voice cracked with defiance, a final refusal of the ghost that haunted her. But the weight of war, of loss, of truth—pressed down until something within her broke.

The surrounding air thickened, alive with energy. A wind swept through the trees, whispering in a forgotten tongue. Fire and ice surged in her veins, something ancient stirring—awakening.

From the shadows, Aurion stepped forward, steady and sharp. His eyes blazed with urgency.

"It's time," he said. "Your power is awakening. The path ahead will either break you… or make you whole."

Seraphina hugged herself tightly. "Aurion... what's happening to me?"

He knelt before her, his voice gentler now. "The magic was always there, buried beneath grief. Pain has unlocked it. Grief is fire, Seraphina. In the right hands, it forges something new."

She shook her head. "But I've never had magic. This is *new*—it's not *me*."

Aurion exhaled, glancing toward the looming treeline. "It *is* you. The pain broke the seal. If you don't master it, it'll consume you. Go. Now."

She hesitated, heart racing. He smirked, nudging her shoulder. "And don't worry—you've got a pocket dragon watching your back. I'm not going anywhere."

Something in her knew he was right. With a last glance at the stars, she rose on trembling legs and crossed the torch-lit threshold. The forest swallowed her whole.

The darkness inside the trees was alive. Shadows slithered on the ground, and the wind carried voices — some familiar, some foreign. The air pulsed thick with ancient power. Each step felt heavier, as though the world itself was testing her resolve.

Seraphina's feet seemed to sink deeper into the earth with each step she took into the forest. The trees towered above her, their twisted branches reaching like skeletal fingers, blocking out what little light remained from the fading campfire. The air was thick, alive with an energy that hummed in her bones. Her pulse thrummed in rhythm with the power inside her, but it was no longer the faint sensation she had felt before. This was something far greater—an overwhelming surge that threatened to crack her apart.

Her head swam as the surrounding air shimmered with heat, then ice, both battling for dominance in her veins. She staggered, barely able to keep herself upright. The forest seemed to pulse in response, shadows closing in around her, whispering words she could almost understand. Her breath came in shallow gasps as she tried to centre herself, to hold on to whatever little control she had left. But she knew now—this wasn't the same power she'd felt before when she lost control with Vaelrik, nor was it like what she had used to save Kade.

This was everything.

"No…" she whispered, her voice trembling as the realisation set in. She dropped to her knees, her hands shaking as they pressed against the damp earth. "I can't—this is too much. I—"

The pain was a gnawing fire, searing every nerve, every thought. Her entire body felt like it was being torn apart and reforged in the flames of her own grief. But there was something else—an ancient, suffocating presence that gripped her heart, pushing her deeper into the madness of the magic coursing through her. This power… it wasn't new. She'd felt it before. She had only touched the surface, playing with embers, thinking them flames. But now… Now, the magic consumed her.

Her heart pounded in her chest as she curled into herself, fighting against the overwhelming tide of power. She gasped for air, but the force inside her pushed harder, stronger.

"Aurion!" she cried out, her voice a mixture of desperation and rage. "It hurts! Please! What is this? What's happening to me?"

Aurion's steady figure emerged from the shadows, his gaze never wavering from her as he sat in his compact form next to her. There was something in his eyes—a flicker of sorrow, perhaps, or understanding. But he did not speak immediately. He simply crouched beside her, his presence grounding her even as the wild energy crackled in the air.

"It's the prophecy, Seraphina," he breathed, his voice low, almost too calm for the storm she was enduring. "The prophecy was correct. This power is yours, but it's controlled through your feelings. And you… you've unlocked something with Kade."

Her breath hitched at the mention of his name. She shook her head, struggling to focus on his words. What Prophecy? What did he mean? "I-I don't understand. What did I do?"

Aurion's eyes softened, but his voice remained firm. "Your emotions—your grief, your love, your anger—they feed the power. When you helped Kade, when you let that moment of you into him, it awakened this." He gestured around them, as if the forest itself could explain what was happening to her. "You used your emotions and power on him, Seraphina.

And now the magic is fully awake. This is the price."

She gasped, her hands clutching at her chest as if she could still the storm within. "I didn't mean it... I couldn't control it. I didn't know..."

Aurion's expression hardened, though there was still a trace of sympathy in his eyes. "It's not about meaning it. The power is always there — waiting for the right moment. And Kade was the catalyst. His presence, his connection to you, pulled it to the surface."

Her mind reeled as she tried to process his words. "So this... this curse I've carried, this... magic, is my fault?" The shame was overwhelming, bitter as it swirled with the pain inside her. She had tried so hard to push it away, to keep it buried, but now it was out of her control. "I can't—"

"No." Aurion's voice was sharp, cutting through her spiralling thoughts. "This was always a part of you, Seraphina. It was never about control. It was always about the cost. And now that you've tapped into it fully, you'll have to live with it. Whether or not you like it."

Her chest constricted as she heard the finality of his words. She had been so desperate to understand, to fix things with Kade, but now she was just here—broken and unravelling.

The power within her surged again, louder, darker. She clenched her fists, trying to hold on to herself, but she could feel the cracks spreading, the walls she had fought so hard to build crumbling around her.

Aurion stood up, his gaze still steady as he looked at her, unyielding. "You wanted to protect him, but this power—your connection to him—will be your greatest undoing unless you master it."

"I don't want this," she whispered, tears slipping down her cheeks as she crumbled forward, her hands splayed against the earth, desperate for something to hold on to. "I don't want to hurt anyone."

"Then you must learn to control it."

Aurion's voice was soft but unyielding, like the quiet edge of a blade. "There is no going back. You must make a choice. None of us can make it for you."

He hesitated, his gaze flicking toward the tree line, then back to her. "I'll tell the others you need space. They'll come looking if I don't. But I won't be far."

He studied her for a moment longer, the flicker of concern in his golden eyes betraying just how deeply he cared. "They don't need to see this, do they?" he added gently. "You don't want them to."

She shook her head once, slowly and broken. No words, just the quiet surrender of a nod.

Aurion reached out, placing a hand on her shoulder—a grounding weight, warm and steady. "You're not alone, Seraphina. Not really. But for now... I understand."

With those last words, he stepped back, fading into the shadows without another sound.

Then she was alone.

Alone with the storm rising in her blood.

Seraphina's mind was a tempest, a maelstrom of magic and emotion threatening to rip her apart. Power surged through her veins—ancient, wild, merciless. Each heartbeat sent another wave crashing against the fragile dam of her will. It felt as if fire was running through her veins.

I can't... I can't do this...

She stumbled, gasping for air as her knees hit the earth. The forest pressed in—alive, sentient, whispering in a tongue older than time. It didn't offer comfort. It demanded surrender.

"No... please..." Her voice cracked, the words torn from her throat like fragments of a prayer too late.

The ground trembled beneath her, resonating with the chaos inside. She clutched the dirt, fingernails carving grooves into the earth, desperate for something real to anchor her.

The air shifted. A quiet hum of power, familiar and fierce, wove around her like a tether. Aurion emerged from the shadows, the light catching in his eyes—golden, knowing, unwavering.

He didn't speak at first. He didn't need to.

His magic reached for her, steadying her storm without smothering it. A silent vow. A promise.

"I told the others I'd return," he whispered, laying before her.

She raised her head barely, eyes glassy with unshed tears. "Why?" she whispered. "Why you?"

"Because I *feel* it too." His voice dropped low with something ancient and aching. "Your pain. Your power. It echoes within me."

Seraphina shook her head, breath ragged. "This... this isn't control. This is a curse."

"It's *you*. Raw and unguarded. And I won't leave you to face it alone."

The words hit harder than any spell. Her body trembled—not just from the magic, but from the weight of his belief. Still, fear twisted inside her.

"The prophecy..." she choked out, clinging to the amulet at her neck. "What is it? How much *do* you know?"

Aurion's gaze flickered—just enough to betray the truth she already suspected.

"No one holds all of it," he said. "Only fragments. What is said to be happening to you is only a part of it."

"But *you* know more," she accused, the fire sparking in her voice again.

"You're not ready," he mumbled, his minor form coming closer. "And I won't let it break you."

"I'm already breaking," she whispered.

Then came the snap.

A surge of power erupted from her chest, wild and uncontrollable—a pulse that tore through the clearing, shaking the trees and ripping through the air like a scream turned to magic. Aurion braced himself, shielding her with a wordless spell, but even he staggered under the force of it.

Seraphina cried out, clutching at her chest, her body alight with energy too vast for one soul to bear. "Aurion—please!" she gasped.

He caught her as she collapsed, his magic entwining with hers to soften the fall. But her vision was already blurring, the edges of the world darkening.

"Stay with me," he said, voice thick with fear.

Her fingers curled around his compact form as he lay next to her head, her lips parting to speak—but no words came.

And the last thing she heard before the darkness claimed her was his voice, broken and soft.

"Seraphina…"

Seraphina floated through the void, weightless in the dark. She felt distant, as if she had left her body behind. Only thought remained—fragmented, flickering.

But something shifted.

The surrounding shadows pulled back like curtains, revealing a battlefield scorched by flame and sorrow. Bodies littered the ground. Smoke curled through the air, thick with blood and magic. At the centre of the chaos stood a woman—tall, fierce, her silhouette ablaze.

Dark fibre shimmered like molten obsidian, wings of darkness and ember fanned behind her, casting firelight across the ruined earth. Her sword carved through the air with grace and fury.

Seraphina's breath caught.

Nyx.

The warrior of legend, the original Nyx, Seraphina had seen statues of her. The name Kade had teased her with—but this wasn't a jest. It wasn't a myth. This was *real*—a truth blooming through her blood.

Nyx fought beside a man cloaked in dusk and silver. His movements were elegant, dangerous. Power pulsed from him like a silent storm. His silver hair streamed behind him like starlight dragged through shadow. His face turned—

And something *struck* Seraphina in the chest.

She *knew* him.

Somehow. Somewhere.

Before recognition could take hold, before the past could catch up, a chorus of unnatural voices cracked the vision like glass.

The gods had arrived.

Their presence thundered like the weight of dying stars. Voices—dozens layered and dissonant—spoke in tones meant for mountains and time, not for mortal ears.

"The blade returns…"

"Born of shadow… shaped in starlight…"

"She must wield it…"

"She must fall like the others…"

"She will rise…"

"It has saved the world…"

"And destroyed it."

And there it was—suspended in the darkness before her.

The sword.

It hovered, as though cradled by the void itself. Worn midnight blue leather, darkened by age and memory, wrapped the hilt. Ancient symbols— etched in silver and forgotten tongues—shifted and slid across the blade's surface like liquid whispers.

The cross-guard arched outward like wings: one side sleek and solid, like sharpened moonlight; the other fractured, drifting into mist as if caught between forms. Blacker than absence, the blade itself was a void consuming all light, yet threaded within were veins of silver starlight, pulsing softly like breath in the dark.

The pommel held a gemstone the colour of collapsed galaxies—obsidian so deep it reflected nothing, not even her.

The sword felt *alive*.

It *watched* her.

A chill rippled down her spine, but she stepped closer, drawn by a gravity beyond magic. The whispers grew louder.

"It knows her…"

"She has worn this soul before…"

"The cycle turns again…"

A final voice cut through like a blade of its own.

"Take it, and the last seal will break. Your transformation is complete."

Her hand trembled as she reached out—drawn by something ancient, something already *inside* her. The moment her fingers closed around the hilt, the world shattered.

Power erupted through her like wildfire and starlight.

Magic spiralled beneath her skin, foreign and familiar all at once. Her body convulsed as light poured from her veins. Behind her, something *unfolded*—a shimmer, a flicker of heat and form.

A wing.

Not flame, not shadow—something in between. It flared once, then vanished.

Seraphina collapsed to her knees, shaking, breath torn from her lungs.

A voice, soft and real, called out to her through the void.

"Seraphina."

She turned. There—glowing softly in the haze of the in-between—stood her mother.

Not a dream. Not a memory conjured by grief.

Her.

Time slipped sideways. Her breath caught in her chest like a wound.

She had imagined this moment so many times in the dark—begging for it in sleepless nights, in bloodstained battles, in the quiet between wars. Ached for her mother's embrace. Ached for forgiveness, she never knew how to ask for it .

Her lips parted, but the words lodged in her throat. The pain swelled too fast.

"I…" Her voice cracked. "Mother… I didn't know. I didn't know what would happen. I never meant for—Alexis—"

The name fractured something inside her, and she broke.

Her mother stepped forward, not hesitating, not judging or punishing. She cupped Seraphina's face with both hands—warm, gentle, real—and Seraphina collapsed into her touch, sobbing like a child who had finally come home after walking through hell.

She couldn't stop.

Years of grief, of exile, of failure—all of it poured out in tears that soaked her mother's shoulder. Seraphina clutched at her as if letting go would unmake the fragile peace between them.

"I should've known. I thought you'd hate me. I

hated *me*. I lost *everything*…"

Her mother shushed her softly, rocking her as she once did in another lifetime.

"I know, my heart," she whispered. "I never blamed you. Not then. Not now. What happened… was never yours to carry alone."

Seraphina shook her head. "But it *was*. I was supposed to protect you. It was my responsibility to stop it. I—"

"You were a girl who had to become a weapon too soon," her mother breathed. "You did what you thought was right. That doesn't make you wrong. It makes you *human*."

The words cracked her open.

For the first time in years, Seraphina allowed herself to be held without guilt gnawing at her bones. For the first time, she let herself mourn—not just Alexis, not just the kingdom, but *herself*. The version of her that had died the day the world shattered.

Her mother kissed her forehead, grounding her in the storm still unravelling inside.

"It was never intended for you to understand it all at once," she murmured. "The prophecy wasn't designed to be a chain. It's a path. One you walk piece by piece, with fire and love and loss."

Seraphina's gaze drifted downward—to the blade still pulsing in her grip.

It was heavy now. Heavier than metal. Heavy with truth.

"Then why me?" she asked, her voice shaking. "Why this power? Why *this* fate?"

Her mother's smile was soft, but her eyes glistened. "Because the world doesn't need a saviour," she said. "It needs *you*. A person familiar with heartbreak. Someone who fights, even when her hands are trembling. Someone who can destroy… but protects."

She reached out, brushing a strand of hair from Seraphina's face.

"I can't give you the whole truth. Not yet. You must find the fragments yourself—in blood, in fire, in time. But this much I know…"

Her form faded, like starlight unravelling.

"You've claimed your destiny now," she said, voice steady even as the surrounding light dimmed. "No one—not even the gods—can interfere anymore."

Panic rushed through Seraphina's chest.

"Wait," she whispered. "Don't go. Please—stay just a little longer. I need you."

Her mother's fading hand pressed against her heart one last time.

"I've always been with you, Sera. I always will be."

Her voice lingered like a lullaby and a goodbye all at once.

"You are no longer who you were. You are who the world has been waiting for."

Seraphina collapsed to her knees, the void around her empty once more.

The blade hummed in her palm. The gods had gone silent.

She stood, breath shaking, heart cracked wide open, sorrow and fire intertwining in her blood.

She was alone. Changed. Nyx.

Then—Darkness.

Chapter 24

When Seraphina awoke, the world felt... different. The wind whispered through the trees, brushing against her skin like a lover's touch, carrying the scent of damp earth and the promise of dawn. The first rays of sunlight bled through the canopy, warm against her aching body, but the pain was distant—drowned beneath the overwhelming sense of something more. Something vast.

Her head throbbed, each heartbeat reverberating like a war drum in her skull, and the memory of last night crashed into her mind like a tidal wave. She sucked in a sharp breath, gripping her head, as if she could hold herself together before she splintered apart entirely. Her thoughts ran with everything that happened; her heart broke at the memory of her mother. Seraphina choked on the sob that threatened to break.

Well, my little human has finally come into her power.

Aurion's voice slithered into her mind, richer, heavier—no longer the sharp, familiar tone of her ever-judgemental companion. It was deeper now, laced with something ancient. Something vast.

Come. Look at yourself.

His huff stirred the air beside her, but it was wrong—hotter, thicker, filled with a weight that made her skin prickle. A rolling breath of steam curled around her, and her stomach twisted. That wasn't right. That wasn't *him*.

Her eyes snapped open.

The creature beside her was *not* the small, sharp-tongued dragon she had known. This was something greater. A towering beast, obsidian scales shimmering like liquid night, shifted under the morning light with a brilliance that swallowed the world whole. Power radiated from him— vast, making the very air tremble.

She scrambled back, heart hammering against her ribs. "Aurion?"

The dragon—*Aurion*—tilted his massive head, the molten gold gaze locking onto hers.

I watched over you. I protected you. You did well, little one. His voice curled through her mind, thick with something almost... reverent. *The sword chose you. You did not dream it.*

Seraphina's breath hitched. A sword. A memory of something ancient, a force calling her name in the darkness. She shuddered, fingers digging into the earth to ground herself.

Slowly, hesitantly, she pushed herself to her feet. Aurion was massive— *bigger than Vaelrik*—his presence eclipsing the surrounding space. "How the hell are you *so big?*"

Aurion exhaled, a plume of smoke curling from his nostrils. *I shall explain later. First, you must look at yourself.* His voice was a command, laced with something unreadable. *You have changed, and you have obtained your true power.*

She swallowed, the weight of his words pressing against her ribs. Slowly, she stepped toward the stream, the cool breeze licking against her skin. When she looked down—she stopped breathing.

The woman staring back at her was... *otherworldly.*

Her ebony hair shimmered in the early light, strands of silver weaving through it like living stardust—shifting and swaying as if caught between this world and another, suspended in magic. Each glimmering thread curled with purpose, not age, but transformation.

Across her skin, delicate runes glowed faintly, as though the stars themselves had whispered secrets into her flesh. Intricate patterns stretched along her arms, elegant and ancient. Some spiralled with curling energy; others cut sharp like warnings etched by time itself. She didn't know what they meant—only that they pulsed with the same rhythm as the blade beside her.

But it was her eyes that stilled her breath.

No longer lake-blue that had once reflected the warmth of sunlit days.

Now they burned with a luminous green—deep, unending, the colour of forest shadows and celestial storms. Power pooled within them, endless and terrifying. Like they had always belonged to something more.

She sucked in a sharp breath. "Gods," she whispered. "Is that... me?"

Aurion rumbled beside her, an indistinct sound thick with pride and mischief.

No, it's Vaelrik.

She shot him a glare over her shoulder. "Oh, hilarious. Did your sense of humour grow with your wingspan?"

He only preened, wings rustling behind him like thunder.

You have done well, he said, voice more gentle now.

But Seraphina didn't hear him.

Her gaze dropped back to the water, to the reflection—her reflection—and something inside her tightened. Not in fear. Not even a surprise.

It was recognition.

This wasn't someone new. It wasn't even a rebirth. The mask peeled away, and it revealed what had always been hidden underneath—the part of her buried by duty, sorrow, and war.

She reached up slowly, fingers brushing the silver threaded through her hair, then trailing the runes on her forearm. She blinked, and in her mind, she saw the woman—the warrior—she had glimpsed on the battlefield earlier. Nyx. The original Nyx.

They shared the same rune. The same storm running beneath their skin.

"Aurion..." she murmured, unsettled. "I—I saw her. The one from before. The original Nyx. And these marks... she had them too." Her voice faltered. "Why do I look like her?"

The great dragon tilted his head.

241

Because destiny works in echoes, Seraphina. And gods work in mysteries. Some paths must return to their beginnings to find their end.

She stared at him. "Wow. That's vague even for you."

He gave a satisfied huff.

You asked a question you weren't ready to hear answered.

She groaned, rubbing her temple. "Why is everyone suddenly speaking in riddles and fate lines? Can't someone just say, 'Hey, you're turning into a divine echo of an ancient warrior goddess, go fetch some ruins and save the world'?"

Aurion's silence was maddeningly smug.

She turned away, jaw clenched, and her gaze fell to the blade at her feet.

It pulsed with quiet power, humming low like a lullaby and a warning. Etched into its surface were the same runes now inscribed on her arms, as if they had grown from it—or it from her. When she picked it up, the metal was cool, and yet... *familiar.*

It felt like slipping into a dream half-remembered.

Like coming home to a place she'd never seen.

Yet... unease twisted in her gut. The blade was still. Too knowing.

Its whispers curled around her mind in broken echoes. Faint voices. Some praising the blade as salvation; others damned it as the world's undoing.

It has saved empires.

It has bled stars.

It has ended, gods.

It will never be clean again.

A shiver ran through her as she tightened her grip. The blade felt alive, watching her. Waiting.

She turned to Aurion. "When did you get so big?" she asked, changing the subject before she unravelled further. She gave the blade a few swings, testing the weight as she waited for his response.

He blinked slowly.

I am a reflection of what you need. Your power strengthens mine. When you blacked out, you willed me into something greater. Probably out of survival.

I shall return to my smaller form when you stop swinging that thing like a madwoman.

She blinked, incredulous. "That's rude."

Yet it is true, he countered.

A ghost of a smile touched her lips. As she sheathed the blade with slow reverence, the weight of it pressing into her hip like a second spine. It was more than a weapon—it was a key, and somewhere out there, the lock waited.

She rolled her shoulders, the mantle of power settling over her like heavy silk. It didn't quite fit yet, but it would.

For now, the ache in her heart remained. The lingering warmth of her mother's touch. The sting of truths half-given.

Her reflection stared back, not as the girl who had run from fire...

...but as the one who had risen through it.

She turned to Aurion.

"We'd better get back to camp," she breathed.

He nodded.

The journey back to camp was quieter than Seraphina expected — but it wasn't silent. It was awareness.

Every sound, every flicker of light through the trees, every breath of wind brushing her skin—it was like stepping into a world reborn. She experienced heightened senses, as if she had lifted the veil between herself and the earth. Each footfall against the mossy ground was sharper, more grounded. Every inhale was a breath of clarity. Whether it was the magic humming beneath her skin or the unfamiliar yet intimate weight of destiny settling into her bones, she couldn't tell. But the world looked different now. Clearer. Brighter. Sharper.

Aurion moved beside her, silent but not unseen. His towering form cut through the forest like a phantom of power, his wings folded tight against his scaled back. Even in his stillness, his presence radiated strength and a deep, quiet vigilance. His scales shimmered faintly, catching threads of sunlight that filtered down between ancient branches, and his massive paws barely disturbed the earth. It was as though he were part of it.

When the scent of smoke reached her nose—char and spice and warm earth—Seraphina paused. Her heart gave a strange flutter. The distant murmur of voices filtered through the trees like ghosts from another life. She exhaled a long, steadying breath and stepped into the soft glow of firelight.

The camp came into view like a memory sharpened by time.

Vaelrik was the first to look up. He stilled mid-motion, eyes narrowing as they landed on her. He didn't move for a heartbeat. Then his gaze swept over her slowly—intensely—cataloguing every detail. Silver runes traced her arms and collarbones. The shimmer in her dark hair, now threaded with silver that sparkled like stars. The subtle shift in her aura, the weight of something older and more immense than the forest surrounding them.

He saw her eyes. That was when his breath caught.

A crooked smirk pulled at the corner of his mouth. "Hell," he muttered, his voice laced with something between reverence and mischief. "You look like you walked through the void and came back with its heart in your hands."

He prowled forward, his movements smooth and predatory. His eyes never left her, gleaming with an unmistakable edge of admiration—and something else. Hunger, perhaps. Respect. Fear. Maybe all of it.

"Well, well," he drawled, cocking his head. "The storm rises."

Seraphina rolled her eyes, the motion automatic, though she felt his gaze like the brush of fire against skin. "Subtle as ever, Vael."

He pressed a hand dramatically over his heart, a devilish grin tugging at his mouth. "Subtlety is wasted on you. You crave honesty. And honestly?" He gave her a look that was almost dangerous. "I've seen many things in my time, but I've seen nothing more devastating."

Aurion rumbled a low snort beside her, his tail flicking. "For a dragon, you lay it on thick."

Vaelrik didn't even blink. "Can you blame me?" His grin widened, bold and reckless.

Seraphina tried—and failed—not to smile. "You're lucky I'm too exhausted to roast you properly."

"Lucky's one word for it," he said with a wink.

But before she could fire back, another figure stirred.

Kade.

He rose from where he sat near the fire, shadows clinging to him like loyal dogs. The flames caught in his silver hair, illuminating the sharp lines of his face—cheekbones carved like stone, mouth tense, brows drawn slightly together. He said nothing, not at first. Just watched her. Watched and studied, as if the girl who had walked away into the forest was not the same one who had returned.

She wasn't.

His eyes, usually calm in their stormy stillness, flickered with something she couldn't quite decipher. Recognition. Concern. Awe. Grief?

Then Vaelrik, unable to help himself, sighed loudly.

"Oh, enough with the brooding," he muttered, waving a hand toward Kade. "If you glare any harder, your face might crack."

Kade shot him a sharp glance.

Vaelrik ignored it and turned to Aurion instead. "You know, I had my suspicions earlier, but now I'm sure. You're compensating."

Aurion slowly turned his massive head, eyes narrowing. "Compensating?" he repeated, voice low and dangerous.

Vaelrik grinned, thoroughly enjoying himself. "Size. Power. What, did you bulk up to impress Seraphina?"

Aurion's nostrils flared. "I am the size she willed me to be. Unlike you, lesser wyrmling, I do not pretend."

Vaelrik raised his eyebrows. "So what you're saying is… she likes her dragons *big*."

Seraphina pinched the bridge of her nose, dragging in a breath. "Size does matter," she said, deadpan.

A beat of silence. Then Vaelrik exploded into laughter, nearly doubling over, while Aurion muttered something sharp and ancient under his breath about "insufferable lizard spawn." Even Kade made a sound—half a scoff, half a reluctant exhale of laughter.

For a moment, everything was almost… normal.

* * *

They packed up camp with the same energy lingering in the air—playful, tense, electric. Aurion and Vaelrik kept up their bickering, taking jabs like old rivals who knew exactly how to get under each other's scales. Seraphina moved among them with quiet focus, letting the banter wash over her.

But she wasn't unaware of the eyes that followed her. She felt the weight of Kade's attention before she saw him move.

He approached quietly, his steps soft, deliberate. His fingers wrapped around her wrist.

She turned, a retort on her tongue—but it died the moment he raised his other hand, brushing his knuckles gently along her cheek. His touch was unexpectedly soft, even reverent. His thumb ghosted just beneath her eye, tracing the edge of the glowing green.

His silver eyes locked with hers, and whatever emotion burned behind them—it was raw.

"I'm going to miss the blue," he murmured.

Her breath caught. Her heart stuttered.

Then, a slow smirk tugged at the corner of his mouth, and his thumb lingered for a fraction longer than it should have.

"But green…" his voice dropped to a low, velvet murmur, "just became my favourite colour."

Then he was gone. He stepped back, all that quiet heat vanishing with him as if it had never been.

She was left standing still, pulse hammering in her throat, lips parted and breath shallow.

Chapter 25

The road ahead twisted through a dense, brooding forest—its canopy thick enough to swallow the sky and drape the world in a half-light that made shadows stretch long and lean. The air felt heavy, not with moisture, but with tension—a humming pressure that clung to Seraphina's skin, like something unseen was watching, waiting. She could feel the shift long before she saw it. The trees whispered differently here. The earth itself seemed wary.

They were close.

The Lycan border was undefined by lines or markers—it was a feeling. A subtle shift in scent, like smoke on the wind and blood in the soil. It prickled her senses and raised goosebumps on her arms. Every part of her was on alert—though she told herself it had nothing to do with the lingering heat ghosting over her skin where Kade had touched her.

She stayed ahead of the group deliberately. Her steed moved in a practised rhythm, but her mind wasn't calm. Not with the memory of his fingers on her cheek, the way his voice had curled low and warm around her like silk dipped in fire.

Damn him.

Aurion, in his smaller, feline-draconic form, lounged across her shoulder like a winged sentinel. He stretched lazily, claws kneading against her as he glanced sidelong at her. "You're remarkably quiet."

Seraphina didn't look at him. "Just thinking."

"Dangerous habit," Vaelrik chimed in, his steed's pace matching hers with effortless ease. His long coat swung around his legs, dark as his grin. "For you especially."

She shot him a half-hearted glare. "Shocking that you can identify danger when you live to flirt with it."

He pressed a hand to his heart, mock-wounded. "I flirt with danger because it flirts back, and had I not been flirting, then we would all still be walking instead of riding."

From behind them came the low, gravelled voice she hadn't wanted to hear again just yet. "How long until we reach the border?"

Seraphina didn't turn. She didn't have to. Kade's voice always wrapped around her, cool and deep, like a midnight wind before a storm. She could feel him behind her—the deliberate weight of his silence, the sharpness in his gaze.

Vaelrik glanced over his shoulder. "Not long. They'll smell us before we see them."

Seraphina's brows pinched. "And what happens then?"

"That," Vaelrik said, his playful tone dipping into something darker, "depends entirely on whether they still remember me fondly."

Kade's voice cut through like a blade. "Do they?"

Vaelrik smirked. "That's the wrong question. The right one is: do I care?"

Aurion huffed, wings rustling, as he resettled his balance on her shoulder. "If they are a threat, we will deal with them."

Vaelrik arched a brow. "All of them?"

Aurion's golden eyes gleamed. "I am not as fragile as you."

Vaelrik made an offended sound. "Oh, please. I'm resilient. You've seen me flirt with death and come out smiling."

"Perhaps death is simply too tired to deal with you," Aurion muttered.

"I take that as a compliment."

Seraphina exhaled, letting their banter distract her for a moment. It was a comforting cadence—danger dressed in sarcasm, the rhythm of companions who'd bled and fought and survived together. Even Kade, though he remained quiet, felt tethered to the moment in his own way.

But then the trees thickened again, their trunks growing close like sentinels, and that simple moment fractured.

Vaelrik broke the silence again, as he always did, his voice laced with dry annoyance. "Remind me again why *I* had to be the distraction to get these noble steeds? Don't get me wrong, they have taken days off the journey, but..."

Seraphina didn't miss the playful flicker in his eyes. "Because you're the only one ridiculous enough to flirt with armed bandits and make them *thank* you for the effort."

He tilted his head, looking smug. "Worked, didn't it?"

"Barely," came Kade's voice, sharp and cold. "You almost died."

"Ah, but *almost* is the key word there," Vaelrik said breezily.

The warmth that had temporarily settled in Seraphina's chest faded, replaced by that constant ache she hadn't yet found a name for. Kade's voice stayed with her long after he fell silent. Sharp and steady. Distant and unrelenting.

She didn't turn around, even when she felt his eyes on her—watching. Weighing.

Let him look.

The forest shifted again; the trees closing in like jaws, and the hum of energy in the air grew louder. There was no mistaking it now. They were on Lycan soil.

Vaelrik's gaze swept the terrain. "This still feels like a mistake."

She arched an eyebrow. "That's never stopped you before."

"I'm usually charming enough to survive my mistakes."

"Key word being *usually*," she muttered.

He turned a sharp grin toward her. "Don't pretend my charm hasn't saved *your* ass a time or two."

Her smirk was faint, amused despite herself. "Only because your mouth confused them too much to finish swinging."

His eyes glittered. "Confusion is a tactic; my ancient knowledge is key to my survival."

"Ancient, my ass," she shot back, snorting. "You're barely a hatchling."

"Flattery," Vaelrik purred, "will get you everywhere, *Nyx*."

The name stopped her cold, slipping through her like a ghost.

Nyx.

It didn't feel the same anymore—not after everything. It used to mean shadow, meant strength cloaked in darkness. Now it scraped against something tender inside her, something not yet healed. It was a name Kade used with reverence. A name from before and now also a name that held more meaning than honouring a warrior of legend.

She stiffened the moment passing sharply. Vaelrik didn't notice—he'd already turned forward, humming to himself.

But Seraphina did.

And so did Kade.

Behind them, a sharp sound broke the rhythm of hooves on earth—a noise caught between a scoff and a growl. Kade didn't speak, but his disapproval was tangible in the silence that followed.

Aurion, who had been uncharacteristically quiet until now, finally stirred. His wings gave a subtle twitch, the scales catching a glint of dying sunlight. When he spoke, it was like a thunderclap rolling over the mountains.

"Do you ever stop talking, Vaelrik?" Aurion's deep voice rumbled, the faintest curl of amusement edging his words. "Or is your purpose in this world solely to ruin everyone's mood?"

Vaelrik gave an exaggerated gasp, clasping a hand to his chest. "You wound me, truly. I'm the life of this sorry little party." He shot Aurion a grin, sharp and smug. "At least I bring personality. All you do is brood and flap around like a haunted cathedral gargoyle."

Seraphina snorted. "He's got a point, Aurion. But so do you." She tilted her head toward Vaelrik, her tone light but dry. "You really need to shut up sometimes."

Vaelrik offered her a wink, utterly unbothered. "Ah, Sera, always the voice of reason. I consider it a gift—being this charming."

Kade's voice cut through the banter, cold and clipped like a blade drawn too fast. "If you're all done with the circus act, we've got a mission to focus on."

Vaelrik's golden eyes sparkled with mischief. "A mission?" he gasped, theatrical horror dripping from every word. "And here I thought we were simply out for a scenic ride through these charmingly haunted woods. How dreadfully serious about you."

Seraphina rolled her eyes, her mouth twitching despite herself. "You're almost as irritating as Kade when he's playing the brooding ice princess."

Vaelrik burst into laughter, the sound loud and bright, then darkened with a dangerous edge as he turned to Kade. "Ice Princess. I like it. Has a regal ring to it, don't you think, sweetheart?"

Kade didn't flinch, didn't rise to the bait. His gaze was steel and silence. That alone made Vaelrik's smirk widen.

"Anyway," Vaelrik drawled, shifting his tone back to mocking ease, "maybe we should ask a few more questions about our mysterious dark fae. He's got secrets stacked taller than his ego."

A low growl rumbled from Kade's throat. "You're pushing it."

"I'm always pushing it," Vaelrik replied, smile unfaltering. "That's half the fun. We've got time to be serious when we're all dead."

Seraphina opened her mouth to shut them both up, but then Aurion's voice curled softly through her thoughts, brushing her mind like a whisper of wind.

For someone so old, you're still an angsty little thing.

She blinked, startled.

I'm not angsty.

Come on, Sera, Aurion's mental voice chuckled warmly. *You are. But that's not the issue. You're scared. Admit it.*

Her jaw clenched. *I'm not scared. I'm just... unsure.*

His tone softened. *Unsure about what? You are more than what someone took from you. More than the broken pieces. Stop pretending you're not.*

For a heartbeat, something tight inside her cracked. Aurion's words wrapped around her chest, not comforting—*anchoring*. A rare thing. She swallowed hard.

Then Kade's presence brushed against her thoughts—cool, restrained, familiar. The ache in her chest returned.

They rode on in silence for a time, the forest thickening around them like a closing fist. Twisted trees, dense shadows, and the scent of earth and moss filled the air. Leaves rustled high above, but the underbrush was eerily still.

Kade leaned closer in the saddle, voice barely audible. "The Lycans won't like us passing through their territory."

From behind, Vaelrik gave a dry snort. "Now there's an understatement."

Aurion sighed dramatically. "She has the social finesse of a rabid wyvern. I'll give you that."

Seraphina smirked. "And yet, you still cling to me like a decorative brooch."

Aurion flared his wings in mock offence. "Please. I'm the only reason you haven't died in a spectacularly humiliating way."

He angled his snout toward Vaelrik and added, "Unlike some, who disgrace the entire Draconic legacy with every word they speak."

Vaelrik growled. "Keep talking, lizard, and I'll make boots out of you."

Aurion gasped. "Boots? *Boots?* The *audacity!* I am a creature of refined elegance! You'd be lucky to have my scales grace your sorry fibre."

Vaelrik muttered darkly. "One of these days…"

Aurion waved a claw, unconcerned. "Yes, yes, we've heard it all before. Let me know when it's *this* day."

Seraphina rolled her eyes as they bickered, but her focus sharpened—because Kade's had.

He scanned the trees with a predator's gaze. "We're being watched," he murmured.

She didn't tense. Didn't give away the sudden spark in her blood. She'd felt it too—the sensation crawling over her skin like an icy breath, the stillness of prey before a strike.

Vaelrik's voice dropped, laced with danger. "Let them watch. Maybe they'll learn something."

Aurion groaned in her mind. *Gods, even his ego has an ego.*

The air exploded into chaos as shapes burst from the trees—fast, savage, a blur of snarling fur and gleaming fangs. Horses screamed and reared, hooves crashing against the earth. The Lycans had come, and they brought death with them.

Seraphina reacted instantly. She hauled on the reins, swung down from her saddle in one fluid motion. As her boots struck the ground, the world seemed to shift.

Time slowed.

The Lycans paused—just for a breath. They could *feel* her. The steel in her bones. The storm in her blood.

The first lunged—massive, snarling, all teeth and muscle. Seraphina spun, blades flashing like silver lightning. Her dagger found flesh—sank deep—and the beast howled, staggering back. Another was already on her.

Vaelrik streaked into the fray, all fire and fury. His golden eyes glowed with violent delight. His blade sang a deadly tune through the night. "Oh well, more things trying to kill us. It's been *hours.*"

Aurion exploded into his true form, a massive black-scaled dragon that tore through the canopy with a thunderous roar. Wind blasted outward as his wings snapped open, sending Lycans tumbling like leaves.

Kade moved in near silence, twin daggers flashing like fangs. He was a shadow slipping through shadows, efficient and brutal. Seraphina felt him—a cold, steady pulse of power near her, a grounding presence amid the chaos.

More Lycans surged forward, teeth bared and claws ready.

They were testing them.

And Seraphina was ready to answer.

Seraphina met the gaze of the largest one—a hulking beast cloaked in silver-streaked fur, its frame carved from muscle and war, its body a tapestry of old battles. Scars crisscrossed its broad chest like history written in flesh. The leader. Its yellow eyes locked onto hers, glowing with intelligence and menace. It bared its fangs—not in a mindless snarl, but in a deliberate show of power. A warning.

Seraphina's grip tightened on her twin blades, the leather of her gloves creaking under the strain. "They're not attacking outright."

"Yet," Kade murmured, stepping subtly in front of her, the tension in his stance coiled tight as a drawn bow. "They want something."

Vaelrik exhaled sharply, flicking blood from his blade with a flourish. "Let me guess. Our charming company?" His gaze flicked to Aurion, who loomed behind them in his full dragon form, wings arched and muscles taut with anticipation.

The lead Lycan took a deliberate step forward. When it spoke, its voice crawled into their minds like gravel scraping over stone. *"You walk on forbidden land."*

Seraphina tilted her head, masking her wariness behind a calm veneer. "We're not here to pick a fight."

"That so?" The Lycan's lips curled into a grim smile, revealing fangs meant to tear, not threaten. *"Then why do I smell death on you?"*

Vaelrik let out an exaggerated sigh. "Well, that's just rude."

Kade didn't rise to the bait. His tone was cold steel. "We seek only a safe passage through the woods. That's all."

The Lycan leader rumbled with amusement, a sound like thunder rolling over broken ground. *"Trouble found you, Dark Fae."*

Seraphina didn't miss the way Kade's jaw tightened—or the way the surrounding Lycans leaned in at those words, eyes gleaming with something more than hunger.

Recognition.

She stepped forward, blades low but ready, and redirected their focus to her. "Let us pass, and there'll be no need for more bloodshed tonight."

The leader's nostrils flared. *"Brave words, little warrior."* Then its gaze slid past her, settling like a predator's weight on Kade. Something darker passed over its face. *"But the fae prince doesn't belong here. And we do not grant sanctuary to the hunted."*

An icy chill rippled through Seraphina's spine like frost spreading across glass.

Kade stood silent, unreadable—but the sharp edge of his stillness was all she needed to know.

The Lycans weren't just patrolling territory.

They were here for him.

Seraphina took a step forward, voice unwavering. "Then you leave us no choice."

The leader's grin stretched wider, savage and eager. "I had hoped you would say that."

Chapter 26

Muscles tensed. Claws dug into the earth. The Lycans poised to strike—but just as the air thickened with the promise of violence, a movement rippled through the pack.

A massive Lycan with deep brown fur stepped forward, slowing as his nostrils flared. His eyes fixed on Seraphina—not with bloodlust, but something more jarring.

Recognition.

He shifted without warning, bones snapping, and skin folding as fur receded into flesh. Where once stood a beast, now towered a man, bare-chested and panting from the shift. His hair was dark and grizzled at the temples; his face was weathered but familiar. Too familiar.

"You…" he rasped, his voice like gravel soaked in disbelief. "You look just like him."

Her breath caught.

Him.

A rush of half-forgotten images surged—flickers from another life, smudged by time and loss. A man laughing beside her father, lifting her into the air like she weighed nothing. Hazel eyes that crinkled with joy. Salt-and-pepper hair that fell into his eyes no matter how he pushed it back. Olive skin like sun-warmed earth. Tall. Gentle.

"Uncle Dylan?" Her voice broke on the name.

His face lit up like dawn breaking after a decade of storm. "By the gods, Sera, look at you," he murmured, stepping closer. His voice cracked with emotion. "I never thought—"

Before she could react, his arms were around her, fierce and trembling. She froze, then melted into his embrace.

For the first time in years, she felt small. Safe.

He smelled of pine bark and wind-swept stone. Like home.

She squeezed her eyes shut, grounding herself in the sensation.

"You used to chase after me through the palace halls," he whispered, his voice thick. "Called me Dyl-Dyl. Drove your father mad that you never followed protocol."

A teary laugh escaped her. "You snuck me sweets when he wasn't looking."

He pulled back just enough to hold her at arm's length, his hands trembling as they cradled her shoulders. "I thought I'd lost you, too."

She saw it in his eyes—the shadow of grief that still haunted him.

A low huff drew their attention. The Lycan Alpha—still in his towering, furred form—stepped forward. His molten gaze flicked between Dylan and Seraphina. "This is the one you were waiting for all these years?" His voice rumbled through the clearing like distant thunder.

Dylan nodded once, firm and proud. "She's blood. She's pack."

The Alpha's ears twitched. Then he gave a slight bow of his head—lesser than a full submission, but more than respect. He declared, "The hunted are not hunted here." His gaze fell on Kade, then on the others. "So long as the fae prince walks with the lost princess... and the niece of Dylan... we will not spill their blood."

The tension in the air fractured like a snapped bowstring. The Lycans behind him lowered their stances. One even exhaled what sounded like relief.

Then, to Seraphina's astonishment, the Alpha turned to her and inclined his head. "You have my apologies, Princess. This land has long been silent without your blood to stir it."

Seraphina blinked, stunned, the weight of the moment catching up to her. She glanced at Kade—whose brow furrowed at the word "princess"—then at Vaelrik, who was already muttering something about needing a drink.

Dylan squeezed her shoulder. "They won't harm you," he whispered. "Not you. Not anyone who walks with you."

Something inside her—something ancient, bone-deep—settled into place. For the first time in a long time, Seraphina wasn't just surviving.

She was home.

But the moment fractured with the sharp edge of sarcasm.

"Well, isn't this just *heartwarming*," Vaelrik drawled, arms crossed and voice oozing sarcasm. "But forgive me if I'm having trouble getting misty-eyed over the family reunion—considering someone once called your kid a *runt* and I was almost killed for it."

He tilted his head with a slow, deliberate smirk, eyes glittering with challenge. "That jog your ancient memory, old man?"

Dylan scowled at Vaelrik. "I almost forgot how frustratingly arrogant you were, Vaelrik."

The word hit like a blade through her ribs. *Runt.*

Her breath hitched—and with it, a memory burst forth, uninvited and raw.

She was small. Barely five. Laughing as she chased after a boy with messy brown curls and sea green-glass eyes that sparkled like the ocean after rain.

Kai.

He had always been faster than her, his Lycan blood giving him an unfair advantage, but that never stopped her from trying.

"You're slow, Sera!" he had laughed, dodging her reach.

"Am not!" she had pouted, hands on her hips.

Kai had grinned, fangs peeking through, before tugging on her braid and taking off again. "Catch me, then!"

She had chased him through the palace gardens, tackling him to the ground when he finally let her win. They had rolled in the grass, breathless with laughter, before he had flopped onto his back, staring at the sky.

"One day, I'll be strong enough to protect everyone," he had said, voice full of childish certainty.

She had plopped down beside him, frowning. "You don't need to. I'll do it."

Kai had turned his head, studying her with those bright green eyes. Then he had smiled. "Then I'll protect you while you protect them."

The memory faded, leaving her with the ghost of his voice and the ache of time lost.

Her throat felt tight when she finally spoke. "Kai was never a runt."

Dylan's green gaze snapped to Vaelrik with dangerous amusement. "You mean the runt who's now one of the strongest warriors in our ranks? And yes, I remember you and everything you did and everyone you hurt, Vaelrik." Dylan gave a pointed look.

Vaelrik's smirk faltered. "Ah."

A slow, dangerous grin spread across Dylan's face. "That same runt who can likely break every bone in your body?"

Aurion choked on a laugh. "Oh, this is delightful."

Even Kade let out a quiet huff of amusement as Vaelrik scowled. "I stand by my statement."

Dylan cracked his knuckles. "Good. He'll be happy to prove you wrong."

The tension broke as laughter rippled through the group—at Vaelrik's expense.

Even Seraphina couldn't stop the grin tugging at her lips.

Vaelrik sighed, rubbing his temples. "I hate all of you."

The levity was brief—but it was enough.

The Alpha had taken Dylan's word as law. With a single nod, stiff with grudging respect, he turned and vanished into the trees, his pack melting away behind him like smoke. They would wait at the stronghold, prepare for their arrival—Seraphina's presence earning them an unexpected reprieve.

But even before the quiet could settle, before Seraphina could ask — hanging in Dylan's gaze—something shifted.

His expression changed. Something knowing. Something *expectant*.

Then—chaos.

The shadows exploded.

A blur of silver and black tore through the clearing, too fast to track, too fast to think.

Vaelrik's snarl cracked the silence like a whip, his blade already half-raised. Kade moved in sync beside him, a dagger blinking into his palm as his eyes went cold, silver sharpened into something feral.

Only Aurion remained still, his dragon form coiled but calm—watching.

But Seraphina had no time to react.

No warning. No breath.

Something slammed into her chest like a battering ram, and she was airborne—weightless for a heartbeat—before the ground surged up to meet her in a jarring, breath-stealing impact. The world tilted. The sky spun.

Then—*warmth.*

Fur, heavy, silken, pressed flush against her chest. A heartbeat thundered against hers, wild and familiar. Clawed paws pinned her down—but there was no pain, no violence. Only… recognition.

Her fingers curled instinctively into thick, silver-black fur, heart lurching as memory rose from the depths like a storm. A muzzle burrowed into the crook of her neck, breath hot with wolf-scent—then a whimper. High-pitched. Desperate. *Childlike.*

Nuzzling.

The massive Lycan—this beast who should have been a threat, a stranger—was *nuzzling* her like a lost pup reunited with home.

Emotion punched through her like lightning.

A laugh broke from her chest, breathless, cracked, and bright with disbelief.

"Kai," she gasped, voice shaking under the weight of it all. *"Kai."*

At her voice, the wolf gave an excited huff, his tail—his damn tail—wagging in rapid, unchecked glee. He pulled back just enough for her to see those eyes.

Those same green eyes.

She remembered them—burning with mischief, glowing with warmth, with trouble. With promises made beneath the sun-dappled leaves of the palace gardens.

Just as effortlessly as he had tackled her, the massive Lycan's form shifted.

The fur melted away, folding into bronze skin, battle-worn but strong. Where a beast had stood, a man remained—taller, broader, his wild brown curls tousled from the wind, framing a face she hadn't seen in twelve years.

He was older now. Harder.

A thousand untold stories etched into the scars on his arms, the roughness of his hands. But the grin?

The grin was the same.

"Gods above," Seraphina breathed. "You grew."

Kai smirked, shameless and sharp. "That's usually what happens in twelve years, Sera."

Her heart clenched painfully at the sound of his voice. Familiar yet different—deeper, richer, carrying a weight it hadn't before.

Before she could gather herself, he reached down and grabbed her arms, hauling her to her feet like she weighed nothing.

Dylan chuckled, arms crossed, as he watched the scene unfold. "Didn't even give her a chance to stand before launching at her, huh?"

Kai grinned, unrepentant. "I was patient. For all of five minutes." His green gaze flickered back to Seraphina, drinking in every detail like he was trying to convince himself she was real. "You really think I was going to wait to see my favourite troublemaker after you sent out a mind link about her?"

Her throat tightened at his words.

Gods, she had missed him.

From the edge of the clearing, Aurion stirred. Not startled. Not aggressive. Calm, watchful.

Seraphina glanced at him, surprised—then understood.

He hadn't reacted because he *hadn't needed to.*

Their bond—unique and soul-deep—had flared the moment Kai came near her. But instead of alarm, Aurion had felt *recognition*. An echo of connection, of *belonging*.

He had *known* she wasn't in danger.

Vaelrik, of course, didn't miss a beat.

"Well, glad *one* of us knew," he drawled, arms crossed, eyes narrowing at Aurion. "Would've been nice to share that little detail before we all went full overprotective bastard mode."

Aurion gave a soft shrug, almost smugly. "You're the ones who reacted before thinking. I simply... didn't."

Vaelrik scoffed. "Yeah, thanks, Wise One. Next time, *use words.*"

Seraphina didn't laugh—but the corner of her mouth twitched, even as the air stayed heavy between the two men before her. Kai still stood close, eyes flicking between Kade and Aurion like he was mentally measuring his odds—and clearly not liking the answer.

The weight of the moment settled in her chest—warm and aching and terrifying all at once.

A cold, razor-edged presence at her back.

Kade. He hadn't moved.

Hadn't spoken.

But the tension radiating from him was suffocating, a storm barely restrained, swirling just beneath his skin.

His fingers curled around his dagger, grip flexing once before he slowly, deliberately, slid it back into its sheath.

Seraphina turned to meet his gaze.

Black.

Endless, starless black. The same black as when his magic was uncontrolled.

His expression was unreadable, but something dark coiled behind his eyes — something fierce, something possessive, and something she couldn't name.

When he finally spoke, his voice was quiet. Flat.

"Who the hell is this?"

Not a question. A demand.

The surrounding air shifted—light and dark colliding, old bonds brushing against new ones.

Kai blinked at Kade, his simple grin faltering just slightly. A fraction of a second. But Seraphina saw it. And something in her told her this moment—this meeting—was about to change everything.

The moment stretched taut as a bowstring.

Seraphina could feel the heat of Kade's gaze burning into her skin, the barely restrained violence curling at the edges of his presence. Kai, for his part, only cocked his head, green eyes flicking over Kade with something unreadable — assessing, calculating.

Then, with the careless arrogance that only he could pull off, Kai smirked. "I'd ask who you are, but I don't think I care."

Kade's fingers twitched, the veins in his arms tightening like a silent warning.

Seraphina sighed, running a hand through her hair. "Kai, don't."

Kai lifted an eyebrow. "What? I'm just saying—"

"You're being an ass."

He grinned, teeth flashing like a wolf about to bite. "And?"

Kade's eyes narrowed. Shadows flickered at his fingertips before he exhaled sharply and crossed his arms instead, muscles coiled tight.

Dylan, who had been watching with increasing frustration, let out a long-suffering sigh. "Oh, for the love of — do we really have time for this?"

Seraphina shot him a look before turning back to Kade. His jaw was tight, the muscle ticking as he watched Kai with something dangerously close to loathing.

"This," she said, clearing her throat, "is Kai."

Silence.

Nothing in Kade's expression shifted. He was an impenetrable wall of shadow and restraint.

Seraphina pressed on, arms folded over her chest. "He's—" She hesitated. Friend? Family? Ally?

She didn't know how to sum it up.

Kai saved her trouble. "Her childhood best friend. And favourite person in the world, obviously."

Seraphina groaned. "Kai."

He grinned wider. "What? It's true."

Kade exhaled through his nose, slow and measured, like he was mentally debating whether he could kill Kai and get away with it. When he slowly opened his eyes, they were back to his dark grey.

Seraphina elbowed Kai in the ribs—easy, but enough to earn a small grunt. "Behave."

Kai muttered something under his breath about her being no fun before finally—finally—taking a half-step back. It didn't help.

The tension in the air remained suffocating, thick with something unspoken.

Kade finally moved, shifting just slightly to stand beside Seraphina, a deliberate motion—possessive, protective, claiming space without words.

Kai, of course, noticed.

And the bastard smirked.

Seraphina could practically hear the unspoken challenge in the silence that followed.

Dylan groaned, dragging a hand down his face. "Seriously? Are we doing this? Right now?"

Seraphina groaned. "You're not helping."

"Oh, I'm not trying to." Dylan gestured between Kade and Kai with an exasperated wave of his hand. "But if we could avoid the inevitable pissing contest, that would be great. Some of us have actual problems to deal with, like the fact you're here for help in this war, and we have a lot to get through."

Kai snorted, Kade scowled, and Seraphina resigned herself to the absolute disaster that was about to unfold.

The path through the dense forest was familiar, yet every step carried the weight of the past. The scent of damp earth mixed with the crisp bite of the night air, curling around them like ghosts of what had been.

Dylan led the way through the forest, rubbing at his temples like he was already regretting all his life choices.

Seraphina and Kai walked in sync beside each other, hands moving in fluid, practised motions—silent words in the stillness of the trees, slipping back into communication they had developed when they lived in a gossiping court.

Kai: *You're really alive.*

Seraphina: *Apparently. I had my doubts a few times.*

Kai's lips twitched. *Of course you did. You were always attracted to chaos.*

Seraphina: *Says the boy who jumped off the training barracks because he 'thought he could fly'.*

Kai grinned. *I almost made it.*

Seraphina let out a breath—something between amusement and exasperation. It felt good—this, him, their effortless communication slipping back into place like no time had passed.

But Kai's hands slowed. *Tell me about them. The dragons and the fae.*

Her fingers hesitated. *It's... complicated.*

Kai arched a brow. *And that means?*

She sighed before beginning to explain—her capture, Kade's transformation, Vaelrik's unwavering presence, her own growing power. She left nothing out, not from Kai.

When she finished, he huffed out a laugh, shaking his head. *Only you, Sera. Only you could end up with two ridiculously powerful, sexy, brooding warriors and still make a mess of it.*

She scowled, elbowing him. He dodged easily, laughing.

The forest trail was calm. The group? Not so much.

Dylan pinched the bridge of his nose for the third time in five minutes. "Okay, I'm trying to give you a tactical overview of the allied forces at the stronghold, but apparently, it's an open mic night for chaos and emotional instability."

Kai, of course, ignored him entirely. "Do you remember the time we fell into the river after you tried to fight those mercenaries with a broken spoon? Gods, the river drenched you. Stunning, but soaked."

Seraphina gave a long, theatrical groan. "Kai..."

Kade and Vaelrik, as if on cue, tensed as if a storm cloud had rolled in and pitched a tent on their shoulders.

"I'm just saying," Kai continued, smiling far too innocent. "It was a *memorable* day. One of many."

"Someone please kill me," Dylan muttered under his breath.

Kai grinned wider, tilting his head at Vaelrik. "You remember that look, don't you? That 'please, gods, don't let her like him' expression? You're wearing it now."

Vaelrik shot him a tight smile that could have curdled milk. "I remember wanting to strangle you."

"Oh well," Kai said brightly, "so nothing's changed."

Aurion, lounging around Seraphina's shoulders like an elegant scarf, lifted his head with a lazy flick of his tail. "I, for one, am enjoying this extra energy. Adds... spice."

Dylan groaned louder. "Of course you are."

Kade said nothing, his expression unreadable as he stalked just behind them, eyes fixed on Kai like he was calculating how many bones were in his body, and how best to break them.

Seraphina didn't bother to look back. "He's fine. He has stabbed no one. Yet."

Kai shot her a wink. "I'm flattered by your faith."

"I'm reconsidering it," she muttered.

Dylan, walking beside her, was clearly trying to pretend none of this was happening. "You all bicker like an exiled noble court. And I am begging the heavens for silence."

Kai leaned toward him, voice a conspiratorial whisper. "Dad. You poor, sweet man. You act like this is new."

"I've repressed most of my memories from the last time you two were together," Dylan snapped. "And you are not helping."

Vaelrik rolled his shoulders, his tone casual but laced with threat. "You know, I've never really enjoyed reminiscing. Especially about old flames with poor survival instincts."

"See? I *love* reminiscing," Kai countered. "So much passion. So many lessons not learned."

Aurion preened, golden eyes dancing. "Oh, this is delightful. Keep going. I want to see who breaks first."

Seraphina blew out a long breath. "You all know we're walking into a war zone, right?"

"You're only calling it a war zone because Dylan was telling you about the Gala and Allies, and you hate that," Aurion purred.

Kade finally spoke, interrupting Aurion, voice low and dangerous. "If you say one more thing about your *past*, Kai…"

Kai held up both hands, grinning. "I'll behave. For now."

Dylan looked like he was seriously debating walking off into the woods. "I'm regretting every life choice that brought me to this moment."

The journey to the Lycan stronghold—Black Hallow—wasn't supposed to be tense, but Kai had other plans. He had latched onto the opportunity to torment Kade and Vaelrik, and, much to Seraphina's exasperation, he was relentless.

As they neared the stronghold, the air shifted—familiar and grounding. The towering walls came into view, a silent promise of safety. Dylan and Kai's home. A place Seraphina had once known well, years ago, on every visit she attended with her father.

She exhaled slowly. Home. At least for now.

And just as things seemed like they were about to calm down, someone met them at the threshold to inform them the Alpha had planned the welcome gala for that evening.

Chapter 27

Seraphina's heart stilled.

A gala—of course.

She'd barely registered the invitation. But attendance wasn't optional. This wasn't just a celebration or a formality it was a strategy wrapped in silk and diplomacy disguised as wine.

The remaining supernatural factions, the remnants of them, gathered. Rebels, stragglers, outcasts from fallen courts and broken pacts. They had responded to quiet signals, whispered calls carried by shadow and flame. Many had aligned with the Lycan Alpha, who had long held the stronghold as a final sanctuary—a crumbling outpost on the edge of war, and now a last hope for unity.

Seraphina knew exactly what this gala was.

A show of strength. A gathering of fractured powers. An unspoken test.

And for her, it was a chance—perhaps the only one—to address those still undecided. To forge the last bonds. Her goal was to convince the last of the willing that they could still win the war.

She took a breath, slow and deep, forcing the weight of it from her shoulders, at least for now. She would walk into that hall like the warrior they believed her to be, no matter how hollow her bones felt beneath the fibre.

But, gods, she wasn't in the mood to entertain a gala.

Not tonight.

Not with everything burning just behind her eyes.

Aurion, sitting nearby, leaned toward her with a playful smile. "Are you wearing the amulet tonight?" He asked, his tone teasing.

She shook her head firmly. "I won't be wearing it. I won't hear you, not tonight."

A chuckle rumbled from Aurion's chest. "I'm pleased to miss all the love triangle thoughts, then." His voice was teasing but understanding.

Seraphina's lips twitched, a reluctant smile tugging at the corners. "If only you knew how exhausting it is to have to deal with it all."

"I'd rather keep those thoughts to myself, if I were you," Aurion replied smoothly. "Some things are better left unsaid."

Her mind turned back to the evening ahead. She had a war to win, alliances to forge, and... a gala to survive. But the amulet could stay hidden for tonight. She stopped listening to the mess of thoughts swirling around her.

Technically, Dylan had honoured that. But as she stood before the mirror, staring at the sapphire blue creation draped over her body, she realised that somehow, this was worse.

The fabric was sheer—delicate wisps of silk that clung to her curves and shimmered like liquid starlight. It wasn't scandalous—not entirely. There were strategic layers, enough to keep her mostly covered. But the slits running up both legs, the way it dipped scandalously low in the back, the way the bodice hugged her waist before flowing like smoke around her...

This was not a dress meant for battle. This was a dress meant to tempt the gods. She didn't let that stop her from strapping daggers to her thigh sheaths, though. To make matters worse, Dylan had left her a tiara. She scowled, turning the delicate silver piece over in her hands. The Lycans were clearly not letting her escape the title of princess tonight. With a resigned sigh, she set it on her head, adjusting it to sit correctly on top of all the braids that some of the Lycan women had come in to help her with, before stepping out.

Kai was already waiting. He took one look at her and whistled. "Now that is an entrance."

She groaned. "If you say one word—"

Kai smirked. "What? That you look drop-dead gorgeous? That if we weren't already attending a gala in your honour, I'd make them throw another one just to see you in this?"

She rolled her eyes but couldn't fight the amused twitch of her lips.

"Come on, Princess." Kai offered his arm with an exaggerated bow.

She smacked him upside the head before taking it. As they entered the grand hall, all conversation stopped. Seraphina swallowed. *Well, shit.*

The grand hall was alight with golden candlelight and the murmur of tense diplomacy. Ornate banners lined the ceiling, each representing factions still loyal—or at least undecided. Music drifted softly, an undercurrent of elegance masking the sharp eyes and hidden blades.

As Seraphina entered, silence rippled through the room.

Every pair of eyes turned to her.

Her gaze swept across the crowd, trained, calm—until she found them. Kade. Vaelrik.

Kade dressed himself in shadow—black on black, tying his silver hair back; his storm-grey eyes locked onto her like a predator. Vaelrik leaned with casual elegance against the wall, dressed in midnight blue and silver, lips curved in a knowing smirk.

The heat of their stares settled like fire along her spine.

But before she could reach them, Dylan appeared at her side. "You'll have time for your admirers later," he murmured. "Come. There are allies we need to secure."

She nodded, pulse steadying, as she slipped back into her role. The battlefield might be different tonight, but it was one she knew how to navigate.

First, Dylan guided her through the crowd, his movements purposeful, his voice an indistinct murmur of names and allegiances.

They approached the Vampire Delegate, an ancient beauty named Lady Virelle. She stood like a shadow sculpted from velvet and blood, her skin as pale as moonlight, her gown a cascade of crimson that shimmered like spilled wine. Her black eyes glittered like obsidian, sharp and unreadable.

Seraphina was silently grateful for Dylan's thorough briefing earlier that day. He had walked her through the intricate political web, outlining the key players and their demands, the tensions simmering beneath their alliances, and the quiet promises made in darker corners. Without that preparation, she would've walked into this room blind. Now, every movement, every word, was part of a careful choreography. These meetings weren't chance—they had come to speak with *her*.

"You're younger than I expected," Lady Virelle said, her voice smooth as silk and twice as dangerous.

Seraphina inclined her head with a poised smile. "And you're just as intimidating as they warned."

The vampire's lips curled faintly. "Flattery is currency, girl. Do you bring anything of actual value?"

"I bring survival," Seraphina replied. "We've mapped secure forest routes your messengers can use to bypass the eastern blockade. But I need your guards at the northern border. If we hold it, we all stand a chance."

Lady Virelle studied her, fingers drumming on her glass of dark wine, rings glinting like tiny bones. "Perhaps... you're not as naïve as you look."

"And perhaps you're not as cold as they say."

A spark of amusement flickered in the vampire's eyes, just enough to soften the edge. She offered a slow, graceful nod—acknowledgement, if not yet allegiance.

Another figure stepped forward from the watching crowd, drawn by purpose. They didn't need to search for the next conversation.

They were already coming to her.

They moved next to the Seelie Fae Delegate, Lord Thalaniel, who looked as if someone had carved him from gold and judgement. His robes shimmered like sunlight on ice, and his wings—faintly visible in the veil between realms—quivered with disdain as his gaze slid past Seraphina and locked onto Kade, still watching from across the hall.

"You travel with darkness," Thalaniel said, each word sharp and slow, as though they tasted sour on his tongue. "That will stain your cause."

Seraphina's jaw clenched. Heat flared behind her eyes—not from insult to herself, but from the sheer gall of dismissing Kade like that. After everything he'd done. After everything, he'd survived. Her spine stiffened, chin lifting with dangerous calm.

"I travel with loyalty," she said. "Loyalty doesn't ask for light or dark. It just endures."

Thalaniel's nostrils flared. His beauty was sculptural—divine even—but his expression soured into something petty. "He is Unseelie filth."

Seraphina saw red for half a second. The fury that snapped chains. Her reply came fast, low, and lethal. "And you're a fool if you think bloodlines win wars. Magic doesn't care how pretty it looks when it dies."

Dylan cleared his throat beside her, quietly horrified.

Thalaniel's glare could've frozen the wine in her glass, but he said nothing. He didn't walk away. He didn't say no.

That was a start.

As Thalaniel turned his head ever so slightly—enough to signal the end of the exchange—Seraphina exhaled slowly, forcing the fire back into its cage.

Maker's breath, she thought. He *got under my skin faster than a blade.*

She hadn't come here to be provoked. And yet all it took was a polished insult aimed at Kade, and she was ready to burn bridges.

Get it together, she told herself. *You're not here to be right. You're here to win.*

And as the next figure approached—drawn, not summoned—Seraphina lifted her chin again, gaze steady, already bracing for the next game of teeth and promises.

A man cloaked in midnight blue stopped before them, and Seraphina steeled herself. Her fury from the encounter with Thalaniel still simmered just beneath her skin, but she pushed it down, donning her practised mask once more.

Smoke curled from the Warlock Ambassador's sleeves, tendrils of mist drifting with each breath like the exhale of an old, smouldering world. The scent of ozone clung to him, sharp and electric, threaded with something older—dusty spell books and burned offerings. Runes shimmered across his hands like veins of living lightning, each pulse a whisper of power waiting to be loosed.

Master Irevon. Mysterious. Mercurial. And notoriously unimpressed.

Seraphina opened her mouth to greet him—but he spoke first, his voice low and crackling with purpose.

"I don't want a kingdom of splintered victories," he said. "Not vampires in the east, fae in the trees, mortals rebuilding dirt roads, while dragons rot in the skies. If we survive this, we do it as one. Or we don't do it at all."

Seraphina blinked. Straight to the point, then.

Unity. Not just alliance. Not just tolerance. Actual unity. A future not made of uneasy truces, but of something rebuilt together.

She'd expected demands. Leverage. Maybe even a veiled threat. But not hope wrapped in smoke and storm.

Still, she couldn't help herself.

"Bold of you," she said drily, "to assume magic will let us all hold hands and sing after it's finished tearing us apart."

That stopped him. A breath. Then a sharp, unexpected laugh burst from his chest—genuine and wild.

Dylan nearly choked on the air beside her, eyes flicking between them. Apparently, Master Irevon did not laugh often.

Irevon's grin curled like flame catching dry wood. "Maybe you're not the diplomat they warned me about."

"I'm definitely not," Seraphina replied, lips twitching. "But I'm the one who's still standing."

He considered her, the mirth fading into something fiercer. Approval, maybe. Or interest sharpened to a blade's edge.

"Then let's see how long you keep standing," he said, and with a nod that felt like a vow, he moved on, smoke trailing in his wake.

Last came the Mortal Delegate.

Elena Marrow stood smaller than the rest, wrapped in a deep burgundy shawl that swallowed her thin shoulders. She didn't wear jewels or weapons—just ink-stained hands and tired eyes that had read too many reports and cried over too many names.

She looked painfully out-of-place amid the gilded chaos, but she stepped forward without hesitation, voice steady despite the tremble in her bones. "We've mapped out troop placements—what little we have. We can share our food stores in the south. And we've coordinated evacuation lines through the river towns. I know it's not much, but—"

Seraphina reached out, gently laying a hand on her arm. The motion was gentle. Too soft compared to the steel she'd shown with the others.

"That's more than enough," she whispered. "You have already given more than anyone should give." The mortals have held the line longer than most. You've endured. That is what matters.

Elena faltered, the mask of professionalism slipping as her eyes shimmered. "But I have nothing to bargain with. Nothing to offer but bodies and broken ground."

Seraphina shook her head, her voice low, almost reverent. "You offer everything. Hearts. Homes. A future that's still worth saving. Keep the humans safe, Elena. That's your part in this. And it's the one that matters most."

A long breath passed between them. A quiet understanding. One born not of politics or power—but of shared history. Of knowing what it was like to be human. To fear. To fight anyway.

Elena gave a single nod, her voice cracking. "Then I won't let them down."

Seraphina gave her a small, aching smile. "Neither will I."

The moment lingered, unspoken and still. Then, Elena stepped back into the crowd, disappearing like a falling leaf.

Dylan watched her go, then turned to Seraphina, his expression unreadable for a heartbeat.

"I forgot," he breathed. "How much I missed while you were growing into all of this."

She arched a brow at him, a little amused. "That a crown doesn't crush everything?"

He smiled faintly. "No. That you still carry so much heart under all that fibre." His voice dropped, warm with something more. "The trials shaped you. But they didn't break you. Gods, Sera... I'm proud of you."

She looked away, just for a moment. Because if she didn't, she might have to admit what that meant to hear.

They made the rounds—drifting between gilded courts, ancient grudges, and the trembling weight of desperate hopes. Each conversation became a thread, slowly stitching together a tapestry of fragile alliances. Seeds were sown amid chaos. Promises whispered in the dark. Hints that maybe—just maybe—this rebellion could become something more than survival.

By the time the music deepened and the scent of sweet wine mingled with the quiet thrum of tension, Seraphina's throat was dry and her spine ached from standing tall for too long.

Beside her, Dylan exhaled slowly, his eyes sweeping the crowded room. "You've done enough," he murmured. "Go to them."

She nodded once, her posture still held by the steel of duty, and turned toward the far table—toward the only place in the room where power didn't feel like a weapon.

Kai met her halfway, falling into step beside her with a familiar grin. "They've been watching you like wolves all night," he said under his breath. "Pretty sure Vaelrik actually spilled his drink at one point."

Seraphina smirked, the weight on her shoulders easing just slightly as she let Kai steer her toward the long table at the head of the hall—toward the ones who didn't need her title to see her.

As conversation swirled around her, Seraphina's attention drifted. The weight of a hundred eyes prickled across her skin, foreign and suffocating. She wanted to disappear into the shadows—but she couldn't. Not tonight.

"You're practically glowing," Vaelrik murmured with a chuckle, breaking the tension at the table. His gaze lingered too long; his meaning layered beneath the compliment.

Kade said nothing. But the heat in his stare was unmistakable—intense, unreadable, seething. His eyes traced the curve of her dress with a quiet fury. Not the kind born of battle—but of pride. Of jealousy.

Kai leaned back with a wolfish grin. "You've stolen the room's breath," he drawled, clearly enjoying the show.

Seraphina shot him a glare sharp enough to draw blood, but he only smirked. She took a long sip of wine, trying to ignore the thunder of her heartbeat and the magnetic pull of Kade's silence.

The air thickened as the laughter faded. Candlelight flickered over the grand table, shadows dancing across tense expressions. She tried to focus on the alpha's speech—but every word blurred beneath the weight of Kade's gaze.

"You should wear that more often," Vaelrik said casually, voice low with implication. "You look like you could walk into any kingdom and bring it to its knees."

Her stomach twisted. Not from the compliment, but from the idea behind it. She wasn't here to be admired. She was here to win a war.

Kade's jaw flexed. His voice, when it came, was tight and sharp. "Maybe I should leave you two to it."

"Why don't you?" she snapped before she could stop herself. She didn't know if she was angry at Kade, Kai, or the entire night closing in on her.

"You've got a temper, Seraphina," Kai teased, his grin playful, but his eyes flickered with something else. "Luckily, I'm here to keep things interesting."

Challenge hung in the air. Seraphina met Kade's eyes again—his hands clenched around his glass, shoulders taut, every muscle straining with something unspoken. The tension between them crackled, electric and volatile.

"Seraphina."

Vaelrik's voice cut through the haze—smooth as velvet, sharp as steel.

He stood a few steps away, confident and unreadable, offering his hand. "Would you do me the honour of a dance?"

She froze. It wasn't the question—it was the way he asked it. Calculated. Intentional. Beside her, Kade was a presence she couldn't escape, couldn't ignore. He'd pushed her away too many times. Still, the idea of stepping away from him—even briefly—felt like betrayal.

But the room was watching. The pressure pressed in, and Vaelrik's offer was an escape. A dangerous one.

Her gaze drifted to Vaelrik—his silver and navy tunic shimmered under candlelight, his hand extended with promise. The music shifted, soft and slow. Kade's anger burned beside her, silent and hot.

Seraphina swallowed, steadying herself. "Fine," she said, voice calm but threaded with quiet defiance.

Vaelrik's smile widened. He stepped closer, brushing his fingers against hers. "Let's make it memorable."

The room seemed to hold its breath.

As she rose, her dress rippled like moonlight. She caught a flash of Kade's expression—tight, unreadable—before he turned away, jaw set hard.

No turning back now.

The floor gleamed like glass beneath their feet. As Vaelrik led her into the slow waltz, the world fell away. His hand rested confidently on her back, the other guiding her effortlessly. He smelled of sandalwood and smoke, danger wrapped in charm.

She didn't know what game he was playing. But gods help her—she couldn't look away.

"You're even more breathtaking in motion," Vaelrik murmured, his voice velvet-smooth, sending a ripple across her skin. "This dress... no one else could make danger look so divine."

Seraphina's lips curled, cold amusement in her eyes. "Dangerous? That's a new one."

"Don't play coy, Princess," he said, gaze steady and sharp. "You've always been dangerous. You just prefer to hide it behind quiet grace."

A shiver trailed down her spine at his words, but she masked it with a pointed look. "Let's keep this simple. A dance. Nothing more."

He chuckled, low and knowing. "Of course. But I can't help wondering what else you're hiding behind all that grace."

The music pulled them into motion; her steps sure despite the pull of his presence. The world dulled around them — until her gaze flicked past his shoulder.

Kade.

Storm-grey eyes locked on her. Jaw tight. He wasn't looking at *her*—he was looking at *Vaelrik*. Fury simmered beneath his cool exterior.

Vaelrik's voice slid back into her thoughts. "Planning to stay distracted the whole dance, Princess?" he teased, warmth curling beneath the words.

Her smirk returned, softer this time. Something about the way Vaelrik spoke, the way he moved, made her feel unmoored. For once, she wasn't the one pulling the strings. She allowed herself to be swept away.

"Maybe I am," she replied, her voice just as light.

His grip tightened slightly at her waist, and for a breathless moment, she let herself fall into the rhythm. But at the edge of her vision, Kade still stood—his expression unreadable, shadows flickering across his face.

A realisation struck her, sharp and sudden.

This wasn't just a dance.

It was a game. And the stakes were rising.

Still, she stayed with it. The quiet between her and Vaelrik shifted— something unspoken passed between them as their bodies moved in perfect sync. His hand settled at the small of her back, more guide than grip. She forgot how much she had loved to dance.

"Another?" he asked, voice low, almost reverent.

She nodded without hesitation.

This time, the silence spoke more than any words could. The music wrapped around them, delicate and haunting. The crowd, the candles, the whispers — they all fell away.

Suddenly, it wasn't *now* anymore.

It was *then*.

A dance beneath a dying sunset. Fingers entwined. No masks, no games—just them.

Vaelrik had smiled then, like he does now. "You know," he'd whispered, "when I look at you, I feel like I've found something I wasn't even looking for."

Her heart had been light back then. Full. She remembered the warmth in the air, the promise in the stars.

Why did we ever let this go?

His fingers had brushed the back of her hand—tender, intimate, full of unspoken things. The memory gripped her chest, heavy and bittersweet.

But it wasn't just *him* she remembered.

It was *herself*—who she'd been back then. Untouchable. Alive. Whole. Before the darkness swept in and shattered everything.

"You remember this, don't you?" Vaelrik murmured now, cheek brushing hers.

She nodded, voice caught somewhere in her throat.

"Nothing was the same after that night," she whispered.

His grip tightened slightly, steadying her. In his silence, she heard it—acknowledgement. Regret.

Then, gently, he leaned in, breath warm against her ear. "I never wanted to leave you," he said. "I never wanted *this*."

Her pulse faltered. His words wrapped around her like the music—soft, mournful, real.

He whispered again, "I never wanted to leave you," as if the second time could rewrite what broke. She closed her eyes and breathed in the weight of him and the past.

But then—

"Sera."

Her body stiffened at the sound of her name—*that* name.

She turned slowly, still locked in Vaelrik's arms.

Kai stood at the edge of the dance floor, expression unreadable, voice a blade.

"You should know… Kade stormed out," he said, eyes flicking toward Vaelrik. "Told me he couldn't stand the sight of it. Especially not now."

Seraphina's heart sank at the words, confusion and disappointment flooding her. She glanced at Vaelrik, his expression shifting, a frown tugging at his lips. The connection they had seemed to slip away, fading back into the past. His hand on her back grew cooler, and the warmth of his whisper faded into the silence.

Frozen, Seraphina looked from Kai to the door Kade had disappeared through. She was torn between the emotions she had for both of them, and his absence weighed on her.

What had felt like a brief, intimate moment with Vaelrik now seemed distant, like a memory fading in the present. She glanced at Kai, noticing the anger in his eyes, and wondered if she was playing with fire.

Vaelrik stepped back, releasing her with a dark flicker in his eyes. "That's enough for tonight," he murmured, a finality in his tone.

Seraphina lingered on him, but the moment had been shattered. The tension between her, Vaelrik, and the distance growing between her and Kade weighed heavily on her. She didn't understand how it had all shifted, but she knew one thing—it wasn't over. She needed to get some fresh air before the room continued to feel as if it was pressing in on her.

Outside, the cool air met her skin as she walked through the quiet garden. Her thoughts were confused. Why did she feel like this? The jealousy and ache when she thought of Kade leaving still gnawed at her.

She stopped under the moonlight, the soft beams filtering through the trees. *I can't do this,* she thought. *I can't keep pretending I'm not torn apart by him.*

A rustle broke through her thoughts. "Kade?" she called softly, her heart skipping a beat.

From the shadows, Kade emerged, looking broken, his usual bravado gone. His storm-grey eyes were tired, haunted. His clothes and hair were dishevelled, as if he had been repeatedly running his hands through it. He stepped closer, his voice low. "Tell me about them. About Vaelrik. About Kai. I need to know. The jealousy... it's killing me, Sera."

Seraphina's breath caught. She hadn't expected this. Kade took another step closer, his voice barely above a whisper. "I don't know how to stop wanting you."

His desperation crashed over her like a wave. She didn't know how to answer, but before she could speak, Kade cupped her face, his touch warm but trembling. "I don't deserve you," he muttered. "But you make me forget that. Forget everything else."

His hands trailed down her dress, his fingertips grazing the silk. Her breath hitched as the heat of his touch sent sparks through her. "You're so beautiful, Sera," he whispered, his voice thick with emotion. "I don't know how to stop this."

The weight of his words made her falter. But before she could say anything, his lips pressed to hers. Tentative at first, then deepening as she leaned into him, her heart raced. The kiss was everything—every longing, every moment of tension between them.

Then, as if reality crashed back in, Seraphina pulled away, breathless. "No," she whispered. "Not like this, Kade. Not when everything's falling apart."

His expression faltered, but before he could respond, Kai's voice sliced through the moment. "Well, well. Look what we have here," he said, stepping into view with a teasing smirk but protective eyes on Seraphina.

Kade stiffened, his voice low, barely a growl. "Don't start, Kai."

Seraphina pulled back from Kade, grateful for Kai's interruption, though the tension between her and Kade still lingered. Kade turned away, his posture guarded. She couldn't help the pang of hurt in her chest.

What are we doing? She thought, the weight of unspoken words pressing on her. "I don't even know what I want anymore."

Kade's eyes met hers, something raw and unreadable in them.

"Well, this has been a blast," Kai said, clapping his hands together. "But I think it's time to get you back to your room, Sera. Enough of the melodrama for one night, don't you think?"

Seraphina let out a small laugh, feeling the weight of the night lighten slightly. "You're probably right," she said, grateful for Kai's presence as he led her through the halls, his lighthearted banter easing the tension.

Chapter 28

Seraphina stood in front of the mirror, her fingers brushing against the cool glass as she reflected on the events of the night. Her mind swirled with a mixture of frustration, confusion, and something else she couldn't quite name. Progress. That was what she told herself she had made tonight—getting through the evening with her composure mostly intact, navigating through the delicate web of emotions she was walking. But that wasn't all of it, was it? No, not at all.

The ache in her chest that had been growing since the night began was still there. She thought she could ignore it, push it down, but each tug of the braid in her hair felt like a reminder that nothing was that simple. The way Kade had looked at her earlier, standing in the hallway, lingering just long enough to remind her of the weight between them—it hurt. But there was no time for that. Not now. She needed to focus, to fight the rising anger that threatened to bubble over every time his name crossed her mind. Irrationally, she reminded herself. It's irrational.

Her hands fumbled with the braids in her hair again, frustrated by the stubborn strands that refused to behave. The complicated weaves of her hair seemed symbolic of everything she couldn't untangle tonight— the emotions, the choices, the memories of a past she wished she could erase. She needed to breathe, to shed the layers of tension that had been wrapping themselves tighter and tighter around her chest.

With a huff of frustration, she gave up on the braid and turned to undo the laces of her dress. Tight. Too tight. They clung to her like the expectations that weighed her down, but she had no choice. She'd worn it for a reason—to hide, to protect herself, or maybe to be seen. But now, in the room's quiet, she just wanted to be herself. She wanted to breathe again.

Just as she was attempting to yank at the last stubborn knot, when there was a knock at the door. The sound cut through the air, making her heart skip. She froze for a moment before the words slipped out of her mouth.

"Come in."

The door opened slowly, and there he was—Vaelrik. He moved with a quiet grace. The shift in his energy was familiar, and yet different. His eyes found hers almost immediately, and a small smile tugged at his lips.

"You look like you could use some help," he said, his voice steady and warm, offering a lifeline without hesitation.

She blinked, trying to push aside the jumble of emotions that came with his presence. "I'm fine," she replied, a little sharper than she meant. "I've just… had a long night."

But despite herself, she didn't protest when he stepped closer, his eyes flicking over her in a way that wasn't judgemental or possessive—simply observant. Seraphina shifted, her fingers still clenched around the laces of her dress, her skin suddenly too hot. Her mind screamed at her to stop thinking about Kade, about him—the stubborn anger that simmered at the edges of her consciousness—but it was hard. Too hard to ignore the tension that had wrapped itself around her chest, strangling her thoughts.

"Here," Vaelrik said, his voice returning her to the present as he gently took the tangled strands of her braid.

"I could help," Vaelrik offered, his fingers gently teasing out the braid's knot, his voice like a steady drumbeat, rhythmic and grounding. "If you let me."

She hesitated, her pulse quickening as she tried to fight the vulnerability creeping into her thoughts. After a moment, she exhaled and nodded.

"Please," she muttered, the words escaping before she could stop them. There was no pride to defend, not right now. "I can't seem to get it right."

He smiled, a soft, knowing curve of his lips that felt like understanding. "It's alright," he said, and she felt the tension in her body slowly ease as he worked with practised hands to untangle her hair. The delicate touch of his fingers against her skin made her heart flutter, but she tried to ignore it.

"Are you alright?" Vaelrik's voice was quiet, but insistent, his hands stilling in her hair as he finished untangling the braids. She didn't notice how long she had been thinking or how much time had gone by.

Seraphina nodded, though her throat tightened. "I'm fine. It's just... everything."

"You've been through a lot tonight," he murmured, his voice carrying an empathy she hadn't expected. She'd always been good at hiding her emotions, but with Vaelrik, it was like he could see right through her walls. "You don't have to talk about it, but if you ever need to..."

Her chest tightened again, but she didn't allow herself to dwell on it. She couldn't. Not now. Kade had made his choices, and she was done chasing shadows. She focused instead on trying to undo the laces of her dress. Quickly realising that it might be easier to cut herself out of the offending garment, and promptly grabbed a dagger to do just that when Vaelrik's hand laid gently against hers on the dagger.

"It would be truly a shame for you to destroy this masterpiece when I can give you a hand." His voice was low as his hands quickly undid her laces on her dress, releasing her from the constraints. His hands lingered at her waist, the warmth slipping through the sheer fabric as Seraphina held the dress against her body to protect her modesty.

She swallowed hard, her breath catching in her throat as she processed his words from earlier. The hollow space left by Kade's absence was still too raw, too fresh, and the unspoken emotions were too tangled. She opened her mouth to say something, but before she could, Vaelrik spoke again, his voice quieter now.

"I care about you. I always have."

The words hung in the air between them, and Seraphina's heart seemed to stop for a beat. She wanted to respond, wanted to say something that would make everything clearer, but all she could manage was a soft, almost imperceptible nod.

"I know," she whispered, though her mind screamed at her to stop thinking about Kade.

"Let's get you into bed, little flame. I think you have had enough excitement for one night."

Seraphina agreed as she quickly ducked behind the screen in her room and changed into her nightgown and climbed into bed with a soft good night spoken to Vaelrik as she heard him slip out her door.

Chapter 29

Kade's point of view

Kade paced outside Seraphina's room, his thoughts a storm of frustration and bitterness. Every passing moment stretched into an eternity as he fought against the primal urge to storm in and drag her out. The silence between them had become unbearable, thick with tension and things unsaid. But something else gnawed at him, something far more primal. *She's different now, isn't she?*

His mind churned with thoughts of Vaelrik. He could feel the weight of their last interaction like a physical presence, lingering in the air. Kade knew the Dragon shifter had his sights set on Seraphina, but it didn't stop the rage that built inside him. He wasn't ready to share her. Not with him. Not with anyone. But damn if he could even admit to himself what that meant.

Then the door creaked open.

Kade didn't even think—his body moved before his mind could catch up. Vaelrik. He emerged from Seraphina's room as though the very air around them had changed. The Dragon shifter's gaze flickered up, and Kade's heart lurched, a feeling he couldn't quite place twisting in his gut.

Without hesitation, Kade stepped forward, blocking the hallway, his body tensed like a bowstring ready to snap.

"You've been in there long enough," Kade growled, his voice a low snarl.

His eyes narrowed, locking with Vaelrik's, raw jealousy and possessiveness bubbling beneath his words. "What were you doing in there?"

Vaelrik met his gaze, a smirk spreading across his face. He was unfazed. Relaxed. He knew exactly what buttons to push, and it drove Kade mad.

"Oh, don't worry, Kade," Vaelrik said, his voice dripping with feigned innocence. "We were just talking. Catching up on old times."

Kade's fists clenched. His patience had worn thin. "Talking?" He scoffed, bitterness in his laugh. "I don't think it was just talking."

Vaelrik raised an eyebrow, the casual amusement in his gaze intensifying. "What's the matter, Kade? Jealous?"

Jealous. The word hit him like a blow, sinking deeper than he'd ever admit. But his chest tightened, his heart pounding with a rage that burned through his veins.

"I don't care what you think you've got with her, Vaelrik," Kade said, his voice low, like a beast ready to strike. "You think you can just waltz in here and pick up where you left off? Things have changed. *She's* changed."

Vaelrik chuckled, his eyes flicking over Kade as though sizing him up. "Oh, I'm well aware things are different," he said. His grin widened, dark and predatory. "But trust me, Kade, I'm not here to make things complicated."

With a leisurely step, Vaelrik continued down the hall, completely unbothered by the tension crackling in the air. But he couldn't resist one last jab.

"By the way, Kade," Vaelrik's voice trailed back over his shoulder, mocking sweetness in every syllable, "I helped her get out of that tight dress. The one that makes her look so... irresistible." He paused for a beat, watching Kade's eyes flare with barely contained fury. "Took my time, too. Untying those knots... a proper test of patience, let me tell you."

Kade's heart dropped to his stomach, his body frozen with disbelief. The words cut deeper than anything physical. *That dress.* The thought of Vaelrik being in there with her—touching her like that—ripped through him, leaving a hollow ache where his pride used to be.

"You're playing with fire, Vaelrik," Kade's voice trembled with rage, but he couldn't bring himself to move.

"Oh, I'm sure I am." Vaelrik's tone was mocking, but there was something more in his eyes now, something darker, that Kade recognised. "But you should know, after helping her out of that dress, I made sure she was comfortable. Took her straight to bed. She was exhausted, after all." Vaelrik's voice dropped, a cruel undertone creeping into his words. "What kind of man would I be if I didn't take care of her?"

Kade's fists were shaking now. He could feel the raw jealousy burning in his chest. It wasn't just about her safety. No, this was something darker. Something deeper. The thought of Vaelrik with her—taking care of her, touching her, holding her in ways Kade could only dream of—consumed him.

"Stay away from her," Kade growled, the words feeling like a plea. It wasn't a command. Not a threat. But damn if it didn't sound desperate.

Vaelrik's chuckle was low and menacing. "I'll do as I please, Kade," he said, stepping closer, his voice lowering even further. "But you should ask yourself—what are you willing to do for her? Because I know what I'm capable of."

The words hit Kade like a punch to the gut. *What are you willing to do for her?*

Kade stood there, rooted to the spot, his body trembling with anger and helplessness. His fists clenched, and he had to fight against the overwhelming urge to lash out. But he couldn't. Not yet.

Vaelrik stepped away, leaving Kade with his thoughts—a swirling mix of rage, jealousy, and a growing sense of inadequacy. Unsure of what to do with it, he paused. He wasn't sure what to do with *her* anymore. He did not know how long he had been stuck there, trapped in his own thoughts.

Suddenly the door creaked open again, and there she was.

Seraphina stood in the doorway, barefoot, bathed in the soft flicker of torchlight, dressed in nothing but a thin, near-translucent nightgown that clung gently to her frame. She wrapped her arms around a pillow, pressing it tightly to her chest like cotton fibre. Her hair—gods, her hair—tumbled down her back in unruly waves, wild and long, catching the light with every subtle movement. Streaks of silver threaded through the dark strands like threads of moonlight woven by fate itself. Kade had always loved her hair. Always. It reminded him of storm winds racing across the highlands back home, of the way clouds churned over the moors just before a downpour—untamed, powerful, breathtaking.

The faint silver runes from her transformation shimmered like forgotten starlight, barely visible now as they faded into her skin, like old scars trying to disappear but never quite letting go. Then there were her eyes—those fierce, luminous green eyes that locked onto his like she could see through every wall he'd ever built. They were the colour of the pine forests after rain, the same shade as the moss-covered stones that lined the riverbanks of his childhood. That same colour had once made him feel safe. Now, it twisted something deep inside him.

Kade's breath caught, sharp and unrelenting. His chest ached, not just with longing, but with the weight of something deeper—something more devastating. She looked... softer tonight. Younger, even. Not the hardened warrior who faced down nightmares without flinching, but the girl he remembered in fleeting moments—when her laugh was still light, when her burdens hadn't hollowed her out.

It had been years since he'd seen her like this—unguarded, almost girlish in the way she held the pillow, in the slight tilt of her head, the vulnerability she didn't hide for once. Yet, it didn't make her seem any less powerful. If anything, it made her more. This wasn't weakness. This was strength dressed in softness. The strength that survives after everything else breaks.

She wasn't the same woman he used to know. She was more—sharper, deeper, scarred and surviving. The fire in her hadn't dimmed; it had condensed, burning low and furious behind those green eyes. Gods help him... he loved her for it. Loved her like a man drowning in a storm loves the glimpse of shore. Fiercely. Desperately. Hopelessly.

In that moment, Kade didn't just see her.

He *felt* her—like an ache in his bones, like the breath he'd forgotten he was holding, like the home he thought he'd lost and now found standing barefoot in a nightgown, looking at him like she still saw him too.

He shook his head. This wasn't a time for weakness.

"What are you doing?" Kade demanded, his voice harsher than he intended. "Wandering the halls like this? *Like that?*"

Seraphina didn't flinch at his tone, but Kade could see the slight flash of irritation in her eyes.

"You don't get to ask those questions," she snapped, her voice low but firm as she stalked off down the hallway.

Kade's frustration boiled over. He reached for her arm, intent on stopping her from heading towards Vaelrik's room.

Behind him, the door to Kai's room swung open. Kai stood there, casually leaning against the frame, his chest bare, his dishevelled hair falling in front of his eyes, and a lazy grin playing at the corner of his lips.

"Sera," he drawled, smooth as silk. "I was wondering when you'd come by. You know this room as well as I do."

Kade's blood boiled, but it was the nonchalant ease with which Kai spoke that got to him. Why did she let him in so easily? Why was this so damn natural for them? The questions burned at Kade, more pressing than anything else in that moment.

"Move, Kade," Seraphina said, her voice calm, almost too calm for his liking. There was no hesitation in her words, no softness. She was as determined as ever. "I'm sleeping here tonight."

Kade's jaw clenched, his fists trembling. What was this? Why was she always so... free with her affections? With him?

"Listen, Ice Princess," Kai's voice dropped, sharp and cutting, his tone now carrying a bit of that protective edge Kade hated hearing. "You can move, or I'll move you. But the lady has spoken."

Seraphina didn't even look at Kade as she passed him. She simply walked past, moving towards Kai's bed without a second thought, as if this were all perfectly normal. Kade's chest tightened, his frustration bubbling over.

"What is this, huh?" Kade finally spat, unable to keep the bitterness from his voice. "You're so damn comfortable with him, aren't you? This—this isn't normal."

Kai raised an eyebrow, his grin only widening as he watched Kade seethe. "Oh, it's *totally* normal. She can't sleep alone for shit, always needs someone. I told her she could crash in my bed one time, and we've been doing it ever since we were kids. It's practically a tradition now."

Seraphina smirked at Kai, tossing a pillow his way with a playful chuckle. "I was not that bad. You're exaggerating."

"Oh please," Kai mocked, catching the pillow with ease and fluffing it dramatically. "You were a mess. You practically begged me to let you stay."

Seraphina rolled her eyes, but there was affection in her expression. "You're impossible."

Kade's blood boiled. Every word, every teasing look between them only made it worse. He felt like a stranger standing outside their world. His voice came out in a harsh whisper. "You think you can just sleep with anyone?"

Seraphina paused, the lightness fading from her face as she shot Kade a scathing glance. A subtle edge laced her tone. "Don't...not again."

"Just like that? You give your trust so easily to him," Kade snapped, gesturing to Kai, who was now lounging on the bed as if nothing in the world could ever bother him. "It's like nothing matters to you. Nothing but... but him. You're always so—" He struggled for the right words, feeling that familiar, unwanted jealousy take root.

Before Seraphina could respond, Kai was there. He had crossed what little space that was between him and Kade in an instant, and now he was standing face-to-face with Kade, his smile replaced with a rare, hard edge.

"No." Kai's voice was low, a warning. "You don't get to talk about her like that." His eyes narrowed, and there was a dangerous edge to his words. "You can pick on me all you want. You can hate me. But Seraphina?" He pointed at her with a possessiveness Kade had never heard from him before. "She's off-limits. You never talk about her like that. Not to me, not to anyone."

Kade's eyes widened at the intensity in Kai's gaze. He didn't know whether to fight back or step back, but either way, the truth was undeniable: He was wrong.

For a moment, the silence hung heavy between them, the air thick with unspoken tension. Finally, Kai leaned back, his shoulders relaxing again as if the confrontation had been nothing more than a casual interruption. He shot Kade a last glance, his smirk returning.

"Now, if you'll excuse us," Kai added, turning away and back to the bed, "we have a sleepover to get through. And I'm not *losing* the blankets again."

Seraphina laughed, her earlier discomfort gone. "You act like I'm going to steal them."

"Oh, you *will*," Kai teased. "I'm not stupid. Last time, you practically yanked the entire duvet to your side."

Seraphina shrugged nonchalantly as she settled in.

Kade's gaze flickered between them. The casual way of interacting drove him mad. He opened his mouth to say something, but Kai spoke first, grinning like he had won.

"Okay, bye babes," Kai called out with mock sweetness, before slamming the door in Kade's face.

Kade stood there stunned, his body frozen in place. The weight of everything—of Seraphina, of Kai, of the feelings he couldn't untangle—crushed him. As he stood taking a deep breath, he heard the unmistakable snort of laughter from Vaelrik. When he turned, Vaelrik was standing behind him in his own doorway with amusement written all over his face. Kade flipped him off, then stormed into his own room. Done with everything.

Chapter 30

Seraphina awoke to Kai crouched beside her, fingers brushing her shoulder with a gentleness that belied his usual bravado.

"Up, princess," he murmured, amusement laced in his voice. "Alpha's ready to talk alliances, and you've slept through half the bloody moon."

Her eyes snapped open. Kai stood next to her, holding her gear from her room. The last threads of sleep clung to her as she rushed to her feet, grabbing it out of Kai's hands and running to the bathroom, throwing on her gear with practised efficiency. Leathers, blades, the amulet pulsing softly with Aurion's essence—all fell into place like a ritual.

Downstairs, Kai waited alongside Vaelrik and Kade, who stood near the doorway with arms crossed and jaws tight, as if already bracing for a fight.

They stepped into the Lycans' domain—and the shift in the world was immediate.

Gone were the warm hues and perfumed halls of the gala. The forest here felt ancient, primal. Moonlight lanced through the thick canopies above, casting silver shafts that turned the undergrowth ghostly. The air was damp, thick with loam and old magic. Every breath was a reminder: this was sacred, deadly ground.

Towering trees bore glowing runes that pulsed faintly, whispering in a language older than memory. The earth trembled subtly underfoot—

alive, aware. Between trunks, moss-draped stone structures rose like the bones of forgotten gods, evidence that Lycans had once ruled not from the shadows, but from thrones of stone and claw.

Warriors led them through this primeval court—hulking Lycans with eyes that gleamed amber and silver. Their expressions were unreadable, but their postures spoke volumes. Tense. Alert. As if one wrong word might end in blood.

At the heart of the stronghold, the Alpha waited.

He stood on a raised stone dais, flanked by two of his eldest guards. A titan of a man, his presence struck like a blow. His dark hair, streaked with silver, fell past his shoulders in thick waves. Scars crisscrossed his bronzed arms, each one a story he'd never need to tell aloud. A great animal pelt hung from his shoulders, clasped with the insignia of his bloodline—one of the oldest in the known territories.

His sharp gaze swept over the group and landed on Seraphina.

For a heartbeat, something softened. Recognition. Memory.

Then it was gone, buried beneath the weight of his station.

Kade caught the flicker, jaw grinding as the Alpha stepped forward, towering and slow, like a storm cloud on legs.

"I see Dylan's niece still walks among peasants," the Alpha rumbled, voice like thunder rolled in gravel. "You were barely past my knee the last time I saw you. Running barefoot through the forest, hair wild, stubborn as the wind, seeing you in the Forrest and at the gala reminds me of everything that has changed."

Seraphina gave a small, respectful bow. "And you still sound like a mountain falling, Alpha Rhian. Although some things have not changed, your presence remains ever intimidating."

The ghost of a smirk played on his lips. "Still mouthy, but with the backbone of a wolf, the pack taught you well. Growing up." But his expression cooled the moment his gaze drifted to Kade—who stood a little too close.

Alpha Rhian's tone dropped, cold steel wrapped in velvet. "Your fae friend hovers like a male without manners."

Kade opened his mouth, but Rhian lifted a hand.

"I respect Dylan, and by extension, I respect you, Seraphina. But do not mistake that for tolerance. You walk with males who look at you with eyes full of things they've not earned. I won't see you reduced to a prize among them."

Kade's fingers curled into fists, but Seraphina simply exhaled. "They walk *with* me, Alpha. Not ahead. Not behind."

That made Rhian pause. His smile returned, small and dangerous. "Then let them prove they're worthy to stand at your side."

The tension cracked as Dylan stepped forward, but before he could speak, the Alpha raised his voice.

"You come for alliance—but the old ways require more than words. The Blood Trials will decide your worth."

Dylan's face fell. "Alpha—"

"Enough," Rhian snapped, voice echoing through the stone. "The proving will not spare her either. Her bond may be of Dylan's line, but her path must be her own."

A chill ran through the group. Even Kai's usual quips died in his throat.

Seraphina's expression never faltered. "So we fight?"

A voice from behind, velvet-smooth and full of smug: "Not fight. Survive."

Vaelrik smirked, arms folded as his golden eyes flicked between Kade and the Alpha. "Try not to die, Shadow. I'd hate to be left alone with Sera."

Kade's glare was lethal, but Vaelrik was already walking off, the rune-lit arch ahead flaring in eerie welcome.

Rhian turned back to Seraphina, his tone solemn. "The trials will test not just strength, but soul. If there is weakness... it will find you. And devour you."

He took one step closer, his voice dropping. "You were always wild, girl. But now you carry a shadow with you. Let's see if they consume or crown you."

Seraphina bowed her head slightly. "Then let them try."

As she stepped toward the arch, Rhian's gaze lingered—not possessive, but heavy with a memory and a warning. A man who once saw a child with stars in her eyes now watched a woman born from war.

And beside him, Kade—tight-lipped, silently fuming—looked ready to punch a mountain.

As the trial began, the Lycans watched in silence and the forest… waited to feast.

Chapter 31

Seraphina stood at the threshold of the trees, where the world shifted. It didn't look different—no sign, no unnatural light, no ominous breeze. Just... stillness. Too still. The kind that pressed against your ribs and waited for your heart to stutter.

She inhaled.

Kade's probably already grumbling his way through something teethy, she thought drily, though the edge of worry tugged beneath the sarcasm. *Vaelrik's probably toying with his opponent like a cat with a mouse.*

But here—here, she felt alone. And worse, watched.

She stepped forward.

The forest swallowed her whole.

It started softly. Like a memory.

A familiar laugh echoed between the trees—Kade's, low and amused. Then another—Alexis, full of light, full of warmth. Her chest tightened. She gripped her blade.

No, that's not real.

But the trees blurred. Shadows shifted. Roots twisted. And suddenly, they were there, surrounding her—Kade, Alexis, and the others she'd led, faces half-cast in shadow. Smiling. Bleeding. Dead.

"You said we'd be safe."

"You promised."

"You don't even know what you are, do you?"

The whispers didn't echo. They *slithered*—curling around her spine, burrowing beneath her skin.

Her sword vibrated in her hand.

You could end this. You only have to listen. Let me in.

She clenched her jaw, ignoring the voice. Her blade—ancient, veined with silver, whispering since the day she accepted it—was always too aware. She had never trusted it. Never dared to draw on its full strength.

Not yet. Not like this.

The illusion before her twisted. Kade stepped forward, but it wasn't him. The angle of the smile. The hunger in his eyes. The wrongness.

It tilted its head, curious. Waiting.

And the others—Alexis, her fallen soldiers, even nameless faces from villages she'd failed to protect—moved in a circle around her, murmuring things she wished she could forget.

"You left us to die."

"You can't save him."

"You'll fail again."

Her breath hitched. Her grip trembled.

Strike now, the blade whispered, *or they will consume you.*

She shook her head. "They're not real," she whispered to herself.

But her heart knew better.

Because a part of her—deep, buried—believed them.

She didn't know the full prophecy. No one had ever revealed her true purpose to her. Some chosen warrior? A sacrifice? A catalyst?

And Kade—gods, Kade. What *was* he to her? A partner? A tether? Something more? Something she might lose again?

The not-Kade stepped closer, head tilted, voice silken. *"You don't even know who you are."*

She raised her blade.

It lunged.

And she met it—steel flashing, slicing through its chest. It screamed, shifting—Alexis, broken and begging; a child sobbing; Kade, wounded and whispering her name.

She faltered. Just for a heartbeat.

Let me in. Let me show you your true power.

Fear clawed up her throat.

Then she remembered—they were already dead. Already lost. Kade was still alive, fighting his own battles. And she was still here.

"Fine," she hissed.

She opened herself to the blade.

Silver runes along the steel flared—light and shadow flashing, pulsing with something ancient. A shriek like shattering bone cracked the air as her sword ignited with raw, untamed power.

She plunged it through the illusion's chest—*through Alexis's face*—and for the first time; the forest screamed with it.

The shadows shattered.

Silence fell.

Seraphina stood panting in the ruins of the trial. Ash drifted like snow. Her blade smoked in her hand, still warm from the unnatural fire.

She staggered back a step, barely staying upright. The tear in her fibre, the blood streaking her arms, and the loose braid with silver and ebony strands falling across her face caused her to stagger back a step, barely staying upright.

She wiped her cheek with the back of her gauntlet, smearing ash and tears together, then looked down at the blade.

Do you see now? It whispered. *You will need me again.*

"Gods help me," she muttered. "I think I might."

The path opened in a slow ripple of light.

She emerged into the clearing.

Kade stood first, leaning back against a tree, giving the impression that he had been there for hours. Someone had roughly bandaged his arm. His brows lifted as he saw her.

"Finally. Thought you'd gotten lost in your own melodrama."

Vaelrik didn't move. Just smirked from where he lounged against a rock, arms crossed, golden eyes gleaming.

"Took you long enough," he said. "Was thinking the forest got bored and just *kept* you."

Seraphina didn't answer.

She just walked past them, eyes forward, shoulders straight. But her grip on the hilt of her blade remained white-knuckled.

And somewhere inside, the blade whispered her name.

Before she could think, Kai jogs into the clearing, grinning. "Oh, you're all alive? That's... unexpected."

Dylan, trailing behind, looks far too excited. "That was amazing! Tell me everything!"

The air in the clearing is deceptively still. Beneath it, tension coils like a blade unsheathed. They think it's over. They've passed. That they've *won*.

A voice—deep, ancient, commanding—cuts through the silence like thunder across the mountainside.

"Now you fight," Alpha Rhian says.

It's not a suggestion. It's a decree.

The Lycans move without hesitation, stepping forward with the fluid menace of a pack on the hunt. They form a loose circle, golden eyes gleaming beneath the moonlight like fire caught in a predator's gaze.

Kade groans, low and exasperated. "Oh, for fuck's sake—"

Aurion chuckles, and the sound vibrates through Seraphina's bond with him like a ripple beneath her skin. It's not just amusement—it's anticipation. He *knew* this was coming.

"Did you really think survival alone would be enough?" He murmurs, voice silk and steel.

Seraphina's throat tightens. No, this wasn't about survival. Not really. This was the true trial.

Vaelrik lets out a long-suffering sigh, as if offended by the inconvenience. His obsidian hair falls like liquid ink across his cheekbones, his features carved in sharp, bored lines.

"More fighting," he drawls. "How original."

Seraphina watches as the tension winds through Kade's body like a pulled bowstring. His silver hair catches the moonlight, his jaw set in iron.

His gaze snaps to Vaelrik's with the weight of storms behind it.

"Careful, dragon boy. Wouldn't want you to chip a claw."

Vaelrik's smirk is infuriating in its ease. His confidence is almost aristocratic—casual, infallible. He looks down his nose at Kade like he's already won. "Pathetic."

That one word is all it takes.

Kade lunges.

Reckless, lethal. But Vaelrik is faster—*always* faster. He sidesteps with effortless grace, not even drawing a blade. Just taunting him.

"Predictable, too."

Kade pivots, a blur of shadow, striking again. Raw force. Rage barely leashed. But Vaelrik? He doesn't break a sweat. He's not even *trying*.

Then—fire.

It erupts from Vaelrik in a golden arc, a radiant inferno that splits the night wide open. Wings unfurl from his back, massive and incandescent, casting shadows that dance and tremble across the clearing. He doesn't shift with violence—he shifts like royalty. Like power incarnate.

His talons gleam, his eyes glowing molten gold. Every movement radiates controlled devastation.

Kade doesn't back down.

"You're a damn dragon," he growls, voice ragged.

Vaelrik's smile is slow and cruel. "And you're still just a man."

Seraphina feels it then—that electric *shift* in the air. This isn't sparring. It's not even posturing. This is blood and history and pride. This is personal.

The Lycans step back, almost gleeful in their bloodlust. They want carnage. They want a leader who dominates.

But this? This is not the way.

Kai appears at her side, watching it all unfold with infuriating calm. His dark hair tousled, mischief danced behind his sharp green eyes. He's too still. Too ready.

"You knew," she says quietly, glaring at him.

He doesn't look away. "Of course I did."

"This was the actual test."

He nods once. "We placed bets. I told them you'd do something reckless."

She glares harder.

Kai's grin widens. "And that it would work."

She doesn't answer. She *moves*.

Her body acts before thought can catch up. Steel in hand, she runs through the chaos with blinding speed. Kade's next strike never lands— her blade is *there*, between them, the force of her interception jarring enough to make even Vaelrik pause.

Stillness.

Seraphina's voice is quiet, but unbreakable. *"Enough."*

The word cuts sharper than her blade. It echoes through the clearing, louder than the fire, heavier than the Alpha's command.

Vaelrik freezes. Kade breathes hard, his fists trembling.

The air shifts.

The Lycans, still and watchful, feel it too. This wasn't about who *won*. It was about who *controlled*.

And Seraphina just took control.

Aurion watches her now with something that might be awe—or maybe recognition. Vaelrik exhales, stepping back with a muttered, "You're lucky she stopped me."

Kade's jaw clenches, but he doesn't retort. Doesn't argue. He *knows*.

The Alpha steps forward at last.

The Lycans part around him like shadows pulled by gravity. His presence alone is enough to hush the world. His dark hair falls around sharp features as he surveys the aftermath with cool calculation.

"Well," he says, his voice a low rumble. "That was entertaining."

He looks at Seraphina.

Not with scepticism. Not even curiosity.

But something colder. Sharper.

Recognition.

"You may not be Lycan," he says slowly, "but you've proven yourself among us, and you have more than earned your place in our pack."

The crowd's murmurs show no surprise.

Because she didn't need to fight.

She *led.*

Aurion hasn't moved. But the gold in his gaze is heavier now. Measured. Calculating.

Kai breaks the silence first, grinning like a devil unleashed.

"Told you she'd do something reckless."

Vaelrik, shifting back into his human form, rolls his neck and mutters, "She didn't stop *me.* She stopped *him.*"

Kade doesn't even look at him. "She stopped a massacre."

The words are quiet. But they land like a thunderclap.

Seraphina keeps her eyes forward. Keeps her voice even. "You're both still standing. That's enough."

And that—*that* is the line that seals it.

The Alpha steps close. Close enough that his presence threatens to swallow the air.

"The bond is clear," he says.

It's not a compliment. It's a *confirmation.*

The pack feels it. The *shift.* She is no longer just a foreign element. She is *Alpha-born* in spirit, if not in blood.

"I don't need a title," she says.

Alpha Rhian smiles—slow, sharp, knowing. "It's not about what you need. It's about what *is.*"

Kai strides in, arms crossed, mock-serious. "I always knew you were a leader, Sera." He lowers his voice to a dramatic whisper. "But the way you put those two in their place? *Majestic.*"

Before they can devolve into an argument again, Dylan wraps an arm around her in a strong, grounding embrace. "That's my girl."

The warmth surprises her—but she leans in.

"You remind me so much of your father," he murmurs, just loud enough for her to hear.

Her breath catches. Just a little. Just enough.

And when Kai claps his hands again, absolutely *thrilled,* the moment is gone—but the impact remains.

"Kade, Vaelrik—" he singsongs, "how does it feel to be completely outclassed by Sera?"

Kade mutters darkly, "I *will* stab you."

Vaelrik's eyes narrow. "I'll help."

Chapter 32

The Lycan stronghold had become a second home to Seraphina. Yet it was not the comfort of a home she had known in the past, but a strange, untamed sanctuary nestled deep in the mountains—a place where the scent of damp earth, blood, and something ancient clung to the air like a persistent memory. The howls that echoed across the wilderness at night had once kept her heart racing, a constant reminder that she was among creatures whose instincts were as sharp and raw as the very earth beneath them. Those howls had once unsettled her, a primal sound that reminded her of the beasts, barely restrained by human skin, and that roamed the dark corners of the stronghold.

Now, however, she had learned to embrace it—their world, bound by the unspoken rules of dominance, loyalty, and the constant pull of the wild, a world where instinct ruled over reason. The howls had become background noise, woven into the fabric of her days as she grew accustomed to the rhythm of the Lycans' lives. She had settled into this life. But the undercurrent of something… waiting remained. Waiting for answers. Waiting for whatever battle lay ahead. Waiting for fate to reveal its hand finally.

Tonight, she thought, might finally bring some answers.

Dylan's quarters were a mess of ancient scrolls, tattered books, and faded maps that sprawled across the long wooden table, curling from age.

The smell of parchment mixed with the faint, acrid scent of burnt embers from the hearth that flickered in the corner. Dust swirled in the dim light, disturbed by the occasional rustle of paper or the soft, impatient rustling of wings. The weight of secrets and things buried in shadows for too long brought the room to life.

On the table, Aurion's tail flicked in irritation, his silver scales catching the dim glow of the torches, shifting like liquid metal as he scanned the ancient script with furrowed brows. His sharp golden eyes traced the lines with a precision that only a creature of his kind could possess.

"This prophecy is incomplete," Aurion said, his voice carrying the weight of his frustration. His wings rustled, a soft, restless sound that filled the silence between their words. "I know the words, but not their full meaning."

Seraphina frowned, her fingers gently grazing the intricate symbols inked onto the brittle parchment. The writing seemed almost alive beneath her touch, the curling strokes of ink whispering something that felt just out of reach, a riddle that begged to be solved.

"What do you mean?" she asked softly.

Aurion's sharp golden gaze met hers, his eyes narrowing as if searching for something in the depths of her soul. "I was bound before I could learn it all. Each supernatural has its own bit. That was all I was told," he admitted, his voice heavy with a burden he had never fully understood. The small dragon's tail flicked again, sending a few loose pages fluttering to the floor. He hesitated for a moment, the silence stretching long between them. "There is more."

The room stilled, the only sounds being the distant murmurs of Lycans beyond the stone walls, the crackling fire, and the rhythmic drip of water from some unseen place. The air seemed to thicken with the weight of what Aurion had just revealed.

Dylan, who had been leaning over his own scroll, tapping his calloused finger absentmindedly against it, finally broke the silence. He leaned back in his chair, his silver hair catching the dim light. "Well, that's just fantastic," he said, his voice dripping with sarcasm.

From across the room, Vaelrik scoffed, his usual amused expression twisting into something far more cynical as he crossed his arms. "Let me get this straight," he drawled. "You've been carrying around an all-powerful dragon who doesn't even know the full prophecy?"

Aurion's golden eyes narrowed, and his tail flicked sharply against the table, the sound like a crack of thunder in the quiet room. "I know more than you, lizard."

Vaelrik raised a single, teasing eyebrow, his smirk sharpening into something far more dangerous. "I am a dragon, you glorified jewellery piece," he retorted, his voice dripping with challenge.

Seraphina sighed and pressed her fingers to her temples, trying to ease the tension that was thickening the air. Dylan chuckled, though there was little amusement in it—just the thin veneer of camaraderie worn from too many hours of searching for answers that might not exist.

"Alright, alright," Dylan said, his voice quieter now, more focused. "Focus. The pieces we have say something about 'fire reborn' and 'the last shadow'—but we're missing the middle lines." His gaze shifted toward Seraphina. "You're the only one who can unlock Aurion's memories and your own. That much is clear."

The weight of Dylan's words pressed down on her chest like a hammer. No pressure then. Seraphina swallowed hard, trying to force the tightness in her throat to loosen, but it only seemed to grow stronger. The fire crackled, casting long shadows across the room, but the warmth couldn't chase away the chill in her bones.

As if on cue, a distant howl echoed through the mountains beyond the stronghold, a reminder of the world that awaited them outside the stone walls. But the questions still hung heavy in the air—questions that would determine the fate of everything they held dear. She couldn't face the world beyond without the answers.

But the answers were slipping through her fingers.

Aurion's sharp gaze remained locked on Seraphina as he spoke again, his voice low and almost intimate. "Little one, your bloodline... it isn't exactly normal." She glanced up at him, brow furrowed, but he didn't falter.

"There is more to you than you fuelled," Aurion continued, his words heavy with the weight of ancient truths. "The origins of magic itself are tied to your bloodline," Aurion stated.

The world seemed to stop, the air suddenly too thick to breathe. It felt as though the ground beneath her feet had shifted, tilting in a way she hadn't anticipated. Memories surged, rushing forward like a flood. Her father, once a proud leader of their people, spoke in hushed tones to her brother Lucanis. The war with the Veilborn took Lucanis, who had been so full of hope. She remembered the way their mother's voice had faltered as she told Lucanis about their bloodline, about the ancient ties that ran through their veins. Bloodlines tied to the origin of magic.

Seraphina's mind spun, the weight of those words threatening to drown her. Her breath caught in her throat, and her thoughts swirled back to the loss of her brother, to the war, to the endless battle that had taken so much. Had they known then? Her family, her people, had always held secrets. But this... this was something deeper. Something she couldn't yet comprehend.

The ancient power that had been dormant in her blood—could it be the key to everything?

A quiet, sharp voice cut through her thoughts as Dylan leaned forward, eyes flickering with concern. "Sera?" he said, his voice laced with concern.

Her thoughts felt fragmented, a jumbled mess of emotions and unanswered questions. She opened her mouth to speak, but the words caught in her throat.

"What is it?" Dylan pressed, his eyes searching hers for answers that she didn't have.

She looked away; her gaze lost in the firelight, her mind unravelling.

The flickering light of the torches danced on the stone walls, casting elongated shadows that seemed to pulse in rhythm with the murmurs of the stronghold. The air felt heavy, laden with anticipation and secrets yet to be revealed. Aurion's sharp golden eyes glinted in the dim light as he perched atop a stack of ancient scrolls, tail flicking lazily behind him. His voice broke the silence, rich, with the weight of history flowing from him as if he were a living monument of ancient times.

"In the beginning, before the kingdoms arose from the ashes of the old world, dragons were the first to walk this land. We were the keepers, the guardians of magic itself. We were born with it, intertwined with it as if the very essence of magic ran through our veins, as much a part of us as the blood that pulsed in our hearts." His eyes gleamed with pride as he looked up at the gathered group, his voice growing stronger with each word. "We protected the world long before kingdoms, before thrones of stone and crowns of gold. Magic flowed freely in those days—untamed, wild. And so were we."

Seraphina's fingers rested lightly on the edge of the table, her mind absorbing every word, every detail. She could feel the weight of history in the air, the reverence in Aurion's tone as he spoke of times long past. Her heart stirred with the pride he conveyed. The dragons, the first rulers of magic... How much of that world had they lost?

Aurion continued, voice a melodic hum of ancient pride. "We were bound to no one—no kingdom, no king. Our only purpose was to protect magic, to keep the balance and to defend its users. We considered the supernatural beings, those tied to magic's flow, our kin. We fought for them, alongside them, against the forces that would seek to corrupt and destroy."

Dylan, ever the scholar, leaned forward with keen interest, his dark eyes bright under the flickering torchlight. His fingers traced the rim of his mug absently, caught up in the weight of Aurion's words. There was something hypnotic about the dragon's voice, like the call of a time long forgotten, but never erased.

"The first guardians of magic... That's incredible." His tone was hushed, almost reverential, as he drank in every detail. "How did it all change?"

Aurion's gaze darkened, and his posture shifted ever so slightly, as if recalling a painful memory. "Civilisation grew," he said with a sigh, his voice tinged with regret. "And with it came the need for control. Kingdoms rose, and kings sought power. They looked to us—the dragons, the ancient ones—and saw our strength, our bond to magic. They wanted us to serve them, to fight for them, to fight in their wars. But not that simple." He met Seraphina's gaze, his golden eyes narrowing with intensity. "They bound us to their cause — through riders."

Vaelrik, who had been silent until this point, snorted loudly in disdain. He pushed away from the wall and crossed the room in several long strides, his sharp eyes flashing as he interrupted with icy bitterness.

"Riders. You speak of them as if they were a blessing, Aurion. But you and I both know the truth." His voice was thick with contempt. "The bond that dragons shared with their riders—this so-called unbreakable bond—it was a curse. A curse that brought nothing but corruption." He spat the words like venom. "Kings, rulers, they wielded a bond like a weapon. They used their dragons to conquer, to slaughter, to control. It was never about honour, never about duty. It was always about power."

Seraphina felt a flare of heat rise in her chest. The words stung, sharp as blades, but there was something in Vaelrik's voice—something bitter — that cut deeper than the words alone. He loathed what Aurion held in such high regard, and for a moment, Seraphina could understand why.

Vaelrik's eyes burned with a fierce resentment as he turned to face Seraphina, a voice laced with disgust.

"Do you really believe it was sacred, Little Flame?" His words were slow, deliberate, as if daring her to challenge him. "Those bonds—those weak bonds—look at what they wrought. Kings and queens corrupted by their own desires, sacrificing their dragons for power, and those dragons bound, tethered to men they could not escape. It was madness."

Seraphina's heart ached as she met his gaze, a storm of conflicting emotions welling inside her. She couldn't help but think of the bond between dragons and their riders as something sacred—something unspoken and beautiful. She had always viewed it as a symbol of loyalty, an unbreakable promise. But now, Vaelrik's words gnawed at her thoughts, turning them into questions.

"But it wasn't always like that," she breathed, her voice betraying the uncertainty building in her chest. "The bond between dragon and rider—

it's sacred. It's not just about power. It's about trust, about knowing that someone has your back, that you fight together—not as master and servant, but as equals."

Vaelrik scoffed, turning away with a shake of his head. "You can believe that if you want, Seraphina. But those bonds led to wars, to betrayals, to kingdoms falling. You humans were the first to abandon what was right for the sake of power. They gave themselves away, one rider at a time. And that's why we're here now, fighting for scraps of what we once had."

Dylan remained quiet, his brow furrowed as he absorbed both Aurion's pride and Vaelrik's disillusionment. He hadn't spoken, but his mind was clearly at work, piecing together the fragmented history that lay before them.

"And now... now, the last of the dragons are bound to something else," he said, his voice steady but filled with unspoken meaning. "The prophecy, obviously, if we don't understand it all, has some truth to it. Fire reborn. The last shadow. And you, Seraphina, are the key to unlocking it."

Seraphina's chest tightened at the thought. The prophecy, the strange magic that stirred within her, the bond with Aurion... It was all coming together, but in a way that felt both thrilling and terrifying. Could she truly unveil something hidden for so long? Could the bloodline she had no memory of — the ancient bloodline she had never known existed—be the answer?

She felt a strange pulse inside her, deep within her veins, a thrum that seemed to resonate with Aurion's presence. It was as if his words had awakened something deep inside her. Something ancient. Something tied to magic itself.

"Then what am I really?" Her voice trembled, her thoughts racing. "If I have this bloodline... if it's tied to the origins of magic, then what am I meant to do with it?" She looked between Aurion and Vaelrik, remembering the cabin as she lay healing from the poison in it. "Vaelrik, you and Kade were discussing me, saying I was more... is this what you meant? You both knew of my bloodline?"

The weight of silence lingered after Seraphina's questions, the flickering flames casting shadows that danced in the stronghold's quiet. Vaelrik had the decency to look away from Seraphina. Aurion's golden eyes gleamed as he looked down at Seraphina, his voice tinged with a quiet reverence.

"Little one, your bloodline is... special. You carry the legacy of a kingdom that was pure, uninterrupted. Your ancestors never succumbed to the corruption of power or greed. Not once did they harm magic or the supernatural beings tied to it. Their bond with magic—its flow — remained unbroken, because they never sought to control it. They nurtured it."

Seraphina's brow furrowed in confusion. "But... how is that possible?" Her voice trembled slightly, the weight of his words settling into her thoughts like a stone sinking into the deep waters of her mind. "How could a kingdom remain untouched by corruption?"

Vaelrik, who had been unusually quiet, let out a surprised scoff, a look of disbelief crossing his features. He crossed his arms tightly over his chest, a wry smile curving his lips.

"Uncorrupted? That's impossible. Every kingdom falls to corruption, even the most virtuous. Power... its poison."

Aurion's gaze never wavered as he addressed Vaelrik, his voice carrying the weight of centuries of wisdom.

"Your disbelief is understandable, Vaelrik. But Seraphina's kingdom... was different. They didn't seek dominion over others. They freely loved, accepted all magic-users, and grew alongside supernatural beings. Over generations, marriages, not manipulation, wove supernatural bloodlines into the royal family. That bond strengthened, not just with each passing year, but with each new connection."

Seraphina's heart beat faster as she processed the meaning of Aurion's words. "But my kingdom... it's gone. It doesn't exist anymore."

Aurion nodded, his gaze sombre. "Yes, little one. They destroyed your kingdom, but your lineage remains. And it is what makes you... extraordinary." His voice softened as if speaking of a long-lost treasure. "Your ancestors, they never sought to use magic for their own gain. Instead, they shared it with others, coexisting with the supernatural beings who lived in this world. It is why your bloodline remains untainted by corruption."

Seraphina blinked, her thoughts racing. "You mean... my family—my ancestors—actually married into these other supernatural families?" Her voice was a mix of awe and confusion, disbelief rising within her.

Aurion's tail twitched, a subtle sign of amusement at her reaction. "Yes. Your people welcomed the supernatural, integrating its power, its gifts, into their lineage. The blood of dragons, vampires, fae, and warlocks runs through your veins. It is a rare thing indeed."

Seraphina's mind whirled, trying to make sense of this information.

Aurion continued, "You dated Vaelrik... a dragon shifter; your best friend even as a child was a Lycan."

She glanced at him, a brief flash of recognition in her eyes.

"They betrothed your brother, Lucanis, to a vampire princess. Your mother was part fae, and your father descended from warlocks..." his voice softened at the end, waiting for her to catch up to information lost to her.

"So, my family was extremely powerful right before its destruction?" She murmured to herself.

Dylan, who had been listening intently, broke the silence with a quiet but resolute statement. His voice was calm, thoughtful, as he met Seraphina's eyes.

"It's because of that generational power, Sera. The power in your bloodline is so potent, so ancient, that it could destroy kingdoms if left unchecked. Your ancestors were careful, cautious with it. They nurtured their alliances, kept their gifts balanced, and never allowed that power to consume them." He looked away, his expression distant. "But others... would see that power as a weapon. A tool for conquest. That's why you didn't fuelled what your bloodline meant until now."

Seraphina's chest tightened at the weight of Aurion's words. It made sense, in a twisted way. Her kingdom's strength had always felt like something more—an ancient fire that burned beneath her skin, a connection she had never fully understood. But now, with Aurion's solemn expression and Dylan's guarded confirmation, the truth wrapped around her like an iron chain. This was no ordinary bloodline. This was a legacy. One that had endured through centuries, whispered through generations, and now pulsed in her veins like a living force.

Then it hit her.

Alexis.

Her vision blurred as she stumbled backward. "I let him in, and he destroyed everything," she rasped, as the realisation slammed into her. His voice echoed in her mind like a ghost: *Give it to me.* The way he'd touched her, trusted her, pretended to love her—only to rip everything away.

"Oh, gods…" She collapsed to her knees, clutching her head as if she could tear the memories from her mind. Her breathing came in quick gasps.

Aurion crouched beside her, his voice gentle but heavy. "Yes, little one… Alexis knew. He knew your bloodline."

"But… why didn't anyone tell me?" Her voice cracked, raw and aching. She turned her face toward him, her tear-filled eyes pleading. "Why didn't I know? Maybe I could have stopped it—stopped *him*—maybe it could have changed something…"

Aurion's gaze faltered. There was sorrow in it, and a quiet, buried guilt. "Your ancestors kept the truth veiled. The knowledge passed only to the heir upon their coming of age. It was tradition… and protection. Secrecy was the only way to keep your bloodline safe—from those who would use it, corrupt it. They did not intend the knowledge to be used for power or conquest. But secrets come at a cost. And though your choices were yours alone, we… none of us foresaw this."

She heard his words, but her heart was unravelling. Vaelrik stood off to the side, arms crossed, his silence louder than any scream. His gaze—dark, wounded—met hers. It struck her like a blade.

She remembered how the dark wizards had torn him from her—how they had been bonded once, and how he had stood between her and death without hesitation. Had that meant nothing? Had their bond been real, or just another piece of some ancient strategy? A cruel twist of fate? In a family of tolerance, there was none for her relationship with him. Sorrow hit her all over again.

She began mumbling through her teeth—half-thoughts, guilt-laced apologies spilling out in broken pieces. "I didn't know... I didn't *mean* to leave you behind, Vaelrik—I didn't know it was all tied to *me*—I'm sorry, I'm sorry. "

Vaelrik stepped forward, then stopped. His jaw clenched, pain flashing in his eyes. "Don't," he breathed. "Don't apologise. Not for this. You didn't choose the lies that were told to you." But his voice cracked at the edges, and despite his words, he looked like a man unravelling. He held her gaze for a heartbeat longer. Something unspoken passed between them—then, he pivoted and walked out without another word.

"Everyone kept this from me." Seraphina fell to her knees. "Everyone important to me kept this from me." She couldn't stop the tears at the betrayal of all the people close to her. Suddenly, she didn't want them near her anymore.

She whispered. "Get out."

Aurion offered a soft, pained sigh. "You were never meant to carry this alone. I am sorry, truly. For everything." He, too, slipped away into the quiet.

Dylan, ever composed, looked down at her with sadness. "We never wanted it to be this way. But some truths... they don't wait for the right time." He gave a gentle bow, more out of guilt than formality, and excused himself with a murmur, disappearing into the hall.

She was alone. Or so she thought. As she heaved giant sobs at all the information she had just been told.

A presence moved behind her, swift and warm. Familiar.

"Seraphina."

Kade.

She hadn't heard him come in. He was supposed to be meeting Dylan. Instead, he was suddenly kneeling in front of her, his voice cutting through the panic that still gripped her lungs. He didn't speak again—he just gathered her into his arms, wrapping her up in that fierce, grounding way only he could. One hand cradled her head to his chest, the other around her back.

"Breathe," he whispered into her hair, his breath steady, soothing. "I've got you."

His scent enveloped her—frost and smoke, like winter caught in firelight. Her heart pounded in her ears, but his heartbeat was steady. *Calm. Strong. Kade.* Always showing up when she thought she would break.

She clung to him, fingers gripping the back of his coat, the sobs finally breaking free.

"I didn't know..." she whispered.

"I know."

"I let him *in*..."

"And you survived him."

She trembled. "There's so much I still don't understand."

"I don't care about your bloodline, or the power, or what anyone expects from you." He gently pulled back just enough to meet her eyes. "I care about *you*. The girl who never gives up. The woman who fights for those who can't. My *Nyx*."

The nickname struck her deeper than expected, and she blinked at the tears welling again.

She leaned into him, and for the first time in what felt like forever, allowed herself to just feel *safe*.

Not as a weapon. Not as a legacy.

Just as Seraphina.

Chapter 33

The candlelight flickered as Seraphina ran a hand through her tangled hair, the once-neat braid now half-undone from hours of restless searching and fidgeting since being overwhelmed with all the information of her past. Kade and left her in her room after she had calmed down enough, and that had felt like hours ago. Her fingers traced the edges of scattered parchment, her desk buried beneath open tomes and faded maps. The scent of ink and old paper clung to the air, mingling with the faint burn of melting wax. Outside, the sky had long since deepened into an inky expanse, the distant hum of the wind whispering against the stone walls of her chamber. But Seraphina hadn't moved since she had left Dylan's room and entered her own.

Aurion's small, ethereal form curled beside her, his golden eyes reflecting the warm candlelight as they skimmed over the open pages. The tiny dragon huffed, his frustration mirroring hers.

Aurion said in an exasperated tone, "I do not understand why you mortals insist on writing prophecies in riddles."

Seraphina exhaled sharply, rubbing her temples. Shadows danced across her face, exhaustion pressing into her limbs, but she refused to stop. Not yet.

"You and me both."

Her fingers skimmed the worn ink, lips moving as she murmured the words again.

"It says my heart is the key. What the hell does that mean?"

Aurion huffed, "If I knew, do you think I would let you sit here stewing in your own thoughts?"

She shot him a look, but the little dragon merely flicked his tail impatiently.

She glanced at him. "So all you dragons knew was this? No one thought to write the full damn prophecy?"

"I did not lose it on purpose." There are pieces missing. Being too young when it was last fully spoken, I don't remember everything.

The frustration burned at the edges of her mind. This was a vital part of who she was, and yet it was slipping through her fingers like sand. She clenched her jaw, shutting the book with more force than necessary.

A knock at the door cut through the thick silence.

"Studying so hard you might actually set something on fire? That's new." Kai smirked.

She glanced up as Kai strolled in, his dark tunic unbuttoned at the collar, loose sleeves rolled to his forearms. His brown curly hair caught the dim candlelight, and a roguish grin tugged at his lips. He carried a plate stacked high with food, kicking the door shut behind him with ease before making his way over to her bed. With a dramatic sigh, he collapsed onto it, sprawling out like he owned the place.

Kai grinned at her. "I figured you'd be in full brooding mode, so I brought back up."

Seraphina rolled her eyes at him. "And by backup, you mean snacks."

"Snacks, sarcasm, and overwhelming charm. A full arsenal." He chuffed.

She snatched a piece of fruit from the plate and threw it at his head. He caught it effortlessly, popping it into his mouth with a smirk.

"So, what's got you all twisted up?"

She hesitated, then sighed, rubbing her forehead.

Seraphina rolled to the side. "It's this prophecy. The prophecy states that my powers are connected to something deeper, but I don't know what. Also, what Aurion knows from the Dragons and the scrolls from the Lycans doesn't even match on the prophecy."

Kai hummed, flipping through one text she'd discarded.

"Didn't your powers first show when your emotions were… overwhelming?"

Seraphina stilled.

She knew exactly what he meant.

Flashes of memories burned through her mind—every time Kade had pushed her away, every time he was in danger. And every time, her power had surged, untamed and unstoppable.

Heat crept up her neck.

She answered too quickly, "Get stuffed, Kai."

Kai grinned, raising an eyebrow. "Ahh, so I'm right. Good to know."

She glared at him, but he only stretched, propping himself up on his elbows as he tossed another book aside.

"So, do we just need to piss you off enough to awaken your true potential? Because I can make that happen."

"I swear to the gods—" She stopped herself, the weight of everything from earlier returning in a rush. She crossed her arms, biting her lip. This wasn't the time for jokes. Kai's teasing, though familiar, felt distant, like a broken link in the chain of everything else that had unravelled. She exhaled slowly, leaning back against the desk, her fingers curling around a tattered piece of parchment.

Seraphina looked at Kai. "I just learned something… something big."

Kai raised an eyebrow, his usual smirk fading into curiosity. "What's that?"

Seraphina hesitated for a moment, then spoke, her voice lower than before.

"Aurion said that my bloodline is… different. My ancestors were the first to keep the magic flowing freely, without corruption. No greed, no power plays. They lived with the supernatural, married into their families, and kept the balance. My bloodline, Kai… it's pure. And that's why this prophecy is so damned complicated. I'm tied to something far beyond just myself."

She glanced at him then, watching as the information sank in. Kai was silent for a beat before he let out a quiet laugh, shaking his head.

"Well, that's... understandable."

Seraphina stared at him, baffled. "Understandable?"

Kai chuckled softly, sitting up straighter and shrugging. "Yeah. I mean, you've always had a little extra... something, Sera. It was just a matter of time before you learned how deep that 'something' runs." His eyes softened with an unspoken understanding, the playful grin now replaced by something more genuine. "Plus, it makes sense. I'm a Lycan, after all. I get the whole 'weird, untold magic running through my veins' thing."

Seraphina blinked, a smile tugging at her lips despite herself. "You're serious, aren't you?"

"Hey, you're not the only one with a lineage packed full of mysteries, right?" He shrugged, but his eyes held a deeper respect. "The supernatural world doesn't exactly make things easy for any of us. But it makes sense that you didn't know about all this. Generational power? That could tear kingdoms apart if it got into the wrong hands. And right now? You're still trying to figure out if you can even control it."

Seraphina exhaled, letting her head rest against the desk as the tension in her shoulders loosened. "I don't know what to do with all this."

Kai was quiet for a moment, the flickering candlelight casting shadows across his face. Finally, he spoke, his voice softer than usual. "You'll figure it out. You always do, but if you would like help, I suggest you look to your brood of brooding men."

Seraphina scoffed. "You can't call them that." She had meant it seriously, but her smile was wide.

"Sera, you have an Unseelie Prince, a legendary dragon shifter, an ancient magic dragon tied to you and us Lycans. You're telling me these men either know nothing about their factions, half of the prophecy, or someone who does?"

Seraphina's smile softened, her eyes meeting his. She couldn't help but feel a little lighter, as if, for the first time in a long while, there was someone who actually understood—not just the power she carried, but the weight of it and gave her solutions to figuring it out.

Dylan stepped inside with the casual grace of someone who was well-accustomed to these chambers. With effortless composure, despite the late hour, he stood with his arms crossed. His deep-set green eyes swept across the room, taking in the disarray—the scattered books, the papers that had slipped to the floor, and the sight of Kai sprawled across Seraphina's bed like a lazy cat. A knowing smile tugged at Dylan's lips as he took in the familiar scene.

Dylan chuckled. "You two haven't changed a bit."

Seraphina raised an eyebrow, her gaze shifting between Dylan and Kai. Her exhaustion, though palpable, couldn't suppress her sharpness. "Meaning?"

Dylan stepped further into the room, his boots clicking lightly on the stone floor as he made his way over to the chair across from Seraphina. He lowered himself into it with ease, his expression softening as his eyes lingered on her, an unspoken understanding passing between them.

Dylan spoke softly. "When you were kids, you'd bicker just like this. Always trying to outmatch each other. And Kai—" (he shot a look at Kai) "—you were always an instigator."

Kai, ever the opportunist, grinned as he lazily rolled over on the bed. "I prefer the term 'motivational strategist.'"

Dylan ignored him with practised ease, his gaze now fixed on Seraphina. The room, so full of their usual banter, suddenly felt quieter, as if the air had thickened with something unspoken.

Dylan looked at Seraphina softly. "But you've always had this fire, Seraphina. You just didn't know what to do with it then."

His voice softened, turning almost wistful as his eyes took on a faraway look. "Your father was the same way."

The air seemed to shift around them, a moment of gravity settling over the room. For a long beat, nothing moved except the soft flicker of the candlelight. The room felt smaller somehow, the distance between them thinning, but the weight of Dylan's words left her feeling unexpectedly exposed.

"He burned bright, just like you."

Seraphina swallowed hard, something tight and unfamiliar curling in her chest. Dylan had never spoken about her father—not like this. Layers of time had always guarded his carefully shielded memories of her father. But here it was, raw and unfiltered, a glimpse into something deeper than just the teasing and easy camaraderie that had defined their friendship. The warmth of Dylan's hand on her shoulder anchored her to the present.

Kai, who usually never missed a beat, sat unusually still, his trademark smirk absent. He watched Seraphina, sensing the shift in the room, and for once, the playfulness was gone from his eyes.

Seraphina exhaled slowly, the tension in her shoulders giving way to the steady rhythm of her breath.

Seraphina looked down. "I wish I could remember him more."

Dylan's expression softened further, his voice low and steady.

"You will. In time. And when you do, you'll understand more about yourself than any prophecy ever could."

His words settled into her bones like a weight she hadn't known she'd been carrying. They anchored her in a way that made the uncertainty of the prophecy, the mystery of her powers, feel just a little more bearable.

She didn't have all the answers. Not yet.

As Dylan got up and left the room, Kai, with his usual flair for breaking tension, slung his legs off the side of the bed and grinned like a wolf.

"So, again I ask, do we just need to piss you off enough to awaken your true potential? Because I can make that happen."

Seraphina's lips twitched, but her tone was razor sharp.

"I swear to the gods—"

Kai shifted, "Or maybe we just need to get the little shadow man back. You know, for experimental purposes."

Seraphina's eyes narrowed dangerously. "Don't you dare!"

Kai grinned, unfazed by her warning.

"I'm just saying, every time Kade's life is on the line, boom—fire, destruction, overwhelming power. Seems like a pattern."

Seraphina launched herself at him, tackling him onto the bed. Kai let out a startled laugh, his hands reaching for her in mock defence as she elbowed him into submission. Their limbs tangled in a chaotic blur, books and papers flying as they wrestled. The room was a mess of laughter, muffled curses, and the sound of bodies colliding.

The door swung open just as Seraphina flipped Kai onto his back. Her knee pressed firmly into his chest as he grinned up at her, utterly unbothered by their playful fight.

Vaelrik leaned against the doorframe, arms crossed, with a look of vague amusement on his face, his usual stoic expression giving way to a rare, fleeting glimmer of approval.

"I don't know what's happening here, but I approve of Kai getting his ass kicked."

Kai, mock-offended, raised a hand to his chest in exaggerated shock.

"Traitor."

Seraphina glanced at Vaelrik, then at Kai beneath her, before her gaze flicked to Kade, who had silently entered behind Vaelrik. He stood there, arms crossed, watching them with the same smirk he always wore. It was the smirk that said I know I'm superior, but there was something different about it today — something warmer, almost affectionate.

There was a beat of silence before both Seraphina and Kai broke into laughter, pointing at Kade like two mischievous children caught in a moment of rare, unguarded joy.

Seraphina laughed, "Look at his face!"

Kai's words came out with a broken chuckle. "He's just standing there, judging us."

Kade raised an eyebrow, his voice dry but tinged with something lighter than usual.

Kade, not at all aware of the situation, "I don't need to judge you. You make it too easy."

Vaelrik, now fully leaning into the doorway, deadpanned in his usual no-nonsense manner.

"They're feral."

Kade sighed, his gaze shifting back to the pair, still tangled in laughter.

Kai, always the provocateur, flashed a grin.

"You love us."

Kade's eyes narrowed, though the flicker of warmth behind his usually cool expression betrayed his words. "Debatable."

Seraphina, with a wide, mischievous grin, shot him a look.

Seraphina, full of laughter, said, "Undeniable."

Kade just shook his head, but despite his outward composure, the corner of his mouth twitched up in a rare, almost imperceptible smile. There was a softness there, a crack in his usual stoicism, and Seraphina couldn't help but feel the weight of it, even if just for a moment.

Vaelrik, still standing in the doorway, crossed his arms again and grumbled.

Vaelrik grumbled, "I still approve of Kai getting beat up."

Seraphina raised an eyebrow, her grin never faltering.

"Well, if that's the case—"

Before Kai could react, Seraphina lunged at him again, and this time, they both tumbled off the bed in another round of chaotic, laughter-filled mayhem. The sounds of their playful scuffle filled the room, a welcome distraction from the weight of their worries and the mysteries that still lay ahead.

"Okay, you absolute menace, get off me. We have training drills in the morning, and I will not be responsible if you did not get enough sleep." Kai grumbled.

Seraphina had forgotten that, had forgotten that she had promised to train with the Lycans so she could learn new skills and train her body differently.

"You're right; I need to be well-rested to kick your ass, but this is a good excuse to kick everyone out of here."

Kade and Vaelrik looked like they both wanted to say something to her, but she didn't care. She had been studiously ignoring them and their complicated emotions.

Yes, because running from our problems has always worked so well, Aurion's voice slipped into her thoughts.

Well, better than me losing control again because I can't control my emotions. I thought at him sarcastically.

Kade was watching her with guarded eyes, like he could read her thoughts, before he nodded and followed Kai out of the room. Vaelrik lingered, with an amiable smile on his face. "Even me, Little Flame?" He murmured.

The nickname sent a shiver down her spine, but she couldn't tell if it was a good thing or not.

"Yes, even you. Out." She commanded.

Vaelrik just laughed as he left.

All this tension, no release. This can only end well. Aurion's voice.

Chapter 34

The sun blazed overhead, relentless and merciless, baking the earth beneath Seraphina's boots. Sweat trickled down her spine, dampening the fabric of her shirt as she tightened her grip around the wooden training sword. Their supernatural endurance kept the Lycans around her fresh despite the gruelling pace of the drills.

Seraphina was running on nothing but sheer willpower.

Kai's squad—six of the toughest warriors among the Lycans—had been running through combat sequences for hours, and Seraphina refused to be the weak link. She matched them step for step, strike for strike, despite the fire burning in her lungs and the protest of her muscles.

"Again," Kai barked, his green eyes sharp as he watched her movements.

Seraphina exhaled sharply and reset her stance. The sparring partner in front of her, a towering Lycan with a scar slashing down his jaw, smirked as he lunged. She ducked, twisting out of the way at the last second, her blade snapping up on a fluid counter. The clash of wood against wood rang out, followed by a grunt of approval from the other warriors.

She knew what this was. A test.

They had strength, speed, and the natural advantage of shifting. Seraphina had none of that—but she had something else. Stubbornness. Strategy. And an iron will that wouldn't break, no matter how many times she got knocked down.

And they knocked her down. Repeatedly.

By the time she hit the dirt for what felt like the hundredth time, her arms trembled with fatigue, and the edges of her vision blurred. The squad murmured among themselves, waiting to see if she'd give up.

She could hear her own heartbeat pounding in her ears.

No.

She gritted her teeth, forcing herself back to her feet.

Kai crossed his arms, expression unreadable. "You've proven your point, Seraphina. You can stop."

She wiped the sweat from her brow and met his gaze with unwavering determination. "I'll stop when you do."

A beat of silence. Then—

Laughter.

Low chuckles from the squad, the kind that carried the weight of approval. Scarred Jaw shook his head, grinning. "She's got fight in her."

Another warrior smirked. "I think she's just crazy."

Kai's lips twitched in something close to amusement. "Both."

Seraphina rolled her shoulders, forcing herself to stand taller despite the aching in her limbs. "So, are we done talking, or are we finishing the damn drill?"

The murmurs turned into nods of respect.

Kai stepped forward, eyes glinting with something unreadable. "Alright, Seraphina. Let's see if you can keep up."

The next round began, and this time—this time, they weren't holding back.

And neither was she.

The moment Kai signalled the start, Seraphina lunged, driving forward with renewed intensity. Every muscle in her body screamed in protest, but she silenced the pain, pushing herself beyond her limits. The Lycans around her moved with terrifying speed, their attacks a blur of strength and precision, but she wove between them like a blade through smoke, evading, countering, and striking.

Kai was faster. Stronger. But Seraphina had spent her entire life fighting against impossible odds.

Scarred Jaw swung at her side—she twisted away, rolling under his attack and springing up in time to parry a strike from another. The impact rattled her arms, but she held firm, planting her feet and shoving back hard enough to break the lock.

Kai advanced next, closing the distance in a blink. His fist shot out, and she barely had time to block. The force of the hit sent her staggering, but she turned the momentum into a spin, sweeping her leg out in a sharp arc.

It caught him in the ribs. Not enough to knock him down, but enough to make him pause.

A flicker of something unreadable crossed his face.

The squad circled around them now, watching with open interest. Seraphina could feel their scrutiny like a weight on her shoulders, but she refused to falter.

Kai feinted left, then came at her from the right. She expected it, dodging just in time. But before she could counter, he twisted, hooking his leg behind hers in a sweep.

She hit the dirt hard, dust kicking up around her.

For a moment, everything stilled.

Then—laughter. Deep, genuine, approving.

Kai extended a hand down to her. "You fight like you've got something to prove."

Seraphina took his hand, letting him haul her up, chest heaving as she wiped the sweat from her brow. "I don't need to prove anything." She smirked. "Just needed to remind you of all that I can keep up."

The squad exchanged looks, then—one by one—they nodded.

"You've got grit," Scarred Jaw admitted, rolling his shoulder. "Didn't think you'd last through the whole drill."

Kai studied her for a long moment before tilting his head toward the squad. "You're running drills with us from now on."

That caught her off guard. She blinked, glancing between them. "You're serious?"

The other grinned. "We wouldn't be wasting our breath if we weren't."

Seraphina exhaled, her body screaming for rest, but beneath the exhaustion, a rush of pride burned hot. She had earned their respect. She smirked, rolling her shoulders. "Then let's go again."

Kai huffed a laugh. "You're insane."

"Maybe." She grinned. "But you're still struggling to land a solid hit on me, so who's really winning here?"

The squad groaned in exasperation, but the energy had shifted—lighter, looser. She had bled, fought, and pushed herself to the edge, but in the end, she had done what she came here to do.

She belonged. And for the first time in a long time, Seraphina felt it.

As they wrapped up the final drill, sweat-drenched and panting, Seraphina rolled her shoulders, feeling the ache settle deep in her bones. She had pushed herself past exhaustion, but it had been worth it. Every fibre of her being was on fire, but she stood tall, chin high, as the squad clapped each other on the back.

Then — "She's human, Kai," Vaelrik's sharp voice cut through the air. "You're pushing her too hard."

The squad went still. Seraphina turned, still catching her breath, as Vaelrik stalked forward, eyes flashing with frustration. His focus was on Kai, but the tension rolling off him was undeniable.

"She's keeping up," Kai said evenly, arms crossed over his broad chest.

Vaelrik scoffed. "For now. But she's going to break if you keep this up." His gaze flicked to Seraphina. "You don't have to keep proving yourself to them."

Seraphina barely had time to process the words before the squad erupted.

"She's not proving anything—she's earning it," Scarred Jaw snapped.

"She's lasted longer than half the recruits we've trained," another added.

"She's one of us," someone else growled, the words carrying an unmistakable finality.

Seraphina's breath hitched. One of them.

Kai said nothing at first, simply watching her as if gauging how she would react. Then slowly he nodded. "They're right," he said. "She's earned her place."

Seraphina stared at them, stunned into silence. Then, of all things—

A laugh. A deep, natural laugh that cut through the tension like a blade.

Seraphina turned to find Kade leaning against the fence, shaking his head in amusement, his laughter rolling through the training grounds like thunder. It was raw, unrestrained—real.

And it shocked everyone.

Even Vaelrik tensed, eyes narrowing. "What's so damn funny?"

Kade wiped at his mouth, still chuckling. "That you think you can win this." He jerked his chin toward Seraphina. "First, because she's unstoppable when she puts her mind to something." His grey eyes gleamed with something almost like pride. "And second, because you're outnumbered, Vaelrik."

The squad grinned, stepping in around her, their agreement nearly palpable.

Seraphina swallowed hard. She had fought for this. Bled for this.

And now — she was apart of their pack. Damn, she thought, I'm going to have to remember more names now.

The path back to the stronghold was quiet, the rhythmic crunch of their boots against dirt filling the space between them. The sky had begun its descent into dusk, the first stars peeking through the veil of twilight. She exhaled, rolling out her shoulders, the ache from training settling in deep.

Kai walked beside her, hands tucked lazily into his pockets, his wolfish gaze flicking toward her with something close to amusement.

"So," he said, breaking the silence, "what's the plan for tonight?"

Seraphina sighed. "Oh, you know. The usual."

Kai ticked the list off on his fingers. "Investigating the prophecy, brooding over my bloodline, questioning everyone who so much as breathed near me if they knew a Jessamine—" she shot him a look "—or, and this is a genuine possibility, climbing Kade like a tree." Kai mimicked Seraphina's voice mockingly.

Kai choked on a laugh, nearly tripping over a root. When he caught her expression, "Gotta say that the last one is the most entertaining option."

She flushed bright red, and before she could retort, a shimmer of blue light flickered in the corner of her vision.

Then—

"Climbing Kade like a tree?" Amusement dripped from the words, thick and unrelenting.

Seraphina groaned. "Aurion."

The little dragon materialised just beside her, flying smoothly, his smirk infuriatingly smug. "I'm linked to an absolute menace," he mused. "Truly, the fates are cruel."

Kai snickered. "I mean, he's not wrong."

Seraphina smacked his arm. "Shut up."

Kai only grinned. "Tell you what—I'll make it up to you."

Seraphina arched a brow.

"There's chocolate cake waiting in your room."

Her steps faltered.

Kai's smirk widened. "And, you know, a bunch of dusty old tomes courtesy of Dylan, but I figured I'd lead with the cake."

Seraphina's eyes narrowed. "You do fuelled I will destroy you if you get to that cake first?"

Kai stretched his arms over his head, already shifting his stance. "Then you'd better move fast, menace."

Then he took off. Seraphina didn't hesitate—she bolted after him.

Kai was fast, but she was determined, closing the distance in a blur of movement before tackling him to the ground. They hit the dirt in a tangle of limbs, Kai laughing as he tried—and failed—to shake her off. "Damn it, Sera!" he wheezed between laughs. "You're actually a menace."

A slow, measured stride. Could be heard approaching. They both froze.

Seraphina lifted her head just in time to see Kade walking past, his silver hair catching the last traces of daylight. He said nothing, didn't even look at them—just kept walking. Back to his brooding behaviour after his brief outburst at training.

But they knew he heard. A beat of silence. Then they lost it.

Laughter burst from them in a wave, their bodies shaking as the realisation of Kade witnessing their absolute stupidity set in.

Aurion groaned. "I am bound to children."

Which only made them laugh harder.

Chapter 35

The night was thick with shadows, moonlight weaving like silver thread through the torn curtains of Seraphina's room. Cool air whispered in from the open window, brushing against sweat-dampened skin. Yet within those walls, the heat was suffocating. It wasn't from the fire—not yet. It pulsed from her, thick and alive, like a second heartbeat. The air trembled around her, too heavy to breathe.

Her breath hitched. The amulet at her throat glowed white-hot, searing into her skin as if trying to anchor her to reality.

It had begun with a dream.

Fragmented, suffocating. Echoes of laughter long silenced, the ghosts of joy turned sour with time. The weight of grief pressed down on her chest like a thousand unseen hands. She couldn't move. Couldn't scream. Then—flames.

The room ignited with a deafening roar, fire blooming from her like a second soul unbound. The bed linens curled into blackened husks, walls flickering with crimson hunger. Wood cracked, the ceiling groaning in agony above her.

And Seraphina? She remained frozen in the storm's centre, eyes wide, hands trembling. The flames didn't touch her. Couldn't.

Because the fire wasn't devouring her.

It *was* her.

The amulet flared again—this time with force.

A voice cut through the blaze. "Seraphina! Wake up, damn you! This isn't just a dream!"

Aurion's silver-white form burst forth from the amulet, his usual calm lost beneath a veil of panic. The tiny dragon's wings beat furiously against the heat as he reached for her with magic, trying to tether her back. But even he flinched as the fire surged, roaring louder at his interference. His golden eyes widened.

"You're going to destroy yourself—VAELRIK!"

The name shattered the dream like glass.

A rush of wind exploded through the room, and with it, a shadow. Massive talons gouged into the floorboards as Vaelrik forced his bulk into the space, his crimson scales glowing like molten steel in the firelight. He moved with impossible grace for something so large, his wings folding tight to avoid further destruction.

No hesitation. He swept forward, his wings unfurling to as full span that could fit in the room—then curled around her in a protective cocoon. The fire snapped in defiance, but his scales extinguished it. Wrapped in him, Seraphina trembled violently. Her fingers dug into his chest of scales, clawing for something real. He lowered his head, nuzzling her temple with surprising gentleness.

Breathe, little flame. I've got you.

His voice was a caress in her mind—deep, anchoring, something primal and safe.

The storm wavered, flickering like it, too, was exhausted. But her power remained too intense and uncontrolled; without grounding soon, it would destroy her.

A calm voice cut in. "She's burning out."

Kai stepped through the blasted doorway, his hair tousled, his expression unreadable and focused.

"Vaelrik, you can't hold her like that. She needs to be cooled before she collapses."

Vaelrik's wings didn't move. His growl rumbled low in his chest—but he

334

knew Kai was right. Slowly, reluctantly, he peeled his wings back, scales crackling with lingering heat.

Kai stepped in. "Let me."

Seraphina barely registered the shift before, arms wrapped around her—strong. Kai scooped her up, cradling her like a flame he wasn't sure wouldn't bite. Aurion whispered a spell beneath his breath, trying to suppress the wild fire magic still simmering in her blood, so she didn't burn Kai.

Her cheek pressed against Kai's collarbone, breath ragged, her magic humming beneath her skin. He adjusted her gently, grumbling with mock irritation.

"If you combust while I'm carrying you, I swear to every god, I will drag you back and kill you again."

Vaelrik snorted behind them, but his eyes were wary.

Kai carried her out into the night, each step sending curls of steam into the air as her fevered body met the chill. When they reached the lake, he didn't stop.

He walked in.

The cold bit instantly, but he didn't flinch. Lowering her into the water with practised care, he held her firmly as her body seized in shock.

She gasped. Steam hissed violently around them as the icy water clashed with her internal inferno. She twisted, instincts screaming, but Kai didn't let go.

"Yeah, yeah," he muttered, voice gentler than his words. "It's freezing. You'll live."

She trembled violently as the magic drained from her, seeping into the lake in golden tendrils. The water glowed faintly around them. Silence settled—except for the soft lap of water and her stuttering breath.

Then Seraphina saw the one person who was drawn to the commotion—"Kade…"

The whisper was hoarse, almost inaudible. But it hit like a blade.

Kai stilled, then turned.

Kade stood at the water's edge, face unreadable. Their eyes met, unspoken understanding flaring. Kai jerked his head.

"Only because she asked," he muttered, passing her over.

Kade's arms wrapped around her before she could fall. She melted into him, her strength utterly spent, her body still trembling from the release.

"I'm here, Nyx," he whispered, voice brushing her ear. "I've got you."

Her fingers curled weakly into his shirt, grounding herself against his heartbeat. She could feel it—steady, warm, real. It soothed her in a way nothing else could.

The lake stilled, moonlight dancing on the steam. Kade's fingers traced slow circles on Seraphina's spine as she rested against him, the fire within her finally dimming, as if her magic was now calm, safe in the arms of someone it recognised.

"Her magic's settling," Kai observed, wading closer. "So what now? You gonna kiss her like some tragic lover, or...?"

Kade shot him a warning look.

Seraphina stirred, a faint smile tugging at her lips. "Shut up, Kai."

He grinned. "There she is."

Kade didn't speak. He just held her tighter.

Vaelrik stood at the water's edge, golden eyes unreadable. His gaze lingered on Seraphina—protective, familiar, territorial.

"Think she'll live, dragon?" Kai called out.

Vaelrik didn't move. "She's too stubborn to die from her own damn magic."

"Thanks," Seraphina croaked, head lifting slightly. She didn't just mean the words he spoke but for coming to her rescue.

"Anytime, little flame."

Kade stiffened at the nickname. So did Seraphina. But she didn't pull away. Not from him.

Kai, ever the chaos-maker, sighed. "Are we done? Or are you going to argue over her while she freezes to death? Or are we going to bring her back to her room?"

"I'm taking her," Kade said simply. Not as a request.

He turned toward the shore, carrying her with a care that belied the tension in his jaw. Kai stepped aside. Vaelrik didn't speak, but his eyes never left them.

Kade didn't let go. Not even when they reached the room hastily prepared for her—fresh linens, unburnt walls, the faint scent of lavender clinging to the space. He placed her gently on the bed, brushing damp hair from her temple.

"You okay?" His voice was a whisper now, rough, almost unsure.

Seraphina blinked up at him, green eyes drowsy but clearer. "Yeah," she murmured. "Just tired."

Kade knelt beside the bed, hands lingering in her hair. He wanted to say more. Wanted to tell her what it meant—that she'd called for *him*.

But before he could, a familiar presence loomed

"She's fine," Vaelrik said from the doorway, voice like steel wrapped in silk.

Kade stood slowly, jaw tight, eyes locking onto the dragon's. Challenge met challenge.

Kai wandered in behind Vaelrik, wringing water from his sleeve. "Relax, we're just here to supervise the next spontaneous combustion."

Aurion's form materialised in the corner, shadows folding in on themselves as he stepped forward. His presence filled the room like thunderclouds rolling in. The tension grew thick.

"Enough. All of you—out." His tone brooked no argument. Even Vaelrik's smirk faltered for a second.

"You're siding with *him* now?" Vaelrik scoffed, pointing at Kade.

"No, I'm siding with the least stupid of you." His eyes drifted to Kai, who blinked, surprised, then smirked quietly and inclined his head.

"I'll take that as a compliment."

Vaelrik scoffed, brushing past Kai with a flick of his coat. "Still playing at guardianship."

He disappeared into the corridor.

Kade hesitated, eyes darting to Seraphina, but he too left her.

Aurion didn't say a word until the door clicked closed behind the others. Then he turned, gaze heavy, assessing, ancient.

Kai moved to Seraphina's side, gently adjusting her blankets, brushing a strand of damp hair from her temple.

"You'll be safe here. I trust him." He glanced at Aurion, something unspoken passing between them. Then he looked back at Seraphina, softer now.

"You are very fortunate that the rooms here accommodate visiting supernaturals; otherwise, Vaelrik's enormous dragon would not have saved the stronghold from burning with your magic. Try not to set the place on fire this time."

"No promises."

Kai gave a wry smile, then stood.

He paused in the doorway, gaze lingering on her. "I'll be in my rooms if she needs anything."

Then he was gone.

The silence felt different now—thicker, but steadier.

Seraphina blinked slowly, trying to gather herself, eyes flicking toward Aurion. "Why did you call for Vaelrik... instead of transforming?"

Aurion's expression didn't change at first. But then a faint flicker of pain touched his eyes—quickly buried beneath centuries of control. "Because I can only shift with your magic."

He moved to her side, kneeling slowly on the bed, his tone low but firm. "You were trapped in that nightmare, Seraphina. Too far under. I couldn't reach you." He bowed his head just for a moment. "I tried."

She stared at him, absorbing the weight of it—the truth of his limits, the way even a dragon could be helpless.

And for once, she didn't have to say anything.

Chapter 36

Seraphina woke to the soft weight of Aurion still curled against her stomach. His steady warmth grounded her, the dull glow of his scales flickering in the dim light. For a moment, she let herself breathe, let the exhaustion ebb before reality came crashing back.

Her power had lashed out again. She'd nearly lost control. Again.

And they had all seen it.

She groaned, covering her face with one hand. "Gods, why am I like this?"

Aurion stirred, lifting his head to peer at her with those glowing golden eyes. "If you are asking me for a long-winded existential answer, I will gladly provide one."

Seraphina huffed, dropping her hand. "I was mostly just wallowing, but thanks."

A smirk curled at the tiny dragon's voice. "I live to serve."

Before she could throw a pillow at him, a knock sounded at the door. She barely had time to sit up before Vaelrik strode in, looking perfectly unbothered as usual.

"You're awake," he noted, like she hadn't nearly set an entire room on fire hours ago. His golden eyes swept over her, unreadable.

"Sharp observation, dragon boy," she muttered.

His lips twitched, but he didn't take the bait. Instead, he folded his arms, wings shifting behind him. "You look—"

"If you say 'better,' I will set your boots on fire," she deadpanned.

"—less charred than I expected," he finished smoothly.

Seraphina rolled her eyes. "What do you want, Vaelrik?"

"To make sure you haven't turned into a pile of ashes overnight." He leaned against the wall, expression deceptively casual. "Also, Kade is brooding outside like a grumpy gargoyle, and Kai is making bets on how long it'll take before you punch someone. I figured I should check in before he sells tickets."

She groaned, flopping back onto her pillows. "Of course he is."

Aurion sighed heavily. "I am trapped in an era of fools."

"You say that like it's a new discovery," she murmured.

Before Vaelrik could retort, the door creaked open again, and Kai slipped inside with his usual catlike grace.

"Oh well, you're not dead," he said brightly. "That means I win the bet."

Vaelrik scowled. "That means I win the bet."

"Nope," Kai said cheerfully, flopping onto the bed beside Seraphina. "I said she'd survive and wake up grumpy. Nailed it."

Seraphina shot him a glare, but he just grinned at her. "How's our little fire hazard feeling?"

"Like setting you all on fire," she grumbled.

"Aw, she's fine," Kai announced to the room. "Crisis averted."

Before Seraphina could kick him off the bed, the door swung open again—this time with much more force.

Kade stood in the doorway, eyes storm-dark, jaw set tight. "Everyone out."

Kai arched an eyebrow. "Well, good morning to you too, sunshine."

"Now," Kade growled.

Seraphina narrowed her eyes. "Excuse me?"

Kade's gaze snapped to hers, the muscle in his jaw flexing. "We need to talk."

Kai whistled low. "Well, that sounds ominous."

Vaelrik, for once, didn't argue. He shot Kade a sharp look, but wordlessly strode past him. Aurion gave a long-suffering sigh, flicking his tail before disappearing in a shimmer of light.

Kai, however, took his sweet time getting up. "I just want you to know," he said solemnly, "that if this turns into a dramatic lovers' quarrel, I will be eavesdropping."

Seraphina shoved him off the bed.

"Okay, okay, I'm going," he laughed, dodging her half-hearted swipe. "Have fun, lovebirds."

The door clicked shut behind him, leaving only the sound of Seraphina's steady breathing and Kade's sharp inhale.

Kade didn't speak at first. Seraphina watched him, uneasy. "Just say it."

He shook his head slowly, as if he were trying to choose the least destructive words. "You nearly brought the ceiling down, Seraphina."

She flinched. "It was a *nightmare*. I wasn't even awake."

"I know," he said. "That's what scares me."

Her throat tightened. "So now I'm terrifying?"

"That's not what I meant."

"Then what *do* you mean, Kade?" She snapped. "Because last night, you were holding me like you gave a damn. Now you're looking at me like I'm some... ticking bomb."

Kade's jaw clenched. "Because I *give* a damn! That's the problem. You could've killed yourself—or someone else. You don't even remember losing control."

Her voice shook. "Do you think I *want* this? You think I haven't fought every damn day to keep it locked down?"

"I think maybe you *can't* anymore."

Silence. Sharp. Devastating.

Something cracked in her chest. "Get out."

"Seraphina—"

"*Get out.*"

Kade's voice rose. "You can't just push everyone away when it gets hard!"

"Watch me."

Then—

"Hey!" Kai's voice rang clear through the door. "I *can* hear the lovers' quarrel, and as *deeply invested* as I am in your emotional catastrophe, we've got places to be!"

Seraphina blinked.

"Also," Kai continued with exaggerated patience, "Sera's got to explain to the Alpha why her room smells like a barbecue pit and looks like the aftermath of a lightning storm. So—less drama, more movement."

Kade muttered something under his breath.

Seraphina just closed her eyes, taking one ragged breath.

Chapter 37

Time slipped past in hushed breaths and frost-bitten silences.

Winter had come with a vengeance—bleeding the world of warmth, burying the fortress and surrounding woods in ice and stillness.

But now… the thaw had begun.

The snow had melted, trickling through the cracks in cobblestone paths, and green shoots curled tentatively from the blackened earth, reaching for pale sunlight like it was a promise.

Still, Seraphina didn't slow down.

If anything, she pushed harder.

Training became ritual. Obsession.

It was easier than dealing with the impossible weight that pressed in from all sides—easier than facing the too-long glances from Kade, or the biting, unreadable quiet that had settled between her and Vaelrik since *that* night.

Easier than remembering the Alpha's voice, sharp and final, like a blade to the gut:

"Power without discipline is a threat, not a gift. You either control it, or I'll find someone who can."

The words had carved themselves into her spine, branding her with doubt. She hadn't argued—couldn't. She couldn't explain the nightmare, and her hands still trembled from it, as the walls were still scorched.

So she trained. Until her limbs ached. Until the wind burned in her lungs. Until her magic obeyed even the subtlest flick of thought.

Because failure wasn't an option.

Not anymore.

Gods, I miss when you used to train for balance and discipline, Aurion's voice drawled inside her mind.

Seraphina moved in a blur, muscles burning as she dodged a clawed swipe aimed at her throat. The Lycan before her was fast—too fast. She barely had time to duck before another attack came from the side. She twisted, deflecting a strike with her forearm, but the force sent her staggering back.

She gritted her teeth, refusing to pause. *I'm training because I have to be better. Now stop being so annoying.*

Her chest heaved. Every inch of her body screamed in protest, but she refused to yield. She had spent hours running drills with the Lycans, each one pushing her harder than the last. They were stronger, more relentless, their endurance damn near supernatural. But she had something they didn't—an iron will forged in fire.

A sharp pain lanced through her side where a clawed hand had grazed her earlier. Blood seeped into the fabric of her tunic, sticking it to her skin. She could taste copper on her tongue, feel the ache in her limbs settling deep into her bones. Still, she gripped her sword tighter, refusing to show weakness.

A snarl to her left—too close.

She spun just as the Lycan lunged, massive and feral, golden eyes locked onto her with predatory focus. The force of the charge sent her skidding across the dirt, her boots digging into the ground to find traction. She barely raised her sword in time, locking it against their forearms. Claws scraped against steel, sparks flashing in the night.

"You're slowing," the Lycan growled, their voice rough with exertion.

Seraphina spat blood into the dirt and lifted her chin, smirking despite the exhaustion weighing her down. "You talking or fighting?"

A sharp, rumbling laugh—then they attacked again.

This time, she was ready.

You're training to avoid him. His tone was maddeningly smug.

Shut up.

Technically impossible, seeing as I live in your head. He sighed. *Honestly, it's mostly just me keeping you company these days while you obsessively pretend your heart hasn't turned into a battleground.*

She ducked under a wild swing, shifting her weight at the last second and slamming her elbow into their ribs. The Lycan grunted, stumbling back a step. It wasn't much, but it was enough. Seraphina seized the opening, twisting her blade in a quick, ruthless arc. The flat of it struck across the Lycan's back, a warning, a claim to dominance.

But they weren't finished.

I said, shut up. Can you not see I am busy?

A clawed hand shot out, slamming into her ribs. The impact sent her sprawling, her back hitting the ground hard enough to knock the breath from her lungs. Stars danced in her vision. She barely had time to register the weight pressing down on her chest, pinning her to the dirt.

The Lycan loomed over her, blue eyes gleaming like the depths of the ocean. "Yield."

Seraphina's fingers curled into the soil.

Touched a nerve, did I? We both know you could have ended this little scuffle ages ago, but no... the distractions. His tone held all the smugness that his age provided, and it was maddening to Seraphina.

Summoning the last of her strength, she twisted sharply, wrenching her arm free. She grabbed the Lycan's wrist and used their momentum against them, dragging them off balance as she rolled. Before they could recover, she sprang onto their back, locking her legs around their ribs, her arm hooked tight under their throat.

The Lycan thrashed, snarling, trying to throw her off, but she held fast, tightening her grip.

Her voice was a low whisper in their ear. "Yield."

A long, tense silence. Then—a low, reluctant growl.

The Lycan's body convulsed beneath her, the thick fur receding, bones shifting with a sickening crackle. Within seconds, the massive beast had melted away, leaving behind the lean, sweat-slicked form of a young woman.

Lyra.

Seraphina let out a breath, pushing herself up and rolling onto her back beside her friend, staring up at the sky. The fight had left both of them spent, their chests rising and falling in tandem as they lay in the dirt, utterly drained.

Lyra huffed a laugh. "You fight like a demon."

Seraphina turned her head, smirking despite the exhaustion gripping her limbs. "And you hit like gods damned war hammer."

Lyra let out a breathless chuckle, rubbing at the bruises forming along her ribs. "One day, I will win."

Seraphina grinned. "Not today."

A moment of quiet stretched between them, the night settling around them in its cool embrace.

Then Lyra sat up, offering a hand. "Come on, let's get cleaned up before someone thinks we actually tried to kill each other."

Seraphina groaned but took her hand, letting Lyra pull her to her feet. Her body ached, her lungs burned, but damn if she didn't feel alive.

They staggered off together, two warriors bound by blood, sweat, and the unyielding fire of the fight.

The cool night air was a balm against Seraphina's sweat-slicked skin as she and Lyra staggered toward the river, their steps slow, weighed down by exhaustion. Every inch of Seraphina's body ached, but it was an ache that felt earned, like every bruise and scrape was proof that she was still standing.

Lyra rolled her shoulders with a wince, muttering, "You ever think we should train during the day like normal people?"

Seraphina snorted. "And let everyone watch me get my ass handed to me? No thanks."

Lyra huffed a laugh. "Please. You're the only one who makes me work for a win. The others just roll over the second I shift."

Seraphina shot her a sidelong glance. "And what, you think fighting at night strengthens us?"

Lyra grinned, nudging her with an elbow. "You tell me. Ever noticed how much sharper your senses get out here? The darkness forces you to feel instead of relying on sight. Every sound, every shift in the air—it teaches you to move on instinct."

Seraphina considered that. She had noticed it—the way her body had learned to expect an attack before she even saw it coming, the way the night forced her to rely on more than just her eyes.

Lyra stretched, groaning as they reached the water's edge. "Besides, if we trained during the day, I'd be too busy showing off for all the pretty boys." She smirked. "And you would be too busy scowling at them."

Seraphina rolled her eyes but grinned as she crouched by the river, cupping the cool water in her hands and splashing it over her face. The cold sent a shock through her system, washing away the sweat and grime. "You know, I'm not completely opposed to the idea of flirting with someone one day."

Lyra gasped, clutching her chest in mock horror. "Seraphina? Flirting? The apocalypse must be upon us."

Seraphina flicked water at her, laughing when Lyra yelped and scrambled away.

They fell into a peaceful rhythm, washing off the dirt and blood, letting the river's steady flow lull them into a comfortable silence.

Lyra eyed Seraphina across the water. "So, where did you learn to fight like that?"

Seraphina hesitated, running a hand through her damp hair. "A little here, a little there. My mother taught me how to throw a punch. My brother was the one who taught me sword skills. My father —" she swallowed, then shook her head. "He taught me how to take a hit."

Lyra frowned but didn't push. Instead, she smirked. "Explains why you fight like you've got nothing to lose."

Seraphina smirked back. "Explains why you fight like a rabid animal."

Lyra gasped, feigning offence. "Excuse you. I fight with precision."

Seraphina gave her a flat look. "You bit me last week."

Lyra grinned. "Tactics."

Seraphina laughed, shaking her head. "You're impossible."

Lyra leaned back on her hands, watching the stars reflected in the water. "You know," she said, more softly this time, "I like this. Just us. No battles, no orders, no expectations. Just... training, talking, making fun of each other."

Seraphina stretched her legs out, letting the exhaustion settle in. "Me too."

And she meant it.

For all the chaos of their lives, for all the war and bloodshed and uncertainty, moments like this—just her and Lyra, aching but alive, laughing under the stars—felt like something worth holding onto. It was a friendship she hadn't expected, but over the weeks of training as winter slowly bled into spring, it was a friendship that had grown to mean everything to Seraphina.

A figure emerged from the shadows—a guard, his armour clinking softly in the night. He paused for a moment, panting, before bowing his head in respect.

"Alpha's orders, Lady Seraphina. You're needed in the war room. Now."

Seraphina straightened, her heart suddenly picking up speed. "What's going on?"

The guard's expression was grim. "The enemy is close. They're drawing near the border—closer than we thought."

Without a word, Seraphina turned to Lyra, who gave her a silent nod, eyes sharp with concern.

"I'll catch up later," Seraphina said. "Stay safe."

Lyra nodded. "Don't get yourself killed."

* * *

Seraphina followed the guard in silence through the camp, her mind racing. As they approached the war room, she could hear voices through the thick wooden doors, a murmur of urgency. The door creaked open, revealing the Alpha, his commanding presence filling the room, and Dylan, standing at attention beside him.

Seraphina bowed her head in respect. "You called for me?"

The Alpha glanced up, his dark eyes narrowing as he assessed her. "It's worse than we thought. The enemy is pushing closer to our borders—and to the villages near the forest that have remained untouched."

Seraphina's heart tightened. The villages in that area were small, peaceful—places she'd once visited as a child. She couldn't bear the thought of their falling. Not to the corruption.

"We'll need to act fast," the Alpha continued. "Dylan, you and I will handle the border. We'll stop them before they get any closer."

Dylan nodded, his expression fierce, ready for battle.

"The rest of you," the Alpha said, his gaze flicking to Seraphina, then to the others gathered in the room, "will split up. Kai, Seraphina, and Aurion will head to the forest near the village and deal with the demon terrorising it."

Kai's lips curled into a small grin. "Looks like I'll get to babysit again."

Seraphina rolled her eyes. "I can handle a demon, Kai. Don't get cocky."

But her teasing was short-lived when Vaelrik spoke up, his voice low, with a hint of tension in it.

"I don't like it," he muttered, his eyes flicking over to Kai. "She's going with him? Not sure I trust him to keep her safe."

Kade, standing next to Vaelrik, crossed his arms with a snort. "Nyx is strong enough to handle herself. She doesn't need a babysitter." His voice was firm, but there was something protective in it, something that made Seraphina's heart flutter ever so slightly.

Before anyone could speak further, Vaelrik shot Kade a sharp look, but the Alpha's voice cut through the mounting tension like a knife.

"I've decided. Sera and Kai will take care of the demon. Vaelrik, Kade, you'll secure the border with us. We leave in a week. Our allies and warriors are currently holding the line, but we will need to end this. Prepare yourselves."

Seraphina's stomach twisted with the weight of it all, but before she could speak, the Alpha's gaze softened, just for a moment.

"Oh, and Seraphina," he added, his voice a little more casual now, "I want you to practice your magic with Aurion. You'll need control if you don't want to set everything on fire by accident."

She didn't know whether to be offended or grateful. "I've got it under control," she muttered, but the Alpha's piercing stare silenced her protest.

"If you say so, but better safe than sorry," he said with a smirk. "Now, get some rest. You'll need it."

Seraphina's heart was still pounding as she made her way out of the war room, her mind racing with the weight of the coming days. But as she turned, she caught Kade's eye. His usual cocky grin was gone, replaced with a rare, softer look.

"You're going to be fine," he said, his voice low, but there was something in it—something that made her breath catch in her throat.

She smiled back, though her heart was still twisted in uncertainty. "I know."

Chapter 38

Only a couple of days had passed since the Alpha's request.

And yet, Seraphina could feel the weight of failure in the air. She had gotten no better at harnessing her magic. Despite her relentless attempts to push forward, the power within her was still as unpredictable and volatile as ever. Each time she tried to grasp it, it slipped through her fingers like smoke.

But she refused to stop.

The sun hung high in the sky, spilling gold over the clearing, the warmth of spring now finally melting away the remnants of winter's bite. It washed over the earth, coaxing the last of the frost from the ground. The trees had budded, their branches light with new life. The once-frozen air was rich with the scent of damp soil and fresh growth—an odd contrast to the frustration that simmered in Seraphina's chest.

Seraphina sighed. "Aurion, we've been at this for hours. Can't we take a break?"

"No," he snapped, his tiny claws digging into the rock beneath him. "You've barely improved, and you're still treating your magic like a wild beast instead of an extension of yourself."

She rolled her eyes. "It kind of *is* a wild beast, in case you haven't noticed. It literally burns things if I don't concentrate."

Aurion exhaled sharply, wings fluttering in frustration. "That's because

351

you *refuse* to listen! You're supposed to *guide* the power, not just throw it around and hope it sticks."

"I *am* listening," she argued, gripping the hilt of her sword tightly. "It's just—"

"The whispers?" Aurion interrupted, tilting his head.

Seraphina's stomach twisted. She hadn't mentioned them aloud, but of course, he knew. He always did.

She glanced at the blade in her hand. It was a masterpiece of obsidian, its edges shifting with an unnatural shimmer, like it was half-real, half-formed from the magic itself. And it spoke—not in words exactly, but in murmurs at the edge of her mind. Soft, steady. It wasn't malicious, but it was *there*, always calling to her, like the power it carried was waiting for something.

"It's disturbing," she admitted, gripping it tighter. "I don't like the way it *feels*."

Aurion sighed, his irritation fading slightly. "It's not trying to harm you, little one. It's part of you. The balance to what you are."

She frowned. "Balance?"

"Yes. You fear it because you don't understand it. But it *chose* you, just as your magic did. Stop fighting it."

Seraphina swallowed hard. She wanted to protest, to tell him that there was something *wrong* about the way the blade hummed with energy, how it felt like it knew her better than she knew herself. But... she *had* felt moments of control when she wielded it, moments where the wildfire inside her didn't feel like chaos, but something focused, something whole.

She exhaled and adjusted her stance. "Fine," she muttered. "One more try."

Aurion watched as she raised the blade, positioning her hands exactly as he had instructed. This time, she *listened*—not just to his words, but to the hum of power running through her. She felt the magic settle, not flaring wildly, not burning uncontrolled, but steady, *balanced*.

A gust of wind rushed through the clearing as she channelled her energy, and for the first time, it didn't explode outward—it flowed, directed into the blade's edge, forming a shimmering arc of raw power. It pulsed once, then dissipated.

Seraphina blinked. "Did I just—"

Aurion sat back, smug now. "Finally," he grumbled. "Took you long enough."

She shot him a glare. "You're nagging again."

"I'm not nagging Seraphina. I am *instructing*," he corrected, preening his wings.

She rolled her eyes. "Fancy way to say nagging." But she couldn't hide the small smile tugging at her lips.

Aurion watched her for a moment before adding in a quieter tone, "Do not be afraid of it, Seraphina. Power without control is destruction, but fear without trust is just another kind of weakness."

Seraphina glanced at the blade again whispers were still present, but... not quite as unsettling as before. She wasn't sure she fully trusted it yet, but for the first time, she didn't *reject* it either.

Maybe that was enough. For now.

It was late afternoon by the time Aurion had allowed her to be released from her training, satisfied she could control her power enough not to burn a forest down. The afternoon sun hung lazily in the sky, casting golden hues over the training grounds as she approached Kai, standing watching as Kade and Vaelrik squared off. The clash of steel rang through the air, each strike echoing with lethal precision. A small audience had gathered—though their attention wasn't entirely on the fight.

Sera leaned against the wooden fence, chin propped on her hand, watching Kade and Vaelrik with a contemplative gaze. Kai sat beside her, their arms crossed as they observed with mild amusement. Aurion, as usual, perched on her shoulder.

They were watching warriors in their prime, their bodies honed by years of battle. Kade moved with raw, unrelenting force—each strike of his sword backed by sheer power, his muscles flexing with every motion. The sun gleamed off his bare torso, highlighting the ridges of his abdomen and the scars that carved stories across his skin. His silver hair, usually

353

bound, had come loose from the exertion, damp strands clinging to his sharp jawline.

Vaelrik was a contrast to Kade's brute force—fluid and unpredictable, his every movement calculated. He was leaner, but no less powerful, his dark hair tied at the nape of his neck, though a few strands had fallen into his strikingly intense gaze. His blade moved like an extension of his body, swift and deadly. The sweat on his skin caught the sunlight, accentuating the corded muscles in his arms as he blocked one of Kade's heavier strikes.

"They're really going at it," Kai mused, tilting his head. "Almost like they have something to prove."

Aurion snorted. "Or someone to impress."

Sera hummed. "I mean... if they want to show off, who am I to complain?"

Kai arched a brow. "Sera. Are you ogling?"

Sera didn't even look away. "No. I'm appreciating."

Aurion chuckled. "Right, right? And the difference?"

"The difference," Sera said, eyes still trained on Kade as he ducked under Vaelrik's blade, "is that ogling is shameless. Appreciation has dignity."

Kai outright cackled. "I'm not sure staring at Kade like he's a prime cut of steak counts as dignity."

Before Sera could retort, a familiar voice chimed in.

"Oh, we're appreciating, are we?"

Lyra appeared beside her, sliding onto the fence with a knowing smirk. She took one look at the shirtless, sweat-slicked warriors before them and let out a low whistle. "Gods, what are they made of? Carved stone?"

Sera grinned. "Right? It's unfair."

Kai shook his head, feigning disappointment. "This is tragic. Two powerful women, reduced to—"

"—just let us have this, Kai," Sera cut in, waving him off.

Lyra sighed dramatically. "I mean, look at the way Kade moves. All power, all control—"

"—and Vaelrik?" Sera added. "Like a storm, all precision and unpredictability."

Aurion held his head up stiffly. "Okay, okay, I think that's enough poetic admiration."

Kai pointed at them both. "I feel like we've learned something valuable today."

"Mm-hm," Aurion agreed. "Our fearless warrior women? Absolute disasters when presented with pretty men and violence."

Lyra placed a hand over her heart. "We are but humble observers of beauty, Aurion."

Sera nodded solemnly. "It's a burden, really."

Kai leaned in. "If I go fight shirtless, will I also get admiration?"

Sera deadpanned, "Only if you survive Kade's sparring first."

Kai immediately leaned back. "Nope. I enjoy living."

Aurion laughed. "Smart man."

Sera looked at her friends and felt a pang in her heart at how peaceful this moment felt and almost felt guilty about the war surrounding them.

Chapter 39

Later that evening, as the sun dipped beneath the horizon, Seraphina found herself alone in the training yard. She was getting some extra practice with her sword. She could feel it whispering to her, at the edge of her mind, *You are not as weak as they believe. You need to take only what is yours.* She startled at the sword, almost dropping it. It unnerved her when it did that. Because of the prophecy and the voices of the gods, on the day she got the sword, she couldn't work out if this was a good thing or an evil thing. The faint amber glow of the setting sun seemed to reflect the ache in her muscles, the burn from the day's sparring settling into her bones. But it wasn't just physical exhaustion that plagued her; it was the quiet storm brewing within, a knot of emotions she couldn't untangle. Especially when they were running out of time before their missions. She couldn't deny that she was worried.

Vaelrik's voice broke the silence, cutting through the stillness with a sharp, teasing edge. "You've gotten better, you know. Remember when you used to trip over your own feet?"

Seraphina rolled her eyes, instinctively retreating into the familiarity of their old banter. "I recall you being the one flat on your back more often than not."

He laughed, and for a moment, it was as though no time had passed at all—like they were back in the carefree days before everything fell apart.

The warmth of his laughter spread through her chest, pulling her in. "Fair point. But I let you win sometimes."

"Sure you did," she shot back, the words tinged with sarcasm, but her heart wasn't in it. Something felt... different. The smile that had once been a comfort now twisted in her stomach.

But then Vaelrik's laughter died, replaced by a quiet seriousness that took her off guard. "You know, I never really apologised properly."

Her chest tightened, and she fought to keep her expression neutral. She knew where this was going. She knew he was going to bring up the past, the betrayal that had torn them apart, and she wasn't ready for it.

"You don't have to," she murmured, forcing her gaze to the ground, anything to avoid meeting his eyes. "I forgave you."

"That's not the same as forgetting," he breathed, his voice laden with something—regret, maybe, or guilt? She couldn't tell. "And it doesn't mean you don't still feel something."

She stiffened, her pulse quickening as she squeezed her fists at her sides. Damn him. "The past is the past, Vaelrik. We both moved on."

His gaze locked onto hers, molten gold flickering with a vulnerability she hadn't seen before. "Did we?" he asked, his voice barely above a whisper. "Because I haven't. Not really."

Seraphina's breath hitched. His words slammed into her like a tidal wave, crashing over everything she'd built up in the years since their separation. She opened her mouth, but no sound came out. What could she say? How could she respond to that?

"I still care about you, Little Flame," he continued, his voice trembling slightly, as though the words were a secret he'd been holding back for far too long. "Not just because of what we were, but because of who you are now. Your fire and fury, strength and stubbornness. And I love you for all of it."

The confession hung between them, suffocating in its weight. Her heart twisted painfully in her chest, and she wanted to push him away, to scream, to deny it all—but she couldn't. She could only stand there, frozen, as the past and present collided in a way she couldn't escape.

357

The tension between them was palpable, thick with everything left unsaid. It curled in the air like smoke, suffocating her, making it hard to breathe. She opened her mouth again, but nothing came out. She didn't know how to handle this. How could she? She was still reeling from the rawness of his words.

"Vaelrik..." she started, voice barely a whisper, but it was too late.

"I needed to tell you before we all left on our own missions. So you knew what I felt." He whispered.

He reached out, his hand warm as he cupped her jaw, tilting her face up to meet his. Her heart skipped a beat, and the pull between them was magnetic, impossible to ignore. She felt her chest tighten, and every part of her wanted to pull away, but she couldn't move her feet.

His touch was hesitant at first, searching for permission. His fingers lingered on her skin, and she felt his hesitation, a silent question hanging between them. She should pull back, she should step away, but she didn't. She didn't know how to say no when everything inside her was screaming to.

His soft but desperate lips brushed hers, and for a moment, the memory of their past and the ghosts of everything they once were overwhelmed her. She let herself remember what it felt like to love him, to trust him. To believe in him.

But then reality crashed back in—a brutal reminder of everything that had happened since. The kiss tasted of betrayal and heartache, a bitter poison on her lips. Her pulse hammered in her ears as Vaelrik's touch made her body recoil, as if she had been burned. Her vision blurred, not from the stinging air but from a flood of memories—pain, loss, the sharp edge of a broken trust that had cut deeper than she'd ever thought possible. She could taste the salt of her own regret, the weight of choices that had led her to this moment, and it felt like a cruel joke.

She pulled away violently, gasping for air, her chest heaving as she staggered backward. Her hands shook, betraying her, as she tried to step away from him, the rawness of everything consuming her.

"Vaelrik, I—" The words caught in her throat, suffocating her, as though her very body refused to let them pass her lips. They were impossible to say—too much, too raw, too broken.

Her heart was splintering as she stared at him, the shadow of their past between them, suffocating what little hope she had left.

Then, the tension shattered with the sudden rustle of leaves, the unmistakable sound of footsteps approaching. Her head snapped toward the noise, eyes wide, and her breath caught in her throat.

There at the edge of the training yard stood Kade and Kai—silent, motionless. The weight of their gaze was a force in itself. It was impossible to look away from Kade, even though she desperately wanted to. His eyes locked onto hers, a void of unreadable emotion, a churning storm that threatened to pull her under. His expression was a mask—stone-cold and unmoving—but she could feel the tension radiating off him. Every muscle in his body was stiff with restraint, as though he was fighting to hold back something wild, something raw. His jaw clenched so hard she swore she could hear the grind of his teeth, and his fists were balled at his sides, knuckles stark and white with the strain. He looked like he was about to break—like he was moments away from unleashing all the anger and hurt that had been building inside him.

But he didn't speak. He just stood there, watching her with that storm-dark gaze—a look that had always unsettled her more than she cared to admit. The silence between them was suffocating, heavier than any words could be.

And beside him, Kai just stood with his arms crossed, wearing that all-too-familiar look of quiet disbelief mixed with just a touch of exasperation. His sharp gaze flicked between her and Vaelrik, then he sighed, rubbing a hand over his face.

Seraphina could almost hear his thoughts—this was the last thing he wanted to deal with.

"Are you okay?" Kai's voice broke through the silence, low and careful, a quiet question that still carried a weight of concern. It was barely more than a whisper, but it hit her like a sledgehammer — a reminder of the surrounding wreckage.

But Kade didn't even look at him. His focus never left her, and when he finally spoke, his voice was low—strained, as if each word had cost him something deep.

"Maybe it's for the best," he muttered, and the words felt like a knife to her chest. He didn't raise his voice. He didn't shout. But the pain in his tone was unmistakable. And it broke her all over again.

Kai scoffed, a sound of disbelief and frustration.

Seraphina couldn't bear it. Her heart shattered in her chest, splintering into jagged pieces that she couldn't put back together. The weight of Kade's words, the coldness that had crept into his eyes—it all felt too much.

She didn't want to look at them. Didn't want to see the disappointment in Kade's gaze, the hurt and resignation that bled through his silence. She couldn't bear to see him like this, couldn't bear to face the mess of everything she had caused.

Without thinking, she turned and ran. Her legs burned as she pushed herself harder, faster, the world blurring around her. She didn't care where she was going—only that she had to get away. She had to escape before she broke down, before she let the overwhelming pain swallow her whole.

Behind her, Kai's voice echoed faintly, calling her name, but she didn't stop. She couldn't stop. Not yet. Not when everything was falling apart.

Vaelrik exhaled sharply, rubbing a hand down his face in frustration. Then he glanced toward the outskirts of the yard, where the sound of footsteps had already made it clear Kade and Kai had witnessed everything.

"Of course you two would hear that," Vaelrik muttered, his voice more exasperated than usual.

Seraphina barely registered her surroundings as she ran, her breath uneven, her chest tight with emotions she couldn't process. Vaelrik's words, his confession, had cracked something wide open inside her— something raw, something she wasn't ready to face.

As she ran, a familiar warmth curled around her shoulders, a presence that anchored her even as her heart threatened to break in two. The soft, silken weight of Aurion's scaled form wound around her, the warmth of his small dragon body pressing into her skin. His tail looped gently around her arm, and his wings tucked neatly against his back as he nuzzled into the crook of her neck, offering silent comfort.

I did not see that coming, Aurion mused, his voice drifting into her mind through their bond—a low, comforting hum. She felt it reverberate in the pit of her stomach.

Seraphina barely managed a breath, her voice weak but still full of dry humour. "Yeah. Me neither."

A gentle pulse of warmth radiated from him. The quiet understanding of someone who had seen too much of her pain already, felt it through their shared connection. Aurion had always been her grounding force, her silent confidant in times like these. He didn't need to ask what she was feeling—he knew just as well as she did. He knew her history with Vaelrik, the hurt Vaelrik had inflicted, and the scars she had never fully healed.

But Aurion was always there. A constant. A reminder that, no matter how broken she felt, she wasn't entirely alone.

Seraphina pressed a trembling hand against his side, a silent thank you.

"Seraphina."

She turned at the sound of Kai's voice, her vision blurred with unshed tears. He had caught up with her, but his presence wasn't the confrontation she had expected. His sharp gaze softened as it swept over her, taking in her state—her ragged breath, the tears that clung to her lashes.

Without another word, he simply pulled her into his arms. No questions. No demands. Just warmth, a comforting presence that wrapped around her like a lifeline.

She broke.

A ragged breath left her lips as she buried her face against his shoulder, her hands clutching him like he was the only thing keeping her upright. The tears came then—hot and unrelenting, pouring out of her as if they had been waiting for this moment to spill. Kai let her cry and didn't stop her. He held her with no expectation, his hands firm but gentle as he soothed her with quiet words.

"It's okay," he murmured, his voice a balm against her frayed nerves. "I understand."

And she knew he did. Of all the people, Kai understood the weight of the past, the ache of something unresolved pressing against old scars. Instead of telling her she was fine, he just held her. He didn't tell her to move on. He just let her feel.

When her breathing finally steadied, she felt Kai pull back slightly, though his hands remained on her shoulders. His usual cocky grin softened into something lighter, something meant to lift the crushing weight pressing down on her.

"Hey," he started, mischief glinting in his eyes. "Want to do what we used to do as kids?"

Seraphina blinked, sniffing. "What?"

Kai smirked, then, in a fluid motion, he shifted—his form elongating, muscles stretching, fur bristling as he fell forward onto four massive paws. His dark-furred Lycan form loomed over her, glowing green eyes gleaming with boyish challenge.

For the first time that evening, Seraphina let out a choked laugh.

Aurion flicked his tail, tilting his head. "Oh, this is going to end in disaster or superb entertainment."

Ignoring him, Seraphina wiped at her damp cheeks before grinning up at Kai's now-wolfish form. "You're ridiculous."

Kai chuffed, lowering himself slightly in invitation. It was an old game, a childhood habit—the thrill of racing under the moon, of escaping reality for a little while.

She didn't hesitate.

She vaulted onto his back, gripping onto his thick fur, and the moment she was steady, Kai bolted forward, launching them into a reckless, wild run through the trees. The cool night air whipped against her face, with the scent of damp earth filling her senses.

Aurion shot into the sky, weaving between branches with effortless ease, his laughter echoing through the bond they shared.

"I can't believe you let her ride you like a common beast," Aurion teased, banking to the side as Kai huffed in amusement, his claws scraping against the earth as he adjusted his speed.

She's the only one who can. Kai's voice resonated in Aurion's mind, rough yet fond, as his massive paws thudded against the ground with controlled power. He wove through the forest; the trees blurring around them as if he were born to move like this.

Aurion, still gliding effortlessly between them, tilted his head, his silver-white scales catching the dim moonlight. "I must admit, Kai, you surprise me."

Kai snorted, his tone dripping with amusement. *That so?*

"Yes." Aurion's voice softened, a rare note of sincerity slipping through the usual teasing. "Because out of everyone, I trust you the most never to hurt her."

Kai faltered, just for a second. It was so subtle that Seraphina almost didn't catch it, but the change in his energy was enough to make her pause. He seemed to hold his breath, if only for a heartbeat.

She squeezed his fur lightly, her fingers brushing through the coarse strands as silent reassurance. In that simple gesture, something profound passed between them—a shared understanding of loyalty, trust, and the fragile bonds that held them all together.

For a moment, everything around them seemed to still, as if the forest itself recognised the depth of the moment. But then, they were moving again—faster now, as the night swallowed them whole.

Aurion took the lead, soaring higher into the sky, his wings beating in a rhythmic, fluid motion. Kai pushed forward, his pace steady and unwavering, the wind howling around them as the world blurred into a mix of shadows and moonlit silver streaks.

But then, something shifted. A strange sensation bloomed in Seraphina's mind, a spark of awareness that wasn't there before. It was subtle at first— just a ripple, a tug—but it quickly expanded, like an invisible thread linking her to something vast and familiar.

You can hear me now? Kai's voice echoed in her thoughts, warm but with a hint of surprise.

She stiffened, her breath catching in her throat. *Wait. What?*

Aurion, who had been flying just beside them, let out a pleased hum, the sound vibrating through their bond like a gentle purr. *I helped you create a bond with Kai,* he said, his voice calm yet filled with something like quiet pride. *Magic makes it possible. Now you can access each other's thoughts—and feelings. But only because I trust him. He can also hear me, like you do.*

Seraphina's eyes widened, her pulse quickening as the weight of Aurion's words settled in her mind. The connection—the one she had with the dragon—was something she had known to be unique. But this? This was something entirely new. The power that had always flowed between her and Aurion had now stretched, woven into the very fabric of her relationship with Kai.

"How?" she asked, her voice almost breathless as she glanced down at the massive form of the wolf racing under her. "How did you do this?"

Aurion's tone was rare, almost wistful. *You and I have shared a bond since the first time we met. But it wasn't until now that you were ready to connect with Kai in this way. Trust Seraphina. It is at the core of the bond between us. Not just trust with me, but trust in him. And more importantly, in yourself.*

Seraphina's mind whirled, trying to make sense of the vastness of this connection, of the intimate trust that had just been established between them all. It was more than just magic—it was a union of hearts, forged through shared battles and unspoken understanding.

A sense of warmth bloomed in her chest as she felt Kai's presence more clearly than ever before. His emotions, his thoughts, even the way his heart beat, seemed to pulse in rhythm with hers. The connection was dizzying in its intensity, but it was also grounding—a tether to something far larger than herself.

She couldn't help wondering how deep this bond would go. Could she feel his pain, his joy, his fears now, as he would feel hers? The thought was both terrifying and comforting all at once.

"Are you okay?" she asked him softly, the words slipping out before she realised it, as if the connection had given her access to his soul in a way she had never expected.

Kai's voice filtered through her thoughts again, gruff but undeniably tender. *I've got your back, Seraphina. Always!*

A small smile tugged at the corner of her lips, her heart lifting at the sincerity in his words, even though he didn't speak them aloud. And in that moment, she knew, without a doubt, that this bond—this inexplicable, magical connection—was something that would define them all and she would definitely need to ask Aurion more questions on the extent it could go and how far it could stretch.

Kai huffed in amusement, his massive paws thudding against the earth. *Guess that makes me special, huh?*

Seraphina groaned, but she couldn't stop the small smile that tugged at her lips. The bond between them pulsed warmly, a newfound connection settling deep within her soul.

Chapter 40

Seraphina's feet shuffled across the dirt as she tried to keep her focus. The sun beat down on her; her sweat mixing with the grit of the training grounds. The air smelled of dust and exertion, but it did little to clear the storm brewing inside her. She had only two more days before Kai and she were to be sent off. Her muscles ached from the last round of sparring, yet her mind was far from the movements of her blade.

Across the yard, Kade was engaged in training with Kai's Lycan squad, his powerful frame moving with unnerving grace. His silver hair shimmered in the harsh light, strands like the brush of moonlight against the sky. He was so damn beautiful it hurt. Despite his turmoil, each swing of his sword and each precise movement seemed to draw her in. The confusion, the guilt, the anger... it all swirled in her chest like a storm threatening to drown her. She knew better than to give in.

But she couldn't stop watching. He still hadn't spoken to her since Vaelrik had kissed her. In fact, he had been ignoring her existence.

Sera, you can't keep staring like this. Kai's voice was soft but insistent, the edge of mischief clear even through their mental bond. She could feel his thoughts slithering through the connection, teasing, nudging, and prying.

I'm not staring at anyone, she bit out, not looking at him. Her grip tightened around the hilt of her sword. Focus. That's all that mattered.

Right, Kai's mental voice purred, his amusement filling her mind. *And here I thought you were going to keep your head in the game.* She felt the mental nudge of his thoughts pointing toward Kade, who was now running through a series of moves with calculated precision, his expression intense. *Is it just me, or does he look even more... delicious when he's angry?* Kai mused.

Seraphina's face flushed, but she quickly suppressed the feeling, trying to focus. *Shut up, Kai.*

Just imagine it, Kai teased, his voice a whisper inside her head, *those arms, the way his shirt clings to his chest, the muscles rippling as he moves... so distracting, don't you think?*

Her pulse quickened, and she tightened her stance. *I said, shut up.*

Kai responded with a mental grin. *You're too fun to mess with. But if you're really trying to ignore him, stop watching him. Every. Single. Time.* His voice dropped to a lower, mocking tone. *I can practically feel your heart racing.*

"Stop it," she snapped, louder than she meant to, and immediately regretted it when she saw Kade glance in her direction. His eyes met hers briefly, sharp and unreadable, before his attention shifted back to his squad.

That's a good sign, Aurion's voice suddenly rang out in her mind, rich with sarcasm. She hadn't noticed him slipping into their mental connection. *It's better for him to see you're struggling. He's probably torturing himself, thinking you've already moved on. Let him stew.*

Her throat tightened. *I haven't moved on,* she thought, though she wasn't sure if she was convincing herself or anyone else.

Kai chuckled, the sound smooth and dark in her mind. *You keep telling yourself that.*

She couldn't afford any of the chaos, the pain, the haunting memories of things that could never be undone.

But Kai, ever the troublemaker, refused to relent. *I think we both know what you really need is a brief release. Maybe spar with Kade—get the heat out, hmm?* He teased again, his voice light.

"Get out of my head, Kai!" she growled, frustration curling in her gut.

Her eyes flicked back to Kade. Every perfect motion of his seemed to pull her in deeper. The way his muscles shifted beneath his dark tunic, the focus in his expression, the way he seemed to move as if nothing in the world could touch him... everything about him seemed so... impossible. How could someone be so full of strength, so devoted to their mission, seem so untouchable, and yet she could still feel the distance between them?

And why did it hurt so much?

Seraphina let out a slow breath, trying to control her racing thoughts. This wasn't about him. It couldn't be. She had to bury her emotions, focus on the training, on the mission, on what came next.

Seraphina's eyes flicked to Kade once more, her stomach twisting in a knot as his muscles flexed with each movement. He wasn't just sparring anymore; he was showing off, trying to outdo every fighter around him. Her gaze locked on his sharp profile, and her thoughts scattered. She couldn't focus on anything but him. Focus on the training, she reminded herself again, but it felt like an endless loop.

Kai's voice slithered through her mind once more, light and teasing. Laughing at her.

"Shut. Up," she growled under her breath. She felt her pulse rising. She couldn't afford to let Kai mess with her like this. Stay composed. Don't let anyone see.

But it was hard when Kai's voice was relentless, filling her thoughts with his observations. *I mean, really. His hair looks so right when it's tussled like that, doesn't it? Almost like he's been through something. It's like... the perfect mix of danger and allure.*

Her face flushed. "Kai, I swear to the gods, I will—"

The voice of one of the squad members, a tall, burly man named Raze, interrupted her outburst. He was wiping sweat from his brow, clearly puzzled by her muttered words. "Is everything okay, Seraphina? You... kind of look like you're about to burn something down."

"Fine," she snapped, glaring at him. He wasn't used to her sharpness. Most of the time, she was stoic, calculated. Raze raised an eyebrow but didn't push it further, though the concern in his expression lingered. He could sense there was something wrong, but like the others, he did not know what was truly going on in her head.

Lyra stepped up to Raze, a sly smile playing on her lips. "She looks way too distracted. Bet she's thinking about someone—probably Kade, right?"

Seraphina gritted her teeth, willing her body to calm down. This is not happening, she thought furiously. But the teasing from Kai didn't stop.

If only they knew she wasn't even hearing her own thoughts anymore— just Kai's commentary on everything she wasn't supposed to feel.

Aurion's voice, low and sultry, joined the conversation with perfect timing. *You know, if you just let him kiss you, maybe all of this would stop. But no... You just keep pretending it's nothing.*

Seraphina's body stiffened. "I'm trying to train," she hissed, hands shaking as she attempted a defensive move. It wasn't working. Her sword was heavier; her movements sluggish.

Lyra caught her slip immediately. "Uh, you okay there?" She glanced over at Kade, who was now effortlessly dodging an attack from one of the Lycans, his eyes briefly meeting Seraphina's. That same unreadable expression. But something flashed in his gaze—something that made her heart skip a beat. She couldn't look at him. Not now. Not like this.

The squad's attention shifted toward her. It was too obvious. They were all watching her—Lyra, Raze, even the stoic Darek, who gave nothing away. But it wasn't just them. She could feel Kade's eyes still lingering on her, the weight of his unspoken thoughts pressing against her like a physical force.

"Okay, seriously," Raze said, his tone heavy with confusion. "What's going on, Seraphina? You're acting weird today. Something has distracted you all morning. Are you hurt? Did something happen?"

She opened her mouth to speak, to brush it off, but her own mind—no, Kai's voice—interrupted her before she could even get a word out.

Not hurt. Just complicated, Kai teased, as if he were watching her unravel in real-time. *You're doing a great job of hiding it though. Just keep it up for the rest of the squad, okay? They're all wondering why you're so tense.* His mental voice dropped lower, darker.

"Shut up!" Seraphina snarled, but her voice was louder than she intended, drawing the attention of everyone around her. Lyra raised an eyebrow. Raze exchanged a glance with Darek. Even Kade seemed to pause for a split second, his gaze narrowing as he registered the sharpness in her tone. But no one knew why she was so unhinged. They didn't understand the mental chaos Kai had woven into her mind.

Seraphina's head was a whirlwind. Every thought, every whisper from the bond with Kai, seemed to amplify her frustration. She had tried to focus on the training, but the constant teasing from Kai—his voice, his presence, his goddamn commentary—was enough to make her lose her mind.

She could feel the eyes of the squad on her. They were watching her, trying to figure out why she was acting so out of character. They did not know about the mental connection with Kai, no idea that he was making her nuts with every sly remark he made in her mind.

But then she heard it again—Kai's teasing tone, the mental thread snaking through her mind, laughing. *Is that the best you've got, Sera?*

Seraphina's patience snapped like a brittle twig. Without thinking, she stormed over to Kai, who was in the middle of demonstrating a series of combat stances with a few other squad members. She couldn't hold it in anymore.

She smacked him upside the head, hard enough that the sound rang out across the training ground. The squad froze. For a heartbeat, there was pure silence. Then, slowly, a few gasps of surprise. Everyone was staring.

Kai blinked in shock, his grin faltering. "What the hell, Sera?" He turned to face her, his eyes wide with exaggerated disbelief. "You hit me!"

Seraphina's lips twitched at the ridiculousness of it all. For a split second, the absurdity of the moment caught her, and her fury faded slightly. But it was still there—just simmering beneath the surface.

"Maybe you deserved it," she shot back, her voice sharp but with a hint of humour sneaking through. She could feel her heart racing, but it was easing now, a bit of the tension melting away. "You've been in my head all day, Kai. All day. I don't care what Aurion says about this bond, but if you keep this up, I swear to the gods I will block you out." She folded her arms across her chest, a half-smile tugging at her lips.

Kai, recovering from the initial shock, placed a hand on the back of his head. "What? You think I'm some kind of—"

"Yes," Seraphina cut him off, her voice dripping with playful mockery. "You're exactly that. And you've been making my head spin with your ridiculous commentary."

His grin slowly returned, with a teasing gleam flashing in his eyes. "Alright, alright. I'll stop messing with you... for now," he added with a wink.

Seraphina rolled her eyes but couldn't suppress the small laugh that slipped past her lips. "Next time, I'll just castrate you," she teased, the words laced with a hint of humour but still holding a little edge.

The squad was silent for a moment longer, processing the exchange. Suddenly, Lyra broke the tension with a loud laugh. "Okay, okay, I didn't see that coming!"

Kai chuckled, holding his hands up in mock surrender. "Hey, hey, I'm not asking for it, alright?"

Raze, still wide-eyed from the unexpected outburst, shook his head. "You guys are something else."

Seraphina flashed Kai a wry smile. "I think I've had enough of your mental games for one day," she added, her voice playful, but still with that spark of warning.

Kai shrugged, still grinning. "Fair enough. I'll lay off for now. But only because you've got me scared now." His tone was light, but there was something genuine behind it, an unspoken understanding between them.

Seraphina gave him a teasing look before turning to the squad. "Alright, enough standing around. Let's get back to it before someone else tests me."

And with that, the training resumed, the tension easing, and the squad's laughter filling the air as if the entire exchange had never happened. Kade stood at the edge of the training field, watching the playful banter between Seraphina and Kai. His brow furrowed slightly as he tried to make sense of what had just happened. One moment, Seraphina had smacked Kai upside the head, and the next, they were laughing as though nothing had ever happened. He didn't know how to read her anymore.

There was something wrong—he knew it; he could feel it in the air.

Kade stepped forward, ready to ask her if she was okay, but Seraphina didn't give him a chance. Without even acknowledging him, she turned on her heel and started walking toward the stronghold, her movements quick and purposeful.

"Kai," she called over her shoulder, barely pausing. "I'm going to handle something. I'll catch up later."

And just like that, she was gone, leaving him standing there in a mixture of confusion and concern. What had just happened? One minute, she was joking with Kai, and the next, she was all business again.

He ran a hand through his hair and glanced around, hoping someone could offer some kind of explanation. Raze was staring at him with wide eyes, still processing the exchange from earlier.

"What's going on with her?" Kade asked, his voice tight.

Raze shrugged helplessly, still looking after Seraphina. "Hell if I know, man." Kade could feel the knot in his stomach tighten. Something told him it had everything to do with that damn connection Seraphina had with Kai. He glanced over his shoulder, but she was already out of sight.

What is she up to?

* * *

Seraphina had barely reached the library before she felt the familiar presence in the air—Vaelrik. He was close. Too close. Her heart rate spiked, and the feeling of his dark, magnetic aura washed over her, like a chill crawling down her spine.

Her footsteps faltered, and for a moment, she froze, her mind racing for an escape. She had no time for his cryptic words, no patience for whatever it was he wanted to say. The last thing she needed right now was another lecture about her potential or her destiny, or, gods forbid, to kiss her again.

There was only one way out of this—her heart thudding in her chest. She turned on her heel and bolted down the hall.

Run. Run now.

Just as she rounded a corner, she saw Kade standing by the edge of the training yard, leaning against the wall, his arms crossed. He looked relaxed, yet there was a flicker of concern in his eyes as he noticed her rushing toward him.

"Kade!" she called, voice a bit too sharp, almost desperate. Her eyes were wide, and her breathing was heavy.

Kade straightened up, sensing her urgency. "Nyx, what's going on? You look—"

"I need to get away," she blurted out, not giving him time to respond. She was looking over her shoulder as she spotted Vaelrik coming towards them. "Please, I need you to come with me. Just—just for a run. Come on, Kade. Please."

Kade's eyes softened, a flash of understanding passing through them. He already knew what this was about. He knew exactly why she was running from Vaelrik. Even though his feelings about seeing them kiss still confused him, he couldn't deny her this. His gaze shifted to the training ground just behind her, and he let out a low breath.

"I've got you," he breathed. He didn't need to ask any more questions — he was her escape. "Let's go."

As they turned and began walking away, Seraphina kept her head down, not wanting to look back. She could feel Vaelrik's presence behind her, could almost hear his footsteps, but she didn't dare glance over her shoulder. Kade was her escape. For now, that was enough.

The moment they were out of the complex, Seraphina let out a breath she hadn't realised she'd been holding. Kade glanced over at her, sensing her relief but also the tension that lingered beneath her calm exterior. "I don't know what's going on, Nyx," he said softly, "but if you need this, we'll do it."

Seraphina nodded, forcing a small smile. "Thanks, Kade. You do not know how much this means."

* * *

Back at the training grounds, the squad had returned to their drills, but the moment Seraphina and Kade left, whispers spread.

"She looked like she was about to explode," Lyra commented, looking at Kai with a raised eyebrow. "What was that all about?"

Raze leaned in closer to Lyra, clearly curious. "Something's up with them, that's for sure. I've never seen her act like that before."

"I know." Kai added, with an amused glint in his eye. "It's Vaelrik. That guy just brings up her past. No idea why, but it's pretty obvious she doesn't want it."

"I don't know," Raze said, furrowing his brow. "Why is Kade always the one to calm her down? You'd think there'd be more people she trusts with that, like you, Kai."

Kai chuckled, shaking his head slightly. "Kade's her anchor. It's always been him since the war. Whenever things get too overwhelming for Sera, she knows Kade's there. She runs straight to him when she needs a breather, unless he is causing the problem, then I'm the one she looks for."

Lyra shot Kai a knowing look. "So that's why they're always so... close?"

Kai nodded, not missing a beat. "Exactly. Sera's got a lot on her plate. Kade's the one who keeps her grounded when the rest of the world is in chaos."

* * *

Meanwhile, out in the open fields, Seraphina was relaxing, her pace picking up as they ran side by side. Kade was right there with her, matching her every stride. It was familiar, almost comforting, despite the turmoil that still churned beneath her skin.

"You all right?" Kade asked, his voice cutting through the rhythmic sound of their feet pounding the earth. He wasn't prying, just asking.

She slowed slightly, finally allowing herself to catch her breath, the adrenaline of the escape still buzzing in her veins. "Yeah. I just... I can't deal with Vaelrik right now. Not with everything else going on."

Kade gave her a sidelong glance, then offered a small smirk. "I think I get it. No one's ever really 'okay' when Vaelrik's involved. "

Seraphina shook her head. "I don't even know. But I just can't let him get in my head today." She looked over at him, her expression a mixture of determination and exhaustion. "I'm sorry to drag you into this."

He grinned back at her. "Hey, you didn't drag me. I'm happy to help you get away from whatever's in your head for a while."

The run continued, the distance between them and the training complex growing as they ventured further into the quiet of the surrounding forest. Kade kept pace, occasionally shooting her knowing looks that she couldn't help but return with a half-smile.

Out in the woods, Seraphina finally felt herself relax, even if it was just a little. She did not know how long she and Kade ran, but for the first time in a while, the world seemed to slow down.

Kade kept the pace steady, not asking any more questions, just running with her—beside her, not ahead or behind. And in that moment, Seraphina allowed herself a bit of peace.

The soft crunch of grass beneath her boots barely registered before Seraphina let herself collapse, arms flopping out to her sides. The cool blades tickled her skin, damp with the lingering touch of morning dew, but she didn't care. She was exhausted, not just from the run, but from everything.

Kade, ever the steady presence, came to a halt beside her. He wasn't winded, not even close, but he slowly released his breath, gazing down at her, one eyebrow arched in mild amusement. "That bad, huh?"

Seraphina huffed, closing her eyes. "If I die here, just bury me under a tree or something. Somewhere peaceful."

Kade smirked before settling onto the grass beside her, leaning back on his hands, his gaze shifting to the sky. They sat in silence for a while, the kind that wasn't uncomfortable. It was just… there. A rare moment of quiet in the chaos of their lives.

Eventually, Seraphina sighed, turning her head slightly to glance at him. "You saw, didn't you?"

Kade didn't need to ask what she meant. His jaw tightened, and though his expression remained neutral, there was something unreadable in his gaze. He exhaled slowly. "Yeah. I saw."

Seraphina turned her face back toward the sky, watching as the clouds drifted lazily above them. Her voice was softer now, tinged with something tired and distant. "My past… Vaelrik… It almost killed me once."

Kade didn't press her, didn't ask for details. He just nodded, listening.

She let out a dry laugh, shaking her head against the grass. "Back then, I turned to Alexis. Thought maybe I could outrun everything if I just threw myself into something else. That was a disastrous situation."

Kade glanced at her at that, his expression unreadable. He knew how that story ended.

Seraphina turned her head again, this time meeting his eyes. There was something searching in her gaze, something almost vulnerable beneath all the walls she kept so carefully in place.

"But," she said, with a small, almost wistful smile ghosting her lips, "at least that's how I met you."

Kade's breath hitched slightly, so slight that most people wouldn't have noticed. But Seraphina did.

For a moment, he just looked at her, the usual smirk absent from his face. Instead, there was something softer there, something real. He said nothing right away, just reached out, brushing a loose strand of hair from her face with the gentlest touch.

Seraphina didn't pull away.

The air between them shifted, heavy with unspoken things. But then, just as quickly as the moment came, she huffed and threw an arm over her eyes, breaking the tension. "Ugh. Why am I even telling you this?"

For a long time, they just lay there, staring at the sky, the weight of everything sitting between them. But it wasn't unbearable. It wasn't crushing. Because somehow, even when she felt like the world was too much, Kade was still there. Despite all the tension that was usually between them, he was still there. Seraphina let out a slow breath, watching the clouds drift. The grass beneath her felt grounding; the air crisp against her skin. It was rare—this moment of quiet. She wasn't sure what to do with it.

Then Kade shifted beside her, lying back fully so his head was beside hers. "You know," he said after a moment, voice casual but carrying something deeper beneath it, "when I was Alexis' bodyguard, I used to watch you with him and think you were strange."

Seraphina let out a short, humourless laugh. "Wow. Thanks."

"I mean it," Kade said, and when she glanced at him, his expression wasn't mocking—it was thoughtful. "You were fire and steel. He was charm and calculation. I didn't understand what you saw in him. But you looked at him like he was the world."

Seraphina swallowed, gaze flicking away. "I was young."

Kade hummed. "Maybe. Or maybe you just wanted to believe in something. I remember the way he treated you. How he twisted things. I remember—" He cut himself off, jaw clenching, before he exhaled through his nose. "I couldn't stand it."

Seraphina's chest tightened. She turned her head to look at him again, eyes searching his face. Kade wasn't one to talk about the past. Not like this.

He glanced at her, and for once, there was no teasing in his gaze. Their noses were close together, his silver hair mixed with her ebony hair as it fanned out around them both. "I changed my whole damn life for you, Sera." His voice was steady, like he was stating a simple fact. "I broke my bonds. Left behind everything I knew. Because I couldn't watch it happen anymore. And I'd do it again."

Seraphina's breath caught in her throat.

He turned fully onto his side, propping his head up with one hand as he watched her, a small smirk curling his lips. "And just in case you're wondering, that includes now. I'll keep you safe, even from yourself."

She huffed, rolling her eyes to cover the way her heart ached at his words. "That's a full-time job."

Kade grinned. "Lucky for you, I'm very dedicated."

Seraphina looked at him for a long moment, something unreadable passing through her expression. Then she sighed, letting her eyes drift back to the sky. She had a question that had been burning inside her after she had been researching supernaturals and their history.

"So, this whole mate thing... with the supernatural, is it all fate? Like... are you bound to a single person by some magic?"

Kade glanced at her, his expression unreadable for a moment before he gave a small shrug. "It's different for each kind of supernatural. For the Fae—both Seelie and Unseelie—it's fated. They don't get a choice. The universe chooses their mates itself, some ancient magic that binds them for life. It's not something they can escape, no matter how hard they might try."

Sera nodded thoughtfully, turning her gaze ahead, trying to make sense of it. "So... the Fae have no say in who they end up with?"

"Exactly," Kade replied, his voice steady. "The bond is there, unbreakable. If they're not already with their fated one, there's this constant pull—an ache, a hunger. It's something they can't ignore."

Kade looked at her, tilting his head slightly with a questioning look on his face.

Seraphina huffed, "I'm wondering if the reason Vaelrik can't let go of me is because of some weird supernatural bond."

Understanding crossed Kade's face. "As Aurion can tell you, dragons form fated mates, but it's more like an instant connection a refusal to be separated. I don't know if that is the same for Dragon shifters but.."

Seraphina looked thoughtfully ahead. Of course, there would be no definitive answer.

"What about Lycans?" Sera asked, genuinely curious now, her fingers brushing against the grass as she stared at the clouds passing overhead.

"Lycans choose their mates based on their wolf's side. Their animal instincts guide them. When a Lycan finds their mate, it's like everything falls into place, the wolf recognising the one it's meant to be with. It's a little more instinctual than the Fae's fate-bound pairing, but still strong." Kade's eyes darkened, as if lost in thought for a brief moment before he snapped back to the present. "Then there are vampires. Their bonds are lifelong too, but it's not fate. They choose their partners—almost like a union, a contract, not a destiny. But once they choose, it's for life."

"Warlocks?" she asked, glancing up at him.

"They choose too," Kade answered with a slight smirk, his tone a little warmer. "There's no magical force behind it. It's more about compatibility, power alignment, trust... and, sometimes, love."

Now intrigued by the various ways supernatural bonds formed, Sera asked, "What about humans?"

"Humans have free will. There's no magic or fate behind their partners— well, apart from their own desires, their own decisions. They can choose who they want to be with and can form a bond as deep as any supernatural connection." Kade's gaze softened as he looked at her. "It's not always easy, but that's what makes the bond so special. They fight for it."

Sera chewed on the information for a moment, then asked, almost without thinking, "The woman who was your partner, the one Vaelrik killed... was she your mate?"

Kade's expression darkened, his jaw tightening as the memories seemed to hit him like a physical blow. He shook his head, his voice quiet but firm. "No. She wasn't my mate. It was an arranged marriage. My family had other plans for me." His words were blunt, but there was a sharp edge of pain beneath them, one that made Sera's heart clench for him.

She stayed silent for a few moments, processing what he had said, then a thought occurred to her, a nagging curiosity she couldn't shake. "But... my bloodline is so unique. It's unlike anything anyone's seen. I'm wondering... " Her voice trailed off, a slight unease creeping into her words. "Do you think I'll have a mate? I mean, with everything... the magic in my blood, the power, all of it... Do you think I'm destined for that kind of bond?"

379

Kade's gaze softened as he studied her. "I don't know, Sera," he breathed, his voice low and steady. "But if you do… it won't be like anything you expect." He paused, looking at her as if searching for something in her eyes. "The bond feels like a pull—a magnetic force you can't explain. It draws you to them in ways you can't ignore. It's a connection that goes deeper than just emotions or magic. It's instinct, it's… everything."

She glanced up at him, her heart racing. Was he speaking from experience? She wasn't sure whether she wanted to ask.

Kade caught her gaze for a heartbeat before turning away, his expression unreadable once again. "But even then, there's no guarantee. The bond isn't always what it seems. It can take you places you didn't expect, and sometimes it's not enough to keep you together."

Sera's mind reeled with the implications of what he said. She wasn't sure if he was speaking about his own experiences, or if he was just talking in generalities, but she couldn't ignore the slight tremor in his voice.

She opened her mouth to respond, but before she could, Kade glanced at her with a soft smile that didn't quite reach his eyes. "It's not about the bond, Sera," he said, his voice tinged with a mixture of sorrow and understanding. "It's about what you do with it once you have it."

Sera swallowed hard, the words hanging in the air like an unspoken promise. She wasn't sure what the future held, or what her bloodline would lead to, but for the first time, she felt a stirring in her chest—a possibility, however distant it might be.

"Fine," she muttered. "But if you ever bring this up again, I'm punching you."

Kade laughed, a warm, low sound. "Wouldn't expect anything less."

And just like that, the moment passed, slipping into something familiar, something easy. But the words lingered between them, settling deep into the spaces they never spoke of. Because no matter what happened—no matter what ghosts from their pasts came back to haunt them — Kade would always be there.

Chapter 41

By the time Seraphina and Kade made it back to the training grounds, the sun had crept higher, casting long shadows over the worn dirt and flattened grass. The scent of sweat and steel lingered in the air.

Kai was the first to notice them, his keen gaze flicking over Seraphina before he smirked. "Well, well. Look who returned from their dramatic disappearance."

Seraphina rolled her eyes. "Don't start."

"Oh, but I must." Kai clutched his chest mockingly. "You ran off, dragging Kade with you—gasping, begging, eyes full of desperation—"

Kade arched a brow. "Gasping?"

"I'm painting a picture here." Kai waved him off.

Seraphina crossed her arms, narrowing her eyes at him. "Keep talking, Kai. See what happens."

Kai only grinned wider. "Ooooh, so touchy. Interesting." His gaze flicked between her and Kade. "What exactly happened on this brief run of yours? Somehow Kade is smiling, and you are brooding. Did you switch personalities?"

Before Seraphina could tell him to shut up, Vaelrik stepped forward, arms crossed, his sharp gaze lingering on her just a little too long. "That's what I'd like to know."

Seraphina stiffened.

Kade, ever the perceptive one, shifted closer, the movement casual—almost lazy—but she knew better. It was protective.

Kai, meanwhile, seemed finally to have pieced together why Seraphina had run off. His smirk faltered for half a second before he whistled under his breath. "Ah. Now I see."

"See what?" Dylan asked, brows furrowed in confusion.

Kai threw an arm around Dylan's shoulders dramatically. "That, my dear father, is Kade doing what Kade does best—being Seraphina's anchor."

Dylan's frown deepened. "Anchor?"

Vaelrik's jaw tightened, but he stayed silent.

Seraphina clenched her teeth, but before she could snap, Kade stretched, all easy confidence, before slinging an arm around her shoulders and turning them both toward the training rings. "I don't know about you all, but I'm in the mood for a spar."

Seraphina glanced up at him, her body still tense. He met her gaze, his expression unreadable, but there was something reassuring in the way he nudged her forward.

Vaelrik said nothing as they walked past him, but she could feel his stare burning into her back.

Aurion's voice curled in Seraphina's mind. *Smooth.*

She barely resisted the urge to groan.

Seraphina rolled her shoulders, stepping into the training ring with measured ease, though her mind was anything but calm. She could still feel Vaelrik's stare pressing into her back, still hear Kai's obnoxiously knowing tone in her ears.

But none of that mattered right now. Not when Kade stood across from her, rolling his wrists, his usual smirk tugging at the corner of his lips.

"Think you can keep up, Nyx?" he taunted.

Seraphina arched a brow. "I should ask you that, old man."

Kai, perched on the fence with Dylan beside him, let out a low whistle. "Oh, this is going to be fun."

Kade laughed, shaking his head. "Alright then." He shifted his stance, weight light on his feet. "Come at me."

The world narrowed. Seraphina lunged.

Their blades met with a sharp clang, the impact reverberating through her arms. Kade was fast—he always had been—but she was faster. She twisted, using her momentum to force him back. He deflected, stepping aside, and instantly, they engaged in a deadly rhythm of strikes, dodges, and counters.

The others had fallen silent now, watching the match unfold. Even Vaelrik had moved closer, arms crossed as his sharp gaze followed every motion.

Seraphina barely noticed.

Steel met steel with a clang, the impact vibrating up her arms as she struck, fast and unrelenting. Kade dodged, parried, and countered — each movement fluid, effortless.

But she wasn't about to let him dictate the rhythm.

She pivoted, forcing him back, their footsteps scuffing against the stone. His tunic clung to him, damp with sweat, the fabric stretching across his chest and arms as he twisted to avoid her next strike.

It was entirely unfair how good he looked when fighting.

Sera grit her teeth and focused.

A feint—left. A strike—right. She was close, so close to slipping past his defence—then he smirked.

A real one. The kind that was more than just amusement, more than his usual mocking grin.

The kind that said he was enjoying this.

It ruined her.

Her step faltered—just slightly—but enough for him to notice.

Kade's blade swept up, twisting her dagger from her grasp in one fluid motion. Before she could react, he hooked a foot behind her ankle and yanked.

Sera barely had time to gasp before she was falling—

Except she didn't hit the ground.

Kade caught her.

With one arm wrapped around her waist, the other gripping her wrist as he pulled her against him, her body flush to his, the heat of his skin burned through her clothes.

For a long, terrible moment, neither of them moved.

She gasped, her pulse hammering as his fingers flexed slightly against her back. He was so close, too close, the scent of him—sweat, steel, something dark and intoxicating—clouding her senses.

His voice was low, almost smug. "Distracted again?"

She could hear the smirk in his words.

She should shove him away. She should say something. Anything.

But her eyes locked onto his lips—just for a second. A stupid, fleeting second.

And Kade saw.

His grip on her wrist tightened just slightly. His expression shifted—smugness fading, something unreadable flickering in the depths of his dark eyes.

Sera swallowed. "Let me go."

His fingers didn't move.

Not immediately.

Instead, his thumb brushed against the inside of her wrist—slow, deliberate.

Her breath hitched.

His gaze flicked up to hers. And gods, he looked—like he was teetering on the edge of something. Like if she leaned in, even just a little, he'd—

He dropped her.

Sera landed with a graceless thud, a small oof escaping her lips as dust kicked up around her.

She gaped at him, stunned. "You bastard—"

Kade only grinned, offering a hand.

She slapped it away, shoving herself upright with as much dignity as she could manage.

Just as Seraphina twisted to land a strike, her muscles coiling for impact, Kade's hand shot out, catching her wrist mid-motion. His grip was firm, his body an iron wall as he twisted her momentum against her. She staggered—just slightly—but it was enough. Before she could regain her balance, Kade's leg hooked behind hers, sweeping her off her feet. In one fluid motion, she found herself flat on her back, Kade's body bracing over hers, his forearm pressing hard against her collarbone, trapping her in a vulnerable position.

A smirk tugged at Kade's lips as he leaned in, his breath warm against her ear. "Pinned you."

Seraphina huffed a breath, frustration and fleeting amusement flickering in her chest. She wasn't angry. Not really. Kade was safe. Kade was *here*. And for a moment, that fragile truth was enough.

Then Vaelrik spoke.

His voice was a dagger wrapped in silk—low, bitter, and cruel. "Well. That didn't take long."

The air turned icy.

He leaned against the doorframe with infuriating ease, eyes glinting like sharpened steel. "Tell me, is this your new thing? Bleed beside them, then warm their bed?"

Seraphina froze.

Vaelrik's smirk deepened, arrogant and ugly. "Or was that just reserved for me? Because from where I'm standing, it all looks *very* familiar."

He clicked his tongue. "Maybe that's what your midnight escape was really about. Couldn't get enough of playing saviour, so you found someone new to fall apart with. Or under."

The words hit her like a physical blow, each syllable a crushing weight that forced the breath from her lungs. The world around her seemed to tilt, the edges of reality blurring as the past rushed in—a flood of sensations she wasn't ready for. Vaelrik's taunting words dragged her straight back to that time when they'd sparred, when everything had been different, when they had been *different*. It had ended in something far more dangerous and passionate than anything she was experiencing now. That memory—of the heat, the stolen moments, the love that had once been—twisted into something darker.

Suddenly, she was there again—back in that cold room, pinned beneath the dark warlocks with force as dark magic tore through her soul. The air had been thick with magic, suffocating. She could still *feel* it—sharp, jagged tendrils of power ripping through her, breaking into something deep within her. The echo of Vaelrik's painful scream flashed before her eyes, the desperate whispers of her pain filling her ears. The memory faded, but the pain remained. How dare he make light of something that had destroyed her as if it had never affected him in the same way?

The pressure in her chest grew unbearable, a storm of magic roaring to life beneath her skin, reacting to the volatile emotions surging within her. The heat was suffocating—her blood burned like fire, like it was fighting to break free. The magic inside her thrashed, desperate for release, desperate for something to tether it.

"Nyx?" Kade's voice was raw with concern as he jumped off her, but even his words couldn't reach her. The pulse of magic that throbbed through her was too much, too strong, and it was *shouting* inside her.

She could hear Dylan's voice, distant and muffled, but it felt like an eternity between each syllable. "Are you—?"

But before any of them could get closer, Aurion's calm, measured voice sliced through the chaos in her mind. *You need to get away. Now.*

The command was firm, and the pressure in her chest intensified. The eyes of too many people were on her now. She could *feel* their gazes—heavy, curious, unspoken. They were *watching*. The weight of it all—of their judgement, their pity—pushed her deeper into the turmoil.

She couldn't stay here. She *couldn't*.

Her magic thrashed wildly, and for a moment, it felt as though her body would simply break under the strain. Then, in a blur of motion, Kai—no longer in his human form—landed beside her with a heavy thud, his massive Lycan form casting a shadow over her. His eyes, fierce and green, locked onto hers, and in that instant, he understood. He *felt* her.

Without hesitation, she moved. Her hand shot out, gripping the thick fur at his shoulders, and as her legs wrapped around him, Kai bolted, carrying her into the woods with a single, fluid motion. The world blurred around them as they fled, the sounds of gasps and shouts from the others fading away into the distance.

For a long moment, the only thing she could hear was the pounding of Kai's paws against the earth, the rushing wind in her ears, the steady rhythm of his breath. The power inside her, the emotions threatening to tear her apart, settled, but it didn't vanish. It simmered, still raw, still *alive* within her. It was only a matter of time before it flared again.

Aurion's voice hummed in her mind, tinged with exasperation but with a hint of amusement. *Smooth.*

Seraphina said nothing. She just closed her eyes and let herself breathe. The wind tore through Seraphina's hair as Kai thundered through the dense forest, his massive paws barely making a sound against the earth. The rhythmic motion of his powerful strides should have been calming, but her pulse still pounded, her chest still ached.

She focused on the sensation of movement, the steady warmth of Kai's fur beneath her fingers, the way the world blurred past in streaks of green and gold. Anything to drown out the echo of Vaelrik's words.

Anything to silence his voice in her head.

Kai didn't slow until they reached a clearing deep in the woods, a secluded space where the air felt lighter and the shadows weren't quite as suffocating. Only then did he stop, lowering himself enough for her to slide off. Seraphina hit the ground and staggered, bracing her hands against her knees as she sucked in deep, uneven breaths.

Kai shifted beside her, his fur retreating, bones cracking as he returned to his human form. "Alright," he said, voice softer than usual, "you want to tell me what that was about, or should I make wild guesses?"

She barked out a hollow laugh, running a hand over her face. "Take your best shot."

Kai folded his arms, eyes scanning her carefully. "Well, considering you looked like you saw a ghost before you freaked out, I'm guessing Vaelrik's brief comment hit a nerve."

She tensed.

He hummed knowingly. "You want to talk about it?"

"No."

Kai sighed, running a hand through his wild curls. "Alright. Then how about this—next time you decide to freak out and run, can you warn me before you jump on my back like a deranged woodland creature?"

That dragged a small, genuine smile from her. "Where's the fun in that?"

Kai smirked, nudging her shoulder. "You're lucky I like you, Sera."

She huffed, but her gaze softened. "I know."

For a moment, they just stood there, the silence stretching between them—not awkward, but steady. Safe. She appreciated that he didn't push her for details.

Then Kai tilted his head, expression shifting. "Kade's probably losing his mind right now, you know."

Seraphina exhaled slowly, the weight pressing down on her chest again. "Yeah. I know."

Kai watched her for a beat, then grinned. "You want me to run more interference, or do you actually plan on facing him this time?"

She groaned, rubbing her temples. "Don't say it like that."

"Like what?"

"Like I owe him an explanation."

Kai arched a brow. "Sera, you ran from him. You jumped on my back and disappeared into the woods like some kind of feral cryptid. I think an explanation is the bare minimum here, especially when he may think this is partly his fault."

She groaned louder. "Gods, I hate you."

"You love me."

Seraphina shoved him, rolling her eyes. "Shut up."

Kai chuckled, but didn't push further. He just stood beside her, waiting.

After a long moment, she exhaled, straightening. "I should get back."

Kai nodded. "Want me to walk with you?"

She hesitated, then shook her head. "No. I need to do this on my own, but I might stay here longer. You know, to make sure I don't start unnecessary fires."

Kai studied her, then gave a small nod of approval. "Alright. But if you need me—"

"I know," she said, offering him a small smile. "You're an annoying pain in my ass, but you're a reliable one."

A voice slid into their minds, smooth and unwavering. *She won't be alone.*

Seraphina exhaled as his presence settled like a steady pulse in the back of her mind. Kai gave a small nod, understanding passing between them silently.

"Alright," Kai said. "I'll go smooth things over."

She snorted. "By 'smooth over,' you mean cause problems, don't you?"

Kai smirked. "Oh, definitely."

Without another word, he turned and shifted mid-step, fur rippling over his form as he sprinted back toward the training grounds.

The training grounds were buzzing with tension when Kai arrived. Conversations halted, eyes flicking toward him as he strode back into the circle.

Kade was waiting. With crossed arms, he fixed a sharp gaze on Kai as soon as Kai appeared. Before he could even ask, Kai passed him, whispering, "She's safe. I left her in the clearing near the ridge. She'll come back when she's ready."

Kade's shoulders eased, but the storm in his eyes didn't clear.

Kai didn't stop walking.

Didn't hesitate.

He didn't slow as he crossed the distance between him and Vaelrik.

Then—

He punched him.

The crack of knuckles against bone shattered the silence, Vaelrik's head snapping to the side as he staggered.

Gasps echoed around them.

Vaelrik blinked, then slowly turned back to face Kai, blood trailing from the corner of his mouth. "...Alright," he muttered, rolling his jaw. "What the fuck was that for?"

Kai's voice was low, dangerous. "How dare you!"

Vaelrik frowned, wiping the blood from his lip. "Going to need a little more context, Wolf."

Kai stepped closer, his teeth bared. "You don't get to bring your past into this. You don't get to say anything that drags her back there."

Realisation flickered across Vaelrik's expression. His brows knit together, but for once, he didn't have a smug retort.

Kai shook his head, stepping back. "You think you know her?" His lips curled in something almost like disgust. "You don't."

And with that, he turned, walking back toward Kade, toward the others — toward the only people who actually gave a damn about the weight Seraphina carried.

Vaelrik stood frozen, staring at the ground, the air around him thick with unspoken words.

And for once, he had nothing to say.

Chapter 42

In the clearing, eyes shut, breath steady. The stars above shimmered like distant embers, a stark contrast to the fire burning in her chest.

Aurion in his dragon form loomed beside her, his massive wings tucked close to his body. His obsidian scales reflected the moonlight, giving him an ethereal glow. His voice rumbled in her mind, smooth and unwavering. Seraphina apparently needed the bigger version of Aurion, her magic transforming him and confusing them both.

You must strengthen your mind against the ghosts that haunt you. Your past is not a weapon to wield against yourself—it is a lesson to guide you.

Seraphina exhaled slowly. "Easier said than done."

Then we start with something simpler. Meditation—not in stillness, but with magic. Focus on your breathing, your heartbeat. Let the power in your veins flow, shape it, and control it.

She inhaled, feeling the steady pulse of magic beneath her skin, like molten light waiting to be harnessed.

Aurion continued, his deep voice wrapping around her thoughts. *Your blade extends from you. Just as your magic is. Find the balance between.*

She rose to her feet, eyes still shut, fingers wrapping around the hilt of her sword. Aurion's presence remained steady in her mind as she took a breath and moved.

The first step was simple—a slow arc of her blade through the air, guiding the energy from her core into the steel. A faint pulse of golden light shimmered along the edge, like the first flicker of dawn. She turned, flowing into the next motion, each step as fluid as a dancer's, the sword an extension of her soul. Her magic pulsed brighter, weaving through the air like threads of liquid fire. Aurion watched with silent pride, the great dragon lowered his head as the surrounding energy grew stronger, steadier.

The world around her faded—there was only the rhythm of her breath, the hum of her magic, the way her blade cut through the air like poetry. Then the whisper on the edge of her mind. The *path ahead is dark, but you do not walk it alone. You have me.* Seraphina didn't have it in her to fear her blade this time. She was using it to find her balance within herself.

She didn't know how long she moved like that, only that it felt right— like something clicking into place inside her. It wasn't until she heard the soft crunch of footsteps that she faltered.

Seraphina turned, breathless, to find Kade standing at the edge of the clearing.

His silver hair caught the moonlight, his sharp eyes locked onto hers with something unreadable—something like awe. He said nothing at first, just watched, as if seeing her for the first time.

"Oh.. Hello," she said, her voice softer than she intended.

"Do you plan on ever returning?" Kade replied, stepping closer, his gaze flickering to the blade still humming with residual magic in her hands. "It's past midnight."

Seraphina blinked, glancing up at the sky. Had it really been that long?

Kade studied her, then the way Aurion stood beside her, radiating approval. "That was… impressive," he admitted, voice quieter now. "I've never seen you move like that before."

A faint flush crept up her neck. "Aurion had a good idea."

Kade's lips twitched, almost like he wanted to smile, but something softer lingered in his eyes. "Yeah," he murmured. "He did."

Aurion huffed, his voice slipping into both of their minds. *Finally, someone acknowledges my brilliance.*

Seraphina rolled her eyes, sheathing her blade as Kade stepped even closer, his gaze still searching her face.

"You okay?" he asked, softer now.

She hesitated—then nodded. "Come on, we should head back," she whispered.

The walk back to her room was quiet, the cool night air brushing against Seraphina's skin like a whisper. Kade walked beside her, his usual imposing presence softened by the silence that stretched between them. The weight of their conversation still lingered, but for once, it didn't feel suffocating.

"You looked good out there tonight," Kade said, his voice low but steady. "With your magic, I mean."

Seraphina huffed a quiet laugh. "You mean I didn't look like I was going to set myself on fire?"

Kade smirked. "Not this time."

They reached the door to her room, the hallway dimly lit by flickering lanterns. She hesitated before opening it, reluctant to let go of the fragile peace that had settled between them. Kade leaned against the doorframe, watching her.

"Are you sure you're okay?" he asked again.

She met his gaze and, for once, she didn't feel the need to lie. "I will be."

Kade studied her, then nodded, as if accepting her words as truth. "Good."

He reached out, just briefly, brushing his fingers against her arm before stepping back. "Get some rest, Nyx."

Seraphina swallowed and gave him a small nod before stepping into her room. The moment the door shut behind her, the warmth from their conversation faded into the stillness. Seraphina made quick work of getting ready for bed and changing her clothes after a relaxing bath, but as she returned to her room and she turned toward the bed. The maids must have changed the bedding, but that duvet—so light, so innocuous—was not a colour she could stand.

And everything shattered.

The sight of the mattress—so simple, so harmless—was like a slap to her psyche. The soft, plush surface was tauntingly normal. But it wasn't. Not to her. Not anymore.

Her breath hitched in her chest as the cold rush of dread filled her veins. It was the same. *So,* like the other bed—the one she had spent countless nights in, helpless, trapped in that foreign, suffocating place. An all-consuming, unstoppable force had once pinned her to the bed. The cruellest hands had violated every inch of her on the bed.

Everything in her mind snapped shut as the memory flooded in, vivid and unforgiving. She was there again, in that dark room. Trapped beneath the pressure of a hand that belonged to someone she had once trusted, her body stiffened with fear. *Helpless.*

Her heartbeat thundered in her ears, each pulse ringing with a deep, agonising echo of what had been. Her limbs trembled—too much, too fast—as the cold, clammy sensation of the past clutched at her. She took a step back, instinctively pulling away, but the walls of that memory loomed over her like an inescapable cage. The blankets, the softness of them—it was *too much.*

She couldn't breathe. Couldn't think. *Not here. Not in this place.*

Desperation seized her. Her hands, trembling violently, reached for the duvet. She yanked it off the bed, her movements frantic, as though the fabric itself might hold the ghosts of the past. She dragged it to the floor, every tug making the room spin around her. She needed it gone.

She couldn't sleep there. The very thought of lying on that bed—of *existing* in that space—was enough to send her spiralling.

Wouldn't. She wouldn't.

A voice cut through the noise in her mind, sharp but gentle, like the touch of a hand that steadied her heart. *Sera.*

Aurion's voice slid in, deep and steady, but there was an edge—a tenderness that carried the weight of understanding, the knowing that this moment was something darker than the simple inconvenience of a changed duvet.

Then he saw it. The memory. No matter the years, her nightmares' thoughts still haunted her. Her reason for hating to sleep alone. The one memory she hadn't meant to share. The flood of horror that had leapt from her mind like an unspoken word.

A low growl, primal and low, echoed in her mind—torn from the depths of Aurion's own soul. The dragon's instinct for protection, for rage, ignited like a flame.

Before she could react, the world around her seemed to shift. The air thickened with power, and the floor trembled beneath her feet. Aurion materialised before her, his obsidian scales shimmering in the dim light, his enormous form unfurling as though the space itself couldn't contain him. His massive wings stretched out, curling protectively around her. Not for the first time, she was grateful the Lycans had built their stronghold with vast rooms intended for all supernaturals in all their forms.

His gaze, glowing with ancient fire, locked onto her with an intensity that rooted her to the spot. His voice reverberated in her mind, the tone dark and soothing, yet fiercely protective. *You're safe now. You are not there anymore, Sera.*

Seraphina's body shook, but the trembling was no longer just fear. It was relief, a flood of both release and sorrow. Aurion was here. Aurion's presence meant she was free. Seraphina quickly ran to the cupboard and grabbed spare blankets and pillows and chucked them in a heap on the floor before grabbing everything off the floor from the bed and throwing it in the bathroom, locking the door behind her on the offending items and her memories.

Warmth radiated from Aurion as he settled, his tail wrapping loosely around her makeshift bedding, his enormous wings tucking in to create a shield. His very presence was grounding, the hum of his magic pressing gently against her own.

Seraphina hesitated, then, with a quiet breath, curled up within the warmth of his form. The tension in her body slowly ebbed as the steady rise and fall of his breathing surrounded her.

She exhaled, turning her head slightly. "No one would believe you did this for me," she muttered, exhaustion creeping into her voice.

Aurion snorted, his tail twitching. *Then it is fortunate that I do not require validation.*

She huffed, but before she could close her eyes, his gaze softened. *Rest, little one. I will watch over you.*

A flicker of awareness brushed against her mind—the bond.

She's safe, little wolf, Aurion murmured, his voice sliding into the connection he shared with Kai.

Kai's presence in the back of her mind hummed with relief. *Good.*

Seraphina closed her eyes. The warmth of Aurion's body wrapped around her, the steady reassurance of the bond with Kai lingering in the background.

For the first time in a long time, she didn't feel alone.

* * *

Kade had intended only to check on her.

The night had stretched long, and though Kade knew Seraphina needed her space, a gnawing weight in his chest kept him from leaving it alone. He had waited until the castle had fallen quiet; the silence broken only by the faint sound of his footsteps as he slipped through the corridors, following the invisible tether that always seemed to pull him toward her. They had only one more night together before their separate missions would pull them in different directions, and he couldn't shake the urge to check on her.

But when he opened her door, what he found stopped him dead in his tracks.

Aurion was curled protectively around Seraphina, his massive form forming a cocoon of darkness and power. His golden eyes glowed faintly in the dim light, a quiet sentinel keeping watch. Seraphina, completely unaware of his presence, slept soundly beneath him, her breath even, her face softened by the peace Kade hadn't seen in years.

Kade stood there, caught between awe and an unexpected pang of emotion, forcing himself to swallow the lump in his throat.

"She hasn't slept this well in a long time," Aurion murmured, his voice low but unbroken, still not lifting his head.

Kade crossed his arms, his voice steady but edged with something unspoken. "And you're playing guardian now?"

Aurion's golden gaze flickered toward him, a low rumble vibrating in his chest. "You should know, Kade, I will protect her. Even from her own memories. From the ghosts of her past."

Kade's jaw clenched. He stepped forward, his voice thick with something raw and unfiltered. "Why do you think I destroyed my soul to help her? Why do you think I fractured my magic, made it uncontrollable?" His words came out like a hiss, full of bitterness and regret. "I did it for her... but I was too damn late."

Aurion studied him for a long moment, his eyes unreadable, before his expression softened ever so slightly. The steel in his voice remained, though, unwavering. "These memories... they aren't your fault, Kade. For once, silver one, they belong to her. To her past with the lesser dragon— and with those dark warlocks and that insufferable husband of hers."

Before either of them could say more, Seraphina shifted beneath Aurion's wing, the slightest hitch in her breath signalling her return to wakefulness. Slowly, she blinked her eyes open, taking in her surroundings with a dazed expression.

Aurion's attention snapped back to her immediately. "Little one," he murmured, his voice now laced with tenderness. "Are you well?"

Seraphina yawned, her mind still sluggish from sleep. She rubbed her eyes, nodding slowly, her voice thick with exhaustion. "Yeah... I think so." Her gaze drifted toward Kade, and the moment their eyes met, something unspoken passed between them. He gave her a look that carried more weight than words, a quiet plea for her to let him in. She didn't have it in her to turn him away. After a long beat, she simply nodded, her expression softening.

Chapter 43

The fire had burned low, its embers pulsing like a dying heartbeat, casting deep shadows against the walls of her room. The night air carried the scent of damp earth after a storm through the open window. Reluctantly, and with a grumble about humans being complicated creatures, Aurion left after Kade gave him a pointed look.

Seraphina sat with her knees drawn up, arms wrapped around herself, as if bracing against a cold that had nothing to do with the absence of Aurion. She had spoken little since waking, but Kade didn't need words to know what was clawing at her. He could see it in the tension in her shoulders, the way she stared into the fire without really seeing it. The way she kept her blade close, but refused to touch it.

Kade shifted beside her, stretching one leg out, keeping the other bent. He tilted his head slightly, silver eyes cutting through the dim glow. "Alright, Sera," he said, voice softer than usual. "Tell me the truth."

She flicked him a glance, her expression carefully neutral. "What do you mean?"

He scoffed. "Don't do that." His tone wasn't sharp, but it held weight. *Knowing.* "Don't pretend. You think I don't see it? So tell me—what's wrong?"

Seraphina exhaled through her nose, turning her gaze back to the fire. A muscle in her jaw ticked. "It's nothing," she said, too carefully.

Kade let out a low, dry laugh. "Liar."

That earned him a sharp look, but it faded almost instantly. Her fingers curled against the fabric of her nightgown, a tell she probably didn't even fuelled she had.

His voice softened, losing its usual edge. "It's your past, isn't it?"

She swallowed, the barest nod giving her away.

Seraphina's fingers traced the edge of the blanket on the makeshift bed, the fabric worn, its edges curling up as if it had seen too many nights like this one. She couldn't quite bring herself to look at Kade as she spoke, the weight of her emotions making her voice feel tight in her chest. The bed on the ground wasn't just a piece of furniture to her—it was a symbol of the time she had spent in the dark corners of her mind, trying to rebuild the parts of herself that had shattered.

She hadn't realised until now how much it all still affected her. Kade's presence beside her, so calm, made her feel safe enough to breathe, but even in that safety, she felt the pull of old wounds. The bed reminded her of what she lost and had to survive.

"I know it's been a long time," she said, her voice barely above a whisper, "and maybe it's silly… but I still don't really understand why this… why this place still feels like a prison." She motioned around, though it was clear the room itself wasn't the issue. It was her.

Kade didn't speak immediately. He was always patient with her; his silences were never uncomfortable but soothing, like the calm after a storm. His presence, his unwavering support, had always been the one constant she could rely on, even in the darkest moments of her past.

She felt his gaze on her, soft and understanding, but it only made the emotions surge higher, rawer. Her hands shook slightly as she continued, looking down at the bedding once again. "It's not just… memories, Kade," she admitted, voice quiet but laced with a tremor of something deeper. "It's what they mean. What they *did* to me." Her eyes closed briefly, as though shutting them could somehow seal away the painful truth.

Kade reached out, brushing his thumb gently over the back of her hand, grounding her with his touch. His presence beside her was unwavering, steady, and it gave her the courage to keep going.

"Every night, I sleep here… and it's not the bed or the place, it's… it's the weight of those moments. The ghosts of them follow me. They… linger." Her voice cracked on the word. She felt it—those memories weren't gone. They were just buried under layers of time and distance.

"Why does it still affect me like this?" She lifted her eyes to meet his, the vulnerability she felt obvious, her heart open and raw. "It's been years, but sometimes it feels like it was just yesterday."

Kade didn't rush to answer, but there was a softness in his gaze, the kind that made her heart flutter despite the heaviness pressing against it. He leaned forward slightly, his voice low and filled with the support she relied on.

"It's not silly," he said, his words firm but gentle. "You can't just move on from something like that, Seraphina. What happened to you… it doesn't just vanish. It's part of you now. But it doesn't mean it controls you." He paused, taking a breath before continuing. "You've carried it for so long, and you've been strong. Stronger than anyone I've ever known. But you don't have to carry it alone anymore. Not now. Never again."

She felt a warmth spread through her chest at his words, but the ache was still there. His reassurance helped, but it didn't erase the scars inside her.

"I don't know how to make it stop," she whispered, her voice small despite her best efforts to sound stronger. "How do you even move past it when it's woven into everything you are? The fear, the doubts, the way it… *changes* you. It's like I don't even know who I am sometimes. Not fully."

Kade's eyes softened, and he reached for her, cupping her face in his hand, tilting her chin up so she was looking at him fully. His thumb caressed her cheek, and his words were steady, a grounding force she could lean on.

"You don't have to know all the answers, Sera," he murmured. "You don't have to know *how*—you just need to know that you don't have to face it by yourself. I'm here. You can be *yourself* again. Slowly. In your own time."

Seraphina swallowed hard, her throat tight with emotions she couldn't fully express. The comfort of his words was a balm, but the pain still lingered beneath the surface. She turned her face into his palm, closing her eyes for a moment, letting his touch calm her.

"I'm tired," she admitted, her voice barely audible. "Tired of pretending that I'm okay when it's... it's still a battle inside me. Every damn day."

Kade pressed a soft kiss to her forehead, his lips lingering there for a moment. "You're not alone in it, Seraphina. You have never been, and you never will be. Let me help you fight it. Let me help you find peace, even if it's just one small piece at a time."

For a long moment, Seraphina let herself lean into his touch, the warmth of his words slowly easing the weight on her heart

Kade studied her for a moment, his gaze tracing over the firelight's glow against her skin, the shadows playing across the tired lines of her face. Then, carefully, he reached out.

His fingers brushed against her wrist first, just a feather-light touch. When she didn't pull away, he slid his hand up, his palm curling over hers, calloused and warm.

"Sera," he murmured, his voice a rough whisper, "you are stronger than you give yourself credit for."

She let out a brittle, humourless laugh. "Am I?"

"Yes." His thumb traced small circles against the back of her hand. "I've seen you fight. I've seen you rise when no one else could. You don't break, Sera." His voice dropped lower, almost reverently. "You *bend.*"

She didn't respond right away, her throat working as she swallowed. Her fingers twitched beneath his, gripping him just slightly. "I'm scared, Kade," she confessed, barely more than a breath. "Not just of the past. Of what it might make me do when I lose control of my magic. I swear the sword whispers things to me. Aurion thinks it is part of my destiny. I don't think we have all the information. I fear for myself."

His jaw tightened, something flashing in his eyes, almost like recognition when she spoke of the sword. Then, suddenly, he shifted, turning fully to face her. Before she could react, his hand left hers—only to cup the side of her face, cradling her as if she were something fragile and breakable.

But there was nothing fragile in the way he looked at her.

"Sera," Kade breathed, her name leaving his lips like a prayer, like a plea. His voice trembled with something fierce, something aching—an emotion he could no longer contain. "You could burn this world to ash, and I would thank the flames for leading me back to you. Become death itself, and I would still choose the fall if it meant chasing your shadow. I tried to fight against this, to fight against you, but I knew I would always lose.

Her breath caught. The words hit like a storm, unearthing a tenderness she'd buried deep beneath scars and silence. But Kade wasn't done.

"Your past doesn't scare me," he whispered. "It built you. It made you this fierce, unbreakable force I've fallen for—completely, hopelessly."

The space between them all but vanished, the air trembling with every breath they took. The tension wasn't just heavy—it was suffocating, the kind that spoke of years of restraint, of holding back something too powerful to name.

His eyes flicked to her lips—a flicker, a heartbeat—he moved.

When his mouth found hers, it was an unravelling. It was need and heartbreak and longing all colliding in one fierce moment of truth. He kissed her like a man who had been drowning without even knowing it, and now—now he was breathing for the first time. His hands tangled in her hair, desperate and reverent, pulling her closer like she was the answer to every question he'd never dared ask.

There was no hesitation. No caution. Only heat and hunger and a desperate worship. Seraphina clung to him, her fingers digging into the fabric of his tunic like she could anchor herself to him—like he was the only real thing in a crumbling world.

Kade tasted like steel and storm, like wildfire barely contained. Each movement was raw, unfiltered, as though he'd broken some dam inside himself and now he needed to show her what it meant to be wanted—truly, irrevocably. A soft gasp escaped her, and he answered it with a low growl, the sound vibrating against her skin as if he was claiming her with every breath.

When they finally pulled apart, they were both shaking—gasping, undone. Kade rested his forehead against hers, his hands refusing to release her, like she was the only thing tethering him to this moment.

Seraphina searched his face, uncertainty trembling in her voice. "Is this real? Is this what you want? Because every time I come close, you disappear."

Something inside him broke at her words, the last of his restraint shattering.

Without a word, his hands cradled her face, gentle now, reverent—like she was both miracle and salvation. "Sera," he said, his voice wrecked with feeling, "you are *all* I want. I've tried to stay away, gods know I've tried. But I can't. Not anymore. I'm done pretending I can survive without you."

Emotion swelled in her chest, her throat tight with the ache of it all.

This time, she was the one who moved.

This time, she kissed him, and it was everything.

It was slower, deeper, an unravelling rather than a collision. She seemed to melt into him, as if something tightly wound for too long had finally given way. Kade responded in kind, his hands sliding down her sides, his fingers tracing the curve of her waist, pulling her closer like he couldn't bear any distance between them. His touch was reverent, as if he were mapping the very shape of her, marking every inch of her skin as though he feared losing her.

Her breath caught in her throat as his hand drifted higher, and an awareness struck her suddenly—the gown she wore, almost entirely sheer, barely offered her any protection. The realisation made her heart thud louder in her chest, but it wasn't fear. No, it was the stark reality of how little she had left to hold on to.

Kade's hand slid through her hair, his fingers threading through the strands as he leaned down, lips hovering just above hers. His voice, when it came, was barely a whisper, thick with emotion that wrapped around her like a heavy weight.

"You're beautiful, Seraphina," he murmured, his words dripping with heat, molten and uncontainable. "More than you know."

It was all too much. She couldn't hold back any longer. With a sudden movement, she pushed Kade back onto the makeshift bed on the floor, her hands working to lift his tunic as she went. She tore it off him in one smooth motion, her heart pounding as she straddled his waist, the feel of his skin beneath her igniting something inside. His breath hitched at the contact, and he reached up, his hands tracing her waist with a reverence that made her skin prickle.

From his chest to his stomach, she traced the muscles of his taut frame, her fingers dancing over his skin, delighting in the soft groans he couldn't suppress. Every touch seemed to pull a new sound from him, and she leaned down, her lips brushing across his in a kiss that was deep and hungry. Kade responded with the same intensity, his mouth matching hers, matching the fire they had sparked. He bit her bottom lip, tugging at it with a ferocity that made her gasp, a moan slipping past her lips.

She couldn't get enough of him. Neither of them could.

Kade's hands wandered over her, his fingertips brushing the soft curve of her collarbone before trailing lower, skimming the edges of the delicate fabric of her nightgown. It clung to her skin, bunched around her thighs, offering little protection. The sheer nature of the material wasn't lost on him. His touch was light, barely there, but the way his silver eyes darkened with desire made her breath hitch in her throat. The pull between them was undeniable now, magnetic, an invisible force that neither could resist.

His hands were warm, rough with calluses that contrasted against her soft skin as they travelled higher, fingers pressing into the delicate skin of her inner thighs. She gasped softly, feeling the heat of his touch radiate through her, his fingers moving higher, caressing her ribs, brushing over the curves of her breasts. Then, without warning, she heard the rip of fabric, the sudden shift of pressure as he flipped her beneath him.

Kade's gaze swept over her, lingering on every inch of her exposed skin, an expression of pure admiration etching his features. The way he looked at her made her stomach tighten, anticipation coiling like a storm inside her. His silver eyes met hers, the unspoken desire between them thick in the air. With the weight of everything between them finally crashing to the surface, he kissed her.

The kiss wasn't soft. It wasn't tentative. It was an explosion, a collision of passion, a hunger they'd both been suppressing for too long. Her body surged against his, the intensity of it taking them both by surprise. Kade groaned into her mouth, a sound born of desperation and longing. Seraphina responded in kind, arms wrapping tightly around him, pulling him closer as if he might slip away if she didn't hold on.

Kade's breath was hot against her skin as he buried his face in the crook of her neck, his lips trailing fevered kisses down to her pulse point. His teeth grazed the sensitive skin there, and a shiver of desire shot down her spine. Her body arched instinctively, pressing closer to him, her hands threading through his hair, pulling him even closer.

"You're mine," he rasped, the words a declaration, a promise, as he pressed his lips to her skin. "And I am yours."

Seraphina's breath caught, her heart pounding against her rib cage. A soft moan escaped her as his lips continued their descent down her chest. His touch was scorching, his breath stirring against her skin, and it sent a wave of heat surging through her. When he traced his finger over the peak of her breast, a tremor ran through her body. Her legs instinctively wrapped around him, grinding against him, seeking that elusive pleasure that had been teasing her just out of reach.

Kade groaned, his voice low and husky. "Fuck, Seraphina." The rawness in his tone sent a jolt of heat through her, sparking something primal in her she hadn't even realised was there.

She couldn't wait anymore. With a flash of need, she reached down, helping him out of his trousers, only for Kade to suddenly stand, pulling her up with him. The speed of his movements took her breath away. In an instant, his mouth was on hers again, fierce and demanding. Kade growled, his hands pressing into the soft flesh of her thighs, lifting her effortlessly. Her legs wrapped around him, locking her against his waist as he pinned her to the wall. The force of it sent a candlestick-holder crashing to the floor, but neither of them noticed. They were too lost in the frantic rush of passion.

Kade's hands roamed, one cupping her breast, thumb brushing over her hardened nipple, coaxing a strangled moan from her lips. The sound pushed him further, his other hand trailing lower, to the heat of her core. His fingers found her, teasing, testing, and Seraphina's breathy gasp echoed in the room's quiet. Her nails dug into his shoulders as she shifted, pushing herself closer, her body betraying her every restraint.

"You don't know what you do to me," Kade muttered, his voice thick with a desperate need.

"Show me," Seraphina challenged, her nails raking down his back, leaving streaks of red in their wake.

Kade growled in response, spinning them both around with a strength that rattled the wooden bed frame beneath them. They collided into the sheets with a force that sent them scattering, desperate hands clawing at each other. Seraphina's power flared in the air, crackling between them like a living thing, sending a shiver down Kade's spine. He answered in kind, his own magic spiralling around them, an invisible force anchoring her to him, making her feel everything, every touch, every shift.

Seraphina's mouth found his neck, kissing, biting, as she arched against him, her hands slipping down to his chest. She flipped them over, taking control, straddling him with a wicked smile playing on her lips as she trailed slow kisses down his torso. Kade groaned, fisting the sheets, his muscles tensing as she explored him with slow, deliberate touches. She was pushing him to the edge with every kiss, every touch, until finally, with a growl of frustration, he flipped her back beneath him, reclaiming dominance.

His hands found the soft curve of her ass, lifting her up as he positioned himself between her legs. Without warning, he thrust into her in one smooth motion, sending a shock of pleasure rushing through her. He stilled, watching her closely, his voice barely a whisper. "Tell me you're okay?"

She could only nod, her body overwhelmed by the intensity of it. The pleasure of having him inside her finally was almost too much. Kade started moving, each thrust slow and deliberate, pulling deep, sending waves of pleasure coursing through her. Her body responded in kind, moving with him, both of them becoming a single, unrelenting force. The headboard slammed against the wall with each thrust, books and trinkets tumbling from the shelves, but neither cared. The air was thick with sweat, magic, and raw need. Each gasp, each moan was a testament to what they were creating together.

Kade gripped her wrists, pinning them above her head as he drove into her, their bodies slick with sweat and power. "Mine," he growled, his voice wrecked, a mixture of possession and reverence.

Seraphina arched beneath him, her legs wrapping around him to pull herself closer, her eyes burning with a fire that only he could stoke. "Yours," she whispered, her voice soft but full of promise, the words carrying something deeper, something only the two of them understood.

That was all it took. The room trembled around them as they both shattered, bodies shaking, magic flaring in one final, explosive release. Seraphina cried out his name, her body clenching around him, a wave of ecstasy crashing over her. Kade followed her, thrusting harder as he came with her, his body shaking with the force of it.

They collapsed in the wreckage of their passion, tangled in the sheets, chests heaving. The bed creaked beneath them, and Kade, still hovering over her, pressed his face into the crook of her neck. He exhaled a shaky breath, his voice rough with exhaustion. "That was a first," he muttered with a soft, tired chuckle.

Seraphina giggled, pressing a lazy kiss to his jaw. "I'll never let you forget it."

Their skin was slick with sweat, the air between them charged with the remnants of their reckless passion. The bed, or what remained, creaked dangerously under them; its wooden frame split in two, and the mattress barely held together. The room was in absolute ruin—the shelves overturned, books scattered, candles melted into puddles of wax on the floor where they had been knocked down. Seraphina let out a slow, satisfied sigh, her fingers chasing the edges of his jaw before drifting up to push the damp silver strands from his face. Her green eyes gleamed with amusement as she studied him.

"We should probably get some rest before we both leave on our missions tomorrow." Her voice was rough but held a tone of amusement before she continued. "Maybe on the makeshift bed I have on the floor. I don't trust this one to hold out." As if to prove her point, the wood creaked again.

Kade snorted a laugh before he stood, scooping her up off the bed and laying them both down on her pile of blankets and pillows.

"Is that better?" he rumbled out with a laugh.

She didn't reply, only snuggled further into him, as his arms wrapped around her, pulling her tight against his chest. He covered them both with a blanket as he kissed her forehead.

"Sleep now, I'll still be here when you wake up."

Seraphina's eyes drifted shut, and for the first time in a long time, sleep came to her easily.

Chapter 44

The morning light slanted through the cracks in the wooden shutters, casting golden streaks across the room. Dust hung in the air, swirling lazily in the quiet stillness. The scent of fire, sweat, and something distinctly them lingered, mingling with the faint, crisp bite of dawn. The room felt heavy with a kind of strange intimacy; the space filled with the weight of unspoken things. It was a mess, yes—but somehow, it felt like it belonged to them in a way that was both fragile and enduring. Sera snuggled in closer, letting sleep take her again.

Kai strolled down the hall, his boots quiet against the wooden floor. The weight of the night was still with him, a dull ache in his bones, though it had nothing to do with exhaustion. Missions at sunrise were never his thing—he preferred his mornings slow, but someone had to keep Sera from doing something reckless. And well, he could hardly let her get herself killed again, could he?

His steps echoed slightly in the hall as he rolled his shoulders, trying to shake off the tension still lingering in his muscles. He lifted a hand, rapping his knuckles against the door.

No answer.

He frowned. Unusual. Sera was normally up by now. Kai sighed, pushing the door open—and froze.

Someone wrecked the room.

Someone shoved the bed, or rather, what remained of it, halfway across the room, leaving sheets tangled in an unholy mess across the floor. Splinters from the bookshelves flew against the far wall; the wood cracked as if someone had thrown something with impressive force. A candleholder had shattered, wax pooling across the floorboards, its flame long extinguished.

But none of that drew his attention nearly as much as the figure in the wreckage.

Kade and Sera.

Sera, tucked in close to Kade's side, her bare shoulder peeking out from beneath the blankets. She was nestled against him, her head resting on his chest, the morning light catching strands of her hair, giving them an almost ethereal glow. Kade was deep in sleep, one arm draped protectively over her waist, the other curled beneath his head. His silver hair—usually so meticulously arranged—was a wild mess, half-matted against the pillow, the sharpness of his features softened by sleep.

Kai blinked.

Then, slowly, a grin spread across his face. "Well, well, well," he drawled, crossing his arms. "Look what we have here."

Sera groaned, her face buried against Kade's warmth, her body instinctively curling tighter into the embrace. But then, as the awareness of her surroundings broke through the haze of sleep, her body tensed, eyes snapping open. Her gaze flicked to the doorway, meeting the smirking figure of Kai.

"Kai," she hissed, her voice still hoarse from sleep, like velvet torn at the edges. "Get out."

Kai couldn't help himself. He let out a low whistle, taking in the room's wreckage with an exaggerated look of disapproval. "Damn, sweetheart, did you two fight or...?" He let the words hang in the air, the wicked grin pulling at the corners of his lips. "Or did you finally give in?"

Kade stirred, exhaling sharply. His brows knitted together as if waking was a personal offence. "What—" His voice was thick, groggy.

Then his instincts kicked in.

411

In a *blur* of movement, he was upright, one arm still gripping Sera, the other reaching for a blade that wasn't there. His eyes, sharp and dangerous, locked onto Kai—

The memory of *why* he was in bed, *who* was with him, and *what* the hell had happened last night *slammed* into him.

"Oh, for fuck's sake," he muttered, running a hand down his face.

Kai was practically vibrating with amusement now, eyes alight with mischief. "Good morning, lover boy."

Kade shot him a glare so venomous that it almost seemed tangible. "Leave."

Kai tsked, strolling further into the room, boots crunching over the broken wood. He gestured vaguely at the destruction surrounding them, his grin widening. "You know, I always wondered what would happen when you finally cracked." His gaze lingered on Kade's expression. "Didn't think it would be *this* though."

Sera groaned again, dragging the blanket higher over her head, half hiding in it like it could protect her from the chaos of the moment. "Kill me," she muttered, her voice muffled and pained.

"Oh no," Kai smirked, clearly enjoying himself. "Not after I've suffered you two eye-fucking across training grounds for months. I deserve this.'"

Kade's jaw twitched. "You don't deserve to breathe if you don't get out in the next five seconds."

Kai pressed a hand to his chest, mock-wounded. "Oh, scary. You really are in a mood this morning." His grin sharpened. "Was she that good?"

Before Kai could react, Kade moved so fast that the air seemed to crackle with the speed. A dagger flew, embedding itself in the wall behind him with a solid thud.

Kai arched an amused brow. "Touchy, but more importantly, where the hell were you hiding that?"

Sera, still hidden beneath the blanket, groaned. "Kai, please. Just leave."

Kai sighed dramatically, giving a resigned shake of his head. "Fine, fine. No appreciation for good humour." He turned, heading toward the door, but just as his hand touched the handle, "One more thing, Sera, that little bond was not as blocked as you thought last night. I knew you were happy but couldn't work out why."

Sera groaned.

"Imagine if mine was muted, what Aurion could feel as he is much more deeply connected with you." Kai laughed, his eyes dancing with his amusement.

The amulet Seraphina wore, hanging from her neck, pulsed faintly—and as if summoned by Kai's voice, Aurion's compact form appeared.

"You know, Kai was at least spared all the details," Aurion's voice emerged, the words vibrating in the air with an eerie calm. His presence was like the cold bite of a winter wind, as if the very atmosphere had changed with his arrival. "But perhaps you, Seraphina, should understand just how much *your* bond was not muted with me."

Kade's eyes went wide, and Sera's body froze as her heart skipped a beat. Neither of them spoke for a moment, eyes wide with horror. The room felt suddenly darker, the weight of Aurion's words hanging heavy in the air like an unspoken threat.

Kai smirked, leaning against the doorframe, his earlier amusement gone. "Well, looks like I'm not the only one in the know, and it seems he is much more in the know."

Sera could only stare, horror etched onto her features. *Muted. Spared no details.*

Sera's voice cracked as she whispered, "What do you mean by that?"

Aurion gave an indignant huff.

Kai let out a wicked laugh.

Sera, still hiding under the blanket, groaned. "Kai. Please. *Leave.*"

Kai sighed dramatically as he turned, sauntering back toward the door. "We leave in a few hours, lovebirds. Try not to *break* anything else before then."

With one last wicked grin, he slipped out the door, whistling as he went.

Silence settled in the room again.

Sera peeked out from beneath the blanket, staring at Kade.

Kade exhaled through his nose, rubbing his temples. "I'm going to kill him."

Sera huffed a laugh, pressing her forehead against his shoulder. "Not before I do."

Kade grumbled something unintelligible, pulling her back against him. Outside, Kai's laughter echoed down the hall.

Chapter 45

The courtyard buzzed with activity as the groups prepared to leave. They saddled the horses, checked their weapons, and the crisp morning air carried the scent of damp earth and the distant crackle of torches.

Kai leaned lazily against his horse, arms crossed, watching Kade and Sera with a smirk that promised trouble. His green eyes gleamed with pure mischief, like a predator about to pounce on its prey.

"So," he drawled, tapping his fingers against the hilt of his sword. "Did you two sleep well in the end?"

Sera shot him a glare, tightening the straps on her pack as if she could pretend he *wasn't* talking. Kade, standing beside Vaelrik, exhaled sharply, his shoulders tensing.

Kai grinned wider. "Actually, scratch that. *Did you two even sleep?*"

Kade's jaw ticked. Sera was seconds away from launching something at his face.

But Kai wasn't done.

"Must've been quite the *battle,*" he continued. "The *destruction* left in your wake—"

Vaelrik, standing just a few feet away, let out a low snarl, his golden eyes darkening as he cast Sera a withering look. "So it's *true.*"

Sera stiffened.

Vaelrik took a slow step forward, towering over her. "I always thought, when the time came, you would *choose* the strongest, the most worthy." His gaze flicked to Kade, full of disgust. "Instead, you destroyed yourself for *him.*"

Kade bristled, shifting slightly, as if ready to place himself between them.

Seraphina met Vaelrik's glare, steady and unflinching. "It wasn't about *choosing.*" Her voice was calm, but the weight behind it was unshakeable. "It was never about that."

Vaelrik sneered but said nothing, spinning away.

Kai, thoroughly enjoying the show, clapped his hands together. "Well, *someone's* bitter."

Vaelrik shot him a murderous look.

Before anyone could say more, with a dramatic *swoop*, Aurion emerged from the amulet, his small, silver-white form materialising in the air. He landed lightly on Sera's shoulder, shaking himself off with exaggerated indignation.

"Oh, *please,*" he huffed. "You're all *concerned* about *who* did what when *I* am the one who suffered the most."

Sera blinked. "Aurion—?"

The little dragon *glared* at her. "Do you have *any idea* what it's like to be magically *linked* to someone while they—" He gestured dramatically with his tiny claws. "—*do things?*"

Sera's face ignited.

Kade looked murderous.

Kai, however, *howled* with laughter, actually *doubling over* in delight.

Aurion wasn't done.

"I *heard* everything!" he continued. "I tried to *block it out,* but no, I was *trapped!*" His wings flared. "You *traumatised* me, little one."

Kai wiped a tear from his eye. "Oh, this is the best day of my life."

Kade pinched the bridge of his nose. "I am *going* to kill you."

Kai only grinned wider. "Wouldn't be the first time you've *tried.*"

Aurion grumbled, curling his tail around Sera's neck, still sulking.

Vaelrik had gone eerily silent, his expression unreadable. Without another word, he turned, stalking toward his horse.

Sera swallowed, shifting uncomfortably.

Kade's gaze softened as he stepped closer, his fingers brushing against hers before fully taking her hand in his. His grip was firm yet reverent, as if memorising the feel of her skin against his own.

For a moment, the world around them blurred—the teasing, the bitterness, and the looming battle. It was just *them.*

His thumb traced a slow, absentminded circle over her knuckles, his warmth seeping into her skin like fire in the chilly morning air.

"Be careful," he murmured, his voice low, intimate, meant only for her.

Sera exhaled slowly, tilting her head up to meet his eyes. "You too."

Kade hesitated, something unreadable flickering in his gaze, before lifting her hand to his lips. But he didn't just kiss it.

His breath ghosted over her skin first, a warm contrast against the crisp air. Then, with aching slowness, he pressed his lips to her knuckles—soft, lingering, like a secret meant only for her to understand. He stayed there for a heartbeat longer than necessary, as if grounding himself in her touch at that moment.

Seraphina's breath caught.

Kade finally pulled away, his fingers giving hers the faintest squeeze before he let go. But the warmth of his touch remained, seared into her skin like an unspoken promise. She reached for him before he could turn fully away, grabbing his wrist and pulling him towards her. Then she stood on her tiptoes to press a kiss to his lips. One that conveyed everything she felt. They finally broke apart at Kai's voice, breaking their moment.

Kai made an exaggerated gagging noise. "Oh, *for fuck's sake,* get on your damn horse before I throw up."

Kade didn't even dignify that with a response. Turning toward his own horse. Sera exhaled, grounding herself, before mounting up beside Kai.

As they set off, Kai *still* couldn't resist.

"So, do you *always* break furniture, or was that just a *special* occasion?"

Sera groaned. It was going to be a *long* ride.

Chapter 46

Seraphina and Kai were assigned this godforsaken mission to find and destroy the enemy. Simple, except it had taken longer and instead of the enemy they hunted, they had a new one to face. Seraphina's nightmares. She had only dozed for what felt like a second when the nightmare took her. Kai had shaken her out of it, concern etched across his beautiful face, his green eyes holding back tears at her suffering. The nightmares had gotten worse, more intense and downright horrifying. Seraphina missed Kade, missed his warmth and his ability to quieten the noise in her mind with calming words.

"Sera! What the hell is happening? I knew you had nightmares, but that was more like you being murdered before my eyes." He let out breathlessly.

She knew she had to explain. The answer she had for everyone was right on the tip of her tongue. "I'm fine; they are just nightmares." But looking at Kai, her heart ached. She didn't want to lie to her best friend anymore. She wanted to tell someone for the first time, and she wanted to ease the burden in her heart.

The fire crackled between them, but Seraphina felt cold. The flames did nothing to chase away the ice creeping through her veins. She stared into the fire, but the only thing she saw was him—his face twisted in mock affection, the lies spilling from his lips like poison, the bruises on her body, the shattered pieces of her soul. Her past was as vivid as the day he had broken her.

Kai had been quiet. Too quiet. The air felt thick with the weight of everything unsaid. She could feel him watching her, waiting, but she couldn't bring herself to look at him yet. To see the pity in his eyes, the shock that would no doubt twist his features when she finally told him the truth.

Finally, she broke the silence.

"You don't know," she whispered, her voice so low it almost got lost in the wind. "No one knows. What everyone remembers of Alexis is that he was suddenly turned evil at the end when he murdered my family, but the things that haunt my nightmares aren't just those last moments."

Kai stayed still, his gaze steady and unwavering, but she could feel the tension radiating from him. He looked poised to strike as they rested by the campfire. Something felt wrong to him. He knew this was more than just the usual haunted silence she carried.

"I didn't know," Seraphina continued, her voice thick with the weight of years she'd buried deep within her. "I thought it was just the war. Initially, I thought it was stress. I know it seems stupid now. What an excuse, but I genuinely believed it was, and that's what he said. That's what he told me when he got angry."

She took a long, shuddering breath.

"When he grabbed my wrist too tight, when he pushed me against the wall. He was a little rough, a little excessive, but I always believed his explanation that it was the weight of the Crown, the pressure of everything falling apart; we were never meant to rule. It was supposed to be Lucanis, so I thought his angry reaction to the weight of it all was justified. That dark, almost sick excitement flashing in his eyes burned itself into her mind. She knew now what it was, but it didn't make her feel better."

"Sera" — Kai's voice was raw with his emotion. It broke off as she inhaled sharply and let the words tumble out before she could stop them.

"He'd hit me," she said, her voice trembling. "Not always at first, but sometimes. A bruise here… a split lip there, a hand print wrapped around my wrist. He'd apologise, hold me like it was nothing, like it didn't matter."

Her voice faltered, a bitter laugh breaking free as she stared at her hands, now trembling.

Kai couldn't speak, his voice frozen with all the words that wouldn't be enough. He just stared, watching Seraphina shake, trembling in the memories of the past as the firelight cast shadows across her face, illuminating her green eyes, haunted by the past.

"I thought it was love... because he would hold me after. He would tell me it was just the war, just the pressure, and that he was just trying to keep control. I thought if I just loved him enough, just gave him enough... I thought it must have been my fault. Was I so wallowing in the grief of losing my brother as not to notice his pain and of everything changing? I thought if I just kept trying.... he'd be the man I married again... But he was never that man, Kai. He was never the same again."

Her eyes darkened. The tears were unshed, filling her eyes with all the pain she experienced at the hands of her husband. As she gazed at Kai, he had wanted to reach out and hold her. The pain she was in was washing over him.

Seraphina's distant expression showed she was trapped in the memory again. "But it got worse, Kai. So much worse. The anger turned into control... he started locking me in rooms, keeping me hidden away like I was some fragile thing to protect. He said it was for my protection in the beginning. I couldn't leave, couldn't do anything. It was like he thought he owned me. No... He did, he owned me." She shook her head at the absurdity of it all. She dropped her head into her hands.

"But it wasn't love, Kai. It was an obsession. He'd force himself on me, touched me like I was a thing, not the woman he swore to cherish. And I allowed him... I allowed him because I feared what he would do if I refused.

Kai had tears silently streaming down his face as he sat there, gazing at her. He saw the pain she suffered, saw the way it clung to her. He couldn't believe this had all transpired between her and Alexis, or really, he felt worse that he could believe it.

She stood suddenly, her movements sharp and jerky, as if trying to shake the weight off. But she couldn't. The pain, the terror, it lingered in her bones, in every scar he'd left on her body. She walked closer to the fire, like she could burn the memory off her if she stood close enough to the flames. Absentmindedly, she traced the scar Alexis had given her on her wrist. She turned back to Kai, as his eyes were drawn to the scar she was touching. A tight smile touched her lips.

"A punishment for crying during one of the many times he forced me." She took a breath. "I couldn't ever escape those moments. He would force me to watch."

Kai's green eyes flicked back up to hers and he held his breath as she continued.

"But I couldn't see it. I couldn't see it until it was too late. Until I stood there, watching him burn my family alive, my kingdom reduced to ash. Watching him stand over the flames, grinning like a madman." Her breath hitched. "I didn't know, Kai. I didn't know it was him. He was supposed to protect us. He was supposed to be my husband... my partner. Instead, he was the monster who made me watch everything I loved burn."

Kai's face twisted with fury, but he kept silent, knowing this was not the time to speak. He couldn't even imagine the horrors she'd witnessed.

She looked at him then, her eyes wide, vulnerable. "My love for him was profound. I still loved him, Kai, right until the moment I killed him. I killed the man I loved, and I still love him... and it breaks me every fucking day. Why do I love him?"

Kai was silent, his chest rising and falling fast with each breath, the weight of her confession hanging heavy between them.

"And the nightmares," Seraphina whispered. "They don't stop. Every night, it's like I'm back there. He's there, watching me, waiting for me to come back to him... to let him own me again. I wake up drenched in sweat, like he's still taking from me, like his hands are still around my neck, still demanding. I feel drained, like he's still there, draining the life out of me." Her voice wavered, like she was trying to hold it together, but the cracks were deep.

Kai gazed at her. He did not know that every time she falls asleep she was back there, in her brutal past, with Alexis hurting her. His hands shook with the restraint he was trying to show. She didn't need his anger, gods she had enough of her own. She needed someone to listen, and he was trying so hard to lock his muscles down and contain his rage at her treatment,

She looked away, her fists clenching at her sides. "But what if... what if he's not really gone? What if he's still out there, waiting? What if those times I hear his voice whispering to me it isn't all in my head?" Her voice was hollow now, empty with the realisation she'd never fully faced.

Kai's voice was quiet, yet intense, as the storm inside him churned. "Did you check the body, Seraphina?" he asked, his words cutting through the silence. "Did anyone check? For sure?"

Her breath caught in her throat, her heart skipping a beat. She shook her head, her eyes wide with horror, and the pieces of the puzzle clicking into place with a sickening finality.

"No... I..." she faltered, her knees threatening to give out beneath her. She didn't want to say the words, but the truth crushed her. "I didn't... I didn't check. I didn't think I needed to. I killed him, Kai. He had my father's sword buried in him where I had stabbed him. I watched him die. But what if—what if I was wrong? What if he's still alive, still waiting to finish what he started?"

Her voice broke on the last word, and she fell to her knees, her hands shaking uncontrollably. The tears fell freely from her eyes as her hair fell into her face.

Kai's anger flared, his hands balling into fists. He was on his knees beside her, grabbing her shoulders so she could look at him. "We're going to find out, Sera. We're going to find out, and if he's still out there, we'll finish it. But you will not let him keep breaking you like this. You hear me?"

Seraphina didn't respond. The weight of her own guilt crushed her chest; the realisation was too much to bear. She had never checked. She had killed him, watched him die in her mind, and convinced herself he was gone. But now... now, she wasn't sure.

The fire between them crackled, its glow casting long shadows across the floor, but it did nothing to keep the chill from spreading in the air. Seraphina had fallen silent, her face pale, her eyes haunted with the memories she'd shared. Kai was right on the ground with her, holding her in a half hug while kneeling on the ground. She hadn't been able to look at him when she finished—how could she? How could anyone look another person in the eye after speaking those words?

But the silence between them grew thick, suffocating. Kai's mind spun with the weight of what she had confessed, the horrors she had lived through, the horrors that she had never even allowed herself to truly see until now. He was rubbing soft circles on her back. Kai didn't know what to say. He knew any words would fall flat in the face of her pain. He was trying to find something, anything, to say—but the words wouldn't come. So he just held her, trying to offer comfort from being near her.

His pulse quickened as the realisation hit him like a wave. His hand stilled on her back. It hit harder than any punch, any blade. Kade. Kade had been there.

Kade had been blood bound to Alexis. He had been there, watching it all. Watching the bruises, the brokenness, the way Seraphina's spirit had withered under Alexis's control. Kade knew the man who called Seraphina his, who twisted her love into a sick obsession. Kade had been right there beside her, bound by blood—compelled to obey.

Kai's hand clenched into a fist, his knuckles cracking under the pressure. Seraphina glanced up at him, feeling the change in his body as he tensed. Her bright green eyes searched his face to understand what made him react this way.

"Kade…" he whispered to himself, but the more he thought, the more the fury built. His gaze flicked to Seraphina, but she looked down.

"Do you have any idea?" His voice broke the silence, harsh and raw. "Do you even understand what Kade saw, Sera? What he witnessed? That bastard saw them break you. He stood there and saw it all — watched you get hurt. He watched Alexis tear you apart."

His chest tightened as his fury blazed in his dark green eyes. He stood up in a rush, and Seraphina shrunk back, not from fear, but from the weight of his words, the anger in them.

"You think you can just... just fall for him and don't tell me you aren't I see the way you look at him? After everything you've been through? After everything he watched you go through?" Kai's breath came out in short bursts. "Doesn't that bother you? Doesn't it make you question what kind of man he is? He was there, Sera! Watching. And now you want to trust him?"

Kai couldn't believe she had allowed this monster near her. He might have done nothing, but Kai knew, knew that Kade would have known something. They all knew Kade had broken his bond with Alexis to save Seraphina that day. But that was it. How far did this go? Kai stared at her, his eyes begging her to explain.

Seraphina's eyes snapped up to meet his, the rawness of the pain in them almost unbearable. "He didn't know everything," she whispered, her voice trembling, as if trying to convince herself more than him. "At least I think he didn't. He was always just there, guarding Alexis. That's all I knew. That's all I believed—until right now. But you're right, I... I don't know everything. I never asked him. I never asked the questions I should have."

The quiet realisation hung in the air, suffocating and cold. With her chest tight, she swallowed hard. She realised she had spent years with this man, fighting side by side, because she had forgiven him the day he saved her, the day he called her Nyx. She thought he had changed sides that day after seeing Alexis kill her family. Was she wrong?

"No," she whispered, more to herself than anything. "I never knew. Not really. All I knew was he was always there, always by Alexis's side, always protecting me. But now..." Doubt creased her features.

Kai's anger boiled over, and he stepped toward her with a seething rage. His voice was low, but the weight hit like thunder. "Now, you don't know if anything is real. You don't know if his loyalty was ever really to you or if he was just bound, forced to be there, forced to watch you fall apart while he stood by and did nothing." Kai tried to soften his anger. He just wanted her to realise that she needed to get answers.

Seraphina looked away, her face a mask of guilt and confusion, but it was the uncertainty in her eyes that cut Kai the deepest. She wasn't sure anymore. She wasn't sure about Kade, about what he'd seen, about what he was still hiding from her.

Her words faltered as the truth crushed down on her. "I thought I knew him. I thought I knew him, Kai. But now... now I don't even know who he really is. How much of him was always part of the lie?"

The air was heavy, thick with their unspoken thoughts. Her gaze dropped to the floor, and for a moment, neither of them said anything. But the tension grew, gnawing at the edges of their conversation.

Kai's voice softened, but his anger still burned beneath the surface. "Sera, you are falling for him. You don't even see it. You don't see it, but I do. And I hate it. I hate him for doing this to you, for dragging you into this mess, but before you hurt yourself more over it, you need to ask him the questions that are burning in your mind."

His words felt like a slap in the face, sharp, and yet Seraphina couldn't fight the truth that was slowly sinking into her bones. She loved Kade. She had almost told him that the night she had tried to save him from himself, and that hurt more than anything. Because how could she love someone who had been so close to the man who had destroyed her? Kai was right. She needed to find out the truth.

Kai turned away, his fists clenched at his sides, the rage still simmering beneath his skin. "What happens when you find out the worst of it, huh? What happens when you find out that the man you trust might have been complicit in everything?"

Seraphina's heart dropped into her stomach. What if Kade was complicit?

"What happens when you realise you know nothing about him at all?" Kai's voice cracked with the weight of his own guilt, his fury, his fear. Not for himself, but for his best friend. "He's hiding something, Sera. And you're standing there falling for him while everything around you burns."

The silence between them stretched unbearably, heavy with unspoken pain. Kai's words still hung in the air like the last echoes of a battle cry, their weight pressing against Seraphina's chest until she could barely breathe. She wrapped her arms around her chest as if she could hold the pain inside.

She wanted to fight back, to deny the truth in his accusations, to tell him he didn't understand—but she couldn't. Because he understood.

And it hurt.

The memories felt like shackles, dragging her backward, drowning her in things she had long tried to forget. But now, she couldn't escape. They curled around her ribs, suffocating, whispering—you will never be free. Her body trembled. With her arms wrapped around herself, curling inward as if she could hold herself together before she completely shattered.

Then—warmth. A voice. Soft, golden, deep as the roots of the world.

She needs you.

Kai stiffened, his breath hitching. Aurion's voice thrummed through his mind, ancient and knowing. Through their shared bond, Aurion had felt it all—seen it all. And now, the dragon spoke only to him.

She doesn't need your fury, Kai. She needs her best friend. Seraphina has just admitted truths to you. She has told no other, and I believe in her heart it has also awoken more dangerous truths as well.

The words struck him harder than any blade ever could.

Kai exhaled sharply, his rage cooling into something deeper, something more painful—grief. His hands ached from clenching them too tightly, from wanting to make it right.

The air shimmered. A pulse of power, soft and radiant, swelled in the room. The amulet at Seraphina's throat pulsed once—twice — before the form of his dragon took shape, woven from moonlight and fire.

Aurion.

The glow of the fire illuminated his silver-white scales and lent him an air of magic. He was small enough to curl into Seraphina's lap, a radiant warmth against the ice in her veins.

Seraphina gasped softly, her fingers instinctively stroking his smooth scales, like silk under her fingers. Aurion let out a slow exhale, his scales glowing softly in the dim firelight.

"You are not broken, little warrior," Aurion murmured, his voice singing of midnight winds and ancient fire.

Seraphina's breath hitched. Aurion's golden eyes held her still, preventing her from denying it, pushing him away, or saying she was broken, though she opened her mouth to do so.

"You are Nyx, warrior of the night," he continued, his voice ancient and unyielding. "You are prophecy incarnate, the storm that does not break, and the flame that does not die. Your past doesn't define you; you are stronger than it. It is a part of your story, but it is not you."

Deep within her, something cracked.

Her hands stilled on his back, her shoulders trembling as she closed her eyes. Not broken. Not something shattered beyond repair.

Just... a story. A history. But not in her future.

Aurion pressed his snout to her chest, right where her heart beat unevenly beneath her ribs. "My little Phoenix, you do not belong to the past. You are not what happened to you. You are what you choose to become."

Seraphina swallowed hard, her throat aching.

Kai knelt back down to her, pulling her against his muscular chest, wrapping an arm around her shoulders. He rested his chin on the top of her head. She leaned into him.

She had spent so long believing her scars defined her. That they were the only thing that defined her. But Aurion's words curled around her soul like warmth after a brutal winter, like the first breath of air after drowning.

She was here. She was alive.

Her fingers started back up, tracing patterns on his scales as she let herself relax against Kai. The weight of her best friend beside her grounded her in a way nothing else could. She felt Kai exhale, his tension slowly unwinding as he was holding her close, wordless, but present.

Then, through the bond, Aurion whispered with something like affection, something like certainty. *You are safe, little Phoenix.*

427

Seraphina stilled. Phoenix.

The name settled into her bones, into her soul.

"Why do you call me that?" she asked, voice barely above a whisper.

Aurion's golden eyes softened. *You rise from the ashes, Seraphina. You always have. And you always will.*

Kai shifted beside her, his voice thick with unspoken emotion. "He's right, you know." He had heard the entire conversation through the bond.

Seraphina lifted her gaze to meet his, and for the first time in a long time, she saw no judgement there. No pity. Only belief. Fierce, unwavering belief.

Kai smirked slightly, brushing his knuckles over her cheek—soft, protective. "You don't break, Sera. You burn and you rise. That's who you've always been."

Her breath caught. She had for so long believed that she was broken. But now, here, held between her dragon and her best friend, she felt something stir within her.

Something bright. Something defiant. She was not in her past. She was something more. Seraphina closed her eyes, exhaling as she leaned into their warmth. "Thank you," she murmured, barely more than a breath.

Kai's arms tightened around her, and Aurion rumbled softly in her lap. "Always," Kai said, and she believed him.

Chapter 47

They had stayed like that for some time until the air had grown thick with a malevolent energy, and Seraphina could feel it in the pit of her stomach—an unease that rippled through her every sense. The ground beneath her boots trembled slightly, as if it too was bracing for what was to come.

Kai stood beside her, pulling her to her feet. His eyes narrowed, the usual banter gone, replaced by the seriousness of what lay ahead. Aurion, curled up in his dragon form on her shoulder, was tense, his sharp eyes scanning the horizon. The mission they were originally sent on had reared its ugly head.

The darkened sky above crackled with energy as the demon emerged, its form an inky void of tendrils and fire, eyes burning like the pits of hell. Behind it came the corrupted soldiers, their faces twisted with madness, armoured in blackened metal, and weapons dripping with malice. Seraphina felt the surge of magic before the first strike. But it wasn't just the raw power—it was the haunting realisation that her past was standing before her, the face cloaked in darkness. Now, here it was—this embodiment of everything she had feared.

The demon's voice cut through the tension in the air. "You'll come with us, woman. Our master demands it. Or we'll take you dead."

That name. Master.

Her heart thudded in her chest, but her eyes hardened. For the first time, she spoke the truth aloud, her voice filled with anger and something deeper, something dark she had buried for far too long. "Alexis is alive. And he can go back to the hell he crawled out of. Tell him that. I'm done with him."

The words felt like a confession—one last breath of defiance. But they sparked something in her chest that wouldn't die. Seraphina could still feel the burn of him beneath her skin, the pull of memories and pain twisted together. Her fury wasn't just about betrayal. It was survival. She was still standing, still fighting. But there was no time to dwell on the wreckage of love and lies.

The soldiers were already charging.

And the demon's laughter—low, cruel—sliced through the air like a blade.

Her voice rang out, clear as a war cry. "Let's end this."

"Sera, get ready! I've got you!"

Kai's form exploded in a burst of raw, primal energy. His Lycan shift was nothing short of violent—bones cracking, sinew stretching, black and silver fur erupting from his skin. He hit the ground snarling, jaws snapping as he launched forward with a roar that shook the trees. He was chaos incarnate, a whirlwind of claws and fangs tearing through the front line of corrupted soldiers like parchment. Steel couldn't hold him. Flesh stood no chance. He moved like a storm, always circling back to her, shielding her from the ones who got too close.

Her words were sharp, final. She could feel the magic swirling in her veins as she called it forth. But it wasn't just her power she channelled—it was Aurion's presence, grounding her, reminding her she was no longer the woman who had fallen into Alexis's trap. She was a warrior who had broken free.

Aurion's voice in her mind was a quiet reminder, but also a challenge. *You are powerful, little Phoenix. Show them who you really are.*

With those words, Seraphina closed her eyes for a moment, her magic building within her. She lifted her arms, and in the space of a breath—

Aurion's true form — rose from the little silver white dragon and changed into his giant obsidian Dragon his massive wings sweeping through the battlefield, creating gusts of wind that sent soldiers flying. His eyes glowed golden with her fury, the magic that coursed through them a mirror of her own soul.

Fury filled the demon's snarl, but Seraphina pressed on. She pulled her daggers from her belt, the familiar weight of them comforting in her hands as she moved fluidly through the fight. With every swipe, she felt the heat of the blade, the precision of her strikes, and the satisfaction of cutting through the surrounding corruption. She was a blur—faster than the soldiers, quicker than the demon itself. Steel clashed against steel. Screams filled the air. She moved like vengeance—silent, precise, unstoppable. Her daggers found flesh, fibre, bone. Blood splattered across her arms, but she didn't stop. She ducked a blade, spun low, and gutted a soldier mid-swing.

Then pain—*hot and immediate*—slammed into her thigh.

A sword had found her.

She staggered, breath catching, teeth bared. Blood ran hot down her leg, staining the earth beneath her.

"That—" she hissed, glaring down at the ruin in her pants, "was my favourite pair."

The soldier grinned, cruel, and jagged, but didn't live long enough to speak. Her dagger found his throat in the next heartbeat. She quickly spun to see the next soldier approaching.

"Come on, give me something to remember you by," she taunted the soldier in front of her, waving her dagger at him. He unleashed a horrible shriek before she took him down in one hit.

Sera, we don't play with our kills. Aurion's voice snaked through her thoughts, but she could tell he was proud of her by the tone.

Aurion, in his massive dragon form, was a beast of destruction beside her, tearing through the corrupted soldiers with ease. With the last soldier fallen and the demon cornered between Aurion's giant dragon form, Kade's hulking Lycan form, and Seraphina, the heat of battle awakened her, pulling her from her nightmares; now she had to end the nightmare.

"You can tell your master that I will, in fact, go nowhere with any of his goons." She pointed her sword at the demon. She knew in her heart Alexis could hear her.

Aurion and Kade stalked closer, ready to attack when she was. She continued,

"If he insists on sending these vermin to get me, then... I don't mind taking his army down one cockroach at a time." She smirked; her gaze held nothing but contempt. The demon hissed, lunging—

But Seraphina moved faster.

She *plunged* her sword through its eye; the blade sliding through corrupted flesh and bone like fire through parchment. The creature screamed—just once—before Aurion's fire engulfed it. The flames roared, curling skyward as the demon crumbled to ash.

Then—nothing.

Only her heartbeat and the smell of scorched earth.

She swayed, the pain in her leg climbing her spine like fire licking bone. Her grip faltered. Her sword slipped from her fingers with a metallic *clang*.

You're bleeding all over the place, Sera.

Kai's voice buzzed in her head, teasing, familiar, rough with affection. *You really should stop doing that. Not a good look.*

Her lips twitched. "Yeah, well," she muttered, limping to a boulder and collapsing against it, "someone had to make a mess. Might as well be me."

Aurion's voice cut through the bond, his sarcastic tone still laced with a certain affection.

You know, we said you'd rise again. We didn't mean to try dying now.

Seraphina winced as she finished the bandage. Her head was spinning from the intensity of the fight and the blood loss, but she felt a familiar sense of relief—of normalcy—as she looked at her friends. Even with everything she'd been through, even with her past creeping up on her, they were still here. They were still fighting by her side.

It's good to see you smiling again, Sera. You've been a real pain in the ass, but... it's good to have you back. Kai's mental voice held a mirthful tune.

Seraphina smirked despite herself, the weight of the moment lifting slightly. She moved to transform Aurion back into his smaller, silver dragon form. He settled onto her shoulder, curling up like he always did. The silver dragon let out a soft huff.

We should get you to the healers. You've done enough for today.

Kai shifted back into his human form and offered a hand to help her up, his eyes softening slightly.

"I can carry you back to the stronghold. You don't have to walk all the way there with a wound like that."

Seraphina raised an eyebrow, clearly not convinced that it was necessary, but after a second of hesitation, she watched him transform back to his Lycan form, as he lowered himself to the ground so she could straddle his back, her legs draped over his back as she leaned into him, grabbing a tuff of fur on the back of his neck to hold on. Kai stood back up as he turned around and started the journey back to the stronghold.

Aurion gave a low, rumbling laugh through the mental bond.

Oh, Kai. You love this. You love the fact you get to play wolf in shining armour? Just admit it.

Kai's laugh was deep and genuine as he started walking, and Seraphina smiled, a warmth blossoming in her chest despite the pain in her leg. They were back to their usual banter, and for a moment, it felt like the past didn't matter.

Shut up, Aurion.

Chapter 48

The day's travel had taken its toll on the group. Aurion was keeping
Seraphina's wound from bleeding out by sheer magic and willpower, but
even he was wearing thin on reserves of magic. Kai's Lycan form was
exhausted from caring Seraphina the entire way without resting, and as
they approached the gates, Kai, with Seraphina still on his back, saw the
stronghold looming ahead and huffed a breath of relief. The air felt thick
with tension, but there was a sense of relief in the air as they neared the
familiar stone walls. The scent of pine and damp earth filled Seraphina's
senses, and despite the lingering pain from her thigh wound, the world
around her felt momentarily safe.

As they approached the courtyard, Kade, Vaelrik, and Dylan came
rushing out to meet them. Kade's eyes instantly locked onto Seraphina,
his face filled with concern. He barely registered the others as he moved
toward her, his footsteps swift and urgent.

Dylan's eyes flickered between his son and Seraphina, his intense gaze
assessing the situation with a practised eye.

Dylan immediately went to Kai, checking him over with quick, thorough
hands down his body, earning him a huff and eye roll from the huge Lycan.
He sighed in relief as he confirmed Kai was whole and in no immediate
danger.

"You're safe, good. But what about her?" His attention shifted to

Seraphina, his face tightening with concern.

"Oh, you know, fought a demon and some corrupted soldiers at the same time. Took a brief stab to the thigh for my trouble, but I'm fine. This isn't my first injury, and I finished the mission, so that demon won't terrorise the villages anymore." Seraphina's lips pulled into a smile, then a grimace as Dylan touched her leg, inspecting the wound.

Through the bond, Seraphina immediately spoke to Kai and Aurion.

Don't you dare say anything about what I said. I'm not ready. Just... let it be for now.

Aurion's voice was like a gentle whisper in her mind, understanding and supportive. *Understood. Your secrets are safe with us.*

Kai hummed in agreement, but his body under her had tensed if he was ready for a fight and locked his muscles down from acting on it.

Vaelrik came up behind Dylan, crossing his arms and smirking. "Well, well, well. If it isn't the mighty warrior. I'm sure you had all that under control, right, Seraphina? But maybe next time, take the right dragon with you. Looks like Aurion could use a little more practice in protecting his chosen."

Seraphina rolled her eyes, her cheeky grin forming despite the exhaustion. It seemed like the weeks they had been apart on their missions and cooled his anger towards her. But there was a flicker of warmth in her gaze when she looked at Aurion. She could feel his power thrumming beside her, grounding her. He didn't need to be told—he already knew what she needed.

"Oh, please. Don't listen to him, Aurion. You're just fine."

Kade shattered the playful moment when he stepped forward, hand outstretched toward Seraphina. Instinctively, Seraphina flinched away, her body reacting before her mind could catch up. The distance between them felt palpable, thick with the unresolved tension, betrayal, and pain. That she had now realised but was yet to tell him. His face pulled with concern at her reaction.

The air around Kai immediately shifted. His hackles went up, a deep growl rumbling from his chest.

The statement, "Touch her, and I'll tear your damn arm off," was implied.

Seraphina's brow furrowed, her voice sharp as she spoke to him through their mental bond.

Kai quit it. I'm fine; I haven't forgotten. His hotness doesn't make me forget, alright? I will deal with it, but you have to stop growling like that.

Could have fooled me! Pretty faces make you forget common sense. Kai's voice was angry as it filtered into her mind.

It's true. Why else would she be friends with you if her common sense wasn't gone? Aurion's voice held a tone of teasing.

Aww, you think I am pretty?

Aurion just rolled his eyes.

Seraphina laughed down the bond, a warmth flowing between all three of them.

Out loud, Seraphina sighed and turned to Kai with an exaggerated, playful roll of her eyes. "Kai, seriously. Everyone's looking at you like you've gone mad. Knock it off."

Dylan raised an eyebrow, the concern still in his eyes as he glanced between the two of them. "Are you okay, son?"

Kai huffed, his posture stiff. His sharp eyes flickered back to Kade before softening slightly. *"I'm fine. Just... protecting her."* His voice filtered into his father's mind through the mind link Lycans shared.

Aurion's voice, tinged with sarcasm but also affectionate, masked the awkward tension between Kai and Seraphina. "He's just being protective of her, Dylan. Wants to take her to the healers. A lot more concern than usual, but it's cute."

Seraphina's lips twitched with a smile at the word cute, but she felt the burn of the wound on her thigh more acutely now. "Can we get to the healers already? I'd really like to avoid further bleeding out. That would be great."

Kai gently set her down, lowering his colossal form steadily despite the turbulent emotions swirling around him. He let her go into Dylan's arms instead of Kade's, the tension between them too thick for him to let go of just yet. With a look that spoke volumes, Kai nodded toward her. He would let her handle it, but he wouldn't trust Kade until she did, and he made that clear.

Before anyone could argue, Kai shifted back into his human form, plastering a smile on. He moved quickly, scooping Seraphina up in his arms and carrying her toward the healer's quarters with a determined expression on his face.

As they passed, his gaze locked with Kade's, and a deep, almost possessive growl rumbled in his chest. He pushed past Kade with a glance that dared him to argue.

Vaelrik, never one to miss an opportunity for teasing, couldn't help himself. "Well, well. Kade must have done something truly horrible this time for Kai to be rattled like that. What did you do, sunshine?"

Dylan, however, wasn't laughing. His eyes flickered to his son. He knew Kai wasn't just angry—he was worried. "Kai's not easy to rattle. But something's got him worked up because nothing gets him that angry unless it's something harming his family, and it's clear Seraphina's family. Whatever happened out there…?" His voice trailed off, the unspoken understanding between them lingering in the air.

Kade, despite his typical confidence, said nothing. His heart was heavy with the weight of his failure, and the worry he couldn't shake about what had happened to Seraphina. And why was Kai so angry with him, and why wouldn't she let him near her?

Chapter 49

Seraphina stepped out of the healer's wing, rolling over her shoulder and wincing at the dull ache that remained. A bandage covered her thigh; she moved carefully, but it did not impede her. The world outside was cool, the wind whispering against her skin, but her mind was a storm of its own. Too much had happened. Too much had been spoken. She just wanted to go back to her room and sleep off the pain. As she made her way slowly to her rooms, she took longer to walk down the corridor, leaning heavily on the wall as she went.

Graceful. Aurion's voice slipped into her mind..

I'd like to watch you get stabbed and bleed for days, then get stitched up and walk a long distance before you can comment. Her tone was sharper than she intended, but she was exhausted.

Aurion's smooth laugh filtered into her mind.

She didn't hear him coming. Too busy conversing in her mind to notice.

"Kai's acting more like a protective mate than a friend."

Kade's voice came from behind her, low and unreadable, but the accusation in it stopped her dead in her tracks. She turned slowly, heart hammering against her ribs as she met his gaze—storm-dark, intense, and searching.

Her lips parted, but nothing came. *Why does it matter to you?* The words were there, burning in her throat, but she bit them back. Instead, she squared her shoulders, forcing steel into her spine. "And if he is?"

Kade's jaw clenched. His gaze flickered, searching her face for something—an answer, a lie, maybe even the truth. "Is that what this is now? What about everything that happened before the mission?" His voice wasn't angry, but it was strained, as if he was barely holding something back. "Because I need to understand. Why is Kai the one hovering over you, ready to burn the world for you, and you won't even let me near you?"

Seraphina's fingers twitched at her sides. The air between them felt thick, suffocating.

Aurion's voice hummed gently in her mind. *You can do this, little Phoenix. Confronting what scares us strengthens us.*

She swallowed, ignoring the way her throat tightened. She didn't want to remember what had transpired between them before the mission. She wanted that night out of her head when she asked what she needed. "I don't owe you an explanation," she said, keeping her voice steady. "Not when I have questions of my own."

Kade went still. There it was—the shift.

The weight in her chest grew heavier as she spoke. "How much did you know?" Her voice barely wavered, but the crack in her armour was there. "About Alexis and me. About everything."

She saw it in his eyes—the flicker of hesitation, the way his shoulders tensed like a man about to face an executioner's blade.

Aurion's presence was solid, a quiet force in the background, but something shifted in the bond. *Kai is close,* Aurion murmured in her mind. *He's listening, but he won't interfere. He knows you need to do this alone.*

Seraphina exhaled slowly.

Kade dragged a hand through his silver hair, the motion trembling more than he wanted to show. He exhaled, sharp and shallow, as if he were forcing the air out just to stop it from turning into something else— something like a sob.

When his gaze finally met hers, Seraphina faltered.

His eyes—those storm-coloured, silver-grey eyes that had always seemed unshakeable—were undone. They were red-rimmed and wide with dread, with the unbearable weight of truths unspoken. The façade had finally cracked.

"You always tell me you're not scared of me," he said quietly.

The shift in his voice caught her off guard. Gone were the cocky bite, the rough confidence. This voice was something else entirely—soft, cracked, vulnerable. It felt like a ghost of a boy she never got to know, whispering through the man he had become.

"You always say you like me as I am," he went on, like the words were unspooling from a wound he couldn't stitch shut. "Broken. Missing parts. A weapon without an edge. You said you cared for me once." His throat worked around the next words like they tasted of blood. "You said you were mine."

Her heart twisted.

"I wonder how long before you change your mind."

Seraphina didn't breathe.

The air between them thickened, too heavy with history, betrayal, and something else—something sharp and final, hanging just beyond her reach.

Kade stood there, wrecked and still proud, his dishevelled silver hair falling into his face, his fists trembling at his sides. He reached out, grabbing onto her wrist. He looked like the battlefield had followed them into this moment, shadows etched deep into the lines of his sharp features. But it wasn't war that had destroyed him this time.

It was the truth.

"I knew."

Two words.

Two words that shattered her.

Seraphina's heart slammed against her ribs. Her vision blurred.

She had suspected. In the farthest corners of her mind, in the quietest hours of her grief, she had *always* suspected.

But to hear it...

Spoken aloud. Without excuse. Without denial.

It broke something fundamental in her.

Her breath caught. Her lungs forgot what to do. Her mouth opened—but nothing came.

"Ten seconds."

Her eyes met his again. The world seemed to slow.

Ten seconds.

That's how long it took to fall out of love with him.

In the first, second, her heartbeat stuttered.

The second, her mind screamed denial.

Third, the memory of him—laughing, broken, beautiful—clawed at her.

Fourth, she searched for the lie on his face.

Fifth, there were none.

Sixth, pain sharp and paralysing, cracked through her chest.

Seventh, she remembered Alexis's dead eyes.

Eighth, she remembered Kade dragging her from the ruins.

Ninth, she remembered trusting him.

Tenth, it all turned to ash.

Her expression shifted. Just slightly. But Kade saw it.

He flinched.

In that tenth second, Seraphina's love for him fractured—not loud or dramatic, but quiet. Absolute. Like a candle guttering out in the wind.

He saw the change in her eyes. The softness gone. The warmth turned to something cold, unreadable.

You need the whole truth. Kai's voice came through the bond, steady, unwavering. *I'll be here if you need me.*

Aurion hummed in agreement. *You are not alone.*

Seraphina exhaled sharply, yanking her wrist from Kade's grip. "Talk. I want the truth from the beginning."

The words sent ice through her veins, and for a moment, she didn't know if she could stand. Her hands clenched at her sides, nails biting into her palms, forcing her to stay upright. She had come into this wanting the truth, but now that it was spilling from his lips, it was like drowning in it.

"I already know what you are," she said, her voice hoarse. "A prince of the Unseelie."

His lips curled bitterly. "The last."

Seraphina blinked.

"The last prince," he repeated, his voice rough. "When the Unseelie agreed with the Veilborn, they ensured their survival. But the price was blood. The price was binding me and Alexis together. Blood and magic." He exhaled, his jaw locking. "I was his right hand, his tether to this world, just as he was mine."

The words turned her stomach, bile rising in her throat.

"You agreed to this?" she asked, already knowing the answer.

"They raised me in a court where pain was currency and suffering was power. I was never meant to be anything else, and after the death of my partner, I saw no reason to fight it." His silver-grey eyes darkened, gaze locked on her like a noose tightening around her throat. "At first, I didn't mind. I grew up with Alexis. We learned to thrive in a world where deception and cruelty were the only truths."

Seraphina's nails dug deeper into her palms. "And me?"

Kade's throat bobbed. "Alexis wanted you."

Something inside her shattered.

She had always known, hadn't she? That Alexis' love had been an illusion, a carefully constructed deception. But to hear Kade admit it—to confirm that Alexis had orchestrated it, had hunted her—

A deep, shaking breath. "You helped him."

Kade closed his eyes for half a second. "Yes."

Seraphina felt like she was standing on the edge of a cliff, the ground crumbling beneath her feet.

Kade's voice was quiet, but the words hit like a blade to the ribs. "I was the one who helped him infiltrate your court. I made sure he fit the part, smoothed over the lies, and ensured no one questioned him."

Seraphina's vision blurred.

"But then," Kade murmured, and there was something fragile in his voice, something raw, "I met you."

Her breath hitched.

Seraphina's stomach turned. "You knew?"

With his jaw clenched, the muscle ticked as he gave a slow nod. "I knew his plans for you."

Her heart stuttered.

Her breathing turned shallow. "And you still helped him."

"I did." Kade's voice dropped, low and strained, like it physically hurt to admit. "At first, I didn't care. I was just another weapon in his arsenal."

Seraphina stared, numb.

"But then—" His throat bobbed. "Then I met you."

Her breath caught, a fragile sound in the silence.

"I was supposed to pretend. Manipulate, lie." He let out a hollow laugh, devoid of humour. "But then I saw you. The way you laughed, loud and fearless. The way you fought, like your soul had claws. The way you cared, even after everything this world did to you." His hands curled into fists. "You were light. And I—" His voice broke. "I was weak."

She let out a bitter, breathless laugh. "No. You weren't weak. You were selfish."

He flinched as if she'd slapped him, but nodded. "Yes."

"I tried to bury it," he said. "Tried to keep my distance. But then Alexis asked me to help him... break you." His voice turned hoarse, brittle. "He wanted me to tear you apart from the inside out."

Her body went stiff.

Kade's fists trembled. "And I couldn't."

Silence wrapped around them like a noose.

"Every time I defied him," he said, breath shaking, "the bond shattered something inside me. It poisoned my power. It tore through my soul like rot." He closed his eyes for a heartbeat. "But I still couldn't hurt you."

She felt as though she couldn't breathe. Her lungs wouldn't obey.

"I refused to kill your family," he continued, softer now. "That was the first time I broke the bond in its entirety. And after that... I did what I could to protect you. To help from the shadows. But it wasn't enough."

Her voice was barely a whisper. "When he chained me to the bed... when he forced me..."

Kade's face went bloodless.

"Did you know?" she rasped.

He didn't answer.

Her voice cracked with venom. "Did you know every time he hit me? Every time he locked me away like an animal?"

Kade's silver eyes brimmed with something worse than guilt—devastation. "Seraphina—"

"Did. You. Know?" Her voice was a whip, laced with agony.

"I am always painfully aware of you."

The words sliced through her like glass.

A choked noise escaped her throat. Her knees buckled, but she didn't fall. Not yet.

"I loved you," she whispered. "I *loved* you."

Kade looked at the ground, unable to meet her gaze. "I knew," he said, broken. "I knew. But I thought if I kept my distance, if I worked from afar, I could protect you in some twisted way. I was already trying to sever the bond."

A sob clawed at her chest, raw and ragged.

"And you knew about my kingdom?" she asked. "You knew he wanted to destroy it?"

His silence was the only answer she needed.

Her legs gave way, and she staggered back, her shoulders hitting the cold stone wall.

"Why didn't you *tell* me?" she whispered, a desperate plea.

"I didn't want to be the reason you broke," he said, and the pain in his voice was real, but it didn't matter. Not now.

"No," she said, breathless, furious. "You just didn't want to *watch* me break."

The air between them shimmered with tension, thick with magic, grief, rage.

"I could have forgiven you," she whispered, "for working with him. If you had told me. If you had given me the truth."

Kade said nothing; his face was unreadable.

"But you *let me suffer alone.* You stood in the shadows while I bled and screamed and *begged* for it to end."

He squeezed his eyes shut.

"You took my choices from me," she continued, shaking. "So you wouldn't feel guilty. So you could pretend you were doing the right thing."

He stepped toward her, face carved in torment. "Sera—"

"Don't," she spat. "Don't call me that."

Kade recoiled as if the word burned his tongue.

"I assumed you were involved with Alexis," she admitted, voice cracking. "I hoped I was wrong. But I could have forgiven that."

Her gaze darkened. "What I can't forgive is that you *knew*—and you let it happen, anyway."

Kade's body shook, then—suddenly—he dropped to his knees.

Seraphina's breath caught.

She had never seen him fall before. Not like this. Not defeated. Not broken.

He knelt before her like a man at his own execution, silver hair a tangled mess, eyes shattered ruins. His fingers dug into his legs, white-knuckled, as if that pain was the only thing keeping him upright.

"This," he whispered, "this is why I never let myself love you."

She didn't move.

"I knew if I let you in, I wouldn't be able to stop." His shoulders trembled. "I tried to do the right thing. But in the end... I let you in anyway."

Silence.

Thick, drowning silence.

Her voice trembled. "You are selfish, Kade."

The words landed like a blade between his ribs. He didn't even flinch.

"I don't know if I can forgive you," she whispered. "Because I don't know how to trust you anymore."

He lifted his head slowly, pain carved into every angle of his face.

She placed a hand over her chest, as if she could hold her heart in place as it crumbled. The pressure there was unbearable. The ache, unspeakable.

Her hand trembled over her ribs. "You were the one thing I thought was mine."

Kade's lips parted—his face a storm of regret, of loss.

Then he exhaled, slow and broken, and stood.

His expression was hollow, unreadable. But his eyes—they were haunted. *Ruined.*

He stepped back.

"Ten seconds."

Her breath stopped.

"What?"

His voice was low. Devastated.

"It only took ten seconds," he whispered, "to watch you fall out of love with me."

Then he turned and walked away.

Seraphina didn't fuelled she was shaking until she felt a warmth against her back.

Kai. He had caught her as she collapsed, his powerful arms wrapping around her as sobs tore from her chest.

She barely registered Kade turning back one last time. The last thing he saw before he disappeared into the dark was the woman he loved breaking apart in another man's arms. And not for the first time in his life, Kade felt truly, utterly ruined.

One moment, Kade had been walking away—his silver hair catching the dying light like a memory she couldn't hold—and the next, she was collapsing into Kai's arms, the world spinning far too fast, far too loud. Her fists clutched the front of his tunic, knuckles white, desperate for something—anything—that felt real.

Her braids had come undone, strands of hair falling across her face, sticky with sweat and tears she didn't even remember shedding. But they must have been falling, because Kai was wiping beneath her eyes with gentle fingers, his usual crooked smirk absent, replaced by something softer. Something real.

"Breathe, Sera," he murmured, voice low and steady as the tremble in her chest threatened to break her in half. "I've got you."

She tried—but the breath didn't come. Her ribs ached too much. Her heart ached too much.

From across the room, Vaelrik lounged against the stone wall with his usual lazy elegance, arms folded, one boot crossed over the other. But his golden eyes were sharp—too sharp—and unreadable, glinting like blades just beneath the surface of calm.

"Kai," he drawled, brushing a hand through his dark hair, "as touching as this is, I think what she needs isn't comfort, but truth."

Kai's muscles tensed beneath her, his hold tightening protectively.

Vaelrik sighed. "You still don't get it, do you?"

Seraphina's stomach twisted, nausea curling like smoke in her gut. "Don't," she rasped, but her voice barely cut the silence.

He ignored her. Of course, he did.

"You know why people hunt Kade?" Vaelrik asked, his gaze locking onto hers like a challenge. "It's not because of Alexis. It's not even about what he's done." He leaned forward just slightly. "They cast him out."

Seraphina tried to swallow, but the lump in her throat stayed stubborn, thick with dread.

"The Unseelie Court doesn't exile people," Vaelrik said, his voice cold. "They *erase* them. His name, his bloodline, his home—gone. Like he never existed. That's what he gave up." His voice dropped a note lower, almost reverent. "For *you*."

Her breath hitched.

"They don't believe in love, Sera. Not really. Not like he does. And believe me," Vaelrik added with a dry twist of his mouth, "I still think he's a reckless, impulsive pain in the ass who's probably not worth your time. But…" He let the word hang in the air. "He's also the first person I've ever seen break a bond forged in both magic and blood."

His words cut deeper than she wanted them to.

"You know what that means," Vaelrik went on, his tone gentler now. "You, of all people, know what it feels like to have a bond shattered—how it tears you apart from the inside out. He broke that bond *himself*. And yes, he should have told you. He should have explained it all from the beginning. But he didn't because he was terrified—terrified of losing the one person he sacrificed *everything* for."

Vaelrik's voice echoed in the hollow space of the room.

"He brought ruin to his own kingdom," he said, quieter now. "All for you."

The silence that followed was deafening.

Seraphina's heart thudded in her ears, too loud. Too fast. Vaelrik—*Vaelrik*—of all people, was defending Kade? After everything? After she had chosen Kade and hurt *him*?

She didn't understand it.

He is right. Even I have never seen a blood and magic oath broken Aurion's voice slipped into her mind filled with wonder at the revelation.

She'd always thought of Vaelrik as smug, irritating, infuriating in ways words couldn't touch—but *never* selfless. Never someone who would speak on Kade's behalf. Her world tilted again.

Then there was Kade's voice—*Ten seconds*, he'd whispered.

Ten seconds to change her mind.

But it hadn't changed her heart. And that was the part she couldn't forgive.

She could *hate* what he had done—hate the betrayal, the silence, the way he'd watched her break without stepping in—but she couldn't hate *him*. Not when her heart still ached at the memory of his face twisted in sorrow, not when the sound of his voice saying her name still shattered something inside her.

He had been her constant.

Now, she wasn't so sure.

Kai let out a long breath beside her. "You're going to forgive him," he said flatly, dragging a hand through his hair.

Seraphina tensed. "I don't—"

"Yeah, yeah." He cut her off, waving a dismissive hand. "You don't know what to do. You're furious. Heartbroken. Betrayed. You feel you can't even breathe without choking under the weight of it. But you're going to forgive him, Sera." He looked at her then, really looked, his green eyes tired and sure. "I can see it already."

He muttered something under his breath. "Stupid, brooding, pretty faces."

Seraphina's lips trembled as she dragged in a breath that hurt all the way down. Her hands clutched the sleeves of her shirt like fibre, like she could hold herself together if she just kept gripping hard enough.

Aurion, small and silver-white on her shoulder, shifted slightly. His golden eyes flicked to her, ageless and knowing.

You are stronger than this pain, Seraphina. But you must choose what you do with it.

The weight of it all pressed down like a second skin.

Vaelrik muttered another snide comment about Kade's brooding, and Kai snapped something about how being emotionally constipated wasn't the same as being mysterious. Their voices faded into the background—noise, distant and unreal.

She was alone. Drowning in a decision only she could make.

Chapter 50

Time didn't heal wounds—it merely eroded them until the pain was worn into the bones. It lingered like the echo of a blade long after the blood had dried, dull and constant, familiar in its torment. Weeks passed. The rage Seraphina once carried like wildfire cooled into something heavier, quieter. A weight in her chest instead of a burn in her throat.

She didn't forget what Kade had done. But the sharp edges of her fury had dulled, ground down by exhaustion and repetition—strategy meetings, late-night patrols, endless negotiations. She moved through her days like a storm that no longer raged, but never stopped looming. Controlled. Contained. But never calm.

Kade remained a phantom at the edge of her awareness—always there, never close. He haunted hallways with sleepless eyes and the tension of a man holding something broken in his hands and unsure how to fix it. Their relationship, once tangled in heat and half-spoken truths, now echoed with absence. A silence so loud it followed her like a shadow.

She became an expert in avoidance. If Kade walked into the war room, she found an excuse to leave. If he stood at one end of the sparring circle, she paired off with someone else. If they were assigned the same mission, she requested reassignment without hesitation. Sometimes, he didn't object. Sometimes, he did—but always quietly.

But life didn't care for broken hearts. Not when prophecies spun on the axis of fate and diplomacy moved faster than grief could keep up.

In strategy meetings, Seraphina spoke with clipped efficiency. Her voice held none of its usual fire—only precision. She kept her eyes fixed on maps and figures, never on him. Kade, for his part, was barely more than a statue—still distant, his tone void of warmth, every word weighted and measured. He looked hollow. Like he hadn't slept in days.

Dylan, bless him, tried to bridge the space between them with soft patience and relentless optimism. He placed himself between them at meetings, cracked dry jokes no one laughed at, and gently redirected tension like someone trying to steer a sinking ship with bare hands.

One night, under the silver cast of the moon, he found her in the training yard, muscles trembling from hours of sparring.

"He's trying," Dylan said softly, holding a towel out to her.

Seraphina didn't reply. She conjured a blast of raw magic and hurled it at the nearest target dummy, sending it flying across the yard with a crack of force. Her chest heaved with the effort, her skin damp with sweat. Dylan didn't flinch.

She stared at the smouldering remains of the dummy. "Not hard enough."

Not all efforts were in vain.

The prophecy—ever elusive, ever coiled in metaphor and fate—had stirred and demanded clarity. It demanded blood and sacrifice. And sometimes, it demanded betrayal.

When Seraphina finally acted on what Kai had said months ago—that there were still pieces of the puzzle locked in mouths that refused to speak—she pushed for answers. Harder. Louder. Sharper. And the cracks showed.

It was Aurion who orchestrated it. Quietly. Precisely. With the ancient patience only a dragon could wield. Kai, for all his volatility, had been the catalyst—agitating like flint until sparks caught fire.

Together, they cornered Kade in the old war room. No one else was allowed inside. No one else would have understood the gravity.

Kade stood at the edge of the obsidian table, tense, hollow-eyed, and defiant. His silver hair was unbound, dishevelled. His jaw locked like stone as Aurion placed the old vellum scroll and an iron-dipped quill before him.

"Write it," Aurion said. Not a request. A command.

Kai paced behind him like a storm barely contained. "You've danced around this long enough. No more riddles. No more silence."

Kade hesitated. Just long enough to speak volumes.

Then, with a quiet breath that sounded too much like surrender, he picked up the quill.

Line by line, he wrote. His handwriting, once fluid and elegant, now looked fractured—shaky under the weight of what he was revealing. He named the hidden sect within the Unseelie Court. The part of the prophecy was buried so deep in secrecy that most thought it a myth, He wrote word for word what he was forced to remember as a child prince who was privy to the most ancient secrets of his court..

As his hand moved across the page, the parchment burned beneath his touch. Wisps of smoke curled from the edges as ancient runes reacted to the magic in his blood—the blood of an Unseelie who had broken one of their oldest laws.

He had spoken the sacred shard.

Eirasé.

The name of the prophecy's lost fragment. A word never meant to be uttered outside the Court's inner sanctum. A shard said to be the heart of the first fae king's legacy—and the key to unmaking or saving them all.

Aurion's eyes narrowed, his wings twitching even in his smaller, curled form. The light in the room shimmered unnaturally, as though even the walls recoiled from the truth being etched into existence.

When it was done, Kade dropped the quill. His hand shook. Not from pain—but from *knowing*. He had just severed his last tie to the Unseelie. Not just defection. Not just betrayal.

He had broken *the pact*.

Later, back in her chambers, Seraphina sat with Aurion coiled loosely around her wrist, his scales cool and smooth, his golden eyes solemn.

"He broke their pact," Aurion murmured, his voice no louder than breath. "The unspoken law of silence. They will feel it. The Court… they always feel when their sacred truths are disturbed."

Seraphina stared at the parchment laid across her desk, now sealed within a barrier of glyph and shadow. Her fingers itched to read it again. To find meaning between the names and allegiances. But she already knew what it meant.

Kade had chosen the truth. Chosen *her*. Or maybe just the cause. She didn't know yet.

Aurion continued, voice thoughtful and low. "There will be consequences. For him. For all of us. But perhaps…" he lifted his head to look up at her, pupils slitted and wise, "…it was not in vain."

A long silence stretched between them.

Seraphina swallowed, the emotion rising in her throat. "You saw what it did to him."

"Yes," the dragon said simply. "But he did it, anyway."

Then came the diplomatic visits.

The Lycan Alpha—gruff, stubborn, and politically inconvenient— refused to budge on the role assignments. Delegations had to be paired, no exceptions. And so, to Seraphina's barely restrained fury, she was assigned to accompany Kade for the entire tour.

They didn't speak as they moved through the outer settlements. She kept her answers clipped and neutral, her eyes always straight ahead. If he tried to speak, she deflected with icy politeness. A nod here. A curt reply there. But she could feel his presence beside her—an ache just out of reach, constant as a heartbeat. He looked different up close. Worn. Hollowed out in ways she hadn't noticed from across a war table. There were new shadows under his eyes, and the sharpness of his usual confidence had dulled to something quieter, almost… cautious.

But she refused to fall for it. Refused to trust what might only be regret masked as change.

It was at the children's centre that the crack appeared.

The building was worn but full of life, laughter echoing off stone walls painted in bright murals. Lycans, humans, and fae young played together in the courtyard—some chasing each other with wooden swords, others weaving spells in the air that shimmered with harmless sparks. A boy, no older than seven, sat on a step near the entrance, trying to fix a broken shoelace with grubby, scraped hands and a crooked little smile that didn't quite reach his eyes.

Seraphina noticed the child, but it was Kade who stopped.

Without a word, he crouched beside the boy, his long frame folding down with ease. His hands—so often used to wield power, to destroy—moved gently, threading the lace with slow, patient precision. He tied it neatly, double-knotted. Then, with a small flick of his wrist, he conjured a swirl of shadow.

The shadows shimmered into shape—soft, glowing butterflies with wings like starlight. They fluttered up, delicate and playful, dancing around the boy's head. The child let out a soundless gasp of delight, then giggled as one landed on his nose and vanished in a puff of silver mist.

Seraphina stood frozen a few steps behind.

She didn't expect it to hit her. The warmth curling into her chest. The sudden ache in her throat. Seeing him like that—not as the war-weary soldier or the bearer of painful secrets, but as something gentler. Something... *good*. It didn't fit into the story she'd been telling herself to keep him at a distance.

Something cracked in her.

She softened. Just for a moment.

He looked up at her.

His expression wasn't guarded. It wasn't smug or pleading. It was open. Quiet. Hopeful in that reckless, stupid way he always had when it came to her.

It was the way he used to look at her before everything burned.

Seraphina's breath caught, Then she turned away.

The warmth hardened in her chest, congealing into something heavier. She stared ahead, jaw tight, every step afterwards purposeful, controlled, cold.

Because one act of kindness didn't undo betrayal. One illusion didn't rewrite the truth.

She didn't see the way Kade's shoulders dropped as he rose to his feet behind her. How he stood for a moment longer, watching the boy run back into the courtyard, the butterflies already fading.

She trained harder than ever.

With Lyra, with Raze, with anyone willing to hit her hard enough to bruise, to burn, to make her forget. Sweat soaked through her leathers daily, her muscles ached in familiar, punishing rhythms, and yet she always asked for more. More rounds. More pressure. More pain. The sting of blades, the crackle of fire spells, the gruelling repetition of parries and counters—it was easier than silence. Easier than thought.

She didn't speak of him. Didn't even glance in his direction when he entered a training ground or stood among the onlookers during a spar. Her walls rose like steel around her, reinforced by every glance she didn't return, every word she refused to offer. Kade might as well have been invisible. But his presence pressed at the edges of her, heavy and insistent like a storm on the horizon.

He never tried to interrupt.

But he was always there.

Then came the party—an opulent, glittering affair thrown in honour of the gathered delegates. The hall was all silver candlelight and soft music, filled with the swirl of silks and shadows, perfumed bodies whispering alliances behind fans and half-empty goblets. Deals were made in glances. Wars were tempered with smiles.

Seraphina stood in the centre of it all, an unintentional beacon.

Her gown shimmered like moonlight poured over shadow, tailored to her strength and grace. Braids threaded with starlight wove through her hair, delicate yet dangerous, much like her. She was every inch the warrior and the weapon, poised and unreadable, her mask flawless.

She didn't seek him out.

But she felt him.

Across the ballroom, Kade leaned against a marble pillar, a drink forgotten in his hand. He wore black trimmed in muted gold, the colours catching faintly beneath the candles, his long silver hair half-tied in the style of the Unseelie court. He hadn't shaved. The dark stubble on his jaw was the only thing out of place, as if he hadn't quite managed to become the version of himself everyone expected to see tonight.

He never approached her.

But his eyes never left.

Not when Vaelrik dragged him into a half-hearted conversation with foreign envoys. Not when the music swelled and couples spilled onto the floor in graceful, spinning waves. Kade remained still, silent, watching her like she was both the beginning and the end of everything he'd ever fought for. Like if he blinked, she'd vanish.

Seraphina pretended not to see.

But her pulse stuttered when she caught his gaze across the crowd, and the wine in her glass suddenly tasted like regret.

And still—she didn't move. Didn't allow herself to feel. Not here. Not now.

Kai's absence had grown longer, more frequent. He was constantly out with his squad—missions that pulled him farther from her side than she liked to admit. Without him, the silence in her quarters was unbearable at first. She didn't fuelled how much he'd held her together until he wasn't there to anchor her.

But she adapted.

She turned to Aurion, resuming her magical training with a focus sharper than ever before. They practised under the stars, in hidden glades and on cliff edges, the air thick with power and memory. She relearned spells she'd once abandoned, her hands no longer shaking when she cast. Her control returned slowly, but with precision, her magic no longer wild with grief, but honed by purpose.

Aurion had noticed the change.

"You're stronger now," he said one evening, watching the earth tremble beneath her feet after a particularly brutal summoning. "And not just with your magic."

Seraphina didn't reply. But she knew what he meant.

Her thoughts were clearer now. Her resolve colder. Where heartbreak once lived like an open wound, there was now only a deep scar—still tender, but no longer bleeding.

Vaelrik, strangely enough, had taken to Kade's side.

It wasn't immediate—nothing ever was with the ever-suspicious dragon shifter—but over time, Seraphina began to notice them together more often. They sparred at dawn, blades clashing in sync like they'd done it for years. They leaned over war tables with their heads bent close, murmuring strategies in low, clipped tones. They argued, of course—loudly, heatedly— but always circled back to some unspoken middle ground.

It was unnerving.

Vaelrik, who had once called Kade a "glorified shadow puppet with too much hair," now stood beside him like they shared something only men forged in betrayal and war could understand. The man Seraphina used to consider the most arrogant pain in her ass—sharp-tongued, impatient, and allergic to teamwork—now seemed... almost fond of the brooding former prince.

When she finally confronted him in passing, catching him after a session as he towelled sweat from his brow, she raised an eyebrow. "You've gone soft," she said flatly.

Vaelrik snorted, slinging the towel over his shoulder. "He's not entirely insufferable."

Seraphina blinked. "That's high praise coming from you."

"Don't get used to it," he grumbled, already turning away. "I still think he broods too much."

She watched him go, unsettled.

Whatever tentative camaraderie had formed between Kade and Vaelrik, it tugged something deep in her chest—something uncomfortable and unresolved. Kade wasn't winning allies. He was... becoming one of them. And that truth complicated everything.

Their world still teetered on the edge of ruin.

The Veilborn moved through the shadows like smoke with teeth, growing bolder with each passing week. Whispers of betrayal clung to every corridor, infecting even the closest of circles. Trust was currency, and they were all running short.

Yet somehow, in the middle of that chaos, the fire between her and Kade had shifted.

It no longer burned hot and uncontrollable, threatening to consume her from the inside out. It didn't make her want to scream or run or fight anymore.

It simmered.

Low. Quiet. Enduring.

Like embers buried beneath ash—still dangerous, still alive, but no longer choking her in smoke.

She didn't know what to do with it. Not yet. That feeling—complicated and jagged—lived somewhere between anger and forgiveness. A place where understanding had taken root, watered by shared grief and the slow erosion of hate.

And there was sorrow, too. Heavy and ancient.

They could have been more. Or maybe they still could be. She didn't know.

But for the first time in what felt like an eternity, the thought of facing him didn't send her spiralling.

She could meet his gaze without flinching. Could listen to his voice without tasting blood and betrayal. Could even admit—quietly, only to herself—that she missed the way things had been. Before.

Chapter 51

The last few months had been nothing but a blur of blood, sweat, and silence. Training sessions that left her breathless. Strategy meetings that spiralled into arguments. And dead ends—always more dead ends. Every supposed lead, every whispered promise of progress turned into a wall, or worse—a door that opened to something monstrous. She threw herself into the grind with unrelenting force, as if sheer determination could break curses and solve prophecies. Morning to night, her world narrowed to the sharp edge of a blade and the hum of power under her skin. It was easier this way—easier to run herself into the ground than sit still with thoughts that gnawed like wolves at her resolve.

She and Vaelrik had formed a solid friendship somewhere in the chaos. Strange, considering he once called her "unhinged by a hero complex" when she had rejected him yet again. But now, he offered sparring critiques, sarcastic encouragement, and just enough honesty to keep her grounded. They'd never be gentle with each other, but there was respect there—something earned, not given. And platonic, to the bone. He didn't poke at her scars. Didn't flinch when her temper frayed. He just showed up.

Which was more than she could say for Kai.

He was still with her—always—but his presence inside her mind had begun to wear on her. His voice filtered through at odd times, echoing her thoughts or interrupting them entirely. A snarky quip. A worried question. A silence that felt too loud. They constantly test the limits of their bond, pushing to see how far apart they can be; their furthest distance is around 20 miles, but such separation severely strains their magic. Sometimes at his most annoying moments Seraphina questions the choice Aurion made in creating the bond, but deep down she wouldn't change it.

Kade hadn't spoken a word to her in weeks. And she hadn't reached out either. Whatever truce they had carved had settled into an uneasy quiet. Not quite peace. Not quite the pain. Just… space.

Oddly, Vaelrik and Kade had grown close in her absence. Closer than she'd expected. They trained together, plotted together, exchanged looks that said more than words ever could. And that unsettled her most of all—because if Vaelrik trusted him, maybe she'd misjudged something. Or maybe she hadn't. Maybe it only made everything worse.

The prophecy still loomed—an impossible riddle, wrapped in shadow and loss. It offered no answers, only more questions. Each step forward crumbled beneath them, every lead on Jessamine dissolving into ash and monsters. Twisted things. Creatures that looked like nightmares clawed free of the Veil.

And Seraphina was tired. Tired of chasing ghosts. Tired of pretending she could fix something when she didn't even know what was broken inside herself.

But none of that mattered tonight.

Not while she was with Lyra.

Tall, stubborn Lyra—her red hair braided tight down one side, fierce eyes that saw too much, and a mouth sharper than any sword. She was fire and grit wrapped in a warrior's skin, and somehow, against all odds, she'd become Sera's anchor.

They had trained together for months—bruised, bloodied, and breathless. Pushed each other past breaking and laughed about it after. Lyra didn't tread lightly. She didn't treat Sera like she was fragile or chosen or cursed. With Lyra, she was just a girl with a sword and a temper. Another fighter in the ring. And gods, it was freeing.

Lyra was the only one who didn't ask about Kade. Didn't stare at her like she might shatter under the weight of prophecy. With her, Seraphina felt... human.

Which is why they'd ignored the curfew, the Alpha's new restrictions, and snuck out into the wild night.

The lake was too perfect to resist.

The summer air clung to their skin, warm and heavy, laced with the scent of pine and distant smoke. The water wrapped around them like silk, cool and rippling with every breath. They were stripped to their underclothes, bare to the stars, moving through the shallows like shadows in motion. They danced between strikes, fists and kicks, echoing through the water. Seraphina twisted away from a blow, only to grunt as Lyra landed a kick to her thigh that sent her stumbling. She lunged, catching Lyra off guard, and they crashed into the lake with a roar of laughter.

When they came back up to the surface, they were soaked and wrecked— bruises blooming like ink across their skin, blood mixing with water in faint ribbons.

"Gods," Lyra wheezed, wiping at the split in her lip. "We look like we got dragged through a battlefield."

Sera rolled her shoulder with a wince. "You might've broken my arm."

"You bit me," Lyra accused, grinning.

Sera smirked. "Then I probably deserved it."

They floated for a while, letting the night settle around them. The lake shimmered under the moonlight, silver light catching in every ripple. It was quiet. Peaceful.

Until Lyra broke the silence.

"You should let your hair down."

Sera blinked, glancing over. "What?"

"Your hair. It's always braided. Let it down."

She hesitated, but her fingers found the plait and slowly tugged it free. Wet strands spilled over her shoulders, floating in the water like black silk.

It felt strange. Exposed.

Lyra whistled low. "Fuck, I love your hair. It's so pretty."

The compliment hit harder than it should have.

Because he had said that too.

Kade. On a night not unlike this one. And just like that, his voice curled through her mind—soft and reverent, like a wound that never truly healed. Her breath caught.

Lyra, ever perceptive, caught the shift in her expression and, mercifully, steered the moment away.

"Remember when we caught Kai and Raze training?" she grinned. "They were going at it—swords clashing, shirts off, totally serious—"

Sera groaned, covering her face. "You mean when we were spying on them like creeps?"

Lyra cackled. "We were admiring their *technique*, thank you very much."

Sera raised an eyebrow. "You were staring at Raze's abs the entire time."

Lyra held up a finger. "I am only so strong."

Sera laughed. "At least I wasn't drooling over Vaelrik and Kade."

"Oh, you *definitely* were," Lyra shot back.

Sera opened her mouth to argue —

BOOM.

A body hit the water like a falling star, waves crashing over their heads. Sera surfaced with a sputter, eyes wide just in time to see Kai emerge from the depths, hair slicked back, grinning like the menace he was.

"I was *not* missing girl time!" he declared, triumphantly.

Lyra groaned. "You *actual* menace."

Kai only laughed, shaking water like a wet dog, before launching another wave toward them. Sera dove under, resurfacing behind him to splash him square in the face. Lyra joined the assault, and soon they were in a full-blown splash war—shrill laughter ringing across the lake, all bruises and joy and something like freedom.

Eventually, they collapsed in the shallows, breathless, shoulders shaking with laughter.

Kai, still grinning, wiped the water from his face. "By the way, saw Kade brooding in the forest on the way here."

The moment froze. The laughter faded. And two pairs of eyes turned to Sera.

She groaned, dropping her head back. "I guess I have to deal with that."

Kai and Lyra exchanged looks.

"Yeah," Lyra said, dragging the word out. "Probably."

Before Sera could reply, a soft, familiar voice curled into her mind. *He's watching.*

She turned her head, scanning the darkened shore—and there he was. Standing at the edge of the tree line, half-hidden in shadow, silver eyes locked on her.

Her breath caught. It had been months.

And yet, when their eyes met, it felt like no time had passed at all. Sera's heart stuttered as she met Kade's gaze across the lake.

Even from this distance, the silver glow of his eyes was unmistakable, burning like smouldering embers in the dark. He stood at the tree line, a statue of shadows and tension, his tall frame half-shielded by the night. He wasn't moving—just watching. The weight of it was heavy.

She swallowed hard. It had been months since they'd spoken alone, since she'd had to stand in his presence without the buffer of some kind. Months since she'd let herself feel anything other than the gnawing ache of exhaustion and failure.

Kade was still Kade. Still too sharp. Still too unreadable. Still him. Unspeakably beautiful.

Lyra sighed dramatically beside her. "Gods, that brooding is exquisite."

Kai snorted. "You think he stands in front of a mirror practising that look?"

"Oh, absolutely," Lyra agreed. "That's not natural. That's calculated."

Sera rolled her eyes, forcing her body to relax despite the wildfire creeping through her veins. She wouldn't give them the satisfaction of a reaction.

"Alright, idiots," she said, shoving herself up from the shallows, water trailing down her body in silver rivulets. "Enough gawking."

Kai grinned, slouching back in the water. "Are you going to go talk to him or just stand here pretending you don't see him?"

Sera scowled. "I hate you."

Kai beamed. "You love me."

Lyra cackled, splashing her. "Go deal with your problems, Nyx."

Sera groaned, shoving her dark hair out of her face before wading toward the shore. The lake water was cool against her heated skin, but the moment she stepped onto land, a different kind of chill swept over her—one that had nothing to do with the temperature.

Kade hadn't moved. He stood where he had before, arms crossed, posture rigid. His long silver hair was loose tonight, shifting slightly in the warm summer breeze. Moonlight kissed the angular planes of his face, highlighting the sharp cut of his jaw, the high sweep of his cheekbones.

For a moment, neither of them spoke. The sounds of Lyra and Kai laughing behind her felt distant, like another world entirely. Here, in the quiet hush of the trees, it was just them.

Sera lifted a brow. "Are you just going to stand there like a creep?"

Kade exhaled, shaking his head. "You're out past curfew."

"So are you."

A muscle in his jaw ticked. "You shouldn't be sneaking out. It's dangerous."

She scoffed. "You shouldn't be brooding in the woods, but here we are."

His lips pressed into a thin line. "Sera—"

"Save it," she cut in, crossing her arms. "I don't need a lecture from you, Kade."

He didn't reply immediately, just let his gaze drift over her—her damp clothes clinging to her frame, the half-dried blood still smeared on her skin from training, the way her hair hung in long, dripping waves.

She hated that his eyes lingered. Hated that even now, after months of distance, she could feel the weight of his stare like a tangible thing, stirring something deep in her chest that she'd spent weeks trying to bury.

"I thought you were supposed to be taking this seriously." The words were quiet, edged in something frustratingly unreadable.

Sera bristled. "Excuse me?"

Kade's gaze flicked back to hers. "The prophecy. The training. Jessamine." His voice was even, measured. "If you're out here playing in the water, I assume you've made progress?"

Something inside her snapped. Because fuck him.

She had been trying. She had been failing. And every day that passed without unlocking the power inside her was another weight pressing down on her chest, another failure stacked on top of the ones before it. She stepped closer, looking up at him with fire in her eyes.

"I have been taking this seriously," she said, voice low and cold. "I have been training, and studying, and chasing ghosts that lead to nothing but monsters."

Kade didn't flinch, but something in his expression shifted.

Sera kept going. "So forgive me," she bit out, "If I took one gods damned night off and spent it with my friends."

Silence stretched between them, thick and suffocating.

Kade's gaze searched hers, and for a brief second—just a second—she saw something flicker behind those silvery eyes. Something that almost looked like regret.

Then—

"I just—" He hesitated. Exhaled slowly. "You're getting reckless."

Sera let out a sharp, humourless laugh. "That's rich coming from you."

Kade huffed, running a hand through his silky hair, it did sinful things to Sera, made her even angrier at the audacity to be this handsome. "Sera —"

Sera barely had time to breathe before Kade stepped closer, heat rolling off him in waves. She wasn't sure if she wanted to slap him or kiss him. That thought alone troubled her.

"You're getting reckless," he repeated, this time sharper, like he thought if he said it enough, it would sink in.

Nope she definitely wanted to slap him.

Sera snapped. "Reckless?" She laughed, but there was no humour in it. Just something jagged, something dark, something that had been building inside her for months. "I have given everything, Kade. Every last shred of myself. Every drop of my gods damn blood. And what do I have to show for it? You standing here acting like I'm some foolish little girl?"

He exhaled through his nose, sharp, frustrated. "That's not what I—"

"Oh, don't pretend," she cut in, stepping closer until they were nearly chest to chest, her anger igniting like wildfire. "You don't trust me. You never have. Not really."

His jaw ticked. "That's not true."

"Isn't it?" She scoffed. "You stand there looking at me like I'm lacking, like I'll never be enough—"

His hand shot out before she could finish. Not touching her. But close.

As if stopping himself. As if afraid of what he might do if he reached for her.

His voice was lower when he spoke. Rougher. "I do not think you're lacking."

The words struck something in her chest. But Sera refused to let them sink in. Refused to let them matter. Because if she let them matter—if she let him matter—she wouldn't survive this.

So she pressed. "If you don't think I'm lacking, then what is it?" she demanded. "Why do you watch me like that? Why do you act like I'm both too much and never enough?"

Kade's expression hardened. "Every time I look at you, I see a force that should never be caged," he murmured, his voice rough with something unspoken. "A storm meant to shake the heavens, a fire meant to burn without fear."

Sera's breath caught.

Kade leaned in just slightly, his voice barely above a whisper. "And yet, I see the doubt that coils around you like chains, the way it tries to steal the fire from your soul." His gaze flicked over her, lingering on the bruises, the battle-worn skin, the exhaustion etched into her bones. "You think I don't trust you?" He shook his head, silver eyes dark with something raw. "I don't trust this world to be worthy of you."

The confession shattered something inside her. Because fuck him. Fuck him for saying that like it was supposed to fix anything. Like it made everything better.

Seraphina let out a sharp breath, hands curling into fists at her sides. She hated that her body reacted to him, that her skin burned under his gaze. Hated that he was beautiful even now, all sharp lines and wild silver hair, his silver grey eyes like liquid silver in the moonlight.

She hated that he could still affect her. So she did the only thing she could do. She turned and walked away. Not back to the stronghold. Not back to him.

Chapter 52

She stormed into the woods, ignoring the bite of cold air against her damp skin. She wasn't going back. Not yet. Not after that. It wasn't until she was deep into the trees that she realised—

She had forgotten her clothes. Sera froze.

Oh. Fuck. She was still in her drenched under things, still barefoot, still half-naked in the gods damn woods.

Her pride screamed at her not to turn back. No. Absolutely not. She would die before she returned with her tail between her legs. Muttering to herself, she pressed on, arms crossed over her chest as the night air curled around her.

"Damn arrogant, pretty-faced, brooding—"

Aurion's voice slithered into her mind. *Your pride will be the death of you.*

Sera scowled. *Oh, shut up.*

If you don't freeze to death first.

She huffed, rolling her eyes. *I don't need a lecture from you too.*

But her steps slowed as she reached a clearing.

It was quiet here, the air thick with the scent of damp earth and pine. The moon hung heavy above the trees, casting silver light over the landscape.

She let out a breath. She didn't want to go back. Didn't want to face Kade. Didn't want to deal with the mess of whatever was between them.

So, instead, she climbed.

The branches bent under her weight, but they held, lifting her higher and higher until she found a sturdy perch overlooking the valley below. She breathed.

Finally.

Far below, movement caught her eye. Kai and Lyra. They strolled back toward the stronghold, their voices drifting up through the trees.

"She'll forgive him," Kai was saying.

Lyra snorted. "Not tonight she won't."

"Think he'll go after her?"

Oh, he's probably already tracking her. You know how he is."

Sera scowled.

Kai hummed. "He looked wrecked, though."

"He should," Lyra muttered. "She's not a damn child. He knows better."

Their voices faded as they disappeared down the path. Sera leaned her head against the trunk, exhaling slowly—

Something warm draped over her shoulders. She froze. Soft fabric, still carrying the lingering heat of someone else's body, slipped over her skin, wrapping her in warmth and a familiar scent.

Frost and smoke and a hint of something darker, something unmistakably Kade. The branch barely moved as he settled beside her. Sera turned her head.

And fuck. He was shirtless. The moonlight cut over his bare skin, illuminating every taut muscle, the planes of his chest, the ridges of his arms. His silver hair was loose, catching the wind. His gaze was dark, unreadable.

They sat in silence for a long moment.

Finally, she exhaled. "...Thanks for the shirt."

Kade's lips quirked. "You forgot your clothes."

She scowled. "I noticed."

He huffed a quiet laugh, but there was something softer in his eyes now.

"How did you find me?" she asked, voice quieter now.

He gazed at her, eyes unreadable but turned back to look over the landscape. The silence settling over them.

The night wrapped around them like a velvet shroud, the wind threading through the treetops with soft whispers. From up here, perched on the thick branch of an ancient oak, the world looked endless. The stronghold flickered in the distance, the torches along its walls mere embers in the dark.

Seraphina exhaled slowly, adjusting Kade's shirt around her shoulders.

"You didn't answer me," she murmured, not looking at him. "How did you find me?"

Kade shifted slightly beside her, one knee bent against the branch, forearms resting on it like he belonged to the night itself. Moonlight kissed his skin, highlighting every carved line of muscle, the shadows dancing in the hollows of his collarbones. His silver-grey eyes flicked toward her, unreadable.

"Because I'll always find you, Sera." His voice was quiet, almost reverent. "Even when you don't want to be found."

Her throat tightened.

Romantic nonsense, Aurion snorted in her mind. *If I had a coin for every time a man spouted useless words in your presence my horde would be huge by now.*

Sera ignored him, shifting her gaze back to the horizon. "You didn't answer me," she said again.

Kade sighed, leaning his head back against the trunk. "I know you, Sera. You like to be above things. To look at the world like you're trying to make sense of it. And I—" He paused, his voice softening. "I can always find your scent."

That caught her attention. Her brows knit together as she turned to him. "My scent?"

Kade smirked, slow and devastating. "Like summer storms and embers. Wild, with a hint of vanilla." His voice dipped lower. "Like something meant to be chased."

A flush crawled up her throat before she could stop it.

Oh, he's good, Aurion drawled. *If I had hands, I'd applaud the bastard.*

470

Sera glared at the little dragon. Mentally, of course.

She cleared her throat, crossing her arms over her chest. "Flattery won't fix this, Kade."

"I know," he admitted. "But I also know I won't get another chance to say everything I should have said months ago. So I'm going to say it all, and you can decide if you want to listen."

She stared at him, heartbeat steady but too loud in her own ears. "Go on, then."

Kade ran a hand through his silver hair, exhaling sharply. "I stayed away because I was afraid. Not of you. Never of you. But of what you mean to me." His voice was raw, scraping against the night like a confession. "I knew the moment I let myself have you, the moment I let you in, I would never be able to let you go." He turned his head toward her, searching her eyes. "I wasn't strong enough to lose you, Sera. And I thought —" He swallowed, voice thick. "I thought pushing you away would keep you safe. Keep you free."

Seraphina felt something inside her crack.

He let out a hollow laugh, shaking his head. "But I was a fool. You were never mine to let go."

Her chest ached.

Damn it, Aurion muttered. *Even I felt that one.*

Sera clenched her jaw, holding his gaze. "You still took my choices from me, Kade."

His expression twisted, his body shifting closer as if he was barely restraining himself. "I know." He raked a hand through his hair again, a habit she knew meant he was losing it. "And I will never forgive myself for that. But gods, Sera, if I had the chance to do it all over, I'd fall for you every time. Even knowing the pain, the sacrifice."

She hated how much she wanted to reach for him. Hated how much those words buried themselves deep in her ribs, making a home in places she thought she had locked away.

She exhaled sharply, turning her gaze back to the landscape. "You don't get to just say pretty words and expect me to fall at your feet."

Kade chuckled, but there was no humour in it. "Believe me, if words alone could have fixed this, I would have written you a thousand letters. And if you demanded the world at your feet, I would have burned everything down just to give it to you."

Her fingers tightened in the fabric of his shirt draped over her.

He shifted even closer, his presence wrapping around her like warmth in the cold. "Tell me what to do, Sera." His voice was barely a whisper. "Tell me how to earn your trust again."

She squeezed her eyes shut, pressing a hand to her chest. "I don't know," she admitted, voice breaking. "I don't know if I can trust you again, Kade. And that physically hurts me."

The silence between them was thick. Heavy.

Kade didn't speak for a long moment. Then, quietly, "Then I'll wait."

She turned to him, startled.

His silver eyes softened, and for the first time in months, she saw him— the man who had been her constant, her rival, her friend. The man who had loved her enough to break them both.

"I will wait until you do," he murmured, "Even if it takes a lifetime."

Her heart twisted violently.

Well, fuck, Aurion muttered. *He really is an idiot.*

Seraphina let out a broken laugh, tilting her head back to stare at the stars. She didn't know what to do with this. With him.

But maybe—for tonight—she didn't have to decide.

For tonight, she could just be.

And Kade, for all his stubbornness, would be waiting.

The wind carried the scent of pine and storm-wet earth, tangling through the trees in restless currents. The stars stretched endless above them, their cold shimmer barely touching the fire simmering between the two figures perched on the thick branch.

Seraphina sat with one knee bent, Kade's shirt wrapped around her shoulders, and Kade... Kade sat beside her, his body all lean muscle and war-forged tension, the moonlight carving over his bare skin like the gods themselves had sculpted him from shadow and silver.

And she was looking. Oh, she was looking.

Kade shifted slightly beside her, one knee bent against the branch, forearms resting on it like he belonged to the night itself. His chest, all smooth, pale skin over sculpted strength, the dark lines of old scars twisting in ways that only made her stare harder. The defined cut of his abdomen, the ridges dipping beneath the loose edge of his pants.

She dragged her gaze back up to his throat, to the sharp line of his jaw, to the silver in his hair that caught the light—like molten moonlight threaded through strands of night.

Sweet merciful dragons, Sera, Aurion whispered in her mind. *You're undressing him with your eyes.*

She ignored him, swallowing hard. She remembered what it felt like to run her hands over those muscles, the memory doing things to her body she wished it wouldn't.

Because Kade was looking right back. And his gaze was dark.

Gods, the way he watched her. It was careful—too careful. Like a man trying not to touch fire even as the heat licked at his fingers. But beneath that restraint was something else, something raw and aching, and something he had not allowed himself to say for months.

And she could feel it now. Every unspoken word. Every held-back confession.

She turned her face away, shifting against the bark, making the fabric of his shirt slip slightly—

Kade moved. Fast. Fluid. Before she could react, he snatched the shirt, gripping it at the collar and yanking it over her head.

Sera gasped, arms tangling in the sleeves as he pulled it down over her frame. Not roughly—no, Kade never handled her roughly. But his fingers brushed her skin as he worked, knuckles grazing her shoulder, fingertips skimming the line of her ribs, heat trailing in his wake. By the time he was done, his hands had settled at her waist, thumbs barely touching the fabric, his breath heavy, uneven.

She was drowning in his scent now—oddly it smelt like home to her.

Then his fingers moved again. Soft. Slow. He lifted her tangled hair,

473

pulling it free from the collar with aching care, letting it spill down her back in a cascade of silk.

Voice hushed like a reverent prayer— "Gods, Seraphina."

Her stomach dropped. "Your hair—" Kade exhaled sharply, fingers slipping through the strands like they were spun from the night itself. "It's like the stars forgot to rise, so the sky itself fell in their place."

Her throat closed.

Oh. Oh, he's good, Aurion admitted. *You might actually be in trouble.*

Kade's fingers traced through the strands again, and his voice lowered, just enough to make her feel it. "Like a moonless night," he murmured, "flowing in silk between my fingers."

Sera had forgotten how to breathe.

Kade suddenly shook his head, as if physically forcing himself back under control. "This—" His hands tore away from her. "This isn't— I didn't come here to—"

"Flirt?" she offered. Her own voice sounded raw, uneven.

Kade let out a strangled sound that might have been a laugh, if laughter could sound like it hurt.

"Oh, make no mistake, Sera." His silver eyes burned. "If this is the last time I get to sit this close to you, I will flirt until the gods drag me to my grave."

Her breath hitched.

He's losing it. Aurion was delighted. *I take back every insult. This is fantastic.*

Seraphina clenched her jaw. "Then leave if you've said all you had to say, Kade."

His humour vanished. The restraint settled back into his body, his hands curling against his knees. He exhaled, long and slow, like a man standing on the edge of a storm.

"For months," he said, voice hushed, "I have been trying to find the right words. I have spent sleepless nights pacing, thinking of how to fix what I ruined." He lifted his gaze, burning through her. "And nothing—nothing— has ever been enough."

She felt those words, sinking deep into the marrow of her bones.

"You don't owe me anything," she said.

He let out a bitter chuckle. "Yet, I owe you everything."

Silence. Thick, charged, breaking at the seams.

Kade inhaled sharply, his gaze flickering over her—her battle-worn skin, the bruises littering her arms, the exhaustion she tried so hard to hide. He exhaled like it hurt him to look at her. "I was afraid," he admitted, voice barely above a whisper. "Because I love you."

Sera's fingers tightened in the fabric of his shirt, her lungs squeezing painfully. She squeezed her eyes shut. "Damn you." tilting her head towards the sky, her feelings mixed.

"Damn me," he agreed, voice rough. As he stared at her in the light of the moon. "Damn me, because I would tear this world apart for you, and it still wouldn't be enough."

"And I will spend every day of my life trying to make it right. But I won't ask for your forgiveness, Sera." His throat bobbed as he swallowed. "I will earn it. If you let me."

Seraphina clenched her hands, pressing them against her thighs. She didn't know what to do with him. With this.

End him, Aurion supplied unhelpfully. *Or kiss him. I can't decide.*

Sera shot him a mental glare.

He exhaled sharply, dragging a hand down his face. "I am out of plans, Seraphina. Out of words." His silver eyes locked onto hers, and it was there—that desperation, raw and open. "If you tell me to leave, I will walk away. If you tell me to stay, I will kneel at your feet for the rest of my damn life. Either way I shall wait to earn your trust. I just need to know whether I can be near you while I wait"

Her stomach twisted.

"I can't undo the past," Kade murmured, his voice like dusk rolling over a battlefield. "But tell me what I can do now—tell me how to fight for you, and I will do it." he finally gave in to wanting to touch her, his hand came up to cup her check. Thumb sliding over it, stroking her face softly. So much promise in his eyes as he gazed at her with bated breath.

The wind whispered through the trees, carrying the echoes of his words between them.

She wanted to throw something at him. She wanted to pull him closer. She wanted—she wanted.

Kade, for all his strength, for all his war-forged arrogance, sat before her vulnerable—waiting for her to decide. She knew in her heart that he had never been this vulnerable with anyone.

Seraphina clenched her hands, digging her nails into her palms.

Well, well, Aurion mused. *Would you look at that? The bastard is actually telling the truth.*

Her throat burned.

She took a breath, then another.

Then—slowly, carefully—she reached forward, pressing her palm against his bare chest, right over the steady, aching pulse beneath his ribs.

Kade went still. Not breathing. Not moving. Just waiting.

Sera swallowed hard. "Stay," she murmured.

Kade inhaled sharply. His heart pounded beneath her touch.

She met his gaze, eyes unwavering. "But you earn your place."

His lips parted—his whole body exhaled, and something deep inside his silver eyes changed.

Then, voice raw and low— "Gladly."

Kade's *gladly* still lingered in the air, like the last breath before a storm.

Seraphina should have felt victorious. She had made him work for it, and gods, watching him struggle, watching the way he struggled—like a man standing in front of an open flame and knowing damn well he would burn—was deeply, deeply satisfying.

But the problem with fire?

It spreads. And now she was burning too.

Because Kade hadn't moved. Hadn't pulled away from her hand pressed over his heart. If anything, he leaned into it, his skin warm beneath her fingertips, each inhale pressing more of him against her palm. And that gaze—the silver-dark depths of it—was devouring her. Not just in hunger, no—worse.

In reverence. Like he was memorising the weight of her touch, like he would carve this moment into the marrow of his bones.

Against every ounce of logic she possessed, she let her thumb move. Just barely. A slow, absent trace over the ridges of his skin.

Kade's muscles locked. His breath hitched.

Then—gods help her—his hand came up. Slow, deliberate, like he was giving her every chance to stop him. His fingers skimmed over her wrist, barely a touch—so faint she almost wasn't sure it had happened at all. But the moment his skin met hers, every nerve in her body ignited. Lower—he dragged his fingers down, tracing the length of her forearm, barely-there, just enough to make her shudder, just enough to make her stomach flip.

She inhaled sharply, ripping her hand away from his chest, as if the action would somehow undo the damage.

It did not.

Because Kade… smirked. And it was not his usual arrogant smirk.

No. It was slow, lazy—a man who had just won a battle, a man who had felt her shake beneath his touch and knew exactly what it meant.

The bastard.

She scowled. "Don't look at me like that."

He hummed, tilting his head. "Like what?"

She gestured vaguely. "Like you—like that."

His smirk only deepened. "Like I've been dying to touch you for months, and you finally let me?"

Her stomach dropped.

She clenched her fists, desperate for something—anything—to ground her.

Then Kade, because he was an ass, stretched, rolling his shoulders back, the moonlight carving over every defined line of his torso.

She swallowed hard.

Gods.

He really was—

Sera. Aurion was tired. *Do not—I swear to all that is unholy, do not give him the satisfaction.*

But it was already too late.

Because Kade's smirk shifted, something darker curling at the edges.

"Oh?" His voice was silk-wrapped steel. "So you have been looking."

Damn him.

Damn her.

Damn the entire gods-forsaken world for making Kade so obnoxiously pretty.

She scowled. "You're in my line of sight. It's unavoidable."

He laughed, low and rough, shaking his head. "That," he murmured, "Is the worst excuse I have ever heard."

Her glare sharpened. "What do you want, Kade?"

His humour faded, his expression turning serious in an instant. "I already told you," he said softly. "I want to fight for you."

A lump formed in her throat.

"You think it's that easy?"

Kade exhaled, shaking his head. "No," he admitted. "I don't."

His voice lowered, turning almost pleading. "But tell me how, Sera. Tell me what you need me to do."

She clenched her jaw, looking away. "I don't know."

Silence.

"Then let me figure it out."

She closed her eyes, inhaling deep.

Because it was dangerous.

It was so dangerous.

This was Kade.

Kade, who had betrayed her.

Kade, who had still been the one to hold her when she shattered.

Kade, who was looking at her like she was his entire world, and he had ruined it, and he would spend forever trying to fix it.

She hated him.

She wanted him.

She wanted to hate him.

Her fingers twitched.

His eyes dropped to the movement, barely breathing.

And gods—gods, if he reached for her again, she might actually—

She jerked to her feet. Balancing with practised strength on the branch.

Kade immediately tensed, watching her carefully, as if any sudden movement might spook her. As he slowly stood next to her.

Seraphina tilted her head, watching Kade through half-lidded eyes, the moonlight catching the sharp planes of his face. He was too still, too controlled, and she hated how much that intrigued her. He was dangerous— not just in the way he fought, but in the way he looked at her. Like he saw too much. Like he wanted too much.

She stepped closer, enough to catch the faint scent of steel and fire clinging to him, mingling with something darker, something uniquely him. "You're still here," she murmured, her voice teasing, daring him to react.

Kade's lips curled slightly. "You haven't told me to leave."

Seraphina exhaled sharply, almost a laugh. "That doesn't mean anything."

His eyes dropped to her lips for the briefest moment, a flicker of heat, then—she moved first.

It wasn't a surrender. It was a taste, a warning, a defiance wrapped in a kiss that burned like embers catching flame. Kade was all tension, coiled strength beneath her fingertips, his breath sharp against her lips as if he hadn't expected her to close the distance. But he didn't pull away. No, he matched her fire with his own, hands ghosting over her waist before he let her go, his smirk returning as if to say, *that's all?*

She scoffed, stepping back, her pulse an irritating drumbeat beneath her skin. "That changes nothing," she said, her voice steady despite the war raging in her veins. "You're lucky I'm letting you stay."

His smirk deepened, but there was something sharper behind it now. "Oh, I feel honoured."

Rolling her eyes, Seraphina reached out through the bond, the familiar presence she sought answering almost immediately. *Kai.*

A moment of silence, then a knowing chuckle rippled through her mind. *Ah, so you've forgiven him?*

Not even close.

Another laugh, but this time more wary. *Dare I ask why you need me?*

No questions. Just be in Lycan form and hurry.

Now I'm nervous. He huffed.

She shut the bond before he could pry further, her gaze flicking back to Kade, who was watching her with a mix of interest and something unreadable.

"You're staring, Nyx."

She arched a brow. "Maybe I am. Or maybe I just haven't decided if you're worth my time yet."

Kade's amusement flickered, just a shade of something darker crossing his features. That reaction alone made her grin. She let a pause stretch between them, dragging it out just to watch him tense, before she shrugged, feigning indifference. "Besides, I can always go stare at someone else." The implication that she wouldn't just stare made him tense.

That did it. The smirk vanished. A flicker of something sharp, territorial, flickered in his storm-coloured eyes.

Before he could respond, a massive black-furred form lunged from the darkness. Kai barely slowed as Seraphina leapt off the branch and onto his back, her fingers tangling in his thick fur as he bolted forward. The wind rushed past her ears, carrying Kade's frustrated growl into the night.

She smirked as Kai shot off toward the stronghold. Kade could burn in his own jealousy. Maybe then he'd finally admit just how much she had him trapped.

Kade's growl followed her, dark and low, a sound that scraped over her skin and made her stomach tighten. But it was the way he cursed under his breath, the sheer frustration rolling off him like a storm that sent a satisfied smirk curling at her lips.

You absolute menace! Kai's voice was rough as it flowed through her mind.

Sera threw her head back with a laugh, gripping Kai's thick fur as he leapt over a fallen log. Oh, this was going to be fun.

Kai huffed beneath her. *You're playing with fire, little moon.* His voice floated in her mind.

Sera only grinned. Then let it burn.

By the time they reached the stronghold, Lyra was already waiting for them, arms crossed and an infuriatingly knowing smirk playing at her lips.

"Well, well," she drawled as Kai skidded to a halt. "Look whose back. And looking positively radiant, I might add."

Sera slid off Kai's back, stretching languidly. "What can I say? I had a very entertaining evening."

Kai shifted beside her, his human form appearing in a ripple of magic. "Oh, she definitely did," he agreed, his green eyes flicking toward the trees where Kade would be emerging any second. "And I, for one, can't wait to see how this unfolds."

The stronghold was alive with the quiet murmurs of the night—flickering torches, the rustling wind, and the distant calls of the nocturnal creatures prowling the dense forest beyond its walls. The training grounds were empty, save for three figures lounging on the cool stone steps leading toward the barracks, their laughter cutting through the stillness.

Lyra stretched her arms behind her head, her short red hair damp from her earlier dip in the lake. "So, Sera, you going to stop sneaking off at night or should I start charging you for my suffering?" she mused, shooting a smirk in Sera's direction.

Sera, leaning against Kai's massive form, raised a brow. "Suffering?"

"Oh, you know," Lyra gestured vaguely. "Having to sit around waiting for you while you're off cuddling mysterious men in the dark."

Kai, sprawled out beside them, immediately perked up, a slow, wolfish grin spreading across his face. "Wait, wait, wait—cuddling?" He turned his green eyes to Sera. "You holding out on me? Who's the lucky bastard?"

Sera shot Lyra a look before shoving Kai's shoulder. "I hate you both."

Kai cackled, clearly unfazed. "Don't deflect, sweetheart. Tell me, should I be worried? Because if I wake up one more time to the scent of someone else all over your bed, I will start taking personal offence."

Aurion, ever the instigator, materialised beside them in his silver white form, legs crossed, looking far too entertained. "Oh, she won't tell you, Kai, but I know."

Sera groaned, head falling back against Kai's shoulder. "I really hate you all."

Kai and Lyra exchanged delighted looks, their grins feral.

"Oh-ho!" Lyra leaned forward, eyes alight. "Kai, you thinking what I'm thinking?"

"Depends," Kai mused, rubbing his chin dramatically. "Are you thinking our dear Sera is a total goner?"

"Oh, absolutely."

Vaelrik's deep voice cut through the laughter as he strode toward them, clearly catching the tail end of their conversation. "Goner for who?"

The moment the words left his mouth, a very distinct presence flickered at the edge of Sera's senses—dark, brooding, tense.

Kade.

Sera barely had time to process it before Vaelrik, unaware of the chaos he was about to unleash, smirked and added, "Because if she's finally accepting suitors, I would like to throw my name in."

Lyra gasped, utterly scandalised. "Vaelrik! I knew you had good taste!"

Sera's mouth opened—ready to deny, threaten, something—but then, she felt it.

The night was cool, but the air between them crackled like fire.

Sera leaned against Kai in the flickering torchlight, draped in Kade's shirt, the fabric hanging off her frame, drowning her in his scent.

And he saw it.

All of it.

The way Lyra smirked as she leaned closer. The way Kai tilted his head, eyes glinting with mischief. The way Vaelrik stood, arms crossed, watching Kade like a predator watching his prey.

Kade had heard everything.

And oh, was he furious.

"You still have my shirt." His voice was low, rough—dangerous.

Sera blinked, tilting her head. "Huh. Guess I do."

Without a single shred of hesitation—she stood and grabbed the hem and pulled it over her head.

Right there.

In front of everyone.

The shirt slipped from her fingers, falling to the dirt.

Silence crashed down.

Lyra choked on air. Kai's eyes widened. Aurion sputtered.

Vaelrik, however, moved first.

With a flick of his wrist, his long coat dropped over Sera's shoulders, covering her from sight before the moment could turn into a war crime.

"Can't have you catching a chill," Vaelrik murmured, smirking as he stepped closer, adjusting the fabric around her like a gentleman.

Kade flared.

Not because of the coat—no.

Because Vaelrik's scent was now all over her.

Kade took a step forward. Then another. Sera didn't move, didn't flinch.

And just as he reached for her, just as his fingers brushed the edge of that cursed coat, she lifted her hand —two fingers pressing against his lips.

Kade froze.

Her voice was calm. Dangerous in its softness.

"I let you stay, Kade," she murmured, staring up at him. "I never said you could have me. My body or my heart."

Something in him fractured.

And just like that, she pulled away.

Kai let out a low whistle, clearly enjoying the spectacle of Kade drowning in his own torment.

Lyra nudged Sera's side, grinning. "Well, that was deliciously brutal. I approve."

Vaelrik chuckled. "Can't blame a man for trying." He looked down at Sera, all warmth and charm. "It's getting late. Would you like me to take you to bed?"

Kade bristled.

Kai barked a laugh. "You? Don't be ridiculous, Vaelrik. If anyone's taking her to bed, it's me. She practically lives in my room anyway."

Vaelrik shot him a look. "And that's precisely the problem."

"Oh, like you're any better," Kai sneered. "Let me guess—you'd love to wrap her up in that damn coat of yours and carry her, wouldn't you?"

Vaelrik smirked. "Well, now that you mention it—"

"Alright, both of you," Lyra interrupted, sighing dramatically. "Clearly, it's my turn."

And before either of them could argue, she linked arms with Sera, tugging her away.

"Come on, love," Lyra cooed. "Let's leave these boys to wallow in their suffering."

Sera chuckled, leaning into her friend as they walked off, the weight of Kade's gaze pressing against her back the whole way.

Just as they rounded the corner and the noise of the boys faded, Lyra leaned in closer and whispered, "Also... surprise, bitch. I have cake and presents waiting in your room."

Sera stopped dead in her tracks. "Wait. What?"

Lyra winked. "You really thought I'd forget your birthday? Please. I may be reckless, but I'm not heartless."

Sera squealed—actually squealed—and took off in a run, her exhaustion forgotten, sprinting down the corridor like a child chasing the stars.

Lyra laughed, trailing behind with a fond shake of her head.

Back in the clearing, the boys stood in silence, dumbfounded.

Vaelrik blinked. "Wait. It's her birthday?"

Kade's face fell. "Shit."

Kai raised an eyebrow, arms crossed. "Wow. Really? You two call yourselves friends?"

Vaelrik frowned. "You didn't tell us."

Kai scoffed. "Why would I need to? How could I possibly forget my best friend's birthday?" He paused, then smirked. "Unlike some people."

Vaelrik groaned. "Damn it."

Kai clapped a hand on Kade's shoulder. "You, lover boy, are *so* deep in the hole right now."

Vaelrik winced. "We're never hearing the end of this."

Kade just muttered another curse under his breath, dragging a hand down his face.

"Fucking hell."

Chapter 53

The first light of dawn spilled through the narrow windows of Seraphina's room, golden and soft, casting long, slanted beams across the floor. She was tugging on her boots, still half-lost in sleep and thought, when a knock came at the door—not loud or impatient like Kai's, or laced with a flirtatious rhythm like Vaelrik's. This one was hesitant. Almost shy.

Curious, she rose and opened it.

Kade stood there, slightly damp from what must have been early drills or a long shower. His silver hair clung to his jaw and neck, darkened by the lingering water. A half-buttoned shirt clung to his torso, his breath held tight in his chest as if the morning itself was fragile.

He shifted awkwardly, something small hidden behind his back.

"Morning," he said gruffly, avoiding her gaze.

She arched an eyebrow. "Morning."

Silence lingered before he finally stepped forward and held out the object: a small bundle, wrapped in deep violet silk, bound with a leather cord braided with care.

"I didn't forget," he muttered, as if defending himself from a crime no one had accused him of. "I was going to give it to you last night, but... you ran off before I could."

A smile tugged at her lips, soft and genuine. Her chest warmed as she gently took the bundle. "You remembered."

His eyes flicked up, meeting hers for the briefest moment. Then he looked away, jaw tightening. "Of course I did. How could I not?"

In the back of her mind, Aurion's voice hummed with dry amusement.

"Ah, the brooding warrior bearing softhearted offerings. How quaint."

Kai chimed in smugly.

"Told you he wouldn't let the others outdo him. He's been sulking all night."

Seraphina ignored them both and carefully unwrapped the silk. Nestled inside was a pendant: a shard of obsidian bound in twisted silver, shaped like a fang. Old magic shimmered faintly across its surface in a soft purple glow, alive and ancient, humming beneath her fingertips.

Her breath caught. "This is—"

"It was my mother's," Kade said softly. "She gave it to me when I first picked up a sword. Said it would protect whoever wore it. I want you to have it."

The weight of the pendant in her hands was nothing compared to the weight of the gesture.

"I... don't know what to say."

"You don't have to say anything. Just..." His voice lowered, rough around the edges. "Wear it."

He stepped closer, so close she could feel the warmth of him. Gently, he lifted the chain from her fingers and reached around her neck, fastening the clasp with care. His fingers brushed the back of her neck, lingering a moment longer than necessary.

She looked up.

His storm-grey eyes held hers—open, vulnerable, a storm quieted. His hands slid down to rest lightly on her shoulders, grounding her.

"Happy belated birthday, Seraphina," he said, just above a whisper.

Their faces were inches apart. For one breathless second, she thought he might kiss her. She almost let him.

Instead, she pressed her fingers lightly to the pendant, now resting against her chest, and stepped back with a crooked smile.

She tucked the obsidian fang beneath her shirt, hiding it away like a secret. "Vaelrik dropped off a gift too, last night. Said it was custom-stitched by some ridiculous merchant from the North. There were feathers involved."

Kade stilled.

The softness drained from his face like colour in fading light.

"He *what?*"

She turned away with a wicked grin. "Don't worry. I told him I didn't have space for another egotistical coat."

Aurion laughed in her mind, loud and wolfish.

"I will never tire of watching them fight over you like wounded crows."

Kai added with a mental cackle.

"Best drama I've had in weeks. I should sell tickets."

—

The clearing was silent, save for the steady beat of her breath.

Seraphina stood at its centre. The world narrowed to the rhythm of power thrumming under her skin. Around her, threads of magic shimmered like constellations pulled close, pulsing with every heartbeat.

Aurion circled her slowly, his steps deliberate, testing. The connection between them flared and pulsed—two halves of something greater moving in unison. The magic didn't burn anymore. It didn't lash or scream. It *sang*, wild and loyal, dancing across her limbs like firelight.

It no longer felt foreign.

It felt like *home*.

She wasn't surviving anymore.

She was becoming.

The others watched from the edge of the clearing—Kade, Kai, Vaelrik, Dylan—all silent, each bearing witness to what she had become.

Kade's gaze never left her. Vaelrik, for once, wore no smirk. Kai gave a low whistle, arms crossed. Dylan's expression was unreadable, but heavy with something that felt like pride. Or a warning.

And in that still, golden light, Seraphina dared to believe.

They had a chance.

The months leading to this moment had been carved in exhaustion and fire. War councils with old enemies. Nights of restless sleep in frost-rimed tents and heat-baked ruins. Endless negotiations with wary sovereigns and reluctant allies. She had crossed shattered kingdoms with Dylan, Kade, and Kai by her side—Vaelrik, when it pleased him—and gathered broken pieces of resistance from the edges of a dying world.

She had bartered for blood-oaths sealed in ancient rites. Shared fires with traitors turned into friends. Found comrades in noble daughters turned spies, in disgraced heirs, in seers who dreamed of truths no one wanted to hear.

Whispers had become councils.

Councils had become unity.

And unity... had felt like hope.

That hope shattered the moment the scout arrived.

He burst into the clearing like a blade of winter wind, fibre torn, eyes wild with horror. Blood smeared down his chest in dark ribbons. His breath came in jagged bursts as he collapsed to one knee, barely upright.

The magic between Seraphina and Aurion vanished, snuffed out like a candle.

"They're gone," the scout rasped. "The vampire stronghold... has fallen."

The world tilted.

Kade was the first to move. "What do you mean, *gone?*"

The scout winced, hand clutching a wound at his side. "Overrun. We didn't even see them coming. Shadow magic... it moved through stone, through us."

Dylan's jaw clenched. "Survivors?"

The scout's pause said everything.

"The Veilborn took those who didn't die. Forced into the Veilborn's army."

Kai cursed. Vaelrik's smirk was gone. Only grim resolve remained.

Seraphina felt her hope unravel, one fraying thread at a time.

Aurion's voice was a quiet snarl.

"It begins."

The vampires had been their strongest defence—fierce, impenetrable, carved into the cliffs like gods carved vengeance into stone. And now...

twisted. Turned.

Her thoughts spun. Lucanis. His partner. The vampire princess. A warrior with fire in her veins and a laugh that could split the heavens.

Was she gone? Or worse… corrupted?

Seraphina's stomach turned.

Dylan stepped forward, tone iron-clad. "We move now. Evacuate the elders. Ready the young. If the stronghold's fallen, we're next."

A storm trembled on the horizon.

Hope hadn't died.

But it bled.

And the war was no longer coming.

It had arrived.

Chapter 54

The sky had not yet turned red, but the earth already knew.

It pulsed beneath their feet, humming with an ancient warning. That pulse moved through stone and soil and bone with the same unspoken urgency now felt by every clan, pack, coven, and circle—groups that, for centuries, had remained apart, separated by blood and history. Now, old grudges were nothing more than ash. Survival had demanded more. Boundaries were offered silently to the flames of necessity.

In the days following the scouts' report—Veilborn legions, countless and merciless, tearing through the old vampire stronghold and razing the Lycan citadel to the ground—chaos surged like a rising tide.

The Lycan stronghold, once a fortress of order and disciplined violence, now breathed like a living beast. Its belly swelled with every kind of supernatural being. Makeshift tents spread across the fields like wildflowers blooming before a storm—shelters not of comfort, but of desperation. Warriors, mages, seers, and sentinels had gathered from every fractured edge of the realm. Fey enchantresses painted sigils in the dirt beside blood witches who murmured runes in long-dead languages. Shifters moved in human skin, their animal spirits prowling just beneath— wolf, bear, falcon, feline—uneasy, waiting.

This wasn't unity born from treaties or oaths. It was forged in necessity. In war.

Evacuations began the moment the Veilborn crossed the Black River. The process was brutal. Time blurred into exhaustion. Each dawn brought lists—who had made it out, and who hadn't. Witches from the southern marshes arrived first, guiding their elders draped in moss-coloured cloaks. Fae children clutched woven baskets and trembling hands. Young Lycans strained under heavy carts, some pulling them with bloodied palms and raw determination.

There was no more room for pride. No more time for old rules.

Seraphina moved through it all like the eye of the storm. Quiet. Focused. Every choice she made now echoed with finality. She checked weapons, reinforced barrier lines, and ensured every faction had the crates and supplies they needed. She walked among the young witches to guide the last civilians through the eastern forest path before nightfall. But no matter how much there was to do, her heart kept drawing her back to the people who had become her family.

She found Lyra by the northern slope, crouched beside a group of wolf pups too young to fight. She had tied back her wild hair, and a sword was strapped to her thigh, but her presence remained soft and calming. The way she eased the children's fear—with gentle words and sweets slipped into tiny hands—spoke of a woman who had mastered both ferocity and tenderness.

When she noticed Seraphina, Lyra stood and pressed her forehead to hers, voice low and warm.

"I'm ready," she murmured. "But you don't get to die. You live—so we can finally talk about your disaster of a love life."

Seraphina huffed a breath that might've been a laugh. "Don't you have bigger concerns than who I kiss during an apocalypse?"

Lyra grinned. "Absolutely not."

Before Seraphina could retort a comeback to her friend. Behind her, Raze appeared like dusk on the horizon—silent, cloaked in shadow. The wind tugged at his black cloak as he stepped closer, and something in his presence tugged at the edges of Seraphina's senses. His gaze met hers. Held. Too long.

Not loyalty. Not fear. Not even protectiveness.

Something else. Something unreadable.

His jaw clenched like he was swallowing words.

She wanted to ask, but the moment passed. Lyra took his hand, grounding him, and the tension in his shoulders fell away like smoke.

Still... something was wrong. She could feel it in her bones.

* * *

Later, she found herself in the ruins on the ridge—where old dragon runes still scarred the stone like whispers of the past. The wind sang low through broken arches, carrying the weight of the battles to come. Aurion lay curled in his smaller form atop a shattered slab, their connection now so strong they didn't need the amulet to access each other, his silver wings folded, tail twitching in dreams.

"Lazy," Seraphina teased, stepping lightly across moss-covered rubble. "Is this your idea of preparation?"

Aurion cracked one golden eye open, voice a low rumble. "Even fire needs to rest. But I doubt you came just to admire me."

She smiled faintly, settling beside him. Her fingers brushed the curve of his snout, comfort in the contact. "I saw Lyra. She's holding on—barely. Raze... he's different. Edgy. Like he's waiting for something to break."

Aurion stirred, lifting his head. "War changes people. Sometimes it breaks them. Sometimes it reveals them."

Seraphina looked out over the valley, quiet for a long moment. "I keep wondering what we'll all look like when this ends. If it ends."

She glanced back at him, something stirring inside her.

"I want to practice. Shifting your form."

He tilted his head. "You've done it before."

"In battle. When I'm panicked or desperate. But I want it to be instinct. Something I *own*—not something I scramble for when everything's falling apart."

Aurion stretched his wings and rose, voice soft with approval. "Then let's teach your body to remember what your soul already knows."

They trained until the stars pierced the veil of dusk. Seraphina summoned him into his great form, wings blotting out the dying light—then called him back, again and again. From mighty dragon to small-winged beast, until her muscles burned and her breath trembled. Yet something shifted. The strain faded. Her movements became smoother. Her magic no longer fought—only flowed.

By the final attempt, she didn't even speak. She simply felt the change, and it happened.

Aurion landed on her shoulder in a form barely bigger than a raven. "You're getting bold," he teased. "You'll change me mid-sentence next."

She laughed—truly laughed—for the first time in days.

If he were human... he could do more.

He could walk the camps freely. Speak to the others. Fight. Be seen.

The magic heard her. Answered before she could second guess.

Light burst from her locket, rippling outward in a pulse that caught him mid-flight. She gasped as magic surged through her, gripping him—twisting, transforming. Aurion flared with golden fire—and vanished.

In his place stood a man.

Tall and broad-shouldered, his skin glowed with a sunlit bronze hue, and his eyes—those molten dragon-gold eyes—remained unchanged. His hair, silver white, tumbled to his shoulders, slightly tousled. He wore a tunic of midnight blue and silver thread, ancient in design, regal in its simplicity.

His voice, still deep and resonant, rumbled softly. "Your magic has grown, Seraphina."

She stepped forward, breath caught. "You're... *you.*"

Aurion nodded, eyes studying her like he was seeing her for the first time. "I gave up this form the day I bound myself to your line. The locket was my tether... and my prison. Only one with magic strong enough to remember me—*truly* remember—could summon this."

Seraphina reached out, pressing a hand to his chest. The warmth of him, the weight of what had just happened, overwhelmed her. "I didn't know I was strong enough."

"You weren't," he said with a rare smile. "Until now."

Magic shimmered in the space between them.

Their bond had deepened—untethered from the locket, no longer needing it to connect. He still relied on her to change forms, but now... he belonged to the world again.

To her.

Aurion's gaze softened. "You've done what many couldn't. Even without finishing the prophecy. Even without finding Jessamine to guide you."

Seraphina's eyes lowered. "If we survive this war..."

"When," he said firmly. "*When.* And when it's done, we'll keep searching—for her. For answers. For the rest of what you are."

A lump rose in her throat. "I'm not ready."

"You don't have to be," Aurion said, voice warm and steady. "You're not alone."

She gave him a look of quiet gratitude, but before she could respond, a distant horn echoed across the hills—short, and familiar.

Training call.

Aurion groaned softly and straightened, stretching his limbs with a lazy grace. "Duty calls. Come on, commander."

Seraphina rolled her eyes, but stood. The sun hung low on the horizon, washing the camp in amber light, casting long shadows across the training fields as soldiers regrouped.

As they walked back, Aurion bumped her shoulder lightly. "You're stalling, you know."

She blinked. "What?"

"You've been avoiding *him* since the birthday gift," he said with a sly grin. "And don't lie—I can still feel the fluster in your chest when someone mentions Kade."

"I'm *not* flustered," she muttered, gaze fixed ahead.

Aurion lifted a brow. "You're wearing the necklace *under* the locket, Sera."

Heat flared in her cheeks, and she instinctively touched the chain at her throat, feeling the press of both pendants—the old and the new, tangled together like a secret she hadn't dared to name.

"I just haven't... had time," she said, a little too quickly. "We've been fighting. Training. Planning."

He smirked. "Mm-hm."

She shoved him lightly with her shoulder. "Don't you have somewhere else to be?"

"Right beside my commander," he said with mock solemnity. "At least until she gets brave enough to face the man who made her blush so hard she dropped her sword last week."

"*Aurion!*"

But he was already laughing, striding ahead, and Seraphina had no choice but to follow but—face warm, heart unsteady, and the weight of both necklaces brushing against her collarbone like a whisper she hadn't yet answered.

Then, just before they reached the edge of the training yard, Aurion paused.

He turned, expression a little more serious now, and walked back to her with long, confident strides. "Hey," he said, quieter this time. "Can you change me back?"

She tilted her head. "Now?"

He nodded. "I'm not ready for them to see me like this. Not all of it. Not yet. If Vaelrik gets even a hint of my history, he'll become *insufferable*. And you know he'll dig."

Seraphina gave a soft laugh. "That's fair."

Aurion glanced around to make sure no one was watching too closely. Then his voice dropped lower, more conspiratorial. "Also... you *have* to turn me into the black obsidian one again."

She blinked, amused. "Why?"

"Because I *plan* to wipe that smug grin off Vaelrik's face when we spar," he said with a glint in his eye. "And the obsidian form hits harder than he expects."

Seraphina laughed, unable to help herself. "So you're hiding your trauma and cheating at training. Classy."

"I prefer 'tactically selective and opportunistically brilliant,'" he said, completely deadpan.

She rolled her eyes and reached out, fingertips glowing faintly as she brushed them along his collarbone. The change shimmered over him like ink spreading through water, shadows coiling until the man she knew melted away into sleek, obsidian scales. Powerful. Regal. Unyielding.

No one else knew she could do this—not even Kade.

Not yet.

And Seraphina, for all the chaos swirling around them, secretly liked that. Just this one thing. Just hers and Aurion's.

A bond forged in blood, shadow, and unspoken understanding.

She touched the spot over her locket once more and whispered to herself, "Go easy on him, alright?"

The obsidian dragon huffed a warm breath that ruffled her hair and stalked toward the training yard, pride in every step.

Chapter 55

That night, the camp finally quieted—just enough for Seraphina to slip away. She ducked into one of the larger tents, where warmth flickered low and steady from the fire pit in the centre. The air smelled of smoke, herbs, and something vaguely sweet—like the promise of a meal and the memory of safety.

Dylan was already crouched near the hearth, stirring a pot of thick stew with exaggerated care. Red rims encircled his eyes, and exhaustion etched deep lines into his face, but he wore a crooked smile when he looked up.

"I made the spicy kind," he announced with mock solemnity, lifting a ladle like a knight brandishing a sword. "You know. Before the world ends."

Seraphina chuckled softly. "You're a hero."

Across from him sat Kai—shoulders hunched, gaze distant, jaw tight. His dark curls hung damp from the mist outside, and a faint bruise bloomed along the edge of his collarbone, likely from training. His wolf's side rarely bruised, but when it did, it meant he hadn't shifted to heal. That in itself was telling.

He looked up at her with tired eyes that didn't quite meet hers. Still, he tried a smile, small and fleeting.

They gathered around the fire, bowls in hand, the silence that followed surprisingly gentle. Dylan filled it with casual talk—rumours from the outer sentries, complaints about the rations, a dramatic recounting of nearly falling into a latrine pit—but the warmth in his voice grounded the moment. His presence felt like a memory of peace, a time before blood and flame.

Kai barely touched his stew.

One of the messengers summoned Dylan away—a soft whistle outside the tent and a brief murmur about strategy updates at the war tent. He kissed Seraphina's head, clapped Kai's shoulder, and vanished into the cold night.

The quiet that followed was heavier.

Kai stared into the fire, fingers absently curling around the edge of his bowl. Then he exhaled through his nose and set it aside with a soft clink.

"Sera," he said lowly, voice rough, like gravel underfoot, "I can't... settle."

She turned to him, brows furrowing. "What do you mean?"

He rubbed the back of his neck, the muscles in his arm taut. "My Lycan side—it's... off. It's like I'm on the verge of shifting, but not. Like I'm waiting for something to hunt me, or... call me. I thought it was just the tension. War. But it's not that."

He paused, looking away from her as though the words cost him.

"It started when Aurion and you showed up earlier today at the training yards after where ever you two had been all day."

Seraphina's breath hitched, though she masked it well. She didn't interrupt.

Kai's voice dropped further, and his next words came like a confession. "There's something about him. The scent of his magic. The way the air feels around him. My instincts keep pulling at me like... like I should *know* him. Or protect him. Or fight him—I don't know. It's like standing too close to lightning, and every hair on my body is standing up waiting for the strike."

She studied him—really looked. His hands clenched on his knees; his knuckles were white, but it wasn't fear. It was confusion. Vulnerability. Something primal straining at the edge of reason.

"You've never felt this before?" she asked softly.

Kai shook his head. "Not even close. Not with any battle. That didn't even happen during my first shift. It's not fear. It's something other than anger. It's like..." He dragged a hand down his face. "Like something in me is trying to remember something I never lived."

Seraphina's pulse stuttered.

Kai had always been literal. Loyal. Grounded like stone. This—this was not like him.

And the old stories came back to her. The ones about soul recognition. About the way Lycans sensed their fated mates—not by logic, or love at first sight, but by instinct so deep it defied explanation. Scent. Soul. Magic. Something *remembered.*

But Aurion hadn't been human before.

The transformation had changed more than his form. It had shifted into something fundamental. Something that might be echoing across threads of spirit and fate now awakened in Kai.

Still, she didn't speak it aloud.

Not yet.

Kai noticed her silence and narrowed his eyes. "You're thinking something. Don't lie."

She blinked, then reached across and took his hand—warm, solid, trembling slightly.

"I'm thinking," she said gently, "that we're all feeling it. Following the war. Pressure is building up. The uncertainty. You're not alone in this, Kai."

He looked at her, studying her face like he might find the answer hidden there.

He nodded, just once.

But something still flickered in his eyes.

Vaelrik's arrival shattered the moment as he threw open the tent flap and stomped in, covered in bruises and trailing dirt across the canvas floor. A gash along his temple was still bleeding slightly, and his tunic was torn at the sleeve.

Seraphina blinked at him.

"He didn't hold back," she murmured under her breath, a hint of pride curling in her voice.

Vaelrik caught it, scowled, and rubbed his ribs. "Your *dragon* is a menace. I think he cracked something just to make a point."

Kai arched an eyebrow from where he sat, one arm draped lazily over the back of his chair. "Why are you interrupting family time, Vaelrik? Did you come to cry about your bruised ego?"

Vaelrik rolled his eyes, too tired to banter. "Seraphina's needed. Now. Kade's losing it again."

Her heart jolted. "What happened?"

Vaelrik hesitated, just long enough to make the silence heavy. "The Veilborn delivered another list of demands. Same as before—complete surrender."

Kai sat forward, growling low. "And?"

Vaelrik's voice turned bitter. "And this time, they named you both. By name. They want *you*, Seraphina—and Kade."

The tent went quiet.

Kai stood slowly, tension rippling through him. "No one would agree with that."

Vaelrik's gaze flicked toward him, then away. "No one from the Lycans would. But there are factions... others. Some who've already lost too much. They're desperate. And that's what set Kade off."

Seraphina's chest tightened. "What are they saying?"

"That you're too powerful to be left unbargained. That sacrificing two might save thousands." Vaelrik's voice was hollow. "Kade's trying to shut it down before it gains traction, but he's not exactly calm about it."

Kai's fists clenched at his sides. "He shouldn't have to be. This is madness."

Vaelrik met Seraphina's eyes then. "You need to talk to him. You need to talk to him before he burns bridges that can't be rebuilt.

They didn't walk—they *ran*.

Boots pounding the packed earth, Seraphina surged ahead with Kai and Vaelrik close behind, weaving between tents as the full moon cast long shadows across the camp. Shouts echoed from the direction of the war tent, and Kade's voice carried above the rest—sharp, furious, unravelling.

By the time they reached the tent, the canvas sides trembled from the energy inside.

Aurion was already there—small in form now, perched atop a supply crate near Kade's shoulder, no longer tethered to the amulet. His eyes glinted as Seraphina approached, knowing where she was through the bond and sensing her need to understand the unasked question of what Kade was yelling for.

Technically, Aurion's voice drifted through her mind, calm but edged. *He's not just yelling about the idea of sacrificing you. He's yelling because he wants to go in your place.*

Seraphina didn't stop to think. Fury flared through her, hot and focused. She shoved the flap open more and barged in.

The inside of the war tent seethed with tension—a living storm of clashing voices, political heat, and barely restrained magic. The thick canvas walls pulsed with the raw power inside, lanterns hanging overhead flickering as if reacting to the room's collective unrest.

Delegates from every faction lined the curved edges of the space. Lycans in dark leathers stood shoulder to shoulder, their broad forms radiating barely leashed aggression. The vampire faction wore crimson and obsidian, their pale features stark beneath soot-streaked hoods. Humans in worn fibre nursed bruises and guarded expressions, while the fae— watched from the shadows with unreadable eyes, draped in silks that shimmered unnaturally with movement.

And at the centre—Kade.

He was fury incarnate.

His long silver hair tousled, fell over eyes that flared like polished moonstone. Veins of magic traced along his arms in subtle flickers, visible beneath the loose folds of his unbuttoned tunic. His hand gripped the edge of the war table so tightly the heavy wood creaked under the strain. A map of contested lands lay beneath his fists, edges curled, ink smudged where someone's magic had already scorched it.

He looked ready to tear the whole damn tent apart.

"Kade," Seraphina snapped, her voice cutting through the noise like a drawn blade.

Every head turned. Every tongue stilled.

Kade froze. His gaze found hers instantly—guilt crashing across his face in a wave so sharp it hurt to see.

"Sera, I—"

"No." She stepped forward, boots echoing on the wooden planks as she met him in the centre, jaw set like iron. Her voice held none of the warmth it did when it was just the two of them. "You don't get to throw yourself into the fire for me."

She turned then, eyes sweeping across the room—a slow, blistering glance that pierced through years of power, politics, and posturing.

"And none of you—*none of you*—will ever again speak about sacrificing anyone like we're bargaining chips."

Silence bloomed. Thick. Awkward. Heavy.

Her voice, when it rose again, was cold steel drawn slow. "I don't care what the Veilborn demand. They've broken every truce. Betrayed every deal. Surrender isn't survival—it's *slaughter delayed.*"

One of the human generals shifted awkwardly. A Lycan muttered under his breath. Another looked away, shame in the angle of his jaw.

Seraphina didn't stop.

"I've fought beside Kade. Bled beside him. I watched him hold the line when others ran. He's no prince to be traded. He's the reason *any* of you are still alive."

She looked straight at the vampire faction.

"So if you think safety comes from handing him over... you've already lost this war."

At the back, the Lycan alpha—Rhian—watched her with folded arms and an unreadable expression. A scar cut through the side of his jaw and disappeared into the collar of his coat. But behind him, Dylan stood proud, a faint grin tugging at his lips. He'd seen this fire in her before, but now it burned with purpose, not just rage.

A voice cut through the silence—bitter and choked.

"We've all lost things," said one of the vampire survivors, stepping forward. His red and ash cloak concealed him; his robe, once regal, was tattered; exhaustion and grief lined his face. "But he's Unseelie. He means something to them. If it's *him* or *all of us*—"

"Don't you *dare*."

Seraphina's magic surged before she could stop it, raw and volatile. The air snapped, gold and obsidian light crawling like fire along her arms. Her irises bled with that same chaotic hue, magic whispering at the edge of destruction.

The fabric of the tent trembled.

Before it could spiral further, Vaelrik stepped up beside her and gently clamped his hands on her shoulders. His touch grounded her like an anchor dropped into a stormy sea.

"Easy, General," he said, voice low and dry. "Can't blow up the allies. Poor form and all."

Aurion's voice in her mind was amused. *Bad sportsman ship to end months of work you put in to these allies*

She exhaled shakily. The magic retracted like a tide, sizzling beneath her skin.

Then—unexpectedly—a fresh voice rose.

"I agree with her."

All heads turned toward the Seelie fae delegate. Thalaniel, tall and severe, had never shown an ounce of kindness toward Kade. His hair fell in intricate braids over one shoulder, and the green gem at his throat shimmered faintly.

He stood.

"I don't like the Unseelie. Especially *him*." He gestured toward Kade with disdain. "But loyalty like hers? That's what wins wars." His eyes didn't leave Seraphina. "We protect our own."

A ripple passed through the room—of surprise, of grudging respect. Of silence that finally... settled.

Seraphina turned back to Kade.

He looked impossibly tired, still beautiful, still infuriating—his silver eyes soft with apology, his stance loosened but not relaxed.

She strode toward him, boots thudding with every step. The crowd parted like they knew better than to get in her way.

"You try to sacrifice yourself again," she said, low and sharp, "and I'll chain you to a post myself. Do you *hear me?*"

"Yes, ma'am," he said, that maddening smirk tugging at his lips.

"Louder."

"Yes, *Seraphina.*" This time, he said her name like it was a promise.

Seraphina tried to hold the shiver back that threatened to trail down her spine at the way he said her name.

From the side, Kai made a strangled noise and flopped back against a crate. "Please," he groaned, clutching his chest, "sort out *whatever* this relationship is. The tension is killing everyone."

He pointed at the tent flap without lifting his head. "Out. Both of you. Now. I need silence. Or peace. Or death. Preferably silence."

Vaelrik folded his arms, still at Seraphina's side. "Ten silver on her blowing him up first."

Aurion, lounging now on Kai's shoulder like a smug cat, flicked his tail and purred, Kai stiffened in response "Twenty on Kade saying something dumb enough to deserve it."

Kade looked around the room, deadpan. "You *know* I'm still right here, yes?"

"Good," Seraphina muttered, grabbing his arm and dragging him out through the flap before anyone could say another word.

Chapter 56

The chilly night air slapped Seraphina in the face the moment they stepped out of the tent. Stars spilled across the velvet sky like ink across parchment, and the smoky scent of distant fires clung to the wind, sharp and raw. Voices and movement from the camp blurred behind them as she dragged Kade further away, their boots crunching over the grass until even the murmur of the soldiers faded into silence.

Kade yanked his arm from her grip but didn't step back. Didn't retreat. He just stood there, silver hair wild under the moonlight, his jaw locked stubbornly in that infuriating line that made her want to both strangle and kiss him in equal measure.

"You're mad," he said flatly, voice low and crackling like a fire starved of air.

Seraphina snorted, the sound brittle. "Mad doesn't even cover it."

They stared each other down, the tension between them as palpable as a drawn bowstring. The charged air crackled louder than any battlefield.

Kade broke first, dragging a hand through his already-tousled hair in frustration. "I wasn't actually going to do it. Just... distract them long enough for you to escape."

"You're an idiot if you think my survival matters more than yours." Her voice shook, despite the fibre she tried to wrap it in.

His gaze softened, something breaking open in him. And gods, she hated it — hated the way he looked at her like she was something precious. Like she was the only thing in this crumbling world worth saving.

"You still wear it," he breathed, almost reverently.

She blinked, thrown off balance. "What?"

He gestured, a little sheepishly now, to the chain at her throat.

Her fingers lifted instinctively, brushing against the thin silver chain hidden beneath the collar of her fibre — a pendant, small and simple: a shard of black obsidian, bound in twisted silver, shaped like a fang and thrumming with old magic.

"I didn't think you'd still have it," he murmured, stepping closer, tentative.

Heat rushed to her cheeks, traitorous and unwelcome.

"It's just a gift. Means nothing," she muttered, hating how weak the words sounded.

Kade gave her a look, maddeningly gentle. "That's a lie. You know what it is. You feel it — the thrum of old magic. It's mine."

Of course she knew. She had always known. It wasn't just a charm. It was protection. A tether. A piece of him, bound to her — cold like frost, sharp like truth, steady as the sunrise.

Every time she touched it, the chill kissed her skin, anchoring her. Every time the loneliness became too much, that shard reminded her: she wasn't alone. Not really.

"I kept it because..." She hesitated, words knotting in her throat. "Because I needed to feel you were still with me. Even when I was too angry... to hurt to admit it."

Kade's hand brushed her cheek, tentative at first, then firmer when she didn't pull away. His touch smelled of frost and smoke, of battlefields and winter nights. Of home.

"It was never like this before," he said hoarsely. "Before you, everything was survival. Duty. Strategy. You were the first thing I wanted — just because I wanted you. Not because I had to. Not because it was necessary."

She closed her eyes, shaking her head. "We're reckless together. Stupid. Emotional."

"And yet," he murmured, thumb tracing the curve of her jaw, "you still dragged me out of that tent like you owned me."

"Someone has to save you from yourself."

A ghost of a smile pulled at his mouth, broken and beautiful.

They shared a breath, the space between them thinning, fraying — breaking.

"I tried," Kade said, voice dropping lower, rougher. "Tried to tell myself it was just battle-bonded loyalty. That I'd feel this way about anyone who bled beside me long enough."

Seraphina opened her eyes — and there it was. The same devastation she carried reflected right back at her.

"But it's not loyalty," she whispered. The truth trembled on her tongue, dangerous and real.

"No," he said. "It's you."

She pressed her forehead to his chest, feeling the cool thrum of his magic against her skin, breathing him in — smoke and frost and Kade.

"I hate you for this. I was supposed to stay mad longer. Make you grovel more." Her words were muffled against him, but they trembled with a fierce, broken kind of love.

"I know," he said, arms wrapping tight around her, as if to hold her together.

Silence stretched, brittle and precious.

Then he teased, voice brushing against her hair, "You're going to make me say it, aren't you?"

"Depends." She smirked against his chest. "Are you going to make it worth my while?"

Seraphina needed to hear this. Needed him to confirm it to her.

He chuckled — a sound she hadn't heard in what felt like lifetimes. Reckless. Dangerous. Alive.

He pulled back enough to see her face, his silver hair messy, his grin crooked. "Remember when you asked if your mixed bloodline meant you might never have a mate? Whether it was even possible?"

Her breath caught. Of course she remembered the conversation.

"I think we're... mates, Seraphina," he said finally, the word tasting wild and raw between them.

She froze, heart slamming against her ribs. Looked up, searching his face for a lie — and found none. Just the quiet certainty that the statement was right. That he felt it too. That this tether between them wasn't new, only finally named.

"I think we were always something," she drawled, voice trembling with the enormity of it. "We just... kept trying to fight it."

"Typical," he said with a soft, rueful laugh. "Lose battles, win wars. Lose hearts... steal them anyway."

She punched him lightly in the chest, but her hand fisted into the fabric of his shirt — unwilling to let go.

Something in her heart locked into place. A long-lost piece slid home like it had been waiting for this moment all her life — a piece of home she hadn't even realised was missing until now.

Kade's hand moved to cup her cheek, and when he spoke again, his voice was barely a breath.

"I don't know when I first noticed it," he said. "That strange pull toward you. Like something old and unspoken was always humming between us. A tether. Invisible. Relentless. The kind of thing that doesn't ask permission — it just *is*."

She didn't speak — couldn't. Her throat closed around the weight of it.

"My magic recognised you before I did," he murmured. "Every time we were near each other, something inside me quieted. Or flared. Like my power knew yours. Like it was... answering."

Seraphina's eyes stung, and not from the cold.

"I felt it too," she whispered. "Even before I had magic. You always felt like... gravity."

He gave a shaky laugh, forehead resting against hers. "Gods, *yes*. Like you were the only real thing in a world that kept trying to burn down around me."

Then a thought struck her, sharp and unwelcome, twisting her mouth into a scowl.

"Wait. You've been around me since I was with Alexis. How the hell didn't you realise? I thought Fae knew their mates instantly."

Kade chuckled, low and slow, the sound curling around her like smoke. He leaned in, his breath warm against the shell of her ear, arms braced on either side of her, caging her in.

"Usually, yes," he murmured. "But when we met... I was blood-bound to Alexis. It muted everything. And you hadn't unlocked the magic in your bloodline yet. The bond couldn't fully manifest. But it was always there, Sera. Always."

Seraphina blinked, her mind spiralling back — to the strange pull between them, the way he had shattered a blood bond for her, the unbearable loyalty, the way his scent had become her anchor after her magic awakened.

"I guess..." she shrugged, helpless, voice breaking at the edges. "After I got my magic, your scent always made me feel like I was home."

Kade smiled — slow, reverent. Something ancient and awed stirred behind his eyes.

"For Fae, the bond pulls. But scents affecting each other? That's a Lycan trait."

Seraphina frowned. "What does that mean?"

He pulled back slightly, his hands still framing her face. "Your bloodline — mixed as it is — intensified the bond in ways neither of us expected. You're not just part Fae or Lycan, Sera. You're generations of supernaturals crammed into one soul, one body. Your magic remembers things your mind hasn't caught up to yet."

He paused, brushing his thumb gently over her cheekbone.

"You're more. *We're* more."

His voice thickened with wonder. His silver eyes gleamed under the starlight, as if she was something miraculous he couldn't quite believe he was allowed to touch.

"We're going to burn the whole damn world down, aren't we?" she breathed, half-wonder, half-dread filling her voice.

He leaned in until their foreheads brushed, a sacred, fragile touch that steadied the chaos inside her.

"Only if you're beside me when we do it."

And for once — Seraphina didn't argue.

Didn't shield herself with anger or sharp words.

She just breathed him in — frost and smoke and something irreproachably hers.

And for the first time in a very long time, it didn't feel like dying.

It felt like finally, finally living.

Kade's thumb traced her cheekbone, feather light, and she tilted her face into his touch without thinking. The moment stretched between them — thick, heavy, inevitable — until she rose onto her toes and pressed her mouth to his.

It wasn't soft.

It wasn't gentle.

It was desperate, bruising, a clash of stubborn hearts finally, finally giving in. His arms crushed her to him, and she fisted his shirt, as if afraid the world might tear them apart again if she let go for even a second.

When they broke apart, breathing ragged, Seraphina rested her forehead against his once more and whispered, "We're not telling anyone. Not until after the battle."

Kade let out a low laugh, his breath ghosting against her skin.

"Afraid it'll make us reckless?"

She snorted. "We're already reckless. But if anyone knew... it would become a weakness they could exploit."

He nodded, the silver of his hair catching the starlight. "Agreed. It's ours. For now."

A beat of silence, then she hesitated, chewing her bottom lip before asking, "How do Fae seal the mate bond? Properly, I mean?"

He leaned back just enough to see her face, his expression softening.

"There's a ritual. Ancient magic woven into our bloodlines. When mates choose to seal the bond, they mark each other — not with a scar, but a symbol. A brand."

"A brand?" she echoed, curiosity flaring in her chest.

Kade smiled, slow and reverent. "It's like a tattoo, but more than ink. It's magic. Our family crests — yours and mine — would merge and create a new symbol unique to us. It appears over the heart... visible proof that we're bound."

Seraphina's hand instinctively rose to her chest, just over her pounding heart.

"And what does it... do?"

His silver gaze darkened, turning molten under the moonlight.

"We'd be able to feel each other. Not just physically — but emotionally. Joy. Pain. Fear. Everything."

Her breath caught in her throat. The idea was terrifying. Beautiful. Terrifying.

"But... there's something else," Kade added, voice rough.

"My powers are fractured after... everything. And your bloodline—" he shook his head in awe, "—your bloodline is something no one's ever seen before. I don't know what sealing the bond might awaken. It could make us stronger. Or it could... change us in ways we can't predict."

Seraphina looked at him, really looked — at the man who had stood beside her through blood and betrayal and war. At the only home she had left.

"I'm not afraid," she said simply.

Kade's smile was sharp and devastating.

"You never were."

He lowered his head again, brushing a kiss against her lips — softer this time, reverent — a promise of everything they hadn't said yet.

"After the battle," she whispered against his mouth.

"After the battle," he agreed.

Their fingers tangled together, holding tight, as if by sheer will they could outrun fate itself.

Together.

Chapter 57

A few days had passed since the stars whispered their promises and Seraphina had kissed Kade like he was the last real thing in a dying world. Since then, everything had moved in that strange, suspended way things do before war — too slow, too fast, like time itself was holding its breath.

The warriors had gathered at the Lycan stronghold. The great hall thrummed with voices and the scrape of metal, fires crackling in hearths carved with ancient runes.

Seraphina stood near the long central table, arms crossed, expression carefully neutral. She was doing her best to ignore the not-so-subtle looks thrown her way.

"Finally," Lyra muttered around a grin, nudging Seraphina's shoulder with her own. "You and Frostbite stopped being morons."

Seraphina arched a brow. "We've always been morons."

"True," Raze said, arms crossed beside them, but not quite meeting her eyes. "But now you're *together,* morons."

"Together?!" Vaelrik barked a laugh from across the table. "Thank the Ancients. The sexual tension was killing the rest of us."

"We're not—" Seraphina started, then shut her mouth as Kade entered the hall, silver hair tied back, a scroll in one hand. He didn't look at anyone else. Just her.

Lyra smirked. "Uh-huh."

Vaelrik groaned. "And once again, I'm the only one not paired off like some rejected side character in a tragic romance."

Seraphina was still stricken with the way their relationship had finally settled and was no longer a cause for her to fret over.

"It's your personality," Lyra and Raze said in unison to Vaelrik.

"Bite me," Vaelrik shot back.

"Only if it shuts you up," Lyra deadpanned. Raze growled softly at her side.

Kade joined Seraphina's side silently, brushing his fingers against hers under the table. No one noticed — or at least, they pretended not to. But it was becoming a thing. Where one of them was, the other wasn't far behind. Shadow and flame. Ice and thunder. Everyone saw it, even if they didn't know the whole truth.

Everyone... except Raze, who still wouldn't look at her for more than a heartbeat, and when he did, it was with a knowing glance. Something about his distance crawled under her skin, but every time she tried to bring it up, he turned the conversation or vanished entirely.

She didn't know what she'd done. And the not-knowing grated.

At the far side of the hall, Kai sat perched on the edge of a stone ledge, arms folded, eyes flicking constantly toward Aurion — who was sitting in the centre of the table, holding a conversation with Lyra about dragons.

Kai's jaw was tense, body wound tight like a coiled spring. He spoke little lately to Aurion even the bond between all three of them was quiet. Seraphina didn't know how to explain what passed between them — only that Kai now avoided Aurion like he was on fire, but couldn't seem to stop watching him burn, and it reminded her of Kade and herself.

The laughter faded into smaller conversations, quieter plans for after the battle. Tension hung in the air like the rising pressure before a storm.

Then—

BOOOOOOM.

The sound reverberated through the stronghold — not a crash, but a call. Deep. Resonant. Ancient.

The alarm sounded.

Everything stopped.

Conversation. Movement. Breath.

Kade straightened beside her, eyes already glowing faintly silver. Across the room, warriors dropped mugs and rose as one. They drew their weapons. Armour snapped into place. This was what they'd trained for. What they'd feared.

"What is it?" Seraphina asked, already moving.

Kade's voice was a low growl.

"They're here."

Seraphina's heart slammed against her ribs. A brutal, frantic rhythm.

No.

Not tonight.

Not when they'd *finally* found peace with each other.

Kade was already gone — out the heavy doors with the Lycans at his back, Vaelrik vanishing like a blade into the night.

She was moving before she could think. Racing through the dim corridors, stone walls blurring at the edges of her vision. Her breath came in sharp bursts, burning her lungs. Seraphina could have slapped herself for how stupid she was for leaving her weapon in her room. She skidded to a halt outside her chambers, fingers fumbling at the latch before she shoved the door open.

There — waiting for her like a patient curse — lay the Blade of Nyx.

The dark sword rested atop the worn oak table, its obsidian edges humming with a low, sinister resonance that she could *feel* in her teeth, in her bones. Shadows coiled along the blade's surface, alive, writhing like smoke.

It called to her.

Whispered to her.

You'll be nothing without me, Seraphina. Nothing but ash and forgotten dreams.

She clenched her jaw so hard it hurt. A bad omen, wrapped in steel and sorrow.

"You should take it," Aurion hissed from his place at her side, his golden eyes catching the dim torchlight, gleaming like molten metal. He looked almost feral. Almost... afraid.

"It's meant for you."

Seraphina tore her gaze from the blade, from the pull that clawed at her chest.

"No," she whispered, the word fragile on her tongue. "It's darkness." She didn't know why today it felt more ominous then other days especially since she had been practising with it for so long but she couldn't bring herself to take it into battle.

Aurion's look was sharp and sad.

"And so are you."

For a moment, a mere heartbeat, she wavered. The weight of fate pressing against her.

But she shook it off, wrenching her will back into place. Not tonight. Not when the stakes were so much more than herself.

She turned her back on the Blade of Nyx, ignoring the heavy ache that settled in her gut as she strapped on her twin daggers instead. Each buckle felt heavier than the last. Each step away from the blade felt like tearing skin from bone.

Still — she moved.

Grabbing her sword — *Kade's sword* — from where it rested against her bedpost, she sprinted for the hall.

Kai was already waiting for her in the shadowed corridor, arms loose at his sides, a familiar reckless grin cutting across his face. His green eyes glinted with anticipation and something harder beneath — something wild, finally the haunted look of the past few days was gone and replaced with the wild look she only saw when his Lycan side was on the hunt.

"Took you long enough," he said, bumping his shoulder against hers as they fell into stride.

"You scared?" she shot back, breathing hard but steady now.

Kai laughed — a short, savage sound.

"Only for them."

They burst into the courtyard together, and the world shattered.

The sky above was torn open — riven like old cloth. Furious winds screamed through the stronghold, carrying the stench of ash and blood. Clouds boiled overhead, bruised black and sickly red, as if the heavens themselves were bleeding.

Through the storm of her thoughts, Seraphina reached for that thread — the one she'd honed in every stolen moment of practice, in every breath of trust and control. She didn't speak. She didn't need to.

Just one thought — fierce, clear, commanding.

Now.

And Aurion *changed*.

In the blink of an eye, his shadow-cloaked form shifted, bones cracking and reshaping with fluid, violent grace. Midnight wings exploded from his back as his massive dragon form burst into the sky like a living eclipse. Moments later, a second roar tore across the heavens — Vaelrik, his crimson scales catching the firelight, joining him in the air.

They were beautiful and terrifying — avatars of rage and power, born of fire and night.

Above them, the sky was no longer just storm. It was war.

Vaelrik's gleaming wings cut through the clouds, each sweep stirring ash and lightning. He crashed into the swarm of airborne demons, claws shredding through flesh and scale. His fire lit up the dark like a sun reborn — an inferno in motion.

Aurion moved like a phantom — darker than shadow, faster than thought. Where Vaelrik was fury, Aurion was precision. He sliced through the air with obsidian talons, smoke and shadow trailing his path like a second skin. Where he flew, demons screamed—then fell, broken and burning.

Together, they lit the sky.

Sera. Aurion's voice wove into her mind — silk over steel. Calm, focused, absolute. *They're coming. And they're not alone.*

Her blood turned to ice.

Below, the battlefield was already unravelling into chaos.

Lightning forked through the storm-choked heavens, illuminating the horror beneath. The scent of rain and fire mingled with the thick iron tang of blood. Screams rose — human, inhuman — and shattered against the howls of the dying.

Seraphina stood on the edge of it all, her sword in hand, eyes burning with storm light.

The ground was slick with mud and death. Bodies—friend, foe, beast, and shadow—littered the field. Magic crackled in the air, sharp and desperate, clashing with steel and fang.

And Seraphina was in the thick of it.

Rain hammered the battlefield, turning dirt into slick, sucking mud that clung to her boots with every step. The air crackled with the raw stench of ozone, blood, and burning flesh. Shadows lunged from every direction—some with horns glistening wet under the fractured sky, others little more than twisted things shaped from nightmares.

Her twin blades moved faster than thought, their silver edges singing through the storm. One slice severed a demon's clawed hand; the next strike buried deep into its throat. It crumpled, black blood spurting across her face in a scalding spray. She barely flinched—already pivoting, already moving—a ghost in the carnage.

Another step forward. Another kill.

Another heartbeat closer to survival.

A flash of claws beside her—then Kai was there, a feral grin splitting his rain-slicked face, his wet fur hanging against him covered in blood. He drove his bloodstained claws through the skull of an advancing corrupted vampire, the creature shrieking as it crumpled.

You keeping count, or am I winning? Kai's voice was a smirk given sound in her mind, wild and reckless, as he kicked the corpse aside.

Seraphina huffed, parrying a blow from a snarling beast before stepping in close, her dagger punching cleanly into the demons throat. Hot blood spurted down her wrist. She ripped the blade free without hesitation.

Do you even know how to count that high? she shot back in her mind, breathless but grinning.

Kai barked a laugh, the sound raw and wild in the chaos. *Sera, darling, are you calling me dumb?*

Before she could respond, Aurion's voice threaded into both their minds—dry and sharp as cracked stone. *She's implying it, Kai. Keep up and both of you focus.*

Overhead, Aurion's massive shadow circled. His dragon form was a thing of terror—dark as a collapsing star, every beat of his enormous wings sending shockwaves through the torrential air. He dove through the clouds, bright fire raining from his maw, carving smoking trails through enemy ranks. His golden eyes—fierce and knowing—never left them.

They were winning. Inch by bloody inch, they were pushing back the tide.

Vaelrik roared somewhere above—a deafening bellow that shook the heavens themselves. His crimson-scaled body cut a burning path through the storm, flames erupting from his maw to consume a battalion of shadow beasts in a single, searing blast. Pieces of charred flesh and shattered bone rained down like cursed ash.

Across the battlefield, Lyra and Raze fought back-to-back, their blades a blur of steel and death. They moved like one—trusted, fearless—slicing down anything that dared step into their reach. Lightning flashed, freezing the carnage in stark relief: Raze's savage grin, Lyra's hair whipping around her like a banner of defiance, Seraphina was shocked they chose to fight in their human forms instead of their Lycans.

Through the smoke, the screams, the writhing hell unleashed around her—Seraphina saw him.

Kade.

He cut through the mass of monsters like a blade through silk. His silver hair, soaked with rain and blood, clung to his face in wild strands. His obsidian fibre, once gleaming and proud, was cracked and battered, deep gouges carved into its surface. Blood—his blood—wept from ragged wounds at his side and across his arms.

But he still stood.

Still fought.

Every movement was violence and grace, his great sword a black arc of death as he cleaved through the enemy ranks. His stance never faltered. His strikes never hesitated. He was a storm wrapped in steel—relentless, merciless.

And now, finally, *whole*.

Shadow poured from him like smoke from a fire, curling around his limbs in living tendrils, lashing out with a will of their own. They surged into the enemy lines—clawing, choking, ripping through the darkness that dared challenge him. Where his blade didn't strike, his magic did. Each swing of his sword was mirrored by a writhing shadow crashing into beasts with brutal efficiency.

The ground beneath his feet cracked with the force of his fury. Energy shimmered in the surrounding air—ancient, wild, and *his*. For too long, Kade had feared what lived inside him. For too long, he'd let shame and grief cage the storm.

But not tonight.

Seraphina's chest tightened. Not just with awe—but pride. He was letting it in. Trusting himself again. Trusting *them*. The part of him that once scared him now moved like a second skin—his power dancing through the battlefield in perfect sync with his blade, She could feel how satisfied he was to be able to use a small part of his magic again even from here she felt it.

She watched one shadow coil up an enemy's leg, dragging it screaming to its knees. Another exploded from Kade's back, a lance of pure dark magic that impaled a demon mid-lunge.

Finally, she thought, her heart slamming with something dangerously close to joy.

He's fighting as who he truly is.

Through the chaos, the fury, the boiling darkness, Kade's eyes found hers, he could feel her watching.

Storm-dark and burning.

For a heartbeat — no, an eternity — the battlefield melted away.

There was no rain, no screams, no blood-soaked ground.

Only him.

Only her.

And the tether that snapped taut between them, a pull that was more than flesh and magic — it was *soul-deep*.

He grinned — feral, beautiful — and lifted his bloodied sword in silent promise.

Seraphina tightened her grip on her blades, the spark of him igniting something savage and unstoppable within her chest.

The world roared back into being — louder, harsher — and they ran to meet it.

The battle was slowing.

At first, Seraphina didn't believe it. She spun, blades ready, expecting another onslaught—but there was only the ragged breathing of the living and the distant crackle of dying fires.

The demons were thinning. The air, once thick with screams and smoke, now trembled with stunned silence. A few final skirmishes flickered at the edges of the field, but the centre — where they stood — was clearing.

Confusion stirred under her ribs.

This isn't right.

This couldn't be the whole army. Had the allied forces crushed more of the enemy than they ever dared hope? Had they managed a miracle in the chaos?

She staggered forward, boots sinking into the blood-muddied ground. Her leathers clung to her skin, heavy with sweat, rain, and blood — most of it not her own. Every step jarred through aching limbs. But she didn't stop.

Because through the haze, she saw him.

Kade.

He moved toward her like gravity itself had shifted — drawn to her with a force too ancient, too deep, to question. His sword dragged at his side, forgotten for now. His fibre was battered, blackened by smoke and splattered with enemy blood, but he still moved with that same relentless purpose.

They met in the ruin of the battlefield, two figures stitched together by war and something far more dangerous — hope.

He didn't speak at first.

Instead, he reached out, bloodstained fingers lifting to brush against her cheek. His touch was rough, calloused, trembling just slightly — whether from exhaustion or something else, she didn't know. He traced the edge of a wound she hadn't even realised was there, the pad of his thumb unbearably gentle against the rawness of her skin.

"You alright, Nyx?" he rasped, his voice a low grind of smoke and steel — battered, strained... but somehow, impossibly, still *home.*

Seraphina's throat closed up. Words abandoned her. She only nodded, leaning subtly into his touch, grounding herself against the feel of him — solid, real, *alive.*

Kade's lips twitched — a ghost of a smile, fragile and broken, flickering across his blood streaked face. His fingers curled around hers, unyielding, unbreakable, as if by sheer will he could anchor her to him.

Above them, thunder rumbled like a distant war drum, the heavy scent of iron and rain thickening the air until it was almost suffocating.

Kade stepped closer, until there was no space left between them. His forehead pressed gently against hers, their breath mingling, and for a single, stolen moment, the battlefield melted away — the screams, the blood, the endless dying — all of it faded to nothing. Just them. Just this.

His breath was warm against her lips as he whispered, rough as gravel and soft as a vow, "If the gods demand your blood, I will slit their throats myself. If the stars try to take you, I will pluck them from the sky and watch the heavens fall dark. There is no fate, no force, no power greater than this—" His fingers tightened around hers. *"I am yours, Seraphina. And I will destroy anything that dares to take you from me."*

A sharp, shuddering breath escaped her. She could feel it — the breaking, the burning, the *everything* — clawing up her throat, threatening to consume her whole.

Then she let go. Let go of fear. Let go of the war still raging beyond the broken edges of this moment.

Let go of everything but *him.*

Seraphina surged upward and kissed him.

It was desperate, searing — a clash of blood and need, a collision of battered souls finding each other again in the ruins. Kade groaned into her mouth, a sound torn from somewhere deep and primal, his arms locking around her, dragging her against the hard planes of his body as if he could weld them together and never let go.

She clung to him just as fiercely, fingers tangling in the torn leather at his shoulders, because this — *this* — was theirs.

And they both knew it might be the last.

When she finally broke away, gasping for breath, Kade's forehead rested against hers once more. His gaze, dark and endless, found hers — and something passed between them. Silent. Eternal.

Mine, his eyes swore. *Always.*

Seraphina opened her mouth to speak — she wasn't even sure what she would have said — when a very familiar, very unimpressed voice shattered the fragile, golden stillness.

"Oh, for the love of the gods, really? A battlefield? That's where you two choose to have a big romantic moment?"

The heavy thud of paws against the blood-soaked earth accompanied the words. Kai loped toward them, his normally sleek midnight-silver fur matted with crimson, his green eyes narrowing in a look of long-suffering exasperation. His tail flicked once, sharp and annoyed.

"Some of us are still trying to *work* here, you know."

Seraphina barked a laugh, the sound raw and unexpected, and Kade only grinned — the first real, reckless grin she'd seen from him in what felt like a lifetime.

Kai grumbled, stalking toward them with a theatrical huff. His massive wolfish head gestured dramatically at the sea of bodies strewn around them. "I've been fighting off wave after wave of bastards while you two were busy making *heart-eyes* at each other," Kai grumbled, stalking toward them with a theatrical huff. His massive wolfish head gestured dramatically at the sea of bodies strewn around them. "Do you have *any* idea how long it's going to take to clean this mess out of my fur? Kade, you owe me a bath. With the *nice oils.* None of that cheap shit."

Seraphina snorted, the tension in her shoulders finally easing. Kade, still holding her like he might never let go, chuckled low under his breath.

"Oh, I don't think so, mutt," Kade drawled. "You're more than capable of bathing your own flea-bitten ass and for the record I preferred when you couldn't communicate with the rest of us outside your mind. Damn Vaelrik for teaching that trick to you."

Kai gave an exaggerated, wounded gasp, as if Kade had personally betrayed him.

"You wound me," he declared, shifting in a shimmer of light back into his human form — tall, muscled, shirtless, and looking every bit like he belonged in a fight. Without missing a beat, he slung his heavy arms over both their shoulders, pulling them into a half-tackle of an embrace, all iron and exhaustion and stubborn, unbreakable affection. His scent — earthy, wild, tinged with blood and storm — wrapped around them, grounding.

"Unbelievable," Kai muttered, as if he truly couldn't fathom their existence. "You two finally get your shit together and I'm the one stuck scrubbing demon gore out of my damn hair."

Seraphina rolled her eyes, amusement tugging at her lips. "Vaelrik, could always help you?" she offered innocently.

Kai recoiled so dramatically it was a miracle he didn't topple over. "I'd rather roll naked in that demon's rotting corpse over there, thanks." But even as he complained, his arms tightened around them for a beat longer — silent, solid, family.

Then, with a sudden seriousness that cut through the banter like a blade, Kai shifted his weight and faced Kade squarely. His green eyes sharpened, losing all humour.

"I'm serious, Kade." His voice dropped low, almost a growl. "I don't know if I forgive you — maybe that's not my choice anymore." His fingers flexed against Kade's shoulder before he finally released him. *"But if you ever let her get hurt again, I will come for you. And there won't be a pit deep enough to hide in."*

Kade didn't flinch. He only met Kai's stare, something grim and solemn passing between them, before nodding — once, firm, absolute. His hand tightened around Seraphina's like a silent oath.

"I won't," Kade said, voice rough with all the things he didn't say aloud.

Before the tension could get too heavy, a deep, annoyed rumble rolled overhead.

Aurion swooped low, his massive, shadowed form blotting out the battered skyline. He landed a few yards away with the heavy thud of ancient power, folding his vast, midnight wings tight to his body. His sharp, bright gaze swept over the scene with clear, unimpressed judgement.

Kai, still riding the wave of indignation, immediately pointed at Seraphina and whined toward Aurion like a dramatic younger brother tattling to a parent. "Would you please get your little *superhuman menace* in line? She thinks a *battlefield* is the perfect spot for romantic dramatics!"

Aurion's wings flared slightly in irritation as he huffed, an unmistakable glower on his face.

"If I could control her actions," he rumbled drily, "She wouldn't be within *five feet* of Kade."

The look he levelled at Kade was nothing short of a threat — ancient, bone-deep, and quietly terrifying.

Kade exhaled a long-suffering sigh and muttered under his breath, "Gods, is every animal in this gods-damned army lining up to threaten me today?"

Seraphina burst out laughing, the sound wild and light and *alive* — and for the first time in what felt like forever, it wasn't weighted by grief.

Kai grinned widely, slapping Kade's back hard enough to make him grunt. "Get used to it, lover boy. Family means protection." He smirked wickedly. "And if you screw up, family means creative revenge."

They bickered and bantered, the three of them exchanging sharp words and sharp smiles with the ease of those who had fought and bled and survived together. For a heartbeat longer, it felt almost normal.

Above them, a chorus of howls echoed across the battlefield — long, triumphant victory cries that rolled like thunder through the clearing skies. Aurion lifted his head, eyes narrowing toward the horizon, his voice a low rumble against the sudden hush.

"It's over," he said. "For now."

Seraphina let out a breath she hadn't realised she was holding, her fingers curling tighter around Kade's.

Maybe — *just maybe* — they had actually won.

Then—A crackling sound split the air—sharp, unnatural, *wrong*.

The hair on the back of Seraphina's neck stood up a second before Kai stiffened beside her, his body tensing like a bow pulled too tight. His green eyes darted over his shoulder—searching, scanning—

Then the world *cracked apart*.

Dark energy, thick and writhing like smoke turned solid, split the very air behind him. The ground itself seemed to *recoil*, the scent of ozone and rot flooding the clearing.

Kai turned, lips parting to speak—

"What now—"

—but the words barely left his mouth.

A wet, sickening *schlkt* tore through the battlefield's fragile peace.

The blade punched through Kai's back in one cruel, deliberate motion. It wasn't a quick strike. It was *patient, savouring*, whispering as it slid between ribs, carving a path through muscle and marrow, before biting deep enough to punch free of his chest.

The sound of it—*flesh parting, bone grinding, breath stuttering*—was louder than the cries of the wind.

Seraphina's heart stopped, the world narrowing to a single, jagged point of agony.

Kai jerked violently, his hands snapping upward as if trying to catch at something—anything—only to claw helplessly at the empty air. His mouth opened in a choked gasp, no sound escaping but a wet, rattling exhale.

His knees buckled.

He collapsed onto the bloodstained earth with a brutal *thud*, the impact rattling through Seraphina's bones. She could feel it in her teeth, in her spine.

Kai's hands scrabbled uselessly against the dirt, nails digging desperate grooves into the ground as his shoulders shook. Blood pooled beneath him, dark and thick, soaking into the soil like a sacrament.

His eyes—those brilliant, mischievous green eyes—went wide.

Not with fear.

Not even pain.

Confusion.

As if none of this made sense. As if some part of him was still searching for the joke, for the trick that would make it stop.

Another sound split the air — a low, wet, *squelch* — as the blade was wrenched free, dragging horribly against bone on the way out. Kai's body jolted with it, a broken, helpless arc, his back bowing, his lips parting in a gasp that was more blood than breath.

Dark blood spilled from the wound, from his mouth, bubbling in thick, glistening streams.

Seraphina tried to move. She *needed* to move — her body screamed to reach him — but her feet felt bolted to the earth.

Kai sagged forward, a puppet with its strings cut, his hands slipping in the dirt as his body struggled uselessly against the inevitable.

The blade, now glistening wet with his blood, hung in the hand of the one who had wielded it so easily.

The one smiling.

The one she knew.

Seraphina's stomach twisted viciously, her throat tightening until she could barely draw breath.

That voice—

"Well, well," the intruder drawled, smooth and familiar as poisoned silk. The smile that curved his mouth was casual, effortless — a mockery of the warmth she remembered.

Alexis.

He stood there, calm amid the carnage, his blood-soaked blade still dangling casually at his side. His golden hair was tied back neatly, his fibre glinting darkly under the dying light — as if he had just stepped out of a memory.

Only his eyes betrayed him.

Those deep, stormy blue eyes — once her comfort, her home — now gleamed with cold amusement as he stared straight through Kai's crumpled form, straight into *her*.

The twisted parody of affection that laced his words made Seraphina's stomach *roil*.

"Did you miss me, wife?"

Chapter 58

Seraphina's scream tore through the battlefield—

A sound so raw, so guttural, it could have cracked the heavens. It shattered through the clang of metal and the roar of dragons, slicing through the chaos like a soul being ripped from flesh.

Dylan's answering howl was just as primal—pain echoing through the pack bond, the grief only a father could know as his son's light faded.

Her feet moved before her thoughts could catch up—

No. No. No.

Her pulse was thunder in her ears. The world blurred at the edges, all colour bleeding out until there was only red. Red on the grass. Red on Kai. Red on her hands.

Kai's knees buckled—but before he could fall fully, a massive shape dropped beside him.

Aurion hit the ground like a meteor, dirt and debris exploding outward in a thunderous cloud. The air warped with the heat of his arrival, his scales glinting obsidian as his enormous snout pushed beneath Kai's body, catching him with impossible gentleness.

His golden eyes, which usually held fierce ancient power, now gazed down at Kai with a look that could only be described as fear.

Stay with me, Kai. Aurion's voice was rough through the bond, ragged with disbelief. *Please. Just stay.*

Kai let out a broken, choking laugh. *Oh, gods, I hate when you sound serious, Aurion.*

It's unsettling.

Seraphina dropped to her knees beside them, barely able to breathe. Her fingers moved of their own accord—desperate—as she pressed down on the wound. Blood surged between her hands, hot and *wrong*, slicking her skin like ink. Her palms couldn't hold it all. It kept *pouring*, as if the earth was drinking him.

"You're alright, Kai," she lied, voice cracking. "You're fine. I've got you."

His smile was crooked, teeth stained red. "I mean," he rasped, "I'm bleeding out like a slaughtered deer but—" he coughed hard, flecks of crimson spraying his lips "—I look good doing it, right?"

Seraphina let out a strangled sound—half sob, half laugh—as she shook her head. "Shut up, Kai. Just—shut up and *stay alive*."

For a moment, his gaze found hers.

And there, in the depths of those wild green eyes, was something fragile. Something that *broke* her.

Goodbye.

"No. Don't you dare," she whispered, pressing harder on the wound. "You're not allowed."

"It's okay, Sera," he whispered, voice barely more than air. "You gave me something worth dying for."

Her chest *shattered*. A cry caught in her throat as she leaned over him, her forehead touching his. Her breath hitched, his already fading.

Then, behind them, Aurion—his great nostrils flaring with panic—nudged Kai gently with his snout, and rolled him slightly, trying to better support him. Kai groaned, barely conscious.

The movement caught *Alexis's* attention from where he was eyeing up the warriors that had surrounded the little group.

He turned his head with idle disinterest—

—and that *smirk* twisted as he looked down at the blood on his blade.

A sneer curled his lips. "Tch. Peasant blood. *Stains everything.*"

He flicked the blade carelessly, crimson spattering onto the broken earth.

And that was the moment Kade moved.

The air pulsed around him, magic rippling with fury as he stepped through it—each motion a study in restrained violence. His silver hair was plastered to his face with blood and sweat, his black fibre slick with viscera, shoulder dented from a blow he hadn't even noticed. The scent of charred flesh and ozone clung to him, his eyes lit with a pale violet glow that promised *retribution*.

He stepped between Seraphina and Alexis, sword drawn. A wall. A weapon.

Alexis raised an eyebrow, spinning his blade lazily. "You always had a flair for dramatics, Kade," he said with mock fondness, like this was all a game. "Tell me, did you miss me? Or did you finally stop mourning what we had?"

Kade's jaw locked, muscles trembling with fury. His voice came low and sharp. "I mourned you," he growled. "The brother I knew died long ago."

"Wrong," Alexis snapped, his eyes suddenly *too bright*, that pleasant facade cracking for a blink. "You were the one who turned your back. You left *me*, remember?"

He stepped forward, slowly, raising his blood-soaked sword to Kade's chest. The motion was intimate. Cruel.

"And now?" he smiled. "I collect."

Kade didn't flinch.

Didn't blink.

Didn't *breathe*.

Then, in one vicious motion,

He lunged.

Behind Kade, a strangled cough splintered through the chaos.

Seraphina's head snapped around, her breath catching like a hook in her chest.

Kai lay crumpled in the dirt, blood blooming across his tunic, soaking through in grotesque, dark patterns. His grin was a shattered thing, thin and trembling.

"Well," he rasped, green eyes flickering like dying embers, "I've had better days."

Tears burned behind her eyes, but she shoved them down ruthlessly.

"Don't joke. Just—stay still," she ordered, voice breaking.

Kai chuckled weakly, a broken, wheezing sound. "I'd argue I *am* pretty still," he quipped, then coughed, grimacing. "Though... bleeding out? Bit anticlimactic. I was hoping for more explosions."

Aurion was beside her in an instant, his massive, scaled body curling protectively around them. His golden eyes were wild with fear, and Seraphina felt the low, desperate thrum of panic pulsing through their bond.

She couldn't lose Kai.

Not here. Not now. Not her brother in all but blood.

She pressed trembling hands to the gaping wound, hot blood slick against her palms. Desperation clawed at her, rising like bile in her throat.

Help him. Save him.

She reached inward, plunging into the ancient wellspring buried deep in her bloodline.

A scorching, blinding heat answered.

Magic howled through her veins, feral and wild, an inferno that wanted to consume her as much as it wanted to obey. Her heart pounded so hard it hurt, the rhythm a deafening roar in her ears.

Stop. You'll break. You'll burn, the old magic whispered, a cruel warning.

She ignored it.

Deeper, she plunged, pushing past the limits that even the oldest blood mages dared not cross. Her vision blurred at the edges, golden light blazing from her hands, the air around them warping and shimmering under the raw force she unleashed.

She barely registered Aurion shifting beside her—his great body shimmering, collapsing inward until he knelt there in human form: bronzed skin, silver-white hair clinging to his brow, tall and fierce and breathtaking. His hands, warm and strong, closed over her wrists.

"Seraphina, stop," Aurion begged, his voice rough with fear. "You're killing yourself—"

"I don't care!" she snapped, shaking him off, her voice raw and wrecked. Her magic was tearing itself apart inside her, tendrils of agony lashing through every bone, every nerve. Still she forced more, tapping even into Aurion's life-force through their bond, yanking at it, desperate.

If she could just hold Kai together, just a little longer—

Blood seeped around her fingers, but it was slowing.

Kai's chest hitched on a ragged inhale.

Aurion's grip tightened again. His golden gaze bored into her, voice cracking. "You have to care. If you fall, Sera, we lose you both."

Seraphina blinked furiously through the tears blurring her vision.

She couldn't lose them. Not Kade. Not Kai. Not Aurion.

Not when everything was already falling apart—

A sound bubbled up beside her. A choked laugh.

Kai, pale and trembling, forced his eyelids open, struggling to focus. His gaze landed on Aurion's human form—haloed by the golden light leaking from Seraphina's hands—and he blinked sluggishly, like he was seeing the sun for the first time.

"Holy shit," Kai breathed, voice slurred but awestruck. "Are you always that pretty, or is the blood loss making you shine?"

Aurion gave a rough, huffing laugh—half relief, half heartbreak.

Kai's cracked lips twitched into a crooked smirk. "You... uh... come here often, handsome?" he slurred, then slumped sideways, unconscious.

Seraphina let out a hysterical, strangled laugh, even as her body sagged forward with the weight of exhaustion.

Aurion caught her instantly, one arm sliding around her waist, the other bracing Kai's limp form with terrifying tenderness.

"You did it," Aurion murmured, voice low in her ear, but the tremble in his arms told her everything.

There was no victory in this. Only survival bought at too high a cost.

Her head lolled against his chest for a heartbeat—only a heartbeat—before the clash of steel yanked her back into the nightmare.

The sound was unmistakable—metal screaming against metal.

Her head jerked up.

Across the battlefield, Kade and Alexis were locked in brutal combat, their blades colliding in showers of sparks.

The air around them was thick with smoke, ash, and blood, the world shrunk down to the vicious dance of death between them.

Kade—

Her heart stuttered painfully in her chest.

Kade, silver hair matted with blood and sweat, his obsidian fibre cracked and dented, fighting like a man possessed.

And Alexis—

Alexis, standing there, *alive*.

Not a ghost, not a memory.

Alive.

And if he was alive—if he had never died—

They were still married.

Seraphina shoved the terror down. She forced herself to focus on Kai, on Aurion, on anything but the man she had once loved now standing drenched in the blood of her people.

Somewhere in the fray, Alexis laughed—a cruel, rich sound that grated against her raw nerves.

Seraphina turned back to Aurion, chest heaving, voice shaking.

"Get Kai out of here. *Now.*"

Aurion hesitated, his golden gaze torn between her and the battle raging beyond.

"I'm not leaving you—"

"You don't have a choice," she rasped. As she crumpled on the ground the weakness hitting her.

Vaelrik landed in a whirl of shadow and smoke, boots slamming into bloodied earth just as Seraphina's magic faltered. Her shoulders sagged, barely holding herself upright, fingers trembling as golden light faded from her skin.

"Gods," Vaelrik hissed, eyes flashing as he took in the carnage around them—Seraphina crumpled, Kai barely breathing, and Aurion... frozen.

Aurion didn't move.

His chest rose and fell in uneven bursts, his expression carved from anguish as he tried—tried—to shift. To take Kai and flee. But Seraphina's magic had leeched his own, the connection between them too deep, too entwined.

He couldn't change.

"No," he whispered, voice cracking. "No, no, no—"

Golden eyes filled with horror. His jaw clenched as raw, primal fury ripped through him.

"I should've stopped her—I should've—"

He roared, the sound a jagged cry that echoed across the battlefield, ragged and wild. It wasn't just frustration—it was grief. Powerless grief.

He fell to his knees beside her, his fingers ghosting over her blood-slicked skin. "You burned everything, didn't you?" he rasped. "Just to keep him alive."

Vaelrik knelt too, eyes flicking between the pair. His voice, when it came, was low but unshakeable. "I'll stay. I won't leave her."

Aurion looked at him, truly looked, and the bond between dragons flared brightly in that moment—raw, ancient trust.

"You swear it," Aurion said, voice ragged.

"On my soul."

That was enough. A dragons word was his law and Aurion knew that Vaelrik wouldn't sacrifice his word.

Aurion gathered Kai in his arms, the unconscious boy limp and drenched in blood, and turned with one last, lingering glance at Seraphina. Every step away from her looked like agony, like his heart was being peeled from his chest.

The battlefield reeled with screams and steel, but all Seraphina heard was the ragged breath of the man she couldn't lose, the scream of a dragon who couldn't save her, and the aching silence of a vow sworn too late.

Vaelrik steadied her against him, whispering something in a language lost to time. She barely heard it—her body was shaking, nerves overloaded from pain and power. But his arms were firm, grounding her as the world bled red and ash around them.

And in the distance, steel met steel—Kade and Alexis locked in a brother's war, as everything else fell apart.

Seraphina barely had time to process the horror—Aurion, stuck in human form because she had drained too much—before the sounds of steel clashing ripped her attention back to Kade and Alexis.

She had to move. She had to.

Pain burned through every limb, a deep, gnawing ache that made her want to collapse right there in the blood-soaked mud. Her vision blurred at the edges, her magic a smouldering ember in her veins, almost gone. *You can't.* A voice whispered. *You're spent. Broken.*

But another voice roared louder inside her, savage and wild: *Get up.*

Vaelrik was at her side in a flash, his hands catching her shoulders. "Sera, you can't—look at you, you're barely standing—"

"I *have* to," she rasped, voice torn and shaking. She shoved him off with a strength she didn't know she had. Her knees nearly buckled. *Kade.* She couldn't leave him. Not with that monster. Not alone.

Somewhere ahead, Kade and Alexis were locked in a brutal dance, blades flashing under the sickly red sky. Kade staggered back a step, and even from here, she could see it—he was losing.

Seraphina's heart twisted painfully.

Her fingers scrabbled against the muddy earth until they closed around the hilt of a fallen sword, half-buried beneath a dead soldier. She yanked it free with a growl of effort, the blade heavy and unwieldy in her trembling grip. She pushed herself to her feet, each movement agony, her muscles screaming in protest.

A wild, reckless glint sparked in her eyes as she turned to Vaelrik. "You better keep up," she said, teeth bared in a feral grin.

Then she *ran*.

It was more a hobbling, staggering sprint, but she didn't care. Every breath was a knife in her lungs, every heartbeat a thunderclap of pain—but she ran for him.

Vaelrik swore colourfully under his breath and sprinted after her, his blades flashing as he tore through corrupted soldiers that burst from the smoke. Dark shapes—grotesque and twisted—rose alongside them, summoned by a figure that landed ahead, shrouded in shadow.

Seraphina skidded to a halt as the figure materialised, blocking her path.

A masked woman, twin blades gleaming like fangs.

Seraphina's heart slammed against her ribs, her blood roaring in her ears. Something about the way she moved—the tilt of her head, the coiled precision of her stance—*familiar*. Too familiar.

The woman lunged. Seraphina parried, but the impact rattled up her arms, nearly knocking her broken body off balance. Pain sparked in her chest, her shoulders, her burning legs. *Not enough. Gods, she wasn't enough.*

Still, she fought. Sheer, brutal instinct drove her, weaving and striking, her sword feeling heavier with every swing. Her breath came in ragged gasps, but she refused to fall.

She pivoted sharply, slashing across the assassin's mask—just like Lyra had taught her.

The mask shifted with the blow, sliding crooked—and Seraphina *froze*.

Those eyes.

Sky blue. Painfully familiar. Etched into her memories.

Her heart cracked. *No. No, it can't be—*

The assassin struck, knocking her feet out from under her. Seraphina slammed into the ground, mud coating her palms, the passionless kiss of steel pressing against her throat.

For a moment, the battlefield faded—the screams, the clash of blades, the stench of blood. It was just her, the woman pinning her down, and the devastating, inescapable truth lurking behind that mask.

In the corner of her vision, Vaelrik fought like a demon, carving through the corrupted ranks that had followed the masked woman. Blood and magic painted the battlefield red and black.

Then—another figure appeared.

Raze.

Except this time, he wasn't at their side. He was beside the enemy.

Seraphina's stomach dropped into a pit of cold realisation as she saw

Vaelrik falter, barely fending off Raze's sudden, savage strike.

Betrayal. It slammed into her chest like a war hammer.

The subtle way Raze had changed, the guarded looks, the missteps. Alexis appearing out of nowhere. *It hadn't been a coincidence.*

It had been *treachery* all along.

"Seraphina!"

Kade's voice, raw and broken with panic, tore through the chaos, snapping her back into the moment. She twisted against the chains biting into her wrists, but the masked woman's grip only tightened, dragging her forward.

Kade fought like a man possessed, hacking his way toward her, but Alexis—*Alexis*—moved with chilling ease.

With a wicked smirk curling his lips, Alexis raised one lazy hand— and the Veilborn army froze. Like puppets with cut strings, they all stopped mid-motion, corrupted soldiers and monstrous beasts alike. The battlefield fell into a sick, unnatural silence.

"I have what I came for," Alexis purred, his gaze locking onto Seraphina. His voice slithered over the broken ground, smooth and cruel. "No need to waste any more of my precious troops."

Vaelrik let out a savage roar and lunged forward—but dark magic coiled out of nowhere, seizing him. Chains of shadow lashed around his limbs, dragging him to his knees. He snarled, his body trembling, fighting to shift into his dragon form—but the chains tightened, spitting sparks of black magic into the air, binding him utterly.

"No!" Seraphina thrashed against the masked woman's hold, heart pounding so hard it hurt.

And Kade—gods, Kade—, sprinting toward her.

Alexis barely spared him a glance. He flicked his wrist, and a blast of dark energy struck Kade like a hammer, slamming him into the mud. Kade groaned, struggling, but Alexis stepped forward, tutting under his breath.

"You lot were fun for a while," Alexis said, sounding almost bored. "But I'm tired of playing." His smile sharpened into something twisted. "I came to collect my wife. I suppose I should thank you for keeping her entertained among the riffraff."

The masked woman dragged Seraphina closer, chains binding her arms, her magic smothered under the weight of dark enchantments and the weakness she already felt. She fought anyway, teeth bared, the raw pain of betrayal burning hotter than any wound.

Vaelrik strained against the chains holding him, muscles bulging, a furious roar tearing from his throat—but Raze appeared at his side, cold and expressionless, as he dragged Vaelrik to Alexis.

Seraphina's heart twisted into knots. *Raze.* Their brother-in-arms. Their family.

Kade, coughing and bloody, staggered upright under the bonds of the magic. His voice cracked with disbelief. "Raze... why?"

Raze's mouth twitched in something like regret—but it wasn't enough. His shoulders were stiff, his hand trembling slightly. "I did it for *us*," he said hoarsely. "You don't understand—this way, we survive. We'll be on the winning side."

The lie hung in the air like rotting smoke.

Lyra appeared then, sprinting across the battlefield, confusion and fear etched on her face. "Raze? What are you doing—?"

Alexis sighed, long and theatrical. "Enough of this."

Before anyone could move, Alexis whipped around and drove his blade straight through Lyra's heart.

She gasped—a soft, shocked sound—and crumpled to the ground, her lifeblood spilling across the ruined earth.

"NO!" Seraphina screamed, the sound tearing from the depths of her soul.

Raze moved without thought, launching himself at Alexis—but the traitor was faster. Alexis twisted his sword free and, with a flick of his wrist, drove a second strike clean through Raze's chest.

Raze's eyes widened in disbelief before he fell beside Lyra, his blood mixing with hers in the dirt.

The world tilted.

Seraphina howled against her bonds, thrashing so violently the chains bit into her skin, but she didn't care. Pain was a distant, meaningless thing compared to the raw agony clawing at her chest. Lyra's blood still stained the ground. Raze's wide, dead eyes still stared at nothing.

Tears blurred her vision, but through the haze of grief, she still saw him—*Kade*—broken, struggling to rise, bloodied but not yielding. Their eyes locked across the ruined battlefield, and the world narrowed to just the two of them.

Kade's chest heaved, every breath a visible battle against despair—but when he spoke, his voice carried across the silence, fierce and unbreakable, a vow stronger than any spell.

"I will find you," he swore, voice ragged with pain and something deeper—*love that would never break.* "I will tear down the skies if I have to, Sera. I *promise.*"

For a heartbeat, something inside her almost steadied—almost believed.

But Alexis yanked her chains, wrenching her off balance.

A low, mocking chuckle left him. "Promises," Alexis drawled, voice thick with venom. He leaned close to her ear, his breath icy against her skin. "Kade once made promises to *me,* too. Swore he'd never betray me. Swore he'd stand by me."

His grip tightened, bruising.

"And he broke *every single one,*" Alexis hissed. "What makes you think this promise will be any different, little love?"

Seraphina recoiled, her breath hitching in horror—but Alexis only smiled wider, relishing her fear. He began dragging her toward a dark rift in the air—a swirling portal pulsing with vile, rotting magic.

"No!" she cried, thrashing harder, heart hammering against her ribs, the world spinning into terror. "Kade! *Kade!*"

Kade roared against his bonds, pure anguish ripping from his throat, but the chains only tightened, magic bleeding the strength from him.

As they neared the portal, Seraphina lost the last of her composure, raw panic clawing through her.

Alexis clicked his tongue mockingly. "Hush now, darling," he crooned, so sweet it was sickening. He reached out and brushed her tear-streaked cheek with the back of his gloved hand, almost tenderly.

Seraphina flinched violently away from his touch, her entire body trembling.

He laughed—a low, cruel sound—and leaned closer. "Don't worry," he whispered, his smile curdling into something monstrous. "I'm bringing your friend too."

Behind them, Vaelrik struggled uselessly against his chains, rage boiling in his glowing eyes.

With a lazy flick of Alexis's wrist, the battlefield itself shifted. The entire Veilborn army—thousands of twisted soldiers, beasts, and shadows— *vanished* in a single breath, like mist scattered by wind.

The power in that small gesture was terrifying. Alexis wasn't just playing anymore. He *was* the storm now.

"Well," Alexis said, flashing a bright, mocking grin at the ruined, bleeding heroes left behind. "This has been *fun*..." He tipped an invisible hat toward Kade, whose face was a mask of broken fury.

"...but it's time to say goodbye."

With a final tug, Alexis pulled Seraphina through the portal—dragging Vaelrik behind her—and the rift snapped shut with a deafening *crack,* leaving nothing but silence.

The last thing Seraphina heard before the world turned inside out was Kade's roar—raw, desperate, a sound so full of rage and heartbreak it seemed to tear the sky itself apart.

Chapter 59

Seraphina woke to darkness so thick it clawed at her throat.

The air was heavy—wet with rot and decay, suffocating, pressing against her lungs with every shallow, burning breath. The coppery tang of old blood saturated the stone, sharp and metallic, sinking into her tongue until it tasted like she was swallowing death itself.

Pain sang through her body in dull, pulsing waves. Her wrists were torn raw where rusted manacles bit into the bone, the iron freezing against her flesh.

Beneath it all, something fouler coiled—*a rot beneath her skin,* wrongness spreading like poison through her veins.

She bit down on the rising tide of panic until she tasted iron.

Not here. Not now.

A low, broken groan snapped her head to the side.

Chains rattled as she twisted.

Vaelrik.

He was crumpled against the wall like a discarded rag doll, breath dragging ragged and wet through his lungs. Blood saturated his tunic, sticky and black in the faint torchlight, the scent of it thick and nauseating. His body was a map of ruin—slashes, burns, cruel carvings etched by a hand that enjoyed the artistry of pain.

But he was breathing. Gods, he was still breathing.

Which meant Alexis hadn't finished playing yet.

The heavy iron door screamed on its hinges.

Seraphina froze, her heart thudding a painful rhythm against her ribs.

Footsteps.

Slow. Deliberate. Each one an executioner's drumbeat.

A figure melted from the darkness, gilded by the flickering torchlight—and the world tilted violently.

Alexis.

He had always been beautiful—too beautiful, like a blade honed to a perfect gleam. But now? Now there was nothing human left to soften the edges.

The sharp angles of his face caught the light like polished marble. His dark eyes, once bright with laughter, were twin voids now, empty and endless. His long black coat whispered across the floor, stitched through with faint threads of silver—power woven into every seam.

He wore death like a second skin.

Seraphina's breath snagged in her chest. The sight of him—the feel of his magic slithering across her skin like oil—sent her stomach lurching.

"Awake at last," Alexis purred, head tilting as he considered her like one might a wounded animal. His voice was soft, almost tender.

It made her want to vomit.

She forced steel into her spine. "Go to hell."

He chuckled, rich and indulgent, like she'd just complimented him.

"Oh, my love," he sighed, stepping closer. His boot nudged against her ankle—a light, almost affectionate touch that made bile rise in her throat. "You still believe in such quaint little endings. I don't die so easily."

Her nails dug into her palms, grounding herself in the pain.

"I watched you die, I killed you!" she rasped.

"And yet here I am." Alexis crouched before her, a graceful, effortless movement that spoke of lethal strength. His dark hair caught the torchlight, a gleaming halo that only made him look more monstrous. "An unfortunate moment in our marriage, true," he said casually, "but you know how well I keep…souvenirs."

His fingers brushed her wrist—feather-light, mockingly tender where the manacles had torn her. She jerked away instinctively, but the chains yanked her back.

"And you," he breathed, reverent, as if confessing a secret. "You were always the most precious."

Old memories—hands held in sunlight, whispered dreams, the taste of a kiss—rose up like ghosts. She crushed them viciously. *She wasn't that girl anymore.*

She wasn't.

Alexis caught her chin between his fingers, tilting her face up to meet his gaze. His grip tightened slowly, nails pressing crescent moons into her skin.

"Tell me, my love," he whispered, voice thick with mockery, "did you really think you could run from me?"

Seraphina glared into the abyss of his eyes. Her voice, though barely above a whisper, struck like a blade.

"I was never yours."

For a heartbeat, he went still.

Then his smile fractured—widening into something unhinged, thrilled.

"Oh, Seraphina," he murmured, lowering his forehead to hers in a mockery of intimacy. "You always were. You just didn't see it."

A choked sound ripped from Vaelrik's throat.

"Interrupting already are we?"

Alexis didn't even glance his way as he rose in one fluid movement, casual and elegant—almost lazily, he pulled a dagger from his belt and *sank it* into Vaelrik's shoulder.

Vaelrik screamed, the sound raw and high, shattering the heavy air.

Seraphina lunged forward, rage and horror burning through her—but the chains jerked her back, slamming her hard against the stone wall.

She tasted blood where she'd bitten her tongue.

Vaelrik sagged against the wall, his breath hitching in broken, pitiful gasps.

Alexis wiped his hands on his coat with a look of disgust, humming under his breath as he landed a kick on Vaelrik's form.

"STOP!" she screamed, her voice breaking against the stone walls.

Alexis stilled mid-motion.

Then—so softly it scraped down her spine like a blade dipped in ice—he murmured, "Oh, Seraphina. I warned you about crying."

The dungeon seemed to shrink around her, every shadow pulsing with the sickening weight of *him*.

He knelt before her again, unhurried, deliberate—savouring every ragged breath she fought to draw. His hand, gloved in blood and cruelty, traced the jagged scar along her wrist, a mockery of tenderness.

"Do you remember how it ended last time?" he whispered, a phantom stirring every old terror.

The tip of his dagger pressed against that same scarred line—slow, taunting, a lover's deadly caress.

Her heart thundered against her ribs. *Not again. Not again.*

"How deep I had to cut," Alexis mused, his voice dripping with twisted affection, "before you finally learned?"

A tremor tore through her body. She *hated* it—hated him—for seeing it.

And he drank it in, eyes gleaming with cruel delight, as if her suffering were the finest wine.

"You think Kade saved you that day?" His dagger slid higher, nicking her skin, a thin line of blood welling to the surface. "You think anyone will save you now?"

His breath ghosted against her throat—hot, suffocating.

"You're mine, Seraphina. Your body. Your power. Every broken, bleeding piece."

The words coiled around her like shackles.

He leaned in, mouth brushing her ear, voice a velvet-wrapped execution.

"And this time," he whispered, "I'm going to savour every moment of your fall."

The dam inside her cracked.

She was on her knees, the cold seeped into her bones, the damp stone gnawed at her skin—but none of it compared to the rotting weight of despair crushing her chest.

Vaelrik groaned beside her, a sound so broken it carved into her ribs. Blood wept from his fresh wound, pooling beneath him, the metallic tang choking the stale air.

Alexis crouched before her, gripping her chin, forcing her gaze to meet his—trapping her, dragging her under.

"You reek of him," he sneered, venom lacing every word.

Seraphina steeled herself. *Don't react. Don't show him.*

But he saw the flicker. He *always* saw.

His grip bruised her jaw. "Oh, Sera," he crooned mockingly. "Did you really think you could let another man touch what belongs to me?"

Vaelrik, despite the agony, surged against his bonds. "Get your filthy hands off her, you *fucking monster—*"

Without even glancing at him, Alexis yanked the blade from Vaelrik's shoulder with a wet, sickening *schhhrrip.*

Vaelrik screamed—a raw, visceral sound that ripped through the darkness.

Seraphina lunged again, rage and grief tearing through her—but Alexis caught her by the hair, yanking her backwards so hard her vision sparked white.

"You care for him?" Alexis sneered against her ear, dragging her tight against his chest. "That's new. I remember when you knelt only for *me.*"

She twisted violently, slamming her elbow into his ribs. He grunted, but his smile sharpened, wicked.

"Good," he breathed. "Fight. Struggle. It makes the breaking sweeter."

He shoved her against the wall; the impact rattling her bones. His palm pressed hard against her sternum, pinning her, chains rattling wildly against the stone.

"You know how this ends," he whispered.

Her power howled inside her—*Run. Fight. Die.*

But she forced her voice through the storm, through the burning wreck of her body.

"I will *kill* you," she rasped.

Alexis tilted his head, almost admiring, before dragging his fingers down her arm, tracing the line of her pulse.

"You'll try," he said, voice velvet over knives. "And I'll love every second of your failure."

Vaelrik's voice, weak but blazing, tore through the gloom. "You think you can take her power? She'll *destroy* you."

Alexis only laughed—a sound dark and rich and utterly without fear.

"Oh, I *hope* she tries," he said, voice thick with anticipation. "It'll be the last beautiful thing she ever does."

Seraphina swallowed the broken sound clawing up her throat and stared him down, letting fury drown the fear.

"You'll never have me," she swore, voice like iron scraped raw.

Alexis' smile faltered, just for a heartbeat. His eyes darkened—something old, something bottomless.

"We'll see," he whispered.

He reached for her.

A shadow moved in the doorway.

A voice, smooth and slicing, cut through the tension like a blade:

"Alexis, darling. Must you waste time with such… peasants?"

Seraphina froze. That voice. No. It couldn't be.

The figure stepped forward, stealing what little breath remained in her chest.

Long raven hair, a face of perfect cruelty. Skin pale as moonlight, lips blood-red.

But the eyes—light, piercing blue—the colour *Seraphina herself* had once worn before everything had shattered and destiny had changed her.

The woman smiled—a slow, poisonous curve that split her face like a wound.

"Hello, sister."

The word struck like a blade twisted deep into Seraphina's ribs.

Sister.

The woman—Elira—moved with silken malice, sliding into Alexis' waiting arms as if she had always belonged there. Her fingers threaded through his hair, tugging him down. She kissed him—slow, possessive, a cruel performance—before pulling back just enough for their breaths to mingle, thick with something obscene.

Alexis exhaled, shuddering like a man starved finally tasting salvation.

Seraphina's soul shattered.

Elira.

Alive. Breathing. Choosing him.

Not the sister who had bled for her.

Not the family she had sworn to love.

No, Elira stood wrapped around the monster who had gutted their world, smiling as if Seraphina's ruin was her finest triumph.

Seraphina staggered back, chains rattling against stone, but the devastation inside her was too vast, too final.

There was no air. No ground.

Only the hollow scream ripping silently through her chest.

Her sister hadn't died.

She had betrayed her.

Epilogue

Kade's Point of view

The battlefield stilled.

Fires guttered low, smothered by the creeping hush of night. Smoke curled around broken bodies, and the scent of blood clung to the wind—thick, suffocating, inescapable.

Kade stood at the heart of the ruin, his sword slack in his grip, silver hair tangled with ash and sweat. Around him, the dead sprawled—warriors, monsters, friends. None of them mattered now.

She was gone.

A ragged sound shattered the silence.

From the shadows, a figure stumbled forward, falling hard to his knees. His hands dug into the bloodstained earth, shoulders heaving, breath broken.

Aurion.

But not as he should be.

Not the dragon who had ruled the skies.

A man.

Soot and gore smeared his skin, and his golden eyes were wild with terror. He clawed at his own chest, desperate fingers digging into the bone, searching.

"I can't feel her." His voice was a raw thing, a tear in the night.

Kade's gut twisted. He knew. Gods, he knew.

Aurion gripped the blood-soaked ground like he could stitch the bond back together, like sheer will could undo the loss. His magic flickered, wild and unstable. He should be shifting, roaring, rising into the air—but Seraphina's magic, tangled in sacrifice, locked him into this fragile, broken form.

Because she wasn't here to release him.

Because she wasn't anywhere at all that they could reach.

A sound tore out of Aurion—half-growl, half a man's sob. His body shook, trembling from a loss too vast for language.

"She's gone," he gasped. "She's—"

Kade was there in an instant, hand clamping down on Aurion's shoulder, grounding him through the tremors.

"You did as she asked," Kade said, voice iron.

Aurion froze.

"You protected Kai. You stayed till the end."

Another sound ripped from Aurion's throat, wounded and raw. His fingers curled into the dirt, into himself.

"I should have saved her—"

"No." Kade's voice sharpened, cut through the grief. "We all should have. But you didn't fail her."

The words were knives because Kade knew the truth.

He had failed. *He* hadn't been fast enough, strong enough, ruthless enough.

Even Vaelrik—the creature made of nightmare and loyalty—had kept his promise. He had stayed at her side to the bitter end.

He had never left her.

And now, he too was gone.

Kade's eyes burned as he looked beyond Aurion — to the broken body of Raze, lying crumpled in the mud.

Aurion followed his gaze.

Disgust twisted Aurion's face, sharp and unyielding. He rose unsteadily, spitting at Raze's corpse, a guttural rejection of everything that the monster had wrought.

"He's not worth the dirt he's rotting in," Aurion muttered, voice shaking with fury.

Kade's chest ached with too much emotion, too many promises unfulfilled. He dragged a hand over his face, exhaling like the act itself might stitch him back together.

"We'll bury Lyra," Kade said, voice thick, hoarse, "By the lake she and Sera loved so much."

Aurion's jaw tightened, something breaking behind his golden eyes.

"I don't know how to bear this," he whispered. "Not like this. Not... human."

His voice cracked, full of despair he couldn't cage.

He lifted shaking hands, staring at them like they belonged to a stranger.

"She was the only one who could turn me back," Aurion said hollowly. "Without her—"

He swallowed, his voice dropping to a whisper. "I'm stuck like this."

Trapped. Half of what he was. Less than he should be.

Kade turned toward him —, and something in his face cracked wide open.

"You think you're trapped?" Kade snarled, the words ripping out of him.

Aurion startled, instinctively bracing.

"You lost your bond," Kade said, his voice splintering — *shattering* under the weight of the words.

His control snapped.

Magic *exploded* around him, tearing through the air in jagged, feral bursts. The ground trembled beneath his boots. Energy cracked and howled, spitting from his fingertips, wrapping around his body like a storm barely contained.

"I LOST MY MATE."

The roar ripped from his chest, *raw, primordial* — not a sound meant for human throats.

The surrounding earth blackened, scorched by the sheer violence of his grief. Stones cracked, smoke curling upward from the ground. Kade staggered, breath rattling in his chest, a broken sob tearing free — wild and guttural, like something inside him had finally, *irrevocably*, snapped.

"If anyone's to blame—"

His fists clenched so tightly blood welled at his palms.

Trembling, seething, magic tearing at the seams of his skin.

"It's ME."

The final word ripped out like a curse, a confession too heavy to carry.

His magic raged in answer — bright, violent, a living thing writhing around him, *hungry*, *wild*, *untamed*. The air itself recoiled, bending away from him.

Aurion stumbled back a step, heart hammering against his ribs — not from fear, but from something far worse.

Understanding.

Mate.

The word echoed in his skull, louder and heavier than any war cry.

He had known Kade loved her — but *not this*.

Not this.

Not a bond stitched into the very fabric of his soul.

Aurion's breath caught.

Through the torn wreckage of Kade's shirt, Aurion saw it — just above Kade's heart.

The *mate brand* of the Fae clans — ancient, sacred — burned into his skin in magic so raw, so achingly beautiful, it almost seemed to *breathe* against the battered flesh.

Dark, intricate lines curled across his chest, sharp and wild — unmistakably Unseelie in design, steeped in the chaotic power of the dark courts.

But woven through the savage patterns, so subtle it almost seemed a part of the chaos — there was something else.

A single, graceful sweep of fire-marked lines.

A curve that spoke not of shadow, but of rising flame.

Of rebirth. Of *light*.

A phoenix wing.

It wasn't obvious — most would never notice it, would think it simply another wild flourish of Fae magic — but somehow, Aurion *knew*.

It was Seraphina.

Her history. Her spirit. Her soul, scorched into the mark that sealed their bond.

In the centre of it all, carved in threads of shimmering silver that pulsed faintly with magic —

Nyx.

Written not just across his heart, but *into it.*

A vow. A brand. A lifeline.

Aurion's breath caught, raw understanding slamming into him like a blade between the ribs.

This wasn't just a bond of love.

It was a covenant of existence.

Kade's hand rose — trembling, desperate — and pressed flat against the mark, as if anchoring himself to it, as if feeling her there could stop the slow collapse of his soul.

For the briefest second, the lines of the brand glowed beneath his fingers, the faintest flicker of magic straining outward — reaching — searching.

But there was no answer.

Only silence.

A broken, shuddering sob ripped from Kade's chest, his magic snapping and crackling like a storm, burning the earth at his feet. It roared around him, a tempest barely contained by sheer will.

Aurion staggered, overwhelmed — because *he finally understood.*

Seraphina had never just been someone Kade loved.

She had been *everything.*

And Seraphina —

Gods above. Seraphina had *hidden it* from him. Had *carried it alone,* protecting them both from the crushing weight of it.

Aurion's knees threatened to give out under the enormity of it — this grief, this revelation, this failure. He wasn't sure what to do except to stand next to Kade in solidarity.

Kade's breathing was jagged, animalistic. His silver hair clung to his sweat-slicked forehead, his hands shaking violently. His eyes—

Gods, his eyes were a battlefield of their own — burning, broken.

The magic flared again, searing hot—with a guttural growl, Kade *wrenched it back* into himself, forcing the raging storm into bloodied chains.

The battlefield around them seemed to shrink, the night pressing heavier against their lungs.

The world felt smaller without her in it.

"I lost everything," Kade said, voice wrecked, shredded down to something *barely human*.

"And I'm going to tear it all apart to bring her back."

He gripped Aurion's forearm—solid, anchoring them both to what came next.

"We'll find her," Kade said, voice low, a storm barely restrained. "We'll tear apart every world, every realm, until we bring her back."

It wasn't a hope. It wasn't even a plan.

It was a *promise* carved into the marrow of him, a vow that would set the heavens ablaze if need be.

Aurion's breathing evened, his golden eyes darkening, matching Kade's unbreakable resolve.

Together, they turned toward the horizon, where shadows stretched long and cruel across the wasted land.

But Kade paused.

He dropped to one knee in the bloodstained dirt, setting his sword down beside him.

The fires hissed and sputtered around him, and still he bent his head, speaking to the night—to the woman who was no longer there but who filled every shattered piece of him.

"Wait for me, *Nyx*," he whispered, voice barely audible. "I'm coming."

The wind stirred, gentle, almost like fingers ghosting through his hair.

Or maybe that was just a wish.

Kade rose slowly, taking up his sword again, the promise burning hotter than the flames.

"They took the love of my life."

"The centre of my universe."

A heartbeat of silence. A shudder in the broken world.

"And now…"

A vow sharp enough to bleed the gods.

"I'll burn their entire world to the ground."

Side by side, battered and hollowed but still breathing, Kade and Aurion stepped into the dark.

And the world shifted, just slightly, like it knew vengeance was coming.